WILD FREEDOM

The rolling plains spread out before her, starkly green and brutal, yet somehow lush and passionate as well. Like a ripe, languid woman, raw and untamed, they lay in soft savage swells beneath the fiercely brilliant yellow sun in the azure sky, untouched, uncivilized like the gunslinger Storm followed. Never had she felt so alone, so helpless as she gazed at the land stretching out forever in all directions. She felt small in comparison—small and humble. Yet had she not been so afraid, the sight might have gladdened her heart, filled it with joy, for this was a land in which a man could breathe, a land in which a man could stand wild and free beneath the unending summer sky and feel he stood in the very hollow of God's palm. Yes, this was God's country, but Storm was not touched by the rugged beauty of the vast terrain. She was used to the neat, enclosed courtyards of the French houses seated elegantly side-by-side in the *Vieux Carré;* the pretty cobblestone bricks of Bourbon and Royal Streets with their clatter of sleek Thoroughbred horses and expensive carriages upon which crisply uniformed Negro grooms sat tall and proud; the plaintive sigh of the wind as it swept in off the Mississippi River and whispered to the rustling magnolia trees. . . .

Rebecca Brandewyne

Love, Cherish Me

LOVE SPELL BOOKS NEW YORK CITY

LOVE SPELL®

March 1999

Published by

Dorchester Publishing Co., Inc.
276 Fifth Avenue
New York, NY 10001

ISBN 0-505-52302-7

Printed in the United States of America.

For my art director,
Gene,
who opened the door at Warner,
who designs such gorgeous covers,
and who patiently endures the Pony Express;

For my editor,
Fredda,
who accepted my first manuscript to begin with,
who edits my work with a kindred spirit,
and who, with each book, has made me a better writer;

For my artist,
Elaine,
who paints my dashing heroes, my romantic heroines,
and my historical setting so beautifully,
always exactly as I have imagined them;

And most especially for my agent,
Max,
who believed in Karma and a struggling young author,
who suffers a writer's temperamental moods
without complaint,
and without whose help I might never have
been published at all.

THE PLAYERS

At Vaillance:
Storm Lesconflair, a
      Southern Belle
Mammy, a slave

At Tierra Rosa:
Gabriel North, a rancher
His children:
      Joe Jack
      Cathy
Ross Stuart, a ranch hand

At Gorda Vaca:
Ma Barlow, a gang leader
Her outlaw sons:
      Luther
      Zeke
      Elijah
      Billy
El Lobo (The Wolf), a
      gunslinger

At the Llano Estacado:
Tabenanika, a Comanche
      Shaman
His wives:
      Woman-Of-The-
        High-Wind
      She-Who-Seeks-
        Wisdom
Masitawtawp, brother of
      Tabenanika's wives
She-Laughs-Like-A-
      Mountain-Stream,
      wife to
      Masitawtawp
Comanche Warriors:
Sons of Ekakura:
      Moon-Raider
      Crazy-Soldier-Boy
Fire-Walker, son of Kwasia
Sons of Masitawtawp:
      Shadow-Of-The-
        Hawk
      Naukwahip
Brother-Of-The-Wolf, son
      of Tabenanika

At the Bon Ton Saloon:
Brett Diamond, a gambler

LOVE, CHERISH ME

From river to range
My heart was bound.
I left soft beds for
Nights on hard ground.
Petticoats and pistols
I have found
In my life.

A bull, a weasel,
A gambling man, and
A savage wolf
Have claimed my hand
With feverish lips
Each scorched his brand
In my life.

One murmured low,
Hot words did croon.
One grinned boldly
In another's saloon.
One held me 'neath
A Comanche moon
In my life.

Till howling winds
Of desire and shame,
With scandals whispered,
Mocking, came
To rage inside
And scar my name
In my life.

Oh, sweet pain
Now dimly sears.
Still I'll recall
Through passing years
A bitter rose
Sunrise and tears
In my life.

Love, cherish me
Chase away all regret,
All those yesterdays
I've tried to forget,
This ache in my heart
That haunts me yet
In my life.

CONTENTS

BOOK ONE
From River to Range

1

Tierra Rosa, Texas, 1866
It was time.

Storm gazed lovingly at the man who lay sleeping so peacefully by her side. There was no need of words between them, no need to tell him of her decision. He would know she had made it the moment he awakened and looked into her eyes. He would know too how very painful it had been and how much it had cost her. Yes, he would understand all that – and more.

She reached out one hand to gently brush away a strand of hair that caressed his cheek. He was here. He was real. He was hers, this man, forever. Only death could separate them now, and they had lived with death too long to fear it. It was as much a part of them as the shadows they cast beneath the fierce Texas sun.

The man sensed Storm no longer slept beside him. He stirred, stretched out one strong, sinewy arm to draw her close once more. She pressed herself against the length of his naked body, laid her head upon his shoulder. This was where she belonged, where she had always belonged, sheltered within his warm embrace. Why had she ever thought differently? The man wrapped his fingers in her cloud of black tangled tresses that billowed out over the pillows. He inhaled the sweet rose fragrance of her deeply, murmured softly in her ear, his breath hot upon her face. One hand stroked her silken flesh languidly: her throat, her breasts, the curve of her slender waist, her hips. His mouth trailed tender kisses across one bare shoulder before he sought her crimson lips, parting them with a gentle ʌsistence sne could not deny, did not want to deny

'Storm,' he whispered huskily. 'Storm.'

Her eyes flew open, meeting his own passion-darkened ones. He knew then why she had been awake. The past had not let her sleep. His hands tightened upon her small frame, for he was afraid for her.

'I'm here.' His voice was low. 'I'll always be here.'

She needed no other reassurance.

'I know.'

Suddenly he forced her lovely countenance up roughly. His mouth closed over hers again, but his tenderness had fled. His lips were hard, hungry, demanding, as though he were branding himself forever on her soul. His tongue shot deep within her, ravishing her mouth as one who knew it was his right. Tasting, taking, he was savage in his desire. She was his. He alone possessed her. He would kill any man who tried to wrest her from his grasp.

She met his searing lips eagerly, not caring that he bruised her own, for she recognized the violent, primitive mood that had come upon him and understood it. His kiss slid across her cheek to her ear and then down her throat to her shoulder. Sparks of fire blazed through her body as his teeth nipped lightly the satin skin that joined her nape in a graceful curve. She moaned and writhed beneath him. The soft hair upon his chest tickled her breasts as he continued his slow onslaught on her senses. She felt her pink nipples stiffen against him, as did he. His fingers teased the taut little peaks to even greater heights before he lowered his mouth to envelope one rosy tip between his lips. His tongue traced tiny swirling circles about the bud, sending shivering tingles from its center in all directions. An aching yearning began to build between Storm's thighs. She arched her hips against him, found his manhood ready. She rubbed the moistness of her flanks along the length of his shaft, but he did not heed her invitation. Instead he bent his head to kiss her pulsating mound, tongue lapping at the honey of her until she made a throaty sound, an animalistic cry that tore from her as though he had yanked it from her very being. Still the man did not stop, but went on driving her to glorious ecstasy again and again, joying in the power he held over her at this moment, thrilled by the knowledge that he alone had brought her such rapture.

'Now, my husband, now!' Her arms sought him frantically.

For one fleeting eternity it seemed as though he would resist her pleas, and his denial further inflamed her. Waves of passion engulfed her. The ache to have him in her reached a feverish pitch. She cried out. With a muffled snarl he flung himself upon her, penetrating her swiftly with a sharp clean thrust that made her gasp aloud and cling to his broad back tightly. His powerful muscles flexed beneath her hands as she held onto him, locked her long lithe legs around his to keep him from escaping. Over and over he plunged into her, muttering words of love and sex against her ear, exciting her beyond belief. Tremors shook her body before she exploded like a volcano beneath his gyrating hips. Rivers of molten lava flowed through her veins. Her blood boiled. She was burning up, and she could not get enough of it.

He was a strong man, however. He pleasured her until she lay exhausted, and the sweat of his strenuous love-making shone with a fine, dewy sheen upon her flesh, marking her as his. He came into her then, gripping the masses of perfumed ebony hair at her temples as he shuddered atop her and finally was still.

They rested, entwined, the silence broken only by the pounding of their hearts as they panted softly together, waiting to float slowly downward from their soaring exultation. The man caressed Storm's cascading locks, then kissed her gently.

'Now you will take a part of me with you when you go.'

'You do not come with me then?'

15

'No, my love, this is something you must do alone.'

She thought about that quietly for a time and knew it was so. She accepted it without question as he continued to hold her in his protective arms. He guessed her anxiety, but said nothing further. If she truly needed him, he would be there. She had only to ask, but she did not, and he was proud of her courage. As she arose he caught her hand and pressed his mouth hotly once upon her wrist.

'I love you, Storm.'

She smiled. With that knowledge to sustain her she could conquer the world. She stretched briefly, like a sinuous little cat, then moved to the tall armoire that stood against one wall of the bedroom. Her husband leaned back among the pillows, lit a cigar, and watched silently, an appreciative gleam in his eyes as they roamed over her naked figure.

Storm opened the armoire, pushed aside the clothes that hung within, then bent down to the coffer area to remove a plain but beautiful gown of gray silk trimmed with black satin. The dress had a low-cut, heart-shaped bodice with short cap sleeves and a narrow waist from which yards of billowing material swept out in a full, flounced skirt. The last had gracefully scalloped edges drawn up in pleats with gray silk ribbons to reveal insets of black satin. There was a matching jacket with tight cuffs that hooked up to the elbows with jet buttons, then puffed out into draped sleeves up to the slightly padded shoulders. The coat flared out over the waist of the frock, when assembled, and fastened up to the collar at the throat with the same ebony studs that adorned the cuffs. There were epaulettes on the shoulders from which hung two loops of black satin braid apiece.

The costume was somewhat outmoded, Storm knew, but it had been well-kept and protected in layers of tissue at the bottom of the cedar-lined chest. There wasn't a frayed seam or a worn spot on it, although the outfit did need pressing. Carefully she laid it on the bed, recalling the last time she'd worn it. Her husband took a drag of his cigar, then blew a

16

cloud of smoke upward toward the ceiling. He remembered too. Ten years ago it had been. Was it really possible so much time had passed? Storm turned once more to the armoire to lift out and unwrap the accompanying bonnet, gloves, and boots. The hat also was of gray silk edged with black satin trim. Two long black streamers dangled from either side, and a wispy black veil tangled round the front, just waiting to be pulled down over the wearer's face. The gloves and boots were of soft black kid.

Storm had designed the entire ensemble herself. It had cost a fortune, but then the expense had not mattered. What had counted had been that the apparel might not arrive in time. She had bought it for a funeral – her own.

She paused to study her figure in the cheval mirror, which had come all the way from the East. She was thirty-four years old, but the reflection that stared back at her was unmarred save for a few fine lines around her keen clear eyes. Her shiny blue-black hair, which tumbled like a waterfall to her hips, was as yet unstreaked with the early gray that seemed to strike so many women in the West. Storm ran her fingers through the wild damp mane, trying to restore it to some semblance of order. Then she cupped her breasts with her hands. Hard work had kept the ripe mounds from falling like most women's after childbirth. Her belly was flat and taut. Her hips, though gently rounded, were slender. Her skin was still flushed with the afterglow of her husband's lovemaking. She smiled softly, meeting his eyes in the mirror, then called for Pilar, her maid.

After the quiet Mexican girl had gone to iron the attire and necessary petticoats Storm stepped behind a hand-painted screen that zigzagged before an intricate cabinet off to one side of the fireplace. When opened, the hinged door of the cupboard lay flat upon the floor to reveal an ornate mosaic set in its inner side. From the cabinet itself Storm withdrew a hammered brass bathtub to rest upon the tiled square. The large basin, the cheval mirror, and her rose scent were the only extravagances and reminders of her girlhood past that Storm permitted herself. Otherwise the East – and the South – were behind her now forever.

She filled the tub with buckets of steaming water drawn from the big black kettle Pilar had set to boiling over the hearth earlier that morning for just such a purpose. Then she poured a small amount of fragrance from a stoppered crystal flacon into the water. After easing herself in she reached for a bar of soft soap and a sponge from the built-in shelves of the clever cupboard and began to lather herself vigorously. By the time she had toweled herself off and spread her hair before the fire to dry, Pilar had returned with the newly pressed clothes. Storm studied them grimly after the maid had closed the door behind her.

Ten years. It had been ten years since Storm had last been to town, to Santa Rosa; but now it was time. She might selfishly keep to the cocoon she had spun for herself, but the boys needed to be exposed to life outside the ranch and the West, as did her young daughter, Anna, who lay resting in another room. They ought to see the East, the South, and Europe, which had been refused Storm. It wasn't fair to deny her children that. Oh, she'd taught them all to read, write, and cipher; but they needed more than that, or they'd wind up little better than the heathens she knew some called them. They were fine, spirited animals, her children, grown tall and dark under the Texas sun, with untamed hair as black as her own. Storm loved them all fiercely, just as she loved the man who'd fathered them, her husband. Impulsively she arose from her stool before the fire and kissed him ro reassure herself that he was real.

'*Je t'aime*,' she breathed.

When her hair had finished drying, Storm wound it into a severe chignon at the nape of her neck, then began slowly to dress. The man continued to watch quietly, but he knew she had forgotten his presence. The past had claimed her

18

again. She was ten years distant from him – or more. He remembered the beginning too. She'd been proud and defiant even then, and he had won her in a card game.

Storm put on the gray silk costume with its black satin trim. Finally only the bonnet remained. She lifted it frozenly, placed it on her head, and jabbed the hat-pin in sharply. Then with trembling fingers she lowered the mask of black net over her countenance, criss-crossed the streamers once around her throat, then tied the ends into a bow beneath one side of her chin. Her hands lingered, still quivering, at the knot. It might have been rope . . .

She drew a deep breath, shaking herself mentally. It was morbid to dwell on such thoughts and stupid when she needed every ounce of her courage and backbone this afternoon. Storm pulled on her gloves, picked up her reticule, and left the room. She moved like a prisoner just released from jail, and only her husband would ever know the price she had paid for her freedom. He lit another cigar and prayed she would not return to him with the terrible scars of her past torn asunder to reveal the wounds that lay beneath – wounds it had taken ten years to heal. A strange peacefulness crept over him as he prayed. Yes, she was strong. She would survive. She had always been a survivor. That was why he loved her so. In the stillness he spoke aloud, but only Storm would have understood the words; and she was gone.

The house in which Storm and her husband lived was a good house, large and welcoming. Rough-hewn split logs of mesquite had been laid one upon another to form the sprawling L-shaped frame, then the chinks of the walls had been carefully filled with baked clay or *adobe*, as the natives called it, to seal the exterior. Three massive stone chimneys jutted up from the slat-board roof turned a dull gray from years of weathering the elements. A wide, railed veranda angled round the entire L, breaking in various places for the steps that led to the range lawn. Glass was impractical and a rarity in the West, but the good-sized windows were covered with the purest of cured rawhide and admitted a soft, pleasantly filtered light when unshuttered. Inside was a *real* floor of puncheon, not just the hard-packed earth that served so many.

Yes, it was a good house, a house that had been built with ruggedness and pride. Still Storm had no doubt some would have considered it sadly lacking. She would have done so – once. Funny, she thought, how time changes us all. She walked on down the hall, passing through the curved archways that led to the salon with its high, beamed ceiling and French doors that opened out onto the back porch. At one end of the stoop hung a swing that had been lovingly carved, sanded, and fitted and that was suspended from giant butchering hooks on heavy iron chain that had been salvaged from a ship's anchor during the Mexican War of 1846. After sitting down Storm rocked idly for a moment, collecting her thoughts, caressing the arms of the swing. There was strength in those arms, just as there was in those of her husband. To her lips she lifted a dipper of cool water she'd drawn from the well outside the kitchen to quench the thirst brought on by her husband's lovemaking. She took small slow sips, knowing from the past that those who swigged their water down in the summer heat either vomited or pissed it out again in a matter of minutes. The sweltering sun would sweat it out of a person soon enough without that!

The brilliant orange ball shone brightly, hotly, directly overhead, beating down upon Storm and the vast, sweeping terrain of the Edwards Plateau fiercely. The blazing sphere was unrelenting in its scorching grip, as though it meant to burn the very life from the land or at least weed out those unworthy of survival. Indeed only the strongest remained alive in West Texas. Storm was one of these.

She gazed out over the rolling plains of buffalo grass

intermingled further on with stretches of dune where the hardy cactuses thrust upward defiantly from the raw red clay-and-golden sand earth: the barrel cactus with its stiff spines, sharply defined ridges, and tiny flowers that ranged in colour from bright yellow to deepest purple; the cholla; the fishhook; the hedgehog; the woolly living rock with its almost thornless rosettes and blossoms of white, cream, yellow, and magenta; the night-blooming moon cactus; the fuzzy old man; and the proliferate prickly pear.

Here and there the agaves, with their pulpy green spike leaves, squatted upon the ground. Their cousins, the taller crowned yuccas, stood regally – like proud kings marching out to do battle – against the stark, barren horizon. Scrubs of many-branched sagebrush with wedge-shaped foliage glinted silver-gray in the distance amidst the tangled chaparral and tarry creosote bushes that sprang up coarsely in haphazard profusion. An odd tumbleweed or two lay brown and lifeless where the dying prairie winds had scattered them earlier that spring. The narrow olive leaflets of the shrubby mesquite trees curled brittlely at the edges. Their dense catkins of cream-colored blooms seemed wilted. The clusters of long, narrow pale yellow beans beneath these hung limply in the summer heat. Even the few silver-barked cottonwoods that nestled forlornly upon the banks of the rivers appeared scraggly and thirsty.

To the west the last of the Rocky Mountains and the beginning of the majestic purple Sierra Madres overlooked the empty, arid savannah mockingly and enticed the basin's inhabitants with cold snowcapped peaks.

One cupped palm traveled to Storm's forehead, shading her eyes against the glare of the sun. At the corral she could see her two sons, Luke and Beau. How like the land they were – wild and savage. The sight of them strengthened her resolve. She stood.

'Luke.'

Storm's eldest son raised his head at once at the sound of

her voice, tossing aside the cloth with which he'd been polishing his saddle upon the split-rail fence of the corral. He was a hard, quiet, steely youth, one who, at age nine, had already shouldered his responsibilities like a man. Well, still waters ran deep, they said; and Storm had more reason than most to know the truth of that. Now Luke stood too, shading his eyes just as Storm had done. He started toward the house. Beau followed his brother at an easy, graceful lope, already beginning to swagger in imitation of the rough men who worked the ranch. At seven, Storm's younger son was a restless boy with a devilish grin that hid well his reckless, gambling nature and hot temper. She had no doubt that one day he would be a drifter, a heart-breaker, and possibly come to a bad end.

They stopped before her, staring with disbelief.

'You look beautiful, mama!' Beau grinned with the careless charm he'd acquired over the years, his eyes glimmering faintly with pride and speculation at her appearance.

'The Shiloh barbecue ain't till next week, mama,' Luke stated flatly, thinking she had mistaken the date. 'Did you forget?'

'No, Luke, I did not. I want you to hitch up the team. We're going into town.'

'Town!' both boys cried, incredulous.

'What for?' Her oldest son was instantly suspicious. 'You ain't ever been to town, mama.'

'But of course I have, Luke. It's just – just been awhile; that's all. And don't say "ain't". I declare, you boys have less grammar than a Georgia Cracker, despite all I've tried to teach you. That's why we're going into town. I'm enrolling you boys in Miss Patton's new school.'

'School,' they groaned.

'I've made up my mind, so you might as well go hitch up the team. *Maintenant*! Now!'

Luke turned away sullenly to do her bidding. Storm's

sons knew better than to argue with her when she spoke French. When they were out of sight, she heard Beau give a whoop of excitement and smiled briefly to herself before she went in to waken the five-year-old Anna.

Storm sat up straight and proud upon the seat of the buggy, eyes looking directly ahead. Her children glanced at her sharply from under half-closed lids. Although she didn't know it, they were thinking they couldn't remember a time when they'd ever seen her spine touch the back of a chair; in fact, they'd often asked each other if she had a steel ramrod running through it. Storm paid no heed to their protests as she began to outline her plans for them in her soft, cultured but determined voice. Rebellious, they advanced every imaginable argument against the scheme, but at last realized resistance was useless. When Storm had her mind set on something, a herd of stampeding cattle couldn't change it.

'You're too stubborn for your own good, mama!' Beau finally laughed ruefully.

Storm gave him a wry smile. Her keen eyes twinkled momentarily.

'So I've been told,' she said.

They finished the remainder of the long hot drive in silence. Storm was apprehensive about entering Santa Rosa and hoped she didn't show it, but somehow her nervousness must have affected the children nevertheless. Luke seemed distinctly uncomfortable as he guided the horses down the wide, dusty main street of town. Anna was cool, as usual – a coolness that masked a spoilt, wilful girl – but her lower lip trembled petulantly, and her dark eyes flashed. Even Beau was strangely subdued.

Santa Rosa, population 547, was a small, lazy town about a hundred and fifty miles west of San Antonio. Its original inhabitants had been of Mexican decent, but after the unrest of 1846, it had been more or less taken over by the hordes of white settlers who had come to Texas to try their hand at ranching, regardless of the outbreaks of cholera and yellow fever that had followed the Mexican War. Those who had failed at cattle-raising (or rustling) had turned to gambling, shopkeeping, or smithing to survive. Santa Rosa had grown from a few adobe huts and one church to a fairly decent town by the standards of the West. It had several stores, two saloons, a livery stable, and even a moderate hotel now. The stage came through once a month, although the Pony Express had been disbanded in 1861, and the circuit judge rode round every six weeks to hear the cases against those who'd been confined to the local jail. Storm tried hard not to think about that.

Here and there a navy-blue-and-brass uniform lounged idly against a post, reminding her of the Civil War that had recently ended, although its ravages had scarcely reached that part of Texas west of the Nueces River. Storm guessed the soldiers were simply men at loose ends, men who'd drifted on after the fighting had ceased. The South had been devastated, she'd heard and wondered if Vaillance had been lost even as Belle Rive had been. She tried hard not to think about that either.

The buckboard rolled on down the road. As the vehicle passed, people on the wooden sidewalks of town stopped, turned, and stared at the four on the buggy. Storm saw a dull red flush of anger begin to creep up her younger son's neck.

'What in the hell are they gawking at?' Beau muttered.

This remark Storm chose to ignore.

'Pull up at Mr Goldschmidt's dry-goods store, Luke,' she directed calmly, but her hands were shaking slightly in her lap all the same. 'You'll be needing some new clothes for school.'

In front of the Crystal Palace saloon across the street two men slouched in chairs, feet propped up on the hitching post, hats pulled down low over their faces, suddenly glanced up with interest at the sight of the two boys helping their mother and sister out of the buckboard. Although she hadn't seen them for a long time, Storm recognized them at once as Farley Smith and Dirk Benteen. She shuddered, feeling sick and faint. How could she ever forget them? She remembered them all, every last one of the ugly, jeering, hate-contorted countenances of the lynch mob that had come for her that horrible night; their vile, vulgar taunts; their loud, angry voices. *Sainte Marie—*

'Lawd a'mighty!' she heard Farley exclaim. 'Wouldya look at that, Dirk! It's her! It's been nigh on ten years or more, but I'd swear on my pore pappy's grave it's old Storm herself!'

Dirk squinted hard at them for a moment.

'Yep, I do believe yore right, Farley. Gawddamm! I never woulda believed it if I hadn't seen it with my own two eyeballs!'

Farley shifted the wad of tobacco he was chewing and spit in the road with disgust.

'Didn't know fer shore she was still alive. Ain't hardly nobody but them friggin' ranchers seen her in a coon's age. I jest cain't understand them bastards givin' her the time of day after all she's been and done, even if her blood be as blue as they claim. Must be that spread and its water rights. Hell! I guess money can buy anythin', even respectability, no matter how low a person's sunk. Jest look at her! Actin' purty high and mighty, ain't she? Thoroughbred, my foot! I never did figger how Gabriel come to pick that loser. Why, she ain't nothin' but a cheap floozy! Shit! Even the dance hall gals are better than that no-count trash, pureblood or no. Got hearts of gold, some of 'em, and that she-devil Storm ain't got none a'tall, nawsir, none a'tall. Oughta consider herself lucky she didn't have that proud neck of hers stretched at the end of a rope! I still think we shoulda strung her up, Dirk!'

Storm's face blushed bright crimson at the stinging words. She tossed the 'proud neck' under discussion with some semblance of arrogance, determined not to let the two men see how badly they had upset her, for she knew they'd intended her to overhear them.

'Ain't it the truth!' Dirk continued the conversation. ''Course, don't nobody know fer shore what really happened and never will, I reckon, 'ceptin' her 'n' Cathy Stuart. I always thought Storm done it, but, hell! You never can tell.'

'Now that's a fact, friend. That purely is a fact.' Farley nodded, stabbing sharply at his piece of whittling wood with his knife. 'But I'm with you, Dirk. I think Storm kilt that boy as shore as I'm sittin' here right now. She's got some nerve, showin' her face in town.'

'Lawd a'mighty!' Dirk's mouth suddenly dropped open for the second time in the space of as many minutes. 'Looks like there's gonna be trouble now!' He jerked his thumb down the road, indicating a slowly approaching blond woman who was clutching the hands of two young children.

Farley whistled softly, then drawled intently, 'I hear they ain't spoke since it happened,' as Storm glanced down the street.

Cathy! Oh, Cath! Storm's heart ached in her breast at the sight. If only they knew!

Drawing in her breath sharply, Storm lifted her skirts to step up on the sidewalk, realizing suddenly since she could hear the two men clearly, so could her children. She did not want them hurt and confused by scandalous talk until she could tell them a story she ought to have told them long before this.

Storm saw the other woman had been aware of her presence, for the tall, graceful blond stopped, hesitated, then squared her shoulders proudly, meeting Storm's clear eyes unwaveringly. Cathy and her children came on, refusing to give way.

Storm was only vaguely aware of her own children

coming to stand at her sides, Luke's hands on little Anna's shoulders, Beau swaggering slightly, hands on hips. She stared at Cathy Stuart measuringly. A decade had come and gone, but although the blond hair was touched faintly with gray, Cathy carried her age well, still retained the freckles and the too-wide mouth with its thin brown cigar.

In that minute the years flew back for both of them, as though time had suddenly stopped for one fleeting moment on the dusty sidewalk of the small hot town. Amidst the onlookers not an eyelash flickered; no one breathed; and still the two women stared.

Luke swallowed hard, not understanding what was going on, but feeling the tension in the air nevertheless. None of her children, Storm felt sure, had ever seen Cathy Stuart in their lives. Beau glanced at the young girl whose hand Cathy held and saw the child was studying him shyly. Her eyes darted away, then back, and then she smiled at him. Beau grinned. The girl's older brother glared hostilely.

Storm observed the children's brief exchange without really seeing it at all. She was still caught, still held by the hands of time, remembering that day it had happened, seeing them all as they had been that summer so long ago, hearing the dreadful sounds of the shots echoing over and over again in her mind, feeling the blood spatter red and warm and sticky upon her flesh in the stifling heat. Which one of them had screamed? It didn't matter now.

The two women had never been and would never be friends, but there was a grudging respect and admiration for each other between them all the same; and so although not one word had passed between them, Storm and Cathy nodded proudly to one another, satisfied with the bargain they'd made so long ago, and moved on. A fly buzzed. A horse whisked its tail. The townspeople breathed again.

'Who *was* that, mama?' Luke asked with barely suppressed curiosity when he could speak once more.

At first Storm was certain her son thought she hadn't

27

heard him; she took so long to reply. She was still looking back on the past, her eyes bright with unshed tears as she remembered a bitter rose dawn and another boy about whom the two men had not spoken, because that boy had been nothing, less than nothing to them.

Then she said slowly, 'When we get home, Luke, remind me to tell you all a very long and foolish, sad story.'

Yes, it was time, Storm thought again, time to tell her children the tale of Cathy Stuart and herself, both of them courageous, brave-hearted women – one of them a murderess.

2

New Orleans, Louisiana, 1848

Somewhere, perhaps, time stood still; but not that summer evening of 1848, and not at Vaillance. The tall white columns of the old plantation glistened as the dazzling lights of the soirée inside streamed through the leaded-glass panes of the sparkling casement windows, windows unmarred by even a single smudge. The black wrought-iron balconies rang with gay laughter and the ripples of melodious music that wafted into the night. The strings of the fiddles harmonized prettily with the plaintive calls of the mockingbirds and the lazy droning of the locusts. The gentle clink of the punchbowl ladle as it filled and refilled crystal glasses with sweet mint julep was accompanied by the low sounds of the darkies' voices as they moved through the throng within the spacious ballroom to be certain no guest wanted for anything.

Long tables at either end of the hall groaned under the weight of their heavy burdens: plates piled high with now-cold beef, ham, and chicken left over from the barbecue that afternoon; green beans that had been boiled slowly for hours with salt, sliced onions, hunks of fatback, and bits of minced ham; ears of sweet roasted corn kept warm by kerosene wicks lit beneath elegant silver chafing dishes; and bisquits so hot the butter just drooled off them. There were cakes and pies too. German chocolate, angelfood, and sticky cherry-and-pineapple creations beckoned scrumptiously, as did the crisp apple crumb sprinkled with cinnamon that fairly steamed alongside cool lemon meringue and tantalizing peach cobbler. An array of cookies and tarts too numerous to mention surrounded a solidly frozen basin heaped high with real vanilla ice cream.

Doors swung smoothly on oiled hinges as the never-ending parade of Negroes came and went with trays heavily laden, some carefully arranged with tasty morsels to replace those already eaten, others stacked high with dirty dishes. Not once was even so much as a fork dropped or a guest on the dance floor jostled; for from the youngest children who shooed the geese and chickens off the front yard, to the field hands who plucked the cotton and harvested the rice, to the virtual army of darkies that served the huge household, the slaves at Vaillance had all been well-trained.

Carrying a large silver tray on which squat glasses of brandy sat neatly, one such Negro made his way unobtrusively toward the blue clouds of smoke that drifted inside from the French doors leading to the terrace. There a knot of fine gentlemen were debating subjects not fit for ladies' ears. In one corner of the ballroom the masculine aroma of tobacco was being patiently waved away by a group of gossiping matrons who were idly speculating about just what it was their husbands were discussing outside.

It was hot and humid that summer evening. Only the constant swish of the palmetto fans held by mammies and maids prevented many of the ladies present from fainting, for the combination of the stifling heat and tightly laced corsets was overpowering. More than one woman pressed a daintily tatted and scented handkerchief to her sweat-dampened temples and wrists, but none thought of retiring upstairs where her modish gown would go unadmired.

Stiff crinoline petticoats rustled provocatively under brightly colored yards of sprig muslin, soft batiste, finely woven lawn, sheer gauze, and elaborate lace. Morocco slippers tapped in time with the musicians, beating a lively tattoo upon the hard oak floor that had been polished until it shone with a rich burnished glow and smelled slightly of the clean fresh beeswax that had been applied by several worn black hands just that morning. Flirting couples clapped and shouted as they executed the intricate steps of a spirited reel, and the walls of Vaillance shook.

The sprawling mansion was not unfamiliar with the sights and sounds of a party in progress, for it had been the setting of many grand affairs in its day; but one would not have expected the same lack of excitement to reside in the breast of its young occupant. Nothing could have been finer than the long, flower-bedecked room filled to overflowing with the crowd of noisy people who had gathered to celebrate the girl's engagement; but the sultry fragrance of the cloying blossoms only made her feel as though she were suffocating, and the raucous clamor of the revelry had given her a splitting headache. Despite being the obvious belle of the ball and having the *Mesdames* Fontaine and Poitier (spinsters to be sure, but staunch pillars of New Orleans society nevertheless) declare stoutly she was the loveliest bride-to-be feted that season, the guest-of-honor longed fervently only for the quiet solitude of her bedroom. The polite smile she wore felt frozen on her face, and she feared any moment she would burst into tears, for her heart was breaking inside her.

Oh, André! How can you let them do this to us? she wanted to cry out, to somehow capture his attention. Of all the fine gentlemen in the hall, however, he alone seemed impervious to the girl's charms; and so despite the many gallant young bucks who flocked to her side, the guest-of-honor could have wept with bitter vexation. She wished desperately she might slip away unnoticed.

This would have been highly unlikely, for at sixteen, Storm Aimée Lesconflair already turned heads with that certain kind of sensual beauty that makes men's hearts beat fast and women seethe with scarcely suppressed jealousy. Knee-deep in would-be beaux, despite her engagement, she was breathtaking in a rose-coloured gown of lace and lawn. Its ruffled décolletage showed just the barest hint of her full ripe breasts. Its velvet sash encircled a waist any of the males buzzing round her like bees to a honey pot could have spanned with his hands. She had that cream-colored skin so greatly prized and zealously protected by Southern women. Her peach cheeks were flushed with pink and glowed enchantingly, but whether this was due to the sweltering crush inside the ballroom, the flattery of her suitors, or her own conflicting emotions, it could not be said. Her long, silky hair, the blue-black of a raven's wing glistening in an April shower, fell in a riotous cascade of curls down her back. Her classic nose lifted haughtily when a moonstruck swain became overbold. Her inviting rose-bud mouth, that lush tint of scarlet men find so difficult to resist, pouted childishly about the corners.

It was really her eyes, however, that held one's gaze riveted upon her countenance. Wide and expressive beneath a pair of swooping jet brows and starred with thick sooty lashes that were so heavy as to seem to pull her lids down at the slightly slanted corners, Storm's eyes were as tempestuous as the hurricane that had been raging the night of her birth and for which she had been named. An ever-changing shade of gray, they could settle softly like blanketing mist in repose, swirl darkly like shattering rain in anger, shimmer brightly like morning dew in laughter, or shadow hauntingly like illusive wraiths in sorrow. Now, however, they smoldered dangerously like cold steel gun-barrels as she jerked her fan shut with a sharp little click at having failed to attract the notice of her cousin, André-Louis Beauvallet. With a veiling flutter of her lashes and a smile that hid her despair Storm turned back to her fiancé and the others at her sides.

The air fairly snapped with heated glances as the sons of the New Orleans planters vied for the girl's attention. Already rude words had been exchanged, for her beaux could not understand why the belle of five counties had chosen a Texas rancher twenty-four years her senior over one of their own. Angry, hurt, and confused, each was determined to discover the reason. To prevent this from occurring and to shield her broken heart from their prying questions Storm was flirting outrageously with each and every one, playing them off against each other. The gossiping matrons in the corner were excitedly examining the possibility of a brawl breaking out any moment. The gentlemen on the terrace were chuckling with amusement as they watched their smitten sons and privately laid bets as to which boy would be the first to cause Storm's prospective husband to lose his temper.

Gabriel North, the girl's fiancé, was no less aware of the emotionally charged atmosphere. He put one hand possessively on his bride-to-be's arm, not liking the drunken flushes that had begun to creep over some of the bucks' dark visages. He felt nothing but contempt for what he thought were the soft, lazy sons of the New Orleans planters. He wouldn't have hesitated to put a bullet through any of them had any been foolhardy enough to challenge him to a duel (he had already killed one in such manner), but he couldn't risk that kind of scandal again – at least not right now. Perhaps then Storm's uncle, Pierre Beauvallet, would not scruple to expose the way in which Gabriel had won the girl's hand.

His eyes hard and calculating, he said, 'Gentlemen, if you will excuse us, I believe my fiancée feels the need of a little fresh air.'

The word *gentlemen* had sounded like an insult. Many of the gay blades stiffened, and the announcement was me with black scowls, instead of the goodnatured jokes and smirks it would normally have received. Still the young men all stepped aside to let the couple pass, suddenly recalling there were other ladies present who were not yet bespoken.

Storm would have protested Gabriel's insolent gesture of dismissal, but his hand tightened warningly on her arm. She closed her half-parted lips, knowing his harsh grip would leave a bruise.

Despite her reluctance to take up his suggestion, the girl found she was glad to escape the crowded, humid ballroom after all, even if it were her intended who escorted her. Summer had come early to Louisiana that year, but the gardens were cool. A small breeze swept in with tangy dampness from the banks of the Mississippi River.

'May I smoke?' Gabriel asked politely.

'If you wish.'

Her fiancé lit a cigar as the two followed the carefully designed stone walkways that wound through the luxurious flowers and were broken here and there by discreet arbors with marble benches and white lattices upon which Yvette Beauvallet's climbing roses abounded. The magnolia and mimosa trees wafted gently in the wind, their white-and-pink-blossomed branches hanging with Spanish moss, filling up the senses and the night air with a sweet, heady fragrance rivaled only by the cape jessamine, the camellias, and of course the roses. There were thousands of these last: red roses, white roses, yellow roses, and Storm's favorite, the dusky pink roses. It was these she snipped lovingly from the bushes, crushing the buds with mortar-and-pestle, then steeping the petals for days to procure the musky rose scent she wore always. This evening, carefully stripped of thorns, they intertwined her mass of black ringlets; one bloom perched seductively behind her left ear. Her aunt's roses were lovely, but Aimée Lesconflair, Storm's mother, had been famous all over Louisiana for hers. The girl's eyes pricked with tears as she thought of *maman*, dead these two years past.

The noise from the ballroom faded into the night as Storm and Gabriel walked on into the hushed gardens where occasionally a high giggle trilled as some sugared compliment was whispered into an encouraging shell ear. The girl smiled wryly to herself. It seemed her admirers had lost no time in consoling themselves. She wondered if

34

André were among them, and her heart ached.

From the distance came the evening cadences of the slave cabins – the quiet singing of old Bess as she rocked rhythmically on one of the log porches:

> *Ah looked ober Jordan, what did Ah see,*
> *A' comin' fo' ter carry me home?*
> *A band o' angels comin' aftah me*
> *A' comin' fo' ter carry me home.*
>
> *Swing low, sweet chariot,*
> *A' comin' fo' ter carry me home.*
> *Swing low, sweet chariot,*
> *A' comin' fo' ter carry me home.*

Tina called her wayward son from the door of her shack. 'Yo, Moses, git in heah. What is yo doin' out der, chile? Doan yo know de boogie man will git yo?'

A sharp crack on the boy's behind punctuated this statement, then the light darkened abruptly in the cabin.

At the kennels a hound scratched a flea in one ear busily, then bayed lowly at the moon hanging down from the sky like a silver halo. In the stables a horse whinnied nervously. One of the mares is in season, Storm thought. Suddenly the gardens seemed overpowering with their aromatic sensuality. The girl glanced up at Gabriel North.

Gabriel. How appropriate was his name. A big, burly hunk of a man with flaming red hair and a bushy beard and mustache, he had a voice that could boom like a trumpet. His dark brown eyes twinkled when he looked at her, but Storm was not deceived. He was stupid and mean! As stupid and mean as one of those old bulls about which he talked endlessly – brawny and beefy, with huge shoulders, muscular thighs, and large hands calloused from years of hard labor. They were strong, those hands, and wide, with thick fingers covered with little mats of red fuzz. Storm shuddered as she wondered how it would feel to have those

35

hands on her body, her breasts.

The girl was not ignorant of the relationship between a man and a woman, although she might have been had it been left up to her aunt to explain the matter, for Yvette Beauvallet never even made the attempt. It was Mammy who prepared Storm for that side of marriage.

'Ah doan know what's wrong wi' white folks, Miz Storm. Dey act lahke lovin' is sumpin' ter be 'shamed o', lahke ain' nobody but de gempmum 'posed ter enjoy it, lahke it ain' nothin' but a buhden fo' de wimmen. Doan yo believe it, chile. Ah ain' neber knowed a man yet what wonted a cohpse undahneath him. Yose gots ter learn how ter handle yore man, honey. Dat's right. Yose gots ter learn how ter make him happy, or he ain' neber gwine hang 'round long 'nuff fo' yo ter find out what's went wrong,' Mammy prophesied darkly.

'Doan yo pay no 'tention ter dem wimmen gos'pin' at dem pahties. Der ain' nothin' dirty or unnat'ral 'bout it. When yo finds yo de right man, yore body's gwine know what ter do, sho' 'nuff. Doan yo worry none 'bout it, Miz Storm. Yo jes' let ole nature take its couhse, an' yo'all be fine, honey, jes' fine. If'n yore man wonts yo ter pleasure him, why, Lawd, chile, yo jes' push dose ole stories from yore purty haid, an' do lahke yore man say. If'n it doan huht yo none, den der ain' nothin' wrong wi' it.' Mammy nodded wisely. 'Yo 'membah what Ah tells yo now, lamb, yo heah?'

Storm shivered as she recalled the words. She just couldn't imagine submitting to Gabriel North. Why, he was so big she'd probably be crushed beneath him! She wiped her damp palms along the sides of her dress at the thought. Her prospective husband observed the nervous gesture and grinned wickedly to himself in the darkness.

'You ought to be decked out in diamonds, Miss Lesconflair,' he purred softly, his eyes roaming appreciatively over her lithe figure. 'When you're my wife, I'm going

36

to put so many diamonds around your pretty neck you won't be able to stop smiling.'

'*Au contraire, Monsieur* North,' Storm returned icily. 'When I am your wife, I shall have nothing whatsoever about which to smile.'

Gabriel only guffawed loudly, for they both knew she despised him, and they both knew why.

Oh, *maman*, papa! To what have I come? the girl's heart cried out silently; but her parents did not answer. They were dead. The horrible yellow fever had taken them both two years ago, leaving Storm alone.

She could still remember the awful sulphuric smell of the tar buckets burning in the streets of New Orleans when she arrived home frantically from the eastern seminary at which she was enrolled. The urgent summons had come too late, however. *Maman* and papa had already been rowed out to the leper colony off the shores of the city and left there to die. Dear God. Would she never forget that accursed day?

Yvett, *maman*'s older sister, took Storm in at Vaillance, for it was unthinkable to permit the fourteen-year-old girl to live alone at Belle Rive, the virtually deserted plantation that had become her premature inheritance.

An only child, Storm was at first grateful to her aunt and uncle for making all the necessary decisions and arrangements for her during her grief-stricken period of mourning; and too her cousin, André-Louis, whom she loved dearly and to whom she had been betrothed since birth, was there to comfort her and ease her sorrow. It was only gradually things changed.

The first inkling Storm had that all was not as it should have been came when she was informed there was no money for her to return to the expensive academy in the East, nor to embark upon the European tour that had been promised her at graduation. Her father had been heavily in debt at the time of his death, Uncle Pierre explained, but was not able to meet his niece's eyes. The Beauvallets would attempt to retain Belle Rive, he continued, but all the slaves except for her faithful Mammy must be sold.

Storm was shocked by the news and could not believe it. Paul-Eduard Lesconflair had been a meticulous, careful, and successful planter. She would have known otherwise! He would have told her, for she and her father had always been close. Still she had no reason to suspect her uncle of lying then. That came later.

The beautiful, ornate furnishings of the old plantation went next in the months that followed, and finally Belle Rive itself was lost. By then Storm had learned the bitter truth as to why she had been made penniless. It was not papa's fault at all, but Uncle Pierre's doing. Her guardian was nothing more than a drunken wastrel who'd gambled himself, his family, and his home to the brink of destitution. Only Storm's inheritance had prevented them all from being cast into wretched poverty; but even that was not enough.

What small profit he somehow managed to turn through the disposition of his niece's estate Pierre Beauvallet soon threw away on one bad business deal after another. Although his friends were too gentlemanly to press him for repayment of their loans, the bank was not. It sent him a nasty letter threatening to foreclose on his mortgage if he did not pay within thirty days.

In desperation Storm's uncle became involved in an all-night poker game at the Quadroon Ballroom on Royal Street in the *Vieux Carré*. There he lost everything he still possessed to Gabriel North, a Texas rancher who had driven his cattle into New Orleans for slaughter and with whom Pierre was slightly acquainted.

Gabriel North was forty years old, a self-made man, proud of it, and used to getting his own way in life. More than anything else he wanted Storm Lesconflair, the belle of five counties, had wanted her ever since he'd first laid eyes on her at the Robitaille barbecue. There she'd snubbed

38

him pointedly as being unworthy of notice when they'd been introduced. Instead of cooling his ardor, Storm's disinterest had only inflamed it. No woman rebuffed Gabriel North and got away with it!

A black sheep cast out by his family, he'd known the Beauvallets would never consent to him paying court to their niece, nor, in any event, would she have received him. Storm had made that quite plain. Now, however, things had changed. Gabriel had Pierre Beauvallet at his mercy, and he had enticed the Frenchman into the card game for no other purpose.

'Well, Mr Beauvallet.' Gabriel leaned back in his chair and grinned. 'That's quite a nice little stack of IOUs I'm holding. Still I'm a fair man. I'll tell you what – I'll give you one more chance to recoup your losses. All or nothing – how will that be?'

'I – I'm afraid I have nothing left to wager, *monsieur*.'

'No?' Gabriel raised one eyebrow quizzically. 'Seems to me like you've got a right pretty niece if I recall correctly.'

'*Monsieur*! You – you cannot be serious!'

'Aw, shit! There's no need for you to pucker up like a prim old maid who's just had her virginity affronted. I didn't mean it *that* way. I have every intention of marrying the girl if I win.'

'But – but she is engaged to my son. And – and what about my – my IOUs? I would still be ruined!'

Gabriel gave him a sarcastic stare. 'Forget your son, Mr Beauvallet. I doubt he'll have any objections to the match – if made. I can drill the eye out of a buffalo at seventy-five yards. As to the other – hell! Do you really think I'd let my wife's family starve?'

'But – but—'

'Deal the cards, Mr Beauvallet.'

Pierre's first thought after the disastrous poker game was to shoot himself with one of his duelling pistols. He was so drunk at the time, however, that his hand trembled violently, and the ball merely grazed the side of his skull.

'You are even a failure at killing yourself!' Yvette hissed upon running into his study at the sound of the shot and finding her husband slumped over his desk abjectly. 'And you the planter every girl in New Orleans wanted to marry! *Sacré bleu!* They should have been so lucky! What is it this time, your drinking or your gambling?'

'Not now, madam, *s'il vous plaît!*' Pierre moaned, his body consumed by racking sobs. 'We are disgraced, ruined, utterly destroyed! Oh, that poor child. That poor child.'

'What – what do you mean?' Yvette's voice was shrill with horrible trepidation.

'I – I have lost everything! Everything! Including our niece! Oh, *Jesù*, what am I going to tell our son? What am I going to tell our son?'

'*Mon Dieu, mon Dieu!*'

Storm was mortified to think she had been gambled away at cards and told her uncle he could wind up in Under the Hill, New Orleans's slum section, before she'd marry Gabriel North. She soon realized, however, she had no other choice unless she wished to end up there also. Her father had no relatives of which she knew, her mother's and aunt's had been taken during the yellow fever epidemic, and her uncle's had long since disowned him for his ne'er-do-well behavior. There was no one on whose mercy she could fling herself. If Storm did not wed the Texas rancher, she would be as destitute as the Beauvallets, who would be bankrupt.

'Oh, Mammy, Mammy! What am I going to do? What am I going to do?' The girl cried her heart out late into the night after her uncle told her what had come to pass.

'Lamb, mah precious honey-chile, Ah doan know. Ah jes' doan know. Dis heah's a mis'ble day, de wustest; an' yose gots a weary load ter tote, child, a weary load. Look ter me lahke yose gwine haf ter marry dat man, Miz Storm, else yo'll gwine stahve, an' dey's gwine sell dis pore ole wuthless nigger down de riber fo' sho'!'

'Oh, no, Mammy! No!' Storm hugged her plump nurse tightly, her throat choked with ragged sobs. 'I won't let them do that! I won't, Mammy! I won't! Oh, Mammy, Mammy, I wish I were dead!'

'Daid?' Nawum, naw, yo doan. Doan yo eber wish fo' things lahke dat, honey. It's bad luck, an' dat ole debil will git yo fo' sho'. Mistah Nawth, he – he ain' so bad, lamb.' Mammy tried hard to lessen the bitter blow. 'Dey say he come from a fine ole fambly in Kaintuck. He gots good mannahs too. He brung yo some flowahs an' a box o' dem bonbons when he come ter call, din he? Yassum. A woman needs dem lil' 'tentions, chile. Ah 'spects he might be a gempmum undahneath all dat Texas talk after all. He sho' do talk big, doan he, honey? Mus' be awful proud o' hisseff. Well, dey say he gots money ter buhn, so Ah 'pose he gots sumpin' ter brag 'bout. Dey say he own a big ole fahm out der in de West, gots lots o' dem bulls an' cows an' whatsech. Dey say he come inter New Awl'ns once a yeah ter sell dem. Dey say—'

'Who says, Mammy? Who says all this about that horrid man?'

'Why, Lawd, Miz Storm. Wheah is yo mem'ry, chile? Eberbody in town knows dat's de gempmum what ruined pore ole Massah Raiford at cahds an' put a bullet in de son's haid when de boy called him out fo' it.'

'*Jesù*,' the girl breathed. 'That *Monsieur* North! Why, how can I marry him, Mammy, knowing that about him? Why, Tommy Lee Raiford was one of my beaux!'

'Yassum, an' yo din care a rap 'bout him none eithah, pore boy. Why, yo din shed one teah ober him at de foon'ral when he was a'lyin' der daid in his cawffin! An', 'sides, Ah doan rec'lect none as how yo was too upset when Mistah André shot pore Miz Letty's husbun', Mistah Raoul, 'cause he 'cused Mistah André o' cheatin' at cahds.' Mammy's face was stern. 'An' Ah'm a'tellin' yo now, lamb, dat if'n yose gots yore haht set on Mistah André, yo bes' put dat out o' yore mind. Ah knows yo love him, an' he loves yo, but he cain' marry yo now, honey. Yo ain' gots no money, an' he's gwine haf ter git hisseff a rich wife to git his fambly out o' dis mess!'

'Oh, no, Mammy! You're wrong! You're wrong! André wouldn't do something like that! I just know he wouldn't! You wait and see. He won't let them get away with this!'

The next morning at breakfast, however, André-Louis announced he was riding over to pay a call on Clarisse Martinique. Storm felt as though the floor had suddenly dropped out from beneath her feet, and she wanted to die. Mammy was right! André had no intention of preventing her marriage to Gabriel North. If she didn't wed him, the Texas rancher would ruin the Beauvallets financially, and their old and proud family name would be disgraced. André couldn't permit that. His father had already done enough damage as it was. No, Storm must marry Gabriel North, and he, André, must find himself a wealthy bride, or they would all find themselves poverty-stricken. It was too bad, but *c'est la vie*.

'I'm sorry, *chérie*,' André apologized uncomfortably after he'd explained the matter. 'But you see how it is.'

'Oh, *oui*, I see,' Storm responded bitterly. 'I see only all too well. What a shallow love you bore me, cousin. I am fortunate to have escaped it!'

The girl came back with a start to the gardens of Vaillance as her fiancé suddenly threw away his cigar and steered her deftly toward one of the more secluded private arbors. To her heartbreak and chagrin she realized it was one she'd often shared with André-Louis in the evenings.

'Let me go!' She struggled against her intended frantically. 'This is most improper, *Monsieur* North, as well you know. Please release me at once so that I may return to the house before we are missed!'

Gabriel only laughed. 'Hell, the whole damned ballroom

42

knows where we are by now. They expect it. They think we're in love, so don't think your unruly tongue and a little resistance are going to put me off, young lady. I like a woman with spirit, as I've told you before. Yeah, I'm going to have a real fine time breaking you to the bit, you wild French filly. You just give me a taste of what I've been promised, and I won't have to use my whip and spurs too hard. Christ! I want you. I guess you're just about the prettiest little gal this side of the Rio Grande.'

'*Mon Dieu!*' Storm's mouth tightened indignantly. 'Do you think I care for your flattery? *Sacré bleu!*' Her voice dripped with scorn. 'How dare you touch me? Take your hands off me at once! Why, you're nothing but a – a cowpoke with some old – old *farm* in some Godforsaken place out West!'

'Maybe so.' He studied her speculatively. 'But that "farm," as you call it, is going to be your home within the year, Miss Lesconflair.'

'I certainly hope you had a full house that night, *Monsieur* North.' Storm tossed her head arrogantly as she tried to yank away from him. 'Because I promise the one I make for you in the future will be empty!'

'You think so, huh? Well, no matter. I still mean to have you for my wife, and nothing is going to save you from that – not tonight or any other night!'

Abruptly he caught her hair with one hand, roughly twisted her face up to his, and ground his mouth down on hers hard. His tongue forced her resisting lips open, ravaging, pillaging, taking that which she refused to give. Storm thought she would swoon. She had been kissed before, but never like this! Even André-Louis had never kissed her like this! The blood sang violently in her ears as she buckled against him. Her heart pounded savagely in her breast pressed up next to his own. Oh, God, how many women had he kissed to learn what he was doing to her with his mouth?

'There.' He suddenly pushed her away, panting heavily as he stared hungrily at her quivering figure in the darkness. 'Take that to bed, you little touch-me-not tease, and think about how it'll be when it's *me* lying next to you!'

Storm turned and ran, still shaking all over from the strange sensations he'd unleashed within herself. Angry and frightened, she wiped her lips off, as though she could somehow eradicate the burning brand Gabriel North had left upon them. The *cochon*! The cad! She hated him! She decided she would rather suffer a fate worse than death than marry him! Too late Storm remembered Mammy's oft-repeated words of warning:

'Chile, doan eber wish fo' things in angah, 'cause yo jes' might git what yo asked fo'!'

3

Gabriel left Vaillance the next day without seeing Storm again. There was no need. He was safely assured of her imminent arrival in Texas. Half the incriminating IOUs he held over her uncle's head had been burned yesterday in the privacy of Pierre's study, but the other half Storm herself would destroy after the wedding, which was to take place within the year at Gabriel's ranch. The Beauvallets had not liked the idea, but Gabriel had been adamant. He'd already laid out the cash for the elaborate engagement party in New Orleans. That was enough. He wanted Storm to become his bride in his own territory. He was sick to death of the haughty Louisianans, had already lingered overlong among them, damned Southerners! They reminded him too much of his father – his father, who had disowned him after a heated argument and banished him from their Kentucky plantation to make his own way in the world.

He stopped in town to pick up the presents he'd ordered for his children: a dress for Cathy, although he doubted she'd wear it, and a book for Joe Jack, although Gabriel doubted his son would read it. Lord! How angry they'd both be when they discovered he meant to marry again. Well, it would serve his children right, the ungrateful whelps! Just itching for him to die so that they could get their hands on his ranch, were they? Well, they'd tread warily in his presence now – with a new bride in the picture, one young enough to give him another heir and cut them out of their shares entirely if he so desired. No, those two vultures wouldn't be at all happy about the forthcoming wedding! Gabriel chuckled to himself at the thought of their faces when they heard the news. Storm Lesconflair was certainly going to be in for one hell of a time as their stepmother!

Joe Jack was a lazy good-for-nothing with a sly cunning his insolent grin masked well. He thought himself a lady's man, and indeed Gabriel was sure many of the women on the ranch had spread their legs for his son's easy charm. Everybody liked Joe Jack. Cathy, on the other hand, was an uppity female with a stride like a man's and the manners of such. She took no pride in her appearance, roaming about the ranch in a pair of breeches and one of her brother's cast-off shirts, a wide-brimmed hat hanging down her back, a thin brown cigar dangling out of one corner of her mouth. Gabriel sighed at the image his daughter evoked, but he could do nothing with her; and his lips tightened into a grim line when he remembered the reason why.

It had happened fifteen years ago, but the real story started even earlier than that, so his mind went back, back to the beginning.

Cathy wasn't born then. Just he, Louise (his first wife), and Joe Jack came to Texas. *Texas!* Gabriel had been intrigued about the place ever since he'd first heard the name. He packed them all up after the argument with his father and set out for the vast expanse of land that bordered on the Rio Grande and to which two nations, the United States and Mexico, laid claim. It took him a long time to find the spot he wanted, but at last Gabriel discovered that for which he was looking nearly two hundred miles northwest of San Antonio. The land lay just outside a dusty one-road town known as Santa Rosa. *Santa Rosa*, Saint Rose. Gabriel almost laughed at the name; it was so absurd! The town was nothing but a few squalid adobe shacks and a small church – or mission really – then. The saint, if she existed and knew of it, could only be offended. But, Jesus, at dusk the land for miles in all directions seemed almost alive when bathed in the flaming, vibrant shade of rose that was the setting sun.

46

It didn't matter to Gabriel that the land already belonged to a dirt-poor Mexican family. He ran them off and settled in the adobe cottage they'd built, keeping their name for the place, *Tierra Rosa*, Rose Land. That was the beginning.

There, that year, Cathy was born, and Louise died giving her life. Gabriel never forgave his daughter for that. He purchased some steer and a bull, and by the time Cathy was two years old Gabriel was one of the richest ranchers in Texas. He sent to Galveston for the finest of lumbers then, not content with the adobe house, and built a huge, sprawling antebellum mansion.

Three years later – he could still recall the very day – the Mexican family returned, proud, defiant, and waving a hard-fought-for deed in their hands, the deed to Gabriel's land. Only it wasn't his land. Some tyrannical government official with a knowledge of settlers' rights and a sharp eye for keeping the restrictions on Texas land to the letter had seen to that, stamping the deed with a seal that was legal all right under Mexican law; but that meant nothing to Gabriel.

He saw red, bellowing like a bull in his rage. 'You Goddamned son-of-a-bitch! I've been here five years now. You think that little piece of paper is going to put me off this place I've worked so hard to build? Why, you frigging bastard! You've got some nerve; I'll say that for you!'

By this time the ranch hands had gathered round to watch the proceedings. Gabriel, however, was not aware of them just yet, nor of his small daughter, who'd crept nearer to see what was occurring, her bright, curious mind far advanced for a five-year-old.

The Mexican man was not to be stared down. 'This is my land.' He indicated the sweeping terrain. 'Which you stole. I have a paper now proving it. You and your men go from here. ¡Ahora! Now!' He waved his musket threateningly.

Gabriel only laughed, a short, ugly sound. 'You see that, boys? This greaser-pig is threatening me. Doesn't hardly seem proper, does it, a no-'count son-of-a-Mexican-whore aiming a gun at a white man?'

'Naw, Boss, it shore don't.' They all nodded in agreement, grinning.

Then before the Mexican man recognized his danger, Gabriel pulled his pistol and shot him right between the eyes. The Mexican man fell to the ground, blood spurting from the mortal wound. His horror-filled wife ran toward her husband's body, screaming in anguish. His son stood rooted to the earth, stunned, disbelieving, and terrified.

'¡*Bastardos*! ¡*Cabrones*!' the grief-stricken woman shouted, tears streaming from her eyes as she glanced upward at the circle of men. '¡*Asesinos de mi esposo*! I'll kill you!'

She suddenly ran toward Gabriel, her fingers curled into ferocious claws. He grabbed her wrists, noting her heaving brown breasts where the ruffles of her loose *camisa* scooped downward, revealing a tiny rivulet of sweat that trickled along the hollow between her melon-ripe mounds in the hot Indian summer sun.

'Jesus! You're a feisty critter. I always did hear you Mexican sluts were a hot, spicy bunch. What do you say, you steaming *tortilla*, is that the truth?' He gazed hard into her frightened eyes, then observed with a shock that they were bright blue, like sapphires. 'Christ! You're not a Mexican! You're a white woman! What kind of a white woman would marry a greaser-pig?'

'Only a whore, Boss.' Gabriel's men leered openly. 'Let's have some fun with the bitch. She spread her legs for that Mexican bastard. She oughta spread 'em for us too!'

'Yeah.' Gabriel licked his lips with anticipation at the thought, his loins aroused by the sight of the struggling woman and the murder he'd just committed. 'I do believe you're right, boys.'

They laughed raucously as, in his bloodlust, he ripped the woman's blouse down to expose her breasts. His free hand cupped one cruelly, fingers rubbing greedily, hurtfully at the dark nipple.

'No, *señor*!' The woman's voice was frantic as she sought to yank away. 'Please do not do this terrible thing. We'll go and never come back. Take the land. Take it! Oh, please, please! My boy—' She nodded toward her silent son, discerning his fear-filled eyes.

Gabriel paid no heed to her pleading sobs. Instead he threw her down upon the hard-baked earth, then shoved her skirt and petticoats up roughly. The last thing she ever remembered was him towering over her, smirking, before he unfastened his pants and raped her savagely. When he was finished, he gave her to the ranch hands, who used her as crudely as their boss had done. It was some time before they realized the woman was dead. After awhile they noticed her son still standing there, vomiting quietly onto the ground. The boy raised his head slowly. His eyes met those of Gabriel's daughter, Cathy, who was still crouched, motionless, on the front porch.

'Hey, Boss,' the men called, 'whaddaya want us to do with the kid? Shall we kill him too?'

'No, he's just a boy,' Gabriel replied as he reached into the pocket of the dead Mexican man's shirt, too intent on removing the fatal deed to pay much attention to the words of his men. 'What can he do – tell all? Who'd believe him? A little half-breed bastard like that?'

Gabriel thrust the piece of paper into his vest, then turned toward the house. It was then he saw his daughter, a witness to the entire ugly episode. He started toward her, but the child shrank away from him, appalled, horrified. For the first time in his life Gabriel was filled with sick revulsion over his behavior.

'Cathy! Cathy!' He held out his arms, stumbling forward blindly; but he was too late. The girl had already run from him.

Afterward Gabriel never really knew for certain how much of the brutal day his daughter recalled, but every now and then he'd feel her eyes on him, arrogant, haughty liquid brown eyes that flashed with contempt and disgust when she looked at him. When he admonished her for her rudeness, telling her she ought to have more respect, her mouth only sneered with derision, curling with distaste as she laughed scornfully and strode off, arms swinging at her sides like a man's.

It did not take Gabriel long to understand that whatever she remembered had affected her greatly, that she despised and abhorred him for it, and that there was nothing he could do about it. The damage had already been done.

Because of this he poured all his affection onto his son, Joe Jack, who knew nothing of the barbarous affair and who, when he learned of it, only grinned slyly and claimed his father had done the right thing.

'I only wish I'd been there to get a piece of that tail, pa,' he droned lazily, his dark eyes gleaming with speculation.

The remark put Gabriel in a temper. 'You wouldn't have known what to do with it, boy!'

The smile left Joe Jack's face, but he was careful to turn away before his father could see he'd been wounded by the cutting jibe. Joe Jack's emotions toward Gabriel were conflicting. On the one hand he admired his father and wanted to be just like him, but on the other he lacked Gabriel's bullish strength and so hated his father for being more of a man than he himself was. Joe Jack *was* clever and cunning, however, and he vowed someday he'd best the old man in one of these encounters, for pa simply couldn't tolerate being beaten at *anything*!

In blithe ignorance of this Gabriel rode on toward Tierra Rosa with two of the worst presents he could have chosen for his children simply because he understood neither of them. He wanted to erase the pain and horror that still lurked in Cathy's eyes and see her dressed like a lady for a change; and he wanted Joe Jack to know more of the world than just the rough realms of Texas. Gabriel knew in his heart neither of his children, despite his disdain of it, would have been acceptable to the Southern society he'd left behind in Kentucky; and while he didn't regret his decision to leave, he did wish for Tierra Rosa to acquire some of the stately grace of his father's plantation. That and his desire to possess her were his sole reasons for forcing Storm Lesconflair to become his bride. For Gabriel North they were reasons enough.

Storm and Mammy had sailed from New Orleans to Galveston. Now they rumbled along a dusty road in the stagecoach that had stopped in Houston earlier that morning and that would take them as far as San Antonio where Gabriel was to meet them. The high wheels of the vehicle seemed to hit every rut and mudhole in their path. Storm, who was used to traveling by steamboat, was decidedly uncomfortable. She clenched her teeth together tightly at the jolting of the carriage and raised her rose-scented handkerchief to her face once more, trying to keep from inhaling the grit that whirled up from the clattering rims of the churning wheels. She wished fervently she'd worn a heavier veil. She pressed her back against the wall of the cushioned seat wearily, glad this was nearly the last stage of her long journey. There was no turning back now. In a few days she would be the bride of Gabriel North. Her heart ached bitterly in her breast at the knowledge and the deeply hurtful thought of André-Louis's vile betrayal.

The elderly couple across the aisle was watching her and Mammy curiously. Storm closed her eyes to avoid their gaze. The woman, Mrs Thatcher, nudged her husband covertly.

'Poor child. She seems dreadfully unhappy. Henry,' she whispered, frowning, 'do you suppose that old Negress is the cause? She certainly looks like a formidable dragon!'

'There now, Naomi. It's none of our business, I'm sure.' Mr Thatcher mopped the sweat from his brow and pushed his spectacles, which had slid down his nose in the heat, back into place. He hoped his wife wasn't intending to meddle. Naomi had a penchant for running other people's lives. 'Besides, the darky is a slave. You know that. I doubt seriously she is the cause of the young girl's distress. Shush now, Naomi. We have problems enough of our own without delving into the troubles of others!'

'Yes, I suppose you're right,' Mrs Thatcher agreed, but was less than satisfied all the same.

Storm opened her eyes. The couple across the aisle were still studying her. They were an odd pair. The husband was short, balding, and had a nervous tic in his cheek. His hands were never still, and he kept poking his head out the window, a worried expression on his countenance. The wife was tall and rawboned, but with the kind of beauty Storm was to learn was predominant in the West – the kind of beauty that stemmed from hard times and hot sun and the type of serenity that came with the acceptance of them both.

The girl sighed audibly.

'I beg your pardon,' Mrs Thatcher said.

'I – I'm sorry,' Storm apologized politely. 'I'm afraid I was only sighing.'

'Miz Storm is a lady. She doan speak ter strangahs what ain' been prop'ly innahduced,' Mammy declared stoutly, her lower lip pushed out twice its normal size with disapproval.

'It's all right, Mammy.' Storm hastened to make amends for her nurse's rudeness. 'I'm sure this nice woman didn't mean any harm.'

'No, indeed not, my dear.' Mrs Thatcher smiled courteously, but her voice was firm, as though it would brook no argument, when she then observed, 'You must be newly come from the East. I think you'll find customs vastly different out here in the West.'

Storm knew it showed bad breeding to continue the

conversation, but she was eager to learn more about Texas, which would be her new home, and perhaps things here were *not* the same, so she ignored Mammy's belligerent glare and spoke again.

'We're – we're from the South actually, New Orleans. I'm Storm Lesconflair, and this is Mammy.'

'So nice to meet you both, my dear.' Mrs Thatcher nodded graciously, although she was a trifle reserved toward Mammy. 'Henry and Naomi Thatcher are the names, from San Antonio. New Orleans is a lovely city. Henry and I visit it often. Henry does all his banking there. Is this your first time out West?'

'Yes – yes, it is,' Storm chatted. 'It all seems so – so strange and – and overwhelming! I'm afraid we know very little about it, so I hope you'll forgive our ignorance.'

'Of course, my dear. I understand just how you feel. Texas *does* take some getting used to, but she'll win your heart in the end, I think. Why, I remember when we first came out in 1836, I thought I'd bake to death, die of thirst, or be scalped by Indians!'

'*Sainte Marie*!' Storm breathed.

'Oh, I didn't mean to frighten you.' Mrs Thatcher permitted herself another small smile. 'It's really not all that terrible. The heat's not so bad, once you get used to it, and there are lots of rivers and springs, so you won't *really* die of thirst. We have a well on our property. Most folks do. And of course the government has pushed the Indians further west, so an attack in town is rare. They're more likely to occur out on the range – where the forts aren't so close – and it's mostly the Apache and Comanche who are dangerous, but even they've been forced from some of their lands.'

'Isn't that – isn't that cruel?' Storm questioned hesitantly, not wishing to offend.

'Cruel? Why, my dear, they're only savages, barbarians really. Why, if you could see some of these red devils a'whooping and a'hollering, all painted up, feathers sticking out all over them, and stinking of bear grease, animal hides and Lord only knows what else, you'd know they're hardly human, although some of them have adapted quite well to civilization and even trade with the *tejanos*, as they call us. No, it's no more cruel than the South's practice of slavery, I assure you.'

Since Storm had not been raised to believe slavery was evil, she thought no more about the Indians being driven from their homes.

Instead she asked, 'Do they – do they really scalp people?'

'Yes, indeed, although why any of them have need of more hair is beyond me. Some of them have it hanging down to their waists! But you needn't worry, my dear. The government will protect you.'

Mammy snorted, as though she considered this highly unlikely, but Mrs Thatcher went on, unruffled.

'And naturally there are the Texas Rangers. They're our lawmen, and Lord help the fool who crosses one of *them*!' She paused a moment, considering. 'Yes, we've survived, and we've done well out West. There's plenty of opportunity out here – for those who aren't afraid to take it. Why, back in Boston, Henry was just a desk clerk, but now he *owns* a hotel in San Antonio.' Mrs Thatcher's ample bosom swelled with pride. 'Don't you, Henry?'

Henry mumbled something under his breath, mopped his brow and pushed up his spectacles once more, then gave another glance out the window, twisting his hands nervously in his lap all the while. Storm watched his fingers entwine, come apart, then clasp together again. She wondered if he ever relaxed.

Beside the girl, Mammy still sat in stony silence, unrelenting criticism written all over her sulking countenance. Now she grumbled under her breath.

'Pull down dat shade, Miz Storm. Dat mean ole sun's

54

gwine make de freckles pop out all ober yore purty skin, and der woan be naw strawburry lotion or mashed coocumbahs out heah fo' me ter fix it. Ah 'spects dey ain' eben gots naw buttahmilk. Dis is de wustest place Ah eber did see, nothin' but dat ole hot sun an' dat dust what's 'bout ter choke me. Yassum, Ah cain jes' feel it a'wukin' its way down inside o' mah ches', an' it sho' is mis'ble, Ah tells yo. Ah cain' eben ketch mah breaf fo' dis dust an' dis heat.

'Miz Storm, what yo brang us ter dis awful place fo', honey? It ain' nothin' lahke New Awl'ns. Heah yo are jes' a'gabbin' away wi' dem ole strangahs an' him nothin' but a wuthless jumped-up portah, eben if he do own a hotel. Ah swan. Yore pore ole mama would a'tuhn ober in her grabe if'n she knowed how porely Ah done raised yo. Wheah is yore mannahs, chile? Ah din raise yo ter talk ter no strangahs what ain' been prop'ly innahduced. Yo is a lady, Miz Storm, not dat white trash riffraff what takes up wi'. dem swamp rats on de riber. Ah 'spects nex' yo'all run off wi' dem Injuns she was a'talkin' 'bout, an' nex' thing Ah knows mah pore lamb woan haf a haih lef' on her purty haid! Yassum, dis heah's a mis'ble day, de wustest, an' Ah'm gwine tell Mistah Nawth dat when Ah sees him. Lawd, Miz Storm, pull down dat shade dis minute!'

'Hush, Mammy! Hush your mouth this instant before the Thatchers hear you!' Storm hissed quietly, mortified. She yanked the blind down impatiently with a sharp little crack, then gave Mrs Thatcher, who was looking at them oddly, a half-smile. The girl cleared her throat, then queried overloudly, 'I wonder how much further it is?'

'Quite a ways, I'm afraid,' Mrs Thatcher answered. 'Texas is a *very* big state.'

Her voice contained a distinct chill that had not been present earlier. Storm was certain the woman had overheard Mammy's remarks.

Some moments later, after a timid glance at the old Negress, Henry rolled the shade back up and poked his head out the window once more. He felt like wringing his wife's neck, but he was petrified of Naomi. Yesterday he'd picked up a huge sum of money that had been transferred from his bank in New Orleans to Galveston where it'd awaited his arrival for conveyance to his hotel in San Antonio. He'd pleaded with Naomi to wait until they could get an armed escort to conduct them and the payroll home, but she'd only laughed at his fears, as she'd done for the past twelve years, claiming they'd be perfectly safe in the stagecoach. After all, drawing attention to themselves was foolish, she'd said. Why invite trouble? she'd said. She wanted to get home as soon as possible, she'd said. She was tired of Galveston, she'd said. No one had ever bothered them before, she'd said, and *he* was a frightened little squirrel.

Since Henry did indeed resemble a squirrel, he'd sniffed, his dignity and manhood seriously affronted, and purchased the two tickets, telling her all the while she would rue the day she'd refused to listen to him. He just knew sooner or later their incredible good luck in transporting their hotel funds was going to run out.

Naomi, on the other hand, thought Henry a fool, a man afraid of his own shadow. Good heavens! One had to take risks, or one never got anywhere! Why, Henry wouldn't even have had the gumption to open up the hotel in the first place if it hadn't been for her. No, *he* would have been content to shuffle along as a desk clerk, and they would have been no better off than when they'd lived in Boston. It had been *her* idea for Henry to ask for a higher position there, and when they'd fired him for the presumption, it had been *her* idea to come West, despite all her misgivings about the horrible stories she'd heard. Yes, *she* had backbone, and Henry was just a frightened little squirrel. What she'd ever seen in him she couldn't imagine. Who could possibly know about the money they were carrying? Who indeed?

*   *   *

Luther Barlow squinted his eyes against the glare of the sun, shifted the wad of tobacco he was chewing, and spit on the ground.

'Zeke,' he drawled to his brother, 'you shore that feller was right about the old geezer bein' on the stage?'

'Yep, shore as I'm sittin' here, Luther.' Zeke Barlow scratched his scraggly, unshaven face with one grimy hand, then wiped a bit of yellow-stained drool from his chin. His aim hadn't been as good as his brother's.

'You'd better be,' Elijah Barlow growled. 'I ain't riskin' my neck fer nothin'!'

'Shut up, 'Lij!' Luther glanced at him sharply. 'You may be my brother, but I'm gonna put a bullet in yore back if you git trigger-happy like you done the last time.'

'Huh!' Elijah snorted, unimpressed. 'Ma'd see you six feet under first!'

'Well, let's make it quick and clean,' Billy, the youngest Barlow brother, spoke up. 'I'm in need of some good likker and an easy female – if you know what I mean.'

Luther gave a hard stare. 'Is that all you ever think about? Damned fool! You'd best keep yore head on this job, Billy, I'm warnin' you. I swear, yore about the silliest pup I ever did see. I dunno what possessed ma to let you join up with us to begin with.'

''Cause I'm her son, same as you.' Billy grinned, unabashed.

The others hooted with disgust.

'Yore jest a no-good punk kid, and don'tcha fergit it!' Elijah sneered.

'Quiet, fools! Here she comes!' Zeke barked.

The Barlows were a thoroughly dangerous gang of men. None of them was bright enough to have carried out any elaborate crimes on his own, but together, with their mother as the brains, they had committed some of the most dastardly deeds on record in various law offices throughout the territory. *Wanted, Dead or Alive* posters were plastered all over the state of Texas, and each of them had a price on his head many lawmen had tried but failed to claim.

Now they pulled their bandanas down over their ugly countenances and drew their pistols. Then they charged after the unsuspecting vehicle.

Storm had almost managed to doze off in the heat to the rhythmic swaying of the stagecoach when she was abruptly jolted from her dazed state by the sound of gunshots and the clattering of horses' hooves beating a furious tattoo over the hard-baked earth.

'*Mon Dieu*! What is going on out there? Why are we traveling so fast?'

Henry Thatcher's squirrel-like face turned a ghastly shade of white at the commotion.

'I warned you, Naomi! I warned you!' he squeaked in a high shrill voice of alarm, not bothering to respond to Storm's question. 'We'll all be killed! Killed, I tell you! I warned you, Naomi, but you wouldn't listen! "You're just a frightened little squirrel, Henry," you said. "We've never been attacked before, Henry," you said. "No one will know about the money, Henry," you said.'

'Money? What money?' Storm managed to ask.

By this time the vehicle was reeling along at such a dangerous, rocking pace Storm could barely keep her seat. She bounced around on the cushioned seat like a piece of driftwood on a madding surf, feeling suddenly very sick to her stomach.

'Henry sometimes carries large amounts of money back and forth between Galveston and San Antonio – for the hotel, you know.' Mrs Thatcher's sun-browned skin had gone as pale as her husband's with fear.

'Do you – do you mean someone is chasing us, is – is going to – to *attack* us for this money?' Storm had not yet grasped the meaning of the shots.

'My dear, I'm afraid that's right.'

Storm gasped with stunned horror as the body of the man who had been riding shotgun tumbled without warning past the window of the stagecoach. His arms were flailing spastically, and blood was spewing from the fatal wound in his chest.

'*Jesù*!' the girl cried. '*Jesù*!'

She tried to stick her head out the opening to see what had become of him, but Henry grabbed her, squealing excitedly,

'Are you trying to kill yourself, young lady? Get down! Get down on the floor of the coach at once!'

'Oh, Lawd, Miz Storm! Oh, Lawd, Miz Storm! We's all gwine ter be killed!' Mammy blubbered as she heaved her considerable bulk off the padded bench to crouch down in the aisle beside the others, who were crammed together like boxed chocolates between the seats. 'We's all gwine ter be killed! Oh, Lawd, oh, Lawd, haf mercy! Ah jes' knowed naw good would come o' us bein' in dis awful place! Fust de heat as hot as de debil, an' den de dust what lahked ter choke me, an' now dis! Dat ole woman din tell yo nothin' 'bout dis, Miz Storm! She jes' rambled on 'bout dem Injuns what would lif' de haih right off o' yore haid an' how not ter worry 'cause de guv'men' was gwine ter perteck yo! But she din say one wud 'bout dis! Nawum, she din. Ah jes' knowed she wasn' tellin' us de truf 'bout dis har'ble place, dat naw-coun' wife o' dat wuthless jumped-up portah what pro'bly doan eben own a hotel in de fust place! Oh, Lawd, oh, Lawd! Dis is de mos' mis'ble day o' mah life! Yassum, de wustest! Miz Storm, Ah ain' neber gwine ter fo'give yo fo' brangin' me ter dis tur'ble ole place! Nawum, Ah sho' ain'! Ah—'

'Oh, hush, Mammy! Hush!' Storm snapped, shaking with terror. Nothing in her life had ever prepared her for anything like this. Why, in New Orleans people had actually laughed at Wild West stories! 'Surely they won't harm us. Three women and a defenseless old man!'

'We – we must try to be brave, my dear,' Mrs Thatcher moaned.

The sobs choked in Storm's throat as she gazed into the elderly woman's wide, terrified eyes.

'*Sacré bleu!*'

Storm heard several loud thuds on the roof and saw two riderless horses careening away wildly from the vehicle, but she did not understand the meaning of it until the stagecoach drew slowly to a halt. Her heart pounded violently in her breast, and the kid gloves on her hands were soaked with sweat.

'You inside. Come out with yore hands up,' a gravelly voice commanded harshly.

Storm looked helplessly at the Thatchers. Henry's tic was twitching so fast in his cheek he appeared to have a hoard of winter nuts stored within. His hand trembled visibly as it moved to the door handle. He gave his wife a glance of utter despair and reproach before he stepped outside and assisted her down from the vehicle. Storm followed them as best she could, hanging onto the sides of the doorjamb to keep from falling before she turned to aid Mammy, who was lumbering out with difficulty.

There were four outlaws. Storm thought she'd never seen anyone as dirty and uncouth in all her life as those four men. Surely not even the New Orleans dock workers or the Cajun swamp rats had been this filthy!

'Well, wouldya look at that!' One of them swaggered forward. 'If it ain't the hotel man and his wife from San Antonio.' He waved a revolver at them insolently. 'All right, you old buzzard. We ain't got time to waste. Where in the hell's the dough?'

'I – I don't know what you're talking about,' Henry stammered nervously.

'You hear that, boys,' the man called to the others. 'Squirrel-face says he dunno what I'm talkin' about.'

'Mebbe you need to refresh his mem'ry a little, Luther,' one of them replied, a leering grin on his gruesome face.

'Now that's a fact, Zeke. That purely is a fact.' Luther appeared to deliberate on this for a moment. 'Whaddaya think it would take to persuade the old coot to talk and quit wastin' our time?'

Before any of them could respond another one of the men aimed his gun at the stagecoach driver, who was standing to one side of the passengers, and pulled the trigger. There was a deafening roar. The driver crumpled slowly to the ground in a pool of blood.

'Gawddamn it, 'Lij!' Luther shouted wrathfully. 'I warned you!'

Storm stared stupidly at the body of the driver, not comprehending the blood seeping languidly across the earth in a rivulet of bubbling crimson. Then she gave a small gasp, muffled quickly by the rose-scented handkerchief she held to her trembling lips before turning away to shield her eyes from the hideous sight.

'So what?' Elijah jeered. 'Why don't you see if the old fool remembers now.'

Luther turned back to Henry. 'Well?'

'Please.' Henry mopped his brow and pushed his spectacles up with fingers that quivered. 'If I – if I tell you where the money is, will you let the rest of us go unharmed?'

Luther chewed his wad of tobacco, then spit squarely in the dust between Henry's feet.

'Shore, squirrel-face, shore thin'.' He grinned.

'In my – my suitcase on top of – of the stagecoach. It has a – a false bottom,' Henry stuttered hurriedly. 'The money's in there.'

Luther motioned with his revolver. 'Billy, git up there, and see if the old bastard's tellin' the truth.'

The youngest member of the gang dismounted and scrambled up the side of the vehicle. Storm watched with dismay as he tossed down her trunks. They split open, spilling her clothes out in disarray. She blushed with shame at the sight of her ruffled corsets, pantalettes, and petticoats lying scattered in the dirt, but the men paid no attention to them. After a moment Billy giggled with delight.

'Whoooeee! It's here, jest like the old man said,' he crowed, throwing the money up in the air as though he'd gone crazy.

'Fool!' Luther snapped curtly. 'Now pick that up. Well, squirrel face, it looks like you was tellin' the truth after all.'

'Now you'll – you'll let us go, won't you, just like you promised?' Henry queried, wringing his hands.

'Shore, squirrel-face, jest like I promised.'

The men started loading the money in their saddlebags. Storm began to breathe a little easier.

'You poor excuse for a man!' Naomi hissed in her husband's ear. 'Are you just going to stand there and let those filthy outlaws rob us blind? That's six months' worth of funding there! We'll lose our hotel and everything else for which we've worked so hard! You make me sick! I don't know why I ever married you!'

'Because, Naomi.' Henry screwed up his courage. 'You – you like to bully people!'

'Why, Henry Thatcher! I don't know how you can say such a thing! Why, I'm one of the kindest human beings who ever lived. I donate my old clothes to the needy; I bake pies for the women's bazaar for the church; and I host a charity ball once every year!'

'You find homes for lost kittens, too, but you're *still* a meddler and a bully. If it weren't for *you*, we wouldn't be in this mess!'

'And if *you* were any kind of man whatsoever, you'd pull out that little pistol you carry in your vest pocket and shoot those dirty criminals before you'd let them take one cent of our hard-earned money!'

'And endanger all our lives?'

'Don't be a fool, Henry? Do you really think those men are going to let us go? They've already killed the driver and the guard! Get out your gun! By God, if you won't, I will!'

'No, Naomi! Stop! Stop!'

'Look out, Luther! The old geezer's gotta pistol!'

Luther whirled, raised his revolver, and blew Henry Thatcher's bald head off.

'Oh, my God! My God!' Naomi screamed. 'Henry! Henry!' His brains and blood spattered across the bosom of her dress and dripped from her outstretched hands. 'Animals! Pigs! Murderers!' She suddenly ran at Luther, crying, wailing, her fingers curled into punishing talons as she clawed wildly at his face, tearing away his protective bandana. 'I'm going to remember you!' she sobbed. 'Do you hear me? I'm going to remember you!'

'Gawddamn it!' Luther swore, trying to fight her off, while the others stood watching and sniggering.

He grabbed her arms, pinioning them roughly behind her back. His eyes narrowed with anger. One hand felt gingerly the shredded flesh her scratches had left upon his cheeks. The tiny furrows stung something fierce.

'You don't value yore skin much, do you, bitch?' He smacked her a ringing blow. 'That ain't the way to handle a man, honey, but I guess yore so damned dried up you've jest fergotten how it's done. Jesus!' He thrust her away in disgust. 'I bet old squirrel-face would druther have got it off by hisself!'

'Hey, Luther,' Billy hallooed. 'Take that stupid hat and veil off the other one so's we can git a look at her. She don't 'pear to be no prune.'

'Naw, yo doan! Doan yo tech one haih on mah lamb's haid!' Mammy warned, a martial gleam in her eye as she moved toward Storm protectively. 'Yo'll ain' nothin' but white trash riffraff, an' Miz Storm is a lady!'

'You hear that, Luther?' Zeke howled indignantly. 'This here nigger done called us white trash!'

'Yassah, Ah sho' did, an' yo sho' is. Yo'all done got what yo come fo', so yo jes' be moseyin' on 'bout yore bizness. Yo'all done kilt dem three gempmums, an' we is jes' three pore ole wimmen what cain' do yo naw hahm.'

'You hear that, Luther?' Zeke huffed again. 'This here nigger is givin' us orders.'

'Yassah, Ah sho' is. Now git! Git on down dat road afore Ah lose mah tempah!'

'You hear that, Luther?'

'Yeah, I hear! I hear! Shut up, Zeke, and let me think!'

'Hey, Luther. I thought you was gonna take off that girlie's hat and veil.' Billy pouted. 'I ain't never had me a real *lady* before.'

'Didn't you hear what I jest told Zeke? Close yore mouth, punk.'

'Well, I don't see what dif'rence it makes if I have her or not. They've seen yore face, Luther. You know we're gonna hafta kill them too.'

'Lawd a'mighty!' Mammy suddenly realized the full import of this statement. With all her strength she raised her satchel and whacked Luther over the head with it. 'Run, Miz Storm! Run, chile! Run while yo cain!'

Storm, who had obeyed Mammy all her life, didn't wait any longer. She turned and ran as fast as her legs would carry her, expecting to be shot in the back any moment. She heard the outlaws cursing, arguing behind her. Then the sound of hard footsteps pelting over the ground reached her ears. She felt a pair of rough hands grab her waist, flinging her body to the earth, and then the blow of Billy's weight upon her own, knocking the wind from her. His breath was hot against her cheek. She gasped as she looked into his eyes and saw the lust that lurked therein. He couldn't have been more than twenty years old at the most. With a whoop he jerked off the offending hat and veil, causing Storm's hair to come out of its neat chignon, sending the pins scattering as the curls tumbled down her back, a mass of ebony tangles.

'Jesus! Oh, Jesus!' Billy breathed. 'I never expected nothin' like *you*!'

'Please.' Storm bit her lip.

He lowered his mouth and would have kissed her had they not been interrupted by the sound of two more gunshots. Storm tensed and jerked her head up fearfully.

'Mammy! Mammy!' she screamed.

'I reckon yore nigger has gone to her maker, *chile*,' Billy said mockingly as Storm's heart wrenched with pain in her breast. 'Along with that other old crone. Elijah jes cain't stand wimmen. But I'll tell you what, you sweet thin', you jest keep yore trap shut, and I'll try to save you.' Then he grinned. 'I can use a woman like you. Whoooeee! I ain't never had nothin' like *you* before!' He yanked Storm to her feet. 'Remember now. Keep yore trap shut, and let me do the talkin'.'

The girl shuddered as he led her away. She knew the uses to which he could put her. Oh, God, she'd rather die than submit to this filthy criminal! Perhaps they'd *all* take turns on her! That thought was even more horrifying. Oh, *Sainte Marie*, she prayed, please let them kill me – and quickly!

'Put that away.' Billy pointed to Elijah's still-smoking gun, while Storm tried hard not to look at the grotesquely sprawled corpses of Mammy and Mrs Thatcher lying in the dirt.

Oh, Mammy! Mammy! You gave your life for me, and I never even had a chance to say goodbye! Tears welled up in the girl's eyes. There was a lump in her throat so big she thought it would choke her.

'You ain't gonna kill this one, 'Lij,' Billy continued as the crystal droplets splashed down Storm's cheeks.

'You gone crazy, fool? Yore damned right I am!' Elijah gazed at his younger brother incredulously and then with mean intent.

'Naw, naw, you ain't. I want her, see? And I mean to have her.'

'Now lookie here, Billy,' Luther spoke up irately. 'We cain't be totin' that female around with us. It's dangerous. She's a – a – whaddathey call it? – a – a material witness to this entire episode.'

'I don't care.' Billy planted his feet apart stubbornly. 'I want her. Hell, I'll share if that's yore problem.'

'*Mon Dieu*,' Storm sobbed quietly upon hearing his words.

'Moan do? What's that?' Billy asked, giving her a little shake. 'You makin' fun of us, gal? What's the matter? You think yore too good fer the likes of us? Is that it? Hey, answer me, girlie!'

Storm was in a state of shock, however, and no longer cared what they did to her.

'Why don't you just hurry up and kill me,' she begged.

Billy ignored that. 'Hey, this high-falutin chit thinks she's too good fer the likes of us. Are we gonna let her git away with that, boys?'

Luther glared at him and, seeing his brother was not to be reasoned with, slyly played his last trump card.

'Ma ain't gonna like it.'

'Ma's gonna like it even less if she finds out we stood around here arguin' over a woman while the posse caught us,' Billy rejoined calmly now that he was sure he'd won.

'He's right, you know.' Zeke glanced down the road anxiously. 'The station master's probably already reported the stage as bein' late. Shit! Let him have the friggin' bitch. We can git rid of her later, when he's tired of her. 'Sides,' he raked Storm's figure lewdly with his eyes, 'I wouldn't mind havin' a piece of that myself.'

Elijah muttered viciously under his breath at the decision, then spat in the dust.

'You'd better keep her outta my way, brother, and the first time she tries to escape she gits it!'

'Whoooeee! Come on, *lady*.' Billy twanged the last word

sarcastically as he mounted his horse and hauled the girl up in front of him.

Storm's armpit ached from the strain of his wrenching grasp. He hugged her tightly, one hand around her waist to keep her from falling off, his fingers already creeping up to fondle her breasts through the thin material of her dress. Storm shivered. To think she, the belle of five counties, was at the mercy of these desperate criminals! To know they were all going to rape her the first chance they got and then kill her afterward! Oh, God!

She did not look back as they trotted away from the disastrous scene, but the girl knew nevertheless that as long as she lived she was never going to forget the sight of Henry Thatcher's bald head blown to smithereens, the red stains of blood across Mammy's and Naomi Thatcher's breasts, and the dark shadows of the buzzards circling slowly overhead in the hot sun as she and the outlaws rode off into the distance.

4

Cathleen Elizabeth North stared hard at her reflection in the mirror and sighed. She was a tall woman, nearly as tall as her brother, Joe Jack, who stood six feet. Her fine straight hair was shoulder-length and sun-bleached blond. The same light-coloured lashes ringed her big brown eyes, eyes that melted like molasses, but didn't sparkle. Brown eyes never sparkled. Her cheeks were flat, angled. Across her slightly upturned nose was splayed a smattering of honey freckles that stood out even more prominently when she'd been out in the sun too long. Her generous red mouth was too wide for her thin face, but could smile prettily when she chose (which was not very often). Her skin was tanned a warm golden hue. Her breasts were small and firm, insolently pert, she'd been told once. Still there was no fault to be found with her long, slender arms and legs and her delicate hands and feet. Besides, men seldom noticed she really wasn't pretty. She had an odd, graceful sensuousness that compelled attraction. It was only when one studied her carefully and critically that one saw even the kindest of persons would not have called her beautiful – and Cathy was studying herself carefully and critically.

She sighed again, gazing at herself arrayed in the dress her father had brought back from New Orleans. It was a lovely enough gown with its ruffles and flounces, but Cathy was not a woman meant for frills. Moreover, the pale yellow silk made her seem wan, washed out. Her mouth looked like a crimson smear in her face! She knew she appeared a fright in the frock, and – what was even worse – she felt like a fool! Angrily she began to undo the little buttons, her slim fingers trembling slightly with rage and frustration. Surely her father could have seen the dress was the wrong style, the wrong color! Of course he could have, just as he had known Joe Jack wasn't interested in reading books. Wrong! Wrong! Everything pa did was wrong because he didn't understand his children and didn't really care to try. He cared only for himself and what *he* wanted. Selfish, that's what pa was!

Cathy ripped off the gown and threw it onto the floor, trampling on it viciously as she reached for her pants and faded checked shirt. It had been stupid to try the frock on in the first place. Whom had she been trying to impress anyway? Her father's bride-to-be? Cathy almost laughed aloud at the thought. Her father's bride-to-be, a girl four years younger than herself and no doubt an uppity miss from the South's high society from what pa had said. Cathy could have kicked her hind end for being such a fool, for unlike most people, she was honest with herself; and she had indeed been trying to impress Storm Lesconflair, a girl she'd never even met. It had been wrong to try. She could be nothing other than what she was, and she was only that in her worn breeches and her brother's cast-off shirts. Cathy hastily attired herself in this ensemble. If the bride-to-be didn't like it, she could go straight to hell!

Cathy thought her father had taken leave of his senses, marrying a chit of a girl younger than his own daughter, but neither she nor Joe Jack had been able to make pa listen to reason. When Gabriel North had his mind set on something, he held on to it like an old dog with a bone.

'Storm Lesconflair is a lady,' he'd said. 'A true Southern belle. She'll give this place class, a woman's touch. That's the only thing it's lacking.'

'I'm a woman, pa.' Cathy had been hurt and defensive.

'Huh!' Gabriel had hooted. 'You could have fooled me!'

Cathy grimaced as she remembered the words. Then she lit one of her thin brown cigars, stalked down the stairs, opened the front door, and went outside. Joe Jack was standing on the porch. He turned at her appearance, frowning.

'I thought pa told you to put on that dress.'

Cathy tossed her head defiantly, the cigar dangling out of one corner of her mouth as she spoke.

'He did, and I didn't.'

'Pa ain't going to like it, Cath.' Her brother grinned. 'You know how all-fired-up the old man is to impress his fiancée.'

'Huh.' Cathy's lip curled into the familiar sneer. 'He's old enough to be her father. Why, she's younger than you and me. What would a chit like that be wanting with an old man?'

'Money.' Joe Jack's voice was suddenly hard.

'You think so? Pa said her family owned one of the finest plantations in New Orleans.'

'That don't mean it ain't mortgaged to the hilt. You know pa. He might have lied, or maybe the girl's so damned ugly no one else would have her, and in that case I don't know why pa would either. I ain't ever known the old man to go a'mooning after nothing in skirts that didn't have a good-looking face to go along with 'em.'

'Nor do you,' Cathy pointed out sharply, her nerves beginning to wear thin.

'I declare, Cath, if you don't sweeten your tongue, you're going to wind up a sour old maid for sure!'

Cathy bit her lip and turned away, stung. Her brother knew being a spinster was a sore spot with her, and he never lost an opportunity to rub it in. She tossed her cigar on the ground, grinding it out deliberately with the toe of her boot. Joe Jack laughed, white teeth gleaming, at her sudden consternation.

Even a stranger would have known the two were brother and sister. Joe Jack had the same blond hair and brown eyes, the generous mouth; but whereas the features on Cathy were only plain, they gave Joe Jack's face a certain lean ruggedness, a sly, cunning cast, although he was handsome enough. Cathy, in her spiteful moments, often likened her brother to a weasel. Joe Jack always laughed at that too, claiming he had indeed slipped in and out of several hen coops while their farmers weren't watching. Cathy always snorted disgustedly in return. She knew what kind of chickens Joe Jack plucked, and they weren't the sort that laid eggs either. She was surprised half of Texas wasn't littered with his illegitimate offspring.

Joe Jack, however, always took care of himself, and now was no exception. It wouldn't do to aggravate Cathy. He might need her help later on.

'Hey, I'm sorry, sis.' He spread his hands disarmingly, the grin on his countenance that had melted so many hearts.

She was not deceived. 'What? Would you repeat that please. I think there must be something wrong with my ears. I thought I just heard an apology.'

'Aw, come on, Cathy. You and I have got to stick together with pa getting married again. It'd be just like the old man to leave Tierra Rosa to this new wife and her kids if they ever have any.'

Cathy seldom agreed with her brother on anything, but this time she recognized he was right. Oh, she knew Joe Jack wouldn't have thought twice about stealing Tierra Rosa from his own sister, but Cathy had sense enough to realize she could handle him and would need his cleverness if they were to prevent the new bride from taking over completely. She nodded.

'All right. Truce then.'

Joe Jack grinned once more. 'I always did say blood was thicker than water.'

'Just don't go getting any fancy ideas, *brother*,' she shot back.

He ignored that. 'I wonder what in the hell is taking pa so long. They should have been here by now.' He squinted his eyes against the glare of the sun, looking for some sign of his father in the distance.

The girl sighed again. 'If they never get here, it will be too soon for me.'

'Hey, Petey, see anything yet?' Joe Jack called to the lookout who was posted on top of the tall entrance arch of the split-railed, white-washed fence that surrounded the immediate vicinity of the house.

'Nope, not yet, Joe – wait a minute. Wait a minute! Boss is comin'! Boss is comin'! Sumpin' musta gone wrong. He's ridin' like a pack of Injuns are hot on his tail!' Petey hollered.

Joe Jack and Cathy started forward to get a better look, but could see nothing save the cloud of dirt Gabriel's horse was stirring up.

'Ring the bell, sis!' Joe Jack commanded, suddenly quick and alert. 'There ain't enough dust for Indians, but the old man's in a devil of a temper for sure to be pushing Buck like that!'

The girl scurried to the far end of the front porch. With its solid metal cylinder she struck the iron triangle that hung there. It clanged loudly several times before she ran back to join her brother.

'I wonder what's wrong,' she mused aloud.

'Don't know.' Joe Jack narrowed his eyes against the sun once more. 'But I don't see Hilton and the buggy. Maybe pa's been jilted!' Then he laughed.

He was not laughing minutes later, however, when Gabriel thundered in, shouting furious orders to the ranch hands who'd answered the iron triangle's summons.

'Stage was held up!' Gabriel sawed on Buck's reins savagely. 'You men get mounted up! They've taken Storm!' Then he kicked the animal's lathered sides cruelly with his sharp spurs and galloped off.

'Jesus!' Joe Jack breathed. 'She sure must be something! Don't hardly nobody accost a lady in the West!' Then he headed for his horse.

Shortly thereafter not a soul remained at the house except for a few servants and Cathy. Her golden visage was horrified as she went inside after watching her brother ride off hell-bent after her father. She had not wanted pa's fiancée to come here, but Cathy had never wished the girl harm. Joe Jack was right. Even the worst outlaws generally treated ladies with respect. The men who'd held up the stagecoach must have been the scum of the earth! Cathy shuddered. She would not have liked to trade places with Storm Lesconflair at that moment.

5

Storm, on the other hand, would have happily switched roles with a dog. Her backside ached from sitting in the saddle. Her face felt as though it were on fire from the hot sun. She suspected her breasts would be black-and-blue too from the sly pinches Billy had given them as they'd ridden relentlessly. She would have traded her soul for a hat and a cool drink of water! Her throat felt raw and parched from the dust that spewed up from the flying hooves of the horses, and her eyes watered continuously from the grit. Surely this wasn't real! Surely this wasn't happening to her, Storm Lesconflair, the belle of five counties! Surely she would wake up presently, safe in her bed at Belle Rive, to the insistent sound of Mammy's voice and find this was all just some horrible nightmare: the yellow fever epidemic; her parents' deaths; the loss of her home; the two years of pain and disillusion-ment spent at Vaillance learning of her uncle's perfidy; Gabriel North's proposal; André-Louis's betrayal; the dust; the heat; the frantic attempt to outrun the outlaws; Mammy's wide, comforting breasts stained with blood; and now this. This!

Oh, surely it couldn't be true! Storm had borne too much already. She couldn't endure any more. It was too much to ask of her; it was just too much to ask! She felt numb and paralyzed with shock and grief. She threw back her head tiredly and moaned. She wished she were dead! Far better to have been lying by the stagecoach, eyes forever closed, than to endure this torturous ride to – where – hell?

They rode on and on until the girl thought surely the horses would drop dead in their tracks of exhaustion. The beasts' sides were lathered with white foam, and they heaved and snorted, instead of breathing.

At last when Storm believed she could take no more, the sun went down. The men slowed their pace, rounding the hills, stumbling along a well-worn path in the darkness until they stopped completely. The girl, sitting upon Billy's horse with the young criminal's arm around her waist, did not realize at first what had occurred. She only knew the terrible jolting had ceased. Luther glanced around warily, then gave a low whistle. From far off in the distance the sound was echoed. Then the jolting began once more.

Storm saw the small crude house then, its one lamp gleaming softly in the blackness. She shuddered. What would happen to her now, when they went inside? She could not bear thinking about it.

'That you, boys?' a woman's harsh voice demanded from the doorway.

'Yeah, ma,' Luther replied.

The woman lowered the carbine she was holding. 'What kept you?'

'Had a bit of trouble, ma,' Zeke answered, since it appeared as though no one else was going to.

'Shut up, Zeke!' Billy snapped nervously, yanking Storm from the saddle.

He shoved her roughly toward the hut. Once inside the girl got her first real glimpse of Ma Barlow. The woman was terrifying, even more terrifying than her sons. Ma was as wide as she was tall, with straggling grey hair and small, evil eyes that seemed to pierce one's very soul. The gross features on her fat, wrinkled countenance were pitted with masses of small pox scars. Her pudgy hands were as big as a man's, as were the massive muscles that flexed in her arms when she moved. She was chewing a wad of tobacco that drooled out one corner of her mean yellow-stained lips when she spat and then spoke.

'Who's that, Billy?'

Billy fidgeted anxiously, his bravado in taking the girl gone now that he was actually face-to-face with ma.

'I asked you a question, Billy!'

'I dunno her name, ma. I – I took her off the stagecoach we held up this afternoon.'

'Oh, you did, did you?' The woman mimicked her son's whining tone, then switched abruptly to her own grizzly voice. 'And jest what was you thinkin' of, you damned fool? How many times have I told you? – NO WITNESSES! If they see yore face, kill 'em! You want yore picture smeared all over them friggin' *Wanted* posters they got plastered all over the place? Well, do you?'

'Well – no, ma.'

'You Gawddamned fool. If this here bitch was to of escaped, she coulda give them Rangers a right good description of you boys. It wouldn't of been like no damned job where you was all masked, and they was all too frightened to remember what they did see, or like no friggin' saloon where they was all too damned drunk to recall yore faces properly. You Gawddamned fool, Billy!'

She pivoted suddenly and dealt him a ringing blow on the ear. Billy fell to the floor like a pole-axed steer. Storm gasped.

'And jest what was you about, Luther,' – Ma turned coldly to her eldest son, who flinched as she approached him – 'to allow that young fool, what ain't got a lick of sense, to keep the bitch?'

'It – it weren't to be helped, ma,' Luther stuttered, shying away a little to keep out of her punching range. 'We couldn't hang around there no longer, or the posse woulda caught us fer shore! We thought—'

'You thought; you thought,' Ma sneered. 'With what? You ain't got brains enuff to think. None of you do. How many times have I told you there ain't a one of you what's too bright? I'm the one who does the thinkin' around here!'

'Yeah, ma,' the Barlow brothers chorused as one.

'You, girl.' Ma stared hard at Storm. 'Come here.'

Storm looked at the woman stupidly, her mind refusing to

comprehend the command. No one had ever spoken to her like that in her life. Ma growled angrily, grabbing the girl's arm in a fearful grip as she hauled Storm into the light.

'Are you deaf?' She shook the girl violently.

'N – no.' Storm managed to speak at last, drawing herself up with some semblance of dignity and trying not to let the old witch see how desperately afraid she was.

Ma grunted. 'What's yore name, girl?'

'Storm. Storm Lesconflair.'

Ma pinched her arm cruelly. 'Not much meat on yore bones, girl. Still I expect if you was cleaned up a bit, you wouldn't be half-bad.'

Half-bad! This to a girl who'd been the belle of the ball in New Orleans. Storm's nerves cracked at last. She laughed, laughed hysterically until Ma Barlow belted her a stinging slap across the face. Blood spurted from Storm's nose. Billy handed her a filthy handkerchief.

'Wipe yore nose, girl, and don't cause no more trouble.' Then he turned to Ma. 'I want her, ma. I ain't never had a woman like her before. She's real quality, a *lady*! You shoulda seen her before we took her off the stage. All gussied up and smellin' so fine.'

Ma grunted again, thinking furiously. She would have preferred her sons have no women at all, although she knew they often picked up sluts in various sordid saloons. She knew too her attitude had driven Elijah to an unnatural dislike of all women except her, although she refused to admit that, even to herself. This incident tonight, however, why, it was open rebellion! Ma couldn't allow that. She was getting old. The boys might turn on her, and she wouldn't be able to handle them.

She debated briefly over holding Storm for ransom. Billy had said the girl was quality, and indeed Ma knew the dress the bitch was wearing did not belong to a saloon slut. Then she dismissed the idea as abruptly as it had occurred. *That* was the way fools got caught, and Ma Barlow had not organized her

76

sons into the desperate gang of criminals they had become just to get caught! For forty years she had been the brains of their operation. For forty years she had outwitted some of the most clever lawmen in the region.

She reached a decision. She would let Billy have the girl. If she gave way to her sons on small points, she could get her own way on things that really counted.

'All right, Billy. But mind you take her into town. I don't want her here. And fer Gawd's sake, keep her outta sight, and keep yore trap shut about today's doin's!'

Billy heaved a huge sigh of relief. He pulled Storm out after him into the night, glad to escape Ma's piercing eyes and sharp tongue, not to mention her beefy fists.

'Foller 'em, boys,' Ma told the rest of her sons when Billy had gone. 'When he's through with the bitch, kill her.'

'Don't worry, ma.' Elijah smiled evilly. 'I'll take care of that friggin' slut!'

'Jest see you don't git trigger-happy in town,' she warned. 'Too many killin's give the gang a bad name. Luther, you 'n' Zeke dump out the rest of the money before you go. I reckon you boys have already taken outta little spendin' cash.'

They shuffled their feet sheepishly. Ma breathed hard, somewhat frightened again. There was a time when they wouldn't have dared to touch a penny of it! Then she smiled.

'That's all right, boys, although you know I've always taken real good care of you, haven't I?'

'Yeah, ma,' they said.

'Well, you jest keep that in mind, and don't go gittin' any fancy ideas.' She looked sternly at them once more.

'No, ma,' they muttered and left her less than satisfied.

After they'd gone she sank to a chair, groaning, feeling the queer pains in her chest starting up again.

Storm thought she had never seen such a filthy pesthole as the small town to which Billy took her. Called Gorda Vaca, it was nothing more than a row of dirty shacks, a haven for criminals of the worst type. Almost everyone in it had a price on his or her head. No lawman who valued his skin would dare venture into it. The last one brave enough to do so had been promptly strung up on the hanging tree. Strangers were usually shot on sight, and no one asked questions of anyone else. Its inhabitants kept their mouths shut, and the outlaws who used it as a hideaway did likewise. The girl would get no help from anyone who happened to see her, and she realized it instinctively, the tiny flicker of hope in her breast a dying ember before it even had a chance to take flame.

'Come on, girlie.' Billy swung her down from the saddle, his laughing self once more now that Ma was no longer present. 'Whoooeee! Are we gonna have fun tonight!'

Storm shivered. How he even had the energy to think was beyond her. She felt ready to keel over from weariness and knew in her heart she would not be able to put up a fight against this young criminal. He would rape her, and she would be powerless to prevent it. He dragged her unprotesting figure into the saloon, disregarding Ma's orders in his eagerness.

The saloon was raucous with laughter and noise as the shuttered doors swung closed behind Storm and Billy. A piano player thumped away unconcernedly in one corner of the room, never missing a note as he banged along, impervious to the fights that sometimes broke out among the guests. Painted women simpered and giggled as they called for the men to buy them drinks. Storm saw a few of the girls, their drunken customers in tow, lurching up a rickety staircase. Her eyes lingered on the seedy hall. That was where Billy would take her, and it was so loud in the saloon no one would hear her if she screamed – or care if they did.

Billy led her to the bar. 'What you need is a good stiff belt,' he said.

Storm cringed. Ma Barlow had already given her a good stiff belt. Her swollen face could attest to that. She put her hand up to her cheek instinctively. Billy saw the gesture and understood.

'Naw, that's not what I meant. Ma shore do have a powerful right, don't she?' he observed, feeling his own throbbing ear gingerly. 'I meant you needed a drink.'

The girl sighed with relief. At least he did not intend to beat her! She could be grateful for that much.

'A bottle of whiskey and two glasses,' Billy hollered, pounding one hand upon the counter. Then he swung around to survey the saloon, a grin of pure delight upon his face. 'No need to hurry,' he told Storm. 'We got all night.' His eyes raked her lustfully with appreciation. 'Yes, ma'am. All night. You'll feel better after you git a lick of whiskey in yore gut.'

Storm took the glass he handed her. Papa had sometimes allowed her to drink spirits at home, as had Uncle Pierre, but never very often and only a few sips at a time. Now she upended the shot, downing its amber contents in one gulp. Immediately she choked, gagged, and felt tears sting her eyes. Billy whacked her on the back rudely.

'Whoa, girl. That ain't no way fer a *lady* to drink! You ain't got the head fer guzzlin' the stuff.' He frowned. 'And I don't want you drunk, you hear?'

The girl nodded tiredly. Of course he would not want her drunk. He would want her to struggle, would probably even enjoy it, would laugh at her pleas for mercy.

I will get drunk, she thought. I will get so drunk it won't matter anymore. Nothing will matter. Maybe I won't even remember this horrid outlaw laying his filthy hands on me. Then afterward I'll steal his gun somehow, someway, and I'll kill him. Then I'll kill myself too, she decided coldly, calmly, feeling better than she had in ages. She took another huge swig from the refilled glass and coughed again. Billy grabbed the shot away from her then.

'Didn't you hear what I said?' he asked impatiently.

'I – I'm sorry,' the girl managed to choke out. 'It's just that I'm so – so thirsty.' Then she felt like biting off her tongue for apologizing to the criminal.

Still his face softened, and he told the bartender to bring her a glass of tea, which was served to the saloon girls (if they wanted it) to keep them from getting as drunk as their customers. Despite herself, Storm was grateful for the cold brew. She gulped it down hurriedly, feeling as though her parched throat would never get enough of it. Billy ordered her some more, then strolled over to where a game of poker was being played.

'Mind if I join you?' he questioned, eager to spend some of the stolen loot and just as anxious to make some more money.

Everybody at the table glanced up at him uninterestedly and said, no, they didn't mind; so Billy pulled out a chair and sat down, being sure to keep Storm as close to him as possible so that the others wouldn't think she was there to spy on their cards. Besides, he didn't want her running away, although she hardly looked capable of even standing.

It was then he noticed the man sitting across the table from him. Billy cursed his luck a thousand times. Shit! If it weren't El Lobo! The young outlaw groaned silently and wished he'd never thought of joining the game. Ma was right; he *was* a fool! El Lobo was one of the most dangerous men in Texas, probably in the entire West and Mexico as well. A gunslinger, a sometime bounty hunter, a man who walked both sides of the law when it pleased him, El Lobo had a draw like greased lightning and was a deadly shot in the bargain. Billy had no desire to play cards with the man, but it was too late now. If he left the table, he'd look like a coward; and it wouldn't do for the Barlow gang to get a reputation like *that*! They'd have every lawman in the region breathing down their necks! With a calmness he didn't feel Billy grinned around the table and tossed in his ante.

Storm sank to the floor beside him, curling her hands around the legs of his chair before she dozed off into a fitful sleep. She didn't notice the rest of the Barlow brothers slink in and take a table across the room. She was just glad for this small reprieve. She knew how men got when they were gambling. They forgot about the time and everything else in their bloodlust for winning. Before she closed her eyes Storm prayed it would be so with Billy, that he would forget about her for just a little while.

The night dragged on, and still Billy played. He was an excellent gambler, and one by one the men in the poker game began to drop out, cursing their luck and their loss of funds. Soon only Billy and the gunslinger El Lobo remained. The young outlaw shifted in his hard chair, trying to obtain a more comfortable position. Storm started awake violently at the motion. For a moment she could not remember where she was, then she recalled all too quickly. She glanced up at the table. From what she could gather an enormous wager was riding on this hand – the final hand she realized suddenly with a sinking heart as Billy pushed the last of his cash forward. Why, the first pale pink streaks of dawn were already stealing across the sky! Storm couldn't believe she'd slept all night propped up against an old wooden chair, but thank God for it. Thank God, Billy hadn't ravished her – yet!

'I'll see that and raise you a thousand more,' the man across from Billy said softly.

The young outlaw stared at El Lobo with sharp dismay. It wasn't fair! It just wasn't fair. Couldn't the man see he didn't have any money left? Oh, Billy just couldn't throw in his hand for lack of funds! He was holding a full house. He bit his lip, thinking hard.

'I – I'm afraid I'm outta cash.' He smiled dejectedly. 'But I've got this gold watch.' Billy held forth the object he'd robbed off some dead man.

El Lobo's steely gaze flickered over the offering without interest. 'I've already got a watch,' he drawled, 'and that one's not worth a thousand. Play or pay.' His strong, slender fingers began to rake in the dollars on the table.

'Wait. Wait!' Billy cried, one hand upon the man's arm. Then at the deadly glint the gunslinger gave him, he snatched his fingers back hurriedly.

'Well?' El Lobo raised one eyebrow coolly, expectantly.

'I – I've got this girl.' Billy reached down and yanked Storm up, pushing her into the light. 'She's a mite dirty and all, but she's real purty cleaned up and quality folk too. She's shorely worth a thousand. Why, you'd git that for a good nigger!'

Storm gasped, outraged that she was being bartered just like a slave, wagered away on the turn of a card – again! The gunslinger's cold eyes surveyed her crudely, insultingly. She suddenly became aware of just how terrible she must appear with her dress torn and grimy, her matted black hair straggling down, and her sunburned face swelling from Ma Barlow's fearful punch. Tears filled her eyes. It was too much to be borne!

'No,' she whispered, and her voice cracked.

Something stirred on the man's hard visage at the girl's soft cry. Storm found herself really looking at him for the first time.

He was garbed completely in black and silver. Black boots with shining silver spurs were upon his feet. Tight black breeches were fastened at his waist with a black leather belt adorned by an intricately carved silver buckle and a knife sheath from which a silver blade glittered wickedly. His black silk shirt, with its pearlized ebony studs rimmed with dull silver metal, was partially open to reveal the dark mat of hair across his broad chest. A black bandana was tied loosely around his neck, and a black flat-brimmed *sombrero* was pulled down over his eyes. Slung low at his hips was a black leather gunbelt bearing two gleaming black-barreled pistols with walnut stocks. Both revolvers were elaborately inlaid with silver and their cylinders engraved with etchings of Indian fights.

When he stretched slightly in his chair, Storm became aware of how tall he must be standing, how the sinewy muscles in his arms and thighs tautened like sinuous thong, giving him the suggestive appearance of a black crouching panther. She could almost feel the physical violence coiled within the man like a deadly snake.

His dark copper-skinned countenance was hard, impassive, as though it had been chiseled out of stone. His nose was straight, proud, and flaring. His cheekbones were high, the cheeks themselves flat and spare. His sneering, dissolute mouth held both warning – and promise. The thrust of his jaw was mocking, self-assured. His glossy mane of ebony hair was shaggy and untamed, as though a wild wind had whipped it freely. It fell just below his shoulders where the ends looked as though they had been hacked off with a knife – something a savage might have done.

. . . why any of them have need of more hair is beyond me. Some of them have it hanging down to their waists.

The girl recalled Mrs Thatcher's words with a shiver. Perhaps the gunslinger was one of *them*! An Indian who had adapted to civilization – and not quite as well as Storm had been led to believe from the looks of him!

With a flutter of trepidation she saw he was still staring at her intently from beneath the brim of his hat. *Jesù*! Those eyes! She had never seen eyes like those before. Deep-set beneath thick, heavy black brows and spiked with dense black lashes, the man's eyes were the most magnetic, penetrating, startling shade of midnight blue the girl had ever seen; and they were unrelenting – as hard as nails.

Storm trembled as they raked her, ravished her, and found her wanting.

The gunslinger took a slow drag of the thin black cigar he had clamped between his teeth, turned back to Billy, and spoke again, his tone silky and deceiving.

'What makes you think I'd take your leavings?'

Billy's young face flushed with quick anger. His hand went for his gun, then stopped in midair, caution overcoming his churning emotions. He wasn't *that* fast, and he wasn't a fool either – at least when it came to messing with El Lobo. He attempted to smile once more.

'I ain't touched her. Haven't had the time.' He pouted and

then brightened. 'But I shore am lookin' forward to it. She's a *lady*!'

El Lobo glanced at Storm again. Despite the chilling fear she felt, an odd tingle of excitement and fascination chased up her spine.

'Is it true – that he hasn't touched you?' the gunslinger asked.

Storm nodded mutely, unaware she had changed the course of her entire life in that moment.

'All right,' El Lobo said to the young outlaw. 'I'll accept the – lady – in lieu of your cash.'

Billy whooped with glee, certain he had won the hand. He displayed his full house with confidence, then began to pull in the money on the table. The gunslinger stopped him slowly, deliberately.

'Aren't you interested in seeing my cards?' the man queried, his voice low.

Without waiting for an answer he turned them over. Billy gasped, then groaned. There against the burn- and knife-scarred wood of the poker table lay five black spades, a royal straight. El Lobo smiled jeeringly as he gathered up the dollar bills, folding them away carefully, calmly. Storm did not realize the full import of this, however, until he took her arm. His touch jolted her like lightning as she looked up into his cold blue eyes and understood she was his now.

It was then Elijah Barlow, still sitting across the room, jumped to his feet, knocking over his chair in his haste, and shouted,

'Billy, you friggin' fool!'

The next minute Storm heard a terrifying explosion, felt a searing pain in her arm, and stared uncomprehendingly at the blood that trickled from the wound, staining her gown. Then the gunslinger shoved her up roughly against the bar, placing himself in front of her. He was holding his two gleaming pistols in his strong sure hands, and one of the black barrels was still smoking. *Sainte Marie*! How had he drawn those revolvers so quickly? Elijah Barlow was sprawled out on the saloon floor, looking just as mean and ugly in death. There had been two shots fired then, almost simultaneously.

'Which one of you boys would like to join your brother?' El Lobo sneered mockingly in the deadly silence that had fallen over the room.

Luther and Zeke drew up sharply, muttering and cursing under their breath, while Billy backed away slowly from the card table, which had been overturned in the fracas. They had no wish to be killed too over a woman. Still there was going to be hell to pay when Ma found out about this night's doings!

'Zeke, Billy, put yore guns away,' Luther ordered reluctantly, returning his own to his holster carefully so that El Lobo could plainly see he did not mean to use it. 'We don't want no more trouble,' he told the gunslinger hastily. 'We'll jest git 'Lij's body and leave quietlike. You go on; take the girl. You won her fair and square.'

'I'll take your brother's corpse too,' El Lobo stated flatly. 'I believe he has a price on his head – dead or alive.'

'But – but—' Zeke stammered.

'Leave him, Zeke.' Luther was already shuffling nervously toward the door. 'He's dead, ain't he? Ain't nothin' we can do fer him now.'

Then the three remaining Barlow boys were gone. The gunslinger turned to Storm, reached up, and tore the sleeve of her frock down to expose the small raw wound in her arm. She flinched at the sudden movement and attempted to pull away, mistaking his intent until he swore at her softly and called for a bottle of mescal. He yanked the cork from the decanter with his teeth, then poured the fiery liquid onto her bleeding flesh. The girl gasped as the stinging alcohol hit the wound. Then she gazed up at him with amazement as the man untied the black bandana from around his neck and bound up her paining arm.

After that he walked over to the card table, picked up the poncho that was draped over his chair, and put it on. It too was black. Both the front and the back of the garment bore the head of a snarling silver-gray wolf. Its hem was bordered all around with long silver-gray fringe. El Lobo turned back to Storm, contemplated her amusedly with his icy dark blue eyes, gave her a wry smile, and shook his head, making a gentle clicking sound of regret with one corner of his mouth. Then without so much as another glance in her direction he heaved the sizable bulk of Elijah Barlow's body upon his shoulder and, spurs jangling, swaggered wordlessly toward the door.

Storm watched him go – so calm, so cool; and abruptly, irrationally the girl who had been the belle of the ball in New Orleans felt a hot, angry flash of stung pride. Why, he was leaving her! He didn't even want her! After all the grief, degradation, and humiliation she'd been forced to suffer, and that contemptible gunslinger didn't even so much as look at her again! Never had a man treated Storm Aimée Lesconflair so. She set her jaw and tossed her head, glaring around the saloon in her fury. Suddenly she was no longer tired; and though she was desperately afraid, the curious, leering, and somewhat hostile stares of the customers and the muffled sniggering she heard from some of the simpering painted women made the girl stiffen her spine with determination. She would not be left here in this horrible place, at the mercy of this cutthroat scum! Her gray eyes narrowed, glinting like steel in the slowly lightening room. Her lips curled into a grim line, not the childishly spoilt pout of old, but a new deadly mask that glittered like diamonds and was just as hard.

My folks are dead, she thought, and Belle Rive is lost to me forever. André-Louis loved his family's name and Clarisse Martinique's money more than me, so I can't go home to New Orleans. The Beauvallets would feel honour bound to send me back to Texas, to keep their despicable bargain with that horrid rancher. No, I've got no place in this world to go, except to Gabriel North. Gabriel North! *He* is the one to blame for all this! If it weren't for him, I'd be married to André by now; Mammy would still be alive; and I wouldn't be stuck here in this filthy pesthole. *Sacré bleu*! I don't even know where I am! I hate him! I hate Gabriel North, the *taureau*, the *canaille*! I'll never go to him, submit to him! Someone will find the stagecoach. My trunks are there. They'll know I was on it at least. They'll guess I was kidnapped, raped, and probably killed afterward. They'll tell Gabriel North. He won't be able to blame the Beauvallets for it. Vaillance will still be secure, and the Beauvallet name will not be disgraced. Gabriel North will believe me dead, and I'll be safe from him forever. He doesn't love me. He probably won't even bother searching for me when they don't find my body. No, I *won't* go to him, the vile pig! I'll never again be used by any man, my uncle, André-Louis, or Gabriel North! I'll die first! – which is most assuredly what will happen if I don't get out of this terrible place – and quickly! *Mon Dieu*! I don't have a cent either! What am I to do? What am I to do?

I'll take your brother's corpse too. I believe he has a price on his head – dead or alive.

There's plenty of opportunity out here – for those who aren't afraid to take it.

Hurriedly, before she could change her mind, Storm ran from the saloon pausing only to slap away the hand of a lecherous drunk who lurched toward her purposefully. When she got outside, she saw the gunslinger had tied Elijah's body onto a pack horse and was mounting a huge *overo* Pinto stallion. Her heart pounded frantically in her breast as she considered what she was about to do, but the girl knew she had no other choice. It was this man or the rabble inside the saloon. The gunslinger at least was clean.

'You there.' She planted her hands on her hips and spread her legs apart in imitation of the stance she'd often seen her beaux take when spoiling for a brawl.

El Lobo glanced around the street, then looked down at her as though she'd been little more than a bothersome, buzzing fly.

'You talking to me – lady?'

Storm took a deep breath, feeling the sudden rush of courage leave her as those midnight blue eyes raked her again. Then she thought, yesterday I survived a stagecoach hold-up, Mammy's death, and those dirty outlaws who would without a doubt have raped and murdered me. I can surely do this!

She pressed on then, heedlessly.

'I – I heard you say there's a reward for that man's corpse.' She indicated the dead Elijah, his head dangling down over the side of the pack horse.

'Yeah, so what?'

'I – I'm claiming half that money,' Storm spoke defiantly. 'After all, that man would not have been in that saloon had it not been for me.'

El Lobo stared down at her as though he surely could not have heard her right. Christ! This – this slut Billy Barlow had dragged off from God only knew where was actually demanding half the reward money from him! He looked into her smoky gray eyes, and for a moment he saw the hopeless despair that lurked behind her brazen façade. Tears trembled on her thick sooty lashes. She brushed them away hastily. He realized then the girl would rather have died than let him see how dreadfully frightened she really was. Haunting images of another face with eyes like that, proud eyes, bitter eyes, eyes that had asked but refused to beg crept into his mind. They'd belonged to the boy who was now the man called *El Lobo*.

It was the man who held out his hand, but it was because of the boy he'd once been that he did so.

Storm studied that hand for a long time. It was dark, strong, and yet curiously gentle, with long, slender fingers. That hand had pulled a revolver from a holster so rapidly she hadn't even seen it. That hand had killed a man for her. That hand had cleansed her wound and bound it with a black bandana. To what kind of a man did such a hand belong, she wondered, and why had he held it out to her? She took it slowly and felt it close firmly over her own before he pulled her up in front of him.

Moments later she was flying through the rose sunrise down the dusty road of Gorda Vaca, tasting her tears bittersweet upon her lips. The gunslinger's arm was around her waist tightly, and Elijah's body was bouncing against the pack horse behind them. Then the town was gone, and there was only the dawn, the cool morning breeze sweeping through her wildly streaming black hair, and the touch of El Lobo's arm to tell her she was free.

Free?

No, she belonged to the dark savage gunslinger now, and she did not even know his name!

BOOK TWO
A Savage Wolf

6

The Prairie, Texas, 1848

His name was Rafael Bautista Delgados y Aguilar, but no living soul knew that; and he had long ceased to be the boy to whom that name had belonged. The White-Eyes, *tejanos*, and Mexicans called him *El Lobo*, The Wolf; and they feared him. The Comanches called him Brother-Of-The-Wolf, and they loved him; and whenever the man thought of himself, it was as a Comanche warrior.

He was the most dangerous kind of man alive, the kind of man who didn't care whether he lived or died. He hadn't always been like that. There had been a time in his secretive, mysterious past when he had known laughter, but then death had come with its icy black fingers to take away so cruelly the things the boy had loved. Charred images of death were forever burned into the darkest recesses of his mind, violent deaths, painful deaths. Whenever the sad slow healing of time crept upon him, the gunslinger would force himself to remember death, and the shattered memories in his soul would harden his heart and strengthen his hate. Death had come to him once. Now he went out to find it.

Scattered pictures of the gentle boy he had once been still haunted him now and then, but they too were for the most part painful.

He was orphaned at an early age and, following the loss of his parents, did not return to the small adobe house that was his home. Neither did he seek out the mission where he attended school and that would have given him aid and comfort had he but asked for it. Instead the quiet, sorrow-filled boy who was devotedly studying for the priesthood lost faith in his God and ran away.

Afraid, stumbling blindly, hopelessly across the Texas prairies, sleeping when he felt like it, and eating whatever roots he dug out of the ground or small game he managed to kill with his only weapon, a hunting knife, the boy was taken captive by a band of Comanche Indians known as the *Kwerharehnuh* of the *Llano Estacado* (Staked Plain). He remembered the year well, for that year a great rain of meteors showered down from the heavens; and thereafter the Indians called it The-Winter-The-Stars-Fell.

At that time there were seven major bands of the *Nermernuh* – The People – as they called themselves: the *Yamparikuh*, the *Kutsuehka*, the *Nawkoni*, the *Tanima*, the *Tenawa*, the *Pehnaterkuh*, and the *Kwerharehnuh*, also called the *Kwahadi*. There were too perhaps as many as ten more minor bands; some of which had already been assimilated by the larger, stronger bands; some of which had, even then, disappeared from the face of the earth entirely; and some of which, like the *Pohoi*, were nothing more than displaced Shoshonis, cousins of the Comanches.

Of them all the *Kwerharehnuh*, who took the boy prisoner, were the proudest, fiercest, and most arrogant of the tribe that reigned supreme over the vast, heart-shaped territory known as *Comanchería*. From them would spring the last and mighty war chief Kwanah, who would be called Quanah Parker by the White-Eyes and who would lead the *Kwerharehnuh* to their bitter, heartbreaking end against their enemies, for the *Kwerharehnuh* would cling to the old ways and be the last of the Comanches ever to surrender.

Who can say why such a band let the boy live? Perhaps it was his youth or his dark coppery skin and jet black hair, or perhaps it was the great courage he showed when they took him to their camp high in the Palo Duro and Tules to kill him. There they beat him cruelly with clubs, tied him to a stake and whipped him unmercifully, then surrounded him with brush and set it afire, taunting him savagely all the while. Through each one of the horrible tortures they boy who'd lost faith in his God uttered not one word of protest, screamed not one outcry of fear, welcomed, in fact, the brutal death offered him by the Comanches, because it confirmed and strengthened his belief that God had forsaken him. Ever a deeply reverent respecter of bravery, however, the *Kwerharehnuh* were impressed by the boy's silent, stoic acceptance of his fate. Before the flames could burn him alive they freed him and claimed him for their own.

Because of the rosary the boy wore around his neck, having been unable to bring himself to throw it away even after he'd judged his god and religion unfit, the Comanches named him *Hisusanchis* – The-Little-Spaniard – associating him with the Black-Robes who carried such beads in their hands. Along with his new name, the Indians also gave the boy a new faith – that of the *Nermernuh* – The People.

He was adopted by Tabenanika, the band's *puhakut*. Tabenanika, whose last surviving son had just been killed in a raid, was a solemn, thoughtful man with much insight into others. Of average height, as were most of the Comanches, the shaman still seemed tall and regal as he sat cross-legged before the fire in his tipi. His red skin gleamed in the flickering light. The smoke from his *awmawtawy* rose in little gray swirls as he puffed in sober contemplation of the boy, his dark piercing eyes studying his new son with care and interest. What did he see in the soul of Hisusanchis, behind the boy's inscrutable midnight blue eyes? A kindred spirit? One that had also known pain and suffering and that had already learned to hate? Perhaps no one will ever know. At last, however, Tabenanika spoke, with his brother-in-law Masitawtawp, who understood the language of the White-Eyes, acting as interpreter.

'Once the *Nermernuh* – The People – were strong and many,' Tabenanika began slowly after he'd finished his pipe. 'They roamed The Land freely, hunted many buffalo, counted many coups, killed many enemies, and took many scalps. None was greater in his glory than The People.

'Then strangers came to The Land – Black-Robes who carried beads in their hands and prayed to a strange god who hung on crossed sticks. They wished The People to give up their own god and pray to this Great-White-Spirit instead. They built lodges to their god and dug up The Land to plant maize, claiming The Land belonged to them. But The People knew The Land belonged to no man. The Black-Robes were weak, and their god had no medicine, so we drove them away.

'More strangers came – hunters who talked through their noses and whose words rippled like mountain streams. They brought giant metal claws to catch small animals and carried long sticks that spoke fire. They brought many presents also – beads and knives for The People – in exchange for buffalo robes. But The People were not deceived. The medicine of the hunters was bad. We drove them away too.

'I had three sons, three brave fierce sons who were bold warriors and fine hunters. I was a proud man to have such sons. But then more strangers came – the *taboh* – White-Eyes – with god-dogs that pulled tipis on round hoops over The Land. With them came very bad medicine – the Spotted-Sickness. Many of The People were taken ill with the sores upon their skin that would not heal. Despite my prayers and power, many died. After that I had two sons.

'The People drove the *taboh* away, as they had done the others, but the White-Eyes were not like the Black-Robes or the hunters. They came back and brought Blue-Soldiers with them. They built many lodges with sharp poles surrounding them. They dug up The Land and scared away the buffalo with their fire-sticks. They gave The People a water that tasted of fire and made their spirits wander, their bellies sick. They wanted The People to make marks on pieces of paper, and many did; but those who made their marks made them only for themselves, for no man can speak for another. The *taboh* did not understand this. They said the papers had been broken. They rode their god-dogs into battle against The People and killed them with the fire-sticks. After that I had one son.

'Still more White-Eyes came – the *tejanos* – with more fire-sticks. Now I have no sons. I ask you to be my son, Hisusanchis, to become one of The People. There is hate in your heart; I can see it. And you wish to die because there is pain also. But this is not the way of a *tehnap'* – a man. This is not the way of The People. The People must live and fight to keep The Land and themselves free. Will you do this, Hisusanchis, my *tua*?'

'Yes, I will,' said the boy who had listened and learned and that day put aside his past to become a Comanche.

Tabenanika was kind to him in a strange way. He put Hisusanchis to work immediately, sensing the boy was still suffering from a sickness of the spirit and needed to be kept occupied so that the cleansing time of healing might begin. At first only small jobs were assigned to the boy, those such as were usually done by young girls and slaves. Because he was new to the band, Hisusanchis did not understand he ought to have rebelled against such tasks, and so he fetched water, gathered nuts and berries, and built fires as instructed. Because of this he was the object of much scorn and ridicule by the Indians and the despair of his father. Tabenanika had hoped the boy would protest such treatment and demand his rights as a *tuibitsi* – a young man; but Hisusanchis did not, so his father watched him silently, shook his head sadly, and went away without comment to his son. Still the boy did not complain, but went about his chores quietly, untiringly, demonstrating his contempt for the others by ignoring them, deigning only to speak to his family once he'd mastered the Comanche language. Proud and stoic, they said nothing to him of their disappointment in his meek acceptance of his lot.

His mother and the chief wife of Tabenanika, Woman-Of-The-High-Wind, was too a'grieved to pay much attention to Hisusanchis at the start. Upon learning of her son's death she had slashed her flesh with a knife and cut off her hair in mourning. She scarcely noticed the boy her husband had taken in to fill the empty void in their lives. Her younger sister and Tabenanika's second wife, She-Who-Seeks-Wisdom, whom the boy also called mother, as was the Comanche way, at last took pity on Hisusanchis, however, and began to find treasured moments to spend with him during the days that passed. If he wished to do women's work, then she would at least be certain he did it well.

She educated him about the plants and herbs to be found in the forests and upon the plains – which were edible and good for seasoning thick, fragrant stews, and which were poisonous and to be avoided. She directed him in the digging of Indian potatoes, wild onions, radishes, Jerusalem arti-chokes and sego lily bulbs; in the picking of persimmons, mulberries, haws, wild plums, grapes, currants, juniper berries, hackberries, prickly pear, and suma; and in the gathering of pecan nuts and, when times were hard, acorns of the blackjack oak. She showed him how to glean wild honey for sweetening. As he progressed in his studies she taught him how to cook; how to dry meats; how to crush the strips of jerky afterward to blend with ground maize (when available), wild berries, cherries, plums, walnuts, *piñons*, and pecans to make pemmican; and how to preserve the mixture with tallow and marrow fat and store it so that it would not spoil for many years. She instructed him in the curing of hides; how to make them supple yet strong; how to smoke them so that they became waterproof; and how to cut and sew the skins to make garments and tipis. She drilled him on erecting the latter properly so that they did not fill with smoke from the fire lit within and on the folding and packing of them to be carried on a travois for many miles.

After a year of her careful and patient schooling she deemed him well-trained and ready to begin his proper studies as a *tuibitsi* of the Comanches in preparation for the day when he would become a *tehnap'*.

'Hisusanchis, it is not right that you continue the work of a young girl when you are a fine young boy soon to become a man,' she told him sternly one day. 'The others mock you and lose the respect they gained for you when you showed such courage at the stake.'

'I do not care, *pia*.' The boy shrugged his shoulders indifferently, although he lied, for he cared very much indeed. 'Father himself has set me to these miserable tasks. If he does not think me worthy of learning those things I should truly know, what else can I do?'

'My husband has done this to test you, *tua*,' She-Who-Seeks-Wisdom chided gently, her normally serious dark eyes twinkling at his obvious discomfiture. 'You should know that by now. Do not bow your head like a coward in defeat. You have learned patiently and well those things I could teach you, but they are the way of a young girl soon to become a woman, and your moccasins should not follow that path. It is time now for you to take your rightful place among The People. Prove to your father you are worthy of such a position so that he will be proud of you, and my sister will cease to mourn Black Bear, who was her favourite son.'

'How, *pia*? How can I do this?'

'Seek out my brother Masitawtawp. He is a great hunter and warrior. I know in my heart he will help you. He will give you a bow and arrows and teach you the way of a *tuibitsi*. Perhaps he will do this in secret so that the others will not learn of it and seek to laugh at your mistakes. If Masitawtawp is not in his tipi, you may take those possessions you desire without his permission so long as you return them afterward. He is your uncle, and this is the way of The People between you. His chief wife, She-Laughs-Like-A-Mountain-Stream, will show you where they are kept. Go now, *tua*, so that I will know my words of wisdom have not been wasted. I will finish gathering the wood.'

Hisusanchis went to the tipi of Masitawtawp. She-Laughs-Like-A-Mountain-Stream bowed her head when he entered and smiled at him shyly, for she was a gentle maid.

'*Hihites, paha.*' The boy greeted his aunt politely, for he did not know her well, even though she was his father's sister.

The People had strict laws governing the conduct between brothers and sisters to prevent incestuous relationships from forming. A man was allowed to kill his sibling without retribution if she violated any of these rules.

'I'm tired of women's work. I must prove to my father I am a true *tuibitsi* – soon to become a *tehnap'* – who is worthy of becoming a mighty warrior of The People. I seek a bow and arrows and any other things I might need to help me do this. She-Who-Seeks-Wisdom has said I might take them without Masitawtawp's permission if I return them later.'

'Yes, that is true, *paha*. I am glad she has spoken to you, for I could not bear you to be scorned when I know in my heart you are a brave young boy who will someday be a good man and a fierce warrior of The People. I will get that which you desire at once.'

Taking the things she offered him, Hisusanchis crept away to a private place in the canyons to teach himself the use of the weapons. All day long he practiced with the bow and arrows, but mastery of them proved more difficult than he had anticipated. The muscles in his right arm ached from pulling the bow string, and the wrist of his left limb pained throbbingly where the thong had seared it raw. Then just as he was about to give up he was grabbed roughly from behind and thrown to the ground. The point of his uncle's sharply honed knife pressed gently against the boy's throat as he stared with fright up into Masitawtawp's dark eyes.

Pia and *paha* lied to me to make a fool out of me, was the boy's first thought. They don't really love me at all!

Still he managed to say calmly, 'I'm sorry, *ara*, if you are angry, but the others said I might take your things without permission. I was going to return them later on tonight.'

'Ah, it is good to hear you address me as family, Hisusanchis, my *ara*,' Masitawtawp replied with a smile, rising, sheathing his knife, and holding out one hand to help the boy up.

'I – I don't understand. You are not – not angry?' Hisusanchis stammered, confused.

'Angry? No, *ara*. Why should I be angry? It is your right to use my possessions as you will.'

'Then – then why did you do such a terrible thing – sneak up on me, attack me, and threaten me with a knife?'

'It was just the first of many such lessons you must master if you wish to be a warrior of The People. Keep your ears open! If I had been a *tabeboh* or an Apache *Inde* – the swine! – you wouldn't be alive right now.'

'Yes – yes, I see. I am sorry, *ara*, that I questioned you, who are far wiser than I.'

'This was my first bow.' Masitawtawp retrieved the fallen weapon, caressing it fondly as he recalled his own youthful training. 'She-Laughs-Like-A-Moutain-Stream did well to give it to you. I must remember to thank her upon our return to camp. I have been watching you for some time, Hisusanchis, since my chief wife told me you had come to our tipi and for what purpose. You have a good eye, but your aim is off because you are impatient, and why do you not wear the wrist band? See how the thong has burned your skin.'

'Oh, I didn't know. Is *that* what that piece of leather is?'

'No matter. You will learn. We will come back tomorrow, *ara*, when you have rested. But for now you have worked hard enough. Come; we will walk to camp together, and there you may choose one of my god-dogs as yours. Every *tuibitsi* should have a pony of his own.'

'*Hu*! Do you mean it, *ara*?'

'*Si-ichka tab-be kaesop*. The midday sun does not tell a lie.'

Hisusanchis studied diligently over the months that passed, for his uncle proved to be a kind but stern instructor. The boy soon grew fond of Masitawtawp, however, and would have done anything to gain the older man's approval. Hisusanchis learned how to break the ponies for which the Comanches traded or that they captured or stole; how to ride bareback with only a single strand of thong looped around the horse's lower lip to serve as a bridle; how to guide his mount with just the slightest gentle pressure of his knees so that his hands would be free to handle his weapons; how to braid his rope in the beast's mane to form a loop through which he could put his leg so that he could hang under the steed's belly for protection and make the enemy think the animal was wild and riderless; and how to become one with his pony.

Unlike most Indians the majority of the Comanches were awkward, not graceful, upon the ground; but on a horse they had no equal in the world.

The boy learned how to shoot his bow and arrows so accurately he could actually split one shaft down its length with another if he wished to hit his target in the same place twice. He learned how to handle his knife in hand-to-hand combat; how to be quick and lithe on his feet, to feint, and to dodge to avoid his opponent's blade. He learned how to throw his *werpitapu'ni* and how to slither quietly through the grass like a snake to bring the battle-ax down upon an unsuspecting victim's head. He learned to hurl his war lance and hunting lance great distances with speed and unfailing precision. He learned how to raid, make war, count coup, kill, and scalp his enemies – the *tabeboh*, the *tejanos*, the Mexicans, and the Apache *Inde*.

The boy learned how to hunt buffalo, antelope, deer, elk, and bears, achieving a great triumph when he brought down an albino buffalo all on his own. His father, Tabenanika, wore the rare robe proudly.

Three years later Masitawtawp told the boy it was time for him to go into the wilderness and seek his vision.

'It is your final test, Hisusanchis, my *ara*. Do not return until you have seen that for which you must search, or you will fail. May the Great-Spirit walk beside you and give you strength.'

High in the Palo Duro and Tules, Hisusanchis waited for his vision to come to him. For four days he waited, without food or drink to sustain his long vigil; and still no vision appeared. Filled with dark despair, he arose on the fifth day and again prayed to the Great-Spirit, to Father-Sun, and to Mother-Moon for guidance and assistance in his quest. That night his prayers were answered, and the following day he returned to camp to relate his vision to the others. That evening the Comaches gathered round the fire eagerly to hear his story.

'According to our custom,' he began, 'I left our camp and walked west into the wilderness until I came to a place that seemed to beckon to me. There I sat and made my prayers and offerings to the Great-Spirit, to Father-Sun, and to Mother-Moon, telling them of my quest and beseeching them for a vision. But for four suns they did not answer, and my heart was heavy in my breast. Then in the twilight of the fifth sun my vision appeared. This is what I saw.

'In my vision I saw a strange barren land, stark and vast, a land filled with naught save fire.'

The others, who were listening intently, gasped. Hisusanchis raised one hand to still their whispering, then continued.

'On the eastern horizon of the fire-land there appeared a White-Eyes, a hunter, a giant of a man who walked in flames as red as the land itself – the Great-White-Devil of the *taheboh*.' There were more gasps. 'In his hands the Evil-Spirit carried a giant metal claw, which he opened and buried in the sand. Then he went away and waited.

'On the southern horizon of the fire-land there appeared a small gray wolf. The wolf was young and ignorant. It ran heedlessly across the sand, straight into the sharp talons of the giant metal claw, which sprang up from its hiding place and snapped shut on the wolf's paw. The wolf tried and tried, but it could not escape from the claw, which only seemed to close more tightly on the wolf's paw as it struggled.

'Many suns passed, then moons, then winters; and still the wolf could not free itself from the claw. The wolf grew older, wiser. It realized at last it must wait for he who had set the claw to return; so it waited, and all the while the flames of the fire-land drew nearer. Soon they even began to singe the wolf's fur. But the wolf was brave and patient, and finally the Great-White-Devil of the fire-land appeared again. The Evil-Spirit saw the wolf's plight and laughed. He laughed so hard the heavens shook. This disturbed the Great-Spirit, Father-Sun, and Mother-Moon and made them angry. They looked down from the sky and saw the hunter towering over the wolf, preparing to kill it with his mighty fire-stick. They took pity on the wolf and opened up the heavens to pour forth a torrent of rain upon the Great-White-Devil and the fire-land. When the storm had ended, only the wolf remained.

'The clouds cleared, and out of the clearing came another wolf. It freed the first wolf from the giant metal claw and licked its mate's paw until the wound that had festered for so many winters was healed, and the first wolf was made whole once more.

'That was my vision.'

Hisusanchis fell silent, waiting for Ekakura, the peace chief of his family, to speak.

At last Ekakura said, 'It is a strange dream, Hisusanchis, this vision of which you speak. Our shaman, Tabenanika, will interpret it for us. Come forward, O' wise *puhakut*, and share with us your words of knowledge.

Slowly Tabenanika arose. 'The vision seems strange perhaps because Hisusanchis is one of us, yet not one of us. Nevertheless it is a true vision and its meaning plain. The land of which he spoke is our land and the fire the blood of the Comanches that has been shed by the *tabeboh* – the Great-White-Devil. We are the young wolf who, in its ignorance, did not divine the cunning power of the White-Eyes and so was caught in the sharp talons of the giant metal claw. But in the end, in the final battle, with the help of the Great-Spirit, Father-Sun, and Mother-Moon, we will prevail, and the *tabeboh* will be destroyed. The second wolf is Hisusanchis himself, who came out of a clearing of dark clouds to befriend the first wolf, The People. When Hisusanchis came to us, he was suffering from a sickness of spirit. Now he is healed and truly one of us. I say to you that from this sun forward he will be known as Brother-Of-The-Wolf, brother of The People. I, Tabenanika, have spoken.'

The boy Hisusanchis died that night. The Comanche brave Brother-Of-The-Wolf took his place. One week later the man moved into his own tipi that his mothers, Woman-Of-The-High-Wind and She-Who-Seeks-Wisdom, and Masitawtawp's chief wife, She-Laughs-Like-A-Mountain-Stream, had made for him during his absence from camp. That afternoon his brother (in the Comanche way) Fire-Walker, who had never liked him, mocked him scornfully.

'Look!' the son of Kwasia jeered. 'The boy who does the work of a *naibi* thinks himself man enough to get his own tipi!'

'Yes, that is true.' Brother-Of-The-Wolf tried to respond calmly, not wanting trouble. 'I am no longer a *tuibitsi*, but a *tehnap*', deserving of my own tipi.'

'You! A *tehnap*'! A *herbi* is more likely! Where is your woman's skirt, little *naibi*? Or perhaps you prefer other *tuibitsis*. Is that it? Should we get you the dress of a *berdache* instead?'

At that Brother-Of-The-Wolf lost his temper. With a cry of rage sounding strangely like a wolf's howl he attacked the other youth. They grappled together on the hard ground amidst a gathering ring of onlookers who urged the two on with their cheers and began betting on the outcome of the fight. Fire-Walker was heavier than Brother-Of-The-Wolf, but the latter's hard life had made him lean and tough. He gained the advantage by blacking Fire-Walker's eye, then hit him brutally in the belly. Fire-Walker doubled over, groaning with shock and surprise, but quickly rallied and, in the sudden stunned silence, pulled a knife. Brother-Of-The-Wolf had suspected such a savage trick, however, and was prepared for it. He knocked Fire-Walker to the earth once more, twisting the knife up to its wielder's throat. The point pressed home gently.

'Know you, Fire-Walker,' Brother-Of-The-Wolf growled through clenched teeth, 'that this day I have fought you, won, and let you live as is the way of The People between themselves. Do not seek to torment me again.'

Then he rolled off the youth's body, knowing from the hate in Fire-Walker's dark eyes that he had made an enemy for life. In fact, Fire-Walker would have killed him when he turned his back, but Moon-Raider, the eldest son of Ekakura, stayed the enraged hand poised to throw the tomahawk.

'Coward!' Moon-Raider hissed. 'The fight was fair, and you lost. Accept it with grace as the warrior I know you to be.'

'He is no warrior, he who would strike a brother in the back.' Shadow-Of-The-Hawk's voice was filled with scorn.

'And Brother-Of-The-Wolf *is* a brother, as well as a man,' Crazy-Soldier-Boy said.

'He has proven so this sun,' Naukwahip added.

Fire-Walker lowered his weapon, ashamed of the disgust he saw in all his relatives' eyes, and walked away. Moon-Raider turned to the rest of the watching band.

'Let it be known that this sun the son of Tabenanika fought well and showed mercy to one of The People. He is truly our brother, as Tabenanika has spoken.'

Brother-Of-The-Wolf glanced up in surprise, for in the past Moon-Raider had treated him with as much hatred as the others. Brother-Of-The-Wolf realized then that by keeping quiet he had indeed earned the comtempt of The People. By defending himself he had gained their respect. His vision and the fight just ended had won his full acceptance by The People. He belonged at last.

That spring he took a Comanche wife. Beloved-Of-The Forest was sixteen, sweet, and shy, with honey brown-red skin, coal black hair, and black eyes that sparkled like jets. Brother-Of-The-Wolf was seventeen and his knowledge of women limited to the few he'd taken captive while raiding other Indian tribes. He was rough with her at first, but she taught him a gentleness he'd seldom known in his lifetime.

106

Before the year was out his cold heart had learned to love again, and Beloved-Of-The-Forest was heavy with their first child.

Whatever love had begun to blossom in his heart, however, died the day Brother-Of-The-Wolf rode home from battle to find his wife of barely eleven moons stretched out on the frozen winter earth, her once-sweet face twisted with pain and the agony of death. She had been brutally beaten and raped. The belly heavy with their child had been ripped open wide by the sharp blade of a knife. He threw back his head and wailed, the piercing howl of a wounded wolf, and shed bitter tears for Beloved-Of-The-Forest and their child – a son who would never see the light of day.

Brother-Of-The-Wolf cut off his long hair and slashed his flesh in mourning. For seven days after the burial he spoke to no one. Not one morsel of food or sip of water passed his lips while he grieved, alone, in the tipi that had been their home. No one, not even Tabenanika, dared enter to disturb him. On the seventh day Brother-Of-The-Wolf pushed open the flap of his lonely dwelling and strode through the camp to his father's tipi, ignoring the curious, awed glances of the rest of the band. He paused outside.

'Enter, my *tua*,' Tabenanika said. 'I have been awaiting you.'

Brother-Of-The-Wolf sat down, taking silently the *awmawtawy* his father offered him. At last he began to speak.

'*Ap*', my heart is heavy in my breast with sadness. I do not understand who did this terrible thing or why. Share with me your words of knowledge and peace, O' wise *puhakut*, that my spirit may find solace in this time of grief.'

Tabenanika puffed thoughtfully on his own pipe before he replied. 'My heart' – he struck his chest – 'is heavy also, my *tua*. We know no more than you who did this terrible thing or why. Beloved-Of-The-Forest had walked to the stream to fetch some water. Some of the children heard her screaming a little while later, but by the time they got there her spirit had already joined the Great-Spirit.' He hung his head in sadness. He was silent for a moment, then continued. 'Once more you suffer

107

from a sickness of the spirit, my *tua*. I say to you that time heals all such wounds. As it did before, so will it do again for you.'

Ap',' Brother-Of-The-Wolf sighed with despair. 'I must leave here. The time has come when I wish to know more of the world and its ways.'

'I shall be sorry to see you go, Brother-Of-The-Wolf.' Tabenanika's eyes were filled with sorrow. 'But you must do as your spirit wills. Go now in peace, my *tua*, and may the Great-Spirit walk beside you and give you strength.'

Brother-Of-The-Wolf's new clothes felt strange and tight, unlike the comfortable, loose-fitting buckskins to which he was accustomed. The gunbelt and pistols were heavy on his hips. Alone on the range, he practiced with the revolvers daily for months until his hands were quick and steady on the draw, his eyes keen and accurate on the target, as precise as they had been with the primitive bow and arrows.

It was hot and dusty the day he rode into a small town just outside the Mexican border. He sauntered into the saloon and ordered a bottle of mescal, the English words as strange upon his tongue as the garments upon his body. He realized then it would take some time to refamiliarize himself with the language and with his native Spanish as well. The bartender had started over the drink when a man standing at the bar, one foot on its rail, turned slowly.

'Think yore big enuff to handle that, half-breed?' he asked jeeringly.

Brother-Of-The-Wolf stared hard at the man, his midnight blue eyes glinting warily.

'You talking to me, mister?'

'Yore damned right, I am!' the insulting stranger responded. 'I ain't drinkin' with no half-breed Injun.'

'Then I suggest you go somewhere else.'

The man swore loudly and went for his gun. Brother-Of-The-Wolf snapped around, wailing his Indian war cry – that savage wolf howl – and shot the stranger in the chest before the man ever even got his revolver out of its holster. The stranger was an outlaw and had a price on his head – dead or alive.

Brother-Of-The-Wolf collected it. That was the day the legend of El Lobo began.

Now, ten years later, he seemed older than his twenty-seven years. His hard life as a gunslinger had left its marks in the fine lines around his coldly calculating eyes and sneering lips. He always fought fairly – if you considered that few men stood a chance against his deadly quick accuracy fair; and when he ran out of money, he turned bounty hunter, stalking the worst kinds of criminals for the prices upon their heads. He was a law unto himself, as was the Comanche way, for he still bore the signs of his Indian upbringing in his silent manner of walking and his usually emotionless face. The latter had stood him in good stead in more than one poker game. A man of few words, he seldom spoke or smiled and never wore anything but the black and silver that had become his trademark unless he was visiting his Comanche family.

A *comanchero* who brought them goods and guns, El Lobo made his way to the camp of the *Kwerharehnuh* several times a year, finding them no matter how often they had moved. Each time Tabenanika shook his head sadly, knowing his son had yet to discover the peace of mind for which he searched.

Driven by his hardness and determination, El Lobo now doubted he would ever find it. The solace he was seeking seemed to slip through his fingers like an elusive soul each time he thought it was within his grasp. Because of this death held no fear for him. He would have welcomed its sweet release. This made him dangerous and often cruel.

His arm tightened in a steely grip around the waist of the girl he was holding. The black hair straggling down her back reminded him unpleasantly of Beloved-Of-The-Forest's dark tresses. For only a moment he was a young brave again, riding into the wind with his Comanche wife. Then he remembered Beloved-Of-The-Forest was dead and that the girl he held was just some slut he'd won in a card game in Gorda Vaca. His jaw set. She meant nothing to him, so just why in the hell had he taken her?

7

The Barlow gang thundered toward the shack they called home, not bothering with the customary warning whistle, and almost got themselves killed for their lack of precaution when Ma Barlow hurried out, firing her carbine at them. Thank God, her eyesight was failing, and she missed!

'Don't shoot, ma!' they yelled. 'It's us!'

'Well, why in the hell didn't you whistle?' she asked angrily when they'd reached the house. 'I mighta blowed yore fool heads off! Where's Elijah?'

'Dead, ma, and it's Billy's fault,' Luther said as he dismounted.

'Was not!' Billy countered nervously.

'Dead?' Ma looked stunned and disbelieving.

'Let's git inside.' Zeke glanced around anxiously. No telling if El Lobo had followed them.

They went into the house and sat down. Ma was breathing heavily. One hand was at her chest where her heart was fluttering queerly again. One of her boys' dead? Such a thing just wasn't possible!

'What happened?' she managed to query. 'It were all that slut's fault, weren't it? I knowed no damned good would come of you bringin' her here.' She turned on Billy.

'It weren't my fault, ma.' He skittered his chair out of her swinging range. 'I had a winnin' hand. El Lobo musta cheated me!'

'El Lobo?' Ma questioned sharply. 'What's *he* got to do with this? How many times have I told you to cut a clean path away from that man? He's got sumpin' bad eatin' on him – don't care whether he lives or dies. A man like that's dangerous!'

'Well, it were like this, ma,' Zeke began to explain since Luther and Billy obviously couldn't. 'Billy took the girl into the saloon after you done told him to keep her outta sight, and he got likkered up and got into a poker game with El Lobo. Me and Luther and – and 'Lij come in and was watchin' from across the room. Well, Billy ran outta money and wagered the chit instead.

'Damn it! I had a full house,' Billy broke in. 'But El Lobo, ma, he musta cheated me, 'cause he turned up a royal straight just as sweet as you please, all spades, damn it!'

'Anyways,' Zeke continued, 'El Lobo won the gal and started to take her away. 'Lij jumped up, mindin' yore orders 'bout killin' her, ma, and fired a shot off at the slut. He winged her, but then that devil El Lobo pulled his guns and killed 'Lij 'fore any of us knew what was happenin'. Damn, but he's fast! Clean too. Shot 'Lij right through the heart!'

'There was three of you left, you cowards,' Ma sneered. 'You coulda killed the man, but, no, I'll bet you was all too damned afraid you was gonna be next!'

The boys shuffled their feet sheepishly, not daring to look at Ma or each other.

'Well, what in the hell are you sittin' here fer? Git after 'em, and git that bitch back!' Ma screamed.

Then she half-rose out of her chair, hands tearing at the bodice of her ragged dress, her breath coming in quick gasps. Her sons stared, horrified, as she gagged and then fell to the floor with a loud thud.

'Ma! Ma!' they cried, springing to their feet.

'It ain't no use.' Luther got up slowly from where he knelt over their mother's sprawled body. 'The shock's killed her.'

Ma gone? No, it just couldn't be! It just couldn't be! What would they do without Ma? She was the brains of everything. Ma had always planned all their crimes, looked after them. She just couldn't be dead! She was, however, and now they were going to have to bury her.

It took all three of her sons to lift Ma Barlow's corpse and

111

lower it into the shallow hole they'd dug for her.

'Oughtn't we to say somethin' from the Bible?' Billy queried.

'Shut up! Yore the one what killed her, shore as if you'd put a bullet in her,' Luther snarled.

'I never did! I never did!' Billy whined.

'Ain't got no Bible anyways,' Zeke pointed out practically, 'and ain't a one of us what can read, 'sides.' He paused, then spoke again. 'Ma, you shore was smart. You was the best damned ma a body coulda had, even if you did hit us now and then. And you shore had a powerful right too. We're gonna miss you, ma, but we won't let you down. We'll git them two if it's the last thin' we ever do, 'cause them was yore last orders, ma.'

Then the three Barlow brothers buried their mother. After that they mounted up and rode after Storm and El Lobo. Not once did any of them look back.

Storm wrinkled her nose. She wished fervently for her rose-scented handkerchief that had been left behind when the outlaws had carried her off. Every time a breeze of wind blew, the odor of Elijah's putrefying body reached her outraged nostrils. Still she did not dare suggest to the gunslinger that they get rid of the corpse. No, the dead Elijah was going to be her unwilling ticket to a stake in this new and harsh land. Besides, the gunslinger himself seemed impervious to the smell.

He was a curious, silent man, Storm thought. She had slept, off and on, her head lolling listlessly against his shoulder, but he had not said one word since they'd left that horrid town. She wondered briefly if she'd been a complete fool to run after a strange man about whom she knew absolutely nothing, then decided she'd had no other choice. God only knew what would have happened to her had she remained in that awful place!

The girl opened her eyes for the last time, knowing from the way the hot sun beat down upon her that she would not sleep again this day. She spied a cluster of trees ahead and thought how nice it would be to rest a moment in their cool, inviting shade. Almost as though he'd guessed her desire the gunslinger rode toward the massive pines and halted the horses. He dismounted and pulled Storm down after him. She was so stiff and sore she almost fell. He put out one hand to steady her. When she'd managed to get herself seated against the side of one of the large trunks, he returned to his stallion. After unlashing one of the canteens looped around his saddle horn he took a small bag from his stash on the pack horse and came to join her, hunkering down on his haunches as he stared at her silently.

The girl winced as he reached out and untied the bandana around her arm. The tiny wound no longer pained her, for it was only a scratch, but it did hurt as the caked blood pulled away with the handkerchief. Without speaking the man cleansed the wound, then handed her the canteen. Storm grabbed it gratefully, spilling the water down the front of her dress as she gulped hurriedly. To her surprise the gunslinger snatched the container away with an angry snarl. She gazed at him in shocked dismay, wondering what she had done wrong.

'Small slow sips,' he growled curtly, 'or you'll be sick. And we can't afford to waste water washing that rag of a gown you're wearing either.'

Storm nodded, somewhat frightened, for his eyes were hard. This time when he returned the canteen, she did as he'd ordered, although she could barely restrain her thirst. Then he gave her what looked like a piece of bark. She glanced at him questioningly.

'Jerky. Better eat it.'

She took a hesitant bite. It was tough and had to be chewed slowly, but at last she managed to get it down, feeling somewhat better when it hit her empty stomach, for she'd eaten nothing since early yesterday morning. The man finished his own small meal of the dried beef, swallowed a few sips of water, then turned to the girl again.

'You got a name?'

'Storm. Storm Lesconflair, *monsieur*.'

'French?'

She nodded.

French, the gunslinger thought, *hunters who talked through their noses and whose words rippled like mountain streams.*

'Suppose you tell me what you were doing with the Barlow brothers and why they tried to kill you.'

'Is – is *that* who they were?' Storm mused with a shudder. 'I only knew their first names. They – they held up the stagecoach on which I was traveling yesterday. They killed everyone else, but took me along with them because – because—'

'I can guess the rest,' the gunslinger said, to the girl's relief.

Damn! he thought. No doubt the Barlow gang would be hot on his heels to get her back – if what she said were true. El Lobo wondered once more just why he had agreed to take her with him. He must have been drunk – or temporarily *loco*!

'Where were you going?' he asked.

'Nowhere,' Storm lied. Gabriel North was rich and a well-known Texas rancher. This man might try and force her to return to her fiancé or, worse yet, hold her for ransom. After all, what did she really know about him? He might be wanted himself. The girl shivered at the thought. 'Coming from nowhere and going nowhere, *monsieur*.'

He studied her curiously at that. The dress she had on looked expensive, despite its tattered condition. Probably stolen, the man decided, if she were just a drifter as she claimed.

'You – you haven't told me *your* name, *monsieur*,' Storm pointed out. She was just as curious about the gunslinger as he was about her, and she intended to find out more about him.

'My name?' He raised one eyebrow as though amused, then drawled, 'I have a lot of them, but most people call me El Lobo.'

'El Lobo.' The girl tried the Spanish words on her tongue. 'What – what does it mean?'

'The wolf.' His midnight blue eyes stared hard at her again.

She trembled slightly. 'Shall I – shall I call you that – El Lobo, I mean?'

'Just plain Lobo will do, or you can call me Wolf if you prefer the English version. I'm afraid I don't know the French word for it.'

'*Loup.*'

'Well, whatever.'

He began to gaze at her silently once more, cursing himself and wondering yet again just why he'd brought her along. Hell! She wasn't even pretty. Well, he'd keep his word and give her half the reward money. Then he'd be rid of her.

'Come on.'

'So soon?' Storm felt weary to the bone.

'Unless you'd rather wait around here for the Barlow brothers.'

'You – you think they'll come after me?' The girl was terrified by the idea.

'Lady, I have no doubt about it.'

At midday they had another brief respite and two hours later reached another town. Called Golaid, it was much larger than Gorda Vaca and certainly not nearly as filthy. It was, Storm thought as she glanced around, respectable – at least decent citizens were abroad. She breathed a small sigh of relief. If Wolf (she had decided on that name for him) were not afraid to show his face here, then he could not be a wanted man as she'd half-suspected and feared. He halted the horses in front of the sheriff's office, which further confirmed her belief that he was not an outlaw, and helped her down from the saddle. Then he pulled a piece of folded paper from his saddle bag.

Sheriff Yancey was seated at his desk, feet propped up on the desktop, his head bowed down over his chest, nodding. He jumped up with a start at the sound of the door slamming shut and the jingle of spurs across the floor. He squinted, spit a wad of tobacco at a spittoon in one corner, swore when he missed, then in a grouchy voice said,

'Hello, Lobo.'

'Sheriff.'

'Ain't seen you around lately. What brings you to Goliad this time?'

The sheriff cast a covert glance at Storm, noted her swollen face and torn dress, and snorted slightly. Another one of Lobo's border wenches, he had no doubt. He wondered if the girl had tried to roll the gunslinger, if Lobo had awakened, caught her in the act, slapped her around a little, then brought her here to be charged. At last the sheriff decided against this. Lobo wouldn't trouble the law with such a petty matter.

'Well?' Sheriff Yancey didn't like to be kept waiting.

'Got Elijah Barlow's body outside.' El Lobo unfolded the *Wanted* poster and shoved it across the desk. 'I came to collect the reward.'

The sheriff frowned disgustedly. Now he'd have to spend the rest of the afternoon filling out reports.

'You shore it's Barlow?' he asked, then could have bitten off his tongue. One didn't question Lobo. 'Sorry, regulations,' he apologized with a crafty smile at the cold stare the gunslinger gave him. 'Well, let's have a look at the bastard.'

They walked outside to the pack horse. Sheriff Yancey grabbed Elijah's corpse by the hair, jerking the puffed head up roughly.

'Yep.' He spit in the dust. 'It's Barlow all right – at least he fits the gen'ral description. I'll hafta take yore word fer the rest. Ugly as sin, ain't he?' He dropped the head with a thud. 'I'll git some of the boys to unload him.'

Once more inside, Sheriff Yancey opened his strong box and counted out one thousand dollars reward money, cursing silently to himself all the while. Lord only knew how long it would take the stagecoach company that had offered the reward to reimburse him; the damned mail system was so slow!

'The funeral – how much?' El Lobo queried.

'Fifteen dollars, same as always.'

The gunslinger peeled off the proper amount from the wad of bills.

'I expect his brothers will be along shortly, Sheriff,' he said.

'Dead or alive?'

'Alive. You'd best prepare yourself,' El Lobo warned, then took Storm by the arm.

After they'd gone Sheriff Yancey sat down to complete the necessary forms and his report, damning all bounty hunters in a whispered mutter to himself. Now, not only did he have to do all this frigging paperwork, but he had to get ready to face down the Barlow gang as well!

'Here.' El Lobo counted off five hundred dollars and handed it to Storm. 'Your share, lady.' Then he tipped his hat politely, grabbed his horses' reins, and swaggered off down the street in the direction of the livery stable.

Storm gazed after him thoughtfully. She just couldn't let him get away! She didn't know the first thing about looking out for herself in this savage land, nor did she know anyone else besides this man Wolf. She realized, in addition to this, that she would have absolutely no way in which to defend herself if the Barlow brothers did indeed pursue her. Wolf would, however. She'd seen how he'd handled those guns in that awful town. Still something told her he wouldn't give her a second glance if she went running after him like a silly, frightened child. Storm squared her shoulders, looked around to get her bearings, then headed for a general store. A tiny bell clanged as the door shut behind her. A small, wry man came hurrying forward at the sound. His grimace of disgust and abrupt manner told Storm well enough how badly she must appear.

'You must be new in town,' the man spoke. 'Witherspoon's shop, down the street, is the place for the likes of you. I run a respectable store here.'

'Are you the proprietor of this establishment, *monsieur*?' she asked.

'Yes. What about it?'

'Then would you be so kind as to take a look out of the window. Do you see that man there' – she pointed – 'the one heading toward the livery stable?'

'Yes, it's the gunslinger – El Lobo.'

'That's right. He's my – my husband,' Storm lied. 'And I don't think he's going to be too happy when he finds out you refused to wait on me.'

The shopkeeper opened his door and shoved the girl through it rudely.

'Don't think you can come in here and bamboozle me with a tale like that, young woman. I've seen your type before. Witherspoon's, down the street. Now get out!'

Storm was furious. To be taken for a common whore and thrown out of this man's store was the last straw.

'Wolf! Wolf!' she called angrily.

The gunslinger turned around just in time to see the proprietor thrusting her out onto the sidewalk. To the girl's relief he started toward the shop with slow deliberation.

'Well, what is it now?' His eyes were narrowed intently with irritation as he studied her, and for a moment Storm was afraid of him again.

Once more she gathered up her courage. 'This – this man refuses to let me inside his store,' she stammered nervously under that impatient frown.

El Lobo leaned back in his saddle and tipped his hat up

slightly to get a better look at the shopkeeper.

'That so? What's the matter? The money I gave you not good enough?'

'Oh, no, sir. No, sir, Mr Lobo,' the proprietor broke in hastily. 'Just a slight misunderstanding; that's all, I assure you. Why, what with the young lady's appearance and all – I'm so sorry, sir. I – I didn't realize she was your – your wife—'

'My wife!'

'Oh, *mon cher*, it's just too terrible!' Storm cried hurriedly before El Lobo could say anything else. 'I told you I looked a fright, and this rude, impertinent little man didn't even give me a chance to explain about our elopement and how I banged my face on the window-sash escaping and how it woke up the whole house and how all my things had to be left behind when we were discovered and how poor papa was so angry he chased us nearly ten miles.'

'Oh, of course I – I – ahem – quite understand then.' The shopkeeper wiped his damp palms on his apron, more flustered than ever.

El Lobo's mouth actually twitched – just once, but Storm was sure she'd seen a flicker of a smile touch those carnal lips. She breathed a small sigh of relief as the gunslinger said,

'Well, Mr—'

'Quigley, sir. Mr Quigley.'

'Well, Mr Quigley, I take it then you now have no objections to selling – my wife whatever it is she desires.'

'Oh, no, sir. None at all, sir.'

'Then good day, Mr Quigley. Don't spend all your money in one place, *paraibo*.' El Lobo's eyes lingered on Storm's slightly trembling figure until she blushed furiously, certain the insufferable gunslinger knew what she looked like unclothed. Almost as though he'd guessed her thought, El Lobo droned, 'No corsets, *paraibo*,' then rode on.

'*Paraibo*.' Mr Quigley tried the word. 'What does it mean, Mrs Lobo?'

'I – I'm afraid I don't know, *monsieur*.'

'You don't speak Comanche then? Well, no matter. No doubt your husband will teach you soon enough. They say he's more Indian than white. Oh! I beg your pardon, Mrs Lobo,' the proprietor babbled, still upset by what he considered was a near brush with death. 'I've got one of the prettiest gowns you ever did see.' He hastily changed the subject. 'Bet it's just your size. Would you care to step this way?'

Storm was momentarily stunned. 'What? Oh, yes. Yes, of course. But I'm not interested in dresses, Mr Quigley. I'm afraid the state of the one I'm wearing has pointed out to me the impracticality of such apparel in the West.'

She followed the man into his shop, still thunderstruck by his earlier words. *More Indian than white*! Wolf *was* a savage – a – a half-breed! *Sainte Marie*! It was a wonder she hadn't been scalped! Oh, just to think one of those 'red devils', as Mrs Thatcher had called them, was the only person Storm knew in this cruel, dreadful land! To think she would still be forced to ask him for help! Storm wanted to die, but it was Wolf or the Barlow brothers; and at least Wolf had not attempted to molest her. She thought of the sly pinches Billy Barlow had given her, his intent plain. Oh, *mon Dieu, mon Dieu*! What was to become of her?

'Well, what did you have in mind then, Mrs Lobo?' The shopkeeper brought her back to the present with a start.

The girl bit her lip. 'Breeches, Mr Quigley.'

'Breeches!'

'Breeches,' Storm said definitely.

'Well, I – I don't know as what I've got will fit you, Mrs Lobo.' The proprietor hid his shock as he appraised the girl's figure swiftly and professionally. 'But we'll see what we can do.'

With the same eye for detail that had allowed Storm to memorize any of the ladies' gowns in New Orleans and copy them later, she now moved to mimic El Lobo's wardrobe.

With Mr Quigley's help she was able to find three pairs of pants and five shirts that might have been made for a fifteen-year-old boy. The breeches were too tight and the shirts somewhat large, but they were the best Mr Quigley had. He coughed and disappeared discreetly as the girl then selected several camisoles and pantalettes, forgoing the corsets as El Lobo had warned. His words, though said mockingly, had been sensible, Storm knew. She would not be able to do anything strenuous laced up so tightly she couldn't breathe, and something told her she would never again be waited on hand-and-foot as she had been in New Orleans. She felt a brief moment of regret for the pampered life she would never know again, then shoved it from her mind. It would do no good to dwell on the past and what might have been. She could never go home again. She must forget New Orleans and do whatever was necessary to survive in this horrid new land and life of hers. With a rather frightened determination the girl continued making her choices.

Mr Quigley returned to help her try on boots. In this area Storm had to settle for a pair intended for a child; her feet were so tiny. Still the hat she picked fit well, and the gloves and stockings were perfect. She also bought what Mr Quigley told her was a poncho for keeping warm at night, two Indian blankets, and a pair of silver spurs.

Then they moved to the glass gun counter. Storm was immediately taken with a revolver that was called a Walker Pistol. It looked lethal!

'Oh, no, Mrs Lobo! You don't want that!' Mr Quigley exclaimed. 'That's the heaviest gun that was ever made! Why, the kickback would knock you flat! I just know your husband wouldn't want you to have that! Here, try this.' He handed her a small pearl-handled derringer that fired two shots.

'No, this won't do.' Storm shook her head. 'I want two revolvers, Mr Quigley, preferably ones that fire six shots each. My – my husband is in a dangerous line of work, and I must be prepared to defend myself.'

'Oh, Mrs Lobo! Surely no one would harm an innocent woman like yourself!' Mr Quigley was horrified.

'I – I hope not, Mr Quigley, but you understand I cannot take any chances.' Storm thought of the Barlow brothers and shuddered.

'Yes, yes, of course. Well, take a look at these Dragoon Colts then. They just came out this year, but I still think they'll be too heavy for you, Mrs Lobo.'

'Why, these are just like my – my husband's, except that his have silver plating on them.'

'Yes, well, something like that would have to be made to order special, Mrs Lobo. No doubt your husband sent back East, to Mr Colt's factory, for his. These are still very nice guns, however. See, the latch is new. The older Colt from which this model was developed, the Walker Pistol with which you were so taken, had a spring cramp latch. This one's much more efficient. If you're determined on a pair of revolvers, I'd take these if I were you.'

'Fine. Would you wrap them up please, along with whatever ammunition and other supplies are needed.'

'I have a boxed package available, Mrs Lobo. Twenty-five dollars for the lot.'

'All right.'

Storm also bought a black leather gunbelt, a deadly-looking knife, two canteens, and, on impulse, some rice powder, a bottle of lotion, and a flacon of rose scent, the fragrance reminding her painfully of New Orleans once more. She also purchased a few essentials such as a toothbrush and tooth powder and a brush and comb.

Peeking through her stack of packages, she then picked her way carefully to the hotel across the street. A short while later the girl had been shown to a room and was ensconced in a hot bath. She scrubbed herself vigorously, lathering her body generously with the hard soap provided. She dunked her head into the water, washing her hair well. Slowly the grime that had covered her began to disappear, and the stiffness in her tired, aching limbs started to dissolve. By the time she'd finished soaking, the meal and the ice cold well water she'd ordered had arrived.

Storm stuffed herself as hastily as possible, feeling only a brief pang of guilt at what Mammy would have said had she seen, for Mammy had always sternly informed the girl that, 'Ladies doan eat lahke pigs!' Storm dipped a small hand towel into the cold water as she ate, then pressed the wet cloth up against her face, hoping to get rid of some of the swelling. Each time the rag lost its coolness she repeated the procedure and thought longingly of the huge cakes of ice her parents had often had floated down the Mississippi River to Belle Rive for some party. If only she had one tiny frozen sliver now! she sighed.

When she had finished her meal, Storm cleaned her teeth, then towel dried her hair and brushed it, doing the best she could to get out the snarls, for Mammy had performed this task in the past. The remembrance brought tears to Storm's eyes. She wiped them away hastily. She was delighted to see most of the swelling had indeed gone down from soaking her face with the cold wet towel. Only a slight bruise remained to remind her of Ma Barlow's fearful punch. The girl slathered some of the lotion on her sunburned face, then patted it gingerly with rice powder. This helped camouflage the purplish-blue mark and some of the redness as well. She examined the tiny wound on her arm, but saw nothing to alarm her, so she left it alone and began to dress herself. The pants were snug and rode her tightly, molding to her slender legs to show the graceful curves of her calves. The breeches were tight and too long as well, but she fixed this by cramming the cuffs inside her boots. The shirt was a little big, so she tied the ends up, making a knot across her belly. She fastened the gunbelt around her waist, clasped on the silver spurs, drew on her gloves, and set the hat on her head, cocking it down over one eye just a little. The extra ammunition belts she draped crossways over her chest. As a finishing touch, she stuck the pistols in their holsters and the knife in its sheath. At last, she was done.

'You look bad enough to scare a swamp rat,' she told her reflection in the mirror proudly.

She glanced longingly at the soft, inviting white sheets of the bed but knew she dared not linger for even a small nap, despite her exhaustion. Wolf might leave without her! Storm gathered up the rest of her things, then headed toward the livery stable, pleasantly surprised to find how much freedom of movement she experienced in her new clothes. Why, if all women discovered such, they'd never be dictated to by fashion and forced into corsets, hoops, and yards of billowing material again!

When she reached the livery stable, Storm glanced around the stalls rapidly, noting with relief that Wolf's horses were still present. Nevertheless, she felt instinctively the gunslinger would not stay the night in Goliad, and she had to be ready to leave when he did.

'I'm interested in buying a horse,' she said as the livery keeper hurried forward upon seeing her.

He scratched his head, staring at her rudely. The girl started to ask if he were deaf and dumb but then realized the poor fellow had thought she was a man at first. Doubtless he'd never seen a female in such attire before. At last, however, he gathered his wits and pointed to a roan in one of the stalls.

'I can let you have that one,' he offered.

Storm opened the half-door and went inside, feeling the gelding's legs and peering into its mouth. Finally, she shook her head reluctantly.

'No, I'm afraid this one just won't do. He's too old,' she stated firmly.

The livery keeper, who'd thought to bamboozle her into a bad bargain, was taken aback by her knowledge of horses, but of course he did not know Storm's father had owned some of the finest Thoroughbreds in Louisiana and that Paul-Edward Lesconflair had insisted his daughter learn to recognize the finer points of a good mount.

'Sorry, ma'am, I don't have anythin' else available, 'ceptin' that little mare over there, and, shucks, you don't want her. She's just an Arab, not much good for anythin' out here.'

The girl glanced over at the dapple-gray the livery keeper had indicated.

'I'll take her,' she decided after an appreciative look.

She knew from hearing her father talk that Arabian horses were sturdy, slow to tire, and could travel long distances without water, something that would be an advantage in this rugged land and something about which the livery keeper obviously knew nothing.

'I'll give you a hundred dollars for her and a saddle – a man's saddle.'

Storm did not intend to try to ride any great distance sidesaddle over the rough terrain of Texas to which she'd already been exposed.

The man scratched his head once more and started to balk, figuring she was not as smart about horses as first he'd thought.

'Well, I don't know—'

'You just said the mare was good for nothing,' Storm pointed out. 'I won't give you a penny more.'

The bargain was struck at last, the livery keeper guessing perhaps it was rather unwise to argue with a female who wore pants and carried two deadly-looking revolvers. Storm considered she'd gotten the better of the deal and had the man saddle the mare and stow her gear neatly in a pack behind the seat. Then she led the horse outside and proceeded to wait for Wolf to appear.

When she got out into the sun, the girl discovered the mare's lovely dapple-gray color was almost blue in the light. As she stroked the animal's velvet nose softly to become acquainted with her new mount Storm decided to call the delicate little horse Madame Bleu. Storm was still chatting gently in French to the mare when presently she saw Wolf sauntering down the street with that peculiar manner he had of walking – a lazy, stealthy, silent stride. Again he reminded the girl of a crouching black panther. He stopped abruptly upon seeing her, his midnight blue eyes travelling the length of her body and back. His icy shards narrowed, and despite himself, he almost smiled. *¡Por Dios*! Why had he ever thought her plain? She was beautiful after all that dirt was scrubbed off and the swelling down in her face. He wondered how she'd accomplished this last. He had to admire the way she'd decked herself out as well. She looked like a sultry Mexican *bandolera*. Much as he wanted to ignore her, El Lobo found himself saying,

'What's the matter? Have you already spent all your reward money?'

'I can drive a hard bargain if I have to,' Storm countered swiftly, breathing a little easier, for she had not missed the appreciative glint in his eyes, nor his inner struggle before he'd spoken.

'Then I take it you still have some cash left.'

'I want to talk to you – please.' Storm looked at him appealingly from under provocatively half-closed, thick sooty lashes.

'Yeah?' He raised one eyebrow. 'What about, *paraibo*?'

'*Paraibo*. What *does* that mean?'

'Chief wife.'

'Oh!' The girl had the grace to flush guiltily. 'I – I'm sorry about that, but that insolent little man—'

'No need to apologize, lady. A Comanche always looks after his woman.'

So it *was* true! He *was* an Indian! Or at least half an Indian.

'I'm not your woman,' Storm spoke through clenched teeth, 'and there's no need for you to rub the lie in.' She was indignant that her charms did not appear to be working on this arrogant, stony-faced gunslinger.

'As you wish. Well, what did you want to talk to me about?' He gazed at her speculatively, a trifle impatient. 'I don't have all dày.'

Oh! He was contemptible! No man had ever spoken to Storm like that. She longed fervently to toss her head and give him an arrogant set-down – one he certainly deserved – but she dared not. She wanted his assistance – needed it desperately.

'I – I saw the way you handled those guns in that horrid town—'

'Gorda Vaca.'

'Yes, well, whatever it was called. If you're a killer, I don't care. I want you to defend me from the Barlow gang. I – I'm willing to pay,' she ended, a little breathless.

'A killer, huh? Well, I suppose that's true. I'm a gunslinger, lady, but I'm not used to working for females, and I don't think you could afford my fee.' He turned to enter the livery stable.

'Wait!' Storm cried, feeling a gnawing fear come over her again. 'You – you just can't leave me here! Those men will kill me! You know they will!'

'Probably; however, you seem well enough prepared.' He noted the pistols at her hips.

The girl bit her lip. 'I – I don't really know how to use them,' she confessed.

'I figured as much.' He led his horses out. 'I wouldn't tell the Barlow brothers that if I were you,' he warned as he mounted up. Then he tipped his hat politely as he'd done before and rode off.

Storm stood there staring after him for a moment, then she swore furiously under her breath. *Par Dieu*! He would *not* leave her here! She would not let him! She mounted Madame Bleu and galloped out of town after him. Wolf gave her an irritated glance as she came alongside of him.

'Lady, I told you I wasn't for hire,' he snapped curtly.

She jerked her chin haughtily. 'It's a free country. I guess I can ride where I choose.'

'Yeah, well, I'm not going to be responsible for you. I don't have time to waste on stupid women.'

'I'm not stupid, only ignorant,' Storm said wrathfully, on the verge of losing her temper and bursting into tears. 'Besides, you already are responsible for me.' She played the last trump card she held. 'You wagered a thousand dollars for me, or did you forget? You'll just have to put up with me until I can buy back my freedom!'

He reined in his Pinto stallion sharply at that, his cold hard orbs raking her lithe figure with sudden intentionally vulgar interest. Damn! If her eyes had been black, instead of gray, she might have been Beloved-Of-The-Forest gazing at him fiercely on their wedding night, asking with angry shyness if he didn't know how to be gentle with a maid.

'You want me to hold you to that?' he asked mockingly.

Storm blushed hotly under his lewd, searing stare, feeling suddenly very queer and confused. Her heart pounded strangely as she turned her head away.

'I thought not,' Wolf jeered, then kicked his spurs into the sides of his horse.

The girl did likewise, not catching up with him this time, but determined to at least keep him in sight. After all, he was all she had.

8

Gabriel North shaded his eyes against the glare of the sun to get a better look at the small shack below. Not a breeze was stirring, and there was no sign of life at the cabin.

'Whaddaya think, Mr North?' Sheriff Martin asked hesitantly, while the rest of Gabriel's men and the posse who'd joined them shifted uneasily in their saddles.

'This is where the trail ends, Lonnie. They've got to be in there.'

'I don't know, pa,' Joe Jack spoke up. 'It looks deserted to me.'

'Yore boy's right, Mr North,' the sheriff agreed.

Gabriel gave them both a curt stare. 'Well, let's go down and see.'

Slowly they started down the rough trail that led to the house. They held their rifles in their hands, ready to fire if necessary, but no one challenged them. The very stillness of the place was eerie, even in broad daylight; and the smell of death that hung in the air made even Gabriel's skin crawl. He pushed open the door of the hut cautiously. The shack was empty. He glanced around, noting the plates on the table where a meal had been hurriedly eaten and left. A cup was overturned. There was a stain on the floor where the coffee had dripped. A horde of ants covered a forgotten or unwanted crust of bread. A large roach scurried around the leg of a chair. Gabriel poked into the cabinets curiously. They were empty too, except for a few cooking utensils and some old newspaper clippings. He rifled through these last.

COACH ROBBED, BARLOW GANG SUSPECTED IN HOLD-UP

A Carstairs stagecoach was held up yesterday afternoon. The coach, enroute from Houston to Goliad . . .

THREE KILLED IN SHOOTOUT WITH BARLOW GANG

Three persons were killed yesterday in a shootout with the Barlow gang at the Last Chance Saloon. Mae Laroux, proprietress of the saloon, said the quarrel broke out when . . .

COMPANY OFFERS REWARD FOR CAPTURE OF BARLOW GANG

The Carstairs Stagecoach Company has posted a reward for the capture of the Barlow gang, dead or alive. Mr Carstairs, President of the line, said . . .

BARLOW GANG HITS SAN ANTONIO BANK, SEVEN DEAD

Seven people, including bank manager Tom Rathbone, were killed . . .

Gabriel tossed the rest of the clippings onto the table, his face grim.

'Well, at least we know who's got her,' he told the men who'd followed him into the cabin. 'It's the Barlow gang, Lonnie, just as you thought.'

Sheriff Martin cleared his throat. 'If that's so, Mr North, they've probably gone on into Gorda Vaca. Leastways, it don't look like they're comin' back here.'

'Pa! Hey, pa!'

Gabriel turned and ran out of the house quickly. 'What is it, Joe Jack?'

'Look here, pa.' Joe Jack pointed to the fresh grave he'd found a ways off from the hut.

Gabriel felt his heart lurch sickeningly. 'My God! You men, get over here. I want this grave dug up. I've got to be sure—'

'Lord, pa, you ain't serious?' Joe Jack stared at his father disbelievingly.

'I've got to know if it's her or not. Don't you understand?' Gabriel shouted angrily.

Reluctantly his men began to search for some shovels. At last they found the ones used by the Barlow brothers. Silently they began to dig. Joe Jack watched, irritated. What in the hell ails the old man? he thought to himself. He's carrying on worse than he did when his prize bull got sick and died. I didn't think pa cared about anything more than that old bull! Well, at least if it's the bride-to-be, we can all go home. I'm sick and tired of sitting in the saddle all day with nothing to eat but a few strips of jerky and no liquor to boot!

'Mr North.'

Gabriel gazed down at the bloated, pox-scarred face his men had finally managed to uncover. He shook his head.

'Thank God, it's not her.'

Joe Jack groaned audibly. Gabriel swung around on his son furiously.

'I've had just about enough out of you, Joe Jack! You get on home before I tan your hide!'

'Aw, pa—'

'Uh, Mr North,' Sheriff Martin broke in hurriedly. 'I think we'd all best be gittin' on back to San Antonio. I'm sorry, sir, but I don't believe we're gonna find yore little fiancée, 'specially if those men have taken her into Gorda Vaca. Why, ain't a lawman alive what'd set foot in that town, not even the Texas Rangers!'

Gabriel looked at the posse's sullen faces and realized the sheriff was right. He'd heard about Gorda Vaca himself.

'I'll pay every man who stays on a thousand dollars,' he offered.

'Sorry, Mr North.'

'It ain't worth it, Mr North.'

'I got a family to think of, Mr North.'

One by one the men turned away.

'Two thousand dollars!' Gabriel upped his price, but still the posse continued to mount up and leave. 'Lonnie, when you get back to San Antonio, you post a reward for my fiancée. I'll pay five thousand dollars for her return or any information leading to her whereabouts.'

'Shore thin', Mr North. Sorry we couldn't be of more help.'

'We going home, pa?' Joe Jack asked hopefully.

'Yes,' Gabriel snarled, realizing he was momentarily defeated. He kicked his spurs into Buck's sides furiously and galloped off, his men following quietly behind.

The next day the Barlow brothers rode into Goliad. They surprised Sheriff Yancey over his morning coffee, questioned him at gunpoint about Storm and El Lobo, then locked both him and his deputy in one of their own jail cells where they remained all day undiscovered. That night the Barlows got drunk and shot up the saloon, killing three people and wounding five more before one decent citizen managed to escape and find and free the two lawmen. By the time Sheriff Yancey arrived at the saloon, however, the Barlow gang had already fled.

That same morning Gabriel North went into San Antonio to be certain Sheriff Martin had posted the reward notice. In his father's absence Joe Jack seduced one of the Mexican women who worked at Tierra Rosa. The girl giggled shyly and tittered, 'Oh, señor,' when Joe Jack pulled her down into the hay in the barn loft. She was new at the ranch and did not yet know about Joe Jack's reputation. She though herself honored to be servicing the Boss's son.

Cathy, as usual, puffed on her thin brown cigar and said nothing.

9

Wolf glanced back over his shoulder. Sure enough, the French girl was still behind him. Despite himself, he began to develop a grudging respect and admiration for her determination. He'd set a rapid pace, expecting she would soon grow tired of following him and quit; but although he knew she must be weary to the bone, she was still hanging on. In addition, the small mare she'd bought showed no signs of flagging either. Wolf felt some measure of surprise at this, for very few horses could keep up with his own Pinto stallion, Pahuraix. He paused, took a drink from his canteen, then rode on.

Storm gritted her teeth in anger to keep from crying out. Damn the man! Had he no compassion at all? Her backside ached from the unaccustomed astride position on the saddle. She was sure her legs were chafed raw from the ceaseless motion. She was hot, thirsty, and tired too – so tired she had twice fallen asleep in the saddle only to lurch into wakefulness, her heart beating frantically, when she had nearly fallen off. She hadn't dared pause to rest, however, for fear of losing the gunslinger, and had only managed to grab a couple of sips of water the few times he had stopped himself for just such a purpose. Had she thought she could hit him, Storm would gladly have fired her pistols at the stubborn man.

At least Madame Bleu appeared to be holding up well. The girl reached down and patted the mare's graceful neck gratefully. Then she wiped the sweat from her face and nape and vowed tomorrow she would put up her hair. It felt unbearably sticky and humid against her neck and back where it clung to her damp shirt plastered between her shoulder blades. She glanced up at the scorching sun and licked her parched lips, trying to moisten them a little with her tongue. I'm going to die, she thought, feeling suddenly overwhelmed and defeated. I can't keep this up. I wasn't born to it like that savage! Oh, *Sainte Marie*, have mercy. Whatever I've done to displease you, surely I don't deserve this. I don't want to die. I've got to stay awake. I've got to keep moving, somehow, someway . . .

The rolling plains spread out before her, starkly green and brutal, yet somehow lush and passionate as well. Like a ripe, languid woman, raw and untamed, they lay in soft, savage swells beneath the fiercely brilliant yellow sun in the azure sky, untouched, uncivilized like the gunslinger Storm followed. Never had she felt so alone, so helpless as she gazed at the land stretching out forever in all directions. She felt small in comparison – small and humble. Yet had she not been so afraid, the sight might have gladdened her heart, filled it with joy, for this was a land in which a man could breathe, a land in which a man could stand wild and free beneath the unending summer sky and feel he stood in the very hollow of God's palm. Yes, this was God's country, but Storm was not touched by the rugged beauty of the vast terrain. She was used to the neat, enclosed courtyards of the French houses seated elegantly side-by-side in the *Vieux Carré*; the pretty cobblestone bricks of Bourbon and Royal Streets with their clatter of sleek Thoroughbred horses and expensive carriages upon which crisply uniformed Negro grooms sat tall and proud; the plaintive sigh of the wind as it swept in off the Mississippi River and whispered to the rustling magnolia trees and the sweet mimosas hanging with Spanish moss; the droning of the locusts in the countryside where white-columned plantations stood guard over the fields of cotton and rice; the jubilant singing of the darkies late into the evening after the day's work was done.

Her sorely grieving heart missed all this that was dear and familiar as she galloped over the land that was strange and unknown and – to her – something to be feared. She felt lost, cast adrift, with only her wits to survive – her wits and the tall dark gunslinger who rode on relentlessly ahead. It was he who frightened her more than anything else – he who was as strange and unknown as the land. How could she put her faith in such a man? How could she not? She wiped the sweat from her forehead with the back of one hand and pressed on.

The day dragged on until at last the sun began to sink on the western horizon. For the first time Texas caught Storm in its grip. Her breath caught in her throat. Surely the entire world was on fire! The flaming red blaze almost brought tears to her eyes; it was so beautiful – the only thing of beauty she had discovered in this harsh land. She missed it when it was over, missed it more than ever as night harried dusk's footsteps, and dark brought the cool air that had waited all day for its release. Storm panicked as she realized she could no longer discern Wolf's tall figure astride his stallion in the distance. I must not lose him! she thought frantically as she pushed on blindly. I must not lose him! Soon she became even more terrified by the wild blackness, for the animals came out, hungry beasts with eyes that glowed in the pale moonlight, hideous creatures that bayed howlingly at the silvery crescent.

She plunged on heedlessly through the dense brush, pushing Madame Bleu as hard as she dared to escape the sparks of eyes melting into the shadows, the frightful wailing sounds. Far and away the girl spied a light flickering strangely on the prairie. She galloped toward it gratefully, almost kicking over the coals of the fire when she reached it in her haste.

Madame Bleu whinnied and reared, sending tiny shards of grass and dirt flying. Storm was almost unseated as she fought the beast for control.

'That was a stupid thing to do,' Wolf snarled at her, appearing out of the darkness with his guns drawn. 'I might have killed you.' He returned the revolvers to their holster, caught the mare's bridle, and yanked Storm from the saddle. 'And what if this camp hadn't been mine? Did you ever think of that, you little fool?' He shook her slightly.

She gasped with fear at the shock of his rough touch, shrinking away from him, looking for some means of protection.

'I – I was afraid – of the – the wolves.'

'Which one?' he mocked, his eyes narrowing suddenly at the play on his name.

'Please.' Her lips parted softly. 'I – I feel so – so strange—' Then she fainted into his arms.

Wolf swore under his breath as he carried her to the fire and laid her out on the ground. Then he rummaged through his pack for the chips of salt block he always carried with him. He raised the girl's head, forcing the slivers into her mouth, then pouring the water from his canteen between her lips. Pretty soon Storm opened her eyes again. She realized she was lying down and that Wolf was hunkered down on his haunches beside her, staring at her in that peculiar, silent way he had.

'Feeling better?'

She nodded her head. 'I – I think so.'

'Didn't have anything to eat, did you?'

'No.'

'You sweated the salt out of your body. That's why you passed out. Are you hungry now?'

'Yes.'

She sat up, not caring to look at the small form roasting on the spit he'd rigged over the fire as he handed her a tin pan filled with steaming meat and beans.

'There's coffee too if you want it.' He indicated a pot sizzling on the coals. 'Go ahead and eat. I'll see to your mare.'

'I – I need a fork please, *monsieur*.'

He gave her a wry glance. 'I'm afraid my utensils don't extend to silverware. You'll have to use your fingers.' Then

136

he turned to lead Madame Bleu away.

Storm had never eaten with her fingers in her life, but outside of starving it seemed she had no other choice. She shivered as she scooped up the hot meat and beans, shoving them into her mouth in a very unladylike fashion. He's a savage, she thought again. He didn't even offer me a spoon! I must have been mad to ride after him – mad! We're all alone here – just he and I – miles from nowhere. God only knows what he might do to me— The girl put her empty plate aside, her fingers trembling, then took another drink from Wolf's canteen. She laid one hand warily on one of her pistols. If he tries to touch me, I'll shoot him, she decided. At this range surely I cannot miss! Her heart began to thump queerly as she waited for Wolf to return, then leapt to her throat as he appeared. Storm saw with a sinking feeling in the pit of her stomach that he was still wearing his revolvers. I'll never be fast enough to kill him, she despaired inwardly. Oh, what have I done? What have I done?

Wolf seemed not to notice her nervousness. He tossed her gear to one side, then poured himself a cup of coffee. After that he sat down a few feet away from Storm, stretching out along the ground, laying his back against his saddle. Casually he lit one of his thin black cigars, blowing a cloud of smoke toward the stars in the sky before at last he spoke.

'Lady, you're worse than a flea on a dog.'

Storm stiffened at the words. Dear God. Maybe he was planning to murder her out here, bury her on this lonesome prairie where she would never be found! Her fingers gripped the stock of her gun tightly.

'I – I told you my name, *monsieur*,' she said, marshaling her courage and wishing this man did not evoke such fear in her. 'You might try using it. I don't see why you have to be so sarcastic just because I managed to keep up with you when you thought I wouldn't.'

She saw at once by the slight narrowing of his eyes that her shot had hit home and felt another tingle of fright run chillingly up her spine. *Sacré bleu!* Why had she deliberately tried to provoke the man when she knew him to be as deadly as a snake? She must be suffering from sunstroke. Yes, that was it. That dreadful sun had done something to her mind!

'What's a green woman like you doing out here?' Wolf asked, that same soft, deceiving note in his voice she had heard when he'd spoken to Billy Barlow. 'You talk like some high class French whore. Did somebody ride you out of town on a rail? Is that why you're "coming from nowhere and going nowhere," as you put it?'

Storm was outraged and if she hadn't been so afraid, she would have tried to kill him right then.

'I am *not* a whore, *monsieur*, and you will do me the courtesy of never repeating that insult. I assure you I am gentle-bred and not used to hearing such language. As for the rest of my past – it's none of your business.'

Coolly Wolf took another drag of his cigar. 'Lady, everything about you is my business if you're going to hang on to me like a wood tick, and I'd better start getting some answers to my questions right now.'

'A gentleman does not ask such questions of a lady, *monsieur.*'

'I never said I was a gentleman.' His voice was low, silky, and threatening as he suddenly threw away his cigar and sprang menacingly to his feet. 'I'm a Comanche, lady. I scalp insolent women like you.'

Terrified, Storm screamed and yanked her pistol from its holster, her hands shaking so badly she could hardly hold the heavy revolver level as she aimed it at his chest. Wolf never even batted an eyelash.

'That wasn't very well-done,' he noted. 'I could have shot you six times before you managed to draw that gun.'

'Don't come near me!' the girl cried as he began to stalk toward her silently. 'I'll shoot! I will!'

'Oh, for Christ's sake! The damned thing's not even

loaded!' Wolf sneered with disgust.

Startled and confused, for she was sure Mr Quigley had loaded it for her, Storm looked down at the pistol she was clutching convulsively. Off guard, she was not prepared for Wolf's sudden graceful, catlike movement as he kicked the revolver from her hands, then fell upon her with an angry growl. She gasped as she felt the jarring shock of his weight, warm and hard and muscular, against the length of her body. She tried to fight him, but she was no match for his steely strength. He grabbed her flailing arms easily as she attempted to claw his face. Then he imprisoned her wrists above her head before he rolled slightly to one side, one leg still pinioning her own to the earth, his free hand resting on her belly. Deliberately he drew his knife. It glittered cold and silvery in the moonlight as he pressed the blade against her throat.

'No, please,' Storm sobbed. 'Don't kill me. Please.'

She bit her lip and looked up at him pleadingly, her soft gray eyes filling with tears. He was so strong, so savage, so compelling. Somehow she knew instinctively he would mate like an animal, wildly, fiercely, exquisitely. There would be nothing of the crude, filthy Barlows in this handsome half-breed. This is your life, Storm! she told herself. He's all you have now, and perhaps he will be gentle with you. Better him than the Barlows. What will it matter if only you stay alive?

'I'll – I'll do anything, *monsieur*, anything—'

Wolf stared down at her, his midnight blue eyes impenetrable and suddenly filled with desire. 'I can think of a lot of things I'd rather do with you than kill you. I never had me a white *lady* before, and since you're obviously so willing—'

With a low mutter he threw away the knife and caught her face with one hard hand, tilting her inviting rosebud mouth up to his own. His lips closed over hers expertly, possessively as his tongue forced its way inside, exploring

139

the sweetness that lay within, ravishing her very soul. Oh, God! How he kissed her, igniting a fire in Storm's blood that rushed to her head and pounded there, making her strangely hot and dizzy. She felt powerless beneath that mouth, swept away by the sheer ecstasy of it, and it terrified her. This was no well-bred Southern gentleman with whom she could flirt and tease with her kisses, who would withdraw politely, if disappointedly, when she asked him to stop. No, this man was a half-bred heathen, a man as wild as the West, a man who took what he wanted without a second thought!

The girl quivered in his rough grasp and shut her eyes more tightly, her breathing ragged as she tried to prepare herself to be raped, as his lips left her mouth to slash across her cheek searingly, like a brand, as his hands began to tear at the buttons on her shirt. A solitary tear trickled from beneath the feathery black fringe of one eyelash as she waited for his violent assault. Wolf tasted the crystal droplet traveling like a rivulet down the side of her face. It was as bittersweet upon his lips as the tears he'd once shed for his mother and father, for his dead wife and son. To Storm's surprise he suddenly swore and released her.

'Well, that answers one question at least,' he said grimly, trying to get himself under control, for he had not realized how much the kiss he'd taken so brutally would affect him. 'You're not a whore.'

Storm gazed up at him incredulously, her mouth still parted tremulously, swollen and bruised. 'You mean you're – you're not going to – to—'

'Rape you?' he asked as she blushed, mortified, and drew the edges of her blouse together with trembling fingers. 'No.' He arose and tossed her gun back. 'Don't ever point that at me again unless you're damned well-prepared to use it. And be careful; it's loaded.'

'Oh.' Storm felt like a fool. 'You – you tricked me.'

He gave her a curt glance. 'Be glad I did, lady. Otherwise

I might have had to kill you.'

'Would you – would you really have done it?'

'Yes.'

The girl shivered at his cold response. 'And – and scalped me too?'

'Well, it would have been a shame to waste all that pretty black hair now, wouldn't it?'

'*Mon Dieu, mon Dieu*!'

'Speak English,' he ordered simply. 'I don't understand French.'

'I – I'm sorry. I said, "my God, my God".'

'The God of the Black-Robes has no medicine, lady. You'd be better off to pray to Mother-Moon.' He indicated the silver crescent in the sky.

Storm wondered at his bitter tone of voice. It almost seemed as though he – he were in pain when he talked about God.

'The Black-Robes, *monsieur*?'

'That's what the Comanches call Catholic priests. And stop calling me "*monsieur*". It sounds damned strange. I told you my name.'

'And I told you mine, *monsieur*, but I have yet to hear you say it.'

'All right then, Miss – I assume it *is* "miss" – Lesconflair, I think you'd better start talking. I don't like not knowing with what I'm dealing.'

Storm studied her hands nervously for a moment. It was useless and foolish to withhold whatever information he wanted. He might change his mind and rape her, try to beat it out of her, kill her. With a deep breath she started at the beginning and told him everything then – everything except Gabriel North's name, for she still feared Wolf might try to force her to return to her fiancé. She sighed when she was finished, feeling oddly relieved. It had been good to get it all off her chest after all.

'Ten years ago, perhaps even five years ago, such a thing

could not have happened, for the French society in New Orleans was very rigid in its rules and closed to outsiders. But as the Garden District grew, and *les Americains* – the Americans – became rich and powerful, we were forced to admit them to our homes, give them our – our women. Then it was no longer a disgrace to wed such a man as I was to have married. But I did not love him; I could not. Now I cannot go home, nor will I go to *him*, the *canaille*! I have no one to whom I can turn but you, Wolf. If – if you do not help me, I am lost,' the girl ended simply.

'This cousin of yours, André-Louis, doesn't appear to have been much of a man. No Comanche would have let his woman go without a fight. Are you still in love with him?' he queried casually, feeling an odd stab of jealousy at the idea.

'I don't know. So much has happened so far I've scarcely had time to think about it. You do not seem shocked by my story.'

'Any reason why I should be?'

'Then do your people also wager their women away at cards as *mon oncle* did me?'

'They are occasionally gambled away, yes, but not at cards and never to an outsider. Nevertheless you belong to this rancher, and I don't have time to waste on the likes of you or the Barlow brothers.'

'Oh, please don't make me go to him! I'd rather die! I hate him – the arrogant pig! He turned André against me and killed Mammy as surely as though he put that bullet in her himself! Oh, please, Wolf, I beg you! I – I know what you are, and even though it frightens me, I don't despise you for it. I'll try not to be of any trouble to you. I promise to work hard, and I won't complain. Oh, please, Wolf. I'll do anything—'

He leaned over and grabbed a handful of her black hair, his dark visage pressed close to hers again, so close she could feel his breath, warm and smelling slightly of the good cigars he smoked, against her cheek.

'So you don't despise me, huh? In fact, you prefer me to your fiancé? So much so that you'd even give yourself to me like a common whore, wouldn't you? Even though you'd die of shame afterward? Oh, yes, I've seen pretty white women like you after they've been taken by red devils like me, haughty white bitches who sweep their skirts aside when I pass them by on the sidewalk, afraid their lily white bodies might be dirtied by my heathen touch! And I've laid with white whores who charged me double because I wasn't quite good enough even for them. But you'd let me put my hands on you all the same, wouldn't you – if I'd take you with me and save your neck? Answer me, damn it!'

'Yes. Yes, if that's what you want!' she cried, ashamed.

'Yeah? Well, one of these days I'm going to take advantage of that.'

He stared hard at Storm once more, his eyes glinting speculatively in the moonlight. She flushed uneasily and turned away with embarrassment. The sight of her, so helpless and vulnerable, stirred the savage Indian in him, and suddenly he found the idea of having this lovely white woman at his utter mercy appealed to him. He despised the white whores who spread their legs for him and took his money, hating him all the while; he despised the rich white bitches who sneered at him as though he were tainted; and most of all he despised the pompous white ranchers who had stolen The Land and killed The People. Yes, he would take this beautiful, desperate white lady with him, and before it was all over she would come to him willingly, wanting him, and beg him to make her his and he would be revenged on them all – the white whores who laughed at him, the white ladies who looked right through him, and the white ranchers who had trampled The Land and spit on its proud inhabitants with disgust.

'You'd better get your bed made up, and get some sleep. We've got a long ride ahead of us tomorrow if we're going to put some distance between you and the Barlow brothers.'

'Does – does that mean you're going to help me?'

'I reckon.'

'Thank you. Oh, thank you, Wolf.'

For the first time since the stagecoach hold-up Storm began to breathe a little easier. Had she known the reason behind his sudden acquiescence she would have been frightened, indignant, and humiliated, but she did not know and so a tiny spark of hope ignited in her breast.

'You'd better save your thanks until you're sure you want to give it,' he drawled. 'I expect you'll end up hating me before this is all over.'

'What – what do you mean?'

'You'll see,' he prophesied ominously, and with that Storm had to be content.

She got her blankets from her pack and made up her bed, using her saddle for a pillow as Wolf instructed her.

'Put your guns underneath the cantle,' he told her, 'so they'll be within easy reach. Might as well start out right, even if you don't know how to use them yet.'

At last Storm was done. 'It doesn't look very comfortable,' she said as she surveyed her handiwork.

'Yeah, well, I'm not running a hotel for Southern belles.'

The girl was crushed by his sarcasm and for one panicky moment felt like fleeing into the darkness. Only the thought of braving wolves far worse than the gunslinger prevented her from wild flight.

'Wolf, I – need to – to have a moment's privacy,' she stammered.

Mercifully he decided to honor her request. 'I'll get some more wood for the fire. Don't wander away from camp. You already know about the wolves out here,' he spoke as though he had read her mind, 'and there are rattlesnakes too.'

Storm nodded. After he'd gone she washed her face and

hands sparingly with some of the water from her canteen and brushed her teeth. She undressed hesitantly, remembering the way Wolf had kissed her earlier and wondering just how much she would have protested, how badly she would have regretted it afterward if he had continued. *Jesù!* Of what am I thinking? Leaving on her camisole and pantalettes, she put on her poncho for an extra measure of warmth and protection. Then she crawled between her blankets and began the arduous task of trying to brush out her hair, which was a mass of tangles from the wind and humidity.

'Are you decent yet?'

'Yes,' she replied, drawing the blanket up hastily around herself, hanging on to it with one hand for modesty's sake, while trying to complete her grooming with the other.

Wolf dumped the wood on the ground and stoked up the fire. Then he finished cleaning up the dishes and made sure they were tidily packed away. At last he lit another cigar and turned to Storm, who was still struggling with her snarled tresses.

'Would you – would you mind helping me with my hair?' the girl questioned timidly. 'It's so long, and I – I'm not used to doing it myself. I lost all my hairpins or it wouldn't be such a mess, and I didn't think to get any more in Goliad. I'm afraid this heat hasn't helped any either.'

'I'm not a lady's maid. Do it yourself.'

Storm lowered her eyes to hide the sudden hurt that shadowed them. I won't ask him for another thing, she thought grimly, feeling more helpless and miserable than she'd ever felt in her life. And once he's killed the Barlows I'll be rid of him. I won't need him anymore then. I'll learn to survive out here – someway, somehow. I'll learn if it kills me, and someday I'll pay him back for being so mean to me! *Mon Dieu!* If I didn't need the wretch so badly, I'd give him the sharp side of my tongue and no mistake!

In an angry huff she yanked at the tangles until her scalp

began to smart, and tears stung her eyes.

'Oh, hell! Give me the damned brush!' Wolf growled after watching her for some moments.

Silently Storm did as he requested. He worked the stiff bristles through the snarled mass expertly, trying not to think of how many times he had performed this same task for Beloved-Of-The-Forest in the evenings after they'd made love. The French woman's hair was blue-black and soft and silky, just as his dead wife's had been. Briefly Wolf's hand tightened in the cascade of curls as he stroked it.

'There.' He tossed the brush into Storm's lap rudely. 'Plait it in the morning into two braids. That's the way Comanche women wear their hair, and that way you won't need any pins.'

'I'm not a Comanche woman,' Storm said stiffly, thinking she'd be damned if she were going to thank him for the assistance he'd so grudgingly provided.

'No, but if your skin were dark and you had on a deerskin dress, you'd pass for a half-breed.'

She lay down without responding and pulled the blanket up around her as Wolf moved to make up his own bed beside her. She studied him stoically, feeling somewhat uneasy again.

'Wolf,' she began hesitantly, 'you won't – won't—'

'Climb into bed with you?' his voice was mocking once more. 'No, not unless you invite me. Here.' He pulled his knife from its sheath. 'Sleep with that if it'll make you feel any better. I just thought you'd be warmer and safer between me and the fire. Rattlesnakes sometimes like to crawl in a man's blanket at night.'

'Oh.' Storm was suddenly ashamed. She gave his knife back. 'I – I trust you,' she stammered, her face red in the darkness.

For the first time since she'd met him he laughed, not a pleasant, joyous sound, but the jeering echo of a demon, showing a flash of even white teeth in the moonlight.

'And besides, you already have a knife, don't you?'

'Yes,' she admitted sheepishly.

He started to unbutton his shirt and pull its ends from his breeches, running one hand across the dark mat of hair on his chest.

'Go to sleep, Miss Lesconflair. That is – unless you'd care to watch me undress? One eyebrow quirked upward with cruel amusement on his copper visage.

With a small, muffled cry the girl turned her back on him and yanked her blanket up over her head, wishing she were anywhere but here on this lonesome range with a man who, though churlishly had offered to help her, obviously scorned and despised her. A long time after she'd fallen into an exhausted slumber Wolf remained awake, smoking a cigar as he stared into the fire and thought about how she was going to look naked and glistening with the sweat of his lovemaking beneath a Comanche moon.

'Miz Storm, Ah declare, youse 'bout de laziest chile Ah eber did see. Git on outta dat bed now, yo heah me? Ole Mistah Sun's jes' shinin', and heah you are jes' a'wastin' dis bootiful mohnin'. Yo git on up now. Miz Storm, yo heah me?'

Mammy's voice faded into the past as Storm's eyes flew open, meeting Wolf's midnight blue ones as he shook her roughly awake.

'Get up,' he ordered curtly.

She sat up then, suddenly startled wide awake as she grabbed his strong arms, not realizing where she was at first. The abrupt contact surprised them both as he caught her instinctively, his face so close to hers he could have kissed again those scarlet lips parted in wild confusion. Slowly he drew away from her.

'Oh,' she spoke, pushing her hair back. 'For a moment I – I thought I was back at Belle Rive, and Mammy was shaking me. It surprised me when I saw you,' she explained.

'I couldn't imagine what a strange man was doing in my room—' She bit her lip, appalled at her mistake.

'There's coffee on the fire if you want it, but hurry.'

She remembered then that the Barlow brothers were after her and that she and Wolf had a long way to ride today. She waited for him to leave, then arose, stretched, and yawned. She relieved herself behind a bush, glancing around rapidly to be certain Wolf wasn't watching. Then she moved toward the fire. Picking up the tin cup she found, Storm poured herself some coffee and sipped it hesitantly. It was hot and bitter, but at least it revived her. When she had finished, she washed the cup and stowed it away neatly in Wolf's pack as she'd seen him do last night.

'Go ahead and rinse out the coffee pot too,' he said, coming up behind here, 'but save the grounds. There's a tin for them.'

'Oh, you – you startled me.' She tried to cover herself completely with the poncho by dropping quickly to the ground, blushing at knowing he had caught a glimpse of her pantalettes.

'Miss Lesconflair.' His voice held that nasty, mocking note. 'We're going to be doing a lot of hard and fast traveling together. I realize you're a gentle-bred lady, but I'm afraid this modesty of yours is going to be very impractical. I can't run around with my back turned every minute to spare you from possible embarrassment. You'll just have to get used to a little less privacy. I assure you the occasional sight of you in your underclothes will not provoke me to – ah – wicked behavior. Now get up from there. You look ridiculous.'

The girl stood up, feeling a trifle foolish since he'd put it that way, but she still couldn't prevent the flush of crimson that stained her cheeks. Wolf appeared not to notice as he continued with his chores. Storm cleaned the coffee pot hastily, dumping the grounds in the tin he'd indicated. Then she brushed her hair and plaited it neatly in two braids, tying the ends with some strips of thong Wolf gave her. After that she dressed herself. She was just getting ready to pull on her boots when Wolf gave an angry shout and strode toward her hurriedly, snatching the shoes from her hands.

'For God's sake, woman! Always shake them out before you put them on in the morning!'

'Why?'

He shook one boot vigorously and then the other, not bothering to respond to her question as a horde of cockroaches dropped out of the latter shoe. Storm stared at the hideous creatures, horrified, for they were monstrous in size.

'What – what are they?'

'Cockroaches,' Wolfe spoke, crushing the ugly things with his boot. 'They carry all kind of diseases.'

Feeling slightly sick, Storm gingerly slid her feet into her shoes, shuddering involuntarily as she did so. Then she rolled up her soiled clothes, poncho, and Indian blankets, tying them neatly. Wolf noted her actions with approval.

'You learn quick. That's good. Now get your saddle.'

'You – you expect me to lift that thing?' the girl asked with amazement.

'And to saddle your mare,' he replied calmly.

'But – but I've never saddled a horse in my life!'

'I'm not your slave, Miss Lesconflair,' he droned a trifle impatiently. 'And if we're ever in a bind, I'm not going to have time to saddle your mount. I told you to save your thanks, that you'd wind up hating me before this was all over.'

Storm saw he was actually serious and sighed, recalling she had promised not to complain. She dragged the heavy leather saddle across the ground to where Madame Bleu was waiting patiently.

'Put the blanket on first. Never forget that; otherwise your mare will have sores on her back before the day's out, and you won't be able to ride her.'

The girl nodded, tossing the woolen square over the horse. That at least was easy. Then she bent down to lift the saddle. It didn't budge. She glanced at Wolf helplessly, but knew by the set of his jaw that he wasn't going to come to her aid. In fact, he seemed to be taking a mean delight in tormeting her – the fiend! Finally, after several more useless attempts to pick the saddle up, she squatted down and managed to haul the weighty burden into her lap. She struggled to stand, pulling muscles in her arms, shoulders, and back she hadn't even known existed. She panted rapidly at the unaccustomed exertion, her face a tight grimace of concentration. I'll show him! she thought. I'll show the bastard I'm not as helpless as he thinks! She shoved upward determinedly, and the saddle dropped with a thud on Madame Bleu.

'See. You're stronger than you thought,' Wolf noted. 'Now throw that stirrup over' – he indicated the left footrest – 'and reach under her belly for the cinch strap. That's right. Loop it through that ring, and pull it tight. Tight, I said.' He paused for a minute. 'Ornery girl.'

'Who, me? I thought I was doing fine.'

'You are. It's your mare that isn't. What's her name?'

'Madame Bleu.'

'Well, she's feeling her oats this morning. See how she's blown her sides up?'

Storm stepped back and saw the mare had indeed puffed her sides out like a pregnant horse.

'Why's she doing that? Is she sick?'

'No. She just doesn't want the saddle on. It's an old trick. You get on a horse that's been saddled like that, and you'll slide right under its belly. Take your knee, and press it into her side, hard. You won't hurt her. Pull on the strap at the same time.'

Storm did as he directed, and Madame Bleu heaved a great gasp as her sides sank back to their normal size.

Quickly, before the mare could blow herself up again, the girl yanked the girth as tight as possible.

'Tie it off now,' Wolf commanded.

When she was done, he checked the saddle to be certain it wouldn't slip.

'Well?' Storm queried, still breathing heavily.

'It'll do.'

The girl thought she had never worked so hard in her life as she did that morning. After her mount had been saddled, and she'd put her pack behind the leather seat, Wolf showed her how to stow their gear on the little gray pack horse, Asenap, so that the weight was distributed evenly. Then she learned how to kick out the fire, covering it with dirt.

'Always, always make sure it's out,' Wolf told her. 'Prairie fire's one of the most dangerous things out West.'

Finally they were mounted up and ready to go. Storm glanced around the camp site wonderingly.

'Why, if I hadn't slept here last night, I'd never have known we'd been here.'

'That's the general idea. Cover your tracks whenever you can.'

Storm stored this bit of information away thoughtfully, along with the rest of the things she'd learned that morning. Already she felt as though her head were about to burst open; there was so much to remember! Whatever would she have done without this man? She had been lucky, very lucky indeed, she realized as they loped along. He might be a gunslinger, a killer but at least he wasn't a wanted man, wasn't like those filthy outlaws – at least she could trust him not to rape her and then slit her throat, for surely he would have done so last night if that had been his intent. She nudged Madame Bleu a little to keep up with his rapid pace.

'Where are we going, Wolf?'

'Corpus Christi.'

'Is it far?'

'About a hundred miles or so as the crow flies.'

'Wolf, why – why are we running away? Why don't we just stay and wait for the Barlows? Why don't you just kill them?'

'Bloodthirsty woman, aren't you? We're not running away. I've got business in Corpus Christi, and I don't have any quarrel with the Barlow brothers. It's *you* they're after. Oh, don't worry' – he laughed shortly, that harsh, devilish sound, as Storm's eyes widened apprehensively – 'I'll take care of them all right if they come after us. I've given you my word, and the word of a Comanche is a sacred honor.'

'I – I guess I've caused you a lot of trouble.' Storm sighed.

'Yeah, well, I've had a lot of trouble before, and I'm still alive.'

Storm was not used to rigorous travel by horseback, and by mid afternoon it showed, despite her attempts to hide it. The strain of the past few days had finally taken their toll of her, and she found herself lagging farther and farther behind as the day wore on, each jolt in the saddle seeming to grow worse and worse until she was forced to clench her teeth together tightly to keep from crying out in sheer agony. Soon her body ached so unbearably she knew she could not ride another mile. Hot, tired, exhausted, aching all over, and defeated at last, she pulled Madame Bleu to a halt, groaning.

After a time Wolf, realizing she no longer followed him, turned slightly in his saddle to see what had become of her. His mouth tightened impatiently as he rode back to see what was the matter.

'Well?' He raised one eyebrow in that horrid manner of his that made her feel as though she were little better than dirt.

'I – I'm sorry, but I just can't go another step. I – I know

I promised not to complain, but please, can't we make camp early just this once?'

For one awful moment she thought he was going to refuse and simply leave her, but finally he nodded tersely, indicating a stretch of trees several yards away.

'We'll make camp there.'

Each movement was like some exquisite torture as the girl eased herself out of the saddle, hanging onto the horn to keep from falling as her knees buckled beneath her, too stiff and sore to hold her weight. Wolf, sensing her predicament, caught her around the waist, sweeping her up with a little low snarl before he dumped her unceremoniously on the ground, then unlashed her blankets and tossed them at her.

'The least you can do is make up your bed,' he stated flatly before turning to lead Madame Bleu away.

Too weary to protest Storm unrolled the bundle and spread one of the brightly colored woven blankets out, then slowly crawled upon it, stretching out gingerly. In moments she was fast asleep. She was wakened some time later by the feel of Wolf's hand upon her, stripping the garments from her until she lay clad in only her underclothes. Half-dazed and physically weakened by her ordeal, she had not the strength to fight him off and sprawled, stupored, beneath him, whimpering softly.

It doesn't matter, she thought. It doesn't matter if he rapes me. *Jesù*, I'm too tired to even care. I just hope he hurries up and gets it over with quickly.

To her surprise, however, he made no attempt to force himself on her, but merely began to massage her aching limbs and joints. The strong pressure of his sure fingers hurt fiercely at first, but gradually as he kneaded her back, her arms, and her legs the pain started to lessen. Dimly Storm realized the tension was leaving her body, draining away as she relaxed beneath his experienced massage. No man had ever before caressed her so intimately, and deep down inside she knew she ought to be mortified by Wolf's doing so; but as his hands continued to roam over her almost impersonally Storm found she was too grateful for the relief he brought her to complain. Once or twice she felt an odd stirring in her loins as he rubbed her down, but she suppressed it hastily, not daring to even think about it. At last she slept again, oblivious to his presence.

As the days and nights passed Storm began to grow more and more aware of Wolf as a man rather than just as a half-breed savage, for despite her initial reservations about him, he exuded a masculine magnetism she found difficult to ignore. Traveling together and sleeping side-by-side in the evenings afforded the girl little privacy or modesty, and though Wolf seldom touched her after those first few nights, Storm would feel his eyes upon her all the same – cold, hard, speculative midnight blue eyes that raked her silently and sometimes hungrily causing her to shiver strangely before she turned away. Sometimes she watched him covertly too, unable to restrain herself when she caught sight of him naked to the waist in the mornings while he shaved. She would study the way the sun played upon his copper skin and the manner in which his powerful, lithe muscles flexed in his arms and back when he moved and feel an odd sense of yearning not unsimilar to what she had experienced during his soothing but disturbing massage of her body. At such times she would blush, horrified by her thoughts, and scold herself mentally; but the straitlaced teachings of her upbringing seemed far behind her now, and often she discovered it was difficult to recall them. The code of the South by which she had been raised was so useless to her in every other way that common sense dictated that its moralities were useless as well, and Storm found herself hesitantly discarding more and more of her natural scruples as time went on. She excused her behavior by telling herself that Texas was hot and that the evenings were too uncomfortably humid to remain fully clothed, that she would have slept in even less at home beneath her canopy of mosquito netting, that many European women, in various stages of undress, were known to permit men into their boudoirs to help them complete their toilettes. Soon she saw nothing wrong in appearing before Wolf half-clothed, without even her poncho for protection, not realizing that to give an inch is often to give a mile.

He noted her inner struggles with secret amusement as one barrier to their intimacy after another went by the wayside, and he knew it would not be long before he had her in his bed. He wooed her so expertly, so subtly that Storm, who was used to the proper gentlemen of the South paying court to her openly, honestly, was only dimly aware of why she was growingly attracted to him. His cool, arrogant treatment of her pricked her vanity on more than one occasion, as he intended, so that without even consciously recognizing it she determined to win him with her many charms, using every coquettish, flirtatious trick she had ever learned in New Orleans to please a man, not understanding she was playing right into Wolf's hands.

The contemptible scoundrel! she thought angrily whenever his eyes ravaged her scathingly for some small mistake. I'll show him!

If he ordered her to sit up straight in the saddle, she stiffened her spine like a ramrod, her breasts straining against the thin material of her blouse enticingly until she was certain he noticed and desired her.

At night when she bathed she allowed her body to dry naturally, donning her undergarments while her skin was still damp so that the filmy material clung to her revealingly, making Wolf's eyes gleam with that hot, heathen hunger that set her blood to pounding.

I'll show him! she vowed to herself over and over as the days passed. I'll make him fall in love with me, and then I'll break his heart! It will serve him right, the rogue!

Unfortunately it seldom dawned on her that Wolf was not hers to command as the boys back home had been, that once she unleashed his barely suppressed passions he would not take 'no' for an answer, that she was playing with a wildfire she would not be able to contain once it had started to blaze uncontrollably. She only knew their strange relationship was racing toward some unknown destiny like thunderclouds across the sky before a storm.

Two weeks later, at midmorning, they reached the Nueces River just north of Lake Corpus Christi. It looked blue and cool and inviting as the dappled water rippled softly beneath the sunstreaked branches of the cottonwoods nestled along its banks.

'We'll go ahead and cross,' Wolf said. 'Then we can follow the river all the way to Corpus Christi so that we'll have plenty of fresh water. Can you swim?' He looked at her doubtfully.

'*Oui, monsieur,*' Storm spoke tartly, irritated, as usual, by the infuriating arrogance of the man. 'That I *can* do. One doesn't live on the Mississippi River all one's life without learning how to swim. My cousin taught me.'

'Good. You probably won't have to, but at least you won't drown if the current gets hold of you.' He eyed her small mare speculatively. 'I reckon that dainty little horse of yours is a lot stronger than she looks. You shouldn't have any trouble. Just spur her on in, and hang on like hell to the saddle horn.'

'As you say,' she answered with more confidence than she felt as she studied the water that only a moment before had seemed so inviting. She wondered why it suddenly didn't appear that way anymore.

I must force myself to do it, she decided. I mustn't be more of a burden to him than I've already been. He might get mad and desert me after all, even if he *does* want me in that – that way.

She took a deep breath, dug her heels into Madame Bleu's sides, and plunged in. The river was freezing, and at the initial shock of the cold water Storm floated right off the saddle and went under as the horse struck out with its front legs and began swimming. The girl broke to the surface, gasping for air as she lunged forward to catch hold of the saddle horn, trying to avoid the mare's deadly kicking hooves. Her fingers gripped the wet leather tightly as she felt herself being yanked along, up and down, up and down, with the motion of the beast. Madame Bleu snorted and tossed her head over and over, trying to clear the water from her nostrils as she swam toward the far side. Storm blinked her eyes rapidly, attempting to dislodge the tiny droplets that clung to her eyelashes, blinding her, but it was useless. The fine spray the mare was stirring up splashed right on the girl. She only knew they'd reached their destination when she felt herself being dragged along solid ground. Numb and exhausted, she released her hold on the saddle horn and dropped to the earth tiredly, panting.

'You'll live,' Wolf remarked sarcastically, dripping water all over her as he towered over her impatiently.

Hurriedly the girl rose and mounted Madame Bleu, not wishing to provoke him into sneering at her again.

It seemed cooler after the river, for trees of every kind grew densely here and provided a welcome shade from the hot sun. Storm's wet clothes helped too, and although they were dry by the time she and Wolf stopped for their midday meal, she was more comfortable than she had been in days.

Birds twittered in the branches, and here and there chattering squirrels and shy rabbits peeped out curiously from their hiding places, scurrying away quickly when they became alarmed. Herds of deer roamed the plains in the distance, lifting majestic antlered heads to stare solemnly at Storm and Wolf when they passed. Sometimes far and away would be heard the wild scream of a panther or puma that had been wakened from its sunny slumber. Once they saw a bear, but it lumbered away after sparing them only a cursory glance. Storm was surprised to see so many animals so close, for with the exception of horses and hounds, she'd had little to do with the creatures of nature.

It was dusk when Wolf at last said they could halt for the night. Storm groaned with relief as she slipped from the saddle wearily, collapsing on the ground in a lifeless heap. Wolf's dark visage was filled with that horrible amusement as he tossed her the tinder box.

'Get up from there, and get the fire started. After that you can put the coffee and beans on to boil. Then you can unsaddle Madame Bleu, rub her down, and feed and water her. When you get all that finished, you can make up your bed.'

'You vile, heartless creature,' Storm moaned, flinging the metal tin back at him. 'My backside aches, and I've never built a fire in my life!'

He ducked as the tinder box flew past his head. 'Yeah, well, that's just 'cause I've been easy on you these past few weeks. You've had enough time on your backside to adjust to this kind of life now. From now on you're going to start pulling your weight.' Storm pouted childishly, refusing to answer. He studied her coolly for a moment, then drawled, 'I thought you wanted my help, Miss Lesconflair, but I see I was mistaken.'

The girl jumped up quickly enough at that, afraid once more that he would become angry with her and leave her to the mercy of the Barlow brothers. He told her how to build the fire, although she'd watched him do it often enough, then picked up his rifle and strode off.

'Where are you going?' Storm called after his retreating figure nervously.

He stopped and turned around, his mouth curled up derisively. 'Hunting of course. Is that all right with you, *paraibo*?'

Storm flushed, realizing she should have known this, and

swore furiously under her breath after he'd gone. How dare he liken her to a nagging wife? She just *knew* that had been his intent! Still cursing him as a henchman of Satan sent to torture her unmercifully she began to search the brush for the hurled tinder box, terrified she would stir up a deadly rattlesnake in the process. At last she found the metal tin without mishap. She took her knife and dug a small indentation in the ground as Wolf had instructed, piled some brush and what pieces of fallen wood she managed to find into the hole, and spent fully an hour attempting to strike the first flint. Finally the flame caught. She blew gently on the tiny spark, in despair that it would go out once more, but it soon blazed up quite nicely. She gathered a few stones with which to surround it so that it wouldn't spread and placed these in a neat circle around the fire.

That done, she hauled her tired body over to Asenap and unpacked the foodstuffs and tin pots and pans they used for cooking. She set up the two forked branches and laid the spit across the fire in the forks. Pouring some of the water from one of the canteens into two pots, she put the coffee and beans on.

Then she stripped the saddle from her mare's back and rubbed the horse down hard with its woolen blanket. She measured out a generous portion of oats for the animal, not knowing how much was enough, which she dumped in a heap on the ground. Then she filled a bucket from the river half-full for the beast to drink. At least she knew better than to let Madame Bleu guzzle a ton of water. She'd learned that back at Belle Rive the only time in her life her father had ever struck a slave. The boy had allowed Paul-Eduard Lesconflair's lathered stallion to swill an entire bucket of water in the space of a few minutes. The horse's belly had bloated something horrible, and it had fallen over with stomach cramps moments later. Only her father's quick actions afterward had prevented the animal from dying. She eyed Wolf's beasts hesitantly, then her mouth hardened.

Let *him* take care of them! she thought wrathfully, the monster!

Finally the girl made up her bed for the evening. She looked at it longingly, but she daren't shut her eyes for even a quick nap. It was already dark, and she could hear the night creatures beginning to stir. She glanced around warily and laid one hand on her pistol for comfort. She wished Wolf would return. How dare he go off and leave her alone like this, the cad? *Jesù*! Perhaps he wasn't coming back, the swine! She jumped, startled, at the sound of a single shot in the distance. She was alarmed for a minute before she realized it must have been Wolf killing some kind of game for supper.

'I wonder how he does it?' she mused aloud to herself. '*Sacré bleu*! That man must have eyes like a cat in the dark.'

Moments later she was shocked and stunned to be grabbed from behind, a rough hand covering her mouth. She struggled wildly until Wolf's silky voice whispered in her ear.

'It's only me, Miss Lesconflair.'

'Well, why in the hell did you sneak up on me like that?' she yelled angrily. 'You scared me half to death!'

'I intended to,' he answered calmly. 'If I'd been a *bandolero* or an Apache *Inde*, you might not be alive right now.' He recalled the similar words of his uncle Masitaw-tawp clearly to this day. 'Never relax your vigil for a moment on the range, and learn to keep your ears open.'

'You might have just told me!' Storm snapped, still frightened and mad.

'By showing you, you learned a much more valuable and better remembered lesson,' he replied, tossing the carcass of a jack rabbit down and dropping his rifle. 'One that might someday save your life.'

The girl bit her lip contritely, knowing he spoke the truth.

'Bring your knife over here. I'm going to teach you how

to skin a rabbit, and then I have a surprise for you.'

'Surprise!' Storm cried, as alert as a child at the word. 'What is it?'

'Huh uh. After you skin the rabbit.'

'I don't want to touch that poor little thing!' She gazed at the pitiful dead beast sadly.

'Nevertheless you *will* do it, won't you, Miss Lesconflair? It'd be a shame if the Barlows were to shoot you just as I did this rabbit.'

The animal was a bloody mess when she'd finished with it – at least what was left of it. It looked nothing at all like the small neat forms she'd seen roasting on the spit the previous evenings. There was still enough meat on the bones for a meal, however, when she skewered it with the sharp stick and placed it over the fire to cook while Wolf took care of Pahuraix and Asenap. At last he was done and came to sit beside her.

'Now, about that surprise—' She smiled at him slowly, tentatively.

Wolf caught his breath sharply at the sight, thinking how lovely she was in that moment, her face glowing from the light of the fire, her gray eyes sparking with anticipation, her white teeth like little pearls in the darkness. For one fleeting eternity she stirred feelings in him he had long thought dead. It startled him, and to hide his sudden consternation he reached inside his shirt, taking out three long fat green leaves with little prickly spines on the sides.

'This – this is the surprise?' Storm stared at the leaves with disappointment as he handed them to her.

'¡*Por Dios*!' he growled more harshly than he'd intended. 'You're the most ungrateful woman I ever did see! If you'll just shut up for a minute, I'll tell you what to do with them.'

'I'm sorry,' the girl whispered chokingly, her eyes downcast to mask the sudden tears that glittered there.

He was right. He didn't have to put up with her, had taken her in when she'd had no place else to go, and was trying to teach her how to survive in this savage land.

'You get one of those tin pans, and mash those leaves up in it with a stone until the juices run out, making a kind of paste. They're from a special plant. They'll help your skin. It's gotten sunburned pretty badly out here, and it's starting to peel now.'

Storm couldn't believe it. This man she had thought a monster and a heathen had actually noticed how badly burned her creamy face had gotten beneath the brim of her *sombrero*. She looked at him gratefully, confused by his unexpected kindness.

'Thank you.'

She could have bitten off her tongue a moment later when he said shortly, 'You can mend some of my shirts in return.'

After supper Storm smeared the paste on her face and sat down resentfully to sew up the rents in Wolf's garments. I might as well have been sold to him, she fumed silently. He treats me worse than a slave, as though I were no better than a common trollop he picked up in some saloon! Then unfortunately she recalled that that was exactly how he had come by her. Mortified, she stabbed wrathfully at the fine silk of his clothes, wishing it were *him* under her needle! To her frustration she only succeeeded in pricking her finger. She sucked the small wound angrily, hating him all the more. When she had finished, she practically threw the shirts at him, then was sorry for it afterward as he stared up at her coldly.

'I – I'd like to have a bath.' She stood up to him defiantly nevertheless in the face of his steely rage.

'Fine. You can do the dirty laundry while you're at it.' He gave her a mocking smile meant to convey that he was getting even with her for the way she'd tossed his garments at him.

Storm wanted to slap the grin right off his face, but she didn't dare. Instead she followed him mutely to the river, muttering very unladylike things to herself under her breath.

'Turn your back,' she ordered crossly, half-afraid, as always, that he intended to sit on the bank and watch her, and while she didn't mind him seeing her now in her damp underclothes, seeing her completely naked was still something else. Obligingly, however, he turned away and stretched out against the trunk of a tree to smoke a cigar.

'Don't wade out too far,' he called unnecessarily. 'You know the water moccasins come alive at night.'

Storm shuddered, wishing he hadn't reminded her. Hurriedly she washed their soiled clothes, then stripped and bathed, not daring to sit down in the water. That done, she donned a clean camisole and a pair of pantalettes. The wet laundry was heavy, but by now Storm knew better than to ask Wolf for assistance. She heaved the bundle up against one hip wordlessly.

'Watch where you tread now in your bare feet,' he warned the girl casually, 'and follow close behind me.'

Perhaps because the bath, though brief, had revived her flagging spirits, Storm snapped impertinently, 'Yassah, Mistah Lobo. Anythin' yo say, Mistah Lobo. Will der be anythin' else, Mistah Lobo?'

He glanced at her meaningfully, his eyes glittering as they raked her in that crude manner of his, making her feel naked and vulnerable.

'There will be, Miss Lesconflair, if your attitude doesn't improve.'

She swallowed hard, realizing she had almost pushed him too far, before picking her way carefully through the trees in the dark as he started toward camp. She was so intent on the path that when Wolf stopped abruptly, she stumbled right into him.

'What is it? What's wrong?'

'We have visitors, Miss Lesconflair.' His voice was low. 'There's no reason for you to be frightened – they're

163

friends, Kiowas – but I want you to do exactly as I tell you – no questions, no complaints. If you in any way by your behavior cause me to lose face before them, you will suffer for it later. Understand?'

'Yes.'

There were nine of them seated silently around the campfire, waiting. Storm trembled when she saw them, for they looked dark and fierce in their fringed leather jackets and bone breast plates, and they all carried firearms, knives, and tomahawks. Wolf dropped his rifle and strode toward them, hands gesturing as he spoke in rapid Comanche. After a moment one of the warriors replied in what sounded, to the girl's untrained ears, like the same language, also using his hands to clarify his words. Then everyone smiled, and Wolf sat down cross-legged before the fire.

'*Paraibo*' – he addressed her first in Comanche, then continued speaking in English – 'in my pack you will find a pipe and some tobacco. Bring it to me at once, then get out the extra plates, and fix them something to eat.'

Quickly Storm tossed down her wet garments and did as he instructed, her hands shaking all the while she searched through Wolf's things. The Kiowas appeared to be impressed by his pipe, for they made sounds of awe and nodded and chattered to one another approvingly as he filled and lit it. He took several puffs, then offered it first to the warrior who seemed to be in charge. The Indian dragged on it solemnly, then passed it to his fellow tribesmen, who followed his example while Storm hurriedly cut thick chunks of what was left of the pitifully small rabbit she'd skinned and cooked earlier. These she mixed with the beans, which were plentiful, and ladled onto the plates.

'Keep your eyes downcast modestly when you serve them,' Wolf commanded, 'and say *nothing*!'

She nodded as she moved hesitantly toward the Kiowas,

handing the plates out to them in the order in which they had smoked the pipe, not daring to look at any of them, even when one glanced up at her speculatively, laughed, and said something to Wolf, who responded agreeably. The warrior continued, still laughing and apparently emboldened by the liquor the Indians had taken out of their packs and were passing around. He gestured emphatically at first himself and then Storm.

This time Wolf shook his head negatively in reply. 'No,' he answered firmly in Comanche, and even the girl understood he was refusing the warrior's request, which obviously had something to do with Storm.

'*Paraibo*, finish your chores then go to bed,' Wolf directed. 'Don't worry about the dishes. You can do them in the morning.'

Slowly the girl moved to lay their wet laundry out to dry, not liking the looks of things at all. The Kiowas were growing louder and more unruly as they consumed more and more of the liquor, seeming to have an endless supply. One warrior had gotten out a pair of dice, and now they were all, including Wolf, engaged in making wager after wager as one after another shook the bones, chanting, then tossed them out upon the ground. There were groans and curses, hoots and hollers as money and other goods began to change hands fast and loose.

After brushing out her hair Storm huddled beneath her blankets, hot, terrified and unable to sleep. She had never seen Wolf like this. He had joined in the unrestrained shouting and laughter as freely as the others. He must be drunk too, the girl thought apprehensively. He's always so quiet and controlled. *Mon Dieu!* Suppose he decided to gamble *me* away to those red devils! Oh, no, surely he won't. He said the Comanches didn't bet their women – at least in games with outsiders. But perhaps that only means whites and Mexicans, not other Indians; and besides, I'm not really his woman. Oh, *Sainte Marie*, have mercy!

Finally, after hours more of yelling, laughing, drinking, and pipe smoking, Wolf at last stripped down to his breeches and, dragging his saddle and blankets over next to Storm, crawled in beside the girl, to her surprise yanking her into the cradle of his strong arms. She could hear the slow pounding of his heart as she lay against his broad chest, too startled and afraid to protest his actions.

'You did real well,' he breathed into her ear, stroking her hair lightly to soothe her, for he could feel her body quivering all over. 'I told you there was no need to be frightened, that they were friends. They're allies of the Comanches. I've known a couple of them a long time. They'll be gone in the morning.'

She realized then the Kiowas were spreading their blankets upon the ground a short distance away. Some were already sprawled upon the earth, apparently having passed out earlier.

'What's the matter? Couldn't you sleep?'

'No, I – I was hot.'

'Yeah, I'll bet.' His voice was thick, husky and slurred. 'So am I.'

The girl blushed, an electric spark running up her spine as she became aware of the hard maleness pressed up against her. She tried to free herself from his grasp, but his arms only tightened around her.

'Wolf, don't! Let me go!'

'Huh uh, baby,' he muttered.

'But—'

'I'm a man, baby. I can't help being aroused. Besides, that's what you've wanted, isn't it, these past few weeks? I've seen tricks like yours before. You're a tease, baby; you like to lead a man on, but you don't want to give him anything in return, do you? Too bad. You don't want old Lame-Horse over there to think you prefer him to me do you? You ought to be grateful to me, baby. I told him you were my wife. Otherwise it might have been him lying between your blankets right now. Hmmm. You smell good – like roses. My mother used to grow roses. Jesus. You feel good too.'

His hand tightened on Storm's waist as he buried his face in her cloud of black hair. Then his fingers swept upward to the lacings on her camisole, pulling at the silken ties impatiently.

'No, Wolf! Don't!' the girl cried, mortified that he should have seen right through her little games and interpreted them in such a manner.

'Shut up, baby.'

He caught her face, turning it to his own. His midnight blue eyes glittered as black as ink as he kissed her lingeringly on the mouth, stilling her whispered outcries as his hand returned to her camisole, pushing the now unbound edges aside to bare her breasts for his exploring fingers.

'You've got pretty white skin, baby, just as I knew you would.'

Storm moaned softly beneath the demanding pressure of his lips, the ravaging insistence of his tongue inside her mouth. A strange half-frightening, half-thrilling shiver seemed to take hold of her, making her whole body shake as he cupped one ripe mound possessively, thumb flicking at the nipple that hardened beneath his touch as though it had a will of its own. Queer tingles raced from the stiff little peak in all directions. Deep in the soft, secret place between her thighs Storm felt a slow, burning ache flicker, take flame, and begin to blaze like wildfire through her loins. His mouth traveled down her throat, pressing hot, gentle, quick kisses along the slender column as he murmured in Comanche, his breath warm and exciting upon her flesh before his lips closed over the tiny rigid bud of her breast that eagerly awaited him. He sucked it with a languid deliberation, tongue swirling, teasing, taunting as Storm writhed beneath him, whimpering quietly, making a half-hearted attempt to free herself again. She was pinned beneath him, however, and he had one of his hands wrapped in her hair, preventing flight. His mouth seared its way across her chest to her other breast, teeth nipping the rosy tip lightly to hold it in place as his tongue fluttered back and forth and all around it while his fingers continued to fondle the swollen crest his lips had aroused just moments before. At last he laid his dark visage upon the satin curve of Storm's shoulder.

'Sweet. Sweet,' he breathed before she realized he had fallen asleep.

Hot in a different way now, confused and quivering all over, wanting something she didn't want to name, and feeling strangely crushed, Storm smothered a little sob of disappointment in the darkness and bit her lip. It was a long time before she too drifted into slumber.

When the girl awakened in the morning, the sun had begun its slow ascent across the sky, and the Kiowas had gone as quietly as they had come. She stirred gently, wondering why she couldn't rise, then became aware of Wolf's arms still wrapped around her tightly. One of his strong hands rested upon one breast that peeked from the lacy confines of her camisole. She lay very still and tried not to think about it, but nevertheless she felt her nipple tingle and harden beneath the slight pressure of Wolf's fingers as she remembered last night. No man had ever used her thusly, and though she was shocked and horrified, there was something else within her too – the desire she did not want to face. The gunslinger slept on, oblivious to the strange sensations he was once more arousing in the girl's body. He shifted positions, burying his face more deeply against her shoulder, his hand tightening on the ripe mound he held. He murmured softly in his sleep. Storm tensed and gave a tiny gasp of surprise. *Beloved*! It had sounded as though he'd whispered 'beloved!'

Her small cry awakened him instantly. For a moment he seemed almost young again, as he must have been before his life had made him hard and cruel. Then his eyes filled with disappointment and pain, and he released her, shattering her half-expectant sense of excitement and anticipation as she wondered who it was he had called beloved.

'They've gone,' she noted dully.

'Who? Oh, the Kiowas. Yeah, they left a couple of hours ago. I figured we could both use a little extra sleep.'

'I know. I – I didn't get much. I was so scared, and you were all drunk and – and—'

'Not too drunk to remember – if that's what you're asking,' he droned wickedly and cocked one eyebrow quizzically. 'I kept you safe, didn't I? You want an apology because I tried to make love to you – or because I didn't finish what I started?'

'Oh!' The girl flushed, mortified. 'How dare you even mention it to me? No gentleman would ever have—'

He stood up, stretching, appearing not to notice the indignant blush that stained her cheeks. 'I thought we already agreed I'm no gentleman. You still haven't answered my question, Storm.'

'So it's "Storm" now, is it? First you force me to submit to the indecent liberties you took—'

'And that you enjoyed as much as I did—'

'Oh!'

'Am I to understand that you wish to share your blankets with someone else then the next time we have visitors?'

'No! I'm leaving you – today! I must have been mad to trust you to begin with. You're just like all the other men I've ever known! You just want to use me!'

Wolf shrugged nonchalantly, infuriating her further. 'Suit yourself.'

She sat up, holding one of the blankets to her chest and studying him covertly as he shaved in the early morning light. He really *was* handsome in a savage way. Naked to the waist, his dark copper skin almost glowed, contrasting sharply with the faint white scars that marked his flesh here and there: burn wounds, knife wounds, bullet wounds – God only knew how many there were. Upon the mat of black hair across his chest hung the ebony-beaded rosary with its solid silver crucifix he wore always. It glinted brightly when the sun's rays struck it. His muscles rippled sinuously in his arms and back as he moved, reminding Storm of some ancient pagan god.

'I thought you worshipped Mother-Moon,' she observed, curious and casting about for something further to say.

'What? Oh, the crucifix. My mother gave it to me.'

'Why? Wasn't she a Comanche?'

'No.'

'That's why you're only half-Indian, isn't it?' the girl persisted.

'Yes,' he responded curtly, not bothering to explain he'd been adopted by the Comanches. 'You'd better get moving if you're leaving me. Those Kiowas might come back here looking for you.'

Storm knew he'd just said it to frighten her, but nevertheless she arose and began her morning chores. She no longer waited for Wolf to tell her to saddle her mare, but performed the arduous task now herself in the mornings after she'd finished dressing (not forgetting to shake out her boots – as though she ever could after the horrible cockroaches) and cleaned up the camp. Once again when they were done, it looked as though they'd never been there.

'Well, I – I guess this is goodbye,' Storm said when she'd mounted up. 'I want to thank you for helping me this far. I – I'm sorry we couldn't be friends.'

Wolf only smiled – that bitter, jeering grin – and tipped his hat politely. Storm's eyes glinted as hard as steel at that, and her mouth tightened. Without another word she kicked her heels into Madame Bleu's sides and galloped off, cursing the gunslinger under her breath.

It was a good day for riding. A light wind was blowing in from the east. It was cool and tasted slightly of salt. It's the Gulf, Storm thought, feeling a sudden pang of homesickness as she recalled how often the breeze off the Mississippi River had had that same sharp tang. I must be close to the Gulf. All I have to do is follow this river to Corpus Christi. I've got money now, and maybe someone will hire me. I'm smart – and attractive. And perhaps the Barlows won't track me down after all. Maybe that heathen just made that up too to frighten me. I wouldn't put it past him, the half-breed devil! Yes, no doubt he just wanted to scare me so that I'd be forced to go along with him, so that he could have someone to warm his blankets at night! I should have known better, despite him treating me so contemptuously, behaving as though he really didn't want me! Well, I'll show him! I'll show him just how well I can fend for myself if I have to!

Unfortunately Storm was not to accomplish this goal, however, for just then her mare balked stubbornly, tossing her head and whinnying as she danced shyingly.

'What's the matter with you?' the girl grumbled, irritated, as she hauled on the reins. 'Get along with you, Madame Bleu, now, before I take a switch to you.'

Storm forced the horse forward but the beast lunged, then reared, neighing shrilly with fear. The girl, caught off guard, was thrown from the saddle. She felt a wrenching pain as her ankle twisted beneath her sprawled body. Tears started in her eyes at the searing agony of the sprain as she tried to crawl toward her mount. It was then she heard the gruesome rattle and dreadful hissing that had so frightened Madame Bleu. Storm looked up and found herself staring right into the face of a deadly rattlesnake. The girl froze, horrified, swallowing hard, her heart pounding fearsomely in her breast.

'Oh, *mon Dieu*,' she sobbed and began to back away as slowly as possible, just knowing the creature might strike at any moment.

'No! Don't move, Storm!'

It was Wolf. Oh, thank God, he had come! He halted his stallion quietly some yards away while the girl waited motionless, for what seemed like an eternity, gazing into the snake's beady black eyes as it continued to hiss and shake its rattle menacingly. A split second later Wolf's rifle cracked, blowing the head of the threatening creature clean away. Its body flung upward at the impact of the shot, lurching crazily in the air for a minute before it dropped to the ground with a thud, twitching spastically. Storm screamed and then screamed again, over and over until Wolf caught her in his arms, pressing her weeping countenance to his chest as he tried to soothe her terrified and shaking body.

'Oh, I was never so glad to see anyone in my life!' she cried chokingly. 'You saved my life! Oh, Wolf! Oh, Wolf!'

'Hush, Storm, hush. It's over now. It's all over, baby. Hush. Everything's going to be all right.'

He walked over to the pack horse and got a bottle of the strong liquor he and the Kiowas had drunk, forcing a couple of sips between Storm's lips. It burned, and she gasped, becoming less hysterical, but even so, it took him nearly half-an-hour to calm her down.

'That stuff's horrible,' she noted with a grimace when she at last could speak again. 'What is it?'

'Mescal. Are you all right now?'

'Yes, yes. I think so, except for my ankle. It got twisted somehow when I fell. *Jesù*. It hurts like the devil!'

'Let me see.' He drew off her boot and stocking as gently as possible, examining the joint carefully. 'It's not broken – just badly sprained. Can you walk?'

With his aid Storm managed to stand, but found she couldn't put any weight on her foot. She clutched on to him helplessly, frantic that she would fall.

'I – I can't make it, Wolf. It hurts too badly.'

'Put your arms around my neck.'

He lifted her easily, for she was as light as a feather in his strong grasp. For a moment their eyes met and locked, and suddenly there was a breathless little silence between them as Wolf's arms tightened around her. Storm's heart began to pound strangely once more as she remembered last night, remembered the taste of his mouth upon hers in the darkness, the feel of his hands and lips upon her breasts. Her eyes fell beneath his piercing gaze, and she buried her head against his chest, not wanting to look at him again, for fear he would read and comprehend all too well the confusion that was written plainly on her face. He carried her to her mare, placing her upon her saddle.

'I reckon it'll be pretty hard for you, on your own now, with your ankle the way it is.'

'Yes,' Storm replied, wishing she didn't suddenly feel like bursting into tears again.

There was a lump in her throat so big she thought it would choke her. Oh, if only she hadn't been so damned proud and stubborn back at camp! After all, Wolf hadn't actually raped her, and perhaps it had been only the mescal that had caused him to behave so – so ungentlemanly. God knows, any other man would have probably forced himself on her several times by now. Certainly those filthy outlaws would have, and they were white! For a savage Wolf had really been fairly decent. And – and she *had* encouraged him, oh, she *had*! How could she have been so stupid? She couldn't make it in this awful land without him. Truly she would have been dead by now if he hadn't come along once more to save her, and she'd only been gone from him about fiften minutes. What would happen to her in an hour, a day, a month without him? Storm shuddered just thinking about it. Yes, she needed him – needed him more than ever now. He walked over to his stallion, mounted up, then nudged the beast up alongside of the girl.

'Wolf—' Storm began, then bit her lip, ashamed to beg him to take her back.

Casually, he said, 'I've decided to teach you how to speak Comanche. I told the Kiowas you were a white captive I'd taken as my wife, and since we were friends, it didn't bother them that I spoke to you in English last night, but it might make other Indians suspicious.'

Storm didn't realize she'd been holding her breath until she exhaled it with relief. He wasn't leaving her. He wasn't leaving her! She looked over at him gratefully, her eyes shining.

'How do you say "friend" in Comanche?' she asked softly.

He studied her quietly for a minute, trying to understand what it was this particular white woman aroused in him so fiercely and why he was suddenly glad to have her back.

'*Haints*,' he said, showing her the symbol with his hands.

'*Haints*,' the girl repeated, making the sign gracefully.

She glanced at him for approval and found it on his face. She smiled at him tentatively, and for the first time since she'd met him he smiled back, slowly, naturally, without any mockery. Somehow the tension between them eased, and Storm felt an odd, uplifting joy in her heart as they rode toward Corpus Christi.

10

Sheltered from the Gulf of Mexico by the Mustang and Padres Islands, Corpus Christi huddled at the mouth of the Nueces River as though its hard life had taught it humility and a certain awe of the West. Founded by Colonel Henry Lawrence Kinney as a trading post in 1838, the town had been the scene of several skirmishes during the Mexican War, and it was obvious Corpus Christi was still trying to recover from the devasting battle. In addition, the town was lashed frequently by hurricanes that blew in from the Gulf which contributed greatly to much of the reconstruction Storm saw underway as she and Wolf trotted slowly down the wheel-rutted main street. Here and there Indians, 'civilized' Tonkawas, Wolf said, lounged on the sidewalks aimlessly, as though dazed or stupored. Some sat stoically smoking. Others were hunkered down in the road, gambling. Several Mexicans, performing the most menial of tasks, were also in evidence; but the majority of the town's citizens were white, and much to the girl's surprise and consternation they stared at her and Wolf hostilely when they passed.

'Wolf.' Storm kept her voice low. 'Why is everyone looking at us so – so – rudely?'

'Because they don't have much use for Indians – or Mexicans – around these parts. These people have fought against both for their lives. The Tonkawas used to control this part of The Land – still do in some places – and they were a fierce, warlike tribe – no friend to the Comanches either by the way. After the White-Eyes managed to kill off or civilize many of them the Mexican War broke out, and the town was pretty torn up by that too. You can see how it is here.' He indicated the street with a stony nod. 'The Tonkawas don't know where to go or what to do, how to fend for themselves now that the whites have destroyed their way of life. They're trying to adapt to an alien civilization, a process made even more difficult by the whites' hatred of them. Oh, sometimes a sheriff or rancher will employ one as a scout or tracker, but otherwise that's about it. The Mexicans can find work at least – as long as they're poor and keep to their place, show the proper amount of respect for the white *patron* or *patrona* who condescended to give them a job.'

'But – but I'm not Indian or Mexican.'

'No, but I am, and I'm a half-breed, which makes it even worse. Everybody in Texas knows it, and even other Indians and Mexicans occasionally despise me.'

'Then you're part – part Mexican too?'

'In a manner of speaking.'

'It must be – very lonely for you.'

'Sometimes. Sometimes it seems as though I've been alone all my life.'

It was one of the few glimpses Storm had gotten of the man behind the mask. It touched her deeply, for she too had known what it meant to be alone – and lonely. This is how he lives, the girl thought as she gazed over at Wolf, just like these dirt-poor Indians and Mexicans – hated and despised because of what he is. That's why he was in that awful town – Gorda Vaca. Those are the kind of people with whom he's forced to mix because he's unacceptable everywhere else. No wonder he hates whites.

In an effort to lighten the dark mood that had settled upon him, she said, 'You have me now, Wolf.'

He glanced at her speculatively, his eyes strangely shadowed. 'Yes, I have you. Come on. We'd better find a place to stay so that we can do something about that ankle of yours.'

'There's a hotel. It looks decent.'

'We can't go in there.'

'Why not?'

Wolf pointed to the large sign in the window. In bold black letters it said: NO INDIANS ALLOWED. Wordlessly Storm followed him on down the street.

At last they came to a big house off one of the smaller side roads on the outskirts of Corpus Christi. It had a saloon downstairs and what Storm realized with a shock was a brothel upstairs. A whorehouse! Wolf meant them to stay in a whorehouse! *Par Dieu*! This is what had come of her allowing the liberties he'd taken with her!

'Wolf, I – I don't want to stay here.'

'Where else would you suggest? I'll go in and see if they have a couple of rooms,' he told her calmly when she didn't reply, appearing not to notice her indignation and distress as he swung out of his saddle.

'No! Just – just one room,' the girl stammered, then blushed as he cocked one eyebrow satirically. 'I – I don't want to be alone in this place.'

'As you wish,' he drawled, raking her with that deliberately crude gaze of his. 'If anyone bothers you while I'm inside, shoot them. Just aim and pull the trigger. At close range even you can hardly miss.'

The girl nodded, swallowing nervously as she glanced around anxiously after Wolf had disappeared.

Boldly Wolf pushed open the shuttered doors of the saloon and swaggered inside. Since it was early afternoon the bar was deserted with the exception of an elderly Mexican man who was sweeping up the remains of last night's debris. Although it had been nearly a year since the gunslinger had visited The Gulf Coast (or what was commonly known as Mimi's Place), the Mexican, Pedro, remembered Wolf without difficulty. He ceased the motion of his broom, his fat, wrinkled face lighting up with delight as he smiled and came forward.

'*Señor* Lobo! Is good to see you again! Come in. Come in. Sit down. I'll tell Madame you are here at once. Juanito! Where is that lazy boy? Juanito! Fetch *Señor* Lobo a bottle of mescal – and quickly! Do not keep the *señor* waiting! My son, *Señor*.' Pedro turned back to Wolf apologetically, his hands spread wide. 'He is good boy, no? But he makes *la siesta* last all day if I let him. Madame will be so pleased to see you.'

'I doubt that,' Wolf droned dryly.

Pedro shrugged noncommittally. 'Is true she no like *los Indios, señor*, but then she no like anybody. Still as long as they have *el dinero* she call them her friends, no? I go get her now, *señor*, or she be very angry with poor Pedro.'

He bustled away, and presently Mimi La Roche, proprietress of The Gulf Coast, appeared. She was a tall, well-proportioned woman with dyed flaming red hair and slanted green eyes, which were always very carefully and heavily made-up, no matter the hour of the day. Of some indeterminate nationality, she had taken the last name of her French lover who had set her up in business before his death in a shooting that had occurred in the very saloon he'd financed for his mistress. The table at which he'd died was always reserved for Mimi and her guests, and she'd never allowed anyone to scrub the bloodstains from the rich burnished oak of the wood. It was said that she'd hated all men since the death of her lover, but she was a consumate actress, and if such were true, she masked it well. Her whorehouse was one of the most successful and exclusive in all Texas – and very expensive. Here well-known white ranchers for miles around mingled with some of the most wanted outlaws in the territory under the cover of darkness. Here wealthy Mexican *haciendados* rubbed shoulders with lace-cuffed French gamblers and fringed-jacketed Indians. Mimi took them all, regardless of race, creed, or color – as long as they could pay; and if she secretly despised them, none knew or cared. Her liquor was the best, and her girls were the fanciest, most exotic of their kind.

Mimi paused for a moment in the hallway that led from her private office to the saloon, patted her hair into place expertly, then stepped forward, her hands outstretched to welcome Wolf, a brilliant (though artificial) smile on her face. She loathed gunslingers – it had been just such a one who'd killed her dear Henri – but only a man as astute as Wolf would have guessed what lay beneath her outwardly calm and slightly flirtatious demeanor.

'Lobo! To what do I owe the pleasure of this unexpected visit, *mon ami*?'

She allowed him to brush her lips lightly with his own, which he did with a wry amusement, discerning the emotions that warred in her breast as he did so. He had lain with her on more than one occasion, and he knew she hated him more than most because he was a half-breed gunslinger who could not only afford her high price, but had more than once tortured her exquisitely in bed and made her beg him to take her.

'I need a room, Mimi – a private room. Move one of your girls if you have to.'

'Why, Lobo, don't tell me you've become jaded and bored with women.' Mimi pouted provocatively.

'Save your – act for someone else, Mimi.' He leaned back in his chair, his eyes raking her lewdly. 'That is – unless you'd care to have me take you up on your invitation.'

She snapped her fan shut with an angry little click, and for a moment her attractively composed mask slipped.

'You half-breed cheapjack!' she hissed.

'Spare me your insults too. Do I get the room or not?'

'Yes, you can have the room, but it'll cost you double, you—'

'I expected that.' He laid a wad of bills on the table. 'Have a hot bath and a pitcher of cold water sent up immediately,' he ordered, then arose. 'And see that you're available tonight,' he drawled mockingly before striding toward the shuttered doors.

'Juanito,' Pedro called loudly, appearing from nowhere as though he had not hidden in the hallway to overhear the entire conversation. 'See to the *señor*'s horses.'

'*Si, mi padre*.'

Once outside Wolf lifted Storm from her saddle and carried her into the saloon and up the stairs to the room Mimi was having prepared for them. Despite herself, Storm glanced around interestedly, for she had never been inside a whorehouse before. She had to admit the place had a certain amount of vulgar class. The saloon had a highly polished wood floor upon which brass spittoons and brass planters with tall, leafy green plants abounded. The tables were solid oak, as were the generous chairs and the long bar with its brass foot rail that ran the length of one whole wall. Above the bar gold-veined mirrors and shelves filled with bottles of liquor and glasses hung and sparkled as cleanly as the glass globes of the oil lamps that rested on each spoke of the huge wagon wheels that dangled from the ceiling. The other three walls were papered with gold wallpaper flocked with red velvet fleurs-de-lis. Plush red carpet covered the stairs leading to the upper story and continued along the hallway and rooms above, just as the wallpaper did. Individual oil lamps were located at strategic points here and there along the corridor, and double-globed lights hung like balances in each of the chambers. Wolf settled Storm on the brass bed in the room they'd been given while the girl glanced curiously at Mimi, who stood hovering in the doorway, staring at them hostilely. Storm was positive the woman's hair was dyed, and she had never in her life seen such heavy make-up or such a shocking gown.

'You should have told me you wanted one of your own kind, Lobo,' the proprietress spoke snidely, her nostrils white and pinched. 'I would have picked one up for you. Half-breed women are a dime-a-dozen.'

Storm gasped and looked questioningly at Wolf, feeling the tension in the air like a knife. Why, the woman thought Storm was a half-breed – like Wolf. The girl started to protest, confused by the woman's hateful attitude and assumption, but Wolf motioned for her to be silent.

'Mind your tongue and your manners, Mimi,' he warned. 'Miss Lesconflair is a lady.'

'Huh!' Mimi snorted, as though she considered this highly unlikely. 'She doesn't look like much of one to me. A French breed, is she? Well, how much do you want for her? Cleaned up and dressed right she might go as high as fifteen dollars. She's got good bones, and a lot of my customers like a touch of the savage in their women, but then there's no accounting for taste. I never did see the attraction myself. Mexicans, squaws, whites – I reckon they're all just about the same when it comes to what's between their legs.'

Storm gasped again, outraged by the woman's crudity.

'I told you to shut your mouth, Mimi!' Wolf snapped sharply, his tone silky and threatening. 'Miss Lesconflair is not for sale – at any price. Where in the hell is that bath and pitcher of cold water? And bring us up something to eat and a bottle of' – he glanced at Storm, frowning – 'French brandy too.'

'Conchita. Ramona. You heard *Monsieur* Lobo.' Mimi turned on the two quiet Mexican girls who had readied the room and were now standing wordlessly off to one side.

They scurried away to do her bidding as Wolf pulled Storm's boot and stocking from her injured ankle, examining it carefully once again.

'That hurt, baby?'

Storm nodded, not trusting herself to speak and wishing the horrible red-haired woman would leave. The girl's head was beginning to ache, and she wanted nothing more than to lie down and rest. Mimi watched them silently, seething but curious, for she had never known the gunslinger to travel with a woman, nor had she ever seen him display such tenderness toward one either. Wolf ignored her, beginning to remove Storm's other boot and stocking.

'What – what are you doing?' the girl asked anxiously.

'Undressing you so that you can have a bath.' He looked

up at her, slightly surprised, for he had felt certain she would want to bathe; she always tried so hard to keep so clean. 'After that you can eat and soak that foot, then get some rest.'

'Make that – woman leave,' Storm commanded imperiously, arrogantly, as though she had been dismissing an ill-favored servant. 'I do not wish her presence in this room.'

Mimi's eyes narrowed even as her ears pricked up inquisitively at the sound of Storm's voice, for it was cultured and her English overlaid with what Mimi recognized at once as a high-born French accent. The proprietress began to retort with a cutting remark at the girl's haughtiness, but Wolf stopped her abruptly, saying,

'That'll be all – until tonight, Mimi.'

Upon being reminded that he had demanded her services this evening the woman quit the chamber in a furious huff, wondering if she dared deny him admittance to her bed later, no matter how much it cost her monetarily. Then she shivered, remembering the one and only time she'd tried to do that. He'd been drunk and surly and had held a knife to her throat and threatened to kill her before he'd taken her coldly, exquisitely, then flung twice her usual fee on the floor with disgust. She'd never refused him again. She knew he took a perverse delight in lying with her, because he hated whites as much as she herself despised men. In a towering rage at being forced to whore for the gunslinger because of who and what they both were Mimi stalked down to her office, cuffing the sleeping Juanito soundly on the ear as she passed. After she'd gone Storm turned on Wolf angrily, all her earlier joy in his nearness vanishing.

'How dare you bring me to this awful place, then attempt to – to make advances to me before that horrible woman, allowing her to think I was no better than she?'

'I didn't do any such thing.' Wolf eyed her impatiently. 'And at least you'll get to sleep in a bed tonight.'

'With you?'

'You were the one who asked for just one room. Now stop complaining so that I can get these clothes off you. You want a bath, don't you?'

'No! Don't touch me, you – you barbarian! I heard what you said. You made an assignation with that – *prostituée*! No doubt you mean to sleep with us both, you animal!'

'Is *that* what's ailing you? Jesus, Storm! First you bitched because I tried to make love to you, and now you're bitching because I'm not. I wish you'd make up your mind. Now take off those clothes! Those girls will be back in a minute with your bath water.'

'No! I won't. I don't want a bath! You're just using that as an excuse to take advantage of me again!'

'Oh, for Christ's sake! If I'd wanted to rape you, I would have done so by now. Now take off those clothes before I rip them off you!'

'You wouldn't dare.'

Wolf gritted his teeth tightly, a muscle working in his jaw. 'You just try me, baby. One way or another you're going to undress and fast. I've got business in town, and I don't have all day to argue with you. All right. You asked for this,' he warned when she thrust her chin out stubbornly and refused to move or answer.

With a low growl he pinned her to the bed and began to tear the garments from her body while she screamed and fought him. The two Mexican girls who'd returned with the copper kettles of steaming water for Storm's bath hesitated anxiously in the doorway, not knowing what to do. Wolf spoke to them in rapid Spanish as he struggled with Storm, and they jumped to carry out his orders, filling the hammered brass tub as quickly as possible and setting the pitcher of cold water on the dresser so nervously that it sloshed over, splashing a little of the liquid on the carpet. Then they fairly ran from the room, closing the door firmly behind them. Wolf stripped Storm naked, his arms tightening around her momentarily before he picked her up unceremoniously and dumped her in the bath. She sputtered indignantly at his rough treatment, cringing in the water as she tried ineffectually to hide her nude body from his appreciative gaze before he tossed her a wash cloth and a bar of scented soap.

'Hurry up – unless you want me to bathe you as well.'

He raised one eyebrow as though the notion appealed to him. Hastily Storm began to scrub herself vigorously, blushing, mortified, horrified, and ashamed. She wanted to die! Never in her life had a male seen her thusly. Even her husband, had she been married to a Southern gentleman, would never have viewed her completely unclothed, would have made love to her beneath the confines of her nightgown, would never have dreamed, surely, of brutally stripping her naked the way Wolf had just done! When she had finished lathing and rinsing herself and unbraided and washed her hair, he lifted her from the tub, sat her on his lap, and toweled her dry, impervious to her shrieks and protests. Even in her rage and embarrassment the girl felt her nipples harden beneath his hands and a strange quiver run through her body as his fingers swept down to dry her inner thighs and buttocks. He grinned mockingly, feeling her, suddenly hot and confused as she had been last night, trembling in his rough grasp, making Storm long to slap his face once more. Then after bundling her into a diaphanous wrapper he yanked from the chest of drawers he poured the cold water from the pitcher into a basin and placed Storm's ankle in it to soak. By that time the Mexican girls had returned with the meal and liquor. Skittishly they placed both on the table, then departed in much the same manner as before.

Wolf tossed the towel aside carelessly, then, still smiling wickedly, flung himself into the chair opposite Storm. He opened the brandy, pouring her a small shot, then ladled steaming meat-stuffed *tortillas*, Spanish rice, and *frijoles* onto her plate. She sat in stony, affronted silence, one hand at her throat where she held the filmy robe together tightly, making no effort to eat.

After about a minute of uncomfortable stillness, he asked, "You want me to force you to eat too?"

The girl swallowed hard. 'No.'

She lifted her fork, scooping up some of the rice, but the mouthful almost choked her. How long had it been since she'd eaten with silverware? Quite suddenly she began to cry.

'Jesus Christ!' Wolf swore, throwing his own knife and fork down with a clatter. 'What is it now?'

'You're just beastly and mean!' she sobbed.

'Yeah? Well, you didn't think so this morning when I saved your life,' he reminded her grimly.

'Well, I wish you hadn't! I wish I were dead! I feel so – so helpless and miserable! I hate this dreadful place! I hate this horrible, hot land! And most of all I hate you!'

'Yeah? Well, that's just too bad, baby, 'cause you need me.' He pushed his chair back menacingly and strode around to her side of the table, gripping her damp hair with one hand, twisting her head up, forcing her to look at him. 'And you ought to be damned grateful that I've kept you around and kept you safe without exacting a fee for my services.'

His cold midnight blue eyes swept the length of her body slowly, then returned to rest upon her face. Storm shivered slightly. Was it only this morning that they had been friends?

'I – I'm sorry. I didn't mean what I said. My ankle hurts, and I have a headache.'

Wordlessly he released her, then moved to finish his meal. Afterward he smoked one of his thin black cigars while the girl stared silently into her brandy.

'How's your foot?'

Storm withdrew it from the water, examining it gingerly. 'Better, I think.'

'Let me see it.'

He prodded at the joint gently, then, taking a sheet from the hope chest at the end of the bed, tore the material into

185

strips and bound up Storm's ankle.

'You certainly seem to know where everything is around here,' she remarked snippishly. 'I wonder why that makes me think you've been here before.'

'Yeah, I wonder,' he said, carrying her to the bed. 'You've got a good view from the window here. I'll have one of the girls bring you something to read if you like.'

'Why? Are you leaving me?' Storm could not hide the anxious note in her voice.

'Don't worry. I'll be back. I have business in town, I told you.'

He pulled his pistols from his holster and began checking them mechanically, as though he'd done it a hundred times before. Storm watched him, startled, then it dawned on her just what his business was.

'You're – you're going to kill somebody, aren't you?' she questioned, horrified, for until this moment the fact that he was a gunslinger hadn't really registered on her brain. He'd shot Elijah Barlow in self-defense, which was something quite different than cold-blooded murder in Storm's mind.

'If I find him.'

'But – why?'

'Because he helped the White-Eyes track down six wounded Comanche braves and kill them.' He walked over to the bed. Turning her face up to his once more, he bent his head and kissed her swiftly on the lips. 'For luck, baby,' he said before he left her.

Storm lay on the bed a long time after he'd gone, trying to sort out her chaotic thoughts. What is it about that man, she wondered, that confuses me so? I would hate him, scorn him for treating me so meanly, taking liberties with me no decent man would dare to take; and yet – I need him so. When he touches me, I know I should want to die; and yet – he makes me feel so strange and unlike myself. My heart pounds, and I quiver all over – wanting him – a half-breed murderer! Oh, if only he were cruel clean through, I could despise him without difficulty; but he has been kind to me in many ways; I cannot deny that. Without him I would surely have been dead by now; and I want so much to live. And he is so alone – so lonely. Somehow I feel he needs me too. Oh, Mammy! Mammy! Is this what you meant when you said my body would know when I had found the right man for me? He is so different from any man I have ever known. Is that why he fascinates me so? Oh, Mammy! If I look into my heart, will I find the answer there? I close my eyes and try to think of André-Louis, whom I loved; but I can no longer recall his face. There is only Wolf: Wolf's icy midnight blue eyes; Wolf's bitter, jeering smile; Wolf's dark copper-skinned body, his hard muscles rippling beneath his flesh like some ancient pagan god – forbidden, unholy, mysterious, and compelling. There is a sadness in him stemming from his past, even as my own holds sorrow. Sometimes he looks at me, and I want to reach out and cradle his head against my breast and ease the pain that torments him inside. Why, Mammy, why? He is nothing to me – a stranger, a savage; and yet – I feel we are alike somehow, he and I; and that frightens me. I am afraid that if given the chance, he would unleash something wild and wanton in me that I do not wish to face. Yes, he a man who would demand every part of me until all that is me would be his too, and I would never be free of him – not as long as I lived. I cannot let that happen! He would use me – as all the other men I've known have used me – and I would be nothing, a storm that blew fiercely, dangerously, electrically alive for a time before it died to a mere whimper and was no more. No! It will not happen! I will not let it! When this is over, I will leave him. Yes, when this is over, I will leave him, Storm thought again as she drifted off to sleep only to dream of Wolf towering over her beneath a glittering full moon, Wolf, like some young savage warrior, some ancient pagan god, naked to the waist, his midnight blue eyes almost black as he knelt by the light of the silvery globe in the heavens and made her his.

187

It was morning when she awoke. Wolf lay beside her in the bed, his arms around her as though he were accustomed now to holding her close while he slept, and for a moment Storm could not remember whether she had only dreamed of him making love to her or if it had really happened. No, it was only a dream, she told herself, nothing more. She stirred gently, slipping out of his grasp quietly so as not to waken him. Tentatively she placed her small weight upon her injured ankle and was pleased to discover the limb would bear it, although it still ached. Then she drew her wrapper tightly around her and moved to the window. Though the sky was light enough to tell her she had slept yesterday and last night away, dark clouds massed on the horizon, foretelling a storm. Already thunder rumbled in the distance, and little droplets of rain splashed upon the pane where Storm had her face pressed close.

A match flared in the half-light, startling her as Wolf lit a cigar and blew a cloud of smoke upward toward the ceiling.

'Come back to bed, baby,' he said softly. 'We're not going anywhere today. It sounds like a real storm's blowing up outside.'

As though dazed the girl complied with his request, moving into the cradle of his strong arms once again, laying her head upon his broad, naked chest where the crucifix he wore always pressed against her cheek. Wolf smoked wordlessly for a time, thinking about how well she fit up next to the length of his body, as though she belonged there. For the first time in a long, long time he felt a still peacefulness invade his soul. Slowly but surely it crept upon him, and suddenly, without him realizing it, the tense wariness that was always a part of him drained from his body as though it had never been. Storm sensed the odd change in him as she felt his muscles ripple and relax. She sighed drowsily and snuggled closer to him as one arm tightened around her. He took a last drag of his cigar, then ground it out, pulling her nearer as the rain began to pitter-patter down upon the roof with a rhythmic, soothing sound.

He made no attempt to make love to her, being strangely content just to hold her close. After a time they talked quietly while the storm lashed around them outside, wrapping them in a soft cocoon, as though only they two existed in the world. Wolf smelled of good cigars and liquor, clean and male, the smells Storm had always associated with her father, who had loved and protected her, and she no longer felt any fear at Wolf's nearness, subconsciously sensing the same caring and security in his arms that she had known in Paul-Eduard Lesconflair's as a child. Oddly enough she felt no shame either at their half-nakedness, for Wolf made no move to touch her as a lover would have done. There was instead a togetherness between them, a simple companionship that Storm had not experienced since the death of her parents and that Wolf had seldom known at all.

Storm asked him about his past, and curiously enough he replied, telling her a little bit about his life with the Comanches – the *Kwerharehnuh*.

'What does that mean?'

'Antelope,' he translated with a smile. 'I told you I was going to teach you how to speak Comanche – Spanish too if you're good.'

'Then I shall teach you French in return. And will you also show me the symbols as well?'

'The symbols? Oh, *mawtakwoip* – hand talk. Yes. See this' – he demonstrated – 'that's a snake going backwards. It means Comanche. Most of my tribe aren't very adept at sign language, however, because Comanche is spoken by the majority of Plains Indians.'

'You've told me of Tabenanika and his wives, who took you in after the deaths of your parents. Do you have any brothers or sisters?'

'Yes, but not in the sense you're thinking. Among the Comanches the children of all one's paternal uncles are considered siblings.'

'Why is that?'

'Because when a man dies, his blood brothers usually inherit his wives and family, and thus their children become one's brothers and sisters rather than what you would think of as cousins.'

'This is what happened with you after your father and mother died?'

'In a sense.' His face was suddenly hard, and she sensed she was prying.

'What about maternal uncles?' She changed the subject hastily.

'They are called *ara*, which is also what they call you in return, and they are one's special friends and companions. Generally an *ara* is one's teacher and disciplinarian. That way *tuas* – sons – don't grow up hating their *ap's* – fathers – for any real or imagined slights, and no chief must worry about his son attempting to kill him and take his place.'

'It all sounds very confusing,' the girl said with a sigh.

'You have a good mind, Storm. You will learn. I will teach you. I will teach you many things. Many things,' he whispered once more, his face very near to hers before he bent and kissed her mouth.

Storm was taken unawares and made no attempt to struggle, being too caught up in the closeness of the moment. His lips were soft upon hers and undemanding, not like the hard, ravaging kisses he'd previously taken by force, and she felt no fright, only a strange yearning to be held tenderly – and loved. She wondered if he had kissed that woman – Mimi – like this last night, if he had held her in his arms and made love to her as he'd planned? If he had, he had bathed the heavily perfumed scent of her from himself before returning to Storm. To her surprise the girl felt something akin to jealousy prick her soul and found she did not want to think of Wolf lying in the arms of another woman. Her hands crept to fasten themselves in his long black hair, caressing the glossy strands that hung down past his shoulders, before suddenly he drew away and swore softly.

'Don't tempt me, baby, not unless you're prepared to finish what you start.'

If she had made one move toward him, he would have taken her then; but she did not, so he rose and dressed silently. Moments later the girl was alone with only the tattoo of the rain upon the roof to keep her company.

Storm lazed away the day, trying yet again to understand herself and Wolf and the strange relationship that had developed between them. *Sainte Marie!* the girl thought. I have known him less than a month and already he would be my lover! It's shocking and scandalous and would not be permitted in New Orleans; but this is not the French Quarter, and Wolf is no French gentleman. Oh, what should I do? What should I do? *Par Dieu!* If only I didn't need him so desperately! If only I didn't find his nearness so disturbing! I wonder why he has not simply taken what it is he desires from me – as he nearly did that night the Kiowas came to our camp?'

At last, finding no answers to her questions, she rose and completed her toilette, then sat down to the meal the two Mexican girls, Conchita and Ramona, had brought. This time the hot, spicy food did not choke in Storm's throat, but tasted good and nourishing. After that she passed the remainder of the afternoon and the evening quietly by reading several horrible (but exciting) pamphlets that would later be known as penny dreadfuls and an old fashion magazine. Then, finding nothing else to amuse her, Storm did something she'd always secretly wanted to do all her life. She smoked a cigar. Wolf had left a couple on the night table, and with guilty delight the girl lit one up and took several puffs. Immediately she began to cough and gag. Tears stung her eyes as she attempted to wave the smoke away, still sputtering and choking. Hurriedly she reached for what was left of her brandy from the previous evening and downed it quickly.

'*Jesù!*' she swore aloud when she at last managed to catch

her breath. 'These things are awful! No wonder women don't smoke!'

She heard the heavy tread of footsteps in the hallway and the jingle of spurs. Thinking it was Wolf and that he would be angry with her, Storm hastily ground out the cigar and tried frantically to dissipate the smoke. Then, pulling the wrapper about her camisole and pantalettes tightly (for she had seen no reason to dress earlier), she tiptoed to the door, opened it a crack, and peeped out, confused that Wolf had not yet appeared.

A strange man, his back to her, was leaning up against the wall of the corridor, a bottle of whiskey held to his mouth. After taking several large swigs he lowered the decanter, wiped his lips with the back of his hand, then staggered on down the hallway. He paused before a door farther down and lifted a hand to knock. It was then he turned his face to the light, and Storm recognized him.

'*Mon Dieu!*' she gasped, frozen with fear as Zeke Barlow looked straight at her and began to grin evilly, showing tobacco-stained teeth.

Storm tried to slam the door shut, but he was faster than she, and in moments he had forced his way into her room. The girl screamed once, a small shrill cry, then backed away from him until she stood cringing against one wall.

'Well, if it ain't Billy's *lady*,' he said with a smirk as he started to walk toward her menacingly. 'Billy's lady – in a whorehouse!' He laughed as though he found the idea highly amusing. 'Go ahead and scream, honey. Ain't nobody gonna hear you above all the ruckus downstairs.'

To Storm's dismay she realized this was probably the truth.

'What – what do you want?' she asked nervously, playing for time and praying Wolf would hurry up and return.

'Well, now. 'Pears to me like you already know the answer to that, girlie.' His eyes raked her lewdly. 'We been lookin' fer you – my brothers and me. What's the matter? Did old Lobo git tired of you and sell you to Mimi? That half-breed bastard!

You shoulda knowed he were no good, honey – no damned good a'tall, the worthless Injun.' He began to edge toward her. 'You jest come on over here to old Zeke now. I'll treat you good, girlie, real good. You don't wanna give me any trouble now, do you?'

With another tiny wail Storm put the table between herself and the outlaw. Oh, if only she could get to her pistols, lying on the dresser! Why hadn't she thought of them in the first place? If only she hadn't been stunned and scared! Her heart pounded furiously, and her palms were damp with sweat. She licked her lips.

'You'd better get out of here, *monsieur*. Wolf will be back any minute, and he'll kill you!' she threatened.

Zeke laughed again. 'Is that right? You know, honey, somehow I jest don't believe that. Lobo ain't got much use fer women, 'specially white women. No, the way I see it he probably fucked you a few times, then dumped your ass off here at Mimi's for a purty profit. I reckon he's clear to Mexico by now or up north with his Injun kin.'

'No! You're wrong!' Storm cried. 'He cares for me! He's *here*, I'm telling you! He'll be back any moment!'

Zeke only laughed some more and moved closer. Feverishly the girl started to throw things at him: her plate, her glass, her nearly empty bottle of brandy; but the outlaw dodged them all expertly and came on. In desperation Storm lunged toward the dresser, hands clawing for her revolvers, her knife, anything! Her fingers just touched the walnut stock of one gun before Zeke grabbed her around the waist and, hauling her across the room roughly, flung her onto the bed. Storm struggled with the outlaw futilely as he fell upon her, leering, drunk and cruel, into her face, the stench of his breath foul with whiskey and chewing tobacco as his hands began to tear at her wrapper and underclothes. She screamed and screamed again hysterically until he ripped the filthy, sweat-stained bandana from his throat and shoved it into her mouth. Then he straddled her to keep her still and yanking his belt from his breeches, bound her wrists to one of the bars of the brass headboard.

'Now you and me got some unfinished business, bitch,' he growled, panting heavily, his fingers wrenching apart her camisole beneath her opened wrapper. His hands fastened on her bare breasts greedily, kneading and squeezing as he grinned down at Storm's wide, horror-stricken and fear-filled eyes. Tears spilled from beneath the girl's sooty black lashes as she moaned and choked on the grimy rag he'd thrust between her lips. 'That feels good, don't it, honey? Yeah, old Zeke knows how to treat his women right.'

One hand moved to unbuckle his gunbelt while the other continued to paw at Storm brutally. He laid the holster on the bed, fingers fumbling with the buttons on his pants. In minutes he had his engorged organ in his hand.

'You see this, girlie? This is what old Zeke's gonna put inside you. I'm gonna shove it in deep and hard, and before I'm through you'll be beggin' me fer it, bitch.' He pushed Storm's legs apart with his knees, then with both hands tore her pantalettes in half, exposing her womanhood. 'I'll bet that sweet little fluff of yours is all hot and juicy jest thinkin' about it, huh, honey?' he jeered down at Storm, who was sobbing silently, shaking with terror and shame.

The girl closed her eyes tightly and prayed for death as she awaited his violent, vicious assault. Moments later she heard a strange gurgling sound and felt something warm and sticky spray and then drip slowly onto her naked breasts and belly. Her eyes flew open just in time to see Zeke Barlow's body topple to one side, a gaping slash across his throat, his blood still bubbling from the fatal gash in a crimson gush over Storm, the bed, and the carpet as he pitched downward to sprawl motionless upon the floor.

'Don't look, Storm,' Wolf ordered grimly, his dark lean visage more fierce and savage in the lamplight than she had ever seen it before; but she couldn't seem to drag her eyes away as he bent with cold, deliberate intent, yanked Zeke's half-severed head up roughly, and with the bloodstained knife he still held in one hand scalped the outlaw expertly and vehemently.

Storm gagged, and as soon as Wolf had taken the bandana from her mouth and freed her, she staggered to the chamber pot and was violently ill. Over and over again she heaved while he held her trembling body and wiped her face and lips with a damp cloth until her nausea had passed. She felt chilled and sick and made no protest when he finished stripping her, lifted her in his arms, and dumped her into the now-cold bath water, which the two Mexican girls had never returned to remove. He scrubbed her all over while she huddled, teeth chattering, in the icy water, her eyes closed for fear she would inadvertently look upon Zeke Barlow's brutally mutilated body. When he was done, Wolf toweled her off and dressed her completely, knowing from her mechanical response to him that the girl was in an almost catatonic state of shock. He forced nearly half a bottle of mescal down her throat, then shook her gently. When he still couldn't get through to her, he slapped her roughly several times until at last she began to cry softly.

'Storm. Listen to me, Storm. I'm going to take Zeke's body down to the sheriff's office. While I'm gone I want you to clean up this place, and get your things packed. The rain's quit. We're getting out of here tonight.'

'Why?'

'You don't want to stay here, do you? Luther and Billy are probably somewhere on this floor,' he reminded her cruelly, trying to shock her to her senses. 'Besides, Rickie Lee Halfhand is on his way to Fort Brown, and I want to catch him before he gets down into Mexico.'

'Who – who is Rickie Lee Halfhand?' Storm asked, still dazed.

'The man I'm after. I thought he was here, but he's already come and gone. He knows I'm looking for him, so he'll be traveling light and fast.'

'How do you know that?'

'He's a half-breed Tonkawa. I – ah – persuaded one of his fellow tribesmen to tell me all about it. It took awhile. That's why I was gone so long. How did Zeke know where you were?'

'I – I thought it was you coming down the hall. I opened the door. I didn't think about this place being a – a bordello and having – other customers—' She began to shake and weep once more.

'Well, he's dead, the bastard, and he'll never bother you again.'

'Wolf, did you – did you have to – to scalp him?'

'He tried to rape you, baby. He deserved that – and more. Nobody touches a Comanche's woman and gets away with it.'

For the first time Storm made no attempt to deny being Wolf's woman. For the first time the girl *wanted* to be Wolf's woman, to know he stood between her and the rest of the world with which she seemed so inadequately prepared to cope.

'Oh, Wolf! It was horrible! So horrible! I – I wanted to die! Oh, thank God, you came! Thank God, you came!'

'Don't think about it now!' he commanded sharply. 'I need you. Now show me some of the guts and determination I know you have inside.'

'I – I'll try.' She wiped her eyes and attempted to smile.

'Good girl. Get this place cleaned up then, and get ready to go. I'll be back in a minute.'

He strode over to the window, shoved open the sash, then dragged Zeke Barlow's corpse across the floor and heaved it over the sill. Storm heard the body roll down the overhanging roof of the first story, then hit the wet ground below with a soft thud. Wolf started to climb out the window.

'Close the door, and lock it, baby. Don't open it for anyone. I'll come back the same way I'm leaving.'

She nodded, feeling a gasping terror grab hold of her once more, as though Wolf were taking all her courage with him. Quickly she stifled the emotion as best she could. After running to turn the key in the lock she moved rapidly and efficiently to tidy up the room, scrubbing the bed and the carpet vigorously to remove the blood before it stained them, forcing herself not to think about what it was she was cleaning up. In minutes her cold bath water was a pool of red. When she had finished, the girl made the bed even though the sheets were damp, then picked up everything she had thrown at Zeke Barlow or that had been knocked over during the struggle. After that she took the basin and made trip after trip to pour the soiled water in the bathtub out the window. This accomplished she dressed, packed her and Wolf's belongings, then sat down to wait, one of her pistols clutched tightly between her hands. It seemed as though she waited for hours, trying to mentally block out what had just happened in the room, to make her mind a blank. It was no good. Over and over she heard Zeke Barlow's jeering voice describing the terrible things he had meant to do to her, saw his scraggly-bearded face leering down at her, felt his calloused hands tearing at her garments, squeezing her breasts. Sobs rose in her throat, and she choked them down with difficulty as the minutes crawled by. When Wolf finally returned, her nerves were screaming silently, and she had started to tremble uncontrollably again. His booted and spurred feet scraped upon the roof before he gained the window. Startled by the sudden noise, Storm cried out and turned, frightened, leveling her revolver straight at his chest. He froze in the misty half-light.

'It's Wolf, baby,' he said quietly, sensing the sheer terror she felt and understanding she might shoot him in her blind state of shock. 'It's Wolf,' he repeated slowly, as though speaking to a stupid child.

Dimly she appeared to recognize him at last. She lowered the gun, letting it slide to the floor before she ran toward him. He caught her in his arms, holding her close against his broad chest for a moment.

'It's all right, baby,' he crooned softly, stroking her hair soothingly. 'It's just like the rattlesnake. It's all right now.'

'You – you ought to be in shining armor.' Storm tried to smile bravely once more.

He smiled back tenderly. 'Because I keep rescuing a certain damsel in distress? It comes with the territory, baby. Do you think you can make it down the roof? Billy Barlow's sitting inside the saloon, gambling. Lord only knows where Luther is, but I'd just as soon not chance the back stairs since we'd have to go through the hallway.'

'Wolf, why don't you just – kill them both now?'

'Because I don't know what kind of friends they might have here, and I don't trust Mimi either. She'd just as soon put a bullet in my back as look at me. Besides, the sheriff was none too happy about the way I carved up Zeke Barlow.'

'But – at Gorda Vaca—'

'That was different, baby. There isn't anybody who holds with a sore loser trying to kill a man, even a bounty hunter, over a game of cards when he's won fair and square. But there are a lot of people who'd like to see me dead, Storm, and there are always a couple of cowardly backshooters in a place like this. If I were to go in there and call the Barlows out, I'd be doing it as a gunslinger, a bounty hunter, and no one would give a damn if I were to meet my maker in the process, no matter how it happened. They'd just figure I took my chances and lost. You don't stay alive in my profession by trying to be a hero, Storm. Besides, I have you to think about now. What would happen to you if I were to be killed? Come on, baby.' He threw some money on the dresser, then tossed their gear out the window. 'Let's get out of here.' he glanced around to be sure there were no traces of what had occurred earlier. 'You did real well. The room looks real clean.'

Storm shuddered as he assisted her over the sill, then helped her slide down the roof that hung out over the back of the saloon and drop the relatively short distance to the ground. The impact strained her ankle, but the girl gritted her teeth and managed to hobble to the stable out back where Wolf had already saddled up their horses. He stowed away their belongings, then helped her mount. Within minutes they were galloping along the Gulf, and Corpus Christi was only a hazy glow of night lights in the distance.

Four hours later they stopped and made camp. By the time their chores were completed Storm was so mentally and physically exhausted she fell into bed and slept as soon as her head hit her saddle. It was a troubled, uneasy slumber, however, one from which she awoke screaming some time later, having dreamed the nightmare of Zeke Barlow's attack so vividly it had seemed almost real again. She struggled frantically in Wolf's arms, grabbing, terrified, at the hand he had placed over her mouth to silence her outcries of fear.

'It was only a dream, baby,' he spoke comfortingly until at last she quieted. Then he gave her a few sips of mescal and told her to go back to sleep.

'Is that a Comanche cure-all?' she asked drowsily after swallowing the liquor. Then she sighed, content, recognizing she was safe in Wolf's embrace, and mumbled, 'You know, I could get to like that stuff,' before he realized she was once more asleep.

He studied her profile in the darkness, noting the shadow on her cheek where her thick sooty eyelash swept downward softly, the straight, slightly upturned nose, the gentle curve of her sweet mouth, the slow rise and fall of her breasts beneath her camisole. The sight of her sleeping so peacefully now, trusting him to protect her, touched him deeply. She was too fragile, too delicate in many ways, but like a weeping willow whose roots grew deep and strong she had a steely backbone too, one that had enabled her to survive where another woman would have failed and died. He admired and respected her courage and determination because they reminded him of himself when he had been lost and alone. Yes, they were alike, he and Storm. Suddenly he remembered the vision that had proclaimed his manhood, the second wolf that had come out of the storm to make the first wolf whole. It filled him with a strange longing he had not felt since the death of his wife.

Without warning he seemed to sense Beloved-Of-The-Forest's presence, saw her gazing down at him from the heavens, in death as she had been in life, so beautiful she took his breath away, her soft dark eyes welling over with love and understanding. He reached out to her, but she eluded his grasp like a will-o'-the-wisp.

'The time has come, my husband, for us to part,' she whispered.

Sadly he understood. 'Kiss me, Beloved. Kiss me one last time before we say goodbye.'

For one fleeting eternity he held her close, tasting her tears upon his lips before she smiled tremulously and drew away, one hand uplifted gracefully as she made the sign of parting. Tenderly, with her blessing, he let the memory of Beloved-Of-The-Forest go, then wrapped his arms around Storm Lesconflair tightly.

11

It was cooler along the Gulf coast where the wind swept in off the waters to mellow the hot sun, and fall hung heavy in the air as well, although Wolf told Storm it was going to be an Indian summer. They made good time, and after the incident with Zeke Barlow, Storm's training began in earnest too. During the many weeks that followed, the girl gradually changed from the frightened green Southern belle she'd been to a cool, capable Western woman highly knowledgeable about Texas and its ways. Wolf taught her well, just as he had been taught by his mother She-Who-Seeks-Wisdom and his uncle Masitawtawp. Whereas before it had taken her nearly two hours, Storm could now build a fire, start supper cooking, strip, rub down, and feed and water all three horses, and make both beds in less than forty-five minutes. She grew strong from the heavy labor she was forced to endure. She could now lift her saddle without the least bit of struggle, and she laughed to herself to think once she'd barely been able to drag it along the ground. When she knew how to recognize which ones were edible, she supplemented their meals with roots she dug out of the hard earth, cutting the tops off as treats for the horses. Others she dried and preserved for eating later on, for towns were few and far between, so one never knew when one was going to be able to get fresh supplies. Waste not, want not: that was the motto of the West, and Storm learned it well, just as she learned the other things Wolf taught her.

She discovered which plants were medicinal and could be used for healing, such as the one from which she made the paste for her skin, which soon tanned dark and gold beneath the Texas sun. She learned which plants were poisonous, that an arrow dipped in a certain juice would bring instant death, that the powder of certain crushed leaves sprinkled on food or in a drink would bring a slow, agonizing end. Wolf told her of a plant that was found only in certain areas of the Southwest and Mexico, a cactus that would cause vomiting and hallucinations when eaten and that was used in special Comanche rituals, about which he also instructed her, steeping her in Comanche religion and folk lore, gradually instilling in her Comanche perspectives, values, and traditions. He departed from this only in that he taught her not only the ways of the Comanche woman, but the ways of a Comanche warrior as well.

He would sneak up on her when she least expected it, so that her ears grew sharp, attuned to even the faintest rustle in the brush. She leaned how to snake through the tall prairie grass on her belly, pulling herself forward with her elbows without making a sound. She glowed with pride the day Wolf said,

'You won't get past a Comanche, but a white man would never hear you at least.' Proudly he told her Comanches were the quietest raiders in the world. 'We can sneak up on White-Eyes' camp when they're sleeping, and even if they've got their horses tied to their wrists, we can cut the ropes and steal their ponies without ever waking a single man.'

He taught her how to use a knife and a tomahawk.

'Come at me!' he would order, and she would choose a weapon and attempt to kill him as he had commanded. The first time she had been horror-stricken by this demand, but Wolf had only laughed. 'Baby, when I think there's a danger of you actually being able to do it, we won't need to practice anymore.'

At night he took her hunting, showing her how to use a lance and a bow and arrows, how to load and prime her two revolvers, and how to shoot.

'If you can hit your target in the dark, you won't miss it in the light of day,' he told her. Relentlessly he coached her as they rode toward Fort Brown after his quarry and then crossed the vast Rio Grande into Mexico when he discovered

Rickie Lee Halfhand had eluded him again. 'Don't try to draw so fast. It won't do you any good if you can't hit what you're aiming at afterward. Accuracy first, then speed.' Storm bit her lip, nodded, and tried once more. 'Keep your eyes on mine, baby! I can smile at you, take a drag of my cigar, grind it out, shift my stance, and hook my thumbs in my belt, and while you're watching all that, I can kill you! But the eyes are a dead giveaway, Storm. When a man's about to make his move against you, they'll change suddenly, for just a split second. That's when you draw! Try it again.' And so it went, day after day, night after night. 'If it's a showdown outside, keep your back to the sun. Inside, keep your back to the wall or the bar, and watch the mirrors out of the corners of your eyes. Move, baby! Move when you shoot! A moving target's harder to hit.'

And so Storm moved, and feinted, and learned how to snap her body around like lightning, how to hit the ground, rolling, and be back on her feet in seconds. She did it all – with one exception. She refused to learn how to scalp a person.

'I can't do it, Wolf. It's – it's too—'

'Savage?' He lifted one eyebrow, amused, but he didn't try to force her, understanding she had not been raised to accept it as natural and expected as he had. 'White-Eyes do it too, Storm. In fact, they started it. In some places the government pays for Indian scalps.'

'Well, I don't care who's doing it; it's inhuman. A person ought to be buried intact.'

'If you're dead, you're dead, I reckon, so I don't know what difference it makes. Sounds to me like pure vanity on your part, baby.'

He grabbed a handful of her hair and pulled her down beside him, spreading the ebony mass in a billowing cloud upon the earth before his fingers caught the tresses at her temples, stilling her struggles before he kissed her lingeringly on the mouth, then wrapped the silky strands around his throat, muttering softly in her ear. Storm's heart pounded rapidly in her breast as she felt herself go limp and hot and shaky all over with expectation, but he didn't press her further.

His eyes glittered hungrily in the moonlight as he gazed at her silently, waiting, wanting, the naked desire evident on his dark visage. Storm swallowed hard and turned away, not yet ready to give herself completely into his keeping, though they had grown closer during the passing weeks. In many ways he was still an enigma to her, and he had not once spoken of loving her, only of wanting her. He was a drifter, a man who lived his life on the run, chasing or being chased. Storm wanted more than that. She wanted roots, a home of her own, children.

'Wolf, don't you – don't you ever want to – to get married and settle down?' she asked hesitantly.

He lit a cigar, assessing her sharply. 'I was married once – to a Comanche woman.'

The words startled her, for she had not known this, and her heart gave a queer lurch. 'What – what happened?'

'She was raped and killed. My unborn son was in her belly at the time.'

'Oh, Wolf! How awful!' Storm cried softly, understanding now why he had never forced himself on her, why he had been so cold and cruel about the scalping of Zeke Barlow. 'I'm sorry. Was it – was it a white man who did it?'

'I don't know. I never found out.'

'Was she – very beautiful? Did you – love her very much?'

'Yes, to both questions. But that was a long time ago, Storm. She's been dead ten years. She – she was only sixteen when she died, the same age as you. I was seventeen. That's when I left the Comanches. I've learned a lot about life since then. I'm older, harder. Maybe someday I'll put down roots again, but I've got – an old score to settle before then, a slate to wipe clean, so to speak. Until then I'll never be truly free of my past, of what I am, a loner, a wanderer. I don't want you to have any false illusions about me, Storm,' he warned her deliberately. 'I'm not going to change, not even for you, baby.'

The girl nodded and turned away once more, wondering what it was that haunted him and why she suddenly felt like crying.

Storm loved Mexico, for it was cool in the mountains, and at night the stars in the heavens seemed so close she felt as though she might reach up and pluck one from the sky. Here too, though Wolf was known in many places, and the name El Lobo was still feared, he was not treated with contempt by the Mexican people, but accepted as one of their own. He was less tense, although wary always, for the land through which they traveled was raided often by various fierce Apache bands and strange Yaqui Indians. *Bandoleros* roamed the hills as well and could strike with lightning speed, terrorizing and murdering their victims with as little mercy as the Indians. Storm and Wolf no longer made camp in open areas, but sought out sheltered *arroyos* high in the rocks where they would have some measure of protection from attack. Often Wolf would stand motionless in the dusk, his eyes scanning the plateaus and sweeping terrain below, his ears listening intently to the sounds of the twilight, his nostrils flaring slightly as he smelled the scents upon the wind. Then sometimes there would be no fire built, and quiet was the order of the evening. The morning following they would find fresh tracks of horses that had passed silently in the darkness, and Storm would marvel at Wolf's sixth sense for danger.

Tonight was different, however. Tonight a fire blazed merrily in the small, cavelike hollow they had found surrounded by brush in a secluded area of the mesa, and Wolf had gone hunting, leaving Storm alone. The girl had at first protested this, claiming they could catch fresh fish in the nearby stream, something she had not eaten since departing New Orleans. Her mouth had watered at the thought of a fat fish baked in the coals until it was soft and flaky and steaming hot, but Wolf had said fish were taboo for Comanches and that he would not eat anything she managed to catch. Storm had sighed and swallowed her disappointment, respecting his religion, although she was mighty tired of rabbit and the other animals Wolf killed for supper, refusing to shoot a deer or bear because they could not eat such a large beast and so the majority of its carcass would have been wasted.

The girl scrubbed and sliced some roots she'd found to supplement their meal, then set them to boiling. After that she fidgeted idly for a time, then suddenly jumped up decisively. There was no reason *she* couldn't eat a fish if she wanted. She had no rod, hook, or bait, but if she were very quiet and very clever, she might manage to 'tickle' one as she and André-Louis had often done in childhood. The thought appealed to her, and she walked quickly to the rivulet to put her plan in action. She stripped down to her underclothes at the bank, then waded in gently, taking care not to disturb the rippling water more than she could help. The brook was cold, but refreshing, and the water clear. Storm bent and dipped her hands in slowly, holding her breath as she caught sight of a good-sized fish. She moved toward it cautiously, intent on her prey, oblivious to her surroundings, forgetting the first law of the West. She had no time to try and capture the slippery, quick creature, however, because just then she was grabbed roughly from behind, a strong arm around her waist to imprison her closely, a calloused hand over her mouth to stifle her screams. Moments later she was dragged from the stream, and the cold steel of a gun-barrel was pressed to her temple.

An oddly accented voice growled in English, 'Don't make me have to shoot you, pretty woman.'

Storm nodded, trying to indicate she would not cause trouble, and ceased her struggles. Slowly she was released. She turned to face her captor. He was young, tall, and muscular, and dressed in an odd mixture of white and Indian clothing; and the features of both races were mingled on his dark coppery visage. He stared at her silently, appraisingly with dark brown eyes, white teeth flashing as he suddenly smiled appreciatively and asked,

'You are Brother-Of-The-Wolf's woman, no?'

'Yes,' Storm replied nervously, recognizing Wolf's Comanche name.

'From what tribe did he steal you, little half-breed?'

'He did not steal me, *monsieur*, and I am French, not Indian.'

The man shrugged and stretched out a hand to tug at one of Storm's braids. 'No matter. He will have taught you well.'

'What – what do you want, *monsieur*?'

'To kill your man, pretty woman, then perhaps you will belong to me, no? Come.'

He indicated with a sharp jerk of his revolver that she was to precede him back to camp. Storm looked thoughtfully at her clothes and gunbelt lying on the ground, then realized it would be foolish to attempt to reach her pistols when her captor already had one of his trained on her. He noted her gaze, bent and removed the revolvers from temptation, slinging the holster over his shoulder.

'Get the rest of your things,' he ordered.

They waited silently at camp for Wolf's return, Storm racking her brain to think of some way to warn him of his danger, but there was none. Her captor had told her calmly that he would kill her if she made a single outcry. At last, after what seemed like hours, Wolf appeared. He took in the situation at a glance. To the girl's surprise he merely tossed the two prairie dogs he had killed upon the ground, then drawled,

'Well, if it isn't Rickie Lee Halfhand.'

It was then Storm noticed the stranger was missing the last two fingers of his left hand. He must have gotten tired of running and decided to confront Wolf.

'Brother-Of-The-Wolf,' the girl's captor acknowledged his foe. 'I heard you wanted to see me, so – here I am.'

'Yeah, well, you sure took your time.'

'This is not a White-Eyes' matter, Brother-Of-The-Wolf, and I had no wish to be gunned down in the White-Eyes' manner. I will fight you, yes, but we will make it man-to-man, hand-to-hand, as is the way of an Indian.'

Wolf nodded curtly, unbuckled his gunbelt and threw it aside, then began to strip to the waist. His opponent did the same, while Storm watched anxiously, realizing the two men intended to fight and understanding this was to be a battle to the death. She felt suddenly sick with fear. It's what Wolf is, Storm, she told herself sternly, a gunslinger, a killer. This is his way of life, and there's nothing you can do about it. He's good at what he does. He couldn't have remained alive this long if he weren't. Still it didn't help to know that in moments he might be lying dead upon the ground, and she would be at the utter mercy of Rickie Lee Halfhand. Oddly enough it was the first thought that caused her heart to ache the worst, and suddenly Storm knew without a doubt she had come to love the savage gunslinger called El Lobo.

Oh, why hadn't she told him before this? Why had she been so stubborn and so afraid of being hurt? He was her savior, her protector, her teacher, her friend. He could have been her lover, would have been had she but held out her arms to him willingly. Now – now it might be forever too late!

Wolf strode over to his saddle bag and took out a long strip of leather he sometimes used to hobble the pack horse. He unrolled it and flipped one end toward Rickie Lee Halfhand, who grasped it deftly and placed it between his teeth. Wolf bit down hard on the the end, and both men drew their knives. The blades glittered cold and silvery beneath the glow of the full moon that rose in the sky as the two men began to circle warily, no more than a few feet apart, voluntarily bound by the rawhide.

The knives slashed through the air, making a soft whooshing sound, as though someone were twirling a lasso in the darkness. Both men bent forward slightly, protecting their chests and bellies from each other's blades as the knives darted outward again and again in swift, cutting arcs. Several times they clashed, ringing steel upon steel and echoing strangely, like a death knell, in the little *arroyo* as the two men danced upon lithe, catlike feet, never losing their grip upon the strip of leather. Once or twice they came perilously close to the fire, even kicking over some of the hot coals as they struggled to haul one another into the flames. Then the battle would become a motionless tug-of-war in which they faced each other grimly, Wolf switching his knife back and forth between his hands with lightning rapidity so that his opponent never knew if he would strike with the left or the right. Then with a leap and a yell from gritted teeth by one or the other the duel would begin again with agonizing suspense.

Storm's nerves screamed silently as she watched and held one hand to her mouth to keep from crying out each time a thin red weal of blood scraped upon Wolf's flesh until it seemed his chest and abdomen were a criss-cross of crimson. Rickie Lee Halfhand bore several bright gashes as well, and the girl began to fear both men would slowly bleed to death before the fight ended. She glanced at her revolvers, lying to one side, but something told her Wolf would never forgive her if she interfered by shooting Rickie Lee Halfhand, so she bit down hard on her whitened knuckles to stifle her sobs as tears trickled from the corners of her eyes, tracing little rivulets from her temples along her cheeks.

The end came so fast she had no warning of it, was unprepared for the horrible thud of a blade driving into a belly, piercing the flesh and internal organs as the knife was twisted deliberately until Rickie Lee Halfhand dropped his own, grabbing the hilt protuding from his abdomen with both hands before he gasped, releasing his end of the rawhide, and toppled backward, dead.

For a moment Storm felt nothing. She had seen men die – too many of them since leaving New Orleans – and perhaps she had become hardened to the sight. She only knew Wolf was alive. That was all that mattered. With a small whimper of relief she ran toward him as he tossed aside the strip of leather, pulled his blade free, then caught her in his arms, holding her close against his bloodstained skin. Suddenly with a soft little snarl, he yanked her head up savagely and ground his mouth down on hers hard, his tongue forcing her lips open, pillaging the sweetness that awaited within. Storm could feel the sweat that beaded his body, feel his muscles ripple and quiver with the power of death that surged within him still, feel the hunger of his bloodlust as he pushed her down upon their blankets and fell upon her blindly. Three times he had killed for her. Three times he had been the victor and kept her safe. *To the victor belong the spoils.* He meant to have her, and this time Storm knew she could not deny him.

She gasped as he rained hot, searing kisses on her mouth and throat, deftly caught each braid and cut the thong that bound it before he loosed the thick plaits to free the ebony cascade, catching great bunches of it with one hand, forcing her to look at him, to yield to him as he pressed the knife against her belly. Storm shook with fear and excitement as he slashed upward with the blade, severing the lacing on her camisole brutally, baring her breasts to his raking gaze. He flung the knife aside, his midnight blue eyes almost black with passion and desire. Storm shivered, for there was nothing gentlemanly about the way those glittering dark shards swept her body, taking in hungrily the sudden smoky gray of her eyes before her lashes half-closed sensuously, the small quiver of her bruised and swollen scarlet lips, the pulse that beat lightly, rapidly at the hollow of her throat, the flushed nipples that had already hardened of their own accord with eager anticipation.

She wanted to speak, to tell him she was inexperienced and afraid – afraid of being hurt by the savage in him, for she knew he had gone pure Indian on her, and afraid of disappointing the proud and arrogant man he was. She opened her mouth to whisper her fears, but it was too late. He was already kissing her half-parted lips again, his tongue darting hotly in and out of her mouth, exploring every curve of the softness that trembled beneath his demanding lips. He ravaged the sweetness of her expertly until she was moaning gently and panting for breath as her arms tightened around his neck, and she kissed him back feverishly, as though swept away by some wild, wanton wind from which there was no escape.

Dimly she realized some part of her wanted this – had wanted it ever since that night he had come to her, drunk with liquor and lust, and put his hands upon her as though it had been his right, arousing her slowly, exquisitely, then leaving her yearning and unsatisfied. Now she would know for what she had longed so badly that evening. Now she would learn those mysteries about which she had only heard whispered secrets, punctuated with sly giggles. Now she would discover those things to which Mammy had only once alluded, remembering at the last moment that 'Miz Storm' was a lady.

It's wrong! We're not married, she thought frantically. *Mon Dieu*! He's almost a stranger to me still and yet somehow I feel as though I've known him all my life, wanted him, needed him, loved him— The South is behind me now forever. I can never go home again, and except for Wolf, I'm so alone. Oh, *Jesù*! Hold me; hold me, Wolf; never let me go—

The girl tingled with excitement once more as Wolf's mouth burned its way across her cheek, up to one temple where he buried his face in her hair and muttered thickly, huskily in her ear, strange words in Comanche, Spanish, and English, all mixed up in some peculiar language of his own making, crude but clear. Storm shuddered, feeling as though the earth had suddenly dropped out from beneath her body. She knew she ought to be shocked by the things he said, things she only half-understood, but she wasn't, for his primitive words aroused her on some instinctive level long suppressed that was rushing to take control of her.

His hands found her breasts, shoving aside the torn camisole until suddenly it was no longer a part of her, but lay in a crumpled heap to one side. His fingers cupped her ripe mounds possessively, fondling them teasingly, tauntingly before he bent his head and covered one rosy crest with his lips, sucking it, sending sparks of quicksilver racing through

211

her veins as his tongue swirled about it caressingly, and his teeth nibbled gently. She was so caught up in the strange sensations he was producing in her body that she was only dimly aware of him yanking impatiently at her pantalettes, ripping them away until she was completely naked beneath him, and one leg was forcing her thighs apart, opening her flanks for the onslaught of his hand as his mouth moved to her other breast, lips pressing tiny circles about its stiff peak, tongue flicking at the little pink bud. His fingers sought her womanhood, brushing her intimately. She cried out in protest, but he covered her mouth with his own once more, silencing her incoherent whimpers as he stroked the pulsating velvet of her tenderly, rhythmically, pulling at silken curls and tracing the swell of satin skin until she was warm and wet where he touched her.

His lips traveled downward once more, mouth murmuring against her throat, then nipping at one shoulder before finding her breasts again. Like a trail of fire he blazed his way to her belly, his hands grasping the little hollows at her hips as his tongue licked the flesh along her sides, then probed her navel before sliding downward to flutter lightly upon her quivering mound. Storm gasped with shock and delight, wrapping her fingers in his hair, instinctively pulling him to her, unable to resist. Oh, God! It was indecent – what he was doing to her! But she was powerless to prevent it and did not want to.

I do love him! she thought wildly. I do! I wouldn't be letting him do these things if I didn't – and yet it isn't like what I felt for André-Louis, sweet, gentle, like some storybook fairytale. No, of course not. Those always ended with a kiss; and there's so much more. I want to know. Oh, Mammy! You said I would know! Is Wolf the right man for me? Is this love? Yes! Yes!

'Oh, God, Wolf—'

Again and again he tasted the length of her soft, honeyed folds while she writhed and strained upward against his lips, feeling a burning ache down deep within her where his tongue flitted, seeking the molten core of her. His hand moved to ease the blind sensation, fingers filling her, exploring her slowly at first and then faster as his mouth continued to titillate her throbbing flower of womanhood, sending earth-shaking tremors through her body that grew stronger and stronger until her hips arched frantically against him, and she felt a million shooting stars explode within her. She cried out once more, over and over, until Wolf raised himself to his knees, towering over her in the moonlight as he unbuckled his belt, then stood and slipped out of his breeches. Tall and proud and naked he planted his feet between Storm's thighs, spreading them further apart before he knelt and, taking her hands, pulled her upward, guiding her fingers over his body.

She touched the dark mat of hair upon his chest, felt the muscles beneath his dark coppery skin, traced the outlines of old scars that gleamed whitely upon his flesh and the new bloodstained scratches across his flat, taut belly made just that evening before tentatively her fingers grasped the hard maleness of him. He taught her the motion, and as she began it on her own, he caught her hair with one hand and started to kiss her mouth again brutally, ravishing her with his tongue. His other hand slid down between her flanks once more, fingers slipping inside her. Gradually he forced her to lower her head, and she understood he wanted her to take his manhood between her lips.

Hesitantly, afraid of angering or disappointing him, Storm's mouth closed around his bold shaft, her tongue imitating in manner the slow, teasing swirls and caresses with which he had tormented her earlier. Minutes later he drew her away and pushed her down upon the blankets again, holding himself poised above her before his sword found her sheath, piercing her savagely with a single jarring thrust. Storm felt a white-hot stab of pain and gave a small, strangled cry wondering why he had hurt her. She looked up at him, confused and suddenly frightened once more, for he was staring down at her intently, his eyes glowing with an odd triumph at knowing for certain he was the first.

'Wolf, no,' she breathed, her heart pounding, and began to struggle against him, wanting to draw back, but it was too late. No power on earth could have stopped him now.

His fingers entangled the mass of ebony tresses at her temples to hold her still while he kissed her, muffling her tiny screams of fear.

For a while he lay motionless atop her, accustoming her to the feel of him inside her while his lips pillaged hers, his nostrils flaring slightly as he breathed in the heady perfume of her rose scent. Then slowly he started to move within her, thrusting upward deliberately, ignoring her efforts to push him away as she fought him. At last her arms ceased to press against his chest and wound tightly around his back instead, feeling his muscles strain and stir beneath her hands as he plunged into her faster and faster with passionate, all-consuming fury.

'Wrap your legs around mine, baby,' he groaned hoarsely against her throat and then, '*Bruja. Bruja.* You have bewitched me.'

Trembling all over, Storm complied dazedly, her head beginning to spin dizzily as he gently bit the sensitive place on her shoulder that joined her nape, as she felt her loins start to churn tumultuously again, like a mass of rumbling clouds building to a thundering peak, before a blaze of lighting burst within her tempestuously, blinding her, shattering her to the very depths of her soul.

Almost simultaneously Wolf plummeted down into her fiercely for the last time, his whole body tense with emotion for one wild, exhilarating eternity as he made that strange savage cry that was his alone and then was still.

Beneath him Storm lay weak and exhausted, mentally and physically drained, her body seemingly limp and lifeless even though her heart still beat too quickly in her breast, and her pulse was racing yet. She could feel Wolf's chest pounding against her own until slowly he raised himself on one elbow to study her in the darkness. She looked just as he had once pictured her, naked and glistening with the sweat of his lovemaking, but oddly enough he felt no victory in the knowledge. The revenge he had planned was forgotten as he kissed her lingeringly on the mouth, then rolled to one side, cradling her in his arms tenderly. He could not hurt her now; she had given of herself too completely.

'You see that' – he pointed to the silvery globe in the Mexican sky after a time – 'that's a Comanche moon, a moon for raiding or making *namaer' ernuh* – something together. Why did you fight me, baby?'

'Because you – you hurt me.'

'There's always pain the first time, Storm. This time you will know only pleasure; I promise you.'

He took her again, more gently, and she found he was right, that there was only a languid feeling of contentment, of being safe, of belonging to him alone as he moved within her, reawakening her body, bringing it to glorious ecstasy once more as he smiled down into her eyes and whispered words of love. And for awhile Storm was sure time hung suspended, that there was only this moment, that only she and Wolf existed, lying close together beneath the starlit heavens, two against the world.

'I love you, Wolf,' she said with bated breath, wondering if he had truly meant the words he'd spoken. 'I am your woman now.'

'Yes, *paraibo*,' he replied softly, stroking her hair. 'You are my woman now.'

12

Like a pale blush of pink across a woman's cheeks dawn was stealing slowly across the sky when they awakened, the sun turning Storm's body to gold with its brilliant rays and making her hair gleam blue-black where it touched her caressingly, even as Wolf did. He wrapped the silken ebony strands around his throat and tasted again the sweet, honeyed flesh of her he had known so intimately last night. Storm was shy with him in the morning light and would have refused his urgent need, but he caught her jaw with his strong fingers, tilted her face up to his, and stated harshly,

'Never deny me, baby.'

She shivered slightly, even though he took her tenderly, for she realized she had given herself body and soul into his keeping and that he was not a man to be ruled by a woman. He would love and cherish her, but he would never be her slave.

Afterward he walked her to the stream where they bathed together, splashing water at one another and laughing before he left Storm to wash her hair while he buried Rickie Lee Halfhand and the two dead prairie dogs they had not eaten after all. When the girl had dressed and returned to the camp, there was no trace of the carnage that had taken place the previous evening. Storm was glad Wolf had not left the matter to her as he had done after killing Zeke Barlow, and to her relief she saw no signs that her lover had scalped the unfortunate Rickie Lee Halfhand either. She busied herself with the remainder of their chores, then at last approached Wolf shyly.

'Wolf—' she began hesitantly.

'Yeah, baby?'

'We must find a priest somewhere.'

'A priest! For what?'

'Why, to – to marry us of course,' Storm stammered nervously, feeling suddenly sick to her stomach, believing she had misunderstood Wolf's intentions toward her. 'Surely you didn't think – I mean – after last night – I – I thought—'

'As did I. Did I not take you willingly – as you came to me? Did I not call you my *paraibo* afterward? And did you not keep silent, making no protest against me?'

'Well, yes, but I assumed we would have some kind of ceremony in a church, that a priest would give us his blessing—'

'Do not speak to me of priests, woman!' Wolf spoke sharply, his voice suddenly cold, his dark visage once more a hard mask. 'I have slept with you and said you are my wife, and you have not denied me. We need no White-Eyes' piece of paper to tell us this. We are married. It is enough! It is the Comanche way. I will announce it to The People when we reach the *Llano Estacado*, and my father will give us his blessing if you wish.'

'But, Wolf,' Storm protested, appalled. 'I – I am a Catholic—'

'You are the wife of a Comanche warrior, and a Comanche woman does not argue with her husband. Now get your things.'

'But, Wolf, it – it isn't legal!'

His eyes narrowed as they raked her icily. 'It is as far as I am concerned; make no mistake about that, baby. You *are* my wife. You belong to me, and if I ever catch you with another man, I'll kill you! Do you understand?'

Storm nodded slowly, shuddering faintly at the thought of Wolf's murderous rage turned loose against her. As though sensing her sudden fear of him he caught her and kissed her roughly, possessively, one hand resting at the base of her throat.

'Last night you said you loved me, and this morning you have already begun to turn against me,' he growled.

'No, Wolf! I *do* love you! I – I just didn't understand; that's all. Oh, please don't be angry with me! I can't bear it!' Tears sparkled on her eyelashes as she pleaded with him.

His face softened, and he kissed her more gently. 'I'm sorry. I am not angry, Storm. You opened an old wound in my past. It wasn't your fault. You couldn't have known.'

'Known what?' she asked tremulously.

'That once I was studying to become a priest.'

The girl's gray eyes widened with surprise. 'You were? What – what happened?'

'Perhaps someday I'll tell you, but not today. It's getting late. Come on.'

Silently she did as he ordered, her heart aching and filled with confusion as she wondered if she would ever truly know this stranger who now called her his wife.

It was nearly a week later when they crossed the Paseo de los Indios, a much-used ford on the Rio Grande just a few hundred yards upstream from the city of Laredo, which Don Tomas Sanchez de la Barrera y Gallardo and a handful of settlers had founded in 1755. Storm drank in the sights eagerly as they entered the town, for in many ways the center of the activity, the San Agustin Plaza, reminded her of home. As New Orleans was a blend of French and American styles, so Laredo was a mixture of Mexico and Texas, curiously interwoven, the old and the new. Here *los Tejanos Diablos*, as the Mexicans called them, the Texas Rangers who had made Samuel Colt successful by adopting his 1836 Paterson Colt revolver, could be seen swaggering down the streets alongside prosperous white ranchers and Mexican small farmers. Occasionally there were Indians, Negroes who had managed to escape their masters, and men who, from the looks of them, were little more than *bandoleros*, whether white or Mexican. Storm barely glanced at these last, having gained confidence in herself and her abilities. Besides, Wolf was with her. She studied him covertly from beneath her eyelashes as they trotted down the street, impervious to the attention they often attracted, for they were a handsome couple, proud, arrogant. Except for the color of their eyes, they might have been cut from the same mold, for there was about the girl now the same wary, steely hardness that marked Wolf's chiseled countenance.

Only for a moment did Storm's face change, lighting up with longing and delight as she caught a glimpse of an outrageous red dress in a shop window. How long had it been since she had worn a gown? And how shockingly delicious this one was. It was cut extremely low at the ruffled neck and had small ruffled sleeves that hung off the shoulders slightly. The swirling, flounced hem was ruffled too, sweeping down around the base of the dummy with a graceful flourish. It would show my ankles, Storm thought ruefully, and perhaps a good deal of leg as well. With a sigh she turned reluctantly away, nearly colliding with Wolf, who had, to Storm's surprise, pulled his stallion up in front of the shop. With the tender courtesy he had shown to her since declaring they were married he helped the girl dismount, then escorted her inside the store. A fat, smiling Mexican woman came bustling forward at the tinkling sound of the little bell on the door.

'Buenos tardes, señor, señora.' She nodded pleasantly. '¿Como estan ustedes?'

'Muy bien, gracias. ¿Y usted?'

'Ah, muy bien tambien, señor. With what can I help you today? Some ammunition for los pistoles? A new pair of boots? Some combs for the lovely señora?'

The woman was very humble and eager to please, and as Storm glanced around the tiny shop she realized it was a very poor store and that great pains had been taken to make its meager merchandise appear as attractive as possible. The shelves were meticulously clean, as though dusted two or three times a day, and the floor was spotless. Brightly colored Mexican serapes hung decoratively on the walls; beautiful hand-made sombreros were displayed neatly alongside hand-tooled leather boots and gleaming silver spurs. A small rack with more frocks stood next to another with men's shirts and breeches. Yards of brilliant material were stacked upon a table in the center of the room. A glass case held guns and knives, fine jewelry and rosaries. Intricately woven baskets and clay pots were arranged fetchingly here and there in heaps upon the floor.

'My wife would like to see the red dress in the window, *señora*,' Wolf said impassively, but his eyes were twinkling all the same as he heard Storm's tiny gasp of pleasure.

'But of course, *señor*,' the woman replied, as though she had guessed this all along. She hurried away, her plump body oddly light upon her tiny feet. Within moments she had returned bearing the red gown in her arms. 'Would you like to try it on, *señora*? I have a small room at the back where I keep my accounts that would be private.'

'Oh, yes!' Storm cried with excitement, praying the frock would fit.

Minutes later she stood arrayed in its satin ruffles, her breasts straining upward from the bodice enticingly, her legs enchantingly revealed up to their calves.

'It is perfect for you, *señora*!' The Mexican woman beamed, then, as though startled, suddenly clucked to herself. '*Un momento, señora*.' She motioned for Storm to stay put, then disappeared only to return once more, her arms heavily laden. 'Here.' She handed the girl a pair of black silk stockings and two red garters. 'You put these on too. ¡*Dios*! You have such little feet, but I think these will do, no?' she asked, indicating a pair of red slippers. 'I told my husband when he bought them that he had wasted our hard-earned *dinero*, that no one would be able to wear them. But see how our Lord does indeed work in mysterious ways, *señora*? They are just right for you! I cannot believe it. Now I will show you how to place the comb in your hair and drape this *mantilla*. Then you will truly look the part of a beautiful Spanish lady, no?' Deftly she unbraided Storm's hair, brushed it, and arranged the lovely comb and red lace. Tilting her head slightly, she studied the girl critically, then frowned impatiently. 'No. This will not do. There is a mystery about your eyes, like smoke; they have seen much more of life than those of a Spanish lady will ever know. *¿Es verdad? Sí*, they have a gypsy cast, secretive and untamed, as though a wild passion lurks within you. Hmmm, yes. Wait *un momento, señora*.' This time when the woman came back she bore a single rose in her hands, its red petals cleverly fashioned from stiff satin, its green leaves from velvet. Expertly she wound its stem into the comb, then positioned it over Storm's right ear. '*Sí*.' She nodded again. 'That is the effect for you, *señora*, and yet – there is still something missing. Wait! I know!' Once more the woman vanished, then reappeared with a pair of silver hoop earrings and several silver bangles. At last she was pleased with Storm's appearance. 'Yes, now I think we are ready for your handsome *caballero* to see you, no? Already he grows impatient, that one, like a panther. Men! They do not understand how much care is needed for a woman to make herself *hermosa* for them, no? Here she is, *señor*,' the woman called, giving Storm a little push forward. 'And worth the wait, no?'

The girl stood silently, her eyes shining as she awaited Wolf's approval. His midnight blue shards raked her intently, possessively.

'*Sí, señora*. Well worth the wait,' he drawled, his voice husky with desire, causing Storm to blush faintly as she thought of the many nights now she had lain within his hot embrace and felt his mouth sear hers demandingly, felt the length of his strong, muscular body pressed passionately upon her own, felt his maleness hard and driving deep inside her, as though he could not get enough of her. Two and three times a night he had taken her under the stars since that first time, teaching her how to make love as expertly as he had taught her how to survive the harsh, savage beauty of Texas and Mexico. 'Choose what else you would like, *paraibo*,' he told her 'and we will have *la señora* wrap everything together.'

Storm selected a few essentials such as lotion and cologne of which she was almost out, then at the last minute impulsively added a black-and-silver rosary similar to Wolf's to her purchases, for her relationship with her lover troubled her conscience greatly. For all that he said so, Storm found it difficult to believe they were truly married when no priest had given them his blessing. Perhaps if she prayed to *Sainte Marie* she would be forgiven for turning her back on the Church and living in sin.

'Now that you have such a pretty costume, *señora*,' the Mexican woman spoke, interrupting the girl's troubled thought, 'you should have some place to wear it. We are having a *fiesta* this evening to celebrate my grandson's birthday. We are poor people, and our house is humble, but we would be pleased to make you and your husband welcome.'

To Storm's surprise Wolf said they would be happy to attend, and after finding out the woman's name and address they left the store to look for lodgings and prepare for the party. Eventually they were ensconced in a room above a Mexican *cantina*. It was small but clean, and although Storm was certain the girls who worked below sometimes worked above, at least the tavern was not overtly a whorehouse. There was a tin washtub in which she managed to bath before a steaming meal was brought to their room, along with a bottle of mescal and a pot of hot, bitter coffee. Storm discovered she had developed a taste for Mexican food, as well as the mescal, and stuffed herself as decently as possible, finding the meal a welcome change from the suppers they usually cooked over a campfire. Wolf watched her with amusement.

'I hope you don't intend to get fat, Storm,' he droned after taking a drag of his cigar. 'I might have to divorce you.'

'Comanches have divorce too?' she questioned curiously.

'Yeah.'

'Well, are you going to tell me how it's done, so that if you

222

ever do decide to be rid of me, I won't be as – surprised as I was upon learning we were married?'

'How do you know we really are?'

'What?' she screeched, horrified that their relationship might not even be sanctified in some pagan manner.

Wolf almost choked on his mescal. 'We are, Storm,' he uttered hastily. 'I was only teasing, baby. Besides, would it really matter if we weren't?'

'It matters to me. Everything I've ever cherished has been taken from me. I would like to think that at least I'm not a – a—'

'Loose woman?' he supplied, casually lifting one eyebrow. 'You'd better not be, baby.'

'You must know I am not,' Storm retorted quietly, indignant.

'I know. I wouldn't have married you otherwise.'

'Why are you talking about marriage? I thought you were going to explain to me how Comanches get divorced.'

'I've changed my mind,' he said, rising from the table. 'I'll never let you go, and I'd never stand for you divorcing me either.' He caught one long tress, pulling her to him. 'Come here, baby.'

Storm shivered with excitement and flushed with shyness as he loosed the towel she had wrapped around herself after her bath. The fluffy material fell to the floor, leaving her naked in his arms. He tilted her face up to his, kissing her deeply on the lips while one hand cupped her breast, thumb flicking at her nipple. His fingers slid downward to tighten on her hip before he gave a low, throaty growl and carried her to the bed. Storm stared up him, unmoving, while he cast away his breeches, then lowered himself over her, beginning to kiss and caress her all over, as though wanting to know each little nuance of her body as intimately as possible. He kissed her eyelids, her temples, her earlobes, the tip of her nose, her scarlet mouth. His lips traveled down her nape to her shoulders, her breasts, and then lower still, to the soft curls that twined between her thighs before his mouth scorched its way back up again, back to bury itself in her cloud of ebony hair while all the time his hands moved upon her, searching, exploring, taking her own small palms in his, guiding her as she touched him, discovered him as he was discovering her, as though it were the first time, every time for them, as though he would never tire of her, or she of him.

'Tell me you love me, baby,' he muttered thickly against her throat. 'I want to hear you say it. Tell me you love me more than you've ever loved anyone before in your life.'

It was as though he hungered for her love even more than her body, as though no one had ever truly cared for him before, and he was starved of affection. Storm had sensed it often in him, especially at times like this when he demanded her words of reassurance, and she wondered again about his dark and mysterious past, who or what had hurt him so deeply, and why? Who had caused him to become what he was? Who had torn from him the love he must have once known for him to be so gentle with her even when he took her so urgently, almost cruel in his passion? Who had turned him into this strong, strange, hard, haunted man who wanted her love so desperately, who could forget his pride in her embrace and ask her for it, the naked desire and longing for her plain within his passion-darkened eyes?

'I love you, Wolf,' she whispered. 'I love you as I've never loved anyone else in my life.'

He groaned and spread her flanks, plunging into her fiercely, as though afraid she might take her words back, as though by the sheer force of his strength and willpower he could make her his forever, imprison her with the virile, hot stab of his manhood as he gyrated down into her until she cried out her surrender, wanting him, needing him, and felt the sudden heady rush of molten ore racing through her blood, setting her afire with its liquid blaze.

'*Mon Dieu, mon Dieu*!' she panted, gasping for breath as her nails tightened on his back, swept down to his hips, cutting little jagged furrows in his skin as she raked at him wildly. He urged her on, his hands beneath her body to hold her even closer as he thrust into her rapidly again and again, sliding down the sweet velvet length of her faster and faster until his own release came tumultuously, leaving him sweating feverishly, his glossy name of black hair damp upon his shoulders as he looked down at her, kissed her, then finally moved to free himself from the tangle of her legs.

Afterward he held her tenderly, seeming to understand she needed to be cradled and talked to soothingly, to be reassured of his caring for her even as he had needed such during their lovemaking; for beneath the hard shell she had built around herself to survive she was a sensitive woman, easily bruised and hurt.

He stroked her snarled curls, smoothing the strands away from her trembling lips, her smoky gray eyes. He lifted a lock that lay upon one breast, then took possession of the ripe mound with his hand, gently brushing its rosy crest.

'There will never be anyone for you but me,' he said. 'No one else will ever know you as I do – like this.' He indicated her nakedness, his fingers sweeping the length of her body jealously. 'You are mine, only mine.'

He kissed her once more, then rose and began to dress while Storm watched him silently, trembling beneath his fiery gaze. He means it, she thought. He will kill me if I ever so much as even glance at another man. *Jesù*! He has a devil in him. Thank God, he is not my enemy!

It was dark when they at last made their way to the *jacale* of *Señora* Ramirez, but the stars lighted their way, and in addition, the small dirt road leading to the *señora*'s house was lined with candles set in little bags of sand. Luminaries, Storm thought with a sudden pang of homesickness as she remembered how she and her father had directed the lighting of Belle Rive's long, winding drive in just such a fashion each Christmas. The *jacale* was indeed poor as the *señora* had

225

warned them, but she made them welcome all the same, bustling forward with a broad grin on her wrinkled but cherubic face, her arms outstretched to draw them into the circle of people who were gathered outside in the street, for the house had no porch or yard, and its meager rooms were too tiny to accommodate all. No one appeared to mind this, however, and those who had found *Señora* Ramirez's *jacale* too crowded had opened up their own humble houses as well. It seemed as though the whole district were present. Everyone knew everyone else, and Storm hung back shyly before the *señora* began to introduce her and Wolf.

'*Atencion, todos. Estes son mis amigos el Señor Lobo y su esposa*, Storm. *Por favor*. Make them welcome, won't you?'

With shouts and laughter the Mexicans displayed their traditional generous hospitality, and soon the girl no longer felt a stranger as she nodded and smiled and watched Wolf proudly as he conversed in rapid Spanish with the others. Storm's language lessons had progressed well enough that she managed to understand several words here and there and to speak slowly herself each time someone approached her. She attracted many admiring glances in her new red gown, although the other young women were dressed similarly, but she was careful not to flirt with any of the men who flocked to her side, for fear Wolf would become angry. Indeed his hard visage darkened once or twice when a suitor became overbold, and finally, when the *mariachi* musicians struck up another lively tune, he led Storm away over the loud protests of her gay cavaliers.

By this time she had drunk several glasses of good red wine and was feeling quite giddy as he swept her into the street among the dancing couples. The hard ground shook with the staccato stamping of boots and slippers, and the air thrummed with the sound of the guitars and clicking castanets. Those watching clapped their hands rhythmically to the wild music and yelled encouragement, which the dancers answered challengingly, whirling faster and faster.

Storm's breath caught in her throat as she found herself twirling along with the rest, the primitive, earthy movements seemed to come naturally, sensuously, needing no thought or experience. She moved like the Cajun women of New Orleans, as all women for centuries have moved when not bound by the dictates of society, never dreaming she could be so free and unrestrained. She closed her eyes and let the beat take hold of her, pervade her very being with its throbbing, wanton essence. The ruffles of her dress swirled about her legs, rippling upward to show a flash of thigh. The heels of her shoes tapped drummingly; her body swayed; her arms lifted, graceful as a swan as she held them out to Wolf imploringly.

She was unaware that she danced alone, that the others had fallen back to watch the pretty French *señora* who spoke Spanish so delightfully and danced so enchantingly. She was the belle of the ball once more, but for the first time in her life she did not care. There was nothing for Storm but the music that pulsated in her soul, draining the life from her, taking away the pain of her past to fill her with love and hope for the future. Every sorrow she had ever known found its way to her face to be gently etched away, her countenance lighting up with pure joy at her release. New Orleans was a million miles away, and the last vestiges of the Storm Lesconflair who had waltzed so beautifully in its plantation ballrooms faded as the untamed West claimed Wolf's woman once and for always.

It was for him whom she danced, the hard, savage, half-breed gunslinger who had taken her in, taught her to survive, stripped away the child in her, and made her his woman. It was then she understood she had been half-dead in New Orleans, a pretty china doll who had smiled and said the proper things; but here, now she was alive! For the first time in her life she was alive! Life tingled in her veins, rushed through her blood to the very tips of her fingers and toes, pounded in her head dizzily, intoxicatingly.

I'm alive! she wanted to scream, to shout to the world. I'm alive! This is what Gabriel tried to tell me about the West, only

227

I didn't understand it then. This is what he meant when he said a man could breathe out here. Ah, Gabriel North, you *taureau*, you have done me a favor after all! You thought you would tame me, but you only succeeded in setting me free!

Her eyes flew open.

'Oh, Wolf! Wolf!'

'I know, *paraibo*. I know,' he said softly before he took her in his arms amidst the enthusiastic applause of the others.

It was getting late, so after the dancing the children gathered round to break the *piñata* someone had strung up on one of the overhanging rafters of *Señora* Ramirez's roof. The *señora* blindfolded each child in turn, then whirled him or her around several times before she released her hold, handing the child a stout stick with which to batter the gaily decorated, brightly colored burro. The children giggled with glee each time a fellow contestant swung wildly and missed, while the adults looked on fondly, calling encouragement.

As befitted the occasion it was *Señora* Ramirez's grandson who finally broke the *piñata* open, sending the lovingly wrapped candy and trinkets inside scattering. With whoops of delight the children ran to collect the treasures, the *señora* making certain no child went home empty-handed.

After that Storm and Wolf thanked their hostess for a wonderful time, then made their way back to the *cantina*. The girl had an uneasy feeling as they wound their way through the dark twisting alleys of Laredo, and once or twice she even stopped to glance back nervously over her shoulder.

'Yeah, I hear it too, baby,' Wolf spoke, his voice low. 'We're being followed.'

Suddenly, without warning, he pushed Storm swiftly into a doorway, pressing himself up against her in the shadows, his hand over her mouth to silence any small outcry she might have made. It seemed they stood like that for hours, breathless, motionless, waiting, their hearts pounding against one another in the starlit blackness. Wolf had drawn his knife, and it glittered, cruel and deadly, where a spray of silver from

228

the heavens struck the blade; but no one came. Whoever had been there was gone.

After a time Wolf pulled Storm from the doorway and sheathed his knife.

'It may have been nothing, baby,' he told her quietly, but her feeling of uneasiness persisted all the same.

Laredo was beginning to stir when Storm awakened in the morning. She lay unmoving for a moment, listening to the sounds of the town coming to life: the rattle of wagon wheels and the clip-clop of hooves over the hard dirt roads; the occasional whinny of a horse; the babble of voices speaking English, Spanish, and various Indian languages; shouts and laughter when a female shrieked at having her dress spattered (whether with the contents of a slop jar or spittoon Storm couldn't tell); the banging of doors. She smiled to herself, for the noises reminded her of Belle Rive and Vaillance in the mornings, and it was good to know some things never changed.

She turned, raising herself on one elbow to gaze at Wolf, who still slept, despite the clatter below. The girl marveled again at how young and handsome he looked in repose. With one hand she stroked his long, shaggy mane of black hair, pushing a strand from his face before she bent and kissed his mouth softly.

Immediately his eyes flew open, and he grabbed her, hauling her on top of him, a smile on his lips.

'Oh, you!' Storm snapped, trying to sound indignant, although her dimples were peeping at the corners of her mouth. 'You were awake all the time!'

'So I was,' he agreed, still grinning wickedly.

She noted how easily he smiled now, not like before when the expression had been bitter and jeering, as though it had caused him pain, but naturally, joyously.

'Wolf, I have made you happy, have I not?' she asked a trifle anxiously, wanting desperately to know she had pleased him.

'Yes, *paraibo*, you have made me happy, very happy,' he said before he kissed her, his hands tangled in her ebony tresses to draw her close. 'You looked so beautiful last night. I was the envy of every man there. You must have been the belle of the ball in New Orleans. Do you miss it, Storm?'

'Not anymore, now that I have you. Hold me, Wolf. Make love to me. I want to know I am your woman, now and forever.'

His eyes darkened, nearly as black as ink as he rolled her over and pressed her down among the pillows, his mouth on hers, his tongue parting her lips, seeking the softness that lay within. Her arms crept up to tighten around his neck, one hand wrapped in his mane of hair as she kissed him back eagerly, wanting him, shivering slightly as she felt the demanding pressure of his mouth on hers. To some extent he frightened her even as he excited her, for always at the back of her mind lay the fact that he was a killer, that the lips that kissed her so hungrily could just as easily have curled into that brutal sneer she'd seen upon his face, that the hands that explored her body so intimately could just as easily have wielded a knife or a gun against her. His muscles quivered and rippled beneath her fingers so that she could feel the sheer power and strength of him even though he held her gently in his steely grip, and she trembled with a strange vulnerability in his grasp as he cupped her breasts possessively, his mouth hot upon her nipples. Tiny tingles of delight raced through her body as his tongue swirled about the engorged peaks, feasting deeply before he sighed with pleasure and buried his face between the soft mounds to feel the rapid pounding of her heart.

His hand swept down to probe between her flanks, stroking slowly at first as he spread her legs with his own, fondling the sweet velvet length of her. She gasped quietly as he caressed her there, her eyes, which had been closed, flying open to meet his as he stared at her, studying the expressions that flitted across her countenance.

'Don't. Don't watch me,' she protested, but he ignored her, continuing to look at her as his fingers moved within her.

'I like to see you,' he murmured, his voice husky with passion. 'I like to know what you're feeling when I touch you, taste you.'

He bent his head and pressed his lips upon the honeyed swell of her that pulsated with little quick flutters as he tongued her deliberately, his eyes still upon her face. Storm gave a small, ragged cry, turning away so that she would no longer have to bear the intensity of his gaze, but she could not escape the intimacy he forced upon her as he caught her hands and drew them down to feel the warm moistness of herself as he continued his onslaught on her womanhood with his tongue. He invaded not only her body, but her very soul until she felt as though he knew her innermost thoughts, her darkest secrets and desires, until she was no longer one with herself, but belonged to him and him alone. She felt as though she were clay, and he was molding her, shaping her, for suddenly she seemed to have no bones, no will of her own. There was only Wolf and what he was doing to her, the feel and scent of him enveloping her, blinding her to everything but him. She was like quicksilver in his hands, growing hotter and hotter, melting beneath him in molten rivers that rushed through her veins as though they had broken from a dam. She arched her hips against him only to discover he was no longer there. She whimpered softly, and her eyes flew open once more.

He was on his knees between her thighs, towering over her briefly before he flung himself upon her with a low snarl, his hard maleness penetrating her swiftly with a deep thrust that took her breath away before she cried out her surrender and gave herself up to him wildly, wantonly, clinging to him tightly as he plummeted down into her again and again, his hands gripping the masses of hair at her temples as he drove her to the heights of rapture and beyond.

'*Bruja*,' he muttered against her throat. '*Bruja*,' and then

'Christ, oh, Christ!'

When it was over, Storm lay quietly in his arms, waiting for the room to stop spinning, for her heart to slow to its normal pace. The sweat of him glistened on her skin, mingling with her own, and the scent of their lovemaking pervaded her nostrils deeply, making her feel as though she were still a part of him and he of her. Wolf kissed her lingeringly, then lit a cigar, holding her close as he blew a cloud of smoke upward toward the ceiling.

'I love you,' she spoke, her head upon his chest.

His arm tightened around her, and he looked down at her strangely, his eyes hard and hungry as they swept the length of her nakedness.

'You say it so easily, so trustingly,' he growled. 'Are you not afraid of being hurt by loving like that?'

'Do you want to hurt me, Wolf?'

'No, but it's been my experience that love brings only pain.'

'Is that why you won't say it?'

'Say what?'

'That you love me.'

'Baby, I've told you that I do.'

'When we – make love, yes, but then you speak of – of loving me – physically. Is that all that is in your heart for me – just lust?'

'Of course not.'

'Then why can't you tell me that?'

'I don't know, Storm. It's hard for me to express what I feel. I wasn't brought up to show emotion. It is not the Comanche way, but I do love you.'

'Tell me.'

'Witch!' He caught her hair, twisting her face up to his roughly, but at her expression his dark visage gentled. 'All right. I love you. I love the feel of you up next to me like this; I love the way you sit up straight and tall on Madame Bleu; I love the glow of your skin by firelight and moonlight; I love the funny little face you make whenever you drink mescal;

232

I love the way your eyes go all smoky when I look at you a certain way – like now,' he whispered intently, crushing out his cigar before his mouth came down on her hard.

'Don't hurt me, Wolf,' she breathed beneath his lips, her eyes wide and suddenly vulnerable.

'Never, baby,' he said, his voice thick before he swore softly and took her again.

Later, when Wolf had left on business, Storm decided to go down to *Señora* Ramirez's shop and thank her again for the wonderful time they had had last evening. The girl had noticed the *señora*'s shawl was extremely tattered, although she had many beautiful lace *rebozos* in her store, and Storm thought she would buy one and make *Señora* Ramirez a present of it. She bathed in the hot water Wolf had had sent up before leaving, then dressed, being sure to check her pistols since this part of Laredo was a rather rough area. After that she went downstairs to the tavern and, ignoring the speculative glances she received from several men below, pushed her way out into the street. Storm had an excellent memory and in no time at all had found her way to the *señora*'s small shop.

Señora Ramirez was delighted to see her again and bustled about cheerfully as she served Storm a cup of coffee and a piece of Mexican bread, then showed her the shawls, chatting contentedly about the *fiesta*.

'Oh, *Señora* Lobo, you break many hearts last night, I tell you. You look so beautiful in the red dress and dance like a gypsy. Your husband, he was so handsome and so proud of you, but he have a temper too, no? I see his eyes flash when the *caballeros* grow too bold, and I cross myself and thank *la Madre de Dios* there is not murder done! He is very good with *los pistoles*, no?'

'Yes, very good. Which one of these *rebozos* do you like best, *señora*?'

'Oh, for myself I like the silver, but for you – the red, *señora*. It will match your gown.'

'But it is not for me, *Señora* Ramirez,' Storm said, selecting the silver shawl and paying for it. 'It is for you, to thank you for a lovely evening.'

'Oh, *señora*, I – I do not know what to say.' The Mexican woman dabbed at her eyes. 'It is too much. I cannot accept it.'

'Please. Take it. My husband and I would like you to have something to remember us by.'

'Oh, *Señora* Lobo, when you put it that way, you make it hard for me to refuse. *Muchas gracias, entonces, para todo el mundo.*'

'*De nada, señora.* It is I who should be thanking you.'

'*Vaya con Dios, señora.*'

'And you also, *Señora* Ramirez. Please wish your grandson "happy birthday" for us again. Goodbye.'

Storm's feet felt as though they had wings as she left the tiny store, the *señora*'s cries of joy still ringing in her ears. It was hard for her to believe that just a few months ago she would never have bothered to enter a shop such as *Señora* Ramirez's, much less have purchased something and then given the woman a gift on top of it. Good gracious, what an ignorant snob I used to be, the girl thought as she wound her way through the twisting alleys back to the *cantina*. I wonder what else I missed as a belle in New Orleans? Certainly the party last night was much more earthy and alive than those dull affairs we used to have at home. Why, yes, they *were* dull! I wonder now how I ever thought them interesting? Why, I could never have danced in New Orleans as I danced last evening, and I'll bet the entire French Quarter would swoon if they could see me now, with my skin as brown as a walnut and breeches that show the shape of my legs! I'll bet André-Louis wouldn't even recognize me, and what's more, I wouldn't even care! How silly and effeminate he seems now compared to Wolf – Wolf, who makes me hot and dizzy with desire.

The girl blushed just thinking about it and how he had made love to her this morning, with an intimacy she would never have dreamed possible. He's changed me, she thought, and I'm glad. He makes me feel like a woman. Why, when I think about how the boys back home used to bore me to tears, I wonder how I ever stood it and how I ever imagined I was in love with André-Louis? *Sainte Marie!* The West was in my blood all along, and I never knew it. Only Gabriel North had sense enough to see it. Poor Gabriel. I wonder if he ever looked for me? Ah, *Monsieur* North, *c'est la vie!*

Storm was so engrossed in her thoughts, the discoveries she was making about herself and finding she liked, and her delight in having 'outwitted them all', as she considered it, she never even noticed the two men slouching in a doorway off the alley, their hats pulled down low over their faces. It was not until she was right up on them, and they began to move toward her menacingly, that she sensed danger. By then they had grabbed hold of her, and it was too late to draw her revolvers. She screamed as she recognized Luther and Billy Barlow and started to struggle against them like a wildcat, biting and clawing and kicking, instinctively using all the tricks Wolf had taught her over the past few months. She caught Billy right between the legs with her boot, and he fell back, doubled over with anguish.

'Gawddamned slut,' he groaned. 'Git her, Luther! Git her!'

'Friggin' bitch!' Luther swore and slapped Storm hard across the face.

The blow sent her sprawling to the ground. She dragged Luther down with her since he was still gripping one of her hands tightly, and they grappled in the dirt, breathing heavily. Storm managed to pull her knife during the struggle and stab her assailant, but the blade only glanced off his collarbone, they were both moving so quickly. The girl did manage to take advantage of Luther's stunned surprise, however, sliding out from beneath him and rolling to one side. Like a cat she was on her feet in moments and had begun to run when Billy, recovering, caught the sleeve of her shirt, ripping her blouse open before he knocked her to the earth, sending her knife flying. Storm heard the blade clatter against the side of an adobe *jacale* and realized dimly she had lost it, but she had no time to think about it before Billy was on her, straddling her body, pinning her hands above her head.

'Gawddamned slut,' he sneered once more, than smacked her another ringing blow as Luther staggered over, one hand pressed against his shoulder to staunch the flow of blood where he'd been wounded.

'Fer Gawd's sake, Billy! What are you waitin' fer? Kill the friggin' bitch before she gits away agin! You want that half-breed bastard of hers to finish you off the way he done Zeke?'

'No, I jest wanna give the Gawddamned slut sumpin' to remember me by on her way to hell!' Billy jeered, tearing at Storm's clothes, stripping off her gunbelt and tossing it to one side before he started to yank at her breeches. 'Hold her hands, Luther. Jesus! Wouldya look at them titties! I wonder if old Zeke got him a taste of those before he died?'

'Stop it! Stop it!' Storm screamed before Billy slapped her again, then yelled,

'Fer Gawd's sake, Luther! Stuff sumpin' in her mouth to shut her up before she brings a pack of Mexicans down on us!'

'I would if I could git my pants unfastened. Hurry up, Billy! I think I'll have me a go at her too after yore done.'

'Any minute now,' Billy crooned, trying to haul Storm's legs apart and pull her breeches down. 'It'd be a helluva lot easier if you'd quit fightin' me, honey. You know yore gonna like it once I git it in you anyways.'

'Wolf'll kill you for this,' the girl moaned, tears running down her face. 'He'll kill you and scalp you just as he did your brother.'

'You think so, huh? Well, we got a little surprise planned fer him too.'

'Come on, Billy. Quit talkin', and git to fuckin', or move aside,' Luther ordered crudely, fumbling with the buttons on his pants. 'I cain't wait much longer.'

'Well, I cain't git her Gawddamned britches off!'

'Here, you hold her then, and let me try.'

'All right, but remember, I'm first.'

Storm wanted to die as they traded places, and Luther went to work on her pants while Billy said he'd get his own off and make use of her mouth in the meantime. She screamed at the top of her lungs as moments later he shoved his organ into her face, trying to get her to take it between her lips. She knew she would vomit if he forced her, that what she had done willingly and lovingly for Wolf, she could never do for any reason for this filthy outlaw.

'I won't do it! You'll have to kill me first!'

She twisted her head this way and that, trying desperately to avoid him, feeling her stomach begin to heave; then suddenly she heard a horde of voices raised in shouts and threats and the pounding of boots upon the hard dirt road as several of the *caballeros* she had met last night came to her rescue, and the Barlows let her go.

Luther kicked her brutally in the ribs a couple of times – 'jest so's you know we won't be fergittin' you, bitch!' – before he and Billy ran as fast as they could, some of the Mexican men chasing them while the others helped Storm to her feet. She swayed shakily against them, clutching onto them frantically for support, crying, trying to thank them, and holding her torn garments together as best she could.

It was this Wolf saw when he rounded the corner in search of her, wondering why she had not yet returned from *Señora* Ramirez's shop. The excited babble of voices faded to a strained silence as everyone noticed him at once, and the *caballeros* started to back off warily at the cold, murderous rage that filled his eyes and distorted his dark visage.

'Wolf?' Storm gasped, finding it difficult to breathe after Luther's battering. 'Wait! Let me explain! It's – it's not what you're thinking.'

Another man might not have listened to her, might have begun shooting or simply walked away in disgust, thinking she had encouraged their advances, but Wolf was not that kind of man.

'Suppose you tell me how it is then, baby,' he drawled, his

eyes as hard as nails as they raked her, and she knew he was remembering that only this morning he had told her he loved her.

'Oh, God, it's not what you're thinking!' She stumbled toward him, her hands outstretched imploringly. 'I swear it! I'd never do anything to hurt you, Wolf!'

Between rasps she told him what had happened, and she thought she never again wanted to see the look that came over his face as he listened. It was terrifying, more terrifying than anything she'd ever seen in her life, and she knew Luther and Billy Barlow were as good as dead right then. If Wolf had had no reason to kill them before, he did now. She could just feel the bloodlust pounding like a torrent through his veins as he pressed her trembling body close to his and thanked the Mexicans quietly for intervening on her behalf. The *caballeros* nodded and dispersed quickly afterward, all afraid of the dreadful look that had come over his blackly scowling countenance.

In an unnerving silence Wolf escorted Storm back to the tavern, upstairs to their room, and left her after informing her harshly she needn't look for him any time soon. She shuddered as she nodded to indicate she understood him, trying not to think about the horrible fate in store for the Barlow brothers and praying Wolf would not be killed himself. Dear God! Was *this* what she had to look forward to the rest of her life? Him walking out and her not knowing if he would return? It was too cruel! She couldn't bear it! She ran toward the door, yanking at the knob, but the barrier refused to budge. Wolf had locked it and taken away the key. Storm pounded on the paneled wood frantically, but if anyone heard, they paid no attention, and soon she ceased trying to escape, sliding down the door to the floor in despair. Racking sobs took hold of her body, making it even more difficult for her to breathe because of the pain in her side where Luther Barlow had kicked her. After a time she realized she would have to get up and tend to herself; the ache was becoming so excruciatingly hurtful.

Damn you, Wolf! You might have seen to me first! she thought, but then recognized the murderous rage that had taken hold of him oblivious to all else, and she had told him she was all right. Gingerly she removed her clothes and began to press the sore spot tenderly, trying to determine if any ribs were broken. Fortunately she appeared to be intact if rather battered and badly bruised. She managed to tear up a sheet and bind herself tightly, which relieved some of the pain, then she examined her face in the mirror. It too was starting to show purplish-blue places where the Barlows had struck her, but at least it wasn't swelling. Apparently the outlaws didn't pack a punch nearly as powerful as their mother's. Storm lay down on the bed, a wet rag over her countenance, and presently, exhausted, slept.

It took Wolf seven hours to find the Barlow brothers, who had managed to escape the *caballeros* who'd chased them, although one had winged Billy's arm with a bullet. Luther, like an animal, had sensed the danger to themselves if they remained in Laredo, for he'd known El Lobo would lose no time in tracking them down; but Billy had whined and complained about the amount of blood he was losing from the gunshot wound and had insisted they hole up for a while in the shabby lodgings they'd found on the outskirts of town. Unable to reason with his brother and the sense of family their mother had instilled in them making it impossible for him to leave Billy, Luther had at last given in to his brother's protests ungraciously and with deep misgivings.

'I don't like it, Billy,' he snarled, pacing the room like a caged panther. 'That Gawddamned half-breed bastard'll be breathin' down our necks before the night's over, and you know it! You pulin' pup!' He stared at his brother with disgust. 'Hell! I lost more blood than that from the stab wound that friggin' bitch gimme! I told you to kill her and have done with it.'

'Well, I ain't never been wounded before like you, Luther. I ain't used to all this Gawddamned pain, and when it's yore own blood gushin' out over the place, it kinda affects you dif'rent. 'Sides, how was I to know them Mexicans would come down on us like a pack of dogs fer a slut like that? I told you to shut her up! No, there's no use to you scoldin' me about it, Luther. You was as hot fer her as me once I started strippin' her. Jesus! She shore is sumpin', ain't she? I wonder if old Zeke *did* git himself a piece of that before he died?'

'I don't reckon it matters much now. He's dead, ain't he? Throat slit by that heathen son-of-a-bitch that's out there right now lookin' fer us!'

'So what? I don't guess even El Lobo and all his fancy shootin' will stand a chance against them kegs of black powder we got, huh, Luther?'

'We gotta find us a way of usin' 'em first, fool! I don't reckon El Lobo's jest gonna stand there while we pour the shit over him and set it on fire! Gawddamn it, Billy! Watch where yore flickin' them ashes! You want us to go up like a ton of firecrackers ourselves?'

'Well, no, Luther. I shorely don't. I guess I jest weren't thinkin'.'

'That's yore whole damned trouble. Ma were right about us. Ain't a one of us got a lick of sense! 'Lij and Zeke gone, and you and me jest sittin' here waitin' fer that friggin' savage to come lookin' fer us.'

'Well, shit, Luther! If yore so all-fire worried about it, why don'tcha jest mosey on outside, and keep an eye peeled for him? Shoot him in the back before he knows what hit him!'

'Ain't easy, shootin' a man like that in the back. He ain't stayed alive this long by bein' a fool! But I think I will slip out and take a look around.'

'That suits me jest fine. Jesus! Yore worse than ma when you got the fidgets. I'm goin' downstairs and git me another bottle of whiskey. Mebbe that'll take my mind off this Gawddamned ache in my arm.'

240

'You stay put, Billy! Ain't no use in you thinkin' yore gonna git likkered up while that half-breed bastard is out there somewhere jest waitin' fer us!'

'Aw, hell, Luther! You ain't never been any fun, no fun a'tall. Shit! I shoot straighter drunk than I do sober.'

'You only think you do, and we already agreed you cain't think period! You stay put, you hear?'

'Oh, all right.'

After giving his brother a sharp glance of warning Luther eased open the window and crept out onto the roof that overhung the first story of the bordello in which they were lodging. He crept across the tiles stealthily, then shimmied down a post at one end before flattening himself against the building in the shadows. From across the yard Wolf watched him coldly, wondering if he shouldn't just shoot Luther now and save himself a lot of trouble. Then he remembered what the Barlows had tried to do to Storm, and his dark visage twisted with that murderous rage. Shooting was too good for the Barlows; they were scum, and they deserved the worst! Quietly he dropped to his belly and began to snake his way across the yard.

Upstairs Billy waited impatiently for his brother's return, growing more uneasy and antsy with every minute that passed. Time seemed to crawl by, and Billy's arm hurt more and more as he dwelled on it. He drained the last drops from his whiskey bottle. Gawddamn it! It weren't right of Luther to leave him here like this when he ached so badly and were so powerful thirsty. He didn't care what Luther thought. He *was* a better shot drunk than sober! Dazedly he staggered from the bed, shaking his head a bit to clear it before he started downstairs.

'Where you going, cowboy?'

He stared stupidly at the girl standing in the hallway, her filmy wrapper concealing nothing. She was black-haired and reminded him of Storm. Billy shook his head again, then grinned.

'To yore room, honey, if you got a bottle of whiskey and sumpin' to ease the pain in my arm.'

'I sure do, cowboy. I sure do.'

Outside Luther edged his way around to the front of the bordello to check the horses lined up at the hitching post. There was no sign of the Comanche's Pinto, but then he hadn't expected there would be. El Lobo was too smart for that. Luther eased himself back around the corner, then sprinted across the yard to the stables. Glancing around quickly to be certain no one was watching, he lifted the latch and slipped inside just as Wolf finished shinning up the post to the roof where he crouched down silently, listening intently.

Satisfied that the Barlows' room was empty, he hoisted himself over the sill and dropped lightly to the floor, keeping his body low so that he wouldn't cast a shadow against the curtain, for the single oil lamp was blazing brightly, as though someone had forgotten to trim the wick. He was gazing around the room warily, trying to decide what was best to do, when his eyes lit on the two small kegs standing in one corner. Black powder! So *that* was the little surprise the Barlows had planned for him. With a devilish grin that would have sent shivers up Storm's spine he pried open one of the tuns and started to pour a trail of sparkling ebony crystals along the floor. It was a corner room. There shouldn't be much damage to the rest of the bordello if he calculated properly. He set the half-empty barrel down off to one side, then grabbing the remaining keg, he ripped its lid off and, still shaking out powder as he went, he let himself out the door into the hallway. He poured what was left of the crystals along the baseboard of the corridor, pausing only once to lean against the wall and hide his face when a drunk came lurching up the stairs, one arm about a raucously laughing red-head. The couple disappeared into a room farther down, and Wolf hurriedly completed the trail, which now led to a window at the far end of the hallway. He tossed away the tun, pushed open the sash, and stepped out onto the roof, then flattening himself against the second story side of the bordello, made his way to the

242

corner of the building where he had a clear view of the back.

Presently he saw Luther come shinning up the post and sneak into his room. Wolf saw no sign of Billy. He picked his way back to the window and peered down the hallway to be certain Luther didn't leave the room and to watch for Billy. A few minutes later Luther came barging out the doorway, looking madder than a hornet. He ran downstairs, then reappeared just as quickly to pound on another door upstairs. Wolf heard the sound of laughter, then Billy yelled something drunkenly to his brother. Luther swore violently and turned away, going back to his own room.

Well, so much for Billy, Wolf thought resignedly, but I can sure get Luther. Casually he lit a cigar, took a few drags, then reached inside the window and touched the glowing tip to the long black snake of crystals that lined the hallway. The powder flickered and then caught, sparkling and fizzing its way down the corridor. Moments later the second story corner of the bordello where Luther's room had been exploded, blowing the two outside walls clean away.

'Surprise, surprise,' Wolf said to himself softly, one eyebrow raised devilishly before he hastened down the roof, dropped to the ground, and walked calmly away amid the confusion of the sudden shouts and hurrying footsteps.

It was nearly dawn when he made it back to the *cantina*. He took one look at Storm's sleeping figure, then shook her roughly awake.

After giving her a few minutes to waken, he snapped angrily, 'I thought you said you were all right.'

'I – I am. Just a little battered and bruised; that's all,' she spoke nervously, drawing up the sheet to cover the strips of bandage around her ribs.

'Don't ever lie to me again, baby,' he warned coldly. 'You need a doctor.'

'No, I'll be fine; really I will. Wolf, are they – are they dead?'

'Billy got away. I imagine they're scraping what's left of Luther off the ceiling.'

Storm shuddered silently and did not question him further.

13

Wolf insisted on taking Storm to a doctor in the morning, although she protested she didn't need one, and the physician who examined her, a kindly German who did not seem to find either she or Wolf at all extraordinary, confirmed her opinion.

'It is as your vife claims, *Herr* Lobo,' Dr Hoffmeier spoke as he packed away his complicated instruments and washed his hands. 'She is only very badly bruised. One or two ribs may be fractured of course, but I can assure you they are not broken. The binding she has done herself vill be adequate until she no longer feels the hurt. I can gif you some laudanum for the pain if you vish, *Frau* Lobo, but really a small glass of brandy, perhaps, at bedtime vould be better. It is my opinion that too many vomen are already addicted to their "drops", as they say. Really, *Herr* Lobo. You must take better care of your vife. This is a rough country, und I'm afraid a very lawless one. For a voman to be set upon by such ruffians—' He made a gentle clicking sound. '*Mein gott*! It's just terrible. I know. I lost my vife to such men in Fredericksburg vhere several of our people haf settled. They broke into our home – ach, vell, it is a long time ago. I could not stay there aftervard, you understand, so I came here. You must not attempt to do anything strenuous for a time, *Frau* Lobo, until the pain has dissipated. I am sure you understand me, *Herr* Lobo, as vell, *ja*? Is good. In a few veeks, perhaps, all vill be vell.'

Storm blushed as she suddenly realized the doctor was advising them to restrain their lovemaking until her side had healed. She glanced at Wolf covertly from beneath her half-closed eyelashes, but his face was as impassive as ever as he shook the doctor's hand and thanked him.

Once outside he put his arm around the girl and gave her a wry smile.

'Frustrating as hell, isn't it?' he asked wickedly, causing her to flush even more furiously.

'Oh, Wolf. You know I could not help it.'

'I know. Damn! I guess this means we won't be going anywhere for awhile. Billy Barlow'll be long gone by now.'

'It – it really doesn't matter, Wolf,' Storm said quietly, trying not to shiver.

'It does to me. However, I'm sure we'll run across him again sooner or later.'

'Oh, Wolf! You've got to stop this! I'm just terrified you'll be killed. I want us to settle down, have a place of our own, raise a couple of children—'

He studied her thoughtfully for a moment. 'I told you I wasn't going to change, Storm. However, fall's coming on. You can already smell it in the air, and it'll be short since we've had an Indian summer. Winter will be here before you know it. I'll take you to The People when you're well, to the *Llano Estacado*, and we'll spend some time together there. Would you like that?'

'Yes, if it means we won't have to be forever on the move, chasing or running.'

'It's what I am, baby. You know that.'

'Yes, I know. It's just that I want something more.'

'Yeah, baby? Well, maybe someday you'll have it, but I'm not making any promises. I've lived too long and too hard to think about tomorrows.'

'Wolf, what is it about your past that haunts you so?' the girl questioned impulsively and at once was sorry, for the jeering mask she seldom saw now dropped into place on his stony countenance.

'Don't ask me to talk about it, baby,' he replied tersely. 'It hurts too badly. There are some things, Storm, that I can never share, not even with you.'

She was hurt he shut her out when she wanted so badly to

help, but she bit her lip stoically and said nothing more.

They left Laredo two weeks later, not alone and on horseback as they had entered it, but with five wagons and a party of hard-looking Mexican men, *bandoleros* Wolf said when Storm questioned him about it, men who raided the vast range lands of Texas, murdering, raping, and pillaging, then retreated across the border into the mountains of Mexico afterward, making their capture nearly impossible. They were rough and crude, the deadliest of cutthroats, men who were not afraid of killing or dying or breaking the law by becoming, for a time, *comancheros* as long as they were well-paid for their trouble.

Storm hated and feared them, but when she protested their presence, Wolf stated flatly he needed them if they were to carry supplies, guns and ammunition to The People high in the *Llano Estacado*.

'This is Apache country, baby,' he intoned dryly, 'and I intend to get through it in one piece.'

The girl trembled at the thought of being taken captive by an enemy tribe, for she knew the Apaches would show her, a Comanche's woman, no mercy; but it did not lessen her fear of the *bandoleros*, many of whom eyed her speculatively and made lewd remarks and offers to her when Wolf's back was turned.

The land through which they traveled was hostile too, not like the soft, rolling plains of East Texas with their forested stretches and cool rivers. This terrain was harsh and arid, almost desertlike in its lack of familiar scenery. Though mountains swelled upward in the distance, and high mesas and buttes cut a jagged edge across the sky, the majority of the area was endlessly flat and barren. For miles in all directions golden sand mingled with red clay until it seemed as though all that was green and lush and lovely had been parched dry by flames, nevermore to be. It was alien and frightening. Storm felt as though she had suddenly been transported to another time, another planet. At night she stared at the stars in the sky to orient herself, reassure herself she was still on Earth, for surely the Big Dipper would have looked differently elsewhere.

Wolf was silent and withdrawn too, the easy laughter they'd shared the past few months gone. Like a whipcord his lithe body was taut and wary now when Storm touched him, needing the physical sense of security his presence always provided; and she knew when he slept, if he slept at all, it was a light, uneasy slumber, one from which he could awaken himself instantly. He trusted the *comancheros* no more than she, but she realized his concern was for her well-being, not his own. He never left her alone if he could avoid it, and on the few occasions he was forced to scout ahead for the party she kept her pistols drawn and resting upon her lap. One of the men at first laughed at this and questioned skeptically her ability to use the guns, a wild, jeering grin still on his face.

High overhead but within range a hawk circled slowly.

'Kill it,' Wolf ordered curtly, his visage closed and unreadable as he rejoined them in time to catch the sneering statement.

'But—'

'Kill it!'

It was a difficult shot, but Storm lifted one revolver and fired. Moments later the bird fluttered gently downward. After that the *bandoleros* kept their distance, and there were no more jokes made as to whether or not the girl knew how to handle her pistols.

Still Wolf took no chances with her safety. In the evenings when she wished to bathe he escorted her himself to the small rivulets or springs by which they camped and stood guard while she lathed herself hurriedly, then dressed, her teeth chattering in the darkness, for the nights had begun to turn cold now. Afterward they bedded down beneath one of the wagons, away from the others, Wolf holding her close, sharing the heat of his body with her, for he was always so much warmer than she.

Storm rested uneasily, however, nevertheless, for there were ten of the *comancheros* against her and Wolf, and she often wondered why they did not kill him and take her for their own use as they so obviously wished to do. She discovered the answer late one evening when they were set upon by a band of Indians – Comanches, who often raided deep into South Texas and Mexico. Had it not been for Wolf, they would probably have all been killed. The band, however, though not his own, recognized him as a brother and left the party in peace after conveying their greetings to his family and chiefs. The Comanches, unlike other tribes, did not war among themselves, and those who belonged to one band were freely accepted by another without question. It was this spirit of tribal unity, even though the bands remained separate, that made them such powerful and formidable opponents and why they would be the last of the Plains Indians to be conquered by the White-Eyes. It was too, Storm knew, one of the reasons the Comanches scorned all Apaches, with the exception of the Kiowa-Apaches, who were also related to the Kiowas and who were allies of the Comanches, as were the Kiowas themselves and the Cheyennes and the Arapahos. The Apache bands – the Lipans, the Jicarillas, the Mescaleros, the Chiricahuas – sometimes fought among themselves, and the Comanches despised them for it and because they ate horse meat, just as the Comanches hated the Tonkawas, who were said to practice cannibalism.

The girl breathed a sigh of relief after the Indians had gone, but she was puzzled too, for they had not resembled Wolf in the slightest. Not nearly as tall as he and built on stockier lines, they had had none of his beauty of movement, but had seemed awkward upon the ground. Only upon their ponies had they reminded her of Wolf, of his pantherish stealth and grace. Their skins had been darker too, even more coppery and leathery than Wolf's. At last she determined it must have something to do with him being a half-breed and gave the matter no further thought. She was just glad to know why the *bandoleros* did not turn on them both. They needed Wolf if they wanted to get out of West Texas alive, for it was as yet untamed by the white man, and settlements were few and far between. Wolf, with his vast knowledge of the Plains Indians and their languages, was an asset with which the *comancheros* could not easily afford to dispense.

Once again Storm's days settled into the pattern of the wilderness as they made their way northeast to Goliad where Wolf would collect the reward for Zeke Barlow with the paper Sheriff Zachary had given him in Corpus Christi as proof of legal claim to the money. Then from there they would go on to San Antonio where Gabriel North had waited for Storm's arrival so many months ago it seemed like years when she thought about it. In San Antonio they would buy more supplies for the Comanches before continuing on to Montell, San Felipe del Rio, and finally the *Llano Estacado*.

Storm rose each morning with the pale pink dawn, stoked up the fire (when Wolf had permitted one), warmed up bitter black coffee, beans, and whatever meat remained from supper the previous evening, then, letting the men serve themselves, saw to her mare, who was tied behind the wagon in which she rode every day. Earlier on the girl had chosen La Aguila's vehicle as her means of transportation, for of all the Mexicans he alone reminded her most of her husband. He was tall and muscular, with hawklike features and a clipped jet black mustache beneath which his white teeth flashed brightly. Unlike the others, who had descended from what Storm suspected was peasant stock mixed with Indian blood, La Aguila's ancestry was noble. He came from a very old Spanish house, from which he had been cast out for his ne'er-do-well ways, and disgraced, had changed his name, although not his bad habits, to protect his family. Very much the gentleman still in his own peculiar manner, he alone of all the *bandoleros* treated Storm as a lady due his respect, perhaps because she reminded him in many ways of what he had once been.

He had known Wolf for many years, although he refused to tell Storm how this was so, saying only that they were cousins.

'I didn't know Wolf had any Mexican relatives.'

'There is, perhaps, a great deal you do not know about El Lobo,' Aguila said gently. 'He is not truly *Mejicano*, *señora*, although he claims that country as well as *Tejas* for his own. The heritage of which you ask is Spanish, but of course to *los Americanos* there is little difference.'

'Then Wolf's blood is – noble also?' the girl asked curiously, determined to discover what she could about her husband's past. 'That's why he look so – so regal for a half-breed, not like the others, the *mestizos*?'

'*Sí*, *señora*, it is so. His mother was pure *Castellano*. His family was once as well-known and respected as my own in the old country.'

'What happened then, Aguila? How did Wolf come to be a half-breed? Did his family immigrate to the New World? Was his – was his real mother taken prisoner by the Comanches?'

The Spaniard shrugged. 'It is for El Lobo to tell you about his – breeding and his mother, *señora*. As to the other – many things happened. Times changed. Men who were once trusted leaders fell from grace and had to flee for their lives. But this is all part of the past, and the past is best forgotten, no? Yes, it is best we do not speak of such things. Sometimes the memories are too painful.'

'That's what Wolf says.'

'*Sí*, and El Lobo is right.'

'El Lobo. That's not his real name, is it? Do you know his true one, Aguila?'

'Alas, that is not for me to say either, *señora*, any more than El Lobo would tell you mine if you asked. I am sorry.'

With this Storm had to be content, being unable to pry anything further from Aguila, who shifted uncomfortably on the hard wagon seat, as though afraid he had already said too much. It was an intriguing glimpse into Wolf's past, however, one that made the girl more determined than ever to find out what it was that haunted him so. Despite their love for each other, there were barriers between them still, and Storm felt certain they were due to Wolf's mysterious past. If only she could discover what demon it was that drove him, she was sure he would be free to love her without restraint and settle down.

Sheriff Yancey had not changed. In fact, he appeared to have been frozen in time since Storm last saw him, for he was still seated at his desk, feet propped up on the desk top, a wad of tobacco in his mouth that he chewed slowly for a minute when she and Wolf entered his office before he spat deliberately, this time hitting the spittoon with a resounding ring.

'Hello, Lobo.'

'Sheriff.'

'Well, what is it this time?'

Wolf reached into his pocket, drawing forth a crumpled piece of paper. 'Got a writ here from Sheriff Zachary in Corpus Christi entitling me to the reward for Zeke Barlow.'

Sheriff Yancey grunted as he took the sheet Wolf handed him. 'That just leaves two, don't it?'

'One. Luther had an – unfortunate experience with a couple of kegs of black powder.'

The sheriff sniggered mirthlessly. 'I reckon I can chalk that one up to you too, huh?'

'I don't have anything to show for it.'

'No matter. The Carstairs Stagecoach Company won't know that, and I reckon they'll be so happy to learn the Barlows have been put outta business they won't mind the cost. 'Sides, long as I hafta complete a report anyhow it won't be no trouble to add Luther's name. Here you go. Two thousand dollars, cash on the barrelhead.'

'I'm much obliged, Sheriff.'

'Don't mention it, Lobo. Say, ain't that the little filly you had with you the last time you was in Goliad?'

'Yeah, this is my wife, Storm.'

Sheriff Yancey's eyes narrowed speculatively. 'Pleased to

meetcha, ma'am. Storm. That's kind of an unusual name, ain't it? Not Indian anyway.'

'My wife is French,' Wolf said coldly.

'That so?' The sheriff was undaunted as he continued to stare at the girl rudely.

'*Oui, monsieur*,' she spoke up hurriedly, afraid Wolf was beginning to grow angry at Sheriff Yancey's prying. 'There was a hurricane raging the night of my birth, so *maman*, my mother, called me Storm.'

'Don't see too many Frenchies around these parts. They mostly like the Gulf areas: Houston, Galveston, Corpus Christi. Whereabouts you from, ma'am, if you don't mind me askin'?'

'I thought one never questioned a person about his or her background in Texas, Sheriff,' Storm replied politely, starting to become rather uneasy, although she didn't know why.

Sheriff Yancey studied her carefully for a moment, then suddenly laughed raucously, slapping his knee.

'That's right, ma'am, and you shorely put me in my place, yessir,' he continued to chortle briefly, then took a deep breath. 'Well, congratulations on gittin' yoreself such a good-lookin' woman, Lobo. Be seein' you now, you hear?'

After they'd gone the sheriff sat up sharply in his swivel chair, yanking the top middle drawer of his desk open with a jerk. Hastily he unfolded the reward poster Sheriff Martin had sent him from San Antonio several weeks ago. He examined it thoughtfully for a minute, pulling on his scraggly whiskers with one hand, then barked loudly for his deputy.

'Cal, I want you to ride out to Tierra Rosa and deliver a message to Gabriel North for me.'

'But – that'll take me more'n a fortnight, Sheriff.'

'Take all the time you need, Cal. Just be shore Mr North gits this letter.'

At the headwaters of the San Antonio River on the Balcones

Escarpment lay the city of San Antonio. Founded in 1718 by a Spanish military expedition from Monclova, it had been built, in the beginning, on the river's west bank on the site of a Coahuiltecan Indian village. Settlers from the Canary Islands had expanded the town in 1731, and over the years it had grown to become one of the largest cities in Texas, second only to Galveston. It was famous for its Mission San Antonio de Valero, commonly known as the Alamo, from the Spanish for cottonwood tree, with which San Antonio abounded. It was there Jim Bowie and Davy Crockett had died, along with the other soldiers who'd defended the post against General Santa Anna and his Mexican troops to the last man during the Texas revolution in 1836. Storm walked through the Alamo's cool stone halls and imagined she could hear the cries of those who'd been so brutally massacred even now, twelve years after they had so bravely battled to the end and perhaps changed the course of history for all time. San Antonio was an old city, one of the oldest in Texas; and perhaps that was why its sense of heritage could not be denied. Storm sat on the bank of the river and thought of the many persons who had traveled the city's streets, pushing westward through the Texas wilderness or eastward to the French trading posts in Louisiana. Here, as nowhere else in Texas, the undaunted spirit of courage it had taken to build such a great state invaded her being, her consciousness, and she began to understand in part men like Wolf, Aguila, and Gabriel North, men who lived off the land, wrested it from its wild savagery, and tamed it, bending it to their wills. Here, had it not been for the Barlows, Storm would have met Gabriel and journeyed west to Tierra Rosa to become his bride.

She wandered through the cobbled streets and quaint shops with red tile roofs and pondered how different her life might have been had the stagecoach on which she'd traveled not met such an untimely end. She glanced at passersby on the sidewalks and wondered how many of them were Gabriel's friends or acquaintances; how many would have journeyed two hundred miles northwest to his ranch to dance at her wedding; how many had sent their condolences when she had not arrived as planned?

She listened to the babble of voices raised in many languages and wondered if Tierra Rosa were as multilingual, if Gabriel hired those whom he scorned – Negroes, Mexicans, Indians – as he scorned all that for which he had no use or understanding, as he would have scorned Storm had not her cultured French heritage born of doors that had remained closed to the Americans for years appealed to his determination to smash them down and take that which was unattainable.

Lost in her reverie, she never knew when she first became aware of the faded posters nailed up here and there along the streets, some torn and dirty, others wrinkled and water-marked by rain, many faint and almost unreadable now. Still, however, she recognized the artist's sketch of herself done from an old daguerreotype she had given Gabriel North. For one horrible eternity the earth seemed to reel under Storm's feet. A reward! Gabriel had posted a reward for her return or any information leading to her whereabouts! Dear God! She had never thought – had never dreamed he would look for her – would even care what had become of her!

The girl climbed shakily onto the wagon seat, knowing from the speculative looks of the *comancheros* and Wolf's hard set mouth that they had all seen the posters too and recognized her. She didn't care about the others. It was Wolf who worried her, Wolf who barely glanced at her as they made their way to a shabby but proper hotel in the winding maze of the town. His stony, impassive silence unnerved her, but she dared not speak before the others, not knowing what he might say, for he was fully capable of turning on her scathingly, and she did not want to be humiliated before the rest. *Sacré bleu!* What was he thinking? No sign of his thoughts shadowed his dark cold visage. He had gone pure Indian on her again.

He said nothing all through dinner, ate little, and drank heavily as he stared at Storm stoically, as though he'd never really looked at her before. The others at the table talked and laughed among themselves, but with restraint as they watched her and Wolf curiously. No one mentioned the posters, or if they did, it was not within Storm's hearing. She wondered frantically if five thousand dollars were enough incentive to cause the *bandoleros* to turn on her and Wolf? As though he too were wondering the same thing, Aguila lounged beside her warily, his eyes black and narrowed watchfully. The girl was grateful for his presence, for she sensed if worse came to worse, he would protect her, even from Wolf if necessary.

It got later and later. The other patrons had long since left the dining room, and still no one moved. They seemed to be waiting. Waiting for what? At last Storm arose.

'If you don't mind, I'm rather tired, so I'll say good night now, gentlemen.'

Still Wolf said nothing.

'I will escort you to your room, *señora*,' Aguila filled the awkward little void smoothly.

'Thank you.'

Storm found she was trembling as they mounted the stairs and walked down the dimly lit corridor to her room. Her fingers shook as she turned the key in the lock and opened the door.

'Oh, Aguila!' She could stand it no longer. 'Why doesn't he say something? It's not as though I were a criminal!'

'No, of course not.' The Spaniard shrugged. 'But perhaps he has his reasons. I'm sure it must be highly disturbing to discover another man – and a very rich and well-known man at that – has posted a reward for one's wife. I'm sure El Lobo must be wondering why you chose him over Gabriel North.'

'He's my husband! I love him!'

'As you say, *señora*,' Aguila responded noncommittally.

'Oh, Aguila! You don't think he'll believe me either, do you?'

'That is not for me to say. Good night, *señora*.'

It seemed like hours before Wolf came upstairs to her. Storm had long since gone to bed, but had been unable to sleep. She sat up, drawing the sheet up to cover her nakedness, and turned up the oil lamp that flickered dimly. Wolf began undressing, tossing aside his gunbelt with a thud and ripping open the pearlized ebony studs on his shirt carelessly. He staggered slightly as he bent to pull off his spurred boots, and Storm realized with a sinking feeling that he was drunk, drunk in a way she had never seen him before. Was he that possessive, that jealous that even the thought of another man wanting her drove him crazy? Or was it Gabriel's rank and riches that disturbed him? Gabriel, one of the white ranchers Wolf so despised, who had trampled The Land and spit on its proud inhabitants with disgust. Storm had to know! They couldn't go on like this!

'Wolf—'

It was all she got a chance to say before he snarled in that strange, wolfish way of his and swore.

'Gabriel North! Gabriel North!' He spat the words bitterly, then laughed harshly, mockingly. 'No wonder you never told me his name! One of the richest white men in the state of Texas, and he wants you, baby. He's still looking for you after all this time! Five thousand dollars, baby. That's a lot of money. Four thousand more than what I offered to be exact. To think that all this time I've had Gabriel North's woman in my bed and never even knew it! Jesus! The irony of it all! I should have stuck to my original plan for you, baby, but I reckon it's not too late.'

He strode toward her menacingly. Storm cringed beneath her fragile cover, not comprehending his words or the rage that drove him.

'Wolf, what's wrong? It's you I wanted, *you* I love!'

'Love! Do you think there could ever be anything like that between us now?' He looked down at her with disgust and something else Storm could not define. He yanked the sheet from her terrified grasp, exposing the length of her naked body to his raking gaze. 'Gabriel North's woman,' he muttered contemptuously before he flung himself upon her drunkenly, cruelly.

He reeked of mescal and cigars, and his hands hurt her as they began to move upon her roughly, tighten on her flesh as he ground his mouth down on hers hard, with a savagery that frightened her. She struggled against him desperately, wanting somehow to make it right between them once again and knowing she would hate him if he took her like this, brutally, without any feeling for her.

'Don't, Wolf! Don't!' she gasped, panting for air. 'Please! Not like this! I'll hate you for it!'

'Yeah? And maybe you've hated me all along, lied to me, used me, and laughed at me behind my back just like all the other white women I've ever known!'

'No! That's not true! You must know that it isn't!'

He paid her no heed, however. It was as though he hadn't heard her, didn't want to hear her. His eyes glittered darkly, almost black in the lamplight, and somehow knowing he could see her, and she him, made it even more unbearable as he forced his crude intimacies upon her, with none of the love and gentleness of the past. He caught her hair in a painful grip to hold her face still as she tried to speak once more, to avoid the demanding pressure of his searing lips and ravaging tongue; and when they started to travel downward to her throat and breasts, she lashed out against his chest with her tiny fists, beating and clawing him wildly before he pinioned her wrists above her head.

Horrible images of the Barlow brothers doing that to her filled her mind, sickening her as he cupped one ripe mound, positioning it for his mouth. He was using her, just as those filthy outlaws would have used her! Just as every other man in her life had used her! His lips closed over the flushed nipple greedily while his free hand moved to her other breast, squeezing it possessively, thumb teasing the tip to a taut little

257

peak. Storm started to protest again, this time almost hysterically, battling him futilely as she tried to free herself of his weight and knowing she was rapidly losing her strength against his own steely power. When his knees began to pry her thighs apart, she screamed. He clapped his hand over her lips with a deft movement, shutting off her breath.

'Would you like to have the *comancheros* take my place?' he hissed. Storm shook her head mutely, horrified that he would even suggest such a thing. 'Then be silent, witch, and open your legs for me!'

Breathless, terrified, and physically exhausted, she did as he'd softly commanded, wanting to die a thousand deaths when his hand left her mouth to slip between her flanks, making her warm and wet, despite herself. He taunted her subtly with his fingers, stroking, caressing, filling her deep inside, arousing her to a feverish pitch as she felt her body responding against her will, against the silent outcries of her mind. He freed her wrists to lower his lips to the throbbing swell of her secret place, but when she would have taken advantage of her release and struck him, he caught them again in a bone-crushing grip.

'Don't even think about it, baby,' he warned silkily. 'I'm a savage, remember? I can hurt you in ways you never even dreamed.'

'*Mon Dieu*!' she whimpered and fell back moaning.

He laughed, a low, jeering sound, like a devil, Storm thought wildly, for the smile did not quite reach the narrowed shards of his icy dark eyes.

His hands grasped her hips as his mouth tasted the sweet honey of her at last, tongue flicking the pulsating flower of her womanhood expertly, exquisitely, torturing her until she began to quiver all over with a burning ache that started deep within her and spread like wildfire through her body, needing that final fulfilment, craving it with a passionate madness. She loved him, hated him, wanted to feel him thrusting inside her.

Over and over his tongue brought her to the edge of climax,

then withdrew, leaving her blind and helpless with desire – and unsated. *Jesù*! What was he doing to her? Was he trying to drive her crazy? Oh, God, what more did he want? Finally she understood dimly what he was after. He wanted her to beg him for it; he wanted to hear her, a lady, a white woman, Gabriel North's fiancée, pleading with him, a Comanche, a savage, a half-breed heathen, to take her and make her his.

No! I won't do it! she thought, but even as she rebelled against the idea she did it all the same; and she hated him for it, despised him as he forced her to beg him and cry out her surrender as he stared triumphantly down into her pleading face.

He entered her swiftly, spiraling down into the soft satin warmth of her again and again while she held on to him tightly and arched her hips to receive him, wrapping her legs around his back.

'I hate you!' she breathed, choking on the words, but he only went on driving into her strongly, deeply, his visage buried in her cloud of black tangled hair, and she could not tell whether or not he'd even heard.

Then there was nothing for her but the waves of passion that swept up to engulf her like a storm – madding, swirling, tempestuous waves that made her feel giddy and wantonly wild, as though she had lost all control of herself, as though a tumultuous mistral were blowing her out to sea, then gently, gently washing her back in to rest upon the golden sands.

Wolf lay still too, his breathing ragged. It was not until he moved from her and saw the tears that stained her cheeks that he felt the first stirrings of shame he'd never known in his life. Her wide, beautiful gray eyes that had held only love for and trust in him were now filled with hurt, sorrow. They gazed at him woefully, wounded, blind, without comprehension. Dear God! What had he done? What had he done? Dazedly he tried to clear his head, opened his mouth to apologize, but it was too late. The damage had already been done. He had destroyed whatever love they had shared. Even as he reached for her to hold her close, to try to explain, her eyes hardened like diamonds, cold, contemptuous, unattainable. She had shut him out, cut him out of her heart.

'You – filthy – half-breed.'

She spoke each word slowly, scornfully, distinctly, so that there could be no mistake, and they fell upon his ears like a death knell. Then she slapped his face. The sharp crack of her hand across his cheek sounded like a gunshot in the hush of the room. For a moment he was motionless, then anger grabbed him in its fist once more. He reached for her wrathfully, but she feinted and eluded him, using every trick he had ever taught her against him. Her fingers curled around the hilt of her knife protruding from her gunbelt, which hung upon the bedpost, and as they grappled on the sheets she yanked the blade from its sheath and brought it up, feeling with a little gasp of shock and sudden awareness the horrible, jarring sensation as the sharply honed point made contact with his flesh, then glanced off a rib-bone. Instinctively she jerked the knife free, watching, horrified, as he pressed one hand to his side to staunch the flow of blood, his eyes unfathomable in the lamplight.

'You've learned well, baby,' he noted softly. 'I don't think we need to practice anymore.'

'*Sainte Marie*,' Storm murmured, unable to believe she'd actually stabbed him, as she backed away warily, taking her gunbelt with her. Frightened, terrified that he would kill her, she pulled one pistol and leveled it at his chest. 'Don't move, Wolf, unless you want to be dead certain about that.'

Hurriedly she dressed, keeping one eye on him all the while, but he made no effort to halt her, being too concerned with stopping the blood that was draining from his body, staining the bed. When Storm had finished gathering up her things, she went through Wolf's shirt, taking half the money he'd gotten from Sheriff Yancey. He studied her impassively, dying inside, knowing she was leaving him and that there was nothing he could do about it.

'Take it all if you want it,' he said quietly, but she only shook her head and turned away so that he wouldn't see the tears that had started in her eyes once more.

'I – I guess this is goodbye,' she whispered, but he heard her all the same.

'I'll come after you. You know that, Storm.'

'To kill me, Wolf?'

'No, to get you back.'

'I don't want to see you again – ever! You're just like all the rest! I hate you!'

Then she backed slowly out the door, checking the hall to be sure it was empty before she fairly ran down the corridor and stairs out into the night.

BOOK THREE
Comanche Moon

14

No one stopped Storm as she entered the stable at the back of the hotel and saddled Madame Bleu cautiously, keeping her ears attuned to the slightest movement outside, for Wolf had stationed two of the *bandoleros* on guard-duty to watch the wagons, which were lined up in the alley. Fortunately the two men were deep in conversation and had sneaked a bottle of liquor from the hotel to keep happy and warm besides. They paid no heed to the girl as she led the mare stealthily down the narrow street, being sure to remain hidden in the shadows as much as possible. Madame Bleu nickered softly once, but Storm laid her hand warningly on the animal's velvet muzzle, as Wolf had taught her, to keep the horse quiet. Only when she was well-away from the hotel did she mount the beast and begin to gallop out of town, Madame Bleu's hooves making a rhythmic clip-clop on the cobbles and then gradually a gentle thud as Storm left San Antonio behind, heading west across the prairie.

She had no idea where she was going. The only thought that filled her mind was that she must get away – away from Wolf. She had money. She wasn't destitute, but she was miserable all the same, more miserable than she'd ever been in her life. Her heart felt as though someone were wrenching it apart within her breast. She couldn't breathe. She couldn't think. She pressed on in a daze, not noticing it had begun to rain steadily, not realizing she was crying until she tasted her salty tears bittersweet upon her lips.

She rode aimlessly for days, like a mindless puppet, eating and sleeping mechanically alone on the range, living off the land as Wolf had taught her. God! He had taught her so many things; it seemed as though everything she did she had learned from him, and she couldn't help being reminded of him every time she shot a jack rabbit or quail or gathered roots and pecans.

The terrain had changed again too, growing rich and forested once more. Ancient cypresses so old and huge ten men couldn't have spanned their trunks stood proudly against the crooked azure sky where hills swelled in the distance once again. Live oaks and pecan trees, tall pines and cottonwoods tangled along bubbling spring-fed rivers that washed their ways through the canyons, clear and cool and blue as they rippled and tumbled in shallow cascades over jumbled scatterings of smooth rocks that thrust upward from the beds. Along the slopes wild persimmons and cherries, madrona and cedar sprung from the ground in haphazard profusion, trailing down to the grassy meadows and ravines where ferns, rock plants, and mosses clung tenaciously, seeking the moisture upon which they fed.

Storm forded the Sabinal and Frio Rivers and crossed the Dry Frio before reaching the small town of Montell. There she begged a few days' sanctuary at the Mission Nuestra Señora de la Candelaria where she knelt in the chapel and prayed with the rosary Wolf had bought for her in Laredo.

Wolf! She couldn't get him out of her mind. She lay awake at night and missed the feel of the length of his body pressed up next to hers, keeping her warm, the feel of his strong arms around her tightly, protecting her from the rest of the world, the feel of his mouth, hard and demanding, upon her lips, branding her forever as his. What she had once feared had become a reality. She was only half-alive without him.

She moved on, restless and without destination. Once she actually cut across a corner of Gabriel North's land without knowing it was Tierra Rosa upon which she trespassed; and it was not until she arrived in San Felipe del Rio that she realized she had been subconsciously following Wolf's route to the *Llano Estacado*, of which he had plotted a rough map for her one day.

I'll come after you. You know that, Storm.

Was she hoping he would?

The girl followed Devil's River north as the days grew shorter, the nights grew longer, and the vast expanse of prairie changed yet again, becoming arid, flat, and endless once more, as though Texas couldn't quite seem to make up her mind as to her terrain. Yet through it all Storm survived, until one dark evening while she traveled beneath the stars the unthinkable happened.

You won't get past a Comanche . . .

They *were* Comanches; she felt certain of that, for they resembled the ones who had come to camp that night and spoken with Wolf, and the fringe on their moccasins was very long, a sure sign of a Comanche, Wolf had told her. There were five of them, and they were painted as though for a raid. They had made camp in a little *arroyo*, but no fire burned to tell her of their presence; and though she had journeyed swiftly and quietly, their sensitive ears had discerned her movements. They melted from the blackness to surround her quickly, and before she could recover from her shock and escape one had yanked her from her horse.

He tugged at her braids and fondled her breasts crudely beneath the woven material of her poncho as she struggled against him helplessly, then he laughed and made some remark to the others.

Storm breathed a small sigh of relief and ceased fighting him, for he had indeed spoken Comanche.

Tentatively she raised one hand in the traditional gesture of greeting and said, '*Hihites, haints,*' then made the symbol of a snake going backward, praying they were not of the *Waw'ai* band, who were said to practice incest.

The Indian who held her glanced at her with surprise. 'How is it you speak our language, *herbi*? Is our blood also yours?'

'No,' Storm spoke truthfully, knowing how the Comanches despised liars. 'But my *kumaxp* is one of The People. I am his *paraibo*.'

267

The Indian studied her stoically. 'To what band does he belong? Perhaps I know him then.'

'The *Kwerharehnuh*.'

'You lie, *herbi*!' the Indian snapped and shook her roughly. 'I am of the *Kwerharehnuh*, and among my people there is no man wed to a woman such as you!'

'Do you not then claim Brother-Of-The-Wolf as one of your own?' Storm asked nervously, trying to remain calm.

The Indian drew a rapid, hissing intake of breath. His hands tightened on her flesh.

'Once more you lie, *herbi*!' He pulled his knife and pressed it against her throat. 'I will cut out your tongue so that you may speak no more untruths!'

'Hold!' another Indian commanded sharply. 'We will hear what the woman has to say first, Fire-Walker. She has claimed kinship with The People, and we do not harm our own. Besides, if she is indeed our brother's wife, he will be most angry if we return her to him tongueless.'

'*Hu*, Moon-Raider! How do you know he will not thank us?' a third Indian teased.

'Be silent, Naukwahip,' the one called Moon-Raider ordered, then turned back to Storm. 'Well, *herbi*, we are waiting.'

'It is true that I am Brother-Of-The-Wolf's wife.'

'Then where is he?' Fire-Walker shook her again, and the girl found she could not meet his piercing eyes.

'We – we quarreled, and I ran away,' she admitted at last.

'*Hu*, Moon-Raider! I told you he would thank us for cutting out her tongue!' Naukwahip crowed triumphantly at this.

'Be silent, Naukwahip!' Moon-Raider repeated, irritated. 'If you have left our brother, *herbi*, then under Comanche law you are no longer his *paraibo*.'

'Oh, no!' Storm cried, dismayed, for if the Indians believed she had divorced Wolf, they would have no compunction about raping her, and evidently their method of divorce was

268

as simple as their ceremony of marriage. 'He did not tell me that! I'm sure he is looking for me even now and will beat me for my disobedience.'

'As well he should,' Moon-Raider observed sternly. 'Then you had intended to return to him?'

'Yes,' Storm lied desperately, praying they would believe her. 'It's just that I was so very frightened. He – he threatened to cut off my nose,' she continued untruthfully, for Wolf had told her many Comanche warriors did indeed punish their women in this manner.

'You see, Moon-Raider. Her nose, her tongue – what is the difference?' Naukwahip questioned cheerfully with a grin.

'Be silent, brother!' Shadow-Of-The-Hawk warned. 'Enough is enough! You are making Moon-Raider angry.'

At this the fifth Indian, who had been softly humming to himself as he watched the entire proceedings, spoke up. 'There is only one way to determine if the woman speaks the truth. We will take her with us to the *Llano Estacado* and wait for Brother-Of-The-Wolf. If he does not claim her, then we will know she has lied, and Fire-Walker may cut out her tongue.'

'I will do more than that,' Fire-Walker growled. 'Remember, brothers, it was I who saw her first.'

'Yes, very well, but release her now,' Moon-Raider instructed. 'She is not yet yours, and if she is truly our brother's wife, his rage will be murderous if he learns you have placed your hands upon her. It shall be as Crazy-Soldier-Boy has suggested. We will take her to the winter camp and wait. How are you called, *herbi*?'

'Storm. My name is Storm.'

For some reason the Comanches glanced at each other strangely at this, as though her name held some significance for them, but they said nothing.

'Brother-Of-The-Wolf has given you no name in our language?'

'No, why?'

269

Moon-Raider shrugged, as though it were of no importance. 'No matter. No doubt he was waiting for his father's approval of your marriage.'

'Yes, yes, he did say he would announce it to The People and ask for Tabenanika's blessing.'

Fire-Walker swore wrathfully upon hearing this and strode off into the darkness with disgust, apparently at last convinced Storm was who and what she claimed to be.

Moon-Raider only smiled, the first warmth he had shown her. 'Welcome to our camp, wife of our brother. We are pleased to have you join us. Come this way. Are you hungry?'

'Famished.' Storm smiled back hesitantly, greatly relieved.

'How was Brother-Of-The-Wolf when you left him? Well, I trust?'

Suddenly the girl recalled the gaping wound in her husband's side, the flow of blood that had stained the sheets upon which he had taken her so violently. For the first time since leaving Wolf, it dawned on her he might be dead. Oh, how could she have failed to consider such before? Her grief and heartache had blinded her to the possibility. She had thought not of her husband, but of herself. Her face blanched whitely. Dear God! He couldn't be dead! He just couldn't be! Surely he had survived far worse wounds! No, he wasn't dead; Storm just couldn't allow herself to believe that. If Wolf were dead, he could not claim her! Even alive he might be so enraged he would not acknowledge her as his wife! But I would not see him dead, Storm realized, even if he no longer wants me.

'Is something wrong, Storm?'

'What? No, oh, no; I'm sorry. It's just that such harsh words passed between us. I – I had almost forgotten until you reminded me. My *kumaxp* was well, Moon-Raider,' the girl said and prayed it was true.

Storm did not fear the Comanches as another white woman in her place would have done, for she had not the ignorance of them that would have caused her to be afraid. Wolf had instilled the knowledge and ways of his tribe in her too deeply for that and so although the Indians were fierce warriors, she knew they would not harm her as long as they thought of her as Wolf's wife. Had she been a captive, things would have been different. Fire-Walker would have forced himself on her brutally and perhaps the others as well. Afterwards, if they'd had no use for her, they would have killed her; at best she would have been little more than a slave. Rape of their own women was rare among the Comanches, however, and punishable by death; and so although she worked hard, the men gave Storm no chores other than what they would have given their own wives had they been present.

As the weeks passed the girl cooked and cleaned and sewed – the major duties she was assigned – and behaved in all ways as befitted a proper Comanche woman, winning the Indians' approval. She was silent unless spoken to and respectful of the men at all times, taking her meals alone after they had finished eating and riding her mare the correct distance behind them when they traveled. Storm was determined they should have no cause for complaint about her to Wolf when they reached the *Llano Estacado*.

At night she slept alone, cold but undisturbed, and the only times she felt the least bit uneasy were those times she would catch Fire-Walker's dark malicious eyes upon her speculatively, filled with naked hate and hunger. Why he despised and yet desired her Storm did not know, but as long as the others were present she was safe and so she took care never to be alone with him.

Moon-Raider was the kindest to her, but since he among them had counted the most coups, perhaps he could afford to treat her more gently without question, for none could doubt his bravery or strength. He told her he was Wolf's brother and also related to her the story of Wolf's double-bowled pipe, with which the Kiowas had been so impressed that night so many months ago.

'It is called a double horseback bowl, Storm,' he explained

271

one evening as he puffed on his own *awmawtawy*. 'It commemorates the heroic deed of a warrior who has ridden through enemy fire to sling a wounded companion over the back of his god-dog and rescue him. Brother-Of-The-Wolf saved my life in such a manner during a battle with the Apaches and so was honored. He is a brave warrior and has counted many coups among The People. You should be proud he has chosen you as his *paraibo*. Among the women in our camp there are many who would gladly share his blanket. Do you not long for him these wintery nights?'

'Yes, Moon-Raider, my *haints*,' Storm replied truthfully.

'Ah, it is as I thought. If you grow too lonely on our journey, you may come to me, Storm, without fear. It is a Comanche's duty to care for his brother's wives in his absence – in every manner if they so desire. There will be no *nanehwokuh* – damages – asked for it.'

'I – I understand, Moon-Raider, and I am honoured, but among my people a woman belongs only to her husband.'

'Yes, that is what I thought you would say. Do not worry, Storm; you have not offended me. I know it is Brother-Of-The-Wolf who holds your heart.'

Yes, the girl thought silently, but does he still want it, and can I find it in myself to forgive him if he does?

It was December when they at last reached the *Llano Estacado* and the winter camp of the *Kwerharehnuh* high in the Palo Duro and Tules. It had turned bitterly cold, for 'blue northers' – freezing winds from the north – swept down through the Texas panhandle and surrounding areas without mercy, bringing a fine layer of white frost to rest upon the land, which was sometimes followed by a heavy blanket of snow. Storm, who only had ever seen snow once in her life before, was grateful for the long warm doeskin dress and furry buffalo robe She-Who-Seeks-Wisdom had given her upon her arrival at camp. The tipi she shared with Tabenanika's second wife was warm too, and at night when the wild winds crawled through the canyons and bluffs with their strange chilling moans, she was thankful to be safe and sheltered within the hide dwelling where a fire burned brightly.

Wolf's family had accepted her presence stoically, with little comment, like the warriors withholding their final decision about her until Wolf's arrival. They were polite to the girl; they saw she was well cared for, but other than this she might not have existed. They spoke to her only when necessary, and she found her attempts at conversation balked whenever she tried to question them about Wolf and his mysterious past. Whatever they knew of his background, they did not intend to share with her apparently, and their silence only made her more curious. Had his real mother, the *Castellano*, been taken captive by The People? Had Wolf's father been a brave Comanche warrior who had boldly made Wolf's mother his even as Wolf had done Storm? Had the *Castellano* gone to his arms willingly even as Storm had Wolf's, or had she been carried off against her wishes during a raid, snatched from her gardens, perhaps? *My mother used to grow roses.* Who had they been, and how had they died, those two who had left nothing behind but their hard, haunted half-breed son?

Storm did not know, and those who might have told her did not. The Comanches rarely spoke of the dead, and when they did it was not by name. Life was for the living, and the spirits of those who had died were sacred, not to be disturbed. Whatever his birth or blood, Brother-Of-The-Wolf was a Comanche warrior now; Tabenanika had spoken, and so Storm remained in ignorance of her husband's origins.

Daily she watched for him, but still he did not come, and she worked hard so that the Indians would not think her an imposition. Some of the women disliked her intensely. A few had mistreated her. One had gone so far as to actually attack her. Wolf's training had enabled Storm to win the fight, however, and afterward there were no further threats of assault against her person. The girl held herself tall and proud as she boldly strode through the camp, and many murmured that Brother-Of-The-Wolf had chosen well in his woman. Several warriors eyed her openly with admiration, but Storm did not encourage their advances, and soon they ceased trying to coax her between their blankets. Only Fire-Walker watched her silently and seethed with his slow, simmering hunger and hate – and waited as Storm did for Wolf to come to the winter camp of his people.

It was a lonely vigil the girl kept, and there were many evenings when she wept silently in the darkness, muffling her sobs so that She-Who-Seeks-Wisdom would not hear the sound of her tortured tears. Night after night Storm lay awake, her heart crying out with anguish as she wondered if her husband were still alive and whether or not he still wanted her. She prayed wordlessly in the blackness for him, her strange brooding gunslinger, for she loved him, regardless of what he had done. Storm vowed if only he would come and claim her, she would forgive him for his brutal treatment of her and beg him to take her back, no matter the price he asked of her in return.

It was nearly Christmas when the joyous shouts of greeting told Storm that Wolf was alive and had finally arrived. She trembled when she heard the cries of welcome, for she was certain it was him and that her time of acceptance or rejection had come at last. Oh, surely he would claim her! He had said he would come for her. Still she hung back as the others crowded forward around the wagons of the *comancheros* and drew Wolf into their midst. It was only when Storm caught Fire-Walker's eyes on her – hard and cruelly eager as they raked her – that she too moved toward her husband. The Comanches, seeing her coming, fell back to make a path for her, and a sudden breathless hush settled over the expectant mass. For a moment the girl thought her knees would buckle beneath her as she walked toward Wolf slowly, feeling his icy midnight blue eyes on her all the way; but somehow she managed to reach him and stand before him, her head bowed slightly in deference as she waited for him to speak.

It seemed like hours before he at last tilted her face up to his and said, 'You are looking well, *paraibo*. I trust my family has seen to your needs.'

'Yes, *kumaxp*, they have been most kind.'

'It is good.' Then he turned away to address his father. '*Ap*', once more I have brought supplies, guns and ammunition for The People. These men' – he indicated the *bandoleros* – 'come in peace and give you greetings.'

'They are welcome, my *tua*,' Tabenanika intoned. 'Masitawtawp will show our honored guests where they may lodge. Come, Brother-Of-The-Wolf. We have much to discuss.'

'Yes, *ap*'. *Paraibo*, see to my tipi. My mothers will help you with what you do not understand.'

'Yes, *kumaxp*,' Storm choked out softly, for Wolf had not looked at her again, and his voice, when he spoke to her, was that of a polite stranger.

Well, what had she expected? After all, she *had* stabbed and deserted him! She was lucky he had even claimed her as his own. He might have kept silent and left her to the mercy of the Comanches. The girl turned away, tears she would not let fall stinging her eyes before she sought out Woman-Of-The-High-Wind and She-Who-Seeks-Wisdom to assist her in erecting Wolf's dwelling. When it was finally standing properly, she built a fire in the center and put a thick, fragrant stew on to cook, not knowing whether or not Wolf would be hungry. Then she stowed his gear away neatly and made up their beds for the evening. After that she huddled nervously on the frozen ground inside the tipi, waiting for her husband to appear.

It was very late when at last he came to her, but Storm had not slept. He paused a moment in the doorway, studying her, before deliberately he allowed the flap of the tipi to drop into place, shutting out the rest of the world. He had changed his clothes, and for a minute the girl did not know him, for she had never seen him dressed in anything but his black silk garments. Now he was garbed like the rest of the Comanches in fringed buckskins. He had plaited a single braid in his long black hair on the left side of his dark visage, and a solitary feather hung, tip down, from the back of his head. Storm gave a small gasp of terror upon seeing him and drew the knife sheathed at her waist quickly, for at first she mistook him for Fire-Walker standing in the shadows. It was only when he moved into the dim light of the fire that she realized it was her husband.

He hunkered down without a word, eyeing the glittering blade dispassionately.

'I see you haven't lost your penchant for knives, baby,' he drawled lazily, seemingly unmoved by the thought. 'If you're planning on using that on me again, you'd best do some hard thinking. Right now I'm the only thing standing between you and those Indians outside. You put that sticker in my gut this time, and I promise you'll beg somebody to kill you before my family has finished with you.'

'I – I know. I'm sorry. I – I thought you were Fire-Walker.'

Wolf's eyes narrowed coldly at that, splintering like shards in the darkness. 'Has the bastard laid a hand on you?'

'No. No one has touched me. You – you didn't seem surprised to find me here.'

'That's because I wasn't. I picked up your trail outside of San Antonio and followed it until you joined up with the others. I knew who had you because of an arrow feather I found. I recognized the markings as Moon-Raider's and guessed you'd be here. I figured you knew enough Comanche to explain you were my wife.'

'Yes, thank you for – for claiming me. I expect it would have been very awkward for me if you hadn't.'

'Awkward, hell, baby. It would have been damned unpleasant,' he spoke grimly. 'I reckon you might even be dead by now if I'd decided not to acknowledge you.'

'Why – why did you then?'

'Because you *are* my wife, and damn it, Storm, you're in my blood like a drug! After San Antonio I thought I could learn to hate you, but I couldn't. And if you hate me, that's just too damned bad, baby, 'cause you're just going to have to learn to live with it. I'm not letting you go.'

'Oh, Wolf!' Storm gave a little cry of anguish. 'Why? Why did you do it – treat me as though I – as though I were nothing to you? And how – how can you forgive me for what I did to you in return? I might have killed you! You might have died that night, and I wouldn't have even known or cared; I hated you so!'

He studied her quietly for a moment, then swore softly. 'I reckon I just couldn't stand the thought of another man staking a claim to you, baby, especially a man like Gabriel North. I was drunk – damned drunk, and I'm sorry. You didn't do anything but try to protect yourself from being hurt by something you couldn't possibly understand. I don't condemn you for that. Hell, I would have done the same thing in your place.' He laughed shortly, bitterly, mockingly. 'Jesus Christ!' he groaned, then shook his head, one corner of his mouth turning downward sardonically. 'It was just too good too fast for us, wasn't it, baby?'

'Yes,' she whispered brokenly.

The word fell awkwardly, beseechingly in the little silence that descended, strangling them both with its choking grip as each tried to understand and forgive and dared to hope they could find once more what they had lost. Wolf's dark eyes locked hers across the tipi.

'I love you, Storm,' he said.

'Oh, Wolf! I love you too!' she cried before she flung herself, weeping, into his outstretched arms.

They wrapped about her tightly, as though half-afraid she was but a dream that would slip away when he reached her, but she was real all right. He could feel the racking sobs that shook her body as she buried her face against his broad chest, just as he could feel the rivulets of her tears that streaked his flesh. He held her close and stroked the tangle of her unbound hair soothingly.

Slowly he twisted her countenance up to his. '*Bruja*,' he muttered. 'Witch! What have you done to me?' he asked before his hands tightened in her ebony cascade of tresses, and his mouth found hers with a passion she had not thought possible.

Storm parted her lips for him eagerly as she felt the tip of his tongue begin to seek her out, then shoot deep inside her waiting mouth to explore the sweetness within as though he had never known it before. Gently, gently his tongue caressed hers, twining hesitantly at first, then swirling with a more demanding pressure when he met no resistance to his tentative onslaught. In every way a man's tongue can know a woman's mouth, Wolf discovered Storm's once more, teasing her to follow where he led before *her* tongue darted swiftly between *his* lips to probe his mouth in kind.

It seemed as though they kissed forever, as though some manner of it might yet remain unfound. It was only later – much later they somehow cast away their clothes to reveal their nakedness to one another.

Wolf's hands touched satin white skin as he laid her down upon the blankets she had spread upon the frozen ground, but Storm was not cold then or afterward when his fingers moved upon her flesh, trailing down her face and throat and shoulders to her breasts where they lingered tantalizingly. Time flew by, but the lovers paid it no heed, for their world was timeless, endless, measured only in each other's desire and need. Storm's nipples flushed like dawn across the sky and hardened to taut little peaks that nuzzled at Wolf's palms enticingly, invitingly. He lowered his head and kissed them both lightly before each one in turn grew more rigid between his lips and tingled beneath his gently nibbling teeth and slowly whirling tongue.

Storm lost her hands in his shaggy mane of hair as she urged

278

him on with tiny moans of pleasure and drew him closer against the soft mounds that swelled upon her chest, round and full and ripe for his taking. And he took and tasted and loved her as he had never loved her before as his tongue licked its way down to conquer that secret place between her thighs, his fingers pulling gently at black downy curls to prepare his way. She quivered when his mouth found her, kissed her *there* – upon that sweet flower of her womanhood whose fragrance only he had ever known, that deep dark well of nectar from which only he had ever drunk and grown dizzy with delight.

The headiness of it filled him, enveloped him, called to him with a siren song from which he could not escape, did not want to escape. He captured the essence of it with his hand, played its haunting melody over and over until he was certain he knew every single note, had heard that dulcet, trilling chord for which he'd searched and listened and waited.

Storm cried out softly as the crescendoes of his music went crashing through her veins, over and over, dying to soft echoes before they rose again and yet again.

And still Wolf played her, twisting his body around slowly so that she might join him in a harmony that made him gasp once, twice with rapture before the rhythm of her lips and tongue and fingers made his head pound with an intoxicating beat and his loins throb to some primitive but never to be forgotten mode.

Her hands crept upward to trace the smoothness of his belly, marred here and there by the white scars of his past and the new arc-shaped wound her own blade had left. Tears started in her eyes once more as her fingers swept the small length of the healing crescent, then glided downward to his muscular flanks before finding his hard shaft again where her mouth still moved with tender passion.

He gasped again and pulled away from her before she made him reach that final measure, righting himself and plummeting deep into the very core of her being. Fiercely he took her, and just as fiercely Storm received him, locking her long lithe legs around his back to draw him even further into herself. Down, down, down into the velvet honey of her he plunged, faster and faster until for one glorious, triumphant moment she was his, all his as she arched her hips against him wildly and dug her nails into his flesh.

'Wolf! Oh, Wolf!' she breathed raggedly, then for one fleeting eternity ceased to breathe at all as a thousand galaxies exploded within her, blinding her with the fiery brilliance of their shooting stars.

As breathless as she Wolf joined her, spiraling into the heavens upon the wings of her ecstasy to find his own. In that moment they were one, and Storm knew, long before the first signs that would tell her for certain, that that night he had given her a child.

15

Cal Tyree, battered hat in hand, shuffled his feet nervously as he glanced around himself in awe. His spurs scraped upon the inlaid white marble tiled floor, and the magnificent hall of Tierra Rosa resounded with an odd little echo. Immediately he froze and looked down cautiously to be certain he had not left scratches where he'd trod. With a sigh of relief he noted the floor still shone with a soft, highly polished gleam, unmarred. Although it was very fine, it could not be as fragile as it seemed. He tiptoed forward hesitantly until he stood upon the bottom step of the flaring staircase that wound upward to the overhanging balcony of the second story. His boots sank into the plush red carpet, and the sound of his jingling spurs was muffled until it was no more. He leaned against the solid oak balustrade, studying the gold wallpaper, which was flocked with red velvet roses, and the immense crystal chandelier that hung down from the ceiling far above. The diamondlike sconces held at least a thousand candles, and Cal found himself wondering how anyone ever managed to get up there and light them. A thousand candles – he had counted them to be sure – and for just one room! He thought of the single oil lamp with which his family had made do when he'd been growing up in the tiny four-room house of his boyhood in the bayous of the Brazos River and was overwhelmed by the evidence of Gabriel North's vast riches.

'Mistah Tyree.' The uniformed Negro butler appeared silently from nowhere. 'Massah Nawth'll see yo now. If'n yo' all follah me. Dis way please.'

Cal jumped, startled, and moved hurriedly from the staircase. His face was flushed with guilt, as though he had somehow committed an unpardonable sin by daring to set one foot upon that which led to the Norths' private rooms upstairs. The darky's countenance was impassive, however, as he led Cal through the entry and down the winding hall to Gabriel's study.

'Mistah Tyree, sah,' the Negro announced him. 'Will der be anythin' else, sah?'

'No, Abel. Leave us. Sit down, Tyree,' Gabriel ordered when the darky had departed.

'Thankee, sir.'

'Care for a brandy?'

'Oh, thankee, sir; I don't mind if I do.'

'Now, Tyree,' Gabriel began after he handed Cal a delicate crystal snifter filled with a small shot of amber liquid and lit a cigar. 'I understand you have some information for me as to the whereabouts of my fiancée, Miss Lesconflair.'

'Yessir, I shorely do – leastways Sheriff Yancey seemed to think so. It's all here, sir, in the sheriff's letter.'

Gabriel leaned across his massive desk for the piece of rather crumpled paper. To his surprise and faint disgust with himself he found his fingers were trembling slightly as he unfolded the missive and read its badly written contents. Afterward he was silent for such a long time that Cal started to grow nervous again. He cleared his throat as quietly as possible to remind Gabriel politely of his presence.

When the rancher finally looked up at him, Cal saw his eyes were as hard as nails. He shivered briefly under the man's piercing stare.

'Is this it?'

'Yessir.'

'Goddamn it! If that fool Yancey knew the girl was my fiancée, why the hell didn't he detain her and take this gunslinger El Lobo into custody?'

'Uh, beggin' yer pardon, Mr North, but El Lobo's a – a dangerous man, real fancy with the pistols and all, and he hadn't committed no crime, leastways none we knew of.'

'Goddamn it, Tyree! The frigging bastard kidnapped my fiancée!'

'Uh, beggin' yer pardon again, Mr North, but it were them Barlow brothers what done that, sir, near as anybody can figger. How El Lobo came by your little gal we dunno, but she didn't object when he said they was married, and he didn't appear to be holdin' her prisoner or nothin'.'

'Married, my ass! Miss Lesconflair is a lady, Tyree! You think she would have wed some half-breed Indian trash with me waiting here for her? My God! For what kind of a fool do you take me? The son-of-a-bitch has taken her captive, I tell you! I can't understand why he hasn't contacted me, demanded a ransom.'

'I – I dunno, sir, 'ceptin' he's a queer one all right, kinda quiet and deadly as a snake – if you know what I mean, sir.'

'And you let him make off with my fiancée!'

'Well, sir, how was we to know you'd want her back once you found out what'd happened? You know what them Injuns do to wimmen. Shit, Mr North, you'd be better off to fergit that little gal of yours, and find you another – one that ain't been quite so used. Hell, the Barlows probably had her too—'

'You shut your mouth, Tyree! By God, I'll have your hide and Yancey's too if you breathe one word of this! You tell him I said so.'

'Yessir.'

'And you get your butt into San Antonio, and tell Sheriff Martin to round up a posse of men and some Indian trackers and get out here *pronto* if he has any ambitions about winning the next election.'

'Yessir, whatever you say, Mr North.'

'That will be all, Tyree.'

'But – but, sir, what about the – the reward money?'

'You tell that frigging sheriff of yours that if he'd have done his job as he was supposed to, my fiancée would be safe at Tierra Rosa by now. Now get out!'

After the quavering and stuttering deputy had left Gabriel clenched his hands together tightly, then banged one fist down viciously on his desk. A whore! Storm Lesconflair was a *whore*! The word stuck in Gabriel's craw. Tyree was right! No telling to what uses the Barlows or that half-breed Indian gunslinger had put her! Oh, he'd like to get his hands on Storm Lesconflair! How dare she make him the laughingstock of Texas by running off with such a man? Even if the Barlows had taken her first, she had obviously managed to escape them. Why hadn't she made her way to Tierra Rosa? Gabriel didn't have to look far to know the answer to that. She despised him of course, preferred a Goddamned half-breed over *him*! That was an insult he didn't mean to stomach. He'd get that whore back if it were the last thing he did. She was his! She belonged to him, Gabriel North, one of the richest ranchers in the state of Texas, just as everything for miles in all directions belonged to him. He would never let her get away, even if she were no longer the pure, unsullied lady he'd thought to marry.

Whore or not, it was the principle of the thing. He'd wagered a sizable sum of his hard-earned money for her, spent a great deal more on her worthless family. Southern belles didn't come a dime-a-dozen, especially to a black sheep like Gabriel North in whose face the South had slammed its doors. Yes, he had bought and paid for Storm Lesconflair, and damaged goods or not he would have her. What did it matter if she were no longer a blushing virgin? Hell, he would like to have been the first, but what was done, was done; and he still wanted her, wanted the undiluted French bloodlines and high-born breeding that were hers, wanted the soft white satin skin he knew lay beneath those yards of crinoline and lace. His loins ached at just the thought of her. Yes, he'd track Storm Lesconflair down, kill her arrogant gunslinger, and make her forget she'd ever thought to revenge herself on him by sharing the bed of a frigging half-breed. Maybe it was even better this way; maybe she wouldn't be so damned high-and-mighty, so haughtily touch-me-not toward him now that she'd been used by the Barlows and that savage. Maybe the red devil had even taught her a few tricks too. Gabriel had only ever had one

Indian woman in his life, but she'd sure been something, a biting, clawing, heathen little bitch. Yes, he'd get Storm Lesconflair back if it killed him. Tierra Rosa would not be cheated of its lady, its hard-won Southern belle; he would see to that. He was rich. He would hush things up all right and tight, gloss everything over, pass Storm off as a respectable widow or something. No one would dare question his story or give his bride-to-be the cut-direct. The water rights he held were too valuable for that!

He leaned back in his massive oak swivel chair and smiled cruelly as he imagined Storm the lady gracing the majestic halls of Tierra Rosa and Storm the whore naked and panting beneath him in his bed.

It was Christmas Eve, and Wolf had remembered. Storm gazed lovingly at the deerskin blouse and long skirt he'd given her to mark the occasion. They had been faded and bleached until they were pure white and were decorated with thousands of brightly colored beads, feathers, and quills, the latter something the Comanches rarely ever used and that made the garments all the more precious. She caressed their soft folds wonderingly, wanting to etch their every detail in her mind. This was her wedding ensemble, and it was as different from what she had imagined years ago in New Orleans as the strange ritual she would shortly undergo. Had someone suddenly offered her a choice between these clothes, however, and her mother's silk wedding dress adorned with its tiny seed pearls and yards of Brussels lace, Storm knew she would still have picked the deerskin apparel. It was the Comanche way, the path in life she had chosen to follow.

She pulled the blouse on carefully over her head, then stepped into the skirt, smoothing out its creases until the uneven hem that was the trademark of a Comanche woman hung gracefully to the ground, its lengthy fringe making a gentle whoosh when she moved. She laced the outfit together at the waist, then donned the *peplum*, a sash that hid the thong. There were two white leather panels also, which were worn over the front and back of the skirt. These were dyed with an intricate pattern of dark blue backward L's, each one symbolizing a war honor Wolf had won in the past. Storm was proud there were so many, for their number signaled her husband's bravery in battle, and all who saw her would know Wolf had counted many coups. Because it was winter, there were, in addition, matching leggings, which she drew on underneath the skirt.

After dressing she unbound her hair, brushed it, and replaited it into two neat braids. Then around her head she tied a narrow white leather headband, which was as painstakingly worked as her wedding ensemble and bore a single down-tipped feather. On her feet were soft white fringed leather boots similarly adorned.

It was time. Quietly she pushed open the flap of the tipi and stepped outside where Wolf awaited her before the central campfire. She had no attendants; alone she walked toward him. When she reached his side, Wolf took her hand in his, turning to his people.

'Before the Great-Spirit, Father-Sun, Mother-Moon, and you, the *Nermernuh* – The People – I claim this *herbi* as my *paraibo*,' he said. Then he took his knife and slashed first Storm's palm and then his own before pressing them together so that their blood mingled as one. 'My *ap*" – he knelt reverently before Tabenanika, pulling the girl down beside him – 'will you give us your blessing?'

Slowly the *puhakut* began to chant, shaking his gourd as he intoned some Comanche words so ancient Storm could not understand them. Then he motioned for them to rise.

'My *tua*, do you recall the vision that proclaimed you a *tenap'*, the storm that swept over the fire-land and brought the second wolf to heal the first?'

'Yes, my *ap'*, I remember.'

Tabenanika made a brief sound of approval. 'It is good for

a man to know he has found the destiny for which he searched. I have looked into your spirit, my *tua*. It is healed. This *herbi*, your *paraibo*, has washed it clean. From this day forward she shall be known as Eyes-Like-Summer-Rain, sister of The People. Go in peace, Brother-Of-The-Wolf and Eyes-Like-Summer-Rain, and may the Great-Spirit walk beside you and give you strength. I, Tabenanika, have spoken.'

'It is done, *paraibo*,' Wolf told her softly. 'No man will part us now. Come, my Indian bride, for I would share your blankets and claim you in another way far older than that of the Comanches.'

Storm knew, long before the men ever reached the winter camp of the *Kwerharehnuh*, who they were. It was as though some strange sense of foreboding had warned her of their coming. Trembling with apprehension, she watched as they wound their way through the canyons to the high bluffs of the Palo Duro and Tules, looking like an army of black ants against the white snow that lay hard and thick upon the *Llano Estacado*. When they were almost upon the camp, she returned, her heart pounding, and ran toward the tipi she shared with Wolf.

It was Gabriel! Even in the distance she could not have mistaken that thick thatch of flaming red hair or the fiery beard and mustache. Oh, God! He had come all this way for her! She covered her face with her hands, weeping silently. Oh, why couldn't he have left her alone? Didn't he understand she didn't want him?

Wolf's eyes narrowed intently as he studied the small party that had halted some yards away from the camp.

'Gabriel North,' he breathed the name aloud, his tone a snarling hiss of rage and disgust.

Still there was an odd hungry pleasure in his eyes too, as though he had been challenged to a battle by an enemy for whose blood he had long thirsted and was already savoring his triumph.

There was some discussion among the men, then the two Indian scouts who accompanied them rode forward. No fear showed upon their stoic faces, for they were Comanches, members of the *Itehta'o* band by the looks of them.

The bastard's smart, Wolf thought to himself. If it weren't for those two, he'd be dead right now. I wonder how he ever managed to convince them to track for him?

One of the Indian scouts spoke, interrupting his musings. '*Hihites, haints.* I am Nayia of the *Itehta'o.* This is my brother, Chikoba. We come in peace and bring gifts for our brothers, the *Kwerharehnuh.* We seek the *paria:bo* known as Ekakura.'

'I am Ekakura.' The peace chief of Wolf's family stepped forward coldly. 'How is it that our brothers, the *Itehta'o,* ride with the White-Eyes and lead them to the winter camp of the *Kwerharehnuh?*'

'The *tabeboh* offered us many fire-sticks and ammunition. They come in peace,' Nayia repeated, 'on a mission of great import to their white chief, Flame-Hair. They seek council with the mighty Ekakura, whose brave coups as a warrior of The People are known throughout *Comanchería.* They are few, and you are many. They bring gifts for the *Kwerharehnuh,*' he stressed again. 'What harm can it do to listen? If they displease you, kill them. They have brought no Blue-Soldiers with them.'

'Very well.' Ekakura nodded at last. 'Let them approach.'

Gabriel glanced covertly about the camp as he strode toward the tipi of Ekakura, but he saw no sign of Storm. The bitch! How dare she attempt to hide from him? He knew she was here; the *comancheros* he and his men had met upon the snow-covered plains had told him that much, thinking they would be rewarded for the information. Gabriel had given them nothing, however, for the news had been old by then. Only the one called La Aguila had said nothing about the girl, merely advising Gabriel and his men that they would be wise to turn back. Gabriel had ignored the man of course, a no-good Mexican *bandolero* if he'd ever seen one.

It was warm inside Ekakura's tipi. Gabriel waited until the *paria:bo* had motioned for them to be seated before he sank to the ground, crossing his thick, muscular legs with difficulty, Indian-fashion. He stripped off his gloves, blowing on his frozen fingers to revive them before he stretched them out to the fire gratefully, while his men began to unbundle the goods they'd brought for the Comanches. Soon hordes of beads, blankets, knives, guns and ammunition lay scattered upon the earth. Ekakura surveyed the gifts silently and was pleased. He got out his pipe, filled it with some of the tobacco Gabriel offered him, lit it, and puffed soberly before handing it to the *tabeboh*. Gabriel also took several drags, then passed the pipe on around the circle.

At last Ekakura spoke. 'You have traveled two moons to The Land of The People, one called Flame-Hair, and have brought the *Kwerharehnuh* many fine presents. What is it you seek in return for your daring and generosity?'

'I search for a woman, O' mighty peace chief of the *Kwerharehnuh*, one who was to be my bride. The stagecoach in which she journeyed to my ranch was held up, and she was taken prisoner by outlaws, bad White-Eyes,' Gabriel explained as Nayia and Chikoba translated. 'Somehow she managed to escape them. Now she belongs to another, one of your people who is called El Lobo.'

Ekakura's dark eyes flickered. 'Yes, there is one among us who is known to the White-Eyes and *Mejicanos* by that name. He is Brother-Of-The-Wolf, son of our *puhakut*, Tabenanika. It is his woman about whom you ask?'

'Yes, O' mighty peace chief. I am here to bargain for her return to her own people, the White-Eyes. She was promised to me and does not belong among the Comanches. Surely you know this.'

Ekakura grunted, his face impassive. 'That is not for me to say, Flame-Hair. The woman about which you ask is Brother-Of-The-Wolf's wife. It is he who must decide whether or not he will let her go. Moon-Raider, my *tua*, go, and fetch your brother to my tipi.'

'Yes, *ap*.'

Wolf had been awaiting Ekakura's summons, so he was not surprised when his brother Moon-Raider called out to him, then entered the dwelling he shared with Storm.

'*Hihites*, my brother. My father asks that you come to his tipi at once. There is a matter the White-Eyes would discuss with you.'

Wolf nodded and rose slowly, casting a reassuring glance at Storm before following Moon-Raider to the dwelling of Ekakura. He pushed open the flap, pausing deliberately in the shadowed doorway before striding softly like a panther to seat himself cross-legged before the fire at Ekakura's right side.

'I have come, *ap*, in response to your summons. What is it you wish of me?'

'The chief of the White-Eyes, one called Flame-Hair, would speak with you, my *tua*. He asks about your *paraibo*, Eyes-Like-Summer-Rain.'

Wolf turned languidly to face Gabriel North, his dark visage revealing none of the thoughts that trampled through his mind at being so close to the hated rancher. Whatever Gabriel had expected, it was not this tall, lithe, handsome half-breed who studied him with such cool arrogance, a faint, mocking smile playing about the corners of his mouth. The icy midnight blue eyes of the man appeared to pierce his very soul, and despite the warmth of the fire, Gabriel shuddered slightly. There was something about this heathen that nagged at him. He didn't like it – not one bit.

'You are the gunslinger El Lobo?' he asked.

'Some men call me that, yēs,' Wolf agreed, to Gabriel's surprise, in perfect English, but then after all, the man *was* a half-breed, so perhaps his knowledge of the language was to be expected.

Gabriel indicated he no longer needed the interpreters, and Nayia and Chikoba lowered their voices, translating in muted tones only for the benefit of the rest of the Comanches present who did not speak English.

'You possess a woman known as Storm Lesconflair?'

'Among my people she is called Eyes-Like-Summer-Rain,' Wolf answered. 'And she is my wife.'

'So the peace chief of your family has said. The woman belongs to me. She was promised as *my* wife. I do not know how you came by her, but I am willing to bargain with you for her return. Name the price you place upon her, and I will pay it.'

'I have told you, the woman you seek is my wife. How I came by her is unimportant. She is mine. I do not wish to sell her.'

'I will give you a hundred fire-sticks and ammunition for her and as many cases of fire-water,' Gabriel offered with insulting ignorance, not understanding there were some things his money simply couldn't buy. 'And that is surely more than she is worth. After all, to you she's just a squaw.'

'You do not listen, White-Eyes,' Wolf noted softly, his voice low and silkily deceiving, something that warned those who knew him well of his quietly suppressed rage, for the Comanches did not use the term *squaw*, which was a White-Eyes base corruption of an East Coast Indian word. 'My *wife* is not for sale, not at any price.'

'Why, you half-breed bastard!' Gabriel spat, foolishly loosing his temper and leaping for Wolf across the fire.

Immediately Moon-Raider and Crazy-Soldier-Boy grabbed the rancher, pressing their knives to his throat while their fellow Indians did likewise to the other white men, who licked their lips nervously and stared at Gabriel with bulging, horror-stricken eyes. For one awful moment the air was as taut as a bowstring. Gabriel considered himself a man of importance and could not comprehend his danger. How dare these uncivilized red devils threaten him, by God?

'You kill us, and the entire United States Army will see you're punished for it. You'll be slaughtered like cattle,' he blustered.

291

'The woman you would have will be one of those massacred by your Blue-Soldiers,' Wolf pointed out practically, unconcerned. The two men gazed at each other unwaveringly, their eyes hard and seething, refusing to give way, realizing they had reached a stalemate. 'Release him, my brothers' – Wolf made a graceful movement with his hand – 'he and his men came in peace and have smoked the *awmawtawy* with our *paria:bo*. He is a chief of great import among the *tejanos*, and for reasons of my own I would see his miserable life spared. *Ara*' – he turned to Masitawtawp as the crackling tension eased – 'have Eyes-Like-Summer-Rain come to Ekakura's tipi. We shall hear from her own lips whether or not she wishes to go with this – *narabuh*.'

The Comanches laughed at the derogatory word, and although Gabriel did not know what it meant, he caught the general gist of the matter. His angry countenance turned a mottled shade of red, and he almost choked on his wrath. By God, if he got out of this alive, he was going to kill this no-good, son-of-a-bitch gunslinger if it were the last thing he ever did!

Storm was pacing the hard earth floor of her dwelling anxiously when Wolf's uncle appeared.

'Masitawtawp!' The girl ran to him with a small sob. 'What is happening?'

'Nothing about which you must concern yourself, little one, if you truly love my *ara* as you have said,' he spoke gently, for he had grown to like Wolf's wife very much. She was a Comanche in spirit, he thought proudly, if not by blood. His nephew had indeed chosen well. 'Come, Eyes-Like-Summer-Rain. Brother-Of-The-Wolf is asking for you.'

Having suspected after Wolf's summons that she would be sent for too, Storm had changed into her wedding ensemble, the best outfit she owned. Now she wrapped the albino buffalo robe her husband had also given her (one of the two he had killed in his life) around herself tightly and followed Masitawtawp to Ekakura's tipi, her boots making soft scraping sounds upon the frozen ground.

Gabriel stared unbelievingly at her when she entered the dwelling behind Masitawtawp, for he was not prepared for her changed appearance and found himself stunned by it. She looked like a savage! The creamy white skin he remembered so well had been tanned to a honeyed brown-gold by the Texas sun during the past several months. The ebony cascade of riotous curls was parted smoothly in the center and plaited into two long thick braids that hung down over her breasts to her hips. She was garbed in a deerskin blouse, skirt, and leggings and was actually wearing a headband and fringed leather boots besides! After his initial shock had passed he began to notice other differences about her too. Though she was still slender, her curves had filled out with a full, exciting ripeness, a maturity they had previously lacked; and the girlish innocence of her eyes was gone, never to come again.

My God! he realized suddenly, she's not only lain with that half-breed bastard; she's carrying his child! He was sure of it.

After one quick, covert glance at the Texas rancher Storm moved unobtrusively to sit on the left side of the tipi, which was the place of a Comanche woman. Her heart beat too rapidly in her breast, and her pulse quivered at the hollow of her throat. This was the man she would have been forced to marry had it not been for Wolf. This was the man who had turned André-Louis against her, wrenched her from her home, and caused the death of her beloved Mammy. This was the man who had sent her running to Wolf's arms and altered the course of her life for all time.

Gabriel hasn't changed, she thought dully; he's as stupid and mean as ever! Oh why did he have to come here, and what does he want of me?

'*Paraibo*,' Wolf said, watching her bowed face closely. 'Do you know this White-Eyes whom the *Itehta'o* call Flame-Hair and who is known as Gabriel North to the *taboh*?'

'Yes, my *kumaxp*,' she replied so quietly he almost didn't hear her.

'Is it true you were promised as his wife?'

'Yes.'

'But the marriage did not take place?'

'No.'

'Why not?'

Storm looked up at her husband curiously, confused. 'You know the answer to that, my *kumaxp*, so why do you ask?'

'I want you to tell me again so that those present may know the truth of the matter.'

Slowly, in a voice devoid of all emotion, Storm started at the beginning as she had so many nights long past that evening on the Texas prairie and related the tale of how she had become engaged to Gabriel North and how she had come to wed Wolf instead. When she had finished, there was silence in the tipi. Gabriel cleared his throat uncomfortably in the hushed stillness, wishing his men had not been present to hear her story, for it had put him in a very bad light indeed. The girl obviously hated him still, but she was his, and he meant to have her.

'You've had a rough time of it, Miss Lesconflair,' he observed, the wheels in his brain whirling quickly as he determined how best to persuade her to rejoin him. 'However, I want you to know I don't hold it against you. You're young, and you've made mistakes. Perhaps we both have. But I still think you're the prettiest little gal this side of the Rio Grande. I want you to come back with me, to Tierra Rosa. We'll get married just as we planned. For God's sake, Miss Lesconflair!' he swore suddenly when she didn't respond. 'You're white! You don't belong here!'

She raised her head then to look at him. Oh, god! Her eyes! Like mist they were, wisps of gray that taunted him, teased him, and deftly eluded him, leaving him lost amid their haunting shadows. And her mouth! Oh, Christ, her mouth! The things he wanted to do to those inviting rosebud lips that trembled slightly at the corners! His felt his manhood grow

hard at just the thought of those things. He must have her back
– whatever the cost!

'You're wrong, *Monsieur* North. This is exactly where I belong.'

'Now look here, Miss Lesconflair,' he growled, starting to become angry again. 'We had a bargain. I've spent a lot of money on you and your family, and in case you've forgotten I'm still holding several of your Uncle's IOUs,' he threatened her warningly. 'I suggest you pack your things, and get ready to leave here.'

'My uncle never cared about me; why should I sell myself to keep him safe? I won't do it, I tell you. I am no longer the confused and unhappy girl I was. Oh, there's no use in me trying to explain to you, *Monsieur* North,' she stated flatly, recognizing impatiently that he was not grasping the words. 'You'd never understand in a million years. I'm not going back with you.'

She was gone before he even had a chance to protest, a chance to realize she had made her decision and that it wasn't in his favor. Stupefied, he stared at his men, not comprehending he had come all this way only to be rejected, him, Gabriel North, one of the richest ranchers in the entire state of Texas!

He sprang to his feet. 'No, you can't do this to me!' he yelled and tried to follow her out of the dwelling, but the Comanches restrained him, growing hostile once more.

'You got your answer, *narabuh*,' Wolf sneered coldly. 'Now take your men, and get out while you still can.'

'You'll pay for this, you bastard! By God, I'll make you pay, you thieving son-of-a-bitch! You're no better than a savage – worse! I'll hunt you down and kill you, you half-breed heathen, if it's the last thing I ever do!'

'Well, while you're looking, you remember who's sharing my blankets,' Wolf jeered, then spat squarely between Gabriel's feet. 'That's how much you worry me, *narabuh*.'

'Come back here, you frigging bastard! Come back here, and fight like a man, you goddamned worthless son-of-a-bitch!' Gabriel howled, but Wolf paid him no heed as he strode from the tipi, afraid if he didn't get away – and fast – he'd throttle the Texas rancher with his bare hands.

His heart was thudding so horribly in his breast Wolf believed it might burst, and even his hands were shaking from the terrible hatred that coursed through his veins, eating him alive. Waves of nausea engulfed him, and for one horrible moment he feared he was going to pass out. I'll kill him. I'll kill him! he raged blindly. But even as the brutal thought took hold of him Wolf knew he could not do it – not here, not now. To murder Gabriel North would be to sign the death warrants of the fifteen men who accompanied him as well. A massacre like that would bring the United States Army down on the *Kwerharehnuh* like ducks on June bugs for sure, and Wolf didn't want the blood of The People on his soul too. There were already too many deaths for which he was going to have to account someday when he stood before the Great-Spirit.

He took a deep breath, trying to calm himself before he went inside to Storm.

She was huddled on their bed, weeping. Wordlesly he took her in his arms, holding her close, rocking her back and forth to soothe her.

'Oh, Wolf, I'm sorry, so very sorry,' she sobbed. 'I – I never dreamed he would look for me, would come after me after all this time. *Sainte Marie,*' she moaned, lapsing into French as she always did when agitated. '*Sainte Marie.* What are we going to do? He's so rich, so powerful; he'll never let me go; I just know it!'

'Hush, baby; hush. It's all right. Everything's going to be all right, I promise you. You mustn't upset yourself like this, Storm. It's not good for the baby.'

Obediently she tried to stem the flow of her tears and managed a tremulous smile.

'That's my girl.'

'He'll come back, Wolf, with more men; you know he will!'

'No, he won't, Storm. After what happened here today he'll

be hard-pressed to find anybody foolhardy enough to brave the *Llano Estacado* and The People. They might all have been killed, you know. I had only to give the signal.'

'Why didn't you?'

'You don't mean that, baby. I might be a killer, but I'm not a murderer.'

'I know; I'm sorry. You think he'll leave us alone then?'

Wolf sighed, not wanting to hurt her, but not wanting her to have any false illusions either. 'No. We made a fool out of him, Storm. He's not a man to forgive or forget that. He won't rest until he's revenged himself on us.'

'*Mon Dieu!*'

'Hey' – he raised her tearstained face to his – 'I've kept you safe before haven't I? He'll have to kill me first to get at you, baby, and killing's what I do best, don't you think?'

'No, it's your way of loving that makes you so special. Hold me, Wolf,' she whispered throatily. 'Make love to me. I want to know you're mine for just a little while.'

With haunted, passion-darkened eyes he pressed her down upon the blankets and took her fiercely, defying Gabriel North to come between them.

16

All those long winter nights Storm lay sheltered in Wolf's strong arms, lulled into a state of false security. Gabriel had not really meant those terrible threats he'd shouted, she decided. He'd had a long, grueling journey for nothing and had simply been tired, angry, and bitterly disappointed. There had been faint lines of strain around his brown eyes, and he'd looked older, thinner. Once her initial shock had worn off Storm found she almost pitied him. He was a proud man, and she had rejected him. Of course he'd wanted to hurt her as she had him. But it was over now, surely. She, Storm, had won. She threw herself into her work and put Gabriel North from her mind.

She joined in the winter buffalo hunt, struggling through the snow along with the rest of The People in strange contraptions Wolf called 'snowshoes', which prevented them from floundering in the treacherous drifts. Her cries of '*A:heh*! I claim it!' mingled with the rest as she surged forward with the other women to take possession of the buffalos Wolf had slain with his bow and arrows.

The Comanches, unlike white men who often stripped the hides and left the carcasses to rot upon the prairies, wasted no part of the beasts they had killed. The brains and small intestines, which could not be preserved, were cooked immediately and eaten. The skins and meat, which would be dried later at camp, were loaded onto sleds, along with the bones of the animals. Only the hearts were left behind, strewn upon the snow-covered ground, for the Indians believed a new herd would spring from these offerings.

Storm was tired and cold on the way back, for the sled was packed full, and she was forced to walk the distance to camp. Uncaring that the other men eyed him with suppressed amusement, Wolf supported her as best he could while leading the team of dogs hitched to the sled. Still no one teased the couple, for they had come to like and respect Storm. If she were not yet quite up to the measure of their own women, she worked hard and seldom complained. More important, she had brought happiness to their blood brother, Brother-Of-The-Wolf, who had come home to the *Kwerharehnuh* at last.

All were content as they waited for the spring that came late to the plains of Texas that year of 1849. The season of fresh beginnings crept upon the land slowly, as though fearing its predecessor would return anew to drive it off. Only the gradual melting of the snow and the green shoots pushing bravely to the surface of the earth here and there gave evidence that, by May, spring had arrived.

She was now five months pregnant, and although her initial morning sickness had long passed, her back had started to ache worse than ever. She felt as awkward as she had upon the snowshoes when she moved, and only the glint of desire that darkened Wolf's eyes whenever they lit upon her prevented her from feeling ugly and graceless.

As he warned her earlier, with the coming of spring the *Kwerharehnuh* left their winter camp high in the Palo Duro and Tules and returned to the flat, sweeping prairies and gently rolling hills below. Wolf said nothing about leaving The People, however, and Storm was pleased he wished to remain at least until the birth of their child. He was so good to her, seeming to understand without question the way her pregnancy affected her temperament, making her moody and easily moved to tantrums or tears. At night, after making love, he held her close, brushed her long black hair, and massaged her aching muscles, whispering soothingly in her ear. In the privacy of their tipi he lightened her burdens by performing many of the chores the Comanches felt should have been Storm's own. He brightened her days in other ways too, bringing her small presents such as a spoon he'd carved, knowing how much she secretly disliked eating with her fingers. Often she would awaken to find a new headband or beautifully beaded necklace lying on her blankets. It was difficult for her to believe Wolf created the tiny treasures, and she knew he did it in secret so that the other warriors of the band would not learn how he spent his spare time and laugh at him. Only She-Who-Seeks-Wisdom saw the objects and smiled to herself, guessing they were gifts from Wolf and not Storm's handiwork, for Wolf's mother recognized several of the designs she had taught her son so many years ago. She said nothing to anyone else, however, realizing Wolf's pride in his manhood would be hurt.

Both she and her sister, Woman-Of-The-High-Wind, took great pains to see Storm was not worked overly hard as well and protected her from the evils they thought might befall a pregnant woman and injure her child.

'You must take care, Eyes-Like-Summer-Rain, that you do not look upon the face of a rabbit, else your *tua* be born with long ears,' they advised the girl solemnly.

Storm's mouth twitched, but she did not laugh, understanding they truly believed the things against which they warned her.

'*Aiee, pabi*!' She-Who-Seeks-Wisdom squealed. 'Our worthless *tua* has forgotten the crow feathers for his son's cradleboard.'

'*Hu*! You are right, my sister,' Woman-Of-The-High-Wind noted with a frown. 'I will speak to him at once lest some misfortune befall our grandchild.'

Wolf was duly chastised, and the crow feathers were obtained and placed carefully around the top of the cradleboard. Storm thought it looked like a war bonnet and said as much.

'It is good,' Woman-Of-The-High-Wind responded. 'Your son will grow up to be a brave and fierce warrior like his father. Is that not what you wish, Eyes-Like-Summer-Rain?'

'Yes, oh, yes! I want him to be just like Wolf. But, mother of my husband, how do you know the baby is going to be a boy?'

'*Aiee*!' She-Who-Seeks-Wisdom squealed again. 'Of course the first of your little ones must be a man-child! How could it be otherwise? Is not your *kumaxp* much a stallion between your blankets?'

Storm blushed furiously at the blunt question. 'Well, yes,' she admitted at last. 'But Wolf will love it, even if it is a girl. He has said as much.'

'Perhaps, but he will be disappointed all the same,' Woman-Of-The-High-Wind observed. 'It is always thus with a man. If the *ona* is a girl, you will call softly to your *kumaxp*: *Ersamop'ma*. "It is a girl,"' she instructed Storm. 'But, ah, if the *ona* is a boy, you will call proudly to your *kumaxp*: *Eh-haitsma*. "It is your close friend." This is the way of The People, Eyes-Like-Summer-Rain.'

Storm nodded. 'All will be done as you have said, mothers of my husband. This I promise.'

'It is good,' Woman-Of-The-High-Wind repeated stoically. 'My *tua* has indeed chosen well in his *paraibo*. Come. We have been serious long enough. Fetch She-Who-Laughs-Like-A-Mountain-Stream, my sister, and we will play the awl game.'

Gabriel galloped away furiously from the winter camp of the *Kwerharehnuh*, his mouth a tight grim line of rage. He was more angry than he'd ever been in his life! How dare Storm Lesconflair and that filthy half-breed make a fool of him in front of his men? How dare that whore scorn him and everything he'd offered, despite her sullied body, for a savage who was nothing, had nothing? How dare that fickle bitch reject him, just as the South had done? It was not to be borne, and Gabriel would not stand for it! By God, he had made his way in the world after his father had disowned him, and he had made it well, had built an empire for which any other woman would have gone down on her knees and begged to be mistress. Of all he might have had, however, he had chosen Storm Lesconflair, the belle of five counties and the pride of New Orleans, a high-born, gentle-bred lady whose pure French

301

bloodlines had been undiluted for hundreds of years, the ultimate in the unattainable to an American black sheep like himself. Yes, he had chosen her and won her, and she would be his, by God! He had never known defeat. He would not accept it now. He had bought and paid for Storm Lesconflair, and he was determined to have her, no matter how much more she cost. Yes, he would have the woman who epitomized everything the South that had cut him off without a penny represented, and before he was finished with her he would see her humbled and humiliated, brought to her knees, the proud hussy. It would be the final *coup de grâce* against all for which she stood! Come summer, after the spring breeding and branding of his vast herd, he would round up his men once more, attack the *Kwerharehnuh*, and take back that which was rightfully his!

'Ishatai, Padoponi, Herkiyani,' Storm called to the children who were playing *nanip'ka* – guess-over-the-hill – a Comanche version of hide-and-seek. 'Do not go too far from camp. Moon-Raider, your father, has said Apache *Indes* have been sighted in the area, and you know they are much worse than the *Sehkwitsit-Puhitsit* or *Piamermpits*.' Storm suppressed a smile as she mentioned the mud men and the big cannibal owl, the bogeys with which the Comanches frightened their children when they misbehaved.

'Oh, Eyes-Like-Summer-Rain, the *Indes* will not attack us, will they?' Herkiyani's beautiful little face puckered up as though she were about to cry.

'Of course not, silly *naibi*,' Ishatai retorted scornfully, swaggering slightly. 'Are not The People the most powerful of all those who roam the vast plains of *Comanchería*? Is not our father a brave and fierce warrior? The *Indes* are cowards. They would not dare to raid our camp, and if they did, I would kill them, scalp them, and count many coups!' The boy brandished a pretend lance threateningly.

'As would I!' Padoponi chimed in, adding his voice of

defiance to that of his brother. 'There is no need for you to be afraid, Herkiyani.' Then, 'Look! Look!' he cried, his attention suddenly diverted from the possibility of an Apache attack. 'It's *Kusehtehmini*. Quick! Catch him! Catch him! We must take him to *ap'* at once!'

The children scrambled hurriedly after the horned toad who, sensing imprisonment was near at hand, was hopping rapidly into the brush. Padoponi made a mad dash for the creature, flinging himself face-down in the dirt.

'Got it!' he crowed triumphantly before he and the others raced away victoriously toward the camp, shouting for their father. This was big medicine indeed!

Storm laughed and shook her head as she watched them run toward the tipis. The Comanches believed the horned toad would tell the location of buffalo herds. If so, they would be off for the first big hunt of the new season. Still smiling and swinging her water bags, Storm continued on to the stream. Someday her child would be among those who played *nanip'ka* and chased after *Kusehtehmini*. The girl placed her hand over her belly where the baby had begun to kick now.

'Ah, my little one,' she said softly. 'You will be as unafraid as the others, will you not?'

Spring was now in full bloom upon the land. Storm gazed out over the gently swelling crests in the distance where the buffalo grass and shrubby mesquite trees rippled greenly in the wind, and the brightly colored flowers of the cactuses shone like splashes of brilliant paint against the red-clay-and-golden-sand earth. The rivulet upon whose bank she knelt bubbled bluely, reflecting the endless expanse of azure sky above in which white cotton candy clouds moved like wisps upon the breeze, and the mellow yellow sun peeped down over its domain with the first real warmth of the season. The water was cold, the legacy of the snow that had melted earlier. Storm shivered slightly as she dipped her bags into the spring-fed brook to fill them.

Once she looked up uneasily, feeling as though she were

being watched, but she could discern no one's presence. She worked faster nevertheless, remembering the reports about the Apache *Indes* and suddenly wishing she had not come alone to the stream. She was just tying the thong about the last bag when she was grabbed roughly from behind. A strong hand was clamped down hard over her mouth to muffle her screams as she was dragged into the nearby brush and thrown to the ground. The girl glanced up with terror at her captor, expecting to find herself surrounded by a band of marauding Apaches.

'Fire-Walker!'

He leered down at her cruelly, his eyes filled with hunger and hate. How he had waited for this moment. For months he had waited, watching the bride of Brother-Of-The-Wolf, wanting her, wanting to feel her struggling against him, wanting to feel his knife driving deep into her flesh after he'd finished with her. Yes, he had waited, and now she would be his. He would take her, use her, and then kill her afterward, and once more Brother-Of-The-Wolf would mourn one he had loved, would cut off his hair and slash his copper skin with grief, would weep bitter tears for another wife –and child who would never see the light of day. Yes, revenge would be Fire-Walker's yet again for that day so many years ago when Brother-Of-The-Wolf had made such a fool out of him before The People.

Slowly Fire-Walker drew his blade. This woman was not like Beloved-Of-The-Forest, who had cried silently and trembled beneath him and begged him for her life and that of her child. No, this woman would fight him; she would not plead for mercy. He could see that in her eyes, those smoky gray shards whence Tabenanika had taken her Comanche name.

He was right. Storm did not wait for him to fall upon her. She knew what he wanted. She had seen that look before on the faces of the Barlow brothers. With a small gasp, once she had recovered from her initial shock, she raised the water bag she still clutched in one hand and struck Fire-Walker across the face with it. As it bashed against the side of his head with a thud the container burst open at the seams, blinding him with water that spewed out in a gush. Briefly he was stunned by the force of her blow, for he had not realized the girl's strength. He grunted, groping for her wrathfully as she rolled away from him, the strange undergarments she wore flashing white beneath the jagged hem of her deerskin skirt. He caught one ankle, yanking her back before she could rise. She kicked out at him with her free foot, striking him squarely in the chest. He released his hold on her and staggered to his knees with a sharp intake of breath. In moments Storm had drawn her knife threateningly from the *peplum* she wore around her waist. *Hu!* Where had the woman learned such tricks? Truly it was as though she were possessed by evil spirits! They circled warily, feinting and slashing at one another with their blades, the girl's lips curled back in an almost feral snarl. Storm was made clumsy by her pregnancy, however, and soon she was flat on her back once more, grappling with Fire-Walker desperately, her breasts heaving beneath her deerskin blouse as she panted for breath. He caught her wrist, slamming it down hard against the earth until she dropped her knife, wincing at the pain of his fingers curled about her in a hurtful grip. Then he pinioned her arms above her head and pressed the keenly honed point of his blade against her throat.

'Do not cry out, *herbi*,' he growled warningly through clenched teeth.

Storm stared at him silently, hatred splintering her steely gray eyes like shards.

'*Bâtard!*' she spat in French, forgetting Fire-Walker would not comprehend her. 'Filthy *canaille*! Let go of me!'

It was true he did not recognize the words she spoke, but he understood enough to guess her general intent.

'Do as she says, Fire-Walker.' Wolf suddenly appeared from nowhere, his dark visage a distorted mask of rage.

Fire-Walker glanced up, his countenance startled but

jeering. 'Do not take another step, Brother-Of-The-Wolf, or I will kill your pretty *paraibo*.'

'I think not.' Wolf's voice held that silky, deceiving note. He made a curt movement with his hand. Immediately all three were surrounded by a group of stony-faced Comanche warriors.

'My people,' Wolf said, 'you have seen with your own eyes that this dog who is lower than an Apache *Inde* would force himself on my unwilling *paraibo*. I claim *nanehwokuh* for it as is my right.'

'Name your price then, Brother-Of-The-Wolf,' Fire-Walker hissed, yanking Storm to her feet and loosing her.

'Your life.'

'It is too much. She is only a White-Eyes *herbi*.'

'She is the *paraibo* of Brother-Of-The-Wolf, whatever her blood,' Moon-Raider snarled.

'Yes, and she was not willing to share your blankets, besides,' Crazy-Soldier-Boy chimed in. 'It is a fair price.'

'Choose your weapons, you *muwaw*,' Wolf sneered as the decision was reached, 'and may the *tabebekut* be upon you.'

The warriors gasped, and even the unrepentant Fire-Walker blanched sickeningly at this last, for the *tabebekut* was a fearsome Comanche curse. Nevertheless he met Wolf's challenge boldly.

'Very well then. I choose *werpitapie'ni* as my weapon.'

Some of the warriors present eyed each other speculatively at this, for it was well-known that Fire-Walker was deadly with his battle-ax, but Wolf seemed unconcerned.

'I choose the *pianer'erpai'i* as mine,' he spoke. 'It is what a dog such as you deserves.'

'Brother, are you *posa*?' Moon-Raider asked, grabbing Wolf's arm angrily. 'You will not stand a chance against him.'

'Moon-Raider is right,' Crazy-Soldier-Boy noted. 'Choose something else, brother.'

'No!' Fire-Walker exclaimed. 'The challenge has been met, and the weapons have been chosen. It is done.'

'What – what is it, Naukwahip?' Storm questioned anxiously, not understanding the meaning of the lengthy word for the weapon Wolf had selected. 'With what has my *kumaxp* chosen to fight?'

'I do not know the English term for it, Eyes-Like-Summer-Rain. I am sorry.' Then, seeing her gray eyes darken with haunted shadows, he turned to his brother. 'Shadow-Of-The-Hawk, can you translate *pianer'erpai'i* for our cousin's *paraibo*?'

'Yes, but perhaps she will wish I had not afterward.'

'No, please.'

'It means "big whip", Eyes-Like-Summer-Rain. I believe the White-Eyes call them bull whips.'

'Oh, God,' Storm moaned, biting her lip. 'Oh, God.'

'This is the Great-White-Spirit of the *tabeboh*?' Naukwahip queried, frowning.

'Yes.'

'You are the *paraibo* of a Comanche warrior, Eyes-Like-Summer-Rain,' Shadow-Of-The-Hawk reminded her tersely. 'If you love Brother-Of-The-Wolf, you will pray to the Thunderbird, so that your *kumaxp* may prevail in the coming battle.'

'Yes, Shadow-Of-The-Hawk.'

'Go now to your tipi, and prepare yourself. This is a fight to the death, and you will belong to its victor.'

'Yes, I – I understand.'

Quickly Storm turned and ran toward her dwelling so that the warriors would not see the tears that had started in her eyes at knowing Wolf was to battle for her yet again. Oh, *Sainte Marie*, have mercy, she prayed as she pushed open the flap of her tipi and flung herself upon her blankets. Why? Why? Why had she brought so much trouble to her husband when she would only have given him happiness? What had she done wrong? She caught a glimpse of her tear-streaked countenance in the little mirror Wolf had bought for her in San Antonio, and suddenly she knew. It was her face – her face that tempted men into wanting her so that they challenged Wolf for her. Yes, her face was accursed; that was it. Without thinking Storm reached for the knife at her waist only to find the sheath empty. Of course. She had left it in the brush in her haste to get away. Frantically she began to search the dwelling for something else that would serve her purpose as well. Her fingers closed over a sharply honed buffalo bone. Yes, it would do. She raised it to her countenance, intending to slash her face to ribbons.

'What in the hell are you doing?' Wolf yelled angrily, then kicked the bone from her poised hands.

Storm flinched, startled, for she had not heard him come in, and cringed from the wrath she saw upon his dark visage.

'I – I was only going to – to cut my face so that a man would never again look upon it with lust,' she whispered.

'Jesus Christ!' he swore. 'You ever try anything like that again, and I'll kill you! Did you ever stop to think your face belongs to me, baby? That I happen to like it the way it is? Oh, Storm, Storm' – he bent to cradle her tenderly as she started to cry once more – 'it wasn't your fault Fire-Walker attacked you. It's me he wanted to hurt, baby. You were only going to be the instrument of his revenge. We quarreled of old, and he has never forgotten, nor forgiven me for besting him in our encounter. Come on now. Dry those tears, and give me a smile. You know I hate to see you cry.'

Tremulously the girl raised her head and tried to smile, but it was a pitiful attempt at best.

'Oh, Wolf, suppose he kills you. How can you possibly hope to win against him with only a bull whip?'

He grinned wickedly, wanting to lighten her dark mood. 'You ever seen me use a bull whip, baby?'

'Well, n – no.'

'And have I ever failed you yet?'

'No.'

'Then try to have a little more faith in my abilities.'

'All right.'

'Will you do something else for me too?'

'What?'

'Here' – he handed her the blade she had dropped in the brush – 'if by some slim – and I emphasize slim, baby – chance Fire-Walker *does* manage to kill me, I want you to take this, and use it on yourself immediately. Your death at his hands would be most – unpleasant, and I don't want you to suffer, understand?'

'Yes.'

'Good. Come on then. They're all waiting.'

Slowly Storm followed him from the tipi to the center of camp where the Comanches had gathered in a circle to watch the forthcoming battle. The hushed murmur of low voices was stilled suddenly as Ekakura raised one hand.

'My people, a challenge has been given and accepted by two among us. Will Brother-Of-The-Wolf and Fire-Walker step forward. Brother-Of-The-Wolf, before witnesses you discovered your brother Fire-Walker with your *paraibo*, Eyes-Like-Summer-Rain. They had come together without your knowledge or permission, and you have claimed *nanehwokuh* for it as is your right. Instead of asking for horses or other worldly goods, however, you have asked for Fire-Walker's life. This is a high price for a *herbi*, Brother-Of-The-Wolf. Why have you claimed it?'

'Because, my *ap'*, Eyes-Like-Summer-Rain was not willing to lie with Fire-Walker, and though he knew this, he tried to force her to share his blankets. Among The People such a crime is punishable by death.'

'Eyes-Like-Summer-Rain, was it as your *kumaxp* has spoken? Did you refuse Fire-Walker, and did he then attempt to take you by force?'

'Yes, Ekakura.'

'Fire-Walker, you have heard the charges against you. Do you refute them?'

Fire-Walker glanced around the circle slyly, but knew from the impassive faces of those who had witnessed his foul deed

309

that there was no way to defend his actions. The warriors who had been his friends now scorned him, for if he would take one brother's wife by force, might he not also take another's in the same manner?

'No, *ap*', I do not refute the charges,' he said boldly.

'Then you do accept the challenge?'

'Yes.'

'The battle will be to the death. If either of you shows cowardice during the fight, I myself will slay you immediately. Is this understood?' The two opponents nodded, knowing that though he was the paternal uncle of them both, he would not hesitate to carry out his words. 'Good. Eyes-Like-Summer-Rain, do you hold yourself ready to be given to the victor?'

'Yes, Ekakura,' Storm replied, trying not to shiver as Fire-Walker's dark eyes raked her crudely. Her fingers closed tightly over the handle of her knife as she recalled her husband's words.

'So be it,' Ekakura stated. 'May the Great-Spirit walk beside you and give you strength. Let the battle begin.'

At this the tom-toms started to pound slowly, mesmerizingly, and the warriors to chant softly. Wolf strode silently to one side of the circle where his father awaited. Tabenanika handed him a length of coiled whip even as Kwasia gave Fire-Walker the battle-ax he would use. Tabenanika folded his arms across his chest as he met his brother Kwasia's eyes unflinchingly, knowing one of their sons would die before this day had ended. In moments the duel had begun.

The two opponents faced each other warily, moving noiselessly on moccasined feet as they circled deliberately, their copper-skinned visages void of emotion. Then suddenly Fire-Walker gave a wild shout and flung himself toward Wolf. Wolf side-stepped gracefully, uncoiling his whip with a flick of his wrist before sending it spinning about Fire-Walker's ankle. Fire-Walker tripped and fell, sprawling face-down in the dirt. Hurriedly he rallied and rolled over, putting up his shield to ward off a sharp, cracking blow as Wolf yanked the whip free and lashed out with its snaky length again. Before Wolf could strike a third time Fire-Walker had gained his feet and put some distance between himself and his enemy. With a low snarl Wolf sprinted forward rapidly, like a bounding animal, the whip snapping repeatedly. Fire-Walker tried to defend himself once more with his shield, but the slithering coil was too quick for him. Wolf ripped open Fire-Walker's flesh, leaving several bright red stripes across his foe's chest and upper arms. With a growl Fire-Walker threw away the useless shield and grabbed the end of the whip as it wrapped about his wrist. He pulled it taut, hacking at it with his tomahawk. Wolf released his hold on the snaky length and hurled himself at his opponent. In minutes the two men were grappling upon the ground, rolling over and over again, entangled by the whip. Fire-Walker raised his hatchet. Wolf twisted to avoid the blow that would have cleaved his head in two, and the ax buried itself in his right shoulder. He grunted with pain as Storm gasped and pressed her white knuckles to her lips to keep from crying out.

Blood spurted, then gushed from the wound as Fire-Walker pulled the tomahawk free to strike again. Wolf lunged upward with his body, tossing Fire-Walker head-over-heels along the earth, then grasped the whip, which lay to one side, as he sprang to his feet. Once more he unleashed a barrage of brutally pelting lashes upon Fire-Walker, this time leaving his enemy's back criss-crossed with deep, stinging wounds. Fire-Walker staggered to his feet with difficulty, panting heavily as he moved to escape the deadly blows. Again he lifted his hachet aloft and with a blood-curdling yell leapt toward Wolf. A split second later Wolf dropped to the ground. Fire-Walker tumbled right over his body and continued to roll. Rapidly he righted himself. This time when he raised his ax, he held it poised, calculating for a moment, before he flung it end-over-end. It hurtled through the air like a bolt of lightning, causing the onlookers to howl and scatter as it flew past Wolf, grazing the side of his head before it clattered against a tipi in the distance.

Storm nearly bit one finger in two as she moaned and stifled her screams of fear. She could taste her blood, bittersweet, in her mouth, but she paid no heed.

Wolf lashed out savagely with the whip once more, sending it spinning about Fire-Walker's throat. With a sharp intake of breath he yanked his opponent to his knees, drawing the snaky length tighter and tighter. Fire-Walker started to choke, grabbing frantically at the slowly asphyxiating coil with clawlike hands as Wolf wrapped it around him several more times, then pulled it even tauter.

'For – what – are – you – waiting?' Fire-Walker rasped. 'Finish it!'

To Storm's horror her husband hesitated. She glanced at Ekakura, terror-stricken, as he suddenly snapped to attention, alert for any sign of cowardice.

Slowly Wolf loosed the coil slightly.

'I want to know if you were the swine who forced my *paraibo* and murdered her and my child.'

'Are you *posa*? Your *paraibo* is alive and well, as is the *ona* in her belly.'

'I'm talking about Beloved-Of-The-Forest, and you know it!' Wolf hissed dangerously, his face distorted with rage as he began to cut off Fire-Walker's breath with the whip again.

Fire-Walker smiled, a terrible jeering grin. 'Yes, I had her, many times, and when I'd taken my fill of her, I killed her and the *ona* she carried.'

Deliberately Wolf's hands gripped the ends of the snaky length he held even tighter, pulling harder and harder as he strangled Fire-Walker with an excruciating finesse. When it was done, he gathered his foe's body in his arms, rose, and made his way to where Kwasia stood in stoic silence. Gently he laid Fire-Walker's corpse at his father's feet.

'You heard?' he asked.

'I heard, my *tua*,' Kwasia spoke, his face showing none of

the pain he felt inside as he lifted his dead son and turned away.

Bit by bit the circle began to break up as Storm moved toward Wolf quietly, forcing herself to walk calmly, proudly, her head held high, as was the Comanche way, although she wanted more than anything to run to his waiting arms. She-Who-Seeks-Wisdom was there also to see the gash in her son's shoulder and the crease near his temple. She spared a slight, reassuring glance for Storm as the girl came alongside them.

'The wounds are not that bad; they will not need *pianahuwait* – big doctoring. You come to my tipi, and I will give you some herbs with which to make a poultice to draw out the evil spirits.'

'Thank you, mother of my husband. Wolf,' Storm questioned once they were alone in their own dwelling, 'why did you force Fire-Walker into admitting it was he who murdered Beloved-Of-The-Forest? Was his shame not already great enough in the eyes of The People?'

'Yes, but I wanted to know the truth, and besides, Kwasia would have felt honor bound to kill me for slaying his son. A life for a life. This is the Comanche way. Beloved-Of-The-Forest's death has been avenged now, and her spirit may rest in peace.'

'A life for a life,' Storm repeated softly. 'I understand, my *kumaxp*.'

Wordlessly she began to cleanse his wounds, wondering what other shadows still haunted him from his past.

17

The Apache came as the first pale streaks of dawn stole in rose-colored wisps across the gray-blue sky, for the hated *Indes* were seldom night raiders like the Comanches.

It was the shouts in the distance and the pounding of horses' hooves over the hard terrain that originally wakened Storm, but dazed with sleep she did not at first comprehend what was occurring until Wolf shook her roughly, his low, throaty voice filled with a commanding urgency that made her sit bolt upright in bed with fright.

'What is it?'

'Apaches,' he answered grimly, hauling on his buckskin breeches and reaching for his weapons. 'Get up, baby, and get dressed,' he ordered unnecessarily, for Storm was already scurrying for her clothes. 'Arm yourself, then go find the rest of the women.'

He kissed her swiftly on the lips, and then he was gone. Storm moved hurriedly to carry out his demands, opening the *nat'sakena* Woman-Of-The-High-Wind had given her to remove her pistols and ammunition belts before lifting the flap of her tipi to step outside. For a moment she could see nothing but a cloud of dust far and away across the sweeping prairie before a herd of wild ponies appeared to stampede straight toward the camp from all directions. Almost simultaneously a series of ear-splitting yells began, and rifles cracked loudly, nearly deafening her with their sharp reports. Storm screamed and dropped to the ground, fearing to be hit otherwise. Through the swirling dirt and smoke she could see the women running frantically for cover in the brush, scooping up wayward children as they went and dodging the Comanche warriors, who had mounted their own horses and were

314

galloping toward the oncoming Apaches. The girl rolled to one side to avoid being trampled in the *mêlée*, then started to snake her way across the sand and grass back to her dwelling. There was no time to join the others.

Gasping for breath and rubbing her scraped elbows, Storm huddled, terrified, inside her tipi, her heart pounding. The baby seemed to sense her distress, for it began to kick inside her belly. She placed one trembling hand over her abdomen, trying to calm the unborn child.

'Shhhhh. It's all right, little one. It's all right.'

She opened the flap a crack to peek out. Confusion reigned amid the camp, which was a maelstrom of flying horses' hooves, fierce painted faces, flailing limbs, clashing weapons, trodden feathers, and blood. Two warriors grappled in the dirt for control of a battle-ax a short distance away. A Comanche woman screamed as the strong copper arms of an Apache warrior yanked her across his pony's bare back. A child crouched piteously, choking on muffled sobs, alongside a tipi. It was Herkiyani, Moon-Raider's daughter.

Without thinking Storm pushed her way from her dwelling, trying to reach the hysterical girl. She tripped over a sprawled body and fell, but was up on her feet again in moments, running, her stride made clumsy by her pregnancy. An Apache *Inde* bore down on her, his dark countenance made all the more gruesome by his chilling war paint. Blindly Storm raised one revolver and fired. He toppled from his horse, catching one foot in the loop of thong that served as a bridle. The pony careened wildly, dragging the warrior along the earth and smashing into a tipi, sending it crashing with a splinter of lodge poles. Storm ducked as the shards of wood flew past her and narrowly missed being struck by a tomahawk. Panting heavily, too scared to even cry out now, and thinking dimly that she had killed a man, she stumbled toward Moon-Raider's daughter.

'Herkiyani! Herkiyani!'

She grabbed the frightened child, cradling the girl against

her breast soothingly for a minute, trying to shield her young eyes from the horrifying sights.

'Oh, Eyes-Like-Summer-Rain!' The child clutched on to her desperately.

'Listen to me, Herkiyani! We can't stay here. Do you understand? We can't stay here. Take hold of my hand.'

Half-crouching, Storm began to make her way across the camp once more, cringing as the bullets and arrows whined past her, and the riderless horses galloped recklessly this way and that. An Apache swooped toward her, attempting to snatch Herkiyani from her grasp. Petrified, Storm clung to the girl, pulling the child's screaming body back with all her strength. The angle of her leverage hauled the warrior from his pony. He grabbed for them both menacingly, then without warning pitched forward, dead, a lance protruding from his back.

Horrified, Storm dragged Herkiyani over the *Inde*'s corpse and then another body, which stared up at them with glazed eyes.

'Look! Crazy-Soldier-Boy!' Herkiyani cried.

Storm glanced to where the child pointed, expecting to find the girl's uncle was dead. Instead he was standing in the midst of camp, humming to himself, seemingly invulnerable to the battle raging about him.

'My God, is he mad?'

'No, *posa* – crazy,' Herkiyani replied. 'That is how he received his name.'

'Crazy-Soldier-Boy! Crazy-Soldier-Boy!' Storm called frantically, thinking he would help them, but he did not answer.

'He cannot hear you, Eyes-Like-Summer-Rain,' the child observed, then suddenly began to bawl once more.

'Hush!' Storm snapped more sharply then she'd intended, shaking all over as she continued to haul the girl behind her.

At last they managed to reach Storm's tipi and crawled inside, lowering the flap hastily.

'There, there. It's all right.' Storm tried to calm the terrified child.

After what seemed like hours there was silence. Storm raised the flap once more and saw the Apaches had been beaten back. She started outside, shuddering as she viewed the number lying dead. She wondered if Wolf were among them, and her heart lurched sickeningly in her breast.

'No, Eyes-Like-Summer-Rain!' Herkiyani caught her hand, tugging at it tightly. 'They'll be back! They'll be back!'

Storm would have protested this, but just then the wild whoops began again, and she realized the girl was right. The brief lull had been but a chance for the attackers to regroup their forces.

The second onslaught was just as bad as the first – worse, for Storm knew by the smell of a new acrid smoke in the air that several of the tipis had caught fire. *Sacré bleu!* Hurriedly she reached for the water bags that hung from one lodge pole and started to damp down her dwelling, fearing the flames would spread and her own tipi burn. The thought had come to her too late, however, for part of her dwelling had already begun to blaze. She wet one of the blankets, beating at the licking orange-and-yellow tongues of fire savagely, scarcely feeling the sweltering heat upon her hands, which soon reddened, blistered, and finally were scraped raw by the scorched blanket as she worked. She stamped the last of the flames out with her moccasins, then paused tiredly to wipe her perspiring face. She pushed back a strand of hair that had become loosed from one braid, turned, and froze as she stared into the dark eyes of an Apache warrior who had crept beneath the hides of her tipi to find his way inside. Herkiyani screamed and screamed again as the *Inde* captured her easily, holding a knife to the child's throat as he motioned for Storm to throw down her guns and approach him.

Slowly she did as he indicated, understanding he thought Herkiyani was her daughter and meant to kill the girl if Storm disobeyed him. When she reached his side, he released

Herkiyani, imprisoning Storm in her place. Roughly he forced her down upon the ground, forgetting the child. Petrified though Herkiyani was, she still managed to bring herself to snatch up one of Storm's pistols. Not knowing how to use it, she simply bashed the Apache over the head with the heavy walnut stock. He groaned and turned angrily, giving Storm a chance to act. Quickly she drew the blade at her waist, plunging it into the warrior's back. He fell forward into the hot ashes that still smoldered from the blaze Storm had battled earlier. The horrible, pungent odor of burning flesh filled her nostrils, making her long to retch. Stomach churning, she fought down the nausea and, body quivering with terror and exhaustion, began to weep silently as she held Herkiyani close to convey her thanks.

Outside the battle still raged. Wave after wave the Apaches came, but as Storm at last marshaled her courage once more to lift the flap on her dwelling, she saw the attackers had dwindled appallingly and were now mainly attempting to recover their dead.

Finally the camp was hushed and still, and Wolf came to her at last. Storm scarcely recognized him through the smears of red war paint with which he had daubed his face and body hastily that morning, the streaks of sooty black gunpowder and gray smoke that clung to his copper flesh, and the fresh, bloody gashes that scored his torso. The wound in his shoulder had broken open and was bleeding freely once more. His blue eyes looked tired, strained, and inscrutable as they took in Storm's horrified countenance, the frightened child she clutched desperately, and the dead Apache sprawled in the dirt.

'Are you all right?'

'Yes. You're hurt. Let me help you.' She put her arms out to steady him, relieved he was alive.

He made no protest as she began to strip his leather breeches, loin cloth, and moccasins from his body as he stretched out upon their blankets. Forcing herself to remain calm, Storm sponged him down, cleaning his many wounds carefully. Fortunately only the one in his shoulder made by Fire-Walker's tomahawk appeared bad. Efficiently she dressed it with the herbs She-Who-Seeks-Wisdom had given her, then bound it tightly. Afterward he rose and, reaching for his *nat'sakerna*, drew forth clean garments and dressed. Then he hauled the Apache's body from their dwelling, and Storm realized there was much work to be done.

'Herkiyani, we must find your parents now. They will be worried about you.'

The girl strode through the camp, searching for some sign of Moon-Raider or his chief wife, Ehkaraw'ro, who was Herkiyani's mother.

'Ehkaraw'ro.' She caught sight of the frantic woman.

'Oh, Eyes-Like-Summer-Rain' – and then – 'Herkiyani! Herkiyani!'

'*Pia*! *Pia*! Eyes-Like-Summer-Rain saved my life!' The child ran to her mother, crying.

'Hush, little one, hush. Oh, how can I ever thank you, Eyes-Like-Summer-Rain? I was so worried—'

'Herkiyani has already returned the favor,' Storm said and began to explain what had occurred.

'How terrible,' Ehkaraw'ro agreed when she had finished speaking. 'My tipi was among those burned.'

'Oh, Ehkaraw'ro.' Storm sympathized immediately, knowing Moon-Raider's chief wife was an orphan with no family on which to fall back. 'Mine has been damaged, but you are welcome to share it if you have made no other arrangements.'

'I am grateful for your offer, Eyes-Like-Summer-Rain,' Ehkaraw'ro thanked her gravely, 'for the tipis of Little-Cloud and Topsannah were also destroyed,' she mentioned Moon-Raider's other two wives. 'They have moved in with their own families for the time being.'

Storm was glad of Ehkaraw'ro's presence, for Woman-Of-The-High-Wind's dwelling had fallen prey to the flames as well, and She-Who-Seeks-Wisdom was busy helping her sister

319

salvage what she could from the ashes. Were it not for Ehkaraw'ro, Storm would have no one to assist her.

By late afternoon order had largely been restored in camp. What *Inde* bodies had not been carried off by the hated Apaches were burned in a huge funeral pyre. The dead of the Comanches were laid out and prepared for burial as well. With the exception of their homes, the losses of the Comanche were relatively few: seven warriors, four women, and two children. Five other women had been taken captive by the Apaches. Already a raid was being planned for their rescue. Storm marveled that Crazy-Soldier-Boy was miraculously unharmed. It seemed he had strong medicine indeed. Families were doubled up in the tipis that remained. In addition to Moon-Raider's chief wife and children, Storm had also taken in Shadow-Of-The-Hawk's second wife, Red-Wing, and her little boy, Tasura.

The Comanches had captured three *Inde* prisoners, warriors naturally since the Apaches' women had not accompanied them, and they were to be tortured slowly this evening. Storm feared their fate would not be pleasant. The Comanches had also seized many of the *Indes'* horses to increase their herd. Storm was stunned when Moon-Raider appeared at her dwelling, leading ten of the ponies.

'They are for you, Eyes-Like-Summer-Rain, for saving my daughter's life,' he said.

'You honor me by your gift, Moon-Raider,' she responded formally, knowing it would be churlish among the Comanches to protest his offering.

'Once more you are a woman of property, baby,' Wolf noted. 'You breed those horses carefully, and come next summer when we go to the fair in Santa Fe, you'll make a lot of money.'

'There's a fair in Santa Fe?'

'Yeah, every summer. The Plains Indians from miles around attend. We won't go this year because the winter was so hard, and especially after this attack The People need to rebuild and replenish their food stores.'

320

Storm studied her new stock expertly. They showed good blood, and she decided at once she would take Wolf's advice and begin to build a sizable herd of her own. Many of the Comanche women had done as much. It was a mark of their importance, wealth, and husband's success and favor. Unlike some Indian tribes and the White-Eyes' way of the times, a Comanche woman's property was hers, to do with as she wished, and even if she divorced him, her husband could not take it from her.

That night the entire camp gathered to celebrate their victory over the Apaches, for although the Comanches had lost many tipis, they had counted many coups, killed many *Indes*, and taken many scalps and ponies. Wolf told Storm to put on her wedding ensemble, which now served as her ceremonial outfit for religious rituals. He himself wore only his leather breeches and loin cloth. He painted himself fiercely with red war paint from his *tunawaws*. There were black palm prints on his broad chest to show he had killed an enemy in hand-to-hand combat, and he wore many feathers and jewelry and carried his charms, coupstick, and shield. Storm saw the other warriors were similarly attired, each with different markings as a sign of his accomplishments in today's battle.

First there was much feasting and dancing, then each warrior rose and, chanting, recounted his brave deeds. If no one disputed the honors he claimed, he was awarded them without question. If there were a disagreement, however, witnesses were called to verify or negate the man's story, and if he had lied, he was disgraced for counting false coups. Storm found it all highly primitive, yet interesting, for she realized the history of the Comanches had been passed down in just such a manner. When the three prisoners were paraded forward, however, the girl discovered she had no stomach for the torture and crept quietly away unseen. Only Wolf guessed that after what she had lived through this day she would not stay. When he was able, he slipped off after her. Somehow he knew where she had gone.

The river glittered as though it were diamond-encrusted beneath the silver halo of the full moon – a Comanche moon, Storm remembered and thought of the night Wolf had first taken her and made her his. The surface of the stream rippled gently as she divested herself of her garments and waded in. The water was cool and inviting, peaceful and soothing after the horrible *mêlée* of the day. Deftly the girl unplaited her long black braids and sank down into the little waves that washed over her restfully, cleansing her body and spirit. Her cascading mass of hair billowed out upon the waters like an ebony cloud before gradually it became heavy with the river, the strands floating slowly downward. Storm threw her head back, letting the stream catch hold of her, lift her softly with its sigh. She closed her eyes.

She had killed two men today, two Apache *Indes*, but nevertheless two human beings of God's creating. Somehow it didn't help to know they would surely have murdered her had she refused to defend herself. Oh, God, where was that girl who only a year ago had flirted and laughed and danced in a rose-colored gown of lace and lawn? Storm's feet touched the cold, sandy bottom of the river. She opened her eyes and stared at her reflection in the shimmering moonlight. The girl she had been was gone as Storm had known she would be. Eyes-Like-Summer-Rain had taken her place.

Wolf studied her quietly from the shadows on the shore, guessing her thoughts. Had he not asked himself the same question after the first time he had killed a man? It wasn't easy – taking a life – and he knew of no way in which to ease her sorrow. How could he tell her that it never grew less difficult, that it was as though a part of her would die too for each life taken if she were decent and honorable? Wolf's dark blue eyes filled with sadness briefly, for he knew the terrible price that must be paid for such; the little death that had come with each notch on his revolvers. Oh, Storm, Storm, I would spare you that. You are too young and innocent to grow hard and filled with hate.

She looks like a madonna, he thought suddenly, remembering the statue of the Virgin Mary that had stood in the chapel at the mission where he'd studied as a boy. How far away it all seemed now. He touched the rosary around his neck, and for a moment the words to the forgotten prayers tumbled to his lips as his fingers stroked the smooth beads, counting off the decades. His jaw set. He forced himself to stop, to shut out the memories that pervaded the very essence of his being. He would not see the young boy who knelt before the altar to receive the priest's blessing. He would not see the young boy who knelt over his mother's body to pull the rosary she had clutched desperately at the last from her stiffened fingers. He would not see the young boy who knelt at his father's grave and wept hot, bitter tears. He would not see the young boy who knelt alone upon the prairie and prayed for death. No matter how hard Wolf tried, however, scattered pictures of the boy flitted across his mind, blurred, and merged, colors running into one another as real and as vividly as though it were only yesterday he had been that boy.

She looks like a madonna, he thought again. I turned my back on God and prayed for death, and He sent me a madonna to ease my pain. Oh, God, where were you when *mis padres* died? he wanted to cry out with anguish; but he did not. They were dead, and it had happened a long time ago.

Storm rose from the water, her skin soft and shining where the moon's rays struck the little droplets that clung to her flesh. Her breasts were round and full with the coming child, their pink crests darkened to a dusky rose. Her belly swelled gently with Wolf's babe. He saw her place her hands upon the mound and whisper something in the night.

Slowly, silently he strode toward her. There was one way to take away the pain that haunted them both – with another type of little death – *le petit mort*, Storm called it – that came from creating life, not killing it.

Tenderly he pressed her down on the wild spring grass beneath the shelter of a sighing cottonwood and showed her that other kind of dying.

18

Summer came once more with its blistering sun that scorched the tall prairie grass until it was the color of old straw. Cathleen North stood upon the front porch of her father's sprawling antebellum mansion, lifting one hand to her forehead to shade her eyes against the glare of the brilliant yellow ball in the blinding blue sky. In the distance, beyond the gently sloping crests of the rippling plains that stretched into the arid, desertlike terrain farther on, she could see a dust devil dancing on the horizon, a whirling dervish of red. Her nostrils flared slightly as she caught the strange, stifling scent of the hot clay that had become the spinning cloud. The air was thick and heavy with it, and she knew a summer storm was blowing up. The sweltering atmosphere almost crackled with ominous foreboding. An odd sense of excitement raced through her veins. Abruptly she strode toward the stables.

Although Gabriel had given the ranch hands strict orders that Cathy was not to ride the range alone – it being dangerous and unseemly, he thought, for a woman of her position – no one tried to stop the girl as she galloped through the tall entrance arch of the white split-rail fence that enclosed the immediate vicinity of the house. Neither did it occur to any of the ranch hands to attempt to follow her. The first few times they had tried, she had actually fired several warning shots at them and yelled that the next bullets would find their marks if they didn't go away and leave her alone. None had doubted she'd meant what she'd said, so on this point only the ranch hands disobeyed their boss and were in tacit agreement to keep him from discovering their insubordination.

'Sides, they argued, if anyone could take care of herself, it were Cathleen North. She could drill the eye outta a prairie dog at fifty yards and were meaner than a rattlesnake too! Didn't she wear them britches and ride astride like a man? the ranch hands asked one another to ease their guilty consciences. Didn't she always have one of them little cigars clamped a'tween her teeth, and couldn't she turn even old Pop Daniels's ears red with her swearin'? Yes, and hadn't she once had a chawin' tobacco match with Lester Jones durin' Gabriel's absence and actually won? Shit, it jest weren't decent, a woman bein' able to spit like that! Nawsir, there weren't no reason a'tall to keep a tight rein on the boss's prize filly. A feller'd hafta be plum *loco* fer shore to tangle with that mannish wildcat. Joe Jack were right. She were a sour old maid and gittin' worse every day! Never a sweet smile or a dewy eye fer a man on the place. Nawsir, Gabriel didn't hafta worry none about that dried up old prune of a daughter of his. Weren't nobody interested in what were inside them britches of hers, no matter how graceful them long legs was. Hell, Miss Cathy were twenty-one years old and probably never even been kissed; she were so damned unappealin'! A feller wanted sumpin' soft and warm 'neath him at night. Makin' love to Cathleen North would be like beddin' a board. Yessir, a man'd jest as well find hisself a knothole for all Gabriel's daughter knew or cared about it.

The ranch hands were wrong, however, and the fact that they found her sexless and without feeling hurt Cathy deeply, for she knew what they all thought. Still how could she blame them? No one ever called on her, and since she was rich enough that her plain looks didn't matter, there had to be some reason for her lack of dates. She was frigid and unyielding, cold and heartless; that was the logical explanation – or so the ranch hands thought. A fellow didn't want a wife who acted like a man, a woman who had a sour face and a sharp tongue and would be as stiff as a ramrod in bed to boot.

What the ranch hands never guessed was that Cathy had so much love bottled up inside her she fairly ached with longing to give it away, but there was no one at Tierra Rosa who wanted it.

Gabriel would never consent to her marrying a mere ranch hand, and his spread was so massive their closest neighbors were nearly a hundred miles away. The few eligible bachelors she'd met, sons of land barons such as her father, had raised no spark of interest in her breast. They'd all been pompous and overbearing just like Gabriel and had talked cattle land and sheep until Cathy had wanted to scream, sitting on the veranda in her best dress and feeling a starched and pressed fool for nothing. Not a one had noticed the stars stretching out in the endless black sky like a cascade of fireworks or said she was pretty. No, they had lounged on the porch with their cigars and glasses of mint julep and pointed out the practical aspects of joining their vast acreages with her father's, of breeding dynasties and building empires. Cathy might just as well have been a brood mare for all the attention they'd paid her. Unceremoniously she'd sent them all packing and made it clear they weren't to come back. Puppets; that's what they'd been, their fathers' puppets – just as Gabriel had tried to make her his; only Cathy wasn't having any. Now she did as she damned well-pleased, hiding her hurt with a brittle façade that would have cracked if just once she'd ever let it; but she never did. She forced herself to stay strong, crushed down her yearnings and weaknesses with a determined fist, and never once shed a tear over her girlish dreams that would never become realities.

Over and over she told herself men were brutes, that they would use her with the callous savageness she'd seen displayed by her father when he'd killed that poor Mexican and raped the dead man's helplessly pleading wife so many years ago. The horrible memory was indelibly etched into Cathy's mind. No matter how hard she tried to forget it, she could still recall it all in lurid detail: the blood gushing from the mortal wound between the Mexican's eyes; the pitiful screams of the woman that had grown weaker and weaker until at the last they'd ceased completely, eerily; the boy shaking with terror and vomiting quietly onto the ground; and Gabriel fastening up his breeches before he'd taken the fatal deed from the Mexican's shirt pocket.

No, Cathy didn't want a man – at least not one like her father. So she stiffened her spine with pride and pretended to be something she really wasn't so that men of Gabriel's ilk and the crude ranch hands would leave her alone; and she dreamed of a gay cavalier who would press her down upon the sweet summer grass and take her gently, lovingly, with none of the brutality she remembered from that day so long ago, a man who would ask nothing of her in return – except herself. She wasn't interested in building a dynasty or an empire. She hated Tierra Rosa and all for which it stood with a passion that seethed hotly just beneath her outwardly calm and brusque demeanor. It was land ill-gotten, land that had been stolen and baptized with the blood of innocents, as though that might somehow wash it clean; but it hadn't. Cathy fancied she could smell the odor of hellfire and decay that lurked just below the surface of the rich clay soil, as though the land knew it had been ill-used and was simply biding its time – awaiting revenge.

Someday, when Gabriel was dead, Cathy was going to let the land take its vengeance. She was going to give her share back whence it had come, let the wilderness claim it as it had before her father had tamed it and bent it to his will. Yes, she was going to stand back and watch all that Gabriel had built crumble to ashes, just as she had watched her own dreams bite the dust as though they had never mattered or even been.

She galloped on challengingly toward the swirling cloud in the distance, a close, secret smile on her face turned headlong into the wind. Already Gabriel was beginning to learn what it meant to be defeated. He'd found his French fiancée and she'd scorned him and everything he'd offered. How angry he'd been, and how Cathy and Joe Jack had sniggered behind his back and raised their estimations of the bride-to-be.

'I'll lay you two to one he gets her in the end,' Joe Jack had wagered, 'or kills himself trying. Lord, pa just can't tolerate being beaten. There's going to be hell to pay before this is over; you mark my words.'

327

'Maybe,' Cathy'd drawled, 'but I'm putting my money on the chit. Anybody who'd rather take up with a half-breed gunslinger than pa can't be all bad. The girl's got guts; I'll say that for her.'

'An iron hand in a velvet glove? Well, well.' Joe Jack had whistled. 'Sounds mighty interesting if you ask me. I'm beginning to hope the old man *does* get her back.'

'More than one way to skin a cat, brother?' Cathy'd lifted one eyebrow coldly, guessing his line of reasoning. 'Yes, that'd be just like you. The final *coup de grâce* – getting the fiancée to lift her skirts for you while the old man's still around for you to throw it in his face. You'd have it all then wouldn't you? Tierra Rosa, the bride-to-be – everything of pa's you've ever coveted.'

'You might be plain, sis, but you sure ain't dumb. You'd better watch yourself if you want to be dealt a hand in this game,' Joe Jack had warned, grinning, then sauntered off.

Remembering the little scene, Cathy was suddenly clutched by a terrible sense of foreboding. Images of her slyly laughing brother and the shadowy figure of the French belle lying together in Gabriel's massive bed filled her mind, making her shiver uneasily in the ominous, hot quiet. Joe Jack was still smiling as he caressed the French girl's breasts, as he poised himself to take both her and Tierra Rosa. No! No! It's mine! Tierra Rosa's mine! Cathy thought wildly. *I'd kill to have it and see it destroyed*! Oh, God, she prayed, don't let pa bring her here. Don't let pa bring his fiancée here. Something awful will happen. I just know it!

As though to accentuate this the wind shifted suddenly; the dust devil Cathy had been following turned to chase her instead. Hell-bent, she rode toward Rosa Pequeño, a small shack high in the distant bluffs. There were two other larger camps, Rosa del Rio and Rosa del Sol, where the ranch hands sometimes bunked overnight when they couldn't make it back to Tierra Rosa proper, but Rosa Pequeño was Cathy's special hideaway. As she raced across the arid, rolling plains the swift summer storm broke at last, nearly blinding her with its fury of unleashed rain. Hurriedly she urged her big Palomino gelding, Sunny Boy, up the rocky, winding path to the leanto, stripped and rubbed him down, then made her way inside the cabin, slamming the door shut behind her.

The place was deserted, for which she was grateful. She paused for a moment to catch her breath, then moved to slip out of her wet clothes as the torrent pounded down upon the rooftop, making her feel as though she were safe and snug within her own private cocoon. Naked, she lay down upon the bed and closed her eyes, sighing. After a time her hands began to slide languidly along the length of her golden body. Her fingers touched her small firm breasts, taunting the dark honeyed nipples to stiff little peaks. Cathy liked the petite mounds; they were insolently pert, she had been told once. She moaned softly, recalling the way Sam had fondled them beneath her shirt and kissed her sweetly, tenderly, as she longed to be kissed. Her hips had strained against his in the summer hay yearningly, and she'd made no protest when his hand had slipped down to unfasten her breeches. She had known somehow that he would be gentle with her. Hadn't he said he cared nothing for Tierra Rosa? Hadn't he begged her to run away with him, leave it all behind? How wonderful it had been – to be sixteen and in love.

But then Gabriel had come and spoiled it for her, just as he'd always spoiled everything in her life. He'd thrown open the barn door with a furious wrench, flung himself up the ladder to the loft, and beaten Sam senseless, then yelled at him to pick up his pay and get out. Despite Cathy's pleading, Sam, seventeen and petrified, had gone. Afterward Gabriel had taken off his belt and walloped Cathy's back until her shirt had lain in blood-drenched ribbons across her welt-covered flesh. She hadn't cried out once or shed a single tear, just stared at her father with liquid brown eyes filled with hate and disgust. She'd never seen Sam again.

Cathy had been coming to Rosa Pequeño ever since, trying

to recapture that feeling she'd known when Sam had kissed her so softly, tentatively, searchingly blotting out the horror in her mind of Gabriel's assault on the dead Mexican man's wife that day so long past. She'd known then it didn't have to be like that – ugly, brutal, but she'd never again found another man who wasn't cut out of the same cloth as her father – or so she thought. Perhaps she just hadn't given them a chance, or perhaps Gabriel had chosen men who'd been carbon copies of himself. Cathy sighed once more. It didn't matter. Nothing mattered as the rain poured down outside as tempestuously as her naked body arched against her slender, suddenly frantic hands.

19

Cholera. The word had hung heavily in the air ever since Tabenanika had called Storm to his tipi to look at a sick warrior he could not cure.

'I have done all I know, Eyes-Like-Summer-Rain,' he had said, 'but my powers are not great enough to fight off this evil spirit of the *taberoh.* Do you know what it is the White-Eyes have brought to The People as they did the Spotted-Sickness?'

And Storm had answered, 'Cholera,' stricken.

It would sweep through the Comanches like wildfire, ravaging them, for the Indians had no immunities to the diseases brought to America by the white men: cholera, yellow fever, syphilis, smallpox.

The warrior groaned, doubling up on the blanket upon which he lay. Storm checked him again, daring to hope she might be wrong, but he was cold to her touch, his pulse faint, his skin withered. His face was drawn with severe pain from the muscle cramping in his abdomen. Even as she examined him he lifted his head weakly to vomit once more, then licked his parched lips before falling back, stupored.

'He must be kept warm, Tabenanika, beneath plenty of blankets, no matter how hot it is outside, and give him lots of water, however much he will drink. Otherwise he will dehydrate and die.'

'De – hy – drate,' Tabenanika repeated slowly. 'What is this, Eyes-Like-Summer-Rain?'

'Dry out. His body will lose too much fluid from the sickness. It must be replaced. He should be given some salt chips as well,' Storm directed, remembering how she had passed out in the heat from lack of salt and thirst that night in Wolf's camp. 'A tonic of boiled wild mint will help the nausea and cramping. Other than this, Tabenanika, I know of nothing we can do for him, except pray. I am sorry, father of my husband, but you must prepare yourself for others to fall ill with the disease. Cholera is truly an evil spirit. It will spread quickly through the camp. Many may die.'

Tabenanika's face was grave as he heard the news. 'Thank you for your honesty, Eyes-Like-Summer-Rain. I will go now and tell The People what you have said.'

The rain had stopped; the dust devil had long since dissipated. Silently Cathy pulled on her clothes and stepped outside. The tension that had built up in her body with the storm had eased. She smiled softly to herself as she saddled Sunny Boy and started down the trail toward home.

The sun had come out and was flaming across the dusk sky in shades of pinkish-orange and gray, pale and washed, like the moist earth into which the shod hooves of Cathy's gelding sank gently as they loped along. It was cooler now. A faint breeze stirred, rippling the tall prairie grass that had been beaten down but not broken by the torrent. Tomorrow the land would be steaming, Cathy knew, but the way it was now, soft and wet in the twilight, was the way she loved it best: hushed, still, seeming to wait breathlessly for its peacefulness to be disturbed, the quiet broken only by the lone cry of a hawk in the distance.

An unfamiliar sound intruded on Cathy's reverie – a low moan. She pulled Sunny Boy to a sudden halt; her ears pricked up cautiously. With a swift movement she bent and slipped her rifle from its saddle holster, then dismounted, creeping toward the brush from which the noise had emanated.

A strange man was lying upon the ground. Cathy made her way toward him slowly as he groaned again. Quickly, spying no wound upon him, she pressed her hand to his forehead. He was burning up with fever. His eyes flew open as she touched him, but he was delirious and did not seem to see her. How blue his eyes were, blue as the pale summer sky, she thought before they closed once more. Whistling for Sunny Boy, she unlashed her canteen and lifted the man's head to force a few sips of water between his parched lips. His dark mahogany hair with just a hint of copper was still damp from the rain, and his close-clipped mustache brushed her fingers like a feather as she placed the container to his mouth. He was soaked to the skin, and though his clothes bespoke him as a drifter, Cathy knew she could not leave him here, for he would surely die. Fortunately she was a strong woman, and her Palomino gelding was well trained.

'Down, Sunny; down,' Cathy ordered.

The horse lowered himself to the earth, rolling on one side. The girl dragged the stranger to the animal, managing to lay him over her saddle as she commanded Sunny Boy to rise, and the gelding sprang to its feet. The man would not be comfortable in his position, but at least Cathy would get him to Tierra Rosa. She mounted up and began the long slow trek back, trying not to jar the feverish drifter more than was necessary.

It was dark when she reached Tierra Rosa, but the house and the main grounds were ablaze with light and filled with ranch hands, many of whom were on horseback or preparing hastily to mount as Gabriel bellowed orders at the top of his lungs. To her dim surprise Cathy realized her father was organizing a search party for her.

'Jesus, sis, where in the hell have you been?' Joe Jack galloped toward her, hauling his stallion, King's Ransom, up shortly. 'The old man's fit to be tied and madder than hell! It won't surprise me none if he wallops your backside raw!'

'I got caught by the storm and rode it out at Rosa Pequeño. I'd have been home sooner, but I found this man lying in the brush. He's sick with some kind of fever. Help me get him inside, Joe.'

'Lord, Cath! He ain't one of ours. Looks like some kind of tramp or something if you ask me. Why didn't you just leave him or send a couple of the ranch hands to bring him in?'

'Didn't you hear me? He's sick. He needs help. He might have died out there.'

'Cathy! Cathy! Where in the hell have you been?' Gabriel thundered as he stormed up angrily. 'Do you realize you've been gone for hours, young lady, without so much as a by-your-leave to a soul, and that you disobeyed my strictest orders to boot? I told you not to ride out without one of the men accompanying you! Do you know all the trouble you've caused me? I was just about to send every frigging hand on the place out to look for you! You think these men have nothing else to do but chase all over the Goddamned ranch after you?'

'I'm sure they've got plenty of other things to do, pa. I don't know why you even bothered. I'm old enough to take care of myself. Hell, I reckon I'm a damned sight better shot than most anybody on Tierra Rosa – including you.'

'Don't you dare sass me, young lady. You're not too old for me to take my belt to your hide. What in the hell is that hanging over your saddle?'

'A man. What does it look like?'

'Don't be impertinent, miss. Is he dead?'

'No, just sick. I found him lying in the brush a little ways off from Rosa Pequeño. I'm taking him inside. He needs help.'

'You send him to the bunkhouse. Pop Daniels'll take a look at him, which is more than he deserves. Damned drifter. He's not one of my men. What in the hell is he doing on Tierra Rosa anyway?'

'How should I know, pa? For God's sake, get out of my way! He could be dying. I found him; he's my responsibility. I'm taking him inside.'

Cathy's jaw was set hard with stubbornness, although why she was suddenly so interested in the sick stranger and determined to care for him herself she couldn't have said. Without warning she found herself recalling the color of his eyes and the feel of his wet mahogany hair as she'd lifted his head. Gabriel noted the mulish lines about the corners of her lips, and his mouth tightened. She'd like nothing better than to

334

make a fool out of him in front of his men with an argument. He decided he wouldn't give her that satisfaction – the scornful bitch. Sometimes Gabriel hated his daughter just as much as he knew she despised him.

'Hilton. Lester. Give my daughter a hand here. The rest of you men get back to what you were doing.'

'Yeah, Boss,' they chorused as one as Cathy shot her father a smug, triumphant smirk.

Grimly he turned his back on her and dug his spurs into Buck's sides sharply.

Once inside Cathy called loudly for Abel. 'Abel! Abel, I want you to see the room next to mine is made up immediately. This man's sick, and he's going to need my attention.'

'Lawd, Miz Cathy.' Abel's eyes rolled skittishly. 'Dat ain' one o' Massah Nawth's gempmums. Does he know 'bout dis? What's he gwine ter say when he finds out yo done brought dat riffraff inter dis house?'

'Shut your mouth, Abel, and do as I say. Hilton, you and Lester get that man upstairs *pronto*. Maria! Luisa! Isabel! Come quickly. Bring some cold water, pitchers of it, and lots of towels and blankets.'

Abel preceded the ranch hands upstairs, grumbling under his breath as he lit the lamps in the chamber Cathy'd indicated and turned down the bed.

'Miz Cathy, yo'all done huht mah feelin's sumpin' fierce. We ain' a 'runnin' naw cheap hotel heah for trash lahke dat, an' Ah ain' naw wuthless portah ter be waitin' on dat riffraff hand-'n'-foot. Dis heah's beneath mah station. Yassum, it sho'ly is. Ah is Massah Nawth's puhs'nal butler an' valet, an' he ain' a gwine lahke yo hafing me fetch 'n' carry fo' dat naw-coun' strangah what's jes' buhnin' up wi' de feber. Lawd, Miz Cathy. What yo brang him inter dis hous fo'? Der ain' naw tellin' what he might haf.'

'Get his clothes off, and put him in bed,' Cathy told the two ranch hands, ignoring Abel's complaints with a practiced ease.

'Lawd, Miz Cathy, yo daddy will tan mah hide if'n he finds

out Ah let yo stay in heah whilst dey's strippin' dat man. Yo git on out now, yo heah me?'

'Oh, for heaven's sake, Abel! I've seen enough stud stock on this place to know what men are like!' Cathy snapped impatiently.

Abel swallowed hard at this and fled the room, while Hilton and Lester exchanged a quick, speculative glance, wondering if they'd missed something about Miss Cathy after all.

If she was so damned frigid, how come she'd been watchin' the breedin' process? their eyes asked each other silently.

They noticed too that although she turned away studiously as they removed the stranger's garments, she stole a covert peek at his nakedness from beneath her fringe of gold eyelashes and blushed faintly upon seeing what a fine figure of a man he was. He was tall and massively built, with hard muscles and darkly bronzed skin. A mat of mahogany hair covered his broad chest, tapering down along his flat belly to his firm thighs. Cathy saw that though his hands were calloused from hard work, his nails were evenly clipped and clean. All of a sudden she thought about those palms cupping her small firm breasts and gave a quick, ragged gasp.

'Get those blankets piled on him, girls,' she said more sharply than she'd intended. 'We'll have to sweat that fever out of him.'

Two hours later the stranger had started to vomit. Cathy wiped his face and mouth and held his head over a basin, trembling with unaccustomed fear.

Joe Jack entered the room crossly. 'You gonna sit up here all night? Pa wants to see you in his study.'

'Oh, Joe, the old man's going to kill me for sure this time,' Cathy breathed, wide-eyed.

'Why? What's wrong?'

'Oh, Joe, I – I think this man's got cholera.'

As Storm had predicted the disease spread through the *Kwerharehnuh* rapidly, sparing some, but attacking too many

336

more. It was especially hard on her to see the children stricken, and against all the Comanches' beliefs that tears were womanish and not to be given into she broke down and cried the day little Herkiyani died. Why had God spared the child from the Apaches only to let her fall prey to cholera? It wasn't fair. It just wasn't fair!

Despite her pregnancy, Storm nursed The People ceaselessly, day after day, night after night, until Wolf ordered her to stop, for she was mentally and physically exhausted, and he feared she would fall ill herself.

Some recovered, but many others died, among them both Masitawtawp's sons, Shadow-Of-The-Hawk and Naukwahip. Storm helped their wives lay them out for burial high in the bluffs where they would be left sitting against the canyon walls, facing the rising sun, their earthly treasures in hand as they waited for the Great-Spirit to come and claim them. She remembered the first time she had ever seen Naukwahip and how he had laughed and kept irritating Moon-Raider by telling him to cut out her tongue. Oh, God, he had only seen twenty-five winters; Shadow-Of-The-Hawk, who'd reminded her to pray to the Thunderbird to give Wolf strength in battle, had been only twenty-seven. Masitawtawp, who'd stood tall and proud, despite his forty winters, now looked like an old man – old before his time. The day She-Laughs-Like-A-Mountain-Stream fell sick Storm insisted Wolf tell him.

'It will break his heart, Wolf; he loves her so. I – I cannot tell him. You must do it.'

After the death of his *paraibo*, although Masitawtawp had not contracted the disease, he took his most cherished possessions and went to the high ground where after several days of fasting he simply died, his spirit broken, his will to live having been buried with his chief wife and sons. Storm thought his passing would kill Wolf, for Masitawtawp had practically raised him, and she knew how much her husband had loved his *ara*, his 'special friend and teacher,' he had said once. Wolf slashed his flesh and cut off his hair in mourning, even as Storm did, as was the Comanche way, and still the final grievous blows had not yet fallen.

Woman-Of-The-High-Wind went next, as stoically as she had lived, without complaint, though she'd been in terrible pain at the end; and the day after that She-Who-Seeks-Wisdom followed her sister to the grave. Wolf closed her eyes silently and carried her in his arms from her tipi, his dark visage void of whatever emotions he had bottled up inside. Storm's heart ached for him, for she knew he was remembering his real mother's loss as well.

'He is a strong warrior, Eyes-Like-Summer-Rain.' Moon-Raider tried to comfort her as they watched him walk away. 'He has known much sorrow in his life. Time will heal these wounds too; do not fear.'

But Storm was not so sure anymore as one by one she saw her husband's family and friends stricken. Only Crazy-Soldier-Boy, with his strange powers, the *posa* medicine with which his special guardian spirit had invested him, seemed immune to the cholera and grief it had brought, humming to himself quietly in his own peculiar world. Sometimes the girl watched him desperately, as though she could somehow fathom what it was that gave him such inner peace, but there was no answer in his dark expressionless eyes.

One morning Storm awoke, feeling as though there were something different about the day. All of a sudden she realized to her horror the chanting of Tabenanika and the rattle of his gourds were missing.

No! No! Oh, *Sainte Marie*, Mother-Moon, have mercy; have mercy! Wolf cannot bear it. *I* cannot bear it! Oh, *mon Dieu, mon Dieu*!

Storm ran to the old shaman's tipi, forgetting in her haste to announce her presence before entering. Tabenanika was lying upon his blankets, his gourds scattered in the dirt beside him. Wolf knelt at his side, one of his father's hands clasped tightly in his own. Wordlessly her husband glanced up at her as she came inside. With a swift motion of his hand Wolf indicated he wanted her to leave. Quietly Storm respected her husband's wishes, knowing the *puhakut* was dying and that Wolf wanted to be alone with his father at the end.

After the girl had gone Wolf turned back to Tabenanika, lifting the shaman's head slightly as he realized his father was trying to speak to him.

'My *tua*.'

'Yes, *ap'*, I am here.'

'My *tua*,' the *puhakut* repeated slowly. 'My spirit shall not roam The Land much longer.'

'No, *ap'*—'

'Do not seek to hide the truth from me, Brother-Of-The-Wolf. A man knows when the time has come for his spirit to join the Great-Spirit, and the Comanches do not fear death as the *tabeboh* do.'

My parents, they killed my parents!

Your parents are not dead, Hisusanchis. Death is but the door that leads to the Great-Spirit and eternal life. It is the door through which we all must pass someday.

I am afraid, ap'.

Do not fear, Hisusanchis, for does not the Great-Spirit who gives us winter also give us spring?

'I know, *ap'*,' Wolf replied solemnly, 'but it does not make our parting any easier.'

'Life was not meant to be easy, my *tua*, for those things that come too easily are empty and without meaning, as is the man whose moccasins have followed such a path. Do not weep for me, Brother-Of-The-Wolf. My life has been hard and filled with the rewards of my struggles. I am an old man, and the old ways are dying. It is right that I die with them. My eyes have seen the future, my *tua*, and my spirit could not be at peace in The Land I have seen. I have fought long and hard, but the White-Eyes are too many and too powerful. Soon The Land will no longer belong to The People, but to the *tabeboh*.'

'No, *Ap'*—'

'Yes, Brother-Of-The-Wolf. In my heart I know this to be

true. It grieves me, my *tua*, for I am a proud man, but this is the way of life. All things must change. All things must die.'

The bird is dead, Rafael.

But why, Father Francisco? Only last night it was so much better.

'*For everything there is a season and a time for every matter under heaven.*' This is the way of God, Rafael. It is not for us to question the Lord.

'Why, *ap*'? Why must things change? Why must they die?'

'So that each man may fulfill his destiny, Brother-Of-The-Wolf. Do you remember when you came to the *Kwerharehnuh* my *tua*?'

'Yes, *ap*'.'

'You had lost your parents and I, my sons. Had your parents not died, you would never have run away from your home, and had my sons lived, I would not have adopted you. The Great-Spirit saw this and knew what must be done so that our lives would intermingle.'

'But why, *ap*'?'

'Because the winds of change are sweeping across The Land, and The People will need one of their own to help them understand the ways of the *tabeboh*. You, who have been one of us, yet not one of us, will teach them these ways, even as The People have taught you the ways of the *Kwerharehnuh*. Yes, when the time comes, Brother-Of-The-Wolf, both The People and the White-Eyes will have need of men such as you if The Land is to survive. This the Great-Spirit saw and so sent you to us. Help The People as they have helped you, my *tua*. Do not cling to the past and allow your bitterness to blind you to the future. As the Great-Spirit took one wife and child from you, so He has given you another, even as He gave us each other in our sorrow. She is a good woman, Eyes-Like-Summer-Rain. She loves you deeply. Be kind to her, for the love of a good woman is to be treasured and cherished. Soon you will be the father of her child, Brother-Of-The-Wolf, and you will raise your son, even as I have raised you. He and the others of his generation will be the *Kwerharehnuh*'s hope for The Land and the future and the new world in which they will live. The Great-Spirit has given you the knowledge, my *tua*. Build a place for The People so that they will not perish, but survive; a place where your son and theirs may learn the old ways so that they will not be forgotten, but will live on in their hearts and spirits whatever paths their moccasins may follow. Do this, Brother-Of-The-Wolf, for me. It is my dying wish of you, who have been my son as truly as those who were of my own blood, you, who have been my joy and solace in this hour I once thought to spend alone, an old man, empty and bereft of all I knew. If I never told you before, I tell you now: I love you, Brother-Of-The-Wolf, my *tua*. Go now, and may the Great-Spirit walk beside you and give you strength.'

I love you, Brother-Of-The-Wolf, my tua.

How long Wolf had waited to hear those words. Hot tears stung his eyes, blinding him, blurring the image of his father's proud still face. *I love you* . . . Wolf did not know how long he knelt there before at last he realized Tabenanika's hand was cold in his. His shoulders shaking with silent sobs, he rose and wrapped his father in the albino buffalo robe he had given Tabenanika so many years ago.

'And I love you, *ap*', who were my father as truly as *Don Diego Ramon Delgados y Aguilar* was,' he spoke softly before he laid his head on the old shaman's breast and wept.

Many of the ranch hands were taken ill with the cholera that had swept through Texas in epidemic proportions. The cemetery at Tierra Rosa was fresh with newly dug graves, but that of the stranger was not among them. Much to Cathy's secret delight and ceaseless vigil, he had survived.

Ross Stuart. She said his name silently to herself over and over as she climbed the stairs to his room, carrying a silver tray laden with hot, nourishing soup. *Ross Stuart.* It was a nice name, she told herself, a good name; and as she remembered the way his blue eyes had gazed at her upon his finally regaining

341

consciousness and how his white teeth had flashed as he'd smiled his thanks weakly, Cathy felt herself tremble with yearning and suddenly wished his name were her own. You've got to stop this! she warned herself sternly. The man's a drifter; you don't know anything about him! Yet deep in her heart she was glad that in his delirium he had called for no one special.

With a soft knock she turned the knob on the door and went in. He was propped up among the pillows in the massive four-poster bed. Washed and shaved this morning, he looked even more handsome than she had imagined. His dark copper-tinged hair had been brushed back in neat wings, and his mouth beneath his mustache was sensuous and inviting. Her thin cheeks flushing faintly, Cathy dropped her brown eyes to the gold piece he wore around his neck and that fairly glittered against his bronzed furry chest.

'Mornin', Miss Cathy.'

She knew if she looked up in that moment, he would be grinning softly at her, his sky blue eyes sparkling and the long furrows of his dimples on either side of his lips showing warmly, enchantingly. He would look like a pirate or a devil-may-care rake, with just a hint of the steely strength and power that lay beneath the surface of his charm. Cathy's heart pounded as she moved to set the tray across his lap and plump up his pillows.

'Good morning, Mr Stuart. I've brought you something to eat – nothing solid yet, I'm afraid. The doctor said to give you a few more days. I hope you like chicken soup. I – I made it myself—' She broke off, suddenly aware she was rambling nervously.

He grasped one of her slightly shaking hands gently but firmly. 'Hey, I thought I asked you to call me Ross, and, yes, I love chicken soup, especially when it's been made by someone as purty as you.'

Cathy raised her eyes to his slowly. 'That's the first time in my life anyone's ever told me I was pretty,' she said quietly. Even Sam had never told her that.

'Well, then, Miss Cathy, I reckon them boys of your father's jest been ridin' the range too long, got too much dust in their eyes to recognize a purty gal when they see one.' Then brusquely he released her hand, turning his attention to the tray. 'My, my, that shore does look good, Miss Cathy. Fairly steamin' outta the bowl, ain't it?'

'Yes, I – I was afraid it might have gotten cold, but it hasn't. Be careful you don't burn your tongue.' Too anxiously she tied the generous napkin around his neck and rearranged the silverware just so, trying to cover up for her lack of poise and only succeeding in making it more prominent. 'I brought you a newspaper too. I – I thought you might enjoy it, even though it *is* a trifle old. We only get one when someone goes into San Antonio for supplies.'

Lord, what was the matter with her, blushing and stammering around like a school girl? Fussing over him like a mother hen? What must he be thinking? Abruptly she fell silent once more, embarrassed and mortified by her behavior.

'Well, Miss Cathy, I ain't much fer readin', but I'd shore appreciate it if you'd stay, and tell me the more interestin' parts while I'm eatin'.'

Glad of something to do with her hands, which suddenly seemed to have a will of their own quite contrary to hers, Cathy pulled up a chair, sat down, and opened up the newspaper. Briefly she cleared her throat, then began to relate the stories she thought he'd want to hear, glancing up now and then hesitantly to reassure herself he was listening and not just being polite. She was petrified she would bore him to tears. As though he understood this, occasionally he interjected a comment or two, his observations making her realize he was a lot more intelligent than he cared to let on. Gradually she started to relax, unaware he was handling her as he would a newly broke, skittish filly, for beneath his warm but elusive façade and naturally suspicious nature he was a kind man. He had taken to Cathy right off and especially after meeting her father and brother had sensed instinctively what lay beneath

343

the image she tried so hard to project and why she felt she had to guard her innermost feelings so fervently. She was deeply afraid of being hurt, laughed at, and rejected. Since Ross himself often employed the same devices for the same reasons, he'd recognized in Cathy a kindred spirit.

He studied her small, slender shoulders and the stubborn set of her chin as she continued to read aloud to him. He marveled at the frailty that lay beneath her outward strength and thought those at Tierra Rosa blind that they could not see it. She might be a defensive little spitfire, but he was willing to wager that deep down inside she wanted nothing more than to find some man who would protect her from her bullish, overbearing father and sly, weasel-like brother – both of whom he'd dismissed immediately as selfish, insensitive schemers.

As outsiders sometimes do, Ross saw the picture at Tierra Rosa far more clearly than those who lived with it on a day-to-day basis, and his heart went out to Cathy. He wasn't a man to rush into things, but he decided then and there to remain at Tierra Rosa. A ranch its size always needed experienced hands, and Ross was good at what he did. Yes, for the time being he would stay on at Tierra Rosa and see what happened.

20

The Great Plains stretched out endlessly before them in tall, rippling waves of pale yellow and brittle green. Storm's heart was heavy in her breast. Several weeks had passed since they had left the *Kwerharehnuh*, and Wolf had scarcely said a word. It was as though a wall had grown up between them. He had shut her out once more, alone with his grief, for it was not his way to share his pain, and she could not reach him.

I loved them too, she wanted to cry out, to somehow capture his attention. Let us share the burden of our sorrow. But she did not speak of these things to her husband, who seemed almost a stranger to her again. His mood was too black, too brooding. She remembered how he had turned against her in San Antonio, and she feared to breach the chasms of his silence.

She felt lost and alone. She missed The People dearly and had not wanted to leave them after the cholera had run its course, but one morning Wolf had come to their tipi without a word, and Storm had known they must go. There'd been no need for him to tell her. His black silk garments and the pistols at his hips had said it all.

They'd traveled purposefully at first, making for Fredericksburg where they'd sold Storm's horses, the animals being too much of a burden for just the two of them to handle on their journey. Though she had been sorry to see the beasts go when she'd had such big plans for the herd, the girl had made no protest in light of Wolf's dark somber manner. Besides, he had given her the profit they'd made, telling her chillingly to save it, that she might need it, and she'd been too filled with foreboding for the future to worry over the loss of her ponies. What had he meant by the cryptically spoken comment? For days afterwards she had pondered it anxiously. At night when they'd lain together untouchingly upon their blankets she had placed her hands over her full round belly and been sick with fear that Wolf intended to leave her and their child.

Ever since they had wandered aimlessly, and sometimes Storm knew he looked at her and saw only the color of her skin. She was sure he despised her for it, for it had been those of her ilk who had brought the cholera to Texas.

'Wolf, I can't help being white,' she had said once, but he had merely stared at her, then turned away without speaking.

And so they rode on, unaware Gabriel North and his men had attacked the *Kwerharehnuh* camp shortly after their leaving and, discovering them gone, had hired his own private band of gunslingers and Indian scouts to track them down. Sheriff Martin had been horrified, claiming it was the posse's business to find Mr North's fiancée, but Gabriel had lost his patience and temper and sneered at the sheriff arrogantly, telling him to mind his own damned business, that he'd had his chance and flubbed it.

'Mr North,' Sheriff Martin had whined. 'I feel it is my duty to remind you El Lobo has done nothin' to break the law. Yore little bride-to-be chose to stay with him out of her own free will. If these hired ruffians of yore'n kill her husband outright without a fair fight, you'll all be guilty of murder, and if she wants to press charges agin you, I'll hafta arrest you.'

'You do what you think is right, Lonnie, and let me do the same,' Gabriel had growled warningly. 'And don't forget I'm a big man in these parts. I've got a long memory, and my arm's got a powerful reach.'

Sheriff Martin had swallowed hard and decided it would be best if he looked the other way as far as Gabriel North and his fiancée were concerned.

Almost as though he sensed he were being followed, however, Wolf traveled swiftly and without any discernible pattern to his movements, so Gabriel's men found nothing, had nothing to report.

'Lord, pa, when are you going to give up this foolishness?'

346

Joe Jack asked snappishly one day. 'Those damned men are costing you a fortune!'

Gabriel stared hard at his son, his eyes narrowed. 'My money's not yours yet, Joe Jack,' he noted curtly.

Afterward Joe Jack told Cathy darkly that the old man had gone off his rocker for sure this time, but Cathy, wrapped up in her dreams about Ross Stuart, had forgotten her ominous sense of foreboding that day of the summer storm and paid no heed.

Fall had burst upon the land with its brilliant splendor. A faint breeze was stirring as Storm gazed out over the seemingly endless terrain. It was vast and empty, and for a moment she felt as though she stood in the very palm of God's hand. Yes, she decided, it was good, a good day, a good place for her child to be born. Slowly she halted Madame Bleu beneath the shelter of a cluster of mesquite trees and dismounted, wincing slightly as another small twinge of pain coursed through her body.

'It is time, my husband,' she said as Wolf looked down at her questioningly.

He nodded grimly, surprised she had managed to continue for as long as she had, for her water had broken several miles back when they had halted for their midday meal.

Silently they began to make preparations, building a fire, setting water to boil, and laying out the clean deerskin rags they would need. Briefly their eyes locked as they unwrapped the cradleboard Wolf had made. Tears filled Storm's momentarily, threatening to spill over as she thought of Woman-Of-The-High-Wind, She-Who-Seeks-Wisdom, and She-Who-Laughs-Like-A-Mountain-Stream who had wanted so much to help with the birthing of this baby. Wordlessly Wolf took the girl's hand in his, understanding her unspoken anguish.

'They are here in spirit, Storm, if not in flesh,' he told her softly.

It was the first time he'd made mention of his dead

Comanche family since leaving the camp of the *Kwerharehnuh*. She was startled and touched, guessing how much it had cost him.

'Thank you, my husband.'

Storm was in her Indian garments, not having been able to fasten her breeches over her extended belly. Now she removed the clean pantalettes and skirt she had put on after her water had broken, as well as her doeskin blouse and *peplum*. Naked, she began to walk deliberately as Wolf's mothers had shown her to ease the pain, the hard ground warm against her bare feet. Wolf bent to spread her blankets upon the prairie grass, then unsheathed his knife and held it to the flames of the fire to sterilize it.

It was as though his solitary mood had never been, for through it all he supported Storm, helping her to stand, holding her, rocking her, massaging her aching back when the contractions became sheer agony, and her legs would no longer support her. At the end she squatted upon the earth over her blankets, bracing herself against the trunk of a mesquite tree, while Wolf knelt down before her, his hands ready to receive their child as she started to bear down, to force the baby from her womb. Sweat ran down into her eyes as she grimaced with pain and concentration. She bit down on her lip so hard she drew blood in an effort to keep from crying out, for it was the way of a Comanche woman to be strong and silent when giving birth.

At last the tiny head with its fluff of black hair appeared. Wolf caught the puckered-up little face gently, his dark visage filled with wonder and awe as he beheld it.

'You're doing fine, Storm,' he encouraged the girl quietly as she paused, panting hard for a minute.

She pushed again and again, and finally the baby's slippery body slid from hers. Deftly Wolf stroked its small chest, forcing air into the tiny lungs. The child gave a lusty cry. Smiling, he pressed the new-born infant into Storm's outstretched arms. She caressed it lovingly, marveling at how small it was as she wiped the mucus from its eyes and nostrils and counted its fingers and toes. Wolf held out one hand tentatively to the baby. Its little fist closed tightly around his finger. The infant quieted, making soft sucking noises as together Storm and Wolf explored it slowly, as though they were scarcely able to believe that between them they had created this tiny miracle, this small bundle of joy that had been born of their passionate union and love.

It is as Tabenanika said, Wolf thought. I have taken his place and my son, mine. '*For everything there is a season . . .*' How much I want to love and protect this child even as Tabenanika did me.

Storm glanced up at her husband shyly, wondering what he was thinking.

'*Eh-haitsma.* It is your close friend,' she spoke proudly, her eyes shining with happiness and unshed tears.

'He shall be called Chance-The-Autumn-Wind, for he has come to us upon the wings of such.'

'It is a good name, my husband.'

Wolf cut the life-giving umbilical cord, tying it off with a piece of thong. Then he bathed the baby and wrapped it in one of the deerskin rags that would serve as its swaddling clothes. After Storm had expelled the afterbirth, he buried it and said a prayer over the mound, asking the Great-Spirit to watch over his new-born son. When all was done as the girl directed, she cradled her child against her breast and slept.

It was as though the coming of the baby breathed new life into Wolf, for gradually his grief began to heal and his black mood to lighten. The Great-Spirit had claimed his Indian family, but spared his wife and given him a son to fill the empty void in his life, just as he had once been given to Tabenanika for a similar purpose. Sometimes he gazed at Storm and Chance, as they called the boy, and it scarcely seemed possible they belonged to him. Love for them both welled up in his heart and spilled over whenever his eyes fell upon them, and his dark past seemed far away, forgotten.

They spent the winter in San Felipe del Rio, Wolf making no attempt to travel to the *Llano Estacado*. Storm did not mention it, knowing his wounds would have been opened afresh by the journey. Someday he would find it in himself to rejoin The People, but the time must be of his own choosing. She knew the *Kwerharehnuh*, with their deep sensitivity, would understand why he did not seek the camp high upon the Staked Plain that year and forgive his absence, just as they had understood and forgiven his leaving. In his heart, no matter what, he was and would always be one of The People. That was all that counted.

The following spring he took Storm deep into Mexico and there, upon a little patch of land she called *Fin Terra*, Land's End, built her an adobe house with a split-rail fence, while she planted a vegetable garden and tended the chickens she'd acquired at the farmers' market in a nearby town. During those two years that followed she was often to wonder how she, the belle of five counties, had come to live in the small thatch-roofed hut she called home and been happy. Had she seen it through the eyes of the Southern belle she had once been, she would have sneered at the shack and called it a hovel, but seeing it through the eyes of the woman she was, she knew it only as the place where on a peg over the stone hearth Wolf had hung up his guns at last to settle down; and life was good.

Storm awoke each morning and bathed in the river that wound through the small valley upon whose gently sloping crest Wolf had built their house. She fed the chickens and later the pigs, goats, and cow her husband bought, then weeded and watered her vegetable garden, picking fresh produce each day for their meals. After that she moved to the kitchen where she baked bread and churned butter. Sometimes there would be a fruit pie simmering over the fire if she'd been to market that week, and Wolf's mouth would water as he watched it cook, knowing it would be hot and good on the table that evening.

At night Storm would light the oil lamp and sew, patching Wolf's garments or making new clothes for little Chance, who seemed to grow like a weed. It wasn't long before he could say '*maman*' and '*ap*" and then all sorts of words in four different languages, for Storm and Wolf communicated in an odd mixture of French, English, Comanche, and Spanish, depending upon their moods.

They laughed when Chance took his first hesitant steps and fell, his face puckering up dreadfully, although he had learned early on never to cry. Wolf had insisted on this, for a crying baby was a danger to the Comanches, giving warning of their presence to enemies and game alike. The first few times Chance had set up a howl, Wolf had told Storm to take him into the brush and leave him there in his cradleboard until he stopped. She had been horrified by her husband's command and at first refused it, but Wolf had been adamant. Someday they would journey again to the *Llano Estacado*, and Chance must be as the other Comanche children, even more so, for he was a breed, and it showed plainly in his features.

'He must be all that I am – and more,' Wolf had said, 'if he is to survive as I have.'

And Storm had gazed at her precious son and wondered what was to become of him.

She loved him fiercely, the bond between them strengthened even more by the fact that she breast-fed him for a year before weaning him. Indian women often nursed their children for even longer periods of time as a natural method of birth control, but this was something to which Storm was averse. She wanted to give Wolf children. He was a proud man. He would expect it, would take joy in each new arrival as proof of his manhood and virility.

He took Storm nightly as he had done before Chance's birth, held her in his arms and whispered his strange words of love, wrapping her long black hair around his throat, binding her to him forever; and if sometimes he glanced longingly at his guns and then disappeared to brood darkly for a time, Storm knew better than to question him. She could only hope their love and their child were stronger than the hold his mysterious past and restless blood had upon him.

'Love me,' he would whisper in the darkness. 'I need you, baby. God, how I need you.'

And she would press herself against him feverishly, wanting to chase away the shadowed demons of the past and the deaths that tormented him so.

'They are only ghosts, Wolf, and we all must live with those. Your father and your mothers would not want you to grieve so for them.'

'And I do no longer, for I know they are with the Great-Spirit. It is the others who haunt me, Storm, the others who do not rest in peace. I have forsaken them for you and my promise to Tabenanika.'

'What others?' she asked, chilled to the bone. 'The ones who are notches on your guns? But surely you cannot hold yourself to blame for them!'

'No, I do not regret them, though their deaths too lie upon my spirit. It is the others.'

Storm could get nothing more from him but this, and she shivered in the blackness as she lay awake and wondered whom he had forsaken for her and his promise.

Dusk settled upon the land with shrouded hush, turning the horizon to a mass of fire as the sun sank slowly in the west. In the distance the cottonwoods whispered with a plaintive sigh, and the cattle moaned lowly. Here and there a meadowlark chirped, but other than this the silence was broken only by the pounding of Cathy's heart.

Two years. Ross had stayed two years, and now he was leaving. She swallowed hard, trying to force down the lump in her throat, fearing it would choke her. For the first time in her life tears stung her eyes, but she raised her chin in that stubborn little gesture Ross had come to know so well and refused to let them fall.

He mustn't think I care, she told herself determinedly. After all, it isn't as though he hasn't been honest with me. He's never spoken of loving me, never tried to lead me on. Oh, if only I hadn't dared to hope—

'I will be sorry to see you go, Ross. You've been a good hand and a good friend,' she spoke, looking at the endless, twilight summer sky, her surprisingly steady hands upon her reins – anything, but him.

'It's a good job, Miss Cathy, foreman of the Chaparral. It's a big ranch, nearly as big as your father's, and Mr Kingston's offered me a mighty nice wage. I figger in about five years I'll have enough money saved up to buy me a place of my own if I'm careful. 'Course, it'll be kinda lonely with jest me on the homestead.'

'Yes, I imagine it will,' Cathy responded, thinking suddenly of Sally, Frank Kingston's pretty daughter, and wishing she hadn't.

'Miss Cathy.' Without warning Ross halted his horse and reached out to take her hand. 'I've a mind to say a piece now, and I'd appreciate it if you'd git down off that geldin', and walk with me a ways.'

'All right.'

Her reply was so low, Ross almost didn't hear it, and she still had her face turned away from his so that he couldn't tell what she was thinking. Cathy prayed he couldn't hear how loudly her heart was beating in her breast as he tied their horses to a mesquite tree and took her arm. They strolled a little way in silence before Ross stopped and, cupping her chin, turned her countenance up to his, his sky blue eyes suddenly dark and serious.

'I'm a proud man, Miss Cathy. My pa run off when I were jest a boy, and ma raised nine of us young'uns in a two-room shack. I've fought and scratched my way up in the world and never asked nothin' of nobody. But there comes a time in every man's life when he's gotta bend a little if he wants sumpin' bad enough. Five years is a long time, Miss Cathy, but I'm – I'm askin' you to wait fer me.' He paused and took a deep breath. 'I ain't never spoke up before, seein' as how you was the boss's daughter and all, and I didn't have nothin' much to offer you. I still don't, but I reckon that don't matter none to you. You ain't cut out fer the kinda life yore leadin'. Shoot, Miss Cathy, you need a home of yore own and a couple of young'uns tuggin' at yore skirts, a man who loves you fer what you are and not what yore pa'd like fer you to be. I know I ain't much, but I love you, Miss Cathy. I love you fer yoreself and not what you stand fer. I love the way yore eyes kinda melt when they look at me and how them freckles kinda sparkle on yore face when you've been out in the sun too long and how yore mouth's too wide fer yore skinny face and how you've always got one of them damned cigars clamped a'tween yore teeth. I wanna wake up every mornin' and see you smilin' at me with that golden hair a'tumblin' down around yore shoulders from my lovemakin' and yore sun-browned skin jest a'glowin' where I touched it. Jesus! I ain't much fer words, and here I am ramblin' on like a fool. I guess the long and short of it is I wantcha fer my wife, Miss Cathy, and I don't want no part of yore pa's land or money. That's why I'm askin' you to wait. Will you – will you wait fer me, Miss Cathy?'

'Oh, Ross, it seems as though I've waited all my life for you. I reckon I can wait a little longer,' she cried before she flung herself into his arms.

Then somehow they were naked, and he was pressing her down upon the sweet summer grass, his mouth on hers hungrily, his hands fondling her swelling breasts, thumbs flicking at the dark nipples that hardened eagerly beneath his palms. His lips found the rigid little buds, sucking gently as his fingers slipped down to caress the dark blond triangle between her thighs. Cathy's legs opened for him of their own accord, her womanhood quivering as he stroked it slowly, taking his time, knowing she was a virgin. Hesitantly he probed her, still kissing her breasts. She was wet and warm where he touched her. He lowered his mouth to taste her.

'Oh, God, Ross, no. No!'

But he paid her no heed.

'Shhhhh. I wanna know all of you, honey – in every way. Ain't nothin' wrong with that.'

He spread her thighs even farther apart with his hands as his tongue found her, making her gasp. Quicker and quicker it darted, hot and hungry upon her pulsating mound, until a burning ache started deep in her loins and began to travel like wildfire through her veins. The secret place between her flanks throbbed, harder and faster, heightening, building until at last she arched her hips and gave a small sob, biting down on the knuckles of one hand to keep from crying out as suddenly his shaft pierced her, spiraling down deep into the very core of her being. He caught her legs, draped them over his shoulders as he plunged into her again and again, his muscle-corded arms rippling with the movements of his body until finally he shuddered atop her and was still.

Afterward he got his canteen and, wetting his bandana, washed every inch of her still smoldering flesh, lingering over those places that still tingled from his lovemaking.

'I love you,' he said. 'I wantcha to remember that tonight when yore lyin' in bed in that big old mansion, and I'm out in the bunkhouse thinkin' about you.

'I will,' Cathy breathed. 'Oh, Ross, I will!'

21

Fin Terra, Mexico, 1852

Morning broke over Fin Terra softly as it was wont to do in the valley that lay beyond the vast Sierra Madres in the distance. The sun crept over the horizon slowly, a pale blush of pink in the purple-and-blue washed sky where wisps of white clouds floated and clung to the peaks high above the land.

Storm breathed in the fresh air deeply, flinging her hands wide, as though to envelop the world in her arms and press it close for just a moment against her breast. She laughed out loud. Chance, by her side, glanced up at her wonderingly. Still smiling gaily, Storm took his hand and began to sing a French ballad as they walked toward the river. Catching her happy mood, the boy suddenly broke away from her grasp and started to run.

'Race you to the bank, *maman!*' he cried.

With joy in her proud gray eyes Storm watched him as he ran, his short little legs pumping up and down enthusiastically as after giving him a head start, she loped after him. He squealed with delight as she pretended she was gaining on him and with a shout flung herself upon him. Together they went rolling down the soft grassy bank to the river's edge. Briefly Storm cradled the boy close before, eyes sparkling, he wriggled out of her grasp and began stripping off his buckskin breeches. In minutes his small brown body was naked, and he was diving into the water, skin flashing like a fish beneath the shimmer of the morning sun. Storm divested herself of her garments more sedately, then waded in after him, trying, without success, to keep her face stern when he suddenly sprang up behind her, splashing her teasingly before he slipped away.

'Don't forget to wash your ears, young man,' she called, 'or

Piamermpits will get you.'

'The big cannibal owl doesn't frighten me,' he boasted back. 'If I see him, I will shoot him with the bow and arrows *ap'* made for me.'

'What about the *Sehkwitsit Puhitsit* then?'

'The mud men do not scare me either,' he said, trying to swagger in the water and only succeeding in thrashing about instead, much to Storm's amusement. 'I am a *paradadeha*, and someday I will be a *tuthuhyet*.'

'So, big boy, you think to be a big war chief, do you?'

'Oh, *oui, maman*! I will lead many raids and count many coups, like so.'

Chance began to prance about as though he were riding a fiery stallion, whooping and hollering, vibrating his hand against his lips to make that odd battle cry that was peculiar to the Indians.

'Heathen little savage, ain't he, that boy of yore'n? Jest like his pappy, huh, *lady*?'

Storm froze at the sound of the voice behind her, that high, whining tone she had thought never to hear again as long as she lived. Still disbelieving her ears, she turned slowly to face Billy Barlow.

'*Mon Dieu*,' she breathed, and then frantically, 'Run, Chance; run!'

The boy glanced up in sudden alarm at her cry, then without hesitation dove beneath the rippling waves as the strange, scraggly man he saw mounted on horseback upon the riverbank started toward him, gelding lunging in the water. Some yards downstream Chance broke to the surface, gasping for air, then floundered quickly toward shore, terrified, his mother's screams ringing horribly in his ears momentarily before there came an even more ominous silence. Petrified, the boy began to run, scarcely feeling the bite of the coarse prairie grass, intermingled here and there with rough sand and cactus spines, upon his bare feet.

'Gawddamn that brat of yore'n!' Billy swore as he rode

Storm down, then hauled her struggling, naked figure up before him in the saddle.

He yanked the horse around, galloping heedlessly through the cottonwoods, pines, and mesquite trees that dotted the valley, trying to catch the escaping boy. Storm spared not a second thought for her own plight. All her concern and concentration was riveted on her own son's safety as she clawed and bit and kicked in Billy Barlow's grasp, tearing wildly at the reins he held in one hand, forcing the horse to careen recklessly this way and that. Low-hanging branches slapped at her face, leaving stinging scratches as the outlaw caught her mass of wet, unbound hair, jerking her head back in an attempt to restrain her. At last, seeing he could not handle Storm and capture her son as well, he swore loudly again, turned his horse, and dug his spurs into the animal's already lathered sides cruelly.

Within minutes the lush green valley Storm had called home for over the past two years was far behind her, and she was once more the prisoner of Billy Barlow.

The girl did not know how many hours or miles they had ridden, except that dusk had long since fallen, and she ached in every bone of her body. It had been a long time since she had done any strenuous traveling. She felt utterly exhausted, dazed with weariness and shock, still unable to credit what had occurred; everything had happened so fast. Her legs were stiff and sore, the muscles in her calves cramped from clinging to the horse. Her naked flesh was chafed raw where it had rubbed against the saddle. She had no idea where she was or where this filthy criminal she had thought long gone from her life was taking her. She was only vaguely aware that the gently swelling crests of the rolling countryside had been replaced by more mountainous terrain.

Billy still held her tightly, one arm about her waist. Every so often he would fondle her breasts, belly, and that soft place between her thighs, breathing hoarse lewd remarks in her ear, giggling when Storm cringed at his touch.

'I'll betcha thought I'd fergotten you, honey, didn't you? I'll betcha thought you was safe from old Billy fer good after what that half-breed bastard of yore'n done to my brothers. But I didn't ferget; no, ma'am. I wouldn't be fergettin' a chit like you now. It jest took me awhile to find you; that's all. Ain't nobody seen that savage son-of-a-bitch in a coon's age. Musta took some doin', yore gittin' him to settle down and lay low like he's done.'

'You're crazy,' Storm spoke tiredly, flatly. 'You know Wolf'll come for me, that he's probably already hot on your trail, and that he'll kill you once he catches up with you.'

'Point is: He ain't gonna catch up with me, not this time, girlie. I'm gonna take you so deep into Mexico he'll never find us.'

'You're a fool, Billy Barlow. He's Comanche, or have you forgotten? Comanche men don't let their women get away. He'll never give up chasing you, and he can track you over solid rock if he has to.'

Billy lapsed into silence at this. Storm could tell her words had made him more nervous than he pretended. Emboldened, she continued to agitate him with gruesome tales of what Comanches did to their captives until he grabbed her hair again and shook her roughly, ordering her to shut her mouth.

She wished they would cease riding, but knew without a doubt what would happen when they did and so made no complaint when they rode on without halting. She'd rather die of exhaustion than submit to the insane criminal, for by now Storm was convinced the man was mad with lust and hunger for revenge that had eaten at him all this time. He must be. He would not have spent over two years tracking her and Wolf down if he weren't. She shivered in the darkness, half from rage and fear and half from cold as the cool night air swept over her naked body.

'The least you might do is give me a blanket for warmth,' Storm said icily. 'I won't be much good to you if I catch a chill and become feverish.'

Billy muttered under his breath at her request, but stopped the horse and unrolled a poncho from his pack.

'Seems a shame to hide all that purty skin.' He grinned as he tossed the garment at her. 'But I reckon I can take me a good long look at it whenever I feel like it now. Ain't that right, *lady*?'

Storm refused to answer, and he sniggered as he assisted her back into the saddle.

'Funny, how you don't 'pear to be so high and mighty now, bitch. Musta been them fine and fancy clothes you was wearin' the first time I seen you that made me think you was sumpin' special. Hell, yore nothin' but a Gawddamned Injun's whore.' His hand crept up under the poncho to pinch her breasts again. 'Whoooeee! I'll bet he's taught you all kinds of heathen tricks, ain't he? Well, I always did have me a hankerin' fer a squaw, as well as a lady, and now I got me both fer the price of one. Shit. I cain't beat that, can I? Jesus. It makes me hard jest thinkin' about it!'

The girl stiffened as he pressed himself against her so that she could feel his swollen maleness through his breeches.

Billy giggled once more. 'Too bad we ain't got time fer you to show me how them red devils do it right now. That's okay though. Once I git rid of that friggin' Comanche of yore'n we'll have plenty of evenin's without interruption together. Yeah, we'll have ourselves a time then. Whoooeee! I can hardly wait!'

He babbled on, not caring that Storm didn't respond. She sighed, closing her eyes and trying to shut out the sound of his whining voice. Presently she slept, her head lolling listlessly against the outlaw's shoulder. When she awakened, the hot sun was beating down upon them, telling her they had ridden all night. As the day wore on she sweltered beneath the poncho she was wearing, but decided foolishly she'd rather suffer a heatstroke than Billy Barlow's eyes raking her naked flesh crudely. Finally, at midday, unable to bear the blistering sun any longer, Storm tumbled from the criminal's arms in a dead faint.

A cool rag was being pressed to her forehead when she regained consciousness, and someone was raising her head, holding a canteen to her lips. Still dizzy, the girl didn't try to move, relaxing and sighing with relief instead. She would have known those strong arms, that clean male scent, and that low, silky voice anywhere. Wolf had come, just as he always had.

'Are you all right, baby?' he asked.

'I am now that you're here.'

'Did he—'

'No. Oh, Wolf!'

She clung to him tightly for a moment, but she didn't cry. Those days of giving in to feminine hysteria were long since past. She took another sip from the canteen, then smiled weakly.

'Water, Wolf? Do you know all the trouble to which I've gone for a taste of that Comanche cure-all of yours?'

He smiled back, the shadows in his blue eyes lightening upon seeing she was well enough to tease him.

'Chance,' he called, 'bring that bottle of mescal over here to your *maman*.'

The boy, who had been standing quietly but anxiously to one side, scampered to his father's unrolled saddle pack lying upon the ground, rummaged through its contents, then hastened back to his mother, relieved she was unhurt. Briefly Storm hugged her son close, ruffling his hair.

'You're a good boy, Chance,' she told him. 'You did exactly as *maman* ordered without hesitation. You saved her life by your quick and brave actions.'

The boy beamed proudly as Wolf yanked the cork from the decanter with his teeth, handing Storm the bottle.

After a couple of swigs the girl managed to sit up and take stock of what had occurred. She found she was no longer wrapped up in the stifling poncho, but was wearing Wolf's shirt instead. Billy Barlow lay very still some yards away. To Storm's horror she saw he was still alive and whimpering softly. He had been stripped naked and stretched spread eagle

361

between four stakes. She knew without asking that Wolf had cut off the outlaw's eyelids.

'*Sacré bleu*,' she breathed. 'Wolf—'

'He had it coming,' her husband spoke harshly, and Storm knew better than to protest, no matter how cruel the criminal's punishment seemed.

She swallowed hard, turning away to avoid gazing at the outlaw any longer.

'Let's go home, Wolf, please.'

'No. We will wait,' her husband stated firmly.

It took Billy Barlow two days to die. Before then he had gone blind from the scorching sun that had blazed relentlessly into the eyes he'd been unable to close, and his tongue had swollen from thirst, silencing at last his pleading moans that had grown fainter and fainter. Storm had been appalled by the slow, torturous agony the criminal had been forced to endure, but Wolf had remained unmoved by the low groans of the outlaw. Even Chance's young face had been curiously stern and stoic throughout the ordeal, and Storm knew the mark of the Comanches already lay upon her young son.

His dark visage grim, Wolf cut Billy's body loose and flung it over the criminal's horse, tying the corpse on securely. Storm watched her husband's movements nervously, feeling a sick sense of foreboding welling up inside her.

'Leave him!' she cried. 'Leave him for the buzzards!'

'Huh uh, baby. He's got a price on his head – dead or alive.'

The girl dreaded hearing those words, dreaded the restless fever, which she had thought forever cooled, she knew was once more racing hotly through her husband's blood. She could almost feel it pounding through his veins. Oh, Goddamn Billy Barlow! Goddamn Billy Barlow to hell for causing Wolf to strap on his guns again and remember what he had been.

All the way to Fin Terra she begged him not to leave her, to think of the life they had made together in Mexico, the home they had carved out of the wilderness, the future haven they would build for the *Kwerharehnuh* when the time came – land the White-Eyes would not be able to take from them; but Wolf made no response. Whatever wounds his strange, mysterious past held had been reopened in some way by Billy Barlow, and neither Storm, nor Wolf's promise to Tabenanika were strong enough to heal them, could keep him at Fin Terra.

He took her once before he left.

Their mating was a savage, passionate, desperate thing, as though somehow it were the last time they would ever come together so. Wolf's mouth closed down over Storm's hungrily, possessively, angrily when she would have refused him in her unspoken fear and hurt, and she trembled upon recalling he had said once she must never deny him. Why had she tried? He was too strong for her; he had always taken what he wanted, and now was no exception. With a low growl he tore the garments from her body, his eyes glittering as they raked her, swept the length of her nakedness before he wrapped his hands in her cloud of unbound hair to hold her still, and his lips found hers again. Like a brand they slashed and seared their way across her face, scorching her cheeks, her eyelids, her temples before they burned down one side of her throat to that soft place where the nape joined her shoulder. The deep rose crests of her breasts hardened beneath the fire of his fingers and then his tongue, as did the swell of her womanhood where he touched her, tasted her, raised her desire to a feverish pitch.

She whimpered her surrender, despising her weakness, but unable to help herself. No matter if he left her a thousand times it would still be so. She had given herself body and soul into his keeping, and even now, when she felt him slipping away, she could not stop wanting him, needing him, loving him. Still her heart ached as she arched her hips to receive him, felt him spiraling down into the sweet moist warmth of her, and she clung to his muscle-corded back fiercely, as though with her arms she could bind him to her, could somehow still prevent his going.

But she could not.

Long after Wolf had kissed her silent tears from her

countenance gently, wordlessly, she lay awake, etching every detail of his sleeping face into her mind. She was still awake when dawn crept over the horizon, and he arose soundlessly to dress, not meeting her haunted eyes as she watched him. Storm was too proud to plead with him again to stay, but in the end one last desperate attempt to hold him was wrung from her lips, words she was to regret for the rest of her life.

'If you leave, don't come back!' she cried.

His eyes locked hers across the room then, darkening momentarily with something she could not fathom before he was gone.

22

Once more Cal Tyree stood, battered hat in hand, in the majestic entrance hall of Tierra Rosa. This time, however, he was not kept waiting, but ushered almost immediately into Gabriel North's presence.

For a moment Cal shivered uncontrollably under the rancher's stare, for now not only were his brown eyes hard and relentless, but they glittered with a strange, piercing, half-mad light that frightened the deputy fearsomely as Gabriel hunched forward eagerly over his desk.

'You've found her!' the rancher said.

Cal did not need to ask about whom Gabriel spoke. Although the deputy had only heard whispered rumors, like everyone else, it was well-known throughout the area that Gabriel North had never recovered from the loss of his pretty French fiancée. The rancher had spent thousands and thousands of dollars in attempts to get her back, gradually growing more and more obsessed by the idea and allowing the reins of management of his vast empire to slip more and more firmly into Joe Jack's grasping hands. No one dared say outright that Gabriel had lost his reason – he was still a very powerful man – but there were many who suspected as much. Cal shuffled his feet nervously, hat twitching between his fingers as he crushed its brim.

'Naw – naw – nawsir, Mr North,' he stuttered, remembering the wild, hushed tales of what had happened to those who'd displeased the rancher with their failure to recover his bride-to-be. 'But – but I do have some good news fer you, sir; indeed I do!'

'Well, what is it, Tyree? Don't stand there like an idiot, keeping me waiting. Out with it, man!'

'It's – it's El Lobo, sir. He came into Goliad two weeks ago with Billy Barlow's body. After the sheriff give him the reward money he got into a poker game at Miss Lily's saloon. There were a bit of a ruckus – seems somebody added a few extry cards to the deck—'

'Get on with it, Tyree!' Gabriel ordered impatiently, his pulse racing.

'Well, sir, the long and short of it were that Sheriff Yancey charged El Lobo with disturbin' the peace, locked him up in jail, and told me to hie my tail out here *pronto* so's you'd know we'd arrested the bastard like you done said to do the next time he showed his face in town. What you want us to do with him, Mr North? We cain't rightly hold him more'n thirty days, and the sheriff's already a might anxious 'bout what that half-breed gunslinger's gonna do once he gits loose—'

'You let me worry about that, Tyree.' Gabriel opened his cash box, carefully counting out a wad of bills. 'This is for you, Tyree; see that Sheriff Yancey gets the rest. You've both done real well. I won't be forgetting it. You tell the sheriff if there's anything he needs, he's to let me know, and – uh – same for you, Tyree.'

'Yessir, Mr North; thankee, sir; mighty obliged to you, sir.'

Cal crammed his hat on his head, tugging at the brim vigorously as he backed out the room, then fairly ran to his horse. Once out of sight of the gleaming white antebellum mansion the deputy gave a whoop of excitement before, grinning, he galloped toward home.

Sheriff Yancey raised his head from his chest slowly at the sound of the door slamming shut and the jingle of spurs across the floor. Craftily he eyed his deputy from beneath the brim of his hat. Cal started to speak, practically bubbling over with his news, but the sheriff motioned imperceptibly for him to hold his tongue. Silently Sheriff Yancey's eyes questioned his deputy and received a small, smiling nod. Deliberately the sheriff swung his booted feet off his desktop, spit a wad of tobacco at the spittoon in the corner, swore when he missed, then stood. Taking a ring of keys from a nail in one wall, he started down the short hall to the cell where Wolf was being held prisoner. The keys jangled as Sheriff Yancey inserted one into the lock, turned it, then growled.

'Yore time's up, Lobo. Don't gimme no trouble, and be outta town before sundown.'

'This an election year, Sheriff?' Wolf drawled with a look that sent chills up the sheriff's spine.

'Never you mind!' he snapped. 'Jest do as I told you, less'n you want thirty days more.'

'No thanks.' Wolf clapped on his hat, then paused in the main room to retrieve his pistols and gunbelt.

'Come on, Peterson; let's move it' – he heard Sheriff Yancey releasing the rest of the men who'd been involved in the saloon brawl (and whom the sheriff had wisely arrested, along with Wolf, to allay any suspicions the gunslinger might have harbored otherwise). 'Haul ass, Bates, or next time you wind up drunk and disorderly I'm gonna leave you to the mercy of yore wife's rollin' pin.'

'Aw, Sheriff,' the man responded sheepishly.

Wolf didn't wait to hear any more.

'Tyree.' He acknowledged the deputy on his way out.

The sun was bright after the relative darkness of the jail cell. Wolf squinted his eyes against the glare for a moment before going round back to pick up his horse. Almost mechanically he checked the beast to be certain it had been well-treated during his incarceration. Finding nothing amiss and the possessions in his saddle bags and blanket roll in order, he mounted up, urging the animal into a brisk trot.

'Well, Cal,' Sheriff Yancey drawled as they watched Wolf go. 'I don't reckon we'll be seeing him fer awhile.'

'Nawsir, I reckon not ever agin. Mr North – he's got twenty men waitin' outside of town fer that half-breed Injun. By the time they git through with him I don't guess there'll be much left, and I 'spect the buzzards'll git that.'

'Yeah, well, it's outta our hands now, Cal. You got my share of the money from Mr North?'

'Shore thin', Sheriff.' Cal nodded, reaching in his shirt pocket for the wad of bills.

'That's fine; that's jest real fine, Cal.' Sheriff Yancey licked his thumb and riffled through the dollars, counting them off efficiently. 'Come on; I'll buy you a drink.'

'Gee, that's mighty kind of you, Sheriff.'

The two men sauntered across the street to the saloon, relieved to have gotten rid of El Lobo at last.

Wolf was ten miles outside Goliad, on his way home to Storm, in spite of her parting cry, when Gabriel's hired gang of ruffians caught up with him. He was unprepared for the ambush they'd laid – after all, it had been over two years since the rancher had threatened to kill him and take Storm back; and although Wolf had never dismissed the menace of Gabriel North as Storm had, he was still taken by surprise.

Warily he surveyed the group of men surrounding him, recognizing several who were gunslingers like himself – or worse, for there were many who had done and would do anything for a dollar. A realist, Wolf did not try to delude himself as to his chances of survival. There were too many of them for him to take them on alone. He was done for, and he knew it. If he went for his guns now, they would kill him instantly. If he waited— Well, hell. He'd always been a gambler.

He allowed no trace of fear to show upon his face as he leaned calmly over his saddle horn, tipping his hat back slightly to get a better look at Gabriel North. Despite his gloating triumph at having captured the gunslinger, the rancher shuddered faintly as he met Wolf's cold hard midnight blue eyes, and once more Gabriel wondered what it was about the man that nagged him so disturbingly. It was almost as though he should have known the gunslinger, but Gabriel was certain, with the exception of that winter in the *Llano Estacado*, he had never seen the man in his life.

Finally, deciding it must be due to the intense way in which the gunslinger stared at him, the rancher dimissed the idea and grinned jeeringly.

'Well, now,' he said, 'I told you we'd meet again, and if there's one thing I am, it's a man of my word.' Abruptly he ceased smiling. 'Where's Storm?'

'That's for me to know and you to find out, I reckon.'

Gabriel swore furiously, then ordered curtly, 'Beat it out of him, boys.'

In moments Wolf had been yanked from his stallion and set upon unmercifully. He was more dead than alive when the rancher at last called a halt to the proceedings, and still Wolf had not given away the identity of Storm's whereabouts.

'Half-breed, you're too stubborn for your own damned good!' Gabriel jerked Wolf's bleeding head up roughly.

Involuntarily the rancher gasped and recoiled a step from the hate he saw upon the dark battered visage of the gunslinger who knelt swayingly in the dirt. Never before had Gabriel seen such animosity on a man's face. The gunslinger's eyes appeared to burn like hot coals. His bruised, swollen, and split lips were parted in a feral snarl. As though Wolf were some putrid, horrifying animal, the rancher loosed his grip on the gunslinger's hair and snatched his hand away hastily.

'Hang him!' Gabriel commanded hoarsely. 'Hang him!'

BOOK FOUR
Oh, Sweet Pain

23

Chance gazed out over the gently swelling valley toward the mountains in the distance, but, like the past three months, saw no sign of that for which he searched. Miserably he turned, sighing, and urged his small pony homeward. Once there he dismounted and, trying hard not to cry, walked slowly toward the house. Storm saw his dejected little figure coming, and her heart went out to him. Briefly she knelt down to hug the boy close. She knew what ailed him, but had no words of comfort to offer.

'*Maman*.' He looked gravely into her lovely, sad countenance, his tiny shoulders squared oddly, manfully, as though expecting a painful blow.

'Yes, Chance?'

'*Ap*' isn't coming back, is he?'

There was a silence for a moment as Storm struggled with her conscience and her own fear before deciding it was best they both face the truth.

'No, son,' she said, 'he isn't.'

'Why not, *maman*?'

'I – I don't know, Chance; I don't know. I told him – I told him – *Mon Dieu*, forgive me! I didn't mean it! I didn't mean it!' the girl sobbed, then pressed her face against her son's chest and wept wrenchingly.

'Don't cry, *maman*. Please don't cry.' The boy patted her awkwardly. 'I'll take care of you; really I will.'

'Of course you will, son.' Storm rose and tried to dry her eyes, reaching a sudden decision. They simply couldn't go on like this. 'Chance, how would you like to go on a journey?'

'To where, *maman*?'

'Oh, San Francisco, maybe. I hear it's a boom town since they discovered gold at Sutter's Mill, and we need a change of scenery. It will do us good to get away from this place.'

'I know. It's awful lonesome here without *ap'*, isn't it?'

'Yes, son, it is. Come on. Let's go inside and get our things packed. We'll leave immediately now, today!' Storm rambled brightly, needing action, fearing she would change her mind otherwise.

In no time at all, it seemed, they had bundled up their few possessions. Storm turned the livestock loose, driving it off to fend for itself, then mounted Madame Bleu. When they had reached the top of the valley, although she knew it was bad luck, Storm couldn't resist one last look at Fin Terra where she and Wolf and their child had been so happy.

Goodbye, she called silently. Goodbye. In a few months the wilderness will take you back, and you'll be gone forever, just like Wolf. Oh, my love, my love! I didn't mean what I said. Why have you deserted our home, our son, and me?

There was no answer save the plaintive whisper of the rustling pines and sighing cottonwoods. Her heart heavy in her breast, the girl dug her heels into her horse's sides determinedly and galloped onward.

It was a sad and lonely time for Storm and her child, for the shadow of Wolf lay between them always, even though they no longer spoke of him. During the day when they would stop for a sip of water from their canteens and a bite of jerky or pemmican from their *awyaw:ts*, they would be reminded of him and the things he had taught them. At night when Chance lay close beside her in the darkness, Storm would study the boy's sleeping profile, and her heart would ache within her breast at knowing Wolf had forsaken the small miniature of himself.

The girl would gaze at the stars in the black sky, brilliant blurs in the distance seen through her tears, and search her soul for answers that would not come. She was but twenty years old, and already it seemed as though she had lived a lifetime.

Sometimes she would awaken during the long, empty nights, certain she had heard the scrape of her father's carriage wheels upon the winding gravel drive leading up to Belle Rive. Then in her dreams she would see herself, a child, running from the tall white-columned plantation down the ribbon of road that lay beneath the canopy of sweet mimosa trees that sheltered it. Her father would step down from his coach and, laughing, sweep her up into his strong arms, holding her close against one shoulder while he kissed her pretty *maman*. In other dreams – nightmares – the scene would change, and the running child would become a running young girl racing frantically through the tangled streets of New Orleans, the sulphuric smell of the burning tar buckets acrid in her nostrils as she searched for her parents in the half-mad mob. Then Storm would see herself standing in the cemetery, her young face streaked with tears beneath the mask of ebony net that covered it. The graveyard would turn into the gardens of Vaillance, the somber black morning clothes change to the pure white wedding dress she had never worn, and she would be dancing with André-Louis, then Gabriel, and then Wolf. She would cling to her husband tightly, only to discover the Barlow brothers or sometimes Fire-Walker had taken his place. Then she would be running once more, running toward the dear haven of Mammy's outstretched arms. Only whenever Storm reached her, the old Negress would be dead, and it would be Ma Barlow's beefy limbs encircling the girl. Storm would break away and run out into the road to be swooped up by Wolf and carried off to the *Llano Estacado* in the distance. She would look up gratefully, lovingly into his face, and by the light of the Comanche moon would see his dark visage twist with murderous rage, the colors of his war paint melting until he became an Apache brave. She would slip from his Pinto stallion in a dead faint, then, dazedly remembering she had forgotten something, would spring to her feet and grab desperately for the child he held in his arms, only to find that her baby was dead.

It was here Storm always awakened in a cold sweat, silent screams tearing from her throat. More than once she clutched anxiously at Chance in the darkness to reassure herself he was alive and real. She became afraid to go to sleep in the evenings, for fear the terrible nightmares would haunt her slumber, and purplish half-circles began to shadow her eyes from her sleepless nights of worry. She grew pale and thin, tired too easily, and often found herself dozing in the saddle.

Thus it was over a month when Storm and Chance, exhausted, finally reached Laredo and begged lodgings with *Señora* Ramirez, who, after hearing Storm's story, was happy to take them in.

'Oh, *Señora* Lobo.' The kindly Mexican woman shook her head and wrung her hands after hugging the girl close. 'Surely something has happened to your handsome *caballero* that he no return to you, no? Such a pretty *mujer* like yourself, and him so in love with you. Oh, *sí*. I remember how you dance that night and how he watch you, so proud you belong to him and him alone. No, a man like that does not leave the woman he loves, *señora*, nor the child she has given him. This I cannot believe.'

'It was my fault, *Señora* Ramirez. I – I was hurt and angry at his going, and I told him not to come back.'

'Ah, *señora*.' The older woman smiled. 'Do you really think a man like that would let such words stand in his way if he wanted you and his son? No, something has happened to him; I am sure of it.'

'You're wrong.' Storm refused to accept this. 'He's too good with his guns for that. He's left us, *señora*; that's all; and we've got to face up to it.'

The elderly woman said no more, realizing the girl's mind was made up, but still *Señora* Ramirez's dark eyes studied Storm pityingly, noting the toll the girl's ordeal had taken upon her.

'You must rest,' the *señora* stated firmly. 'I will take the little *muchacho* into the store with me and watch him. It will be no trouble at all.' She stayed Storm's protests with an upraised hand. 'He can play with my grandson. I will stop by my daughter's *jacale* on the way. Indeed she will be happy to be rid of Manolito for the day. He is – how do you say? – much a handful, that one! Come, Chance; your *madre* is very tired. We will leave her to get some sleep, and I will take you to my shop and teach you how to break a *piñata*.'

'What's that?'

'¡*Dios mio*! Have you never had a *fiesta para tu cumpleaños* – a birthday party?'

'Only very small ones, *señora*, at home, at Fin Terra, with *maman* and – and *ap'*.'

'Gracious, child, how many languages do you speak? You sound like the Tower of Babel, Never mind.' *Señora* Ramirez flung her hand up wildly, shaking her head at the questioning expression on the boy's face. 'If you have not been raised by the Good Book, I don't want to hear it. A *piñata* is like a treasure chest, filled with surprises. Would you like that, Chance?'

'Oh, yes, *señora*, very much.'

'Well, then, come along.'

They stayed with *Señora* Ramirez for nearly two weeks, during which time Storm recovered much of her strength, although her spirits remained depressingly low, much as she tried to hide it. Nevertheless she was determined on her plan of action, which was to continue on to Corpus Christi and then Galveston, from where she would travel by ship around Cape Horn to San Francisco. The journey would take longer by sea, but would be less strenuous than following the overland route. Why she had settled on San Francisco, Storm didn't know, except that something in her was crying out for a new place, a new beginning, and the West was in her blood now.

Remembering the hostility of the *taboh* toward Indians, she had purchased new garments for Chance and herself, White-Eyes' clothes, things she had not worn since leaving New Orleans so many years past. She studied her reflection in the mirror and didn't recognize the woman who stared back at her so regally. From the jaunty plumed hat perched upon her neatly coiled hair, down the length of her severely tailored riding habit, to the stylish kid boots that buttoned up the sides of her ankles, Storm looked every inch a stranger to herself. The change in Chance was even more dramatic. Storm had cut off his unkempt, shoulder-length hair and forced him into a small neat suit, despite his struggles and howls of displeasure.

'You must learn to be a little man, Chance,' she told him sternly.

'A White-Eyes!' he spat.

'Their world is ours now, and you must accept it as such if we are to make our way in it. *Entends?*' she asked sharply in a tone he'd never heard before.

It frightened him. This was not the mother who'd laughed and chased him down the riverbank. His face fell. '*Qui, maman.*'

'*Bon.* Besides, Chance, *maman* is a White-Eyes.'

'You never seemed so before,' he protested, hurt and defiant once more.

'Nevertheless it is so,' she said, giving his bow tie a final tug. 'There. No one will guess now you are part Indian.'

'No, indeed, *señora*,' *Señora* Ramirez spoke up. 'Why, he looks almost noble, like a Spanish *grandee*, no?'

'Yes,' Storm responded slowly, suddenly startled as she gazed at her son.

What the elderly Mexican woman had said was true. There was nothing at all Indian about Chance's appearance now. He could indeed have passed for a full-blooded Spaniard or Frenchman, with his black hair and dark skin. His blue eyes stood out brilliantly above his high cheekbones, and there was an arrogant thrust to the set of his jaw, as though he had been born to the silver. Almost mechanically, as though fearing the results, Storm mentally stripped Wolf of his Indian trappings and imposed his visage over that of her son's.

His mother was pure Castellano. *His family was once as well-known and respected as my own in the old country.*

Why, Wolf isn't a half-breed at all, she thought suddenly. It is only his hair and manner that make him seem so, just as they did Chance. Why then does he call himself such and suffer its indignities? Is there something in his past for which he is punishing himself? It doesn't matter now. I'll never see him again anyway.

Quickly she turned away so that her son would not glimpse the tears that glistened without warning in her haunted gray eyes.

Corpus Christi had changed little since Storm had last seen it, although it had grown and prospered. Several new buildings had sprung up sprawlingly here and there, and the air was filled with the pounding of hammers as a group of men in the distance worked at laying additional sidewalk. Wagons, many with their beds fully loaded with construction materials, rumbled down the busy main street, lurching precariously now and then when their wheels collided with the numerous mudholes that pitted the road. Horses wove their ways carefully through the milling mass, hooves making a loud clip-clop that rang in counterpoint to the rhythmic sound of the hammers.

Storm drew Madame Bleu to a halt before a small, quiet hotel. It was nothing fancy, but since she didn't know how much the passage to San Francisco would cost, the girl was wisely hoarding her money. A young women traveling alone with no escort save for a child was bound to raise eyebrows, but Storm was prepared for the questions she had realized would be asked. In a low voice that trembled slightly she explained to the innkeeper that her husband had been bitten by a rattlesnake and died enroute to Corpus Christi from Laredo. As she had taken Wolf's pack horse, Asenap, whom Wolf had left behind, with her upon leaving Fin Terra, her story seemed plausible enough.

'You're a brave young woman, ma'am,' the innkeeper said. 'Most women wouldn't have known how to survive out on the range alone, especially a lady like yourself. You were lucky you and your son managed to get here on your own, real lucky. Room number seven, ma'am. Straight up those stairs and to your right. If there's anything you need, just let me know. I'll have one of the boys take your horses round back to the livery stable.'

'Thank you, *monsieur*. You're very kind,' Storm replied. 'Come, Chance.'

Once inside the room Chance gazed steadily at his mother. 'Why did you lie to that man, *maman*, and tell him *ap'* was dead? He's not, you know.'

'I know, son, but decent white women don't travel alone.'

'You're not alone. You have me.'

'I know, son,' Storm repeated, 'but it's not the same as having a husband to protect me.'

'But *maman*, you shoot better than most men. *Ap'* said so. You are able to take care of yourself.'

'Yes, Chance, but white women aren't supposed to know how to take care of themselves.'

'That is foolish,' the boy noted gravely. 'I do not think I like the ways of the *tabeboh*. They are stupid. They wear too many clothes. This thing around my neck – this – this tie – it is useless and uncomfortable. And why would they want their women to be ignorant? A woman must have knowledge of many things. How else is she to care for herself and her children when her man is away hunting or raiding?'

'White ladies have servants or slaves to see to their needs, Chance.'

'Slavery is evil.' The boy frowned. '*Ap'* said so.'

'That's enough, Chance. The world is not always as we would like for it to be. You must learn this and accept it or become a renegade like your father.'

'Ren – e – gade. What is that?'

'A person who does not belong – someone who defies the world into which they were born.'

'If it means not wearing this awful thing round my neck, then that is what I will be.'

Storm sighed, not knowing what else to say and wondering why things always seemed so simple to children, who saw only black and white and never shades of gray.

Mimi La Roche stared hard at the woman and child waiting at the depot to board the stagecoach. The saloon proprietress had an eye for faces, and although the girl's appearance was drastically altered, Mimi was certain the woman was the same one the gunslinger El Lobo had brought with him that time at The Gulf Coast. Mimi would never forget the girl's haughty carriage and arrogant manner or that high-born French accent that even now wafted to the proprietress's ears as the woman said something to the driver. Mimi's eyes narrowed speculatively, for she knew now the girl was Gabriel North's missing fiancée, rumored by some to have been abducted by first the Barlow brothers and then El Lobo, although others claimed the bride-to-be had jilted the Texas rancher and married someone else instead. Gabriel North was an occasional customer of hers, and the proprietress was certain the shrewd Texas rancher had deliberately obscured the real facts of the matter to prevent anyone from learning the truth. Her eyes sparkling with greedy anticipation, Mimi turned and started across the street to the sheriff's office.

Storm continued giving instructions as to the loading of the two trunks, which she'd purchased earlier that morning for herself and Chance, to the driver, unaware she had been maliciously observed and identified.

'There now, ma'am. I think that'll hold 'em,' the driver said, giving the ropes that bound the cases to the top of the stagecoach a final tug. He clambered to the ground. 'Here, ma'am. Let me help you there. Watch yore step now, you hear? In you go, son.' He swung Chance up after Storm. 'It'll be jest a few more minutes, ma'am,' he spoke and tipped his hat politely.

'Thank you, driver,' Storm replied, settling back onto the cushioned bench inside. 'Here, Chance. Let me straighten your tie.' The boy made no response, just gazed out the window, trying hard not to cry. Storm sighed, thinking how like his father he was when he brooded. 'I'm sorry about your pony, son, but there was no help for it. Even if we'd ridden the horses to Galveston, we would still have had to sell them. We couldn't have taken them with us to San Francisco, Chance.'

The boy still didn't answer. Storm sighed again and gave up trying to lighten his dark mood. After all, it wasn't as though she didn't sympathize with the child. She'd wept herself over having to part with the faithful little Madame Bleu, but there had been nothing else to be done. Storm had needed the money – not the horses.

Wishing she didn't feel so terribly depressed, the girl closed her eyes tiredly as the stagecoach gave a sudden lurch, then jolted out of Corpus Christi.

24

San Francisco, California, 1853

The trip by stagecoach to Galveston and from there by sailing ship to San Francisco had passed without incident. Now Storm and Chance stood on the deck of the vessel as it pulled slowly into the harbor, manuevering carefully around the deserted ships that still choked the bay, remnants of the Gold Rush. The captain had told Storm that in 1851, more than eight hundred of the vessels had been anchored in the cove, abandoned by their crews. Many were gone now, but several still remained, floating up and down listlessly as the waves slapped against their empty hulls.

The wharf itself, as the girl and her son disembarked, was a filthy mass of small crude buildings, which sprawled along the rutted roads in close, haphazard clutter. Persons of every nationality crowded the area: Englishmen, Irishmen, Frenchmen, Germans, Spaniards, Italians, Chinese, and an occasional Negro. The voices raised in loud clamor babbled in every language imaginable as their owners hurried on about their business, sparing little more than passing glances of disinterest for Storm and Chance. To the girl's surprise she realized it would have made no difference had she and her son been garbed in their Indian clothes. No one would have noticed or cared if they had.

She gazed about helplessly, dismayed, as her large trunk and Chance's smaller one were unloaded. This was not what she had expected. She had been led to believe San Francisco was a thriving metropolis. From what she could discern it was little more than an overgrown slum. Chance clutched her hand tightly, awed and afraid by the immense activity going on around him. He shrank back against her skirts as two Chinese men, pulling strange, two-wheeled contraptions, came running up to them, heads bobbing as they bowed, then started to chatter almost unintelligibly to Storm in pidgin English.

She stared, unable to prevent her rudeness, as she tried to comprehend them, for she had never seen a Chinese before. They both wore odd little hats upon their heads, and their hair was as long as hers, hanging in neat queues down their backs. What she could see of their skin not hidden by the folds of their colorful robes had a yellowish tinge, and their dark eyes slanted upward, like slits in their excited, beaming faces.

'Missy need lide?' one asked. 'Missy have money fo' hotel? Take Missy and small boy velly nice place. *Chop, chop.* Only fifteen Amelican dollahs—'

'Me take Missy,' the second Chinese broke in. 'Cost only twelve Amelican dollahs.'

He grasped Storm's trunk and began hauling it to his vehicle. The first Chinese protested indignantly, grabbing the handle on the opposite end of the girl's case, yanking firmly. Each started yelling at the other rapidly in their own language as a tug-of-war ensued. Storm, confused, bewildered, fearing a fight between the two men would break out any moment, and realizing at last that no one intended to come to her aid, finally agreed to let the first Chinese take her and Chance up in his rickshaw, as he called it, with the second Chinese following with their luggage. Despite her best bartering, she wound up paying the two men ten dollars each. She was horrified by the cost, not yet knowing enough about San Francisco to understand what she thought a staggering price had been relatively cheap in a city where eggs sold for a dollar apiece. She counted what little money she had remaining in her reticule worriedly, not sure now she had even enough left for a hotel room. She leaned forward to tell the Chinese she had changed her mind, to take them to a wagon yard instead, but he only smiled and shook his head.

'No place fo' lady, Missy.'

The rickshaw jolted on up the steep hills amidst the din,

dodging other vehicles and people expertly. Storm glanced down at Chance anxiously as they rumbled along, for he had his hands pressed tightly over his ears against the noise.

'We'll get used to it, son,' she told him firmly, not wanting him to know she was as upset as he by the continual racket, which was seemingly worse in San Francisco than any other town to which Storm had ever been.

Everything appeared to be louder here: the clatter of horses' hooves and carriage wheels, the pounding of hammers by the construction workers, the voices raised in so many different languages, the bustle of people on the sidewalks, the fights that broke out here and there, the banging of shop doors and saloon doors. It was dreadful – and dirty, oh, so dirty. Hordes of grimy, unshaven men filled the streets, thousands of would-be miners who had come to San Francisco too late to get rich and now wandered about dazedly, their dreams shattered, their hopes crushed, their money long gone. Many were camped in tents where buildings had not yet been erected. Some, who had a few belongings left, were peddling their wares alongside the roads. Storm heard tin pans being hawked for five dollars or more, shovels for twelve at least. The cost of a horse or mule was unbelievable, and the girl grew sick at the thought of the price she might have gotten here for Madame Bleu, Asenap, and even Chance's little pony. She gripped her reticule, refusing to dwell on the matter. What was done, was done. She had learned a long time ago there was no use crying over what was past.

The rickshaw slid to a halt at last before a hotel that, though shabby, seemed fairly decent. The first Chinese helped her and Chance alight, while the second Chinese unloaded their trunks from his vehicle. Storm paid them both, then, after instructing Chance to stay with the baggage, went inside. As she had feared she did not have enough money left for a room. Moments later she was back out on the street, thoroughly bereft and discouraged.

'What is it, *maman*? What's wrong? Won't they give us a

room? Is it – is it because they know I'm part Indian?'

'No, Chance. I don't think that matters here,' she spoke tiredly, not bothering to explain she had come to the conclusion that he hadn't a drop of Indian blood in him. 'I don't think anything matters here, except money, and I'm afraid we have very precious little of that remaining.'

'Well, then, we must do what *ap'* does.'

'What's that, son?' Storm asked absently, distraught.

'Kill a bad man.'

'*Mon Dieu*, Chance!'

'Oh, don't worry, *maman*. It shouldn't be hard. They must have a lot of them here. I saw two stabbed to death while you were in the hotel.'

'*Sainte Marie*!' Storm swore again, appalled.

To what kind of a place had she brought her son? Even the women were cheap and tawdry. One such had just flounced out of the saloon across the street, carpetbag in hand. Now she turned and raised one fist, shaking it threateningly as she began to hurl vulgar epithets at the well-dressed gentleman who'd followed her out. He smiled and spread his hands disarmingly, but the woman only continued berating him loudly. Finally he shrugged and went back into the saloon. The woman bent, picked up a rock, and hurtled it angrily at his retreating figure. It crashed through the saloon doors noisily, but the man did not reappear. The woman hesitated for a moment, then grabbed her satchel and stomped off down the road, ignoring the hoots, hollers, and whistles directed toward her by some of the vagrant miners.

Storm watched her go, then, biting her lip, turned her attention back to the saloon, her eyes lingering on the large sign nailed to the upper story. It read: THE BON TON. After a time she squared her shoulders determinedly. They could not stand in the street all day – already passing men were beginning to notice her and the boy, their eyes lustful with appreciation as they raked Storm's slender figure crudely – and she was desperate for funds. The girl accosted one man who appeared more decent than the others and paid him five dollars to carry her and Chance's trunks across the road to the saloon. Once more she told the boy to remain with the luggage, then pushed her way inside.

The Bon Ton was as raucous as the rest of the city and reminded Storm of the saloon in Gorda Vaca where she had first met Wolf, for it was a hellhole, not the elaborate establishment The Gulf Coast in Corpus Christi had been. There was the usual bar (its mirror cracked in several places), blowsy dance hall girls, impervious piano player, and a stage where a grotesquely fat harlot was singing a naughty ditty, much to the amusement of the customers. Several eyebrows raised faintly in surprise at Storm's entrance, but she lifted her chin haughtily, ignoring the sudden, speculatively leering glances she received as she made her way to a table in one corner where a game of poker was being played.

'Is this game closed?' she asked. 'Or can anybody play?'

The men at the table looked up interestedly. A few of them smiled. Only one objected to her being dealt in, and the others quickly overruled him, two jumping to their feet to pull out a chair for the girl. She sat down, then a trifle nervously tossed in her ante.

You're good at this, she tried to still her anxiety. Wolf taught you well at cards, just as he did everything else. You know every cheating trick in the book, Storm!

Nevertheless the girl took a deep breath, for Wolf had taught her those tricks only so that she would know what to watch for during a game. He had rarely ever employed them himself and had cautioned her against it, saying there was nothing a man hated worse than a card cheat.

I reckon there's been more men killed over a poker table than anywhere else in the West, baby.

I don't care! Storm thought wildly. I've got to win! What will happen to Chance and me if I don't?

Carefully, secretively she slipped the hideout pistol she'd bought in Laredo from her reticule into her lap for protection, then picked up her cards. She *was* good, damned good, so good, in fact, that only one man in the entire saloon watching her realized she was cheating and knew just how she was doing it. He leaned back against the bar and smiled, saying nothing, for he appreciated seeing a real expert at work and, after all, it wasn't *his* money she was winning.

The hours dragged on, and the pile of bills and coins before Storm grew. She glanced up occasionally now and then to look through the saloon doors to be certain Chance and their trunks were safe, but other than that she was impervious to her surroundings, her concentration riveted on the game. She scarcely noticed the attention the poker table was beginning to attract. She was unaware she was just about to clean out one of the meanest, most dangerous men in San Francisco, the miner who'd originally protested against her joining the game. His ugly face gave her an evil leer as he tossed in the last of his cash to call. Without waiting for Storm to show her hand he laid his cards on the table.

'Four ladies, *lady*,' he sneered, reaching for the pot.

'Four gentlemen' – Storm deliberately let her eyes roam over his filthy, seated figure – '*mister*.' She spread her kings over his queens.

'You Gawddamned bitch!' he roared, suddenly springing to his feet. 'You cheated me; that's what! I dunno how you did it, bitch, but I say you cheated me!'

The man at the bar quit smiling and snapped to attention as Storm's diamond-hard gray eyes stared coolly at her ugly-faced accuser, although she was shaking like a leaf inside. Surely no man would gun down a woman, especially before witnesses!

In the deadly silence that had fallen over the saloon the girl said softly, 'And I say you're a poor loser.'

'Is that right?' the miner drawled, deliberately lighting a cigar.

Keep your eyes on mine, baby! I can smile at you, take a drag of my cigar, grind it out, shift my stance, and hook my thumbs in my belt, and while you're watching all that, I can kill you! But the eyes are a dead giveaway, Storm. When a man's about to make his move against you, they'll change suddenly, for just a split second. That's when you draw!

Her heart pounding in her throat, nearly choking her, Storm kept her eyes on those of her accuser. Nervously she wet her lips. The miner took another drag of his cigar, then abruptly threw it away. His eyes changed.

Now, Storm! Now!

Her accuser went for his gun. The man at the bar went for his gun. Storm went for her gun – and she was the fastest of the three.

. . . Keep your back to a wall or the bar, and watch the mirrors out of the corners of your eyes. Move, baby! Move when you shoot!

She fired and fired again and again in rapid succession, moving, diving, rolling. In moments the miner lay sprawled upon the floor, blood spurting from the bullet holes she'd pumped in his belly. The girl sprang to her feet, her back against the wall as she, wide-eyed and trembling, faced the terribly quiet, awestruck saloon.

For an eternity, it seemed, no one moved. Then the man at the bar, seeing it was not needed after all, put his small but deadly derringer back in his coat pocket and shouted,

'Li Kwan! Li Kwan!'

A Chinese man came running into the saloon, his queue bobbing. 'Yes, Missah Brett?'

'Take that man's body out into the street, and dump it. *Chop, chop.*'

'Yes, Missah Brett.'

'All right, folks,' the man at the bar continued as the Chinese began to drag the corpse from the saloon. 'The show's over.' He turned to the bartender. 'Drinks on the house, Riley.'

'Aye, Mr Brett.'

The customers whooped with glee, crowding forward for the free drinks, the gunfight forgotten. The man at the bar strolled over to Storm, who, seeing no further trouble in the offing, was now leaning against the wall for support, fearing her knees were about to give out any minute. She felt desperately ill and choked down with difficulty the vomit that rose to her throat.

I just can't be sick, she told herself irrationally. I just can't be sick before all these people!

'Are you all right, ma'am?' the man asked.

She gazed at him stupidly for a moment, not registering the question. Dimly the girl noted his prematurely silvered hair (for she guessed him to be in his early thirties) combed back in neat wings, his sparkling jet black eyes, hook nose, and the silvery mustache that hung down cavalier fashion around his sensuous mouth and was curled up debonairly on the ends. He was wearing a gray pinstriped suit of expensive broadcloth, above whose waistcoat a frothily ruffled and starched white shirt was buttoned up to an artfully arranged cravat. Blindly Storm's eye focused on the diamond stickpin there that appeared to be winking at her. This was the man she had seen outside the saloon, smiling at the painted floozy who'd yelled at him so irately. Dazedly the girl realized he had asked her something and was still waiting patiently for a reply.

'I – I'm sorry. What – what did you say, *monsieur*?'

'I asked if you were all right, ma'am,' he repeated gallantly. Slowly she nodded. 'Yes – yes, I think so.'

'You look a bit shaken – understandable under the circumstances. Here, ma'am,' he said, pulling out a chair for her. 'Won't you sit down?'

'Yes – yes, I will. Thank you. You're very kind, *monsieur*.'

'Not at all. It's my pleasure. Allow me to get you something to drink, a brandy, perhaps?'

'Yes, thank you.' Storm tried to recover her composure. 'A brandy would be fine.'

'Riley, bring a brandy for the lady,' the man called. 'Here, take a few sips of this, ma'am,' he spoke gently when the drink had arrived.

The fiery amber liquid burned as Storm downed the glass swiftly, accustomed now to spirits. Gradually some of her color began to return.

'Feeling better?' her benefactor queried.

She nodded again, then suddenly glanced up anxiously once more. 'My son!'

'The small boy outside? Li Kwan is with him. See?' he pointed through the saloon doors to where the Chinese was chatting amiably with a beaming-faced Chance. 'No doubt Li Kwan is telling him a dragon story. Allow me to introduce myself, ma'am. Brett Diamond, proprietor of this establishmentt, at your service.'

'Storm – Lesconflair, *monsieur*,' the girl replied, extending her hand.

His lips just brushed her knuckles, courtly fashion. 'Pardon me, ma'am, but if you ask me, your mama should have named you Lightning instead. That was one of the damnedest pieces of shooting I ever saw in my life!'

'I – had a good teacher,' Storm rejoined, suddenly feeling as though she were about to cry. She tried hard not to think of Wolf, but found it difficult indeed as the quick tears of late again started in her eyes. She reached into her reticule, withdrawing a clean handkerchief. 'I – I'm afraid you must excuse me. I fear I'm still a trifle overwrought—'

'That's quite all right, ma'am.'

A few minutes later Storm, more herself and realizing she was still clutching her revolver tightly, dropped the gun back into her reticule, then carefully raked up her winnings.

'You've been very kind, *Monsieur* Diamond. If I could impose upon you just a moment further – would you mind directing me to the sheriff's office so that I can report what's happened and pay for that man's funeral?'

'Well, now, that's right decent of you, ma'am, but you must be new in San Francisco. We don't have any law of which to speak, and as for funerals – Jesus! There's so many killings in this city I guess they just pitch the bodies in the Bay.'

'Why, that's horrible!'

He shrugged nonchalantly. 'A fact of life, ma'am.'

'Then if you would be so good as to find someone to assist me with my baggage to the hotel across the street, I would be most grateful. I – I must confess that my son and I just arrived in San Francisco this morning, and I'm afraid all this has been a little too much for me. I'm very tired.'

'I don't mean to pry, ma'am, but your – your husband is not with you?'

'No, *monsieur*. My husband has' – Storm faltered, then plunged on – 'deserted myself and our child. We came to San Francisco to begin a new life for ourselves. I – I know you must be wondering why I entered your saloon and involved myself in a poker game. It – it wasn't very ladylike; I realize that now, but I – I was desperate. I know no one in town, and our passage tickets were quite expensive, and I – had no idea how very costly things were going to be here—'

'Forgive me, ma'am, but am I to understand you are quite without funds or friends in San Francisco?'

'*Oui, monsieur*. Please – I've taken up enough of your time with my troubles—'

'Now just hold on a minute, ma'am.' Brett laid a restraining hand upon Storm's arm as she rose to take her leave of him. 'San Francisco's a rough city. I just can't let you walk out of here like this – with no friends, no money—'

'I have money now, *monsieur*.'

'Yes, but that won't last long, I assure you.'

Worriedly, Storm glanced down at her now-bulging reticule, then bit her lip. Mr Diamond was probably right, she decided, suddenly anxious and distraught once more.

'I'll – I'll manage somehow. I've just got to!'

'Well, now, ma'am, if you're interested, I just might have a proposition for you.'

Storm's eyes turned to ice. Her voice froze. 'I'm not interested in propositions, *Monsieur* Diamond, and I apologize if my unseemly behavior has given you cause to think—'

'Forgive me, Mrs Lesconflair—'

'Lesconflair is my maiden name, *Monsieur* Diamond.'

'Then forgive me, Mrs—'

'Lobo,' Storm supplied, wondering why she hadn't just said so in the first place.

'Lobo, but my proposition has nothing to do with whatever you may have imagined, and I certainly didn't mean to give offense. Any fool can see you're a lady born and bred. What I was going to say was that my hostess left my employ this morning, and I was intending to offer you the position if you'd care to have it. The pay is a hundred dollars per week, plus room and board – for both you and your son. I guess he won't take up too much space or eat too much.' Brett smiled at her. 'Besides, I think he's grown rather attached to Li Kwan.'

Storm looked out the saloon doors again to where Chance was still chattering excitedly to the Chinese. The girl paused, considering. Here was a way out of her dilemma. She'd be a fool not to grab it. She knew nothing about San Francisco; what she'd seen was not encouraging. Lord only knew what other prospects she had. At least Mr Diamond was a gentleman and had offered her a proper job, albeit in a saloon. She took a deep breath, sending a silent prayer of thanks to God for her salvation.

'What would my duties entail, *monsieur*?'

'Greeting the customers, seeing that everybody's taken care of as far as drinks go, managing the girls, dealing cards – that sort of thing. It's not too hard, and it kind of gives the place a little class.'

'I am *not* a whore, Monsieur Diamond.'

'I never said you were, Mrs Lobo. I don't expect you to entertain upstairs. I've got other women for that.'

'I'll accept your offer then, *monsieur*, on two conditions. The first is that you give me a free rein in cleaning up your saloon. Your place is cheap, and your girls are trashy. I won't allow my son to be reared in a hellhole. If it's class you want, I'll see you get it. The second is that I – I won't be your mistress.'

Brett smiled once more. 'Fair enough, Mrs Lobo.'

'Please – call me Storm,' she instructed, wishing now she had not told him her married name after all. 'I – I don't want to be reminded of my husband.'

'How about if I call you French Lightning instead? All the girls have nicknames, and I kind of like that.'

'All right.'

'Shall we have a drink to celebrate? Riley, a bottle of brandy and another glass please. Well, here's to a mutually satisfactory relationship' – he raised his snifter after the order had come. 'Oh, and, Lighting, when you work for me' – Brett winked – 'you deal from the top of the deck.'

That night Storm and Chance had a hot meal and slept with a roof over their heads, much to the girl's relief. After Brett's crack about her cheating she was momentarily afraid he intended to expose her. She held her breath for the longest time, mentally feeling the heavy strands of a rope choking her throat – for she had no doubt the friends of the ugly-faced miner she'd killed would be quick to hang her under the circumstances. Brett only laughed, however, and told her not to worry.

'I admire a woman with guts, Lightning,' he said. 'And if you hadn't been so quick with your pistol, I would have shot Hawkins myself. Men don't gun down women – whatever the provocation – at least not in my establishment.'

Storm thanked him gratefully for his protection, then went upstairs to the room she was to share with Chance. The boy was fast asleep, a smile curved upon his peaceful face, a tiny carved dragon clutched in his little fist. The girl smiled gently to herself.

The Bon Ton isn't home, and Brett isn't Wolf, she thought but Chance and I will build a new life here, and together we will find a way to be happy; I swear it.

The following morning Storm began her duties as hostess of Brett's saloon. The first thing she did was to shut the place down. Over the still sleepy-eyed employees' protests (for they were not used to being wakened so early) and Brett's indifferent shrugs when they complained to him, the girl had Riley hang a huge sign out front that read: CLOSED FOR REMODELING. Then she called all the help together to explain the new rules and procedures of The Bon Ton. Many eyed her hostilely; some spoke up loudly to ask what right she had to give them orders, but they soon quieted when Brett, smiling amusedly in one corner, arms folded over his chest, made no move to countermand Storm's authority.

The girl did not of course know anything about running a saloon, but she *had* been reared to manage a huge plantation, and she quickly applied her knowledge to The Bon Ton, thinking it could not be all that different. There were still accounts to be kept, chores to be done, and people to be overseen. She faced Brett's employees squarely, took a deep breath, and began her speech.

'As you all are aware, *Monsieur* Diamond's' – she nodded respectfully toward Brett – 'hostess quit yesterday. I am her replacement – French Lightning.' There were a couple of grins at this, for they all knew how she'd acquired this nickname.

'Damned fine shootin', ma'am,' one man hollered to a smattering of applause.

Storm smiled, acknowledging the compliment, then sobered once more. 'Now I don't know how Saucy Sal ran this place, and I don't care. Monsieur Diamond has given me a free hand to make whatever changes I see fit, and from now on things will be done my way. Those who do not feel they can comply with my demands should pick up their pay right now, and leave. *Monsieur* Diamond will give you your wages.'

Only one woman stepped up to where Brett awaited, cash box in hand. Storm was relieved to note it was the grotesquely fat harlot who'd been singing the dirty ditty yesterday, for the girl had planned to fire her anyway. All the others remained as Storm continued.

'From now on the motto of The Bon Ton will be "class and

cleanliness". I will not tolerate a slovenly appearance or behavior. Both draw scum like flies, and that is no longer the type of clientele this establishment wishes to attract. I intend to make The Bon Ton one of the most exclusive saloons in San Francisco, open only to the *crème de la crème* of the city. *They* are the people with real money to spend. By having such as our patrons The Bon Ton will naturally have more money to spend, and you will receive raises accordingly, depending upon your performances here. Those who do well will be rewarded. Those who do poorly will be fired immediately. No second chances will be given to those not willing to do their jobs properly. If there are any of you who now feel you cannot comply with my demands, you should pick up your pay, and leave.'

Four more persons left, grumbling under their breath. Storm ignored them imperiously and went on.

'Now the first thing I will do this morning will be to interview each one of you personally, inspect your rooms and wardrobe, and make a list of your needs as I see them. When I have finished interviewing you, you will change into your oldest clothes, and report for work. We will spend the next several days scrubbing down this saloon with turpentine from top to bottom. I have discovered it is infested with lice and bedbugs. What garments I allow you to keep, you will deliver *pronto* for boiling to Li Kwan in the kitchen. You will all, in addition, bathe yourselves scrupulously to rid your hair and bodies of these insects. I have no doubt some of you are fairly crawling with them.

'When all this has been accomplished, I will start the men to work making needed repairs and the women to sewing. The harder you work and the less you complain, the sooner The Bon Ton will reopen for business. Are there any questions?' There were none. 'Good. Then we'll get started immediately. Whiskey Annie,' Storm called out, glancing down at her roster of names, 'I'll see you first, then China Doll, Golden Garters, Flamenco Rose, Brass-Hearted Kate, and so on down this list, which I'll post over the bar. Let's go, ladies, gentlemen.'

Within two months Storm had The Bon Ton whipped into shape. The night of the grand reopening she walked gracefully down the staircase from the upper rooms, surveyed the saloon, and took pride in her accomplishment. The Bon Ton gleamed. Storm had made good use of what she'd seen in Mimi's Place in Corpus Christi. The brass lamps perched upon the wagon wheels hanging from the ceiling fairly shone. There wasn't a single smudge on the gold-veined mirror that had replaced its cracked predecessor over the bar, and the glasses lined up on the shelves across the mirror sparkled in the glow of the soft, cheery light. The bar itself had been sanded down, stained, and polished with beeswax until it shimmered with a dark burnished gleam, as did the hard wooden floor, the stage, and the furniture. The walls had been stripped and repapered with a pale gold wallpaper. Elegant red silk curtains hung at the two front windows and upon the stage, complimenting the plush red carpet on the stairs and upper story. Potted green plants and brass spittoons completed the downstairs picture. Storm knew the upstairs floor looked just as fine.

'It's beautiful, *maman*,' Chance whispered by her side.

'I quite agree,' Brett spoke, only he was staring at Storm.

She blushed prettily, highly aware of how lovely she was this evening. Her yellow gown with its ruffled neck and tiny cap sleeves that hung off her shoulders was cut shockingly low, exposing a daring display of her full ripe breasts, which were once more like pale cream now that she no longer spent her days beneath the harsh Texas sun. Her tightly corseted waist was as slender as a young girl's where her sash, adorned with a satin yellow rose, encircled it, then tied in a bow at her back. The hem of the dress was ruffled too, drawn up in flounces here and there to show a glimpse of her frothy white lace petticoats. Yellow ribands threaded their ways through her mass of unbound black curls. A hand-painted fan finished the ensemble.

'Run on down to the kitchen, son, and tell Li Kwan I said to give you your supper now. Then off to bed with you. I'll be up later to tuck you in.'

'*Oui, maman.*'

'He's a nice kid,' Brett said, stepping forward to offer the girl his arm as they watched Chance scamper off.

'Yes, he is.'

'You've done a wonderful job, Lightning. I can hardly believe this is the same place. I'm very proud of you,' he breathed, his black eyes glittering as he gazed down at her approvingly. He pressed her hand. 'Have supper with me tonight to celebrate.'

Storm's heart beat fast as she replied. 'All right.'

She knew she should have rejected the invitation, for over the passing weeks Brett had made it quite plain he desired her, would try to seduce her at the first opportunity she gave him, and the girl's love for Wolf was still too deep for her to allow that to happen. Nevertheless she felt it would have been churlish to refuse supper. Brett had been very kind to her, had taken her in and offered her his protection when she'd had nowhere else to go, and it was not as though he would force himself upon her. He was too much of a gentleman for that. No, it was herself Storm did not trust. Brett was too handsome, too debonair, too polished, too cultured, too reminiscent of all the things she had left behind in New Orleans; and she was too terribly lonely. Deep in her heart the girl knew only her love for the man who'd deserted her stood between them. Had the shadow of Wolf not separated them, Storm realized she would have been Brett Diamond's mistress by now. All San Francisco thought she was, and she had not disabused them of the notion. A woman alone was fair game for any man – or so they all believed. Though by profession a gambler, Brett still had a fast draw and was known to have no qualms about using it. The rumor that she was his woman helped keep Storm safe from the unwelcome attentions of other men, for there were many who could not credit her own skill with a pistol, despite the tale of her gunfight with the ugly-faced miner.

'Lightning, Lightning, where are you?' Brett asked gently, bringing her back sharply to reality.

'Standing right beside you,' she responded lightly, avoiding his question. 'Shall we go open up?'

'Whenever you're ready.'

'I'd like to say a few words to the help first. They've all worked very hard.'

'Of course.'

Slowly Storm approached the stage where the employees had all gathered, awaiting her instructions. She smiled, proud of and pleased by what she saw. No longer were the girls painted, cheap, and tawdry, the men grimy and unshaven. By treating them like ladies and gentlemen, instead of whores and ne'er-do-wells, Storm had given them back their pride and self-esteem. The girls were artfully made-up to enhance their natural beauty, rather than their faces looking like jesters' masks. Instead of the vulgar, knee-high dresses they'd previously worn, each girl was garbed in the costume of her origins. China Doll was exotically beautiful in her colorful silk kimono with its wide obi and her hand-painted fan. Flamenco Rose was breathtakingly sultry in the traditional ruffled gown worn by Spanish dancers. The men too were clean right down to their fingernails. Each one had been outfitted with a proper, garter-sleeved shirt and dark trousers, although no-one's clothes were as expensive or elaborate as the broadcloth suit Brett was wearing. Only the two bouncers, twin cousins of Li Kwan and whom Storm secretly suspected were members of one of the Chinese Tongs, were naked to their sashed waists, their legs encased in Oriental breeches. The girl thought the effect was startling and more than enough to deter trouble-makers, for the twins guarded the door like two Chinese dragons. They even frightened Storm to some extent. Their faces were impassive; their massively muscled arms were folded across their broad chests; and each had a wicked-looking dagger thrust into his sash.

Storm cleared her throat. 'I just wanted to take a moment to tell you all how wonderful you look this evening and how much I thank you for all the hard work you've accomplished during the past two months. The Bon Ton's success will be greatly due to your efforts.' Everyone applauded this. Storm let the cheers go on for a few minutes, then raised one hand for silence. 'Ladies, I want to remind you that you are under no obligation to go upstairs with any client who does not take your fancy. If a customer gets nasty, call one of the gentlemen or the bouncers for assistance. This goes for you too, Little Italy. No stilettos in any of our guests, all right?'

The girl mentioned blushed, then sheepishly raised her skirt to remove her knife from her garter.

'Sorry, Miss Lightning,' she apologized, handing the blade over.

Storm smiled once more. '*Maintenant, mes amis*. Let's make *Monsieur* Diamond proud.'

25

Joe Jack gazed down at the Indian lance that had been driven into one of the fence posts of the corral and swore.

'Goddamned Comanches!'

With another loud oath he yanked the offending spear free, broke it over one knee, and threw it into the dirt.

'I wish you'd never attacked those Indian bastards, pa. We're short six more head from last night's count. Jesus! They get more brazen with every raid. The next thing you know they'll be burning down the frigging house – with us in it!'

'You're talking nonsense, Joe Jack, as usual,' Gabriel retorted dryly. 'I've got too many men guarding the place for those red devils to come within a mile of it.'

'Yeah? Then how come they managed to make off with six of our cattle right underneath our very noses?' Gabriel had no answer to this. 'Well, Goddamn it, pa,' Joe Jack continued impatiently. 'This has been going on for over four years now and all because of your frigging fiancée, who never wanted you to begin with!'

'You shut your mouth, boy!'

'No, I won't. Goddamn it, pa! Those Comanches are costing us a fortune. I reckon they've done us out of about five hundred cattle since you raided their camp that summer – not to mention the horses they've stolen – and some of it was damned good breeding stock too. Now just when are you going to put a stop to it, pa?'

'When I get good and ready, and not before. I've got other things to worry about besides those frigging cattle.'

'Well, Jeeeeesus Christ! Knock me down with a feather! I never thought I'd live to hear you say *that*! Shit! 'Pears to me like what folks have been saying's true. You've gone plum *loco*, pa; that's what. That frigging French bitch has driven you clean out of your mind—'

'Goddamn it, Joe Jack! I told you to shut your mouth!'

'Well, hell, pa. That's what they've been saying, and what else am I supposed to think when you waste more time trying to find one French chit, who didn't give a damn about you in the first place, than you do protecting the interests of Tierra Rosa?'

'Don't you mean *your* interests, boy? Huh!' Gabriel snorted, then smirked. 'The ranch isn't yours yet, Joe Jack: I don't know how many times I have to tell you that to get it through your thick skull. And I'll tell you something else too, smart mouth: you'd better watch your step with me from now on. You're already treading on thin ice, boy, and by the time I return from San Francisco, you might just have fallen through it.'

Joe Jack's eyes narrowed cunningly. 'And just what do you mean by that, pa?'

'That got you, didn't it, boy? Just why do you think I'm driving the cattle into San Francisco this time for slaughter, instead of New Orleans?'

'Why, I hadn't really thought about it, pa. I guess I figured the price of beef was higher in California than Louisiana.'

'Huh! A lot you know about it then. See; you're not as smart as you thought. I've located my bride-to-be,' Gabriel spoke triumphantly, 'in San Francisco – and when I get back to Tierra Rose, I'm going to throw the biggest wedding party this state's ever seen.'

'Jesus, pa! You just won't give up, will you? You just can't admit you've been defeated, can you?'

'Nobody beats Gabriel North, boy. Nobody! You remember that now, you hear?'

'You're crazy!' Joe Jack called angrily to his father's retreating figure. 'She won't have you! Aw, shit!' he cursed, then kicked the fence post so hard he nearly broke his toe.

*   *   *

The reopening of The Bon Ton was a grand success. It seemed as though everybody who was anybody in San Francisco came, even if only out of curiosity. Word of the notorious gunfight had spread, and there were many who desired a glimpse of the woman who was rumored to have gunned down mean Coleman Hawkins and was now Brett Diamond's mistress.

'I'll say one thing for you, Brett,' one man spoke up, gazing with appreciation at Storm in the distance. 'You've got damned fine taste in women.'

Brett only smiled that strange, enigmatic grin, and went on playing cards as usual; and as usual, his jet black eyes watched the saloon like a hawk. Before they had done so because Saucy Sal had been a haphazard hostess at best, prone to drunkenness and being cheated by the customers. There was nothing incompetent about Storm, however, and Brett knew his watchfulness stemmed from wanting to protect the woman he'd named French Lightning. Momentarily he frowned. It had been a long time since he'd truly cared for a woman, although he'd treated all his mistresses courteously and parted with a smile when he'd tired of them.

How ironic, he thought, that I've never even so much as kissed the woman all San Francisco believes my new mistress, that I should have fallen like a fool for a woman in love with another man. What kind of a man was he, I wonder, and why did he desert her when she loved him so, still loves him? Only a fool would have tired of French Lightning, and only a cad would have left her destitute, without friends or funds, to make her way alone in the world with the child he gave her. Ah, we are all fools, we men, made so by a glance, a kiss, and our own desires.

He looked down at his cards and shrugged, seeing he had won the hand. He always did. Carelessly he raked in his winnings, determined French Lightning would be his too in the end.

Gracefully, slipping away just once to tuck Chance in as

promised, Storm moved among the tables, nodded graciously to the clients as she passed, pausing now and then to speak to the few she'd met while out driving with Brett to choose the new furnishings for the saloon. Everything was going well, and she was pleased. There had been only one minor incident, when a customer had gotten ugly with Outlaw Red, an Irish girl rumored to have fled her homeland after killing a man. A quick glance toward the twins, Li Chiang and Li Fang, had taken care of the matter immediately. The man involved would not be admitted to The Bon Ton again.

Certain all was progressing smoothly, Storm relieved Brass-Hearted Kate, who was dealing at one of the tables, and signaled Riley to bring her a small brandy.

At last it was closing time. The girl rose, bidding everyone good night before slipping down the hall to Brett's office where Riley would deliver the cash box after locking up. Minutes later Brett joined her, a bottle and two glasses in hand.

'What's that?' Storm asked.

'French champagne for French Lightning,' he spoke as he uncorked the decanter. 'Only the best for the best. To your success, my dear.'

'And yours,' the girl replied, downing the bubbly contents of her glass. 'After all, it's your saloon.'

'Ah, yes, but *you*, my dear, have truly given it *bon ton*.'

There was fire in his eyes when he looked at her. Storm blushed, wishing her heart would stop beating so fast. He took the empty glass from her hand. Their fingers touched, did not disengage. An odd little silence fell over the room. The door opened. The tense spell of the moment was broken.

'Well, Riley' – Brett dropped Storm's hand and turned – 'everybody gone home?'

'Aye, the last o' the lot be gone, sir. Faith and *begorra*, 'Twas a night to remember – in more ways than one, sir.' Riley heaved the heavy cash box up onto Brett's desk. 'Sure and I'll wager this thing weighs more than the Blarney Stone, Mr Brett.'

'Well, let's count it out and see, shall we?'

Brett's slender fingers flicked through the bills expertly, while Riley stacked the coins into neat piles and Storm made careful entries in the ledger. Over the past two months she had learned that Brett, who won so easily, valued money the less for it and was extremely careless about his bookkeeping, so she had taken over the tiresome chore herself. Two hours later they had reached a final figure.

'*Mon Dieu*.' Storm leaned back in her chair, weary but exuberant. 'We made *thousands* of dollars.' She had never seen so much money in her life.

'Twenty-five thousand, to be exact, and we'll do even better than that tomorrow night,' Brett said, locking the funds away in his safe. 'Come, Lightning. I'll wager you're starving, and I *did* promise you supper.'

They dined on Chinese food, painstakingly prepared by Li Kwan in the kitchen, and washed it down with more of the champagne. Storm sighed as she savored the last morsels.

'Hmmm. That was delicious. Thank you.'

'My pleasure.'

The girl glanced up with surprise at his suddenly brooding tone of voice. 'You've been very quiet this evening, Brett. Is something bothering you?'

'No, not at all.' He roused himself. 'I'm sorry. I was just thinking.'

'About what?'

'Can't you guess?' His intense black eyes burned her like hot coals again, fire flickering in their mysterious depths. He reached out one hand to draw her close, his fingers wrapping themselves in her tangle of ribanded curls. 'I want you, Lightning,' he whispered.

His mouth was warm on hers. His soft mustache tickled her gently as his tongue parted her lips. It seemed as though he kissed her forever before he swept her up from her chair and carried her to his bed, laying her down tenderly, and Storm, dizzy from the champagne and filled with longing for a man's touch, did not protest.

Wolf's gone, she told her aching heart, and you'll never see him again. Life has to go on for you, and Brett has been so very kind . . .

He cupped her breasts through the thin satin of her dress, fondling them until the nipples strained upward rigidly, their taut little peaks outlined clearly beneath the smooth, shiny yellow material. Then slowly, caressingly he slid the tiny sleeves of Storm's gown down the length of her arms until the ripe, naked mounds lay exposed to his hungry gaze. He lowered his mouth to cover one rosy bud with his lips as the girl moaned quietly, the champagne and the languid love-making having taken their toll of her.

Dazedly she breathed, 'Wolf; oh, Wolf!'

Immediately Brett stiffened and drew away. Storm never even realized her mistake. She had fallen asleep, tears streaking her cheeks. Silently Brett rearranged her gown, then left the room, closing the door softly behind him.

Months passed, but after that night of the grand reopening of The Bon Ton, Brett never again attempted to make love to Storm. Sometimes she would catch his jet black eyes watching her longingly, hungrily and know he still wanted her, was waiting for her to come to him, but the shadow of Wolf stood between them, would always stand between them. The girl knew that now, for she had awakened that morning in Brett's room, alone, and remembered whose name she had murmured so piteously in the darkness. Brett had never once confronted her with or reproached her for that name, but Storm realized nevertheless he had been deeply hurt. Not knowing how to explain, she had not attempted to apologize. Thus in tacit agreement they had never spoken about that night. Still it taunted them both and never more so than when they bid each other good night in the upstairs hall to retire to their respective chambers. Often Storm lay awake in the blackness, listening to Chance's gentle breathing beside her, and wondered why she could not bring herself to slip away to Brett's waiting arms; and always she would find the answer in Wolf's dark visage, his midnight blue eyes smoldering with passion as he took her in her dreams.

Gabriel glanced about curiously, for he had never been to San Francisco before, but he saw little to interest him. The place was a slum, filled with worthless foreigners, all for whom he had no use. He noted an obviously wealthy Chinese being carried past in a rickshaw and snorted to himself. Damned upstarts, all of them! He shook his head. It was a sad day indeed when those who weren't white forgot their place in the world. Jesus! To what were things coming?

Well, he'd sold all his cattle, had, in fact, gotten a better price for them in San Francisco than he would have in New Orleans. All that remained now was for him to find Storm Lesconflair. Then he'd be quit of this city.

Muttering under his breath, he started down the street, occasionally stopping passersby or going inside a shop to inquire about his bride-to-be. It seemed no one had heard of Storm Lesconflair, however, and at last Gabriel returned angrily to his hotel. By God, if Mimi La Roche had sent him on a wild-goose chase, he'd see her out of Corpus Christi on a rail!

Galveston, Mimi had said. *Your Frenchie took the stagecoach to Galveston. Told the driver she was bound for San Francisco . . .*

She *had* to be here! Somewhere in this frigging town was the woman for whom he'd waited and searched over five years, and Gabriel meant to have her. Storm Lesconflair wasn't going to get away from him again – not now, not ever.

'Rough day, Gabriel?' Montgomery Niles greeted him as he entered the lobby.

Shit. Gabriel had forgotten he'd accepted an invitation to supper with several of the cattle buyers this evening.

'Sorry, Monty. Dawson, Ed, how are you, boys?' He shook hands with the three men. 'Have I kept you gentlemen waiting?'

'Not at all, Gabriel. Not at all,' Monty responded, grinning.

'Hell, we just figured you were afraid to face us after the way you cheated us on your cattle. Shit. I never saw a man drive such a hard bargain in all my life. Dawson here's been crying about it all afternoon.'

They all laughed.

'My boys get you all taken care of?' Gabriel asked.

'Sure thing, Gabriel,' Ed Wilkins spoke up. 'They're damned fine men, your hands. We didn't have a bit of trouble.'

'Glad to hear it. Glad to hear it,' Gabriel replied, forcing himself to present a jovial façade, although he was champing at the bit inside. Damn! He wished he hadn't agreed to have supper with the three, even though they were some of the most important men in San Francisco. He was too anxious to find Storm Lesconflair, now that his business had been concluded.

'Well, gentlemen, shall we go?' Dawson Sinclair suggested.

'Any time you're ready,' Gabriel asked.

'Damned fine meal.' Monty leaned back in his chair, took a drag of his cigar, and winked at the waitress who was pouring him a cup of coffee. 'You just can't beat The Golden Nugget for good food. Well, Gabriel, did you get the rest of your affairs settled today?'

'Unfortunately, no.' The rancher's face darkened.

'Here, honey.' Ed grabbed the waitress's bottom. 'Bring us another round of drinks.'

'Yes, Mr Wilkins.'

'What's the problem, Gabriel?' Dawson queried.

'I'm looking for a woman.'

'Aren't we all?' Monty laughed.

'Boy, don't let your wife hear you say that,' Ed teased. 'She's liable to take a knife to your balls.'

'Oh, Fanny's all right, just a bit wild, I guess. What kind of a filly did you have in mind, Gabriel? Dawson here knows 'em all. Ain't that right, Dawson?'

'The ones worth knowing anyway.' Dawson grinned.

'Cut it out, boys.' Gabriel frowned. 'Storm isn't that kind of a woman.' And even if she is, he thought silently, nobody's going to know about it but me. Tierra Rosa's going to have its Southern belle, that high-born French bitch I bought if it's the last thing I ever do.

'Shit,' Ed drawled. 'They all got a price. Some just come a little dearer than others; that's all.'

'Yeah? Well, this one's already cost me a pretty penny, and I still haven't gotten what I paid for.'

'Storm,' Dawson mused. 'Storm what, Gabriel? Tell me her last name, and I'll see if I can't help you out.'

'Lesconflair.'

'Storm Lesconflair. No.' Dawson shook his head. 'I can't say as that rings a bell. Name mean anything to either of you boys?' he inquired of the others.

'No, can't say it does,' Monty answered.

'Me neither,' Ed chimed in.

'Tell you what, Gabriel: has she got a handle of some sort, you know – a nickname?' Dawson clarified, seeing the rancher's puzzled expression.

'Damned if I know.'

'Well, hell. What does she look like, Gabriel?' Ed asked. 'Dawson's had so many he can't remember half their names anyway. Ain't that right, Dawson?'

The three cattle buyers all laughed again.

'I doubt if Dawson's Storm's type,' Gabriel intoned dryly, irritated. 'She's about so high' – he demonstrated with his hands – 'smallish build, figure that would knock your eyes out, long black hair, gray eyes – bedroom eyes, and a lush scarlet mouth that kind of pouts at the corners. Well, here, I've got a picture of her, since you're all so frigging interested.' He reached into his vest pocket and pulled out the battered daguerreotype of Storm he carried always.

'Jesus Christ!' Dawson swore, then whistled. 'Why didn't you say so? That's French Lightning, Brett Diamond's mistress.

*   *   *

She was wearing a pale rose dress that reminded Gabriel of the first time he'd ever seen her – at the Robitaille barbecue – and of their engagement party in the gardens of Vaillance. Her blue-black hair was hanging down her back in a tangled cascade of curls and ribands. Her gray eyes were sparkling like morning dew as she shuffled a deck of cards, spread them across the table at which she was seated, flipped them over expertly like a stack of dominos, then back, then swept them into a neat pack once more. Her dimples peeped at the corners of her inviting mouth as she smiled and handed the deck to the gentleman on her right for the cut, then began to deal the cards out one by one.

My God, Gabriel thought with grudging admiration. There is no end to the whore's talents!

'Place your bets, gentlemen; place your bets,' he heard her say.

'Well, Gabriel' – Monty clapped one hand on the rancher's shoulder – 'is that her?'

'Yeah, it's her all right.'

'Well, what are you waiting for?' Ed piped up. 'Go on over, and say hello.'

'I want to know which one's Diamond first.'

'That well-dressed, silver-haired gentleman in the corner.' Dawson pointed.

Gabriel took a long hard look at the man. 'Pretty fancy, isn't he?'

'Don't let it fool you. He carries a derringer in his coat pocket, and he's damned fast with it too,' Dawson warned. 'He's already killed three men over that French chit.'

'Yeah, well, I'm not too bad with a gun myself, and death and I are old friends. Bartender, give these boys a drink on me. They've earned it,' Gabriel called to Riley, then turned back to study Storm once more.

French Lightning. Brett Diamond's mistress. Dawson's words hammered in Gabriel's brain as he watched her. The Goddamned slut! How had she dared scorn him and all he'd offered for that frigging half-breed Indian he'd hung, then made her way west to San Francisco to become the whore of a fancy-pants gambler rather than seeking him, Gabriel North, the richest rancher in all Texas, out? Well, by God, she'd pay; he'd make her pay if it were the last thing he ever did. He'd see her on her knees, begging him for mercy, before he was through!

Storm paid no heed to the four men at the bar; in fact, she never even noticed them. The Bon Ton was crowded, as usual, and she was too busy concentrating on the game at her table.

'Place your bets, gentlemen; place your bets,' she said.

To the girl's surprise someone tossed a cowboy hat on the table amidst the dollar bills and silver coins. She glanced up wryly, intending to tell the prankster off. Instead the words died on her lips and her heart lurched in her breast. Stunned, she closed her eyes tightly for a moment and shook her head to clear it, thinking she had drunk too much brandy, but when she again peeped out from beneath her fringe of black lashes, the man was still present. One hand went to her throat. Her gray eyes flew open wide.

'I don't believe it!' she breathed. 'I don't believe it!'

There stood Gabriel North, grinning bold as brass and saying,

'Miss Lesconflair, I still think you're about the prettiest little gal this side of the Rio Grande.'

26

Storm's mind was in a turmoil, torn between three men, one who had deserted her, one who had pursued her relentlessly, and one who had offered her his protection and asked for nothing in return. Ever since that night when Gabriel North had first walked through the doors of The Bon Ton, it had been so, and Storm knew sooner or later she was going to be forced to make a choice between them. It was not a decision to which she was looking forward. Her heart lay with Wolf, but Wolf was gone – she would never see him again – and her head dictated practicality. The past was too painful to recall. The wound of Wolf's betrayal had grown more bitter with the passing of time. Beneath Storm's bright, brittle façade she ached deep inside with hurt and resentment, and she realized at last she could not go on in such a manner. She would destroy herself if she did.

Gabriel's arrival in San Francisco had made her recognize her life at The Bon Ton was like a frantically spinning carousel at a carnival gone mad and that she had plunged into it with a pitiful desperation in order to prevent herself from having to think – to remember. She had filled up her days with the hustle and bustle of Brett's business affairs and her nights with laughter and lights, cards and brandy – frivolous things that had served to keep the world at bay and loneliness from her evenings. She had not really wanted a new life; she could have built one with Brett had that been true. She had only wanted to keep on running, to find a place where all was illusion, and reality could not intrude.

Now she knew she had only been fooling herself. There was only one way to escape life – and it was final. The avenue she had chosen was but a blind alley in a maze, a dead end from

411

which she must retrace her steps back to the living if she were to survive. In that moment Storm hated Wolf and all for which he had stood.

She tossed her head defiantly. He gray eyes smoldered. Her lip curled. He had used her, had awakened her heart and body with his whispered words of love, the fiery caresses of his hands, then he had scorned her, cast aside both her and their child without a second thought. She must force herself to be just as hard and uncaring, to put Wolf from her mind as coldly and cruelly as he had done her. She would never think of him again. She would go crazy if she did.

Storm glanced down at the desk before her where a scrap of paper lay, upon which she'd idly written the three men's names.

Deliberately she obliterated Wolf's.

She stared at the remaining two. Brett and Gabriel. Slowly she chewed the tip of her pen as she considered them. *Mrs Brett Diamond*. Was there not just a touch of flash to Brett's elegance? Just a hint of vulgar commonness beneath his gracefully acquired class? For Brett's debonair manner *was* acquired. He was the bastard son of a drunken gambler and a dance hall girl – as at home in the hellhole The Bon Ton had once been as he was now since Storm had reformed it. Money meant nothing to him. He won and lost fortunes at poker tables, and he cared not on which side of the tracks they were located. True, he liked the finer things in life, but if he did not have them, he simply shrugged his shoulders in that careless way of his and made do with what he had. Whereas his seamy childhood would have made another man ruthlessly ambitious, it had left Brett with the attitude that life went on, regardless of the circumstances, and only death was to be avoided at all costs. He was kind, and he cared for Storm in a languid fashion, but he would never sweep her off her feet in a savage blaze of uncontrollable passion as Wolf had done. No, Brett's lovemaking would be lazily sensuous, tender, unhurried. There was no fire in Brett. He was too cool, too suave for that, and Storm knew if she left him tomorrow, though he would mourn her loss, he would easily find another to take her place. He would not pursue her with grim determination as Wolf had once done, as Gabriel had done.

Mrs Gabriel North. How solid and respectable that sounded, but was it not just a trifle matronish? Just the slightest bit fusty? The girl imagined herself gracing Gabriel's table, smiling graciously at all his business acquaintances, making polite chit-chat with their wives. Her days would begin with a silver tray in bed, a hot bath, and an appropriate selection of gowns. Her morning would be taken up with approving menus and writing proper notes on delicately edged stationery at a fragile-legged desk. Her afternoons would be spent in a round of teas and shopping sprees, her evenings in attending those social functions at which it was necessary the 'right' people be seen. And her nights— She and Gabriel would have separate bedrooms of course, but he would enter her suite like a man who knew it was his right to be there and her duty to submit to him, whatever his desires. Unlike Brett there was no tenderness in Gabriel, only an overwhelming brute obsession to take and possess, to conquer utterly, while giving as little as possible in return.

Only Wolf had understood a woman's strange need to stand on her own two feet beside her man, yet feel his arm about her small shoulders as well, protecting her when the world became too cruel. Only Wolf had understood a woman's deep longing for trust and faithfulness in a relationship, her yearning for the knowledge that her man placed too high a value on their intimacy to ever share it with another. Only Wolf had understood the desperate fragility of a woman's surrender, had sensed that for her man to take her all without honestly cherishing the gift she offered of herself was to destroy her love for him in the end.

Oh, to be Eyes-Like-Summer-Rain again for just a little while.

Blindly Storm reached out and tore the scrap of paper in

413

half, then crumpled the two pieces in her trembling hands before she laid her head on the desk and wept bitterly for the past she had lost and the uncertain future that was staring her in the face.

It was too late, and Brett Diamond was restless, too restless to return to The Bon Ton to be tantalized by Storm's aloof nearness, the rose scent of her perfume, the full ripe curve of her breasts swelling from the low-cut bodice of her gown. Brett felt his loins quicken at just the thought of her and inhaled sharply.

The smells of the wharf assaulted his nostrils, but he felt no distaste at the unpleasant odor of fish mingled with smoke and spindrift. It reminded him of the New England docks upon which he'd grown up, and somehow the aroma was touchingly familiar.

He sauntered on down the wooden planks, his walking-stick in hand, his brandy-tinged lust increasing as his thoughts continued to dwell on the woman he'd named French Lightning. She'd been different of late, more elusive than ever since the man called Gabriel North had come to the city. Gabriel had asked her to marry him – of that Brett was sure – but Storm had refused him. Still the Texas rancher was persistent, and of late Brett had noticed Storm wavering, beginning to realize the life Gabriel offered would provide a much more proper upbringing for her son than that which Brett had to give. He sighed. Storm understood his careless attitude about worldly possessions. In a strange way, perhaps, she even shared it; but what woman had ever lived who had not wanted more for her child than she had had herself?

Brett sighed once more. He didn't want to lose her. Not only did he desire Storm, but she had become invaluable to him in his business as well. She had made a success of his once haphazardly run saloon, and for the first time in his life he no longer wondered if tomorrow he would wake up in the gutter out of which he'd crawled time and again. Though not essential to his well-being, he had to admit the feeling *was* pleasant. Brett made up his mind; he would ask her to marry him. She would not be his mistress, but perhaps now she would become his wife. She had brooded too long over her husband. Her hurt at his desertion had begun to turn to hate, and more and more her body had been craving the physical release of lovemaking to which her husband had wakened her. Brett had heard her prowling her room late at night, long after they'd closed The Bon Ton, and had known what ailed her, though Storm had refused to admit it to herself. She needed the feel of a man inside her again. She was too sensual a woman not to long for such.

Yes, Brett would make her a proposal of marriage. He should have understood a woman like Storm would never consent to being his mistress. Despite the setbacks she'd suffered in life, she was still a lady – and proud, so very proud. Surely she would prefer him to a blustering bull like Gabriel North. Brett smiled. Of course she would. He had seen the way she shuddered at the Texas rancher's nearness, though she had hidden her feelings well. The thought of selling herself to Gabriel North for her son's sake appalled her.

Certain he would triumph in the end, Brett continued on down the wharf. His mind lay at ease now, but his body did not, and he remembered a Chinese girl he'd seen earlier in one of the cribs lining the docks. His footsteps hastened in that direction, but not in time to prevent the three men who'd been following him from seizing him roughly. Brett cursed himself a thousand times for being so lost in his thoughts he'd forgotten to remain aware of his wretched surroundings, then he lashed out with his cane, there being no time to draw his pistol. The heavy silver knob of the walking-stick cracked open the skull of one of his assailants with a sharp, satisfying report, but in moments Brett found himself being overpowered by the remaining two men. His heart sank as he spied the large burlap bag the fallen man had carried, for the sight of it told him he was not merely being robbed as he'd first suspected, but shanghaied as well. He renewed his struggles valiantly, but his efforts proved fruitless. He caught an earth-shattering blow to one temple and crumpled to the wooden planks in despair, knowing he would awaken on a slow boat to hell.

The Bon Ton was chaos and becoming more so with each day of Brett's absence. Storm was just certain something horrible had happened to her gallant gambler, and she shivered uncontrollably as she thought about the numerous murders that occurred daily in San Francisco and how Brett had joked about how people just pitched the bodies in the Bay. Dear God! It was terrible – just terrible living in a city that had no law and order! Even Texas, for all its harsh ruthlessness, had had its small-town sheriffs, its feared Texas Rangers, and an occasional US marshal. Here people took the law into their own hands. A man would kill a stranger for less than looking at him with a crooked eye. It was dreadful, simply, dreadful, and Storm grew more and more afraid with each passing day.

With Brett's disappearance the atmosphere of The Bon Ton had changed subtly, and the clientele had steadily begun to worsen. Despite the watchful presence of Li Chiang and Li Fang, rough miners and cutthroats were once again beginning to filter inside the saloon. Already there had been several fights and three killings, and a group of coarse men thrown out into the street by the two Chinese bouncers had actually smashed the expensive glass-paned windows that lined the front of The Bon Ton. Storm had had to board up the gaping holes four times since when the scum she'd previously banned from the saloon had come by to rip the planks off and jeer at her insultingly. Moreoever, she'd started to receive scrawled notes threatening her life, and she knew, despite her ability with her revolvers, she was no longer safe in San Francisco. She'd scorned too many men, secure in the knowledge that they'd thought her Brett's woman. Now Brett was gone, and his reputation alone could not protect her. *Sainte Marie*! What had happened to her gallant gambler?

'Surely you must see you can't go on this way, Miss Lesconflair,' Gabriel North told her over and over. 'The Bon Ton is too much for you to run alone, even with your Chinese watchdogs.'

Storm still persisted, not yet willing to concede defeat and marry the man who had relentlessly pursued her for the past six years. Even now there was something cold and hard in Gabriel's eyes that nagged her, made her shudder when his lips brushed her hand. Things had been going so well before he'd arrived in San Francisco; now suddenly everything was all wrong, and she wondered briefly if he'd had something to do with Brett's strange disappearance.

That night someone set fire to the saloon. The kitchen, storeroom, and Brett's office were destroyed before they managed to put the blaze out. Thank God, Brett's safe was made of heavy metal and had refused to burn! At least Storm was not left destitute. Nevertheless the latest incident so badly frightened several of the girls that they packed their bags and departed, seeking employment with The Bon Ton's competition.

'It's not that we want to leave, Miss Lightning,' they said nervously when Storm pleaded with them to stay, even offered them higher wages, 'but all the money in the world ain't worth our lives, and someone's got it in for you real bad since Mr Brett's disappearance. We can't risk staying on. Lord only knows what might happen next.'

Storm could not argue with them – not when the same fear was plaguing her own mind. She sighed and reluctantly let them go, wishing them the best. The following morning she approached Li Kwan and told him they must have help.

'If people knew we were under the protection of a Tong, they'd leave us alone, Li Kwan! You know they would! Please, Li Kwan; it's the only way! There must be *someone* you know who would be willing to assist me for a price!'

His black eyes were unfathomable, but at last he nodded. 'Velly well, Missy. I go and allange such a meeting, but I plomise nothing, you unnahstan'?'

'Yes, yes, just do the best you can.'

The next day Li Kwan hitched up Brett's buggy and team (which, mercifully, had not been stolen in his absence) and told Storm he would take her into Chinatown. She clutched her open reticule tightly, fingers wrapped anxiously about the hideout pistol within. She wasn't taking any chances. Things had gotten too violent, and she was desperately frightened. Beside her Chance wore a worried frown on his small face. He bit his lip as the vehicle started down the hill, dodging the noisy traffic.

As usual, the raucous hubbub overwhelmed them both. Snarled drays and carts pushed and shoved their way through the street, battling each other for the limited openings in the tangled, wheel-rutted lanes until little semblance of orderly progression remained. Drivers hauled on their reins and shouted epithets at horses and pedestrians alike. Whips cracked; wheels scraped; and vehicles jostled one another and splintered on impact. Up ahead a beer wagon had overturned, several of its broken and bashed barrels spilling their frothy contents onto the road. Storm hoped it wasn't her delivery, but had a sickening feeling at the pit of her stomach that it was. She watched in dismay as the yellow liquid bubbled and soaked its way into the ground. The driver's team neighed piercingly and lunged, chafing at their restraints as the barrels continued to roll and shatter and gush, spewing foam like geysers. At last the horses broke free of their shafts, galloping mindlessly down the street, trampling passersby and adding to the general pandemonium.

To Storm's petrified shock someone chose that exact moment to fire a shot at her. The report echoed loudly over the din, and at first the girl only dimly realized there'd been some sort of explosion. Then she felt the bullet sear past her in a sharp, heated whir, nearly grazing her cheek, and saw Li Kwan flail spastically for a moment before slumping to one side on the seat ahead of her, blood pumping from his back, spraying her and Chance with its warm, sticky red wetness.

She screamed and screamed again as Brett's team reared and plunged forward uncontrollably, whinnying shrilly as the wildly careening horses belonging to the driver of the beer wagon swerved toward them. With a jolt Brett's buggy suddenly bounced onto the sidewalk, tilting dangerously and pitching Li Kwan's body into the street before the vehicle righted itself to clatter with a furious, pounding roar down the wooden planks. Horrified pedestrians scattered and ran for their lives, yelling and screaming at the tops of their lungs. Storm lost her reticule as she grabbed blindly for Chance to keep him from being thrown out. Her revolver was flung free. It struck the side of a building, discharging. There were more shouts and screams as someone fell, and Storm did not know if the unfortunate woman had been hit by the gun's deafening blast or had merely tripped and sprawled trying to escape the runaway buggy. There was no time for the girl to wonder further, however, or feel any pity for the poor woman's plight, for her own had worsened considerably.

Brett's team had spied an opening in the long stream of hitching rails. The horses lurched through the gap precariously. The vehicle sprang forward, smashing crazily against a post, then clearing the sidewalk to land with a wrenching thud upon the ground. Mud and manure flew. The pillar toppled. The overhanging roof that had been supported by the post collapsed, sending shards of wood flying. The terrified team thundered on heedlessly, dragging the helpless buggy with it.

At last the harness frayed and snapped, and the rampaging horses yanked free of the vehicle, leaving it to collide briefly with a peddler's cart. Pots and pans soared into the air, then hammered with a resounding ring as they hurtled to the earth and clashed upon the sidewalk. Storm felt a heavy iron skillet slam against her arm bruisingly as the buggy raced on down the hill, narrowly sideswiping a hastily abandoned buckboard in the process. Buildings flashed by in a blur as the vehicle gained impetus, rolling and rocking as the shafts splintered along the pitted lanes.

To Storm's utter horror she saw a heavily loaded freight wagon pull out from a side road at the bottom of the hill, directly blocking the path of the onrushing buggy. She crushed Chance to her tightly, burying his head against her breast.

They were going to die.

'Jump, Storm! Jump! For God's sake, jump!'

It was Gabriel. Somehow he was galloping dangerously alongside them, sawing cruelly at the reins of his petrified stallion. The horse screamed, rolling its white eyes as the rancher forced it closer and closer to the vehicle. Gabriel's mouth set in a grim, determined line, and for the first time in her life Storm gave thanks for his masterful, brute strength that enabled him to retain control of the animal.

There were only moments to spare. Terrified, she flung Chance from her grasp with all her might toward Gabriel's body, saw with relief the rancher's outstretched arm close about her son's whimpering figure, saw the boy, despite his fear, had sense enough to cling to Gabriel's neck tightly, freeing the rancher to grab for Storm herself. The buggy reeled on ceaselessly toward certain doom. The girl took a deep breath and jumped. Gabriel's strong hand gripped one of her wildly flailing arms tightly, nearly wrenching it from its socket as Storm slammed hard against his stallion, snatching desperately at the saddle horn to prevent herself from being dragged under the horse's deadly, cutting hooves.

The vehicle rammed into the freight wagon just as Gabriel managed to swerve at the last minute to avoid the terrible collision. Slowly he pulled the animal to a halt, allowing Storm to slide to her knees. She was scratched and battered and gasping for air as she fell upon the ground. She feared she would vomit any minute. She almost did when she saw the top half of the buggy had been sheared clean off by the freight wagon before Brett's entire vehicle had shattered to pieces.

Her stomach lurched sickeningly at the sight, then, mercifully, she fainted.

'You what?' Storm shrieked disbelievingly, then fell back moaning against the pillows as her head spun dizzily.

'I said I sold The Bon Ton,' Gabriel repeated calmly, not in the least perturbed by her angry glare. 'Let's face it, Storm: you would have had to get rid of the place sooner or later. It was simply too much for you to run alone, and I doubt seriously if Brett Diamond is planning to return.'

The rancher thought smugly of how cleverly he'd managed to dispose of his rival. Gabriel sincerely hoped Diamond liked Chinese food, since if he'd survived the strenuous journey, he was halfway to Macao by now, a much better scheme, the rancher thought, than having Brett's body turn up and Storm begin to ask rather unpleasant questions.

'You had no right to do that, Gabriel,' the girl spoke, her words clipped with cool rage, for ever since the accident a week ago, the rancher seemed to have taken complete charge of her life. Despite the fact that she was alive due only to his daring intervention, Storm resented his control over her. 'The Bon Ton wasn't yours to sell, and people don't just disappear. Brett's alive somewhere; I just know he is—'

'Even so, there was nothing else to be done, Storm. The doctor said you needed to have absolute rest and quiet. That didn't mean running a saloon. Besides, the place was a mess when I got there. Most of the help ran off after hearing about your accident, and the vandals in this town naturally had a heyday helping themselves to anything that wasn't nailed down. Serves Diamond right for deserting you the way he did. Now when are you going to stop this shilly-shallying around and agree to marry me? I've got to get back to Tierra Rosa before Joe Jack steals me blind.'

'Gabriel, I've told you before I don't want to wed you,' Storm said wearily. 'I don't love you, and, besides, I already have a husband.'

'Huh!' the rancher snorted. 'One who abandoned you and your child. Besides, as *I've* told *you* before, you weren't legally married to that half-breed savage, and even if you were, you aren't anymore.'

'Why? What – what do you mean?'

'Nothing.'

'No, go on; tell me.'

'Aw, hell, Storm! I've been trying to keep it from you, because I didn't want to hurt you, but it's common knowledge around Texas that that gunslinger of yours got in a fight over some arrogant black-haired woman and tried to best one man too many. I hear they hung him for it,' Gabriel stated truthfully. 'He's dead, Storm. I'm sorry.'

'Dead? No! It isn't true! It just *can't* be true!'

The rancher shrugged, turning away so that the girl couldn't see his face. 'That's what they say, but believe what you will, Storm. It's up to you. I'm going downstairs to the dining room for some supper now. When I come back, I want you to give me your final answer one way or the other about marrying me, because I don't intend to ask you again. I'm not a patient man, and I've waited six years for you. I think that's long enough.'

With these ominously prophetic words Gabriel left her.

The silence, after he'd gone, seemed deafening. It drummed in Storm's head and rang over and over in her ears. *Dead!* *Dead!* *Dead!* No! It wasn't true! It just wasn't true! Wolf was too vital, too vibrantly alive to have been cheated of that life by a hangman – and because of an argument over a woman. A woman! Storm wondered what haunting face had taken the place of her own? What trembling lips had kissed the mouth that had once belonged to her? What soft curves had molded themselves against Wolf's body late in the moonlit evenings? That the woman had been her, only her, always her, did not occur to Storm. Instead she imagined a stranger's head pillowed against the cradle of her husband's shoulder, another cascade of long black hair billowing across his dark copper chest. Now she knew why he had not returned to her. He had found another to take her place in his heart. The knowledge was bitter, more bitter than his desertion had been. For a moment Storm was glad Wolf was dead.

It was only later, much later that the reality of his death swept over her, and she wept uncontrollably – for Wolf and perhaps for the girl in his arms she'd once been.

After a time she forced herself to rise, surprised to find the dizziness in her head had gone. She had cried it away, and now there was only a dull, throbbing ache in its place – and in her heart as well. She rubbed her temples briefly, then wet a rag with cool water from the basin on the dresser and pressed the cloth to her swollen red eyes. It soothed her, and after a minute she laid it down and stared into the mirror before her, scarcely recognizing the ravaged woman reflected therein. She was twenty-two years old, and she felt as though she were a hundred. The world seemed to have settled the heavy burden of its weight on her small, sagging shoulders. Valiantly Storm attempted to square the blades in her back, but she was too weary, too tired of trying, too emotionally drained, wrung out. Her shoulders slumped after the slight, exhausting effort.

She gazed around the luxurious hotel suite Gabriel had engaged for her after the accident. The rooms were all rose, sleek and plush with satin and velvet. Perhaps if she refused to marry him, the rancher would make certain the management presented her with the bill for the suite – and Chance's smaller room next door too. Storm pressed her hands against the sides of her head once more. How would she ever pay such a bill? She thought of Brett's safe, filled with money, then realized the men who'd vandalized the saloon would have broken the strong box open and stolen its contents. Perhaps Gabriel would even refuse to give her the proceeds from the sale of The Bon Ton. After all, the saloon had not belonged to her, and what was her word against that of the rancher? All San Francisco believed her a kept woman, Brett Diamond's mistress – and when had a man's mistress ever had any rights?

Oh God; oh, God! Why had Wolf abandoned her for

another woman? Why had he died? What had happened to Brett, and what was to become of Storm and her child?

The girl lurched unsteadily back to bed, feeling sick with despair and grief. Once more fate had charted the course of her life and left her no choice. Storm would have to marry Gabriel North, no matter her feelings toward him. He was rich. He would take care of her and Chance. They would never have to worry about the future again. Right now, becoming Gabriel's wife seemed a small price to pay for that security.

27

Galveston, Texas, 1855

'*Maman*, may I please have one of those?'

'Don't point, Chance; it's not polite,' Storm reprimanded the boy automatically as she looked over toward the next table where two young children, seated with their parents, were busily dipping spoons into small silver dishes of ice cream. 'Gabriel, would you mind?' She glanced up at her fiancé appealingly.

'Not at all,' he responded courteously, although inwardly he seethed. 'Waiter.'

'*Gracias, Señor North*.' Chance thanked the rancher when the order came. 'Hmmm. It is very good, *très bon*.'

'Papa, Chance. You are to refer to *Monsieur* North as papa,' Storm reminded the boy gently. 'And speak English. *Monsieur* North doesn't understand Spanish or French.'

'I don't know why not. *Ap'* spoke four languages after you taught him French. And why are you marrying *Señor* North anyway, *maman*? *Ap'* isn't truly dead, you know, whatever *Señor* North says.'

'Don't be impertinent, Chance!' Storm snapped more sharply than she'd intended. '*Monsieur* North has no need to speak any other language but English, and your real father *is* dead – gone to the Great-Spirit. *Entends*?'

'*Oui, maman*.' Chance's face fell. His lower lip trembled petulantly. He stabbed at his ice cream despondently, making a mess of the expensive treat. 'May I be excused?'

'Yes, you may.'

The boy slid off the chair, started to walk away, then suddenly turned back defiantly. 'I wish *ap'* and Li Kwan and

Brett were here! They'd fix you for treating me so mean! *Chop, chop*! I hate you, do you hear? I hate you both, and I'm not wearing this stupid tie anymore either!' He jerked off the offending bow and flung it onto the floor.

'Chance-The-Autumn-Wind! You go upstairs to your room immediately, and don't come down again until you can apologize to *Monsieur* North and me for your rude and wicked behavior! I'm sorry, Gabriel.' Storm turned to her fiancé after the boy had gone. 'Everything's just been too much for him, I guess. He just can't seem to adjust.'

'Well, Jesus Christ, Storm! How much time does he need? It's been over nine months since we left San Francisco.'

'I know, but he was sick on the ship a lot too, remember? We should have traveled overland with your ranch hands, I guess, as you suggested. But I'd forgotten how ill Chance was on the way to San Francisco and thought the trip would be easier by sea. I should have recalled how the waves affected him. I've just had so much on my mind— Oh, Gabriel, do try to have a little patience with the boy – for my sake if nothing else. I know he's just a – just a half-breed bastard to you – but he's my son, and I love him dearly.'

'All right, Storm. I'll try. You'd better go upstairs now, and get packed. The boys will probably be here today to escort us home.'

The girl sighed. 'It seems like an awful lot of trouble for them, coming all the way from Tierra Rosa for us. I don't know why we didn't just take the stagecoach to San Antonio.'

'Huh uh. If you think I'm taking any chances on you getting away from me this time, you're crazy. Besides, the wages I pay those frigging hands, they ought to be willing to go to the moon for me if I tell 'em so.'

'Gabriel, I do wish you'd try to watch your language,' Storm spoke, getting to her feet as he rose and pulled out her chair. 'Remember, you have a lady in your life now. You'll have to give up your old bachelor ways.'

She kissed him coolly on the cheek, then moved gracefully through the dining room to the lobby of the hotel, seemingly impervious to the admiring glances she received from passing men.

The bitch! Gabriel thought wrathfully when she had gone. The hypocrite! Lady, my ass! She's nothing but a whore, a half-breed Indian's woman, Brett Diamond's mistress! And still she dares to call herself a lady to me! My God! The very audacity of the slut! Well, after the wedding I'll make it clear she's to play the part of a lady only for the public's benefit, not for mine. It's Storm, the whore, I want in private, and I'd better get my money's worth too! Jesus! I get hard just thinking about it! And she never let me touch her once on the ship, the dissembling bitch! Well, I'll get even with her, the proud hussy! I'll see her humbled yet! We made a bargain, and I mean to see she keeps it! Still I'll have to be careful. She's learned a lot besides her whore's tricks since she was just a girl in New Orleans. They said she killed a man in San Francisco, gunned him down just as cool as you please when he accused her of cheating at cards. I wouldn't put it past her to try to do the same thing to me if she ever finds out it was me and my men who hung that savage gunslinger of hers – and me who sent her those threatening notes and fired that shot at her in San Francisco, killing that slant-eyed Chinese bastard. Jesus! That was close; but how in the hell was I supposed to know the damned team would bolt like that? I only meant to scare her just a bit; she's so frigging stubborn. Oh, well, I'll keep the little slut fooled. But the boy—

Gabriel felt the throbbing in his loins ease, his manhood shrinking slowly to normal once more at the thought of Storm's son.

I haven't tricked the boy. He knows. Somehow he knows! I can see it in his eyes, those cold hard midnight blue eyes of his frigging Indian sire. The little half-breed bastard. Every time he looks at me, he accuses me of murder with those eyes. He hates me. He'd like to kill me, just as I did his worthless, son-of-a-bitch father. I've got to get rid of him. Somehow I've just got to get rid of that brat!

The blinding yellow-orange sun shone hotly, fiercely, beating down with relentless fury upon the buggy that spun over the vast sweep of the Edwards Plateau toward Tierra Rosa. Storm closed her eyes for a moment to shut out the glare, licking her lips to moisten them. She had grown soft, had forgotten how the blistering Texas sun scorched the land and its inhabitants without mercy. She sighed, opened her eyes once more, adjusted her parasol, then leaned forward to wet her handkerchief with a bit of water from her canteen. She pressed the damp, lacy square to her temples and wrists for the hundredth time that day, it seemed. The vehicle rattled onward.

The cooler stretches of forest had long since given way to the tall prairie grass that covered the rolling plains. Now even that too was forced to yield its place as gradually the gently swelling crests flattened, leaving an endless, arid horizon in the distance. A fire-land, Storm thought, for here the only traces of green were the hardy cactuses and scrubby mesquite trees that rose upward in stark silhouette against the sun-washed blue of the sky. Other than this the terrain was a brilliant, overwhelming blend of red clay and golden sand.

'Pull up! Pull up, Hilton!' Gabriel called, cantering up to the buggy as the foreman obediently brought the vehicle to a stop.

'What is it, Gabriel? Is something wrong?' Storm inquired a trifle anxiously.

'No. I just wanted to see your face when you got your first glimpse of Tierra Rosa.'

'Are we nearly there then? Show me where your property begins, Gabriel. I want to see it.'

'Hell, Storm. We've been on Tierra Rosa land for the past two days now. It's the house itself to which I was referring; Tierra Rosa proper, we call it. Look over there.' He raised one hand and pointed.

'I thought you said it wasn't polite to point, *maman*,' Chance noted with a studied innocence that failed to deceive his mother.

'Hush, son,' the girl said, suppressing a smile, then turned to observe the house rising up regally just beyond.

The majestic antebellum mansion glistened like some rare white jewel in the summer heat. The tall columns lining the massive front proch stood like sentinels guarding the precious gem. Behind these the ranks of mullioned casement windows gleamed, wide-eyed and alert at their posts. Above them black wrought-iron balconies perched like crow's-nests, keeping watch afar. On either side square neat wings flanked the house in an orderly fashion, for there was nothing sprawling or disorganized about Tièrra Rosa. It had been well-planned, laid out, and built precisely down to the last detail. It was awesome, compelling, overpowering, breathtaking, but there was something disturbing about it all the same.

'It's lovely, Gabriel,' Storm murmured, not quite able to put her finger on what it was that nagged her about the house, for it was surely more beautiful than any Southern mansion she had ever seen.

'It's wrong,' Chance stated flatly beside her, spoiling Gabriel's triumphant expression. 'It doesn't belong here. It's not part of The Land.'

Storm knew she ought to have reprimanded the boy once more for his sullen behavior, but this time she said nothing, for Chance, deeply sensitive, was right. The house *didn't* belong. It was out of place in the savage setting where buffalos had once roamed, and Indians had died to be free.

'Drive on, Hilton,' Gabriel barked curtly, galloping on ahead again, leaving Storm and Chance to finish the remainder of the journey in silence.

'Boss is comin'! Boss is comin'! Petey hollered down from where he sat upon the tall white entrance arch of the split-rail fence. 'And he's got his fiancée with him!'

Deliberately Joe Jack lit two thin brown cigars, handed one to Cathy, then took a deep drag of his own. His eyes narrowed speculatively as he gazed off into the distance.

'Well, well,' he droned. 'I don't believe it. So the old man really *is* bringing home the bride-to-be this time.'

'I hope she's as ugly as a sow and has teeth that could eat corn through a picket fence!'

'Now, now, Cath.' Joe Jack grinned.

'Well, I do!'

'Why? You afraid your beau might set his sights on pa's fiancée, instead of you?'

'What beau?' Cathy asked defensively.

'"What beau?"' Joe Jack mimicked mockingly her high, girlish voice. 'You know damned good and well what beau I'm talking about. Ross Stuart, Frank Kingston's foreman at the Chaparral. Shit, Cath. I thought you had better sense than that. The old man will hit the roof for sure if he ever finds out where you've been sneaking off to and what you've been doing. He ain't about to let you throw yourself away on some two-bit ranch hand. Jesus!' Joe Jack whistled. 'I'd sure like to know what Stuart has in his breeches to have gotten into yours.'

Cathy flushed.

'That's none of your frigging business! And just how do you know so much about it anyway, Joe Jack? You been spying on me? I swear, if you have, I'll kill you! You're the nosiest damned bastard God ever put breath into!'

'Now, now, sis. There ain't no need for you to get so all-fire riled up. A man's got to take care of himself, look out for his interests. There ain't nothing wrong with that. How's a man to get ahead if he don't know who's making money, who's frigging whom, and who's going toes up?'

'You Goddamned weasel! If I ever catch you spying on me, *you're* the one who's going to be pushing up daisies, brother! I mean it, Joe Jack! You breathe one word about Ross to the old man, and I'll tell him Nathan Davies *was* right, that you *did* seduce his daughter, that she *was* carrying your child, that you knew it and *still* refused to marry her, and that that's why she killed herself! Pa and Nathan have been friends for a long time, Joe Jack. The old man wouldn't take kindly to learning the truth about Ellie May's death.'

'Well, hell, Cath. You couldn't hardly expect me to settle for that small-time crap Davies would have given Ellie May. Shit. Not when I've got a shot at Vanessa Granville.'

'You're dreaming, Joe Jack. Her daddy can't stand you. I heard him say so at the Lazy W barbecue, and the Bar G's just as big a spread as Tierra Rosa. The Granvilles don't need you,' Cathy sniffed, 'so don't think your prospects of inheriting the old man's ranch are going to do you any good with that stuck-up miss.'

'Right about now I'd say my prospects of inheriting the ranch were looking pretty dim,' Joe Jack replied, his face a cool, calculating mask as he watched the buggy rolling in beneath the tall entrance arch of Tierra Rosa.

Then, plastering on his best smile, he stepped forward to greet his father's bride-to-be. There was more than one way to skin a cat, and after seeing his prospective stepmother, Joe Jack didn't mind changing his plans in the least.

Dinner that evening was a highly strained affair, with Gabriel being the only one present who enjoyed it. All through the meal he needled both his hostile children unmercifully with sly remarks about having to see his lawyers after the wedding to make some changes in his Will, much to their obvious chagrin. Neither could help but blame Storm for this, as she was well aware, and she wished violently Gabriel would cease harassing the two, for he was only making matters worse. Cathy had hated Storm on sight and was making no attempt to hide it, for Storm was everything Cathy was not and secretly longed to be. Storm tried hard to engage the girl in pleasant conversation, but received only cool stares and monosyllabic replies for her pains.

Joe Jack, on the other hand, if he despised his father's

431

fiancée, concealed his emotions expertly, causing Storm to suspect he liked her only far too well and in a manner that was *not* what a son's feeling for his father's bride-to-be ought to have been. He entertained her mockingly throughout dinner, his brown eyes roaming over her low-cut gown's display of décolletage admiringly, devouring the ripe mounds pushing upward from her tight bodice. He insulted her repeatedly with oblique references to her past and crude double entendres, but grinned engagingly when he did it, so that she was unsure of whether or not it was done with the express intention of offending her – or piquing her interest.

'Do you ride, Miss Lesconflair?'

'Yes, I do, Joe Jack.'

'Oh?' One eyebrow raised. 'What kind of horse are you accustomed to riding, ma'am?'

'I had an Arabian mare, but was forced to sell her. I am presently without a mount; however, your father has mentioned giving me one of your geldings as a wedding present. I understand Tierra Rosa is quite famous for its Palomino stock.'

'Why settle for a gelding, ma'am, when you could have a stallion instead?' he asked meaningfully.

Thank God, Gabriel was at the opposite end of the table and did not hear these low-voiced exchanges!

I won't let Joe Jack ruffle me! Storm told herself angrily. I won't let him see how uncomfortable he's making me! *Jesù!* I wish he'd stop looking at me like that – as though he's – undressing me with his eyes. It's horrible! A son ought to have more respect for his father's fiancée!

Storm's only consolation was that she now felt less guilty about Chance's attitude toward Gabriel, for his own children were behaving just as dreadfully. The girl was only too happy to escape the dining room, leaving Gabriel and Joe Jack to their brandy and cigars when the meal was finished. Somehow she managed to get through the awkward silence in the salon with Cathy until the men joined them, then as soon as she was

432

politely able she bid them all good night, hurrying upstairs to the privacy of her own chamber. Her head was splitting, and Storm felt as though it were going to come off if she didn't lie down and get some rest.

She closed her door firmly behind her, bolting it with trembling fingers, then moved swiftly to the connecting room to be certain Chance was all right. He was sleeping soundly, the tiny carved dragon Li Kwan had given him clutched tightly in one small fist, as usual. Thank God, Gabriel had insisted the boy was too young to join them for dinner. The strained atmosphere in the dining room would have caused him to be more resentful of their new life than he already was. He'd had his supper up here, in the nursery.

Storm's face softened as she studied the sleeping boy. She had been too hard on him of late. He was only a child. She tiptoed from his chamber, resolving to do better in the future.

The girl's own room had been intended for the governess, had Gabriel employed one, but Storm was glad now she'd remained adamant about having it in order to be near Chance, for it was located in the west wing, away from the others. After the wedding of course Storm would move into the suite connecting with Gabriel's own in the east wing, but for now it was somehow comforting to know Joe Jack slept on the other side of the house. Briefly the girl considered what Gabriel would do if he knew his son had been making advances to her over dinner and shuddered.

He'd kill him, Storm thought, for there's no love lost between them, nor Cathy either for that matter. Poor Gabriel. It must be terrible knowing his children despise him and wish he were dead, but perhaps he doesn't care. After all, he's marrying me, knowing *I* don't love him either. *Sacré bleu!* I wish I hadn't come here. There's something evil in this household. I can feel it. I'll have to be on my guard every minute. Cathy hates me and Joe Jack will stop at nothing to get his hands on his father's ranch, even if it means taking me in the process, although why he thinks Gabriel will leave Tierra Rosa to me, I can't imagine. Gabriel doesn't love me any more than I love him. He only wants me.

The girl shivered at the sudden image of the rancher's mouth and hands possessing her body. How could she bear it? Well, she'd just have to; that was all. Gabriel North wasn't about to bestow his name and riches on her without something in return; she had known that when she'd agreed to marry him. Besides, he *had* saved her life, and at least she and Chance had a proper roof over their heads now. For what more could Storm ask?

She thought of Wolf and love – and cried.

28

It was only eight o'clock in the morning, but Storm, unable to sleep, had already been up for two hours. It was a fine August day; the brilliant sunlight streaming through the mullioned French doors of her room made patterns of fine, hazy gold upon the rich blue of the plush carpet. The pale white walls gleamed, and the dark burnished furniture glowed where the rays touched them.

Fall was in the air, that first hint of the coming autumn that would mellow the fierce Texas sun until winter swept down from the *Llano Estacado*, bringing the bitter 'blue northers' in its wake. Today, however, summer still reigned supreme, its balmy warmth flooding the room and Storm's naked body as she stepped from her bath water. She paused, motionless for a moment before a window, letting the sun's beams caress her bare flesh intimately, sighing with pleasure as the heat radiated over her skin.

Today was her wedding day, but she did not hug herself girlishly at the thought, for she felt no anticipation at the prospect. She had come a long way from the frivolously romantic dreams of her childhood. She glanced toward the bed where her wedding gown lay pressed and ready in stiff silk and lace folds. It had been made for Storm seven years ago. To think Gabriel had kept it carefully wrapped and waiting all this time. He must have been very sure of himself.

The rattle of carriage wheels below brought the girl back to reality with a tiny start. *Sainte Marie!* What was she doing, standing here in a daze like a fool? Several of the wedding guests had been at Tierra Rosa a day or more. Many others were beginning to arrive. She had to hurry, but she made no move to do so as she donned her chemise and pantalettes, then

435

called for the maid with whom Gabriel had provided her.

'Pilar! Pilar!'

'*Sí, Patrona.* I'm coming. I'm coming.' The young Mexican girl arrived breathlessly.

'I'm not "*Patrona*" yet, Pilar,' Storm reminded her, trying to smile, for she liked the maid.'

'No, but soon, soon.'

'Not if you don't lace me up – and quickly. *Sacré bleu!* I did not realize it was getting so late—'

'I will hurry, *señorita*. If you will please take hold of the bedpost, and inhale—'

Frowning slightly, Storm braced herself, sucking in her breath. *Sainte Marie!* She'd been just sixteen when the wedding dress had been made, and she'd borne a child since. What if Pilar couldn't get her waist laced small enough to fit into the gown? The maid jerked vigorously on the strings of the stays; at last the whale-bone girdle drew tight.

'Ah, there we go, *señorita*.' Pilar smiled with satisfaction, then turned, lifting one of the three billowing petticoats Storm would wear beneath her wedding dress.

Efficiently the maid pulled the undergarment down over the girl's head and tugged it into place securely before reaching for the next and then the last. Finally she hooked Storm up into the gown itself.

'Now, *señorita*, if you will please be seated, I will fix your hair, no?'

Pilar brushed the girl's long black tresses expertly, then deftly began to force them into a mass of tangled ringlets with the aid of a curling iron. When the maid had finished, she threaded several creamy white ribands through the cascade, then placed Storm's scattered-seed-pearled veil upon her head, arranging the net so that it fell in filmy folds about the girl's face. Then Pilar stepped back to survey her handiwork. Her brown countenance beamed.

'*Perfecto, señorita. El patrón* will be so proud.'

Oh, Señora *Lobo, you break many hearts last night. I tell you.*

You look so beautiful in the red dress and dance like a gypsy. Your husband, he was so handsome and so proud . . .

No! I won't think about Wolf; I won't! I won't!

Tears started in Storm's eyes. She brushed them away hastily.

'Oh, go on. Cry a little, *señorita*. It is your wedding day, is it not? A time for tears of happiness, no?'

'Yes, Pilar. Oh! It's time!' Storm cried, suddenly glancing at the clock on the mantle. 'Everyone will be waiting for me—'

She cast a final look at her reflection in the mirror, squared her shoulders, then, chin held high, began her slow descent downstairs to the veranda out back where Gabriel was standing impatiently.

In no time at all, it seemed, he was lifting her veil and kissing her amid the cheers of the onlookers who had come from hundreds of miles in all directions for the wedding. It should have been the happiest day of Storm's life, but she trembled when her husband's beard and mustache grazed her face lightly, and her hand was cold in his. She took a deep breath, summoned up her courage, and forced herself to smile up into his triumphantly twinkling brown eyes brightly.

The fiddlers struck up a spirited reel, and the next thing the girl knew Gabriel was leading her down the steps and whirling her out beneath the gay white canopy that shaded the lawn against the sweltering sun. The guests began to whistle, clap, and stamp their feet in time to the music, then soon after Storm and her husband had taken a few turns alone other couples joined in the dancing. Before long the girl was swept away by a new partner, and then another, and then another until the rest of the morning faded into a blur with the onslaught of the afternoon.

Breathless, Storm at last insisted on a respite, making her way to a shady place on the lawn beneath a mesquite tree. Someone handed her a glass of sweet mint julep. She sipped it gratefully and was reminded, for a moment, of Belle Rive. Her heart ached. How far away her childhood seemed.

The vast barbecue pits, which had been burning since late last evening, were now long troughs of glowing red embers. The sauce, which mingled with the juices of the tender beef slowly turning on the spits, trickled down onto the hot coals hissingly, sending little puffs of acrid, tangy-smelling smoke swirling upward to the azure sky. The pungent aroma of the gray wisps made Storm realize she had not yet eaten. She made mention of this, and immediately several of the gentlemen surrounding her offered to fill her a plate. Years ago she would have smiled, dimples peeping as she studied them coquettishly from beneath her fringe of lashes, then flirtatiously tapped the one she chose lightly on the arm with her fan. Today, however, the bevy of admirers she'd attracted meant nothing to her. She did not even notice the faces that fell in disappointment as she rose and walked away.

Reluctantly, Storm mounted the stairs to her suite in the east wing, into which her belongings had been moved earlier that day. Everything had gone well, and Gabriel was pleased; for Storm had played her part to perfection, and no one had dared question the story the rancher had given to account for her past. The girl's head should have been swimming with the thrill of success, but instead it only throbbed dully from heartache and the amount of liquor she'd drunk. Her feet lagged on the steps, and though she was worn out and longed to lie down and rest, she wished only that the tiring day had not yet ended. The moment of truth was upon her, and she found she could not bear to face it after all. She turned hesitantly to her husband by her side, opened her mouth to plead her excuses, and got no further than his name.

'Gabriel—'

'I was very proud of your performance in front of our guests today, Storm,' he noted smoothly, as though aware of her intent to elude him. 'I hope I won't be disappointed by your showing in private.'

The girl flushed, and her heart sank, knowing there was to be no escape for her – not tonight or any other night. Gabriel was her husband, and he meant to exercise his rights as such.

Somehow, even now, it was difficult to think of herself as the rancher's wife, despite the fact that she, in her proper white wedding dress, had knelt beside him to receive the priest's blessing. Storm glanced down at the heavy gold ring Gabriel had placed upon her finger, something Wolf had never done, and knew then what Wolf had told her was true. Outward trappings did not make a marriage. It was how one felt in one's heart that did that. With a sudden little sense of panic the girl realized she had wed a man about whom she knew almost nothing – despite the nine months they had spent together aboard ship from San Francisco to Galveston – a man whom she did not love and did not want. Tonight would be like sharing her bed with a stranger. The thought appalled her.

'I'll – I'll need some time, Gabriel,' she murmured hesitantly, wishing she were a frightened virgin who might delay the moment of her taking for nights with her fears.

'Naturally, I'll knock on your door in – shall we say an hour, my dear?'

Somehow his endearment seemed to mock her. She lifted her chin.

'I'll be waiting,' she said.

'As shall I,' he replied, his eyes gleaming with anticipation.

Slowly, with Pilar's assistance, the girl bathed and changed into the sheer white nightgown the maid had laid out on the huge four-poster bed. After that Storm blew out all the lamps but one and slipped between the cool linen sheets that beckoned to her weary body invitingly. If only Gabriel weren't going to be sharing them with her. She shivered at the thought.

He *is* your husband, Storm, she told herself firmly, attempting to calm her fears. What else did you expect? And – and surely he will be gentle with you—

'How charming you look, my dear.'

He had not knocked – she was certain of that – but simply entered her bedroom like one who knew it was his right. He was wearing a brown satin dressing gown, bound loosely at the waist, and his dark eyes raked her with a strange, enigmatic hunger the girl could not fathom. It was almost as though he were – were *gloating* at the idea of possessing her. Storm shuddered faintly once more, for there was no love – as she had once known love – in his eyes.

His slightly contemptuous glance making her feel suddenly cheap and self-conscious, she leaned forward to blow out the remaining lamp.

'Don't. I want to see you, my dear,' he purred. 'I want to see every pale inch of that creamy white skin for which I've waited so long.'

Deliberately, almost menacingly, it seemed, he walked toward her, drawing the coverlet and sheets back slowly, revealing the length of her to his glittering gaze.

'Such modesty, my dear,' he chuckled reprovingly, noting her negligée. 'I had hoped to find you completely naked.'

The bed creaked as he settled his weight upon it, straddling Storm's body and bending over her with a peculiar little smile on his face as his hands moved to untie the ribands that laced her nightgown. Dimly she noticed his fingers shook with barely suppressed excitement as he fumbled with the silken bows. Then he was pushing aside the filmy material, exposing her nude flesh to his appreciative stare. After a minute Storm closed her eyes tightly, unable to bear his lingering appraisal any longer.

She expected him to kiss her, as Wolf had always done, but instead Gabriel's palms grasped her breasts, squeezing them possessively, his thumbs rubbing her nipples firmly until the rosy tips blushed and hardened of their own accord. He lowered his mouth to them, sucking eagerly. Slowly the girl became aware of his now-swollen manhood jutting from the confines of his robe, pressing into her belly. As though he sensed her awareness of him, Gabriel rose to his knees, loosing his dressing gown and tossing it aside.

Storm opened her eyes.

He was massively built, as she had known he would be, with powerful, thick, beefy arms and a big belly that had started to run to fat from rich indulgence. Lower still his throbbing maleness protruded from a coarse red bush. The girl could not help herself. She shuddered again as she mentally compared the rancher's body unfavorably to the remembrance of Wolf's hard, lean, muscular flesh. Dismayed, she swallowed the lump in her throat and gritted her teeth, steeling herself to accept without protest what must follow.

Gabriel chuckled as he observed her brief scrutiny.

'Now you know why all my friends call me the bull, my dear.' He winked. 'I might be getting on, but I'm still the biggest stud in the corral!'

He slid down a ways, slipping his hands under Storm's knees, pulling them up to open her legs so that he was now on his haunches between them. Languidly, as though he were contemplating the finer points of a prize heifer, he studied the sheath of ebony curls so crudely and vulnerably laid before him. Then he ran his fingers up the insides of Storm's thighs. Involuntarily she quivered at the light touch.

'That excite you, my dear?' Gabriel asked, watching her face.

When she didn't respond, he chortled once more and cupped her womanhood with one hand, stroking her soft folds with his thumb. Then leisurely, still watching her and continuing the rhythmic movement he had begun, he started to explore her inner sweetness with his fingers, penetrating her deeply. He grunted with satisfaction.

'Jesus, you don't know how long I've waited to do this to you, my dear. How does it feel, Storm?' He panted heavily, not caring that she didn't answer, then reached down to caress himself with his free hand. 'In just a little while it's going to feel even better,' he promised, indicating his hardness.

After a time he leaned forward to fondle her breasts once more, still watching her. Storm found it all very disturbing and wished he hadn't ordered her to leave the lamp lit. It somehow made it all the more awful, him being able to see her reactions to what he was doing to her, lewdly inspecting her, probing her, debasing her as though she were nothing – less than nothing.

The rancher groaned and, fingers still in her, moved to lie down beside her, catching her hair to twist her lips up to his. His tongue plunged deeply into her mouth, ravishing her, nearly suffocating her. Then suddenly he rolled over on his back, hauling her with him, and instructed her to kneel by his side. Hesitantly, half-afraid because she found his manner of lovemaking so troubling and unnerving, Storm did as he commanded.

Gabriel's hands found both her and his manhood again.

'Take off your negligée,' he demanded hoarsely.

Slowly she shrugged the nightgown from her shoulders, allowing it to fall.

'Now touch yourself.'

The girl only looked at him, distraught and perplexed.

'Oh come on, Storm. You know what I mean.' The rancher frowned a trifle impatiently when she continued to stare at him uncomprehendingly. 'I reckon that half-breed Indian lover of yours didn't teach you as much as I thought. I guess I'm going to have the pleasure of breaking you to the bit after all, my dear. Put your hands on your tits as I did earlier. I want to watch you—'

Storm gasped in sudden understanding, his words rousing her at last from her dazed, slightly drunken state. Her eyes widened with shock. Why, Gabriel wanted her to – to – stimulate herself for him, while he went on invading her with his fingers and manipulating his maleness with his hand. And – and after that—

'I – I can't, Gabriel! I just can't!' she sobbed, stunned and horrified as he had known she would be.

'Oh, hell! Come off it, Storm. There's no need for you to play the lady in private with me, and it's certainly not my desire. I want you to amuse me with some of your whore's tricks. What's the matter with you anyway? You used to be a damned good tease – with your sultry bedroom eyes that promised and yielded nothing. Jesus! You nearly drove me insane that night at Vaillance when I kissed you.'

'What – what do you mean? What – what whore's tricks? I never led you on; I never teased you! Oh, Gabriel, I don't understand you,' the girl cried, no longer silent and accepting. 'Why – why are you doing this to me, asking such things of me, as though I were – were a common trollop?'

'Well?' He raised one eyebrow. 'Aren't you? Oh, not that I'm complaining, my dear. Please don't misunderstand me. Virginity has seldom held any interest for me although I would have liked to have taken yours. However, I'm sure there'll be other compensations – at least I thought there would be. After all, it's not as though you haven't had ample opportunity to learn . . .' His voice trailed off meaningfully.

'*Jesù! Jesù!*'

'Do as I told you, Storm,' he ordered softly, grinning at her agonized consternation. 'Do it, you Goddamned tease. I'm not about to let you deny me what you gave to the Barlows and that half-breed Indian lover of yours and that frigging gambler—'

'None of them ever touched me but Wolf! Oh, Gabriel—'

'You expect me to believe that? Christ? For what kind of fool do you take me, Storm?'

'It's true; I swear it! Oh, Gabriel, why won't you believe me?'

'All right. I believe you. It really doesn't matter anyway. One or a hundred, you're mine now, and that's all that counts. I bought and paid for you, bitch, lock, stock, and barrel, and I intend to get my money's worth. Put your hands on your tits before I think of something even more – interesting for you to do.'

'No, I won't!'

'Do it, or by God, I'll make you wish you had!'

Sainte Marie! If only she had a pistol or a knife! She would kill him! But she did not. She was at his utter mercy, for there was no one at Tierra Rosa who would come to her aid if she struggled – and if she ran, where would she go?

Tears of anger and humiliation streaming down her cheeks, Storm bit her lip and did as he'd commanded, vowing silently to make him pay, someway, somehow, for her shame after it was over.

'*Maman! Maman!* Help me, *maman!* Come quickly, *s'il vous plait!*'

The screams pierced the night and Storm's ears dreadfully, echoing through the entire house.

'Chance!' the girl yelled, frantically trying to yank away from her husband. 'Chance!'

'Goddamn that frigging little bastard!' Gabriel swore, feeling his hardness soften and shrivel as it had that day in Galveston at the thought of the boy's cold, accusing blue eyes. Jesus Christ! The kid couldn't have picked a worse time for the interruption. It was almost as though he'd known what the rancher had been doing to his mother . . . 'Go on!' Gabriel snapped, realizing he was momentarily impotent. 'Go see what that Goddamned brat wants, then get back here, *pronto!*'

Without hesitation Storm sprang to her feet, threw on her dressing gown, and ran hurriedly from her suite down the long corridor connecting the east and west wings.

'Chance! I'm coming, Chance! What is it, son? What's wrong?' She burst into his room.

He was sitting up, shaking, wide-eyed in bed. '*Piamermpits,*' he breathed, petrified. '*Piamermpits* has come to get me. Oh, please don't let him take me.' His voice rose to a wail. 'Please don't let him take me, *maman!* I didn't mean it when I said I hated you! I didn't mean it! I'll be good from now on, I promise!'

'I know you will, son. Where is he?'

'Out there.' With a trembling hand Chance pointed to his balcony. 'Oh, be careful, *maman!*'

Stealthily, one finger held to her lips, Storm moved toward the open French doors. She sighed with relief when she saw the owl perched on the black wrought-iron railings, its dark eyes studying her curiously.

'Whooooo,' it said. 'Whooooo.'

'Is it *Paimermpits*?' Chance queried, creeping timidly to her side.

'No, son. It's *Dohate*,' Storm spoke reassuringly, 'the owl prophet, come to tell you something.'

His eyes began to sparkle. 'Really, *maman*?'

'Of course, Chance. Now – back to bed with you, young man. You've wakened the whole house, I have no doubt.'

'I'm sorry, *maman*.'

'I'm not,' Storm said, ruffling his hair. 'Give me a kiss. There's a good boy. Good night, son. Pleasant dreams.'

Quietly she closed his door, then informed the anxious household hovering in the long hall that the child had merely suffered a nightmare. Grumbling, they returned to their rooms in the servants' quarters. Storm continued on down the corridor, thanking God for her son's intervention on her wedding night. It had given her time to marshal her wits and courage. How had she ever thought she could submit to Gabriel North, even in return for saving her life? She must have been mad! He had not merely wanted her – he had wanted to humble her pride and humiliate her body and soul as well! Well, she would not stand for it, would not suffer the indignities with which he had tormented her this evening, wifely duty or no. She had made a mistake. She would ask Gabriel for a divorce in the morning. Somehow she and Chance would make their way in the world, even if she were reduced to scrubbing floors for a living.

'I told you not to settle for a gelding, stepmama,' Joe Jack drawled impertinently from his doorway, startling her.

'What are you doing up?' Storm hissed, wrapping her robe more tightly around her as his eyes raked her lithe figure through the thin fabric appreciatively.

'I heard the brat scream of course, just like everybody else. Jesus Christ! I thought we were being attacked by Indians or something.'

445

'Well, we're not. Go on back to bed.'

'Care to join me, stepmama?'

'No! How dare you even suggest such a thing, you – you—'

Joe Jack shrugged, grinning. 'When you get tired of the gelding, let me know,' he whispered, then disappeared.

Farther down the long hall Cathy shut her door noiselessly, her heart pounding in her breast as her ominous foreboding that day of the dust devil returned to haunt her with its shadowed images.

29 ·

Gabriel North had cursed the Almighty, threatened Him, bargained with Him, and finally pleaded with him, but to no avail. No matter how hard the rancher swore, menaced, bartered, or prayed, the fact remained: He was impotent and unable to consummate his wedding vows.

He ground his teeth in wrath and frustration when he remembered how Storm had returned to her suite the night of their marriage, taken one look at his still shrunken maleness, laughed mockingly, and jibed,

'What's the matter, Gabriel? Did *Piamermpits* scare you too?' Then her steely gray eyes had narrowed dangerously, and she had spat, 'Get out! Get out, you poor excuse for a man, before I scream this house down around your ears! *Jesù*! To think you sneered at Wolf!' She'd stared pointedly at the rancher's limp maleness, then laughed once more, a short, jeering sound that had made him feel as though her half-breed lover were there in the room with them, gazing at Gabriel triumphantly from over Storm's shoulder. 'He was more of a man than you'll ever be!'

God, how the rancher had wanted to kill her! Had wanted to put his hands around her throat and choke the scornful life from her body! He had not, however, of course. Even *he* wasn't rich enough to get away with murdering a white woman, but he had wanted to do it, had wanted to see her down on her knees, begging him for mercy before he'd raped and killed her.

The following morning the girl had coldly asked him for a divorce. When Gabriel had refused, smiling mockingly at her distress, Storm had hissed,

'Very well then. Have it your way. But I'm warning you, if you ever touch me again, I'll take my knife to you and see you

447

gelded like one of your old steers!'

He hadn't taken her threat seriously of course, but nevertheless whenever he'd laid his hand on her doorknob, intending to force himself upon her, despite her unwillingness to receive him, Gabriel had discovered his manhood refused to respond to his desires.

It's the boy, the rancher thought irrationally for the hundredth time. Every time I think about raping the slut I married I see that brat's eyes; I hear him screaming as he did on our wedding night; and I know he knows – everything: what I did to his father, what I tried to do to his mother . . . It's almost as though he'd been *there*, at the hanging, *there*, in Storm's room looking out at me from behind his father's dark icy blue accusing shards.

God, what was it about that half-breed Indian's eyes that even now they nag me, haunt me through his bastard kid? The man was just a gunslinger, a son-of-a-bitch gunslinger whom I hung – nothing more. So why in the hell have I dwelled on him to the point where I can't even get my Goddamned pecker up? Shit!

It's the boy, Gabriel thought again, angry, frustrated, humiliated, and unable to admit to being thwarted by his own body. If I didn't have that frigging brat around me to remind me of that half-breed Indian laying hands on Storm before I hung him, I wouldn't have any trouble at all bedding that haughty, hypocritical French bitch I married! Somehow I've just got to get rid of that brat and make his whore mother rue the day she ever laughed at me, threatened to cut off my balls! And I've got to do it fast, before the dissembling slut betrays me with my own damned son! I know Joe Jack wants her. Oh, yes, I know what he's up to, sniffing around her skirt and petticoats like some dog in heat. He'd like nothing more than to cuckold me with my own frigging wife! The bastard! I'll tan his hide good if he tries to trifle with her when I haven't even had her myself yet – the bitch! Playing up to him, leading him on, trying to make a fool out of me, anger me into letting her go! Well, I won't. She's mine, and by God, I mean to see she stays that way! I'll strangle her if she spreads her legs for Joe

Jack, let's him— Goddamn it! I wonder where in hell they've disappeared together this time?

'Damn it!'

'What is it, Joe Jack? What's wrong?'

'Those frigging Comanches have been raiding our land again. See those tracks. They belong to unshod horses – Indian ponies. I wonder how many head of cattle the Goddamned thieves stole last night?'

'Does it matter? It seems to me you've got more than enough to spare.'

'You're damned right it matters. I've warned pa and warned him that if he lets it continue, the next thing you know they'll be burning down the house – with us in it.'

'Oh, Joe Jack.' Storm laughed. 'How you do run on. Surely Tierre Rosa's much too well-guarded for that.'

She sobered, and her eyes clouded slightly as she thought of the men Gabriel had set to watch her so that she and Chance couldn't escape from him. Ever since she'd asked her husband for a divorce it had been so. Even now a ranch hand lingered in the distance, pretending to search for strays, but Storm knew he was spying on her, would report her every movement to Gabriel.

The girl tossed her head, then leaned down a little closer to Joe Jack.

'Yeah, well, maybe,' he was saying. 'Still I wish the old man had never attacked those red devils. We've had nothing but trouble ever since.'

'Gabriel – Gabriel attacked the *Kwerharehnuh*?'

'Yeah, a long time ago, looking for you.'

'He – he must have wanted me pretty badly. Perhaps he does love me after all, in his own strange way.'

'Aw, shit, Storm! If you'd believe that, you'd believe anything,' Joe Jack said with disgust. 'Pa don't love anybody, not me, not Cathy, and least of all you. The old man just can't stand being beaten; that's all.'

'Yes, I guess you're right.' The girl sighed, wondering how she had come to make such a mess of her life.

449

'Hey.' Joe Jack stood, helping her up. 'When are you going to forget pa, and give me a chance? I know damned good and well he don't come to your room nights—'

'*Merde*, Joe Jack! Cathy's right. You *do* spy on people! You ought to be ashamed of yourself—'

'And so should you, stepmama.' He grinned wickedly. 'Letting that fine young body of yours turn to ice when I'm just dying to set it on fire. Aw, come on, honey,' he crooned hotly, suddenly taking her in his arms and pressing searing kisses down the length of her throat and then her lips as he caught her hair, forcing her mouth to his. 'Jesus! I've just been aching to do that,' he muttered, claiming her lips passionately once more.

Storm's head spun dizzily. Her body flushed feverishly with sudden wanting. She could feel the hot flash of moisture that dampened the curls between her trembling thighs, reminding her that it had been a long time since she'd had a man.

'Stop it, Joe Jack! Stop it!' she cried, succeeding in pushing him away at last. 'Lester will see us and tell your father!'

'So? I ain't afraid of pa. Are you?'

The girl made no reply. She was shocked by his actions, and mortified by her own response, for she had not meant things to progress so far. She had meant only to flirt with him a little – to irritate Gabriel and ease her own pangs of loneliness and misery. As though she could somehow eradicate what had passed between them, Storm wiped her mouth off with a hand that shook noticeably.

'That won't do you no good, honey.' Joe Jack's eyes were suddenly serious with intent. 'I've put my brand on you now. Aw, shit, Storm. You were made for loving, and you know it. You wouldn't be here with me now if you didn't. I warned you not to settle for a gelding, didn't I? You made a mistake, marrying the old man, and now you're tied to him, with no escape and all those bitter, empty years ahead staring you in the face. Just how long do you think you can stand it, Storm? A month, a year? When pa might live twenty or thirty more? Just how long are you going to toss and turn all alone in that big cold bed of yours, itching for the feel of a man between your thighs? I felt you go all hot and quivering like a mare in heat when I kissed you just now. Ain't nobody who can give you what I can, honey. Pa'd kill anyone else who tried to touch you. Shit, he might even kill me, but what the hell? I'd risk it for you, Storm. I ain't ever seen a woman I wanted as much as I want you. And I know you want me too. So how long are you going to make me wait, stepmama, before you let me scratch that itch of yours?'

'Till they nail down the lid on your coffin,' the girl spat, horrified by his vulgar language, his lewd suggestions, and, most of all, by the fact that he'd read her all too well.

Oh, why had she ever taken up with him? If only she hadn't felt so desolate and unhappy because of Gabriel. If only she and the rancher could have made something of their marriage, Storm would never have turned to Joe Jack, been attracted by his lean, hungry looks and confident swagger. But he alone had been her friend at Tierra Rosa, and now he had wakened her body with his hot kisses and caresses, wanting to arouse her, please her, not humiliate her as Gabriel had done.

'Yeah? Well, I ain't figuring to be pushing up daisies any time soon, stepmama.' Joe Jack grinned again, as though sensing her inner turmoil. 'So you're going to have a long, lonesome wait. I'll just bide my time. When you get to itching real bad, you feel free to call on me.'

For a moment the girl was almost tempted. It had been so long . . . And instinctively she knew Joe Jack would make it good for her. Why then did she hesitate? The memory of Wolf had kept her from Brett Diamond, but Wolf was dead and had left her for another before he'd died—

'Gabriel would kill us both,' she breathed, her heart pounding strangely in her breast before she turned and ran from the all too inviting desire in Joe Jack's dark brown eyes.

Fall came and went, and winter settled early over the land, bringing with it the bitter 'blue northers,' which swept down from *Llano Estacado* with icy fury.

Outwardly, to those who knew them, the Norths were the perfect family: the successful, middle-aged rancher; his elegant, dashing second wife; his, lean, handsome son; and his plain but graceful daughter, all a credit to Tierra Rosa and Texas.

Inwardly, however, the household seethed. Gabriel and Storm had become falsely polite, wary strangers, smiling at each other before guests, only to retire, unspeaking, to their separate suites in the evenings. The girl did not realize it was not her threat to take a knife to him that kept the rancher from her room, for she made certain Gabriel knew she slept with the blade under her pillow. It was enough that he left her alone. Had she guessed her husband had become permanently impotent, understood how deeply his absence of virility had affected him, known how irrationally Gabriel blamed Chance, instead of himself, for his failure to consummate their marriage, Storm would have taken her son and fled Tierra Rosa someway, somehow, in horror. But she had no inkling of the rancher's continued inefficacy or the lengths to which he was willing to go to restore his manhood and make her his. So she stayed, oblivious to the impending doom that seemed to be closing in on them all.

Only Cathy knew it was racing toward them like the dust devil that day of the summer storm. She could see it in Gabriel's brooding stare when he watched the boy, Chance; in Joe Jack's hungry gaze when his eyes raked his father's wife; and in Storm's increasingly reckless glances as she began to look back at her husband's son.

'Oh, Ross, Ross! How much longer do we have to wait?' Cathy cried out and clung to her lover tightly one day at Rosa Pequeño. 'Something dreadful is going to happen at Tierra Rosa; I just know it!'

'Well, I reckon as how yore right then, seein' as how yore sech a sensitive gal, but, darlin', I jest cain't leave the Chaparral right now, not in the dead of winter, when there ain't nobody lookin' fer work, and not with spring comin' on. You know breedin' and brandin' time's our busiest season. Mr Kingston's been too good to me, Cathy, to leave him short-handed. Cain't you hang on jest a little longer, honey? Then next summer, I promise, I'll marry you and take you away.'

'Oh, Ross! I'm so worried. Pa will find some way to stop us; I just know he will!'

'No, no, he won't darlin', and I don't want you to fret yore purty head none about it, you hear? Yore of legal age, and there ain't nothin' he can do about it.'

'There'll be a scandal, you know. It isn't every day a rich rancher's daughter runs off with a foreman.'

'Do you care, Cathy? I've got a lot of pride, but still I know I ain't much. I – I haven't got a lot of money, and I haven't had any book-learnin' like you either—'

'Oh, Ross! Do you really think I care about *that*? My God! For what do you take me anyway? A stuck-up miss like Vanessa Granville? You've worked your way up to something from nothing, and I've got a hell of a lot more respect for you than I do any wealthy, educated fool. I don't care about anything as long as I can have you, Ross. You're my strength, my port in every storm. I know when the world beats me down, I can come and lay my head on your shoulder, and you'll make everything all right again. That's all I care about, Ross: having you beside me, loving me, sharing our lives together, holding each other close late at night, talking – really talking to one another, and laughing over little things together. All the money and education in the world can't buy that, Ross. That comes straight from the heart, and it's free – for those who want to take it and give it in return. That's all I've ever really wanted out of life, all I've ever really asked. To quote a wise poet named Marlowe, "Come live with me and be my love/ And we will all the pleasures prove . . . If these delights thy mind may move/Then live with me and be my love."'

'That's beautiful, Cathy. Yore beautiful. And I do wanna live with you and yore love, fer jest as long as you want me.'

'Forever is a long, long time, Ross. Hold me for just a little while longer until we can be together always.'

It had been a long and tiring three days, with first the lengthy journey to the Chaparral, then the supper and All Hallow's Eve costume ball that had dragged on into the wee hours of the morning, and then the seemingly even longer trip back to

Tierra Rosa. Storm sighed tiredly, shifting the burden of Chance's sleeping figure cradled in her arms. Things had been made, if possible, even more unpleasant by Cathy's disappearance late the evening of the Kingstons' party. Storm had received a raging dressing-down from Gabriel on her lack of competence as a chaperone for his daughter, and her head had been aching severely ever since.

'Oh, for God's sake, Gabriel!' she'd finally cried in desperation. 'Cathy's twenty-seven years old and neither wants nor needs my supervision. Besides, do you know how many women came as dance-hall girls?'

Nevertheless Gabriel had persisted, and Storm had been forced to question Cathy sharply upon her return, only to receive no satisfactory answers. Wherever Cathy had been, it had been obvious she'd had no intentions of telling her stepmother.

Things had gone from bad to worse when Joe Jack had followed Storm out into the Kingstons' preciously cultivated and carefully irrigated gardens to press his attentions on her again. Since the trees had shed their fall leaves, Storm had been furious at her stepson, fearing they'd be seen through the naked branches. She'd managed to be rid of him before they'd been discovered, but had been made highly aware of the fact that she would not be able to put him off much longer and – worse yet – that she did not want to. She was physically attracted to Joe Jack, and now he claimed to be in love with her. Storm realized, however, that as long as Gabriel was alive, their situation was hopeless. If she took Joe Jack as her lover, the rancher was bound to find out about it sooner or later, and there was no telling what he might do in retaliation against them both.

Oh, if only Gabriel would drop dead of a heart attack, the girl thought uncharitably, petulantly biting her lower lip.

Then she was immediatley contrite, for Mammy had often warned her it was bad luck to wish someone ill, no matter how badly you hated them.

Doan neber hope sumpin' awful'll happen ter a puhson, Miz Storm, 'cause more'n lahkely yo'll be de one what gits it!

How true, Storm was to think afterward, for it was then the Indians attacked.

The girl, confused as to what was occurring at first, started instinctively at the sound of the first arrow thudding into the side of the buckboard. Then suddenly everything seemed to happen at once. The Comanches began yelling the war cry she recalled so well; shouts broke out among Gabriel's outriders escorting the buggy home to Tierra Rosa; and gunfire erupted in short, staccato blasts as horses reared and whirled, kicking up clouds of frost. The rancher lashed out at the team with his long, snakelike whip, and soon the vehicle was jolting precariously over the frozen ground.

'It's too far, pa! The house is too far away!' Joe Jack yelled over the uproar. 'We can't make it!'

Apparently Gabriel agreed, for presently with a snarled oath he yanked the buckboard to a halt. In a thundering voice he ordered everyone out, then he and Joe Jack unharnessed the team and turned the buggy over on its side to offer them all some protection.

Storm shook as she crouched between the padded seats, crushing Chance close to her body as the arrows, lances, and bullets whizzed past them, and an occasional horse cleared the vehicle itself, causing them to duck to avoid being struck by sharp, flying hooves. The rancher's men had taken what cover was available, and both Gabriel and Joe Jack braced themselves against the buckboard. All were firing their weapons rapidly at the shadowed, painted figures of the Indians. After a time the rancher flung his rifle down angrily and drew his pistol.

'For Christ's sake!' he cursed Storm briefly. 'Didn't that goddamned half-breed lover of yours teach you *anything*? Quit huddling down there like a frigging fool! Grab those ammunition belts, and get busy reloading for me!'

Some of her shock and stupor receding, Storm did as he commanded, slightly exasperated she hadn't thought of it herself especially when she saw how coolly Cathy was already jamming shot in Joe Jack's carbine.

There was no time to think or argue after that, for Gabriel

and Joe Jack were both too occupied firing again and again until the steel barrels of the guns grew hot in their hands, and the chambers clicked dully, empty, to be tossed aside for reloading. Time after time as Storm's fingers fumbled with the shot in the darkness she saw Gabriel's aim strike true, watched a Comanche warrior fall, and tried desperately not to wonder if it had been Moon-Raider or Crazy-Soldier-Boy or any of the other proud braves she had once known and for whom she had cared. She forced her mind to stop worrying about it. It hurt too badly.

They're the enemy, she told herself. They'll kill you if Gabriel and Joe Jack don't kill them first.

But somehow that didn't help matters.

Once Storm saw Cathy eyeing her with a sort of grudging admiration. 'I'll say one thing for you,' the girl spoke, wiping the grime from her forehead. 'You've got guts. I thought you'd have swooned by now, being a Southern belle and all.'

Storm smiled her appreciation wryly, but there was no time to pursue what might have developed into a friendship otherwise, for just then Chance gave a wild cry, sprang from beneath the buggy where he'd been crouched, and ran toward the open plains.

'Chance! Chance!' Storm screamed, dropping Gabriel's rifle to follow the boy, scarcely feeling the pain when she twisted her ankle in her haste. 'Chance! Come back! Come back!'

The night was chaos, reminding her of the Apache attack upon the camp of the *Kwerharehnuh* that spring so many years ago. Fearsomely painted warriors on horseback pounded by the girl frighteningly, hollering their peculiar battle cry at the tops of their lungs. Storm was only vaguely aware of threading her way between them, of dodging a tomahawk, which flew past her dangerously close, of eluding dark copper-skinned arms that grabbed at her as she ran on.

'Chance!'

Moonlight streamed down from the starry winter sky, casting hazy mists of silver beams upon the land. It was a full moon, Storm noted dimly, *a Comanche moon, a moon for*

456

raiding or making namaer' ernuh – *something together*. Oh, God! Why should she think about that now?

'Chance!'

At last she spied his small figure, his chubby legs pumping up and down steadily as he wove his way through the *mêlée* toward a powerful Pinto stallion. It was then Storm realized what word had been wrung from the boy's lips before he'd gone racing from the cover of the vehicle.

Ap'! It had been *ap'* he'd shouted.

'*Sainte Marie*,' Storm murmured. 'He saw the horse and thought it was his father. Chance!'

Breathless, she ran toward the boy, sweeping him up into her arms just as he reached the warrior mounted on the *overo* stallion. Terrified, she looked up into the brave's fiercely painted face, nearly fainting as he stared down at her, his cold eyes diamond-hard – those midnight blue eyes Storm had thought never to see again as long as she lived. Dear God!

It was Wolf!

BOOK FIVE

Love, Cherish Me

30

Tierra Rosa, Texas, 1855

Wolf gazed down at Storm and his son forever, it seemed. It was as though he saw them and yet did not see them, as though his mind were far away . . .

Hang him! Hang him!

Rough hands grabbed him from every direction, tearing at what remained of his black silk shirt, yanking him savagely to his feet. It did not matter that his knees were weak and would not support his weight. The hands held him up, dragged him brutally over the sparsely forested prairie to a nearby oak that stood apart from the other trees. Bits of sand and prickly burrs ripped at his legs, dug their sharp spines into his flesh, but he scarcely felt the harsh scratches and stinging punctures.

The hands divested his Pinto stallion of its saddle and trappings, so that there would be no stirrups to which Wolf's feet might cling. Then they stripped him down to his breeches, taking even his black silk socks and silver-spurred black leather boots, and tied his wrists behind his back. When they had finished, the hands tossed a length of rope over a sturdy branch of the oak, then flung him onto Pahuraix's broad back and dropped the coiled noose around Wolf's neck, drawing the loop so tightly it burned his skin and choked his throat, nearly suffocating him. He gasped raggedly for breath.

Slowly, my ara. When you fear, breathe slowly and deeply, and your dizziness and nausea will pass. Do not be ashamed, Brother-Of-The-Wolf. A man feels thus many times in his life.

Wolf forced himself to remain calm, to take slow deep breaths. The choking sensation eased. His dizziness and nausea passed.

The hands slipped the bridle from his *overo* horse. Any

461

moment now Wolf would be dead. He closed his eyes, emptying his body and soul of fear and pain. He was a Comanche warrior. He would die as such.

Images from Wolf's past began to fill his mind, moving in slow motion, some sharp and clear, others blurred at the edges like misty vignettes. Bright hues became transparent, like the pentimento sometimes found on old canvases, fading into softer tints that ran together like watercolors in the rain.

He saw himself as a boy, kneeling as the darkness of death closed in around him, even as it did now. He saw himself racing Masitawtawp to retrieve their fallen arrows. He saw himself as a young brave, riding into the wind with his Comanche wife, Beloved-Of-The-Forest. He saw himself as a man, bending over Storm with fierce tenderness as he made her his beneath a Comanche moon. He saw himself weeping against the white buffalo robe in which he had shrouded Tabenanika. He saw himself kneeling once more, this time on the autumn-swept plains as he held out his hands to receive his son, and all was sweetness and light.

These were the treasured moments Wolf remembered in his life as he waited for death to clutch him in its fist. These were the cherished memories of which even the blackness that swirled up to engulf him could not rob him.

He opened his eyes, wondering why the hands had not yet slapped his stallion to send it flying from beneath him, had not yet jerked the rope to set his spirit free from the battered body that chained it to the earth.

And then he understood.

Oh, cruel! Cruel, the hands were as they wrapped the loose end of the rope around his horse's neck and tied it. Wolf would not die quickly, not unless the stallion suddenly galloped from beneath him. No, the end would come slowly, with excruciating agony as each movement of the horse gradually hauled him upward toward the branch and finally over it so that his dead body (if God were merciful, and he *were* dead) would be dragged along the ground as a last indignity.

The hands left him. Alone, Wolf waited for his oldest foe to claim him.

He waited, but not in resignation. He had a chance – one chance of which Gabriel North, the hated rancher, had not known. Pahuraix was well-trained. The horse would not move without its master's command. Wolf strained at the rope drawn tightly around his neck, leaned his body forward slowly until he thought the noose would choke him. Then he eased himself back to his original position once more. Again and again he repeated the motion so that the rough bark of the oak's limb grated against the coarse hemp of the rope above, weakening it.

The minutes seemed like hours, the hours like days, and the days like years. The scorching sun beat down upon him relentlessly. The sweat ran down his face into his eyes, blinding him before the rivulets trickled on to his mouth. His parched lips parted gratefully so that his tongue could lick the few droplets of salty moisture that lingered there. Over and over as the restless, thirsty stallion snorted and pawed the hard ground Wolf whispered the same hoarse command in Comanche: stay; stay; stay. Time and time again he dozed in the heat only to lurch into wakefulness. He couldn't allow himself to fall asleep; he would die if he did. His mind began to wander. Wolf jerked it back to reality painfully. It would have been so much easier to let it snap. Desperately he forced himself to concentrate on the rocking motion that was sawing at the rope above. It was his only chance—

Darkness fell, and he was still alive. The rhythmic movement had become automatic: lean forward; ease back; careful; be careful! One slip, and you're dead! Keep awake; damn you! Keep awake! Stay, Pahuraix; stay!

The night was endless. Wolf felt debased, degraded. Gabriel North had stripped him of silent pride and dignity, leaving him less than a man. He moaned.

Morning came. The second morning? The third? He didn't know. Wolf realized his mind was wandering again. Mentally

463

he yanked himself back to reality once more, losing the iron control he'd had over his body. That was when it happened. That was when he suffered what to him was the greatest humiliation of all. The bladder he had held achingly for so long emptied, sending its contents spilling down one leg. He felt the wetness soaking his breeches, and his hatred for Gabriel North intensified. Silently Wolf vowed that if he survived his ordeal, he would kill the despised rancher, would kill him very slowly, with excruciating finesse.

On the evening of the third day it rained. The corded muscles in Wolf's neck bunched and tightened as he strained against the noose, forcing his head back to swallow the droplets that shattered down from the heavens, drenching him. The shower ended as quickly as it had begun, leaving him feverish and chilled. He shivered. His teeth chattered.

Pahuraix moved.

Wolf's knees tried in vain to retain their grip around the horse's sides. His lips parted futilely to croak out a command, but he was too late. He dangled until he lost consciousness, praying for death.

He awakened on the seventh day to find himself lying on the earth. He groaned. He was alive! He had won! Somehow he was still alive! Dazed and yet ill, he examined himself with difficulty. He was covered with vomit, soiled with urine and excrement. There was a gash on his forehead where he had struck the branch just as the rope, taxed by his efforts, had given way, sending him hurtling to the ground. Three of his ribs were fractured, and one of his arms hung at an odd angle. It was broken. His right leg bore a long deep gouge. His left ankle was sprained. His body was a mass of scratches, cuts, and bruises. Wolf did not know how he had survived. Only the miracle of the coarse hemp snapping, instead of his neck, had spared his life.

Nearby Pahuraix whickered. Painfully Wolf raised his spinning head at the soft neigh. Sensing the man had awakened, the stallion walked over and nudged him, sending shards of agony shooting through his body. Wolf tried to rise and fell back, moaning again as once more the blackness enveloped him.

Three days passed before he again regained consciousness. This time he made no effort to get up, but instead, knowing he must have water, crawled to the edge of a stream that wound its way tantalizingly through the trees some distance away. It took him nearly an hour to travel roughly twenty feet, hauling his body along like an inchworm. Weakly he lapped at the bubbling brook like a dog. Five minutes later, his empty stomach rejecting its contents, he vomited, but at least his thirst had been quenched. Exhausted, he slept.

The next morning Wolf drank again, this time managing to keep the water down. Feeling somewhat better then, he set about to free his bound wrists by rubbing the imprisoning rope against a sharp rock. Every movement was sheer torture. Twinges of white-hot pain needled through his injured arm each time he jarred the broken bone, nearly causing him to swoon once more. He gritted his teeth and worked on. At last his fingers felt the coarse hemp begin to unravel. With a final jerk his hands parted. The blood rushed like pricking pins to his numbed wrists, which were now chafed raw from his efforts. He tried to remove the noose coiled around his neck, but found it had been drawn too lightly for him to loosen it with only his one good arm. Feebly Wolf pulled on the length of rope, then clenching the slack between his teeth, determinedly he began to chew. It took him two days to gnaw through the coarse hemp, but finally he had the piece he needed. Grimly he dragged himself to one of the cottonwood trees, which huddled in clusters on the bank of the stream. There he wrapped one end of the rope around the trunk, tying it as firmly as he was able, then wound the other end about the wrist of his injured arm. Setting his jaw hard, he twisted his shoulder with a sharp jolt, yanking the rope taut. With an ear-splitting crack the broken bone set.

Wolf cried out once, his brow beaded with sweat. Then after

panting raggedly for several minutes, his body racked with pain and relief, he gradually allowed the rope to slacken and untied it from his wrist. Cradling his injured arm, he eased himself forward toward the edge of the brook again. He waited four hours before at last a piece of driftwood that would serve his purpose bobbed sluggishly to shore. Desperately Wolf grabbed at the limb. Wet, it slipped from his fingers. Moments later it rippled back to the bank, and he tried once more, this time with success. He laid the branch down beside him, then returned awkwardly to the cottonwood tree where he raised himself to a sitting position, bracing his back against the trunk. His head swam briefly, causing him to feel faint. He leaned his head back and closed his eyes until the sensation passed. Then tearing the legs of his breeches into long strips, Wolf placed the crude splint along the length of his injured arm, binding it as tightly as he could. After he was certain it was properly set, he wrapped up his ribs and sprained ankle and attempted to stand.

His knees were shaky, and his ankle hurt like the devil as his weight bore down upon it, but he managed somehow to stay on his feet and hobble to the stream again. There he stripped with difficulty, washing every inch of his soiled body and what remained of his breeches. After that he slept.

The following day he felt stronger and was able to dig some roots with his good hand and eat them, although they came back up almost immediately. Wolf realized he was still sick, guessed that, in addition to the fever and chills, the nausea and dysentery, which had persisted, he was probably suffering from the aftereffects of a slight concussion as well. He searched the area for medicinal plants he knew would aid his recovery; wild mint for his queasy stomach, yarrow for his cuts and bruises, Indian turnip for the ache in his head, and tiny pine cones for the horrible soreness in his throat. He also discovered a slope filled with wild persimmons and cherries, on which he subsisted, along with the roots, until he was well enough to catch small game in the snare he fashioned out of the rope. He thought it ironic that the would-be instrument of his death now served in so many ways to keep him alive.

Weeks passed. Wolf did not know how many, for he had lost all track of time in his battle for survival. He did not care. He was like a hurt animal, needing time to lick his wounds, like the haunted boy he had once been, alone, living off the land; only this time he had not even a hunting knife to sustain him. He did not need it. The Land was in his blood now, as it had not been during his childhood. Wolf *was* The Land. His keen eyes were like those of the hawks that soared in the night sky in search of prey. His discerning nostrils breathed and identified every scent of the wind. His body could slither through the tall prairie grass like a snake's, with only a hushed, passing rustle in the darkness. Yes, he was The Land, and like The Land he would grow strong again.

Eventually his body healed, and there was only – once he had torn away the noose – a terrible scar around his throat where the rope had burned and bitten into his flesh to remind him of his grueling ordeal. By the silvery light of a Comanche moon Wolf mounted Pahuraix and turned the horse southward, toward Mexico, toward home, toward Storm and the child she had given him.

He was struck dumb by the sight of Fin Terra, for if ever there was a place more desolate, it existed only in his heart. The haven toward which he'd hastened was gone. Storm's arms were not there, eagerly outstretched and waiting to hold him close and ease the anguish of his torment. Chance's small face was not there, at the window, watching expectantly, excitedly for his arrival. There was nothing but the deserted house they'd shared, void of even a trace of their existence.

His first thought was that Gabriel North had discovered their whereabout and taken them, but Wolf saw no signs of a struggle, and surely Storm would not have gone without a fight! Feeling oddly detached, he gazed around the house curiously, as though he were a stranger to it. It had not been inhabited for some time, for everything was covered with a fine layer of dust, which had been allowed to settle undisturbed. There was the table where they'd eaten their meals, the washtub on the counter where Storm had rinsed the dishes, and Chance's little bunk to one side. Beyond the curtain dividing the one room there was the bed Wolf had built and in which he and Storm had slept and made love. His eyes fell upon his belongings, stacked neatly in one corner, and then he knew.

If you leave, don't come back!

When he hadn't returned, Storm had thought he'd taken her at her word, abandoned her and Chance, and she and the boy had gone. For a long time Wolf's tortured soul refused to accept the conclusion it had reached, fought against it, thought of a thousand other reasons for his family's absence; but in his heart he knew the truth. Oh, God! Oh, God! How could she have done this to him?

After awhile Wolf took off his tattered breeches and changed into his Indian garments, then quietly he left the house.

The tracks that would have told him where to search for his wife and son had long since been obliterated by time and nature. Heartsick, he rode toward the one place he knew would always be there waiting for him, the one place where Storm would seek him if she loved him still. He rode toward The Land, The People.

They gave him the welcome Storm had not, took him into their arms without question. It was enough that he was home. If he wished to tell them what had caused the torment in his eyes, he would do it in his own way, his own time.

Somehow, when Wolf had rested, he found the words to explain his agony and discovered his enemy Gabriel North to be The People's own. Ekakura and Kwasia were dead, slain by the white chief Flame-Hair many winters past. Moon-Raider and Crazy-Soldier-Boy thirsted for revenge, even as Wolf himself did. With a frenzied vengeance he threw himself into the attacks on Tierra Rosa. Piece by piece he would see the hated rancher who had cost him his wife and son destroyed.

The maidens of the camp who would gladly have shared his blankets found themselves turned away with no more than a passing glance of disinterest. There was only one woman Wolf wanted, and she had left him . . .

He stared down into her stricken, disbelieving gray eyes and those of his son, whom she clutched in her arms.

Oh, God! To find them now, *here*, on *this* land, Gabriel North's property, defending all that which Wolf had vowed to lay to waste, murdering The People—

'Storm!' he breathed before she turned and ran from him as though she had seen a ghost.

31

Storm was shaking all over when she somehow reached the buckboard. *Jesù! Jesù!* Wolf was alive! Alive! Oh, God, it *had* been him; she just knew it! *Sainte Marie!* Had she been wrong about him deserting her and the boy? Had Wolf gone back to Fin Terra, found them gone, and searched for her and Chance after all? No, of course not. He'd been on Tierra Rosa land because the Comanches – The People – were raiding it. Surely that was all. Oh, dear God, what had he thought when he'd found his wife and child here – of all places? and – worse yet – what would he do?

'*Maman. Maman.*' Chance brought Storm back to reality with a start. 'It *was ap*', wasn't it?'

'*Oui*, Chance; it was. *Sacré bleu!*' the girl spoke in rapid French so that the others wouldn't understand if they heard. 'You mustn't say anything to the others, Chance. Do you understand me? You mustn't tell them *ap*' is alive. *Monsieur* North, papa, will kill him, do you hear?'

'*Monsieur* North is *not* my papa,' the boy said calmly, also speaking in French. '*Ap*' is, and *ap*' is a much better shot than that horrible old man. I *told* you *ap*' was alive, *maman*. Why would you not believe me? I knew he would come for us. I just knew he would! *Dohate* told me so, but you would not believe me. *Ap*' *will* come back for us, won't he, *maman*? Now that he knows where we are.'

'*Oui*, Chance,' Storm replied, somehow certain of this and growing cold with fear at the thought. Oh, God, Wolf would kill her! Hadn't he warned her often enough about what he would do if he ever caught her with another man?

'What's the matter, *maman*? Don't you want *ap*' to come for us? Don't you love him anymore?'

'I don't know; I don't know. Hush, Chance, and let me think. Oh, how dare you run away from *maman* like that, scaring her out of her wits? You might have been killed!'

'Oh, no, *maman*. The People don't kill those of their own blood. *Ap'* said so.'

'And just how did you think the *Kwerharehnuh* were going to recognize you, you wicked little boy?' Storm's voice rose hysterically. 'Because *ap'* told them to look for you? *Ap'* couldn't care less about you! He abandoned you, do you hear? He didn't want you anymore! He didn't love you, didn't love me— Now quit talking about *ap'*! I don't want to hear any more about him, ever, do you understand me?'

Chance turned away, crushed, unable to comprehend his mother's hurtful words. His tiny shoulders sagged.

'Oh, Chance! Chance! I'm sorry, son, so sorry,' Storm apologized, hugging him close. 'I didn't mean those terrible things I said. Of course *ap'* loves you. It's *maman* he doesn't want—'

'Is that why you're crying?'

'No. I – I got something in my eye, a speck of dust—'

'It's winter, *maman*. The ground is frozen, and there isn't any wind, besides,' Chance noted softly, wise beyond his years.

'Goddamn it, Storm! Stop coddling that brat, and give me a hand here,' Gabriel roared.

Tears streaming silently down her cheeks, the girl picked up her husband's rifle, wondering if he would kill Wolf with it.

The Comanches had gone as swiftly as they had come, taking their wounded and dead with them. A stout wagon sent from Tierra Rosa had conveyed the Norths and Gabriel's injured outriders back to the house. Those men who had lost their lives during the Indian attack had been strapped to their horses and taken to the stables to be laid out for burial on Gabriel's picnic tables. Storm had shuddered at the idea, knowing, come the summer barbecues, that she would be unable to sit at the long benches and eat from the wooden planks that had once been laden with Tierra Rosa's dead.

The night was quiet now. Storm scarcely dared to breathe in the stillness of her room. Wrapped in the dressing gown she had thrown over her negligée earlier, as though it might offer some protection against what was to come, she waited in the darkness, her heart pounding. In an hour, perhaps less, when he was sure the house slept, Wolf would come back; she was certain of it. It made no difference that he had deserted her and Chance; he would still consider them his, would still kill her for daring to begin a new life with another man.

The girl clutched her knife convulsively.

The arrogant bastard! Had he thought Storm would have no more pride in herself than to wait complacently for a man who'd had no intention of returning to her from the moment he'd strapped on his guns again? She had seen that strange look in his eyes when she'd told him not to come back, and she'd known then Wolf had chosen his restless way of life over her — and his son, had made his decision long before that final parting cry had ever been wrenched from her lips in despair. She and Chance had become a burden to him, had forced his strong will to bend to a way of life for which he'd had no use or desire.

Baby, I told you I wasn't going to change, not even for you. I've got a restless fever in my blood. I like to roam. It's all I know.

All right; Goddamn you, Wolf! You tried to meet me halfway and couldn't. I accept that. You went your own way; now leave me and my son to go ours!

But he wouldn't; Storm knew that. She had seen it in his eyes on the flat, frozen plains of Tierra Rosa. He would come back — tonight.

The girl imagined him creeping through the brush outside, slipping into the house through one of the windows on the first floor, gliding through the hallways, up the long, curving flight of stairs, stealthily opening up room after room in search of her. She pressed her ear to the paneled wood of her door to listen for the gentle whisper of moccasin fringe that would tell her he had come. Her fingers curled and uncurled about the deadly blade she held in her hand.

There! She was sure she had heard something!

The next minute Wolf had grabbed her roughly, clamping his palm over her mouth before Storm could scream and twisting the knife from her grasp. The steel glittered cold and silvery in the moonlight that streamed in from the now-open French doors leading to her balcony. He had not come through the house at all! Wolf pressed the blade's sharp point gently against her throat.

'I see you still have a penchant for knives, baby,' he muttered against her ear, then growled, 'Shall I kill you, you adulterous bitch, or merely cut off your nose as punishment instead?'

Terrified, the girl struggled against him, only to be halted by the prick of the finely honed steel.

'Well?' Wolf asked, then swore as he realized she could not possibly answer with him choking off her breath. 'You cry out one time, Storm, and it will be the last sound you ever make,' he warned, then slowly released her after she had nodded to show she understood.

He turned her around to face him. Still holding her knife and placing his hands on either side of her so that she couldn't escape, he forced her up against the paneled door. Storm shivered at the nearness of him, at the warmth that emanated from his body so close to hers.

Wolf had changed. Whereas before he had been quiet, suppressed, now he seemed tense, lethal, ready to spring at any moment, like a dangerous, lithe panther just released from a cage. Storm had never been more aware of the murderous violence coiled within him.

'Well?' he reiterated, his voice low and silky, with that deceiving note she had come to know so well.

The girl swallowed hard. 'How – how did you find me?'

He shrugged. 'The layout of a house like this is fairly simple to determine. The room next door is the master suite, so obviously this chamber had to be yours. Stop stalling for time baby, and answer my question. Which is it to be: death – or disfigurement?' Grimly he indicated the blade he held poised in his hand.

'I – I don't want you to do either of course.'

'Of course.' He smiled jeeringly, relaxing slightly to allay her wariness of him, then said casually, as though they were making polite conversation, 'Do you want to tell me what you're doing here?'

'Oh, Wolf! I – I thought you were dead; Gabriel told me you were—'

'And you believed him – the treacherous bastard!' Wolf suddenly had the knife at Storm's throat once more.

'I – I had no reason not to. Besides' – her voice faltered – 'it – it didn't matter anyway.'

His eyes narrowed frighteningly at that. 'What do you mean – it didn't matter anyway?'

'You ask me that – after leaving us, abandoning me and our child? *Mon Dieu*! Do you know what we went through, waiting there for you? Do you even care? Chance rode his little pony to the crest of the valley every day to watch for you, and you never came, weren't there to see the anguish in his eyes as I was—'

'You were the one who told me not to come back—'

'You must have known I didn't mean it; you must have!'

'Keep your voice down; damn you!' Wolf snarled harshly, pricking her with the blade again threateningly. 'Do you want to waken your lover'?

Storm did not need to ask whom he meant. 'He's not my lover,' she spoke, praying Wolf would believe her.

'No?' One eyebrow raised mockingly. 'What then?'

'He's my – my – Gabriel is my husband.'

Wolf inhaled sharply, stunned. 'No, he can't be, you lying bitch!'

'Why would I lie? Answer me that then.'

There was a tense silence in which Storm thought surely Wolf would kill her. She could see a muscle working in his jaw as he fought himself for control.

'How?' he snapped curtly, making her shrink away from him in fear. 'Why? Goddamn you, Storm! I could have borne anything but that!'

Pale and shaking at the petrifying wrath she saw in his eyes, she told him, told him all about leaving Fin Terra, sailing to San Francisco, marrying Gabriel, everything.

'By God!' he cursed when she had finished. 'I ought to kill you! Cutting off your nose isn't good enough for you, bitch! How many times – how many times have you lain with that no-good bastard? Tell me!'

'Never.'

'Jesus Christ! For what do you take me? Don't lie to me, you whore!' He shook her roughly.

The girl cowered at his rage, for she had never seen him so angry, and he was the one man in the world who truly frightened her beyond belief. He could be so cold, so deadly – and she was so vulnerable to him.

'For God's sake, it's the truth, Wolf! Gabriel couldn't – couldn't – has never been able to – to—'

'Fuck you?' He supplied the words crudely, cruelly.

'Yes,' she replied with quiet dignity, drawing her dressing gown more tightly about her in an attempt to shield her body from the way his midnight blue eyes were now speculatively raking the length of her.

'Well, well,' he drawled, suddenly tossing away the knife and placing one hand upon her throat, allowing it to rest there possessively for a moment before it slid down to join his other hand in shoving aside the edges of her robe, baring the soft swell of her creamy breasts to his hungry gaze. 'How fortunate for us both that I won't have to kill you after all.'

Storm gasped as she realized what he was saying – wanting. *Jesù*! It was so difficult not to remember the brush of his lips upon her cascading black tresses, the husky murmur of his voice in her ear, the taste of his carnal mouth upon her own eagerly parted one, the touch of his fingers caressing her velvet flesh so very intimately, the silky ripple of the muscles in his back beneath her hands, the feel of the hard, muscular length of him weighing her down, driving into her senses, filling her with yearning. Even now desire for him flickered deep inside her and took flame, burning her secret place to its core.

She trembled with its fire. Wolf's eyes darkened, their lids sweeping downward lazily to veil his thoughts, and Storm knew he was remembering too . . .

No! I won't let him touch me!

Her mind rebelled against the idea as she forced herself to recall how he'd left her, allowed another woman to take her place in his heart.

'Take your hands off me!' she hissed, infuriated by his easy assumption that she was once more his for the taking. 'Do you think I would let you touch me now, you *bâtard*, after the way you deserted Chance and me and took another woman to your blankets?'

'What other woman? There has been no woman but you for me since the night we were married, *paraibo*.'

For a minute the old, familiar endearment brought tears to her eyes. Then wrathfully the girl dashed them away.

'Liar!' she cried. 'No – I don't want to hear your stupid explanations,' she went on, dismissing whatever it was he'd been about to say. 'You're just like all men! You just want to use me! I don't know what I ever saw in you. You're nothing but a liar and a cheat, you dirty half-breed!'

It was the wrong thing to have said.

Oh, if only Storm had told Wolf she loved him still instead, had gone willingly into his waiting arms, had admitted she'd made a horrible mistake in marrying Gabriel North, had begged Wolf to take her and the boy away. But she did not. Her pride and hurt at being rejected, unwanted, were too great, as great as Wolf's own at knowing she really believed he had abandoned her and the boy. He, who had loved them both more than life itself.

Oh, if only he had told her so. If only he had spoken then, despite her not wanting to hear, had forced her to listen to what

Gabriel North had done to him, had shown her the dreadful scar around his neck – how different things might have been. But he did not.

They were like two strangers, two people who only pretended to be hard and uncaring, two people who loved and tragically lost one another because both were afraid of being even more deeply wounded if they revealed their true feelings. Oh, if only they had known the terrible price they would have to pay for their foolish pride and silence. *If only*. How many lifetimes of pain could they have prevented by never having to say those two small words of regret: *If only?*

'Am I to understand you no longer want me then, Storm?' Wolf asked, stung, infuriated, and embittered to the core that she had loved him so little. 'Am I?' He gave her another savage shake, wanting to hurt her for what she had called him and the things she had said.

'Why *should* I want you? You didn't want me!'

'Oh, God, where was your love for me when you thought that?'

'I had none,' she stated coldly, 'just as you had none for Chance and me. Where are your guns, Wolf? Where are those cold bits of steel for which you traded your son and me?'

'I want to see the boy,' he intoned dully, ignoring her question, realizing it was useless now to try to explain.

'No! Haven't you done enough as it is?'

'I – want – to – see – the – boy,' he repeated through clenched teeth. 'Take me to him, Storm, now, or by God, I'll kill you with my bare hands!'

She hesitated briefly, then nodded. 'All right, but you're not to wake him up. He's adjusted now to you having deserted him,' she lied, 'and I don't want him upset again.'

The look Wolf gave her at that would have caused her to faint in sheer terror if she hadn't been so determined to protect her child. Nevertheless Storm quivered as she led the way on cautious, hushed, bare feet down the hall and opened the door to Chance's room softly. Then she turned and barred the entrance with her body challengingly so that Wolf was forced to look over her shoulder to see his son. Storm didn't think Wolf would take the boy, that the thought would even occur to him, for the place of a Comanche child was with its mother, but the girl couldn't be sure and wasn't taking any chances.

Chance was sleeping, as she had known he would be, his tiny carved dragon clutched in one fist, as usual. For a time, as Storm and Wolf gazed at him, each remembered that hot autumn day of the boy's birth upon the plains; how they had shared the delivery of him together; how they had held him afterward and marveled over the little bundle of joy their love had wrought; how they had counted his fingers and toes; relieved and laughing at their foolishness when there had been ten of each; how they had bathed him from a canteen and swaddled him with soft deerskin; how Wolf had lain beside Storm while Chance had suckled at her breast. Their eyes met, bared and pleading for a fleeting instant. Oh, God, what had happened to the love they'd known that special day? Then Storm turned away, recalling the woman who had taken her place in Wolf's heart, and tossed her head defiantly. Whatever they might have said was left unspoken.

Silently they returned to the girl's suite.

'I want you to go now, Wolf, and leave me alone. You've gotten whatever it was for which you came.'

'Have I, baby?' he queried, his voice low as he started to walk toward her purposefully, his eyes dark once more with desire. *'Te quiero, bruja. ¿Comprendes?'*

Understanding his intent, Storm backed away, her heart pounding queerly in her breast.

'No,' she whispered. 'No.'

Wolf only smiled strangely, ignoring her soft, whimpered pleas, and yanked her to him roughly.

'No, don't scream, Storm,' he purred with deceiving pleasantness. 'I promise you won't like the results.'

Then he bent his head to kiss her.

Oh, how dare he presume to make love to her after

abandoning her and taking another woman to his bed?

The girl lashed out at him, enraged, struggling wildly in his arms, clawing at his face, kicking at his shins. Caught off guard, Wolf stepped back to avoid being struck, trying at the same time to restrain her vicious blows. Somehow they spun about as they grappled, then tripped and fell, sprawling upon the bed. Storm inhaled sharply as she felt the shock of Wolf's warm weight upon her. Her dressing gown had loosened in the fight, exposing her creamy flesh beneath the transparent negligée she was wearing. She shuddered at the hunger on Wolf's copper visage as his eyes swept the length of her, then settled on her angry, frightened face. Briefly, the midnight blue shards softened, Storm thought, but it must have been a trick of the light, for the next moment they were as hard and merciless as ever.

'Let me go!' the girl spat.

'There was a time when you had no objection to sharing my blankets, Storm.' Wolf arched one eyebrow in mock surprise at her protest.

'Well, not anymore.'

'Too bad. I mean to have you anyway, baby. Not, however, here, I think,' he said, indicating the bed. His harsh grip like a vise, he dragged her to the floor and pinioned her wrists above her head. 'A bed always squeaks, doesn't it?' he noted jeeringly with a tight, hateful grin that didn't quite reach his narrowed eyes. 'And I really don't want to be interrupted by your – husband. Funny, isn't it? For some strange reason I thought *I* was your husband.'

'*We* had no priest, you vile *cochon*! Now let me go!'

'But you and Gabriel did, huh, is that it? I'll bet you even wore a pretty white *pitsikwina* too, even though you were no virgin!' he sneered. 'You fool! Do you really think somebody mumbling a few words in Latin over you made you Gabriel North's wife in my eyes. You're mine, Storm, *mine*! And I'm going to take you now to prove it.'

'No, you can't. You have no right—'

'No right? Baby, you're my wife, whether *you* think so or not. Jesus Christ! You're lucky I haven't killed you for what you've done. I'd be within my legal rights, you know. There *is* such a thing as a law against bigamy, Storm, in case you haven't heard. Now stop fighting me, baby. You know you want it as badly as I do.'

'No, I don't!' the girl denied him sharply, mortified. 'Don't touch me!'

Wolf only laughed, a low, leering sound. 'Shut up, you liar, or I'll slit your throat,' he threatened softly, pulling his knife from its sheath at his waist. He smiled again, that horrible, derisive grin. 'I reckon it would be kind of pointless to be polite and ask you to undress,' he stated wickedly before brutally but expertly cutting the garments from her cringing flesh, then somehow casting away his own clothes.

Naked except for an Indian collar with masses of beads that hung down upon his bare chest, mingling with those of the rosary he wore always, Wolf's body covered Storm's. Then there was nothing but the feel of his mouth on hers, hard and possessive as one hand wrapped itself in her mass of hair hurtfully to hold her still, and the other cupped her breasts, fondling first one and then the other as he continued to kiss her savagely. Storm beat on his chest and back with her small fists until she tired of her futile struggles and his fingers tightened in her cascade of curls, jerking her head back painfully.

'Do you want me to break your damned neck?' he growled against her lips. Immediately she relaxed beneath him. 'I thought not.' His voice was smug, and she wanted to kill him.

'I hate you!'

'Do you think I care – now?' His midnight blue eyes stared down into her gray ones with cold amusement. Still something else, something like pain clouded their depths, and for a minute Storm longed to reach up and caress his copper visage lovingly to take away the hurt.

'Wolf—' she breathed, but it was too late.

He was already kissing her fiercely again, parting her

resisting lips for his ravaging assault. Roughly he teased the inner sweetness of her mouth, exploring it with taunting swirls of his tongue and gentle nibbles of his teeth. On and on he kissed her until she began to feel hot and dizzy with passion. A slow, burning ache started deep within her womanhood, heightening as he continued his onslaught on her senses until she yearned to have him touch her there, between her thighs; but he did not. Instead his lips blazed across one cheek, leaving a trail of fire to her ear where he muttered Comanche and Spanish words of love and sex huskily, his thick voice and warm breath sending little tingles of shock and anticipation down her spine. She shivered involuntarily, feeling somehow helpless and vulnerable in his arms, as though he could do anything he wanted to her, and she would be powerless to prevent it. He sensed the odd thrill of fear mingled with desire she felt, and in a strange, primitive way it excited him. She was his – his for the taking – and, God, how he wanted to take her, wanted to feel himself driving down into her, conquering her in every way.

Slowly he loosed his grip on her tangled tresses, knowing even if she wished to fight him now, she could not. Her body had betrayed her, had responded to his mouth and hands. Even now he knew she ached to have him in her. She gave a low moan as his fingers swept down to cradle her breasts, rub her dark rosy nipples until they stiffened eagerly. He took his time playing with them, wanting to arouse her to a feverish pitch. Lingeringly he let his lips roam over the rigid little buds, sucked them, took them between his teeth, flicked them with his tongue. And all the while his hands moved on her flesh; his weight leaned against her own; one leg rode between her flanks tormentingly, knowing she was waiting breathlessly, expectantly for his knee to slide up and spread her thighs. He could feel the hard throbbing of his own loins as his fingers slipped down her belly to brush lightly along the insides of her legs, still torturing her until at last he found the soft swell of her pulsating mound. He stroked her dark damp curls rhythmically, wanting to feel the sweet, honeyed moistness of her.

He glanced up at her face, wondering what she was thinking. Storm's gray eyes were closed, her lips parted from her ragged breathing. As though she sensed he were looking at her, her eyes flew open wide.

'Don't,' she pleaded softly. 'Don't.'

Wolf only smiled, for he knew his watching her made her feel as though he were invading her soul, as well as her body.

Still he asked, 'Why not?' wanting to hear her admit there was no part of her he could not have.

'You know why.'

'Do I, baby?'

When she didn't answer, he laughed and bent to kiss her mouth once more.

'*Bruja*,' he breathed. '*Bruja*.'

Then his lips were licking her breasts again, devouring their way down her belly to the soft fluff that twined between her thighs. He tongued her slowly until she was writhing beneath him, arching her hips against his mouth and probing fingers.

'*Mon Dieu*; *mon Dieu*!' she gasped.

Her bones were melting inside her. She could feel them, feel them turning to hot, molten ore that seared through her veins like flashes of quicksilver, and then she was exploding, over and over, like a keg of black powder to which he had struck a match. Moments later he was spiraling down into the sweet velvet length of her with a tender fury that made her cry out once before he muffled her whimpers with his lips. Again and again his hard maleness plummeted into her, faster and faster as he put his hand beneath her hips, lifting her strongly to receive his rapid thrusts. She could no longer think. Her mind had gone blank, spinning into a wild blackness filled only by Wolf, the scent of him, the feel of him; the essence of his being whirled about her, engulfing her with its raging tide of fire. She could feel the beads of the Indian necklace and rosary around his throat pressing into her soft breasts, but she didn't care. She trembled beneath him with passion, quivering all over as she felt herself begin to burn once more, hotter and hotter until she was sure she would die from the ecstasy of the sudden, all-consuming blaze that swept through her body. Then there was nothing but her surrender as she clung to him feverishly, letting the flames envelop her.

Mad with desire, with the feel of her warm, yielding flesh beneath him, molding to fit the length of his hard, muscular body; spurred on by the sound of her ragged breathing in his ear as she climaxed, Wolf drove into her powerfully until his own triumphant release came, and he filled her with his seed.

Slowly, still panting, he raised his head, knowing that no matter how much she now hated him, he had left his brand inside her, marked her as his. He kissed her mouth once more, deeply, lingeringly before he rose, his eyes veiled against her. They did not speak. There was nothing left to say. On silent feet he strode over to the pitcher and basin that sat upon the dresser. He wet a rag, wrung it out, then returned to sponge off the sweat that shone upon Storm's skin with a fine, dewy sheen. He smoothed the damp, tangled strands of hair away from her face, then bathed himself and dressed.

At last he turned back to her.

'Good evening, Mrs North,' he said jeeringly, smiling. 'It's been a pleasure.'

What had happened between them might never have been. Whatever Storm had expected, it was not this. The small hope within her that he might love her still was crushed. *Gabriel North's wife*! That's all she was to Wolf now. The girl shuddered at the thought, remembering the way it had been between them in San Antonio when he had discovered her to be the despised rancher's fiancée. All her hurt and hatred toward Wolf at being deserted, rejected, and now used and scorned returned. Oh, God, what had she done? What had she done? She had let him possess her, humiliate her – Storm sprang to her feet, yanking out the drawer of her night table and grabbing the hideout pistol she kept within. She leveled it evenly at Wolf's chest.

'Don't you ever come here again, you filthy half-breed, or I'll kill you,' she warned him feverishly, half-mad, like a cornered animal, with pain.

'Is that right?' His eyes narrowed, glinting hard like steel at her insult. 'We shall see, Storm,' he promised, 'when I return.'

And then he was gone.

Wolf did come again, as he had vowed. He came as he had come that first time stealthily and on the wings of night. When Storm least expected it, she retired to her room one evening to find him waiting for her in the darkness, waiting to force himself on her unwilling body and soul, waiting to laugh at her futile struggles to prevent him from doing so, for despite her threat, the girl discovered she could not kill him after all. He was stronger than she and had found a means of besting her and insuring her silence, besides: Chance.

Wolf had arrived while the boy had been still awake and had played with the child in the nursery, bringing him a small gift to remind him of his Indian heritage. Storm was angry and terrified upon discovering this, but Chance, oddly enough, had accepted the secretive but joyful reunion calmly, understanding without being told that he was not to inform the remainder of the household about his father's late night call.

'How dare you?' the girl spat at Wolf upon being told of the visit. 'I told you to keep away from the boy! He's mine, and you'll only upset him, confuse him by coming here. He doesn't understand – Oh, Goddamn you, Wolf—'

'You listen to me, baby,' he snarled, wrapping his hand in her hair and yanking her head up to his. 'Chance is my son, and I'll come to see him any time I choose, just as I'll take you whenever I please. No, don't cry out, baby, and don't try to deny me. It will only be worse for you if you do, I promise you.' He slipped his hand inside her bodice, cupping one breast possessively. Storm trembled slightly, her face flushing as her nipple hardened against her will at his touch. Wolf grinned, continuing to fondle her as he went on softly, menacingly.

484

'Really, Storm, how dare you instruct my son to call that worthless piece of shit you married papa? Perhaps I should cut off your nose after all. I wonder how Gabriel North would like seeing his very costly bride disfigured?'

'You wouldn't!'

'Wouldn't I? Take off your clothes, Storm.'

'If you think you can threaten me into whoring for you, you're wrong, Wolf! I don't care if you kill me! I hate you! I won't let you touch me again!'

'Oh, but you will, baby; you will. You see, strangely enough I find myself still wanting your body, despite the fact that it's now missing a heart. Love; hate.' He shrugged. 'I told you once I didn't care. Take off your clothes, Storm.'

'No, I won't, I told you!'

'You *will*, baby. You will do whatever I want you to do, and keep silent about it as well, or you'll never see Chance again.'

'*Sainte Marie! That's* why you haven't tried to take him away from me! Not because under Comanche law his place is with me, but because you want to hold him over my head in order to use me to satisfy your desires! *Sacré bleu!* How could you be so cruel? Take your lust to one of your saloon sluts, Wolf, and *leave me alone!* I wasn't enough for you before; why should now be any different?'

'Let's just say I like the idea of bedding the woman who belongs to Gabriel North,' he drawled insultingly, making her shudder once more as again she recalled how he'd taken her so brutally that time in San Antonio for the very same reason. 'Now take off your clothes, Storm, unless you want me to use my knife on you as I did the first time I came here.'

Mute with anger and humiliation, she obeyed.

Time after time Wolf came to her at night and forced her to lie with him; forced her body to respond to his demanding mouth and hands; whispered '*bruja, bruja*' against her throat; laughed at her struggles, her hatred, and her fear; terrified her with a quiet, frightening intimidation when she called him a half-breed. Storm saw nothing to do but submit. If she told

Gabriel, Wolf would take Chance away from her as he had threatened, and she would be powerless to prevent it. She couldn't watch the boy every single minute, and Comanches were notoriously successful raiders. Wasn't Wolf's getting into the house without being discovered proof enough of *that*?

Besides, Gabriel himself would never believe Wolf had forced himself on her. No, the hated rancher would think Storm had scorned and betrayed him once more for her 'half-breed Indian lover' and would kill her in a blind rage for it this time; the girl was sure. Joe Jack was right. Gabriel couldn't stand being beaten. It was why he had married her, in spite of the fact that by then he'd thought her a whore. Winning was everything to Gabriel, no matter what he had to do to achieve it. No, Storm could not tell him about Wolf; it would be like signing her own death warrant. So she submitted to Wolf and kept silent and despised him for the way in which he treated her.

Oh, if only he had not deserted her and Chance; if only he still loved her; *if only—*

32

'Well, what do you say, Joe Jack?'

'I say you're mean, pa, mean and cold-hearted. I just never realized how much so until today.'

'I'm not interested in your opinion of me, boy. I want something done; I've asked you to do it; and I've offered you half Tierra Rosa in return.'

'Shit! That ain't nothing! I'm likely to get that much anyway – if not more.'

'By God! I wouldn't be too sure of that if I were you, Joe Jack. I just might leave it all to Storm—'

'Like hell!' Joe Jack grinned wickedly. 'Who do you think you're fooling, old man? I know how matters stand between that good-looking bride of yours and you, and don't think I don't! Shit! The only reason you married her was because you couldn't stand to be whipped. You don't love her, and she don't love you. It's *me* she wants. So go on, pa. Leave the ranch to Storm. See if I care. I'll still get it all in the end anyway. Yeah, old man, you just do that, and while you're having Oakley draw up the papers, you think about me upstairs in your bed, showing your rich widow that at least one of us North men has balls.'

'And what makes you think I don't? Goddamn you, Joe Jack! You're always so damned sure of yourself, aren't you?'

'Yeah.'

'Why is that, I wonder?'

''Cause I got something you don't, pa.'

'Yeah? What's that, boy?'

'A pecker that gets hard.'

The rancher's face turned a mottled shade of red with rage. How in the hell did his son always know everything that went on at Tierra Rosa?

'By God! I'll fix you for that, Joe Jack!' Gabriel bellowed. 'You wait and see if I don't! I'll leave the whole frigging ranch to Cathy; that's what I'll do! And if I know that uppity miss in man's breeches, she'll see you never get a single square inch of my land.'

Abruptly Joe Jack stopped smirking. He debated briefly over telling his father about Cathy and Ross Stuart, then realized the old man would still leave Cathy Tierra Rosa just to spite him because he'd guessed Gabriel was impotent.

The rancher laughed shortly.

'That got you, didn't it, boy? That got you good! Well? Are you ready to talk business now, or aren't you?'

'Yeah, I'm ready, but I ain't champing at the bit about it. Why in the hell don't you have one of your hands or hired guns do it?'

'And be blackmailed for the rest of my life by some punk who knows *I* gave the order? Come off it, Joe Jack. I didn't build Tierra Rosa into one of the finest ranches in Texas to see it sucked dry by some two-bit cowhand or some scum of a gunslinger. Killing a Mexican or a half-breed Indian's one thing. No court in Texas would convict a white man for that. But this— This is something else. Folks aren't likely to take too kindly to it, especially the womenfolk, no matter what the sorry bastard is.'

'Then why in the hell don't you do it yourself? That way nobody'd know about you, and, shit! Even if you did get caught, I reckon you're rich enough to get away with just about anything in this state if you wanted to—'

'I just can't; that's all. Not this time anyway. The frigging son-of-a-bitch doesn't trust me. I couldn't get near him with a ten-foot pole. He's damned smart; I'll say that for the bastard.'

'Well, I ain't risking my neck for nothing; *that's* for sure,' Joe Jack droned slyly, as greedy and calculating as always. 'If I do it, I'll make it look like an accident, and I want the whole damned ranch in return. I want Storm and Cathy *both* cut out of their shares.'

That way, Joe Jack thought, Storm would *have* to give in to him at last or wind up destitute, and Ross Stuart could just damned well take care of Cathy since he was frigging her anyway.

'You do this for me, Joe Jack' – Gabriel leaned forward intently in his swivel chair – 'and I promise I'll leave you every frigging bit of Tierra Rosa.'

Joe Jack grinned. 'Consider it done, pa.'

You do this for me, Joe Jack, and I promise I'll leave you every frigging bit of Tierra Rosa.

Cathy's heart pounded horribly at the words she'd over-heard standing in the hall outside of Gabriel's study. Dear God! What was Joe Jack going to do? What was Joe Jack going to do that was so terrible Gabriel had promised him all Tierra Rosa for doing it?

I've got to find out! Cathy thought frantically. Somehow I've got to find out what it is and put a stop to it before that weaselly brother of mine gets his hands on pa's ranch! Dear God! It'll destroy us! I just know it! Whatever it is, it'll destroy us all!

'The time has come, my brothers, to attack the great white lodge of the one called Flame-Hair,' Moon-Raider said, his dark eyes hard as he gazed off into the distance reflectively. 'We are strong again now – and many. Already our *tuibitsis* grow as young eagles, proud and brave. Look you at Kwanah.' He turned, indicating the half-breed boy listening intently to his words. 'Only ten winters has he seen, and already he hungers for war against the *taboh*, thirsts for revenge against the White-Eyes for desecrating The Land with their strange tipis and surrounding barriers, for killing The People with their fire-sticks and sicknesses. Such despoliation must not go unavenged!'

There were loud murmurs of anger and assent from the warriors and younger boys who had gathered to hear their war chief Moon-Raider speak. He raised his hand to still them, motioning for silence, then clapped Wolf lightly upon one shoulder.

'It is a thing that must be done, my brother, for your father and mine. We have waited long enough to see Flame-Hair brought to his knees. I will give orders that your wife and son be not harmed, but taken prisoner instead. This will satisfy you, banish the doubt that clouds your eyes and the fear for them I know is in your heart? You love them so.'

'Yes, Moon-Raider, that will satisfy me.'

'It is good then.' Moon-Raider's voice rose slightly. 'My brothers, you have heard my solemn promise to Brother-Of-The-Wolf. Let no man here bring harm to our brother's wife, Eyes-Like-Summer-Rain, or his child, Chance-The-Autumn-Wind, upon pain of death. They are Flame-Hair's captives. Their rightful place is among The People. Go now, my brothers, and make ready to attack the great white lodge of our enemy. This time we will have enough fire-sticks, like the White-Eyes, to prevail.'

Storm was roused from slumber by a hand clamping down hard over her mouth. Dazed she struggled wildly at first against the intruder until she heard Wolf's harsh voice ordering her to be still.

'Get up. Get dressed,' he commanded imperiously, releasing her.

Still frightened and confused Storm clutched the coverlet and sheets to her breast convulsively, her gray eyes wide with apprehension.

'Why? What's wrong? What's happening?'

'The People are attacking Tierra Rosa in full force. They mean to kill every *tabeboh* they see and burn the house to the ground.'

'*Mon Dieu!*'

Wolf snatched the bedding from her hands. Angrily he snapped, 'Didn't you hear what I just said? Get up, and get dressed! We've only moments to spare.' He yanked her from the bed, then strode her over to her wardrobe, flinging open its doors and riffling through its contents. Cursing under his breath, he paused to light a lamp, then continued his inspection of her garments. 'Here.' He tossed a fancy riding habit to her. 'Put that on, and for God's sake, hurry!'

With trembling fingers the girl slipped off her negligée and stepped into the camisole and pantalettes Wolf had thrown at her too after dragging them from her chest of drawers. Then she moved to don the riding habit and her stockings and kid boots.

Seeing she was dressed, Wolf grabbed her hand, hauled her impatiently across the room, then swiftly down the corridor toward the west wing, disregarding his usual caution in his haste.

'Oh, I've got no use for women; a true one may never be found,' Joe Jack sang drunkenly as he staggered up the stairs. 'They'll stick by a man for his money; when it's gone they'll turn him down. They're all alike at the bottom, selfish and grasping for all. They'll stick by a man when he's winning and laugh in his face when he falls.' He swayed against the bannister, giggled, then hiccuped. 'Oh, my pal was a straight young cowpuncher, honest and upright and square, but he turned to a gambler and gunman, and a woman sent him there— Hey!' He paused abruptly, lifting his lamp a little higher. 'What the devil— What's going on up there?'

Wolf stepped back from the landing into the hallway, slamming Storm's body hard against one wall, but it was too late. Joe Jack had already seen them.

'Indians!' he bellowed at the top of his lungs. 'Them Goddamned Comanches are attacking the house! I warned you, pa! I warned you! One of 'em's got Storm!'

Then he pulled his revolver and fired off several rounds.

As though on signal, the Indians outside began whooping wildly as they charged the house, and all hell broke loose. Gabriel came roaring out of his room, buckling on his gunbelt, and farther down the corridor Cathy appeared, holding her carbine. Wolf glanced grimly down the shadowed hallway and swore. Even now he could hear Joe Jack pounding up the staircase. If Wolf didn't move – and fast – he'd be trapped. It never occurred to him to use Storm as a hostage for his safe exit. Gabriel North didn't love the girl and probably wouldn't care if she were killed. Wolf let go of her hand, then flung himself across the landing, hitting the floor and rolling to avoid being struck as the hated rancher began shooting at him. Gabriel didn't recognize him in the darkness, but Wolf knew the rancher intended to kill him nevertheless. Storm screamed hysterically, hugging the wall as the bullets spun past her with resounding echos, burying themselves loudly into paneling. This just couldn't be happening! This just couldn't be real!

There was no time for Wolf to get his son. With another muttered oath he barged into the closest room, shattered the glass French doors, and dropped from the balcony to the front porch below, nearly killing himself in the process.

Outside, the Comanches were already battling furiously with Gabriel's men, who'd been roused from the bunkhouse by the shots, and the night air rang with the horrible sounds of the *mêlée*. Wolf hurled his hatchet, burying it in the back of a ranch hand's head. Then he drew his knife and slit another man's gullet before whistling for Pahuraix and making his escape on the animal's bare back to join the others circling the house. Moon-Raider spied him and, seeing he was now weaponless, tossed him a rifle, which Wolf caught deftly.

Inside Gabriel, Cathy, and the servants were already breaking out the mullioned casement windows downstairs to return the Indians' fire. Of Joe Jack there was no sign, and Storm thought fleetingly, he must have passed out somewhere, before she finished jamming shot into an empty carbine and returned it to its owner. Reloading for the others was her only contribution to the fight, for she found she could not bring herself to shoot the Comanches. Wolf was out there. The girl knew she shouldn't have cared – but she did.

The night wore on, and still the battle raged. Storm could hear the terrified screams of the Mexican women who served the household, as they were captured by eager braves and borne away on horseback. She shivered, for she knew it meant the Indians had managed to invade the kitchen where most of the women had been huddled. Gabriel realized this too, for immediately he sent men to investigate. A few minutes later Pilar, who had somehow gotten away from her would-be captors, came running into the salon, yelling that the house was on fire. Storm thought of the huge woodburning stoves in the kitchen that were never allowed to die out and shuddered as she understood what had happened. The Comanches had opened them up and scattered their burning contents. Oh, God, why hadn't Gabriel had sense enough the build the kitchen separate from the main house, instead of insisting on having it connected to the dining room by a hallway so that his food wouldn't have a chance to get cold?

'You men: Smith, Benteen' – the rancher turned to some of his hands who'd sought cover inside Tierra Rosa – 'go help Timothy, Pop, and Lester put out that blaze.'

Obediently they scurried to do his bidding, but Storm noted drops of sweat beading Gabriel's forehead all the same. He and his men were losing the fight. They couldn't hold out much longer. Already shouts warned them that other parts of the house were being penetrated by the Comanches. Two even managed to gain the salon. Storm gasped as rough hands grabbed her hair, yanking her head back to sever her throat with a blade.

'Crippled Elk – no! It's Eyes-Like-Summer-Rain!' she cried, then nearly fainted as she realized she'd spoken in English and that he hadn't understood a word she'd said.

His companion, Idahi, had however. Just in time he ordered his fellow brave sharply in Comanche to stop.

Then he spoke rapidly to Storm in the same language. 'Eyes-Like-Summer-Rain, get your child, and come quickly. Brother-Of-The-Wolf is waiting for you.'

She had no time to do as he'd commanded, however, for just then Gabriel observed the two Indians helping her to her feet. His pistol reported several loud bursts, and the Comanches crumpled to the floor in pools of blood. Storm screamed, horrified. Crippled Elk and Idahi had lost their lives trying to save her and her son.

The rancher snaked his way to her side, then rose, shoving her away from the shattered windows where they would be easy targets. His brown eyes glittered with a strange, triumphant gleam as he studied her tear- and powder-streaked face.

'They want you alive, don't they?' he barked victoriously. 'For some reason they want you alive.'

And then it happened. Gabriel couldn't believe it. He could feel his manhood swelling in his breeches, growing harder and harder as he pressed against Storm's quivering body.

'Jesus Christ,' he groaned. 'Why does it have to be now?'

He couldn't resist. His mouth swooped down to cover hers ravishingly as he fumbled with her bodice, forced his hand inside to fondle one ripe breast.

'No!' Storm struggled against him furiously, beating on his chest with her small fists.

Her resistance seemed to bring him to his senses. He swore again, panting heavily, but ceasing his assault.

'You sweet bitch,' he whispered thickly. 'I'll get an heir on you yet.'

'*I'm* your heir, pa, or have you forgotten?' Joe Jack swaggered into the salon, his dark eyes coldly sober and speculative. He must not have been as drunk as he'd appeared earlier. 'We made a bargain, remember? And I've kept my half.'

'It's done then?' Gabriel asked eagerly.

'It's done.' Joe Jack nodded. 'But it ain't going to do either one of us any good if we don't get out of here – and now. The fire's spreading, and I'd rather take my chances with those red devils outside than fry in here.'

'Chance!' Storm rasped, suddenly recalling her son sleeping above. She picked up her skirt to run.

'Pilar went after him,' Joe Jack said, and when Storm would have hastened upstairs after the boy anyways, Gabriel grasped her wrist tightly.

'I need you outside, my dear.'

Roughly he pinioned her arm behind her back, then shoved her forward. When they reached the front porch, he drew his revolver and jammed it up against her temple.

'Gabriel! My God! What are you doing?'

'Getting us out of this mess, my dear. I don't intend to see Tierra Rosa burned to the ground or my scalp hanging from one of those Comanche bastards' lances. So you just speak up real loud, my dear – in their lingo – and tell them I'm going to put a bullet through your head if they don't clear off – now!'

Shaking all over, Storm did as he'd demanded, and at last the Indians heard her yelling above the *mêlée*. One by one the warriors fell silent, looking to Moon-Raider and Wolf for instructions.

'Eyes-Like-Summer-Rain is your wife, my brother. The decision is yours. What do you want me to do, Brother-Of-The-Wolf?' Moon-Raider queried.

'Call your braves off,' Wolf spoke without hesitation. 'The one called Flame-Hair is capable of killing her otherwise. There will be other nights with Comanche moons.'

'So be it then.' Moon-Raider turned to the others, lifted his lance high, and motioned them away from the blazing house.

The entire first floor of the west wing was now afire, although Gabriel's men were working frantically to douse the flames, and to Wolf's horror, as he began to ride away, he saw the second story above had ignited. His heart lurched queerly in his breast. Chance! It was Chance's room from which the smoke was pouring! Oh, surely Storm had gotten the boy out! She loved him so.

'*Patrona*! *Patrona*! Oh, God help us, *patrona*!' Pilar's screams reached Wolf's ears clearly.

'Pilar! What is it?' What is it? Oh, *Sainte Marie*—' Storm sobbed in sudden understanding. 'Where's Chance? *Where is my son*?'

'Oh, *patrona*! The door to his room – it is jammed. Oh, sweet *Jésus*! Forgive me! I – I could not get it open—'

'*Mon Dieu*!' Storm's eyes flew upward to the burning second story of the west wing. 'No! No! The fire just couldn't have spread that fast! It just couldn't have! *Jesù*! *Jesù*!'

She turned, yanking away from Gabriel and running toward the front doors of Tierra Rosa only to be stopped by Joe Jack.

'Let me go! Let me go!' The girl lashed out at him like a madwoman.

'For God's sake, Storm! You can't go back in there! The place is an inferno! Hilton! Benteen! Jones! Get a ladder—'

The three men raced toward the stables, while Joe Jack dragged Storm's crazily protesting figure out onto the range lawn. She gazed helplessly at Chance's balcony, searching for some sign of the boy.

'*Mon Dieu*,' she whimpered, and Joe Jack gasped.

The child was pounding on the French doors, trying desperately to get out. Storm could see him coughing and choking, tugging futilely at the doorknobs, beating fruitlessly on the glass panes. His small face looked pinched and pitiful, petrified with fear. Tears were streaming down his cheeks, although manfully he kept brushing them away.

'*Jesù*! *Jesù*! He can't get the doors open!' Storm screamed. 'He can't get the doors open! Break the windows out, Chance! Break the windows out!' she yelled hoarsely and then frantically, 'Dear God; dear God! He can't breathe! He can't breathe—'

There was a smashing of glass. A sudden billowing of smoke poured from Chance's room as he pressed his face to the shattered pane, rasping horribly for air. The timbers of the house creaked ominously, and someone shouted,

'My God! The whole west wing is going to go!'

Storm screamed again hysterically as she heard Chance cry,

'*Maman*! *Maman*!'

Then there was a massive, groaning shudder and a crackling burst of flames as the first floor gave way, and the second story toppled.

'Oh, Great-Spirit! No! No!' Wolf gave an agonized cry, savagely digging his heels into Pahuraix's sides and galloping back toward Tierra Rosa before Moon-Raider or Crazy-Soldier-Boy could prevent him from doing so.

Deep in her heart somehow Storm knew then. Still she would not believe it, refused to accept it, kept on hoping desperately, praying for a miracle right up until the time she reached Chance's little copper-skinned figure sprawled pathetically on the frost-touched ground where the wing's collapse had flung him. The Chinese dragon was clutched tightly in his tiny hand. He'd used it to break the glass . . .

For an eternity she froze. Her heart stood still. Her body went deathly cold, and her stomach heaved, as though the earth had dropped without warning from beneath her feet. Then a queer sense of unreality, as though the world had suddenly stopped spinning, took hold of her, and she seemed to see everything in a daze, like a feverish person.

It can't be true! she thought angrily, irrationally, trying to force the hollow sick feeling from her insides. It just can't be true! I won't let it! I won't let it! I'll turn back the clock somehow, someway, for just a few hours, a few minutes, a few seconds and everything will be just as it was before. Surely God will understand. Surely just this once He can make exception. I have to force myself to believe that. Yes, I've got to believe that. Otherwise I'll go crazy – I'll scream again. I'll start screaming again, and I'll never stop. Oh, God! Oh, God! I'll do anything, anything at all— Oh, please, God, ask anything – ask anything of me – but this—

Chance was cold, oh, so cold somehow, despite the heat of the fire that flushed his body. Storm cradled him tenderly in her arms, trying to warm him up, trying desperately to bring the child's life back to him with her own.

Why, he's only sleeping, the girl thought as she brushed a strand of hair from his little cheek, for there was no mark on him, except for the streaks of soot that stained his flesh. He had not been burned. Only a faint bluish hue tinged his flesh, especially around his tiny, pinched nostrils. That's it. He's hurt himself somehow, bruised his small sweet face. Any moment now he'll awaken, and everything will be just as it was—

She hugged him close to her breast, rocking him gently as she began to sing the soft Comanche lullaby he had loved so well. A crystal droplet splashed down upon his skin as she sang. Storm saw the shining bead through blurred eyes. She wiped it away tenderly, for it would not do for the boy to get wet and catch a chill when he was already so cold. More droplets fell. Dimly Storm glanced up at the sky where the pale rose sun was sweeping across the horizon, lightening the dull slate gray of the heavens.

Why, it's not raining at all, she thought. I don't understand—

Then slowly, painfully she realized the glistening beads were her own bitter tears. Chance was dead. Her son was dead, and nothing was ever going to bring him back to her.

Six years. Six all too fleeting years were all she had been given to share with her firstborn child. How unfair it seemed when it ought to have been a lifetime, a lifetime to watch him grow and become a man She remembered carrying the weight of him in her body, caressing her belly, round and full, and weaving a thousand dreams over his cradleboard. She remembered the pains of childbirth she'd suffered, his small body slithering from her womb, and the sight of Wolf bending over him, forcing the first breaths of air into his tiny lungs. She remembered her awe at touching him, holding him, counting his fingers and toes, placing him to her soft breast, and the feel of his precious little mouth sucking firmly at her nipple. She remembered the clutch of his tiny fist around her finger, his first genuine smile, and his first awkward, shaky steps. She remembered, even more agonizingly, the first word he'd ever spoken – and the last: *maman*.

Oh, Chance! Chance!

She tried to stop the memories from coming, but they filled the chasms of her mind anyway, a thousand bright pictures, sharp and clear in every detail. His first pony ride. His first bow. His laughter ringing sweetly, joyfully as she chased him down the riverbank, rolling over and over together, his diminutive figure close and warm against hers. How he'd grinned when he'd splashed her, then slipped quickly beneath the rippling water of the stream, like a fish as he'd dived and swum. How bravely he had run, never questioning her command, when Billy Barlow had wrenched her from her home. How calm he had been when he'd told his father what had happened, although he'd been so terribly frightened. How manfully he'd tried to bear up, thinking his father had abandoned him, and how courageously he'd entered into their new life in San Francisco, though he had been awed and afraid. How he'd clutched the tiny carved dragon at night and named it 'Li Kwan Too' (meaning 'Li Kwan also') to tease his Chinese friend. How he had cried out in the night, scared by *Piamermpits*, giving her time to gather her wits and prevent Gabriel North from using her as the hated rancher had so desired. How he had shouted, *'Ap'! Ap'!* and run from the overturned buckboard to his father's arms, never doubting Wolf's return for an instant. How his bright face had beamed excitedly at some new discovery, and most painful of all, how he had kissed her dearly each evening and said,

'I love you, *maman*. You're the best *maman* in the whole wide world.'

Oh, how could God have been so cruel as to take that from her? How swiftly those six short years with which she had been blessed now seemed to have passed. Oh, God, he'd been only a child! Too young to die! It was so unfair!

Oh, God, why couldn't you have taken me instead? Storm thought vehemently. I've lived a hundred lifetimes, while Chance – Chance had only just begun to live—

Heartsick, Wolf strode through the silent stunned crowd

surrounding his wife and son. He walked tall and proudly, as though daring Gabriel North or the ranch hands to challenge him, but oddly enough none did. The hated rancher was too shocked at seeing the half-breed, whom he'd hung, alive; and the rest were too afraid the Comanches would resume their attack if they harmed this warrior.

Tears glistened on Wolf's cheeks as he knelt down beside Storm, managing at last to pry Chance's body from her blind, convulsive grasp.

'He's dead, *paraibo*,' he said gently. 'The boy is dead.'

Oh, how Wolf wanted to cling to her, love her, share her terrible grief and anguish and his with her. He would take her away – now. No one would stop him. He and Storm would bury Chance together, weep for the child they had made and loved together, and perhaps someway, somehow, they would find what they had once had and lost and ease the pain of their child's death a little – Wolf held out one hand to Storm, knowing she would understand, would forgive and forget the past now.

'Give me my son, whom you murdered, you filthy half-breed.'

'What?' He stared down at her disbelievingly.

'Give me my son, whom you murdered, you filthy half-breed,' she repeated through clenched teeth, her gray eyes narrowed like shards of steel.

Wolf's heart sank with despair.

'Storm – you – you don't know what you're saying— The fire couldn't have spread that rapidly. Something happened – something's not quite right somewhere— Oh, baby, baby, you know I would never have done anything to hurt Chance—'

'Oh, yes, yes, you did. You killed him! You and The People, and I'll never forgive you for it, not as long as I live! *Now give me my son!*'

Wolf's midnight blue eyes were fathomless. His voice, when he finally spoke, was flat, without emotion.

'Madam,' he spoke coldly, 'you have no son – and no

500

husband either.'

Then slowly he turned and walked away, clutching the boy's dead body tightly against his chest, leaving Storm alone, with only the Chinese dragon for comfort.

Empty. The girl felt vast and empty and old – oh, so very old; and she knew it would be a very long time before she would ever laugh again, before the sweet, searing pain of that bitter rose dawn would dim, and she would begin to live again. How strange it seemed that even now her blood went on circulating; her heart went on beating; her lungs went on breathing. How strange it was that they didn't understand she was dead, that some horrible mistake had been made, that they had misinterpreted her brain's signals and gone on functioning, instead of ceasing to operate, keeping the hollow shell of her body alive, instead of letting it die as it had wanted.

Even now they forced her numb limbs to begin moving, forced her to stand and face the crowd around her and the dawn that was so very quiet, except for the hissing of hot embers that still glowed here and there.

The entire west wing had burned. In stark black silhouette those timbers that had not collapsed rose in ruined outline against the pale pink blush of the sky, a dark ugly flaw in what had once been Gabriel North's perfect white jewel.

The rancher stepped forward, mindful of his position, to offer Storm his arm, but she slapped it away wrathfully.

'Don't touch me!' she spat.

Gabriel had done nothing to try to save Chance. It had been Joe Jack who'd sent his father's men for a ladder, Joe Jack who would have climbed it to the blazing second story had the first floor not given way. It was for Joe Jack's arm Storm reached, turning her back on Gabriel North.

33

Spring came early to Tierra Rosa that year of 1856. It came with a soft, soughing wind that rippled the tall prairie grass gently and rustled the leaves of the mesquite trees huddled in clusters on the banks of the Nueces River. Its mellow golden sun shone down upon the land with lazy warmth, as though it had only just awakened after its long winter slumber, and quietly aroused the brightly colored blossoms of the cactuses, prodding them to bloom. The animals crept from their hiding places and after cautious sniffs to be certain spring was truly in the air frolicked gaily upon the rolling plains in the distance and performed their intricate mating rituals like graceful dancers. As the season wore on proud mothers gave birth to delicate, shaky-legged fawns and fat, roly-poly cubs. Frisky foals scampered skittishly in the corrals of Tierra Rosa; little butterball calves trudged awkwardly upon the range.

Storm's heart ached at the sight of the young animals nursing at their mothers' sides, and for the first time in her life spring depressed her. She was, perhaps, a trifle mad those warm, budding days, for she was a woman with passionate emotions. Her heights were glorious, her depths agonizing, and Chance's death had affected her deeply. Sometimes it seemed as though she had died with the boy, for often she moved blindly, dazedly, like a sleepwalker, as though the world around her did not exist. She took to riding farther and farther away from Tierra Rosa proper, galloping aimlessly over the vast terrain, a sorrowful, solitary figure against the sweeping azure sky.

Often she returned to the house with her face flushed, her cheeks tearstained, and her black hair a wild, tangled mass where the wind had whipped it freely. Her wide gray eyes would be glittering strangely, as though she saw things others could not see, and sometimes a sad, wistful half-smile at some memory would be curved upon her lips, causing the ranch hands to shake their heads grimly when she passed. Storm cared nothing for her appearance those days, however, or the fact that people whispered about her behind her back and thought her slightly touched in the head. She had withdrawn into herself, allowing Cathy to resume managing the house and hostessing its grand affairs, which Storm now refused to attend, no matter how often Gabriel berated her for her absence. Once, when the rancher was unusually insistent, Storm went downstairs clothed in her Comanche wedding ensemble. A dreadful hush fell over the ballroom as the shocked guests ceased chattering and turned to stare at her. She gave them all that odd little smile, looked pointedly at Gabriel, then silently disappeared. After that the rancher left her alone, not knowing what she might do next. Sometimes he was half-afraid the girl would kill him.

After Chance's death he'd found he was no longer impotent, but when he'd attempted to exercise his marital rights upon Storm, she'd stabbed him with her knife as she'd threatened. The blade had buried itself into his thigh, narrowly missing his sexual organs. Gabriel had been stunned, for it had never occurred to him that she'd really meant what she'd said. Thereafter, when he'd found her door locked against him, he'd made no effort to force it open, fearing he would get a bullet through his heart the moment he walked through it. Storm had told him as much, no longer caring if she lived or died. She would rather be hung for murder than permit the hated rancher to touch her ever again.

So they went on as before, with Gabriel not only sexually frustrated by his wife, but now socially thwarted by her as well. After a time he realized this last didn't matter, that although people talked about Storm, they pitied her and sympathized with him for being what they perceived as so kind and understanding of her tragic loss. It raised Gabriel's estimation in many women's eyes, and he discovered several who had previously been coolly polite to him after his marriage now sought to 'comfort' him in his hour of need. When they approached him, the rancher grinned knowingly and reveled in their brand of hospitality. After being ministered to by the ones he'd desired, Gabriel finally selected Maggie O'Brian as his mistress, simply because her husband had tried to outwit him in a business deal.

She was red-haired, green-eyed, and buxom, and she pleased him well enough, but she was not Storm; and though she eased the ache in the rancher's loins, Maggie did nothing for Gabriel's increasing rage at being bested by his wife. To divorce Storm would be to admit defeat, and so with each passing day he become more and more determined to see the girl brought to her knees and destroyed instead.

Storm, on her way to the stables, paused, glancing over at the corrals with the first sign of interest in life she had displayed since Chance's death. It was branding time, and the ranch hands were shouting at one another teasingly as they chased elusive calves around the enclosure. Uproarious laughter arose each time an animal managed to squirm free of its captor. Cheers and applause rang out whenever one of the frantically lowing beasts was finally ensnared and hogtied.

Joe Jack, stripped to the waist, his darkly tanned skin glistening with sweat in the summer heat, was doing the branding. Storm studied him intently as he worked, noting the way his lean muscles rippled in his back and arms each time he knelt over a calf and seared the hot TR brand to its hide. For a moment the girl felt a quicksilver flash of forgotten desire tingle through her body. How handsome Joe Jack was. One of the ranch hands made some remark to him, and he grinned, white teeth flashing as he flung his head upward, his brown eyes crinkling against the glare of the sun. It was then he noticed Storm. The smile left his face as he got to his feet, handing the branding iron to one of his father's men before he strode over to where the girl stood leaning against the corral. He took off his hat, running his fingers through his blond, sun-streaked hair.

'You going riding?' he queried.

Storm nodded.

'Wait a minute and I'll go with you.'

'No,' she replied hurriedly, reluctant to let him accompany her after being aroused by the sight of his bare chest. 'You look awful busy.'

'Just making sure we don't have any stray mavericks running loose; that's all. Hilton can finish up. I've done my bit for the day.' He grabbed his shirt and hoisted himself over the fence. 'Let me get cleaned up, and I'll be right with you.'

Storm waited, not knowing how to gracefully decline his company. She watched him covertly, unable to help herself, as he sluiced himself off in a water trough, then donned his shirt and buttoned it, stuffing the ends into his breeches. For some reason just seeing how his firm flat belly tautened and how his hands slipped beneath the waist of his pants, drawing them tight across his loins as he fixed his shirt and adjusted his belt, caused the girl to inhale sharply and turn away. Joe Jack buckled on his gunbelt, then put his hat back on, as though unaware of the effect he was having on her.

'Ready,' he said, taking her arm.

'Why do you call unbranded cattle mavericks?' she asked nervously, trying to make conversation to hide the anxiety she felt at going riding with him. It would be the first time they had been alone together since Chance's death.

'Well, it's kind of funny actually,' he explained, sensing her unrest and attempting to put her at ease. 'The term came about because of a man called Samuel A. Maverick. This fellow owed him some money and couldn't pay the debt, so old Sam agreed to accept some of the fellow's cattle instead. Well, old Sam was kind of a careless, devil-may-care rascal – like myself' – Joe Jack grinned – 'and not knowing what to do with the cattle after he'd gotten them, he put 'em in the charge of this Negro he knew.

505

Now the Negro knew as much about cattle as a rooster does a freight train and neglected to brand them. Of course all of old Sam's neighbors, being such meticulous ranchers, found this hilarious and started joking about it to each other. After that every time they'd see a stray running loose without a brand they'd holler, "Hey, fellers, there goes one of Maverick's!" and pretty soon things got out of hand, and the word "maverick" came to mean any unbranded stock.'

Storm laughed, the first time she had done so since Chance's death. Today was a day for firsts, it seemed.

'Poor old Sam Maverick. Imagine your name being immortalized in such a fashion! Are you sure that isn't one of your tall Texas tales, Joe Jack?'

'Of course not, and even if it had been I'd have told it to you anyways. It made you laugh.' His eyes, sparkling with amusement, darkened, suddenly serious. 'It's good to hear you laugh, Storm. I've missed the sound of your laughter. I've missed being with you.'

'I – I wanted to be left alone,' Storm told him softly, staring off into the distance so that he couldn't see her face.

Joe Jack sighed. 'I know, honey, but you're alive, and you've got to go on living. All the tears in the world aren't ever going to bring that boy back.'

'I know; I know, but, oh, Joe Jack! It's so hard to accept that.' Storm bit her lip. 'I – I can't even take any flowers to his grave. I – I don't even know where he's buried.'

Tears stung her eyes bitterly, and all of a sudden Joe Jack understood the reason behind her solitary rides. She was searching for her son's grave. No telling where that God-damned half-breed had buried the kid – if he'd buried the child at all. Indians were strange about that sort of thing. Joe Jack hadn't particularly cared about Chance one way or another, but his heart *did* ache for Storm, and he wished she'd get over her grief. It made him distinctly uncomfortable.

'I'll tell you what,' he spoke kindly, 'why don't we just ride along until we find somewhere you like, somewhere special, and I'll put up some sort of memorial there for the boy.'

'Oh, Joe Jack! Would you?' Storm cried, for Gabriel had never even offered to hold a religious service or buy the child a headstone for Tierra Rosa's cemetery.

'Yeah. It's the least I can do.' His voice sounded odd, as though overcome by emotion, and the girl was touched. 'In fact,' he continued, 'I know just the place.'

'Thank you, Joe Jack,' she breathed.

The spot to which he led her was quiet, peaceful somehow, and lovely. Storm had never seen it before, for it was set upon the crest of a hill some distance away from Tierra Rosa proper and was sheltered by a small grove of mesquite trees. From it one could look out over the vast expanse of land and see the deep rose beauty of it, cast by the setting sun, for miles in all directions.

'It *is* a special place, Joe Jack. I couldn't have chosen a better spot,' Storm murmured and then, 'Why, there are already graves here too.'

'Yeah, that's why I picked it.'

'To whom do they belong? Why aren't they in Tierra Rosa's cemetery?'

Joe Jack shrugged. 'I don't know; no one does. They're just here; that's all.'

'Perhaps they were special people – like – like Chance.' She gazed down at the three lovingly carved crosses that marked the burial sites, thereby missing the peculiar expression on Joe Jack's countenance. 'Yes, I'd like to think that: a special place for special people. I'd like to think of – of Chance lying here somehow, beneath one of these crosses. I'll choose one for him.'

She picked some wildflowers, then knelt, laying them carefully on the three graves before she said a small, silent prayer for her son and the unknown persons buried in the ground beneath her.

All that summer Joe Jack was Storm's constant companion.

She did not love him, as he claimed to love her, but he made her laugh again, filled the emptiness in her life she had refused to share with Wolf. *Wolf.* She scarcely thought of him now. He had killed her son, and she had sent him from her side for it. As though sensing whatever love they'd shared between was finally and truly destroyed, he had not returned. There was only Joe Jack – and Gabriel, who watched his wife and son expectantly, waiting with bated breath for them to betray him. So far they had not; he was certain of that from the reports given to him by the ranch hands he had spy on Storm. He sneaked a quick glimpse of the two from behind his newspaper. They were sitting at the game table, playing poker. Gabriel frowned disgustedly for both were cheating outrageously and laughing whenever they caught one another in the act. Joe Jack's head was bent close to Storm's, whispering in her ear, and she was blushing.

'Come on, Storm,' Joe Jack purred softly, so that Gabriel couldn't hear what was being said, even though he strained to listen. 'You know you want to, and all summer long you've just been putting me off.'

'I'm just not ready,' she hissed, glancing covertly at her husband. 'It's too soon after – after Chance's death, and – and I just wouldn't feel right about it. Besides, Gabriel would kill us both if he ever found out!'

'Jesus Christ! Is *that* what's really bothering you? Hell, honey. I can outshoot the old man any day of the week!'

'Joe Jack! He's your father!'

'And a damned poor one at that. Aw, come on, Storm,' he crooned hotly once more. 'I'll make it good for you; you know I will. And you need a man in your life right now, someone to hold you close and chase away the shadows haunting you; you know you do. You can't keep your grief bottled up inside forever.'

Oh, it would be so good to lay her head on Joe Jack's chest, to let him shoulder some of the terrible burden of her anguish, to let him love her as she was meant to be loved – as Wolf had

508

loved her once. Oh, Wolf! Wolf! How did it happen? Where did it all go wrong? At last Storm shook her head.

'I – I can't, Joe Jack; I just can't.'

'I'll tell you what,' he coaxed slyly, unwilling to take 'no' for an answer, 'why don't we let the cards decide? We'll cut the deck. High card wins; low card loses. If you win, I promise I'll leave you alone until you tell me different.'

'And if I lose?'

'You meet me at Rosa Pequeño tomorrow.'

Storm inhaled sharply, shaking her head again. She just couldn't bring herself to do it.

'Coward!' Joe Jack jeered, grinning.

'I am not!'

'Then cut the cards, honey.'

The girl took a deep breath, starting once more to refuse, then asked herself: Well, why not? She'd been gambled away to Gabriel and Wolf. Why not do the gambling herself this time? After all, what did she have to lose? She was nothing but an empty shell anyway. Maybe Joe Jack would make her feel alive again, as he had made her laugh. Her fingers trembling slightly, she laid her hand on the deck and smiled.

'Queen of hearts,' she spoke, turning the card face up on the table.

'You are that, Storm, but *I*, my sweet lover-to-be, am the king,' Joe Jack crowed triumphantly, placing the king of hearts over her queen.

Storm gasped. 'You cheated me!'

Still grinning, he drawled, 'Yeah, I did, but all's fair in love and war, honey.'

34

It was a summer she would never forget as long as she lived, but Storm did not know that as she rode toward Rosa Pequeño, her heart pounding with fear and excitement in her breast. She knew only that Joe Jack was waiting for her, waiting to make her his.

The flat, endless horizon, broken here and there by swelling hills and the jagged buttes in the distance, stretched out before her starkly, its beauty wild, savage, clean, and uncluttered save for the tall crowned yuccas, the shrubby mesquite trees, and the few forlorn cottonwoods. The sun beat down from the clear blue sky hotly, as though seeking to wilt the brightly colored blossoms of the cactuses it had brought to bloom earlier.

Storm skirted the patches of prickly plants and agave carefully. It wasn't for naught that one of the spiny flora was called horse crippler.

Soon she was making her way up the winding path that led to Rosa Pequeño. For a moment she hesitated, panting from the exertion of her canter in the heat. She licked her lips nervously, then wiped the sweat from her brow. After a time she set her jaw determinedly and dug her heels sharply into her golden gelding's sides. She had come this far; she would not turn back now.

King's Ransom whickered welcomingly as the girl approached the cabin. Inside, Joe Jack's ears pricked up expectantly at his stallion's neigh. Casually he lifted the curtain at one window, thanking God that Gabriel had arrogantly insisted on expensive glass panes in all his buildings, instead of the cheaper and more practical rawhide. At least Joe Jack could see out.

She had come! She was here as promised. He felt his loins quicken throbbingly at the sight of her. It was difficult for him to believe that in moments Storm would be his. God! How he'd wanted her, wooed her, waited for her. Never had a woman led him such a chase! And for the first time in his life Joe Jack knew he was in love. He could understand now why his father had been so obsessed with her, would have done anything to possess her, had done it – just as he, Joe Jack, had.

His face darkened momentarily. His eyes clouded. He hated to see Storm grieving so over her son. Joe Jack wanted to make her happy, make love to her, and give her another child – his. His countenance lightened. Yes, he would give her another child to replace the one she had lost. She would be all right then. Everything would be all right. He envisioned her belly soft and full with his baby in it and smiled. It was all he could do to keep from ravishing the girl the minute she walked in the door.

He strode swiftly to her side, taking her in his arms.

'You came!'

'Did you think I would not?' Storm asked archly to hide her nervousness.

'I didn't know. Oh, God, Storm! You don't know how badly I've wanted you, how long I've waited for you – for this—'

He bent his head and kissed her fervently, his tongue parting the lips he'd taken by surprise, his hands ripping off her riding hat and tearing the pins from her hair.

At first Storm struggled against him, but gradually, as Joe Jack's mouth continued to cover hers insistently, his tongue exploring the innner sweetness of her lips expertly, she relaxed in his embrace, feeling a sudden, hot pulse of desire race through her body. She moaned gently, and at last he released her, panting hard, his eyes dark with passion and triumph.

He'd learned a long time ago that a woman was always a trifle anxious with a new man and that it was best to give her no time to think, to simply sweep her off her feet. Storm's breath was coming in small quick gasps now, and her earlier unease was gone. He smiled and poured the girl a drink, which she downed hurriedly before holding out her glass for another. Joe Jack refilled it, then slowly began to unbutton his shirt.

Storm watched him, mesmerized, remembering the way the lean muscles had rippled in his naked back and arms that day he'd been branding the cattle. He shrugged off the garment, draped it over a chair, then ran his fingers through his blond hair, flinging his head back as several strands fell down over one eye. After that he unbuckled his gunbelt, hanging it casually over one of the short footposts of the bed. He hesitated over his boots and breeches, finally deciding it was too soon. He inhaled sharply and placed his arms around Storm once more.

Without a word his lips closed down hard over hers again.

'Oh, honey,' he sighed, lifting his head at last to study her face. He smoothed the tangled tresses of her ebony cascade away from her temples, stroking the silky, snarled mass as though it were precious to him. 'You're beautiful – simply beautiful,' he said.

His hands slid down to her shoulders and then her breasts where his palms rubbed her nipples gently until they stiffened, showing plainly against the thin summer fabric of her riding habit. Deftly his fingers moved to her throat, starting to unfasten the buttons on her jacket. They were tiny and difficult to undo, but he managed them with a practiced ease, obviously highly skilled as to the intricacies of a woman's clothes. When he had them undone, he slipped the jacket from her body and tossed it aside. Then he groaned and without warning swept Storm up into his arms, carrying her to the bed. He laid her down tenderly, his eyes never leaving her suddenly vulnerable countenance as he towered over her.

'Oh, honey,' he breathed, 'I wanted to do this right, but I just can't wait to undress you, to feel your naked body up against mine.'

With that he caught the high, delicately laced collar of her blouse and yanked, rending the cotton material into shreds,

512

exposing the ripe curve of her breasts above her camisole.

'Thank God, you're not wearing a frigging corset,' he muttered before jerking feverishly at the ribands that kept the soft mounds of flesh from view.

Then hungrily he pressed his mouth to one firm rosy crest.

Cathy bit her lip indecisively as she stared anxiously out the window of her bedroom, watching first Joe Jack and then Storm ride off into the distance. They were going to Rosa Pequeño! They had to be; there was nowhere else for them to go. And there they would betray her father; Cathy was sure of it. Never before had they galloped off separately in the same direction a little while apart. They could only be trying to avoid suspicion, to throw off Gabriel's men, which meant they had reached a decision about becoming lovers. Always before they had ridden openly together, for they'd had nothing to hide – but today—

Cathy shivered suddenly. She had to stop them! She had to stop them now! Now – before it was too late! She just couldn't let Storm become her brother's lover, no matter how much she disliked her father's wife. It wasn't right. It just wasn't right! Storm was Joe Jack's stepmother, for God's sake! And besides—

Her brown eyes closed tightly as Cathy recalled her ominous foreboding that day of the dust devil so long ago and the horrifying conclusion to which she'd come just recently, not wanting to believe it at first. Her heart fluttered frighteningly with trepidation.

Oh, God! Oh, God! To what had pa and Joe Jack brought them? They would all be destroyed if what Cathy suspected were true. And Storm – if Storm found out she would hate herself afterward if she went through with what she'd planned today. Cathy just *couldn't* let that happen. It wasn't right. It just wasn't right!

Her mind made up, she raced downstairs to the stables, cruelly spurring Sunny Boy to a reckless gallop toward Rosa

Pequeño, praying she was not too late.

Storm screamed and tried frantically to cover her naked breasts as Cathy burst into the cabin, panting heavily from her long hard ride.

'Storm!' Cathy yelled. 'You can't do it! You just can't, do you hear me?'

'What the devil—' Joe Jack snapped his head up in disbelief as he rolled off his stepmother's body and onto his feet. 'Just what in the frigging hell do you think you're doing, sis?' he shouted angrily.

'Storm, listen to me,' Cathy went on intensely, ignoring her brother. 'You can't go through with this—'

'Get your Goddamned ass out of here, Cath!' Joe Jack ordered warningly, beginning to move toward her menacingly. 'This is none of your frigging business—'

Cathy shied away from him nervously, but she didn't stop the torrent of words pouring from her lips. 'Storm, you can't do it! He killed your son!' she blurted before her brother could shut her up. 'Joe Jack murdered your son—'

'You shut your goddamned mouth, Cathy— Don't listen to her, Storm,' Joe Jack turned frantically to his stepmother. 'She's obviously gone off her frigging rocker—'

'No, I haven't! Oh, for God's sake, listen to me, Storm, please! I heard them talking, pa and Joe Jack. Pa hated Chance. He wanted to get rid of him, but he couldn't do it himself because the boy didn't trust him, so he – he promised Joe Jack all Tierra Rosa if Joe Jack would kill the child instead—'

'Goddamn you, Cathy! You shut your frigging mouth!' Joe Jack roared, grabbing his sister cruelly and giving her several vicious slaps. 'You're a raving lunatic; that's what! Pa's going to have to put you away for sure—'

'No! It's true! It's true!' Cathy cried, continuing to babble on raspingly, despite the savage blows and the tears now streaming down her cheeks.

514

'I saw you that night the Comanches attacked Tierra Rosa! I saw you go up to Chance's room after the fire started! You – you had an oil lamp in your hand— Oh, God, Joe Jack! You're my brother! Do you think I wanted to believe it?' Her head jerked back and forth painfully as Joe Jack shook her brutally, then hit her again and again, cursing her at the top of his lungs; but still she didn't stop talking. 'When you came out, the oil lamp was gone. I thought you'd left it for Chance, because he – he was afraid— And then I saw you – saw you fumbling with the latch on his doorknob, but I – I never dreamed you were locking him in— Oh, God! Oh, God, Storm, forgive me! Forgive me! I didn't want to tell you! I didn't want to believe it was true—'

'For Christ's sake, don't listen to her, Storm! She's crazy! Crazy, I tell you!'

Storm was shaking all over as her trembling hands clutched the torn edges of her blouse and camisole together raggedly. Terrible sobs choked her throat, strangling her. Tears stung her eyes as she stared at Joe Jack in horror.

'Is it true? Is it?' Her voice rose piercingly.

'Oh, God, Storm! I love you! *I love you!*' he repeated, as though she would forgive him anything because of that. 'You'll have other children! I'll see that you do—'

'*Is – it – true?*' she screamed hysterically.

'Yes! Yes! For Christ's sake, yes! But I did it for us, so that the old man would leave us Tierra Rosa— Aw, shit, Storm. The kid was only a half-breed Indian's bastard—'

. . . *only a half-breed Indian's bastard—*

The words hammered relentlessly into Storm's heart and mind as she thought of Chance's pitiful little figure sprawled lifelessly on the hard, frozen ground, his small sweet face pinched at the nostrils, his dark blue eyes forever closed. *Maman!* Chance, her son, and Wolf, the only man she'd ever truly loved in her life. Wolf, who had given her their child and then taken the boy away that bitter rose dawn, never to return . . . *Maman! Maman!*

She went crazy then, running at Joe Jack like a madwoman, her hands clawing at him horribly, leaving bloody scratches down one cheek and his bare chest before he dealt her several ringing smacks, and she fell, sprawling painfully upon the hard wooden floor, blood spurting from her lip.

Dazed, she attempted to rise, managing to get up on her hands and knees. It was then she saw Joe Jack's gunbelt hanging on the bedpost. Blindly she staggered to her feet and yanked the pistol from its holster. It was the last thing she ever remembered clearly, for everything seemed to blur after that, to move in slow motion as she raised the revolver and fired again and again until the dull click of the hammer told her the chambers were empty.

She was only dimly aware of Cathy screaming as the shots ripped through Joe Jack's body, slamming him up against the far wall of the cabin. He jerked spasmodically several times, his arms flung wide and flailing spastically before he clutched his belly, trying to staunch the blood that was spewing from his insides. The frothing liquid was warm and red and sticky in the summer heat where it sprayed upon Storm's face and hands until at last Joe Jack toppled in a crumpled heap.

Cathy stared at her brother's body and then at her stepmother, horrified, choking and gasping for air as her violent, stunned, and disbelieving emotions overwhelmed her. Then she turned and ran from the cabin, crying and screaming once more with shock and incredulity.

After a time Storm sank down on the bed, letting the gun slide through her fingers to the floor.

She was still sitting there, motionless, when Gabriel and his men found her.

35

They took Storm into Santa Rosa, and there they locked her in the tiny, one-room adobe hut that served as the local jail. It was dark inside, and it took a few moments for the girl's eyes to adjust to the lack of light after the glare of the blinding summer sun. Then numbly she gazed without interest at her surroundings. The cell was stifling in the August heat, for there was only one small high window, which was barred, barely permitting the sun's rays to enter, much less any breeze. The four white-washed walls were gray with grime, and the dirt floor was filthy, covered with traces of old vomit and excrement and crawling with vermin. Two narrow wooden bunks took up one side of the room, their hard rough planks unadorned by even the most meager of pallets. Mutely Storm sat down upon the lower one. Her hands touched the splintered wood numbly.

This would be her bed until they hung her. *Hung her*. Yes, she would surely hang. She had murdered Joe Jack, shot him down in cold blood for killing her son; and Gabriel had insisted on bringing her into Santa Rosa where the only law was his. The town was too small for even a sheriff. There was only old Luis, who had turned the key to the cell nervously under the hated rancher's triumphant smirk.

Storm shuddered slightly as she recalled the expression on her husband's face. He had not grieved for his son as she had grieved for hers. Instead Gabriel had only gloated over the circumstances of Joe Jack's death, the circumstances that would enable her husband to see Storm brought to her knees and destroyed.

The girl glanced once more at the locked door, the four gray walls imprisoning her, and the barred window. No, there would be no escape for her. Here she would stay until the circuit judge summoned by Gabriel came to preside over her trial, and the jury chosen by Gabriel convicted her of her crime. *Guilty. Guilty! GUILTY!* There would be no other verdict. The despised rancher would see to that, and Storm would be defenseless against his power and riches. It wouldn't matter that Joe Jack had murdered her son. She had no way of proving it, and even if she had, she'd taken the law into her own hands, instead of allowing the court system to punish Joe Jack for the deed. *Punish Joe Jack.* Storm almost laughed aloud dementedly at the idea. No court in Texas would have convicted the legitimate white son of a well-known and respected rancher of killing a half-breed Indian's bastard. No, if Storm hadn't shot him, Joe Jack would have gone free, despite his dastardly crime, and Chance's death would never have been avenged.

I'm not sorry! Storm thought wildly. I'm not sorry! I don't care if they hang me! I'm not sorry for what I did! Oh, Chance! Chance! I did it for you, son, for you – and for Wolf! Oh, God, Wolf! I wronged you so. You, whom I loved, still love, have always loved. Oh, God! Oh, God! What happened to us? What happened to our love, our life together? Oh, Wolf! Wolf! My love; my life! I'd give anything, anything at all to be Eyes-Like-Summer-Rain again for just a little while . . .

Storm heard the lynch mob coming for her long before it ever reached the awful adobe jail, but at first she did not understand what was happening. It had never occurred to her that Gabriel might not wait to see her tried by a jury, but would subtly incite his men to riot, to string her up before she had a chance to expose what he had ordered and Joe Jack had done. It was only when the crowd's loud, angry voices, their vile, vulgar taunts reached her ears, and she ran to the barred window, hoisting herself up on tiptoe to see out into the night, that she realized what was going on outside.

Her heart beat frantically in her breast at the sight of the torches – and the men who carried them.

'We all seen how she were a'carryin' on with the Boss's son, a'flirtin' with him, a'leadin' him on, didn't we, boys?' Hank Hilton called.

'Yeah, we shore 'nuff did!' the men hollered in agreement.

'A'promisin' herself to him with them bedroom eyes of hers. The Boss weren't enuff fer her, was he?' Lester Jones ranted. 'Nawsir, she didn't care a rap about him and never did! It were Joe Jack she wanted, and when he rightfully spurned her, 'cause she were his daddy's wife, she killed him, the blueblooded bitch!'

'Blueblooded, my ass!' Farley Smith shouted. '*Cold*blooded is more like it! I never did figger how the Boss come to be so taken in. She fooled him good; that's what! Jest like she done the rest of us! Shit! She ain't nothin' but a whore! A Gawddamned *Injun's* whore! We all seen the way that friggin' half-breed come to git his little bastard that night!'

Storm's stomach heaved. Oh, what did they know about Chance and how he'd died? Or of Wolf and how he'd loved her – as Gabriel never had?

'A cold-blooded murderess! That's what she be!' Dirk Benteen took up the hue and cry. 'Shot Joe Jack down with his own damned gun, she did!'

'Yeah! Miss Cathy seen the whole friggin' thin', and we all know it shook her up so bad she ain't been able to say a word since!' Young Timothy Williams, who was sweet on Cathy, joined in.

'I say, why wait fer a trial? We all know the heartless whore is guilty! Guilty as sin!' Hank Hilton urged the mob on. 'We don't need no damned jury to tell us that. Let's git her! Let's git her now!'

'Yeah! Yeah!' the men chanted.

'Farley,' Lester Jones hallooed. 'Go wake that sorry old greaser-pig Luís up. Tell him to haul his fat ass out here with the key to the jail, *pronto*! Dirk, you and Timothy go git us some rope so's we can string that whore up proper—'

'*Mon Dieu*,' Storm whispered, her face blanching whitely as the senseless, madding crowd began marching toward the jail. '*Mon Dieu!*'

Her eyes searched the cell frantically for some means of escape, but there was none. After a time she stared down at her torn riding habit, feeling oddly detached. She was going to die. In moments she was going to die, and all she could think about was that she didn't want to go wearing the garments Joe Jack had ripped open to expose her breasts to his hungry gaze. She felt sick as she remembered the thrill of desire that had raced through her body when he'd pressed his mouth to her hardened nipples. Dear God! How could she have let him touch her, the murderer of her son? To think she had almost given herself to him, *would* have given herself to him if Cathy hadn't arrived in time to stop her!

Then all of a sudden it didn't matter anymore. Nothing mattered as the lynch mob flung open the door of the jail and leered at her triumphantly.

'Brother-Of-The-Wolf is a good man,' young Kwanah said thoughtfully to his brother, Pecos. 'For despite his grief, he has taken time to mend my bow and fix the feathers on the shaft of this arrow.'

'That is because you are one of his favourite *tuibitsis*,' Pecos observed correctly. 'And because you – we' – he corrected himself – 'are like him. We are all half-breeds.'

'Brother-Of-The-Wolf is not a half-breed.' Kwanah gave his brother a look of disgust. 'He is like the Black-Robes. He told me so. He was taken prisoner by The People, just as our mother was. He had only seen twelve winters at the time. That is why he seems more Comanche than white.'

'Yes.' Pecos nodded. '*Pia* is like that too. She had seen only nine winters when she was captured. Her name was Cynthia Ann Parker then, and she was the niece of a great white chief. That is why our father and chief of our family, Peta Nawkoni, chose her for his bride.'

'Yes, yes. I know all that.' Kwanah frowned impatiently. 'You are missing the point.'

'Which is?'

'*Pia* is happy. *Ap'* has made her so. Brother-Of-The-Wolf is not. The one called Flame-Hair has stolen his *paraibo*, Eyes-Like-Summer-Rain, and killed his *tua*, the little *tuinerp*'.

'Yes. It is a great sorrow to us all.'

'Pecos.' Kwanah's eyes glittered with daring and excitement. 'We must try to help Brother-Of-The-Wolf, to thank him for his kindness to us. Go, and fetch your god-dog. We will ride to the great white lodge of the one called Flame-Hair. Perhaps if we tell Eyes-Like-Summer-Rain how deeply Brother-Of-The-Wolf grieves for her and their dead *tua*, she will return to him, and he will be happy once again.'

'No! *Ap'* will be angry if he discovers we have left camp for such a purpose. He has said the one called Flame-Hair is an evil spirit, like the one who tried to kill the wolf in the fire-land of Brother-Of-The-Wolf's vision. *Ap'* has said of all the *taboboh* who have come to The Land the one called Flame-Hair is the worst and must be destroyed. For us to venture to the great white lodge of such a one would be bad medicine indeed. We must not go.'

'Yes, we must! We will say we are going hunting, and then none will suspect our true destination. Oh, very well then. If you are afraid, I will go alone.'

'No, Kwanah!' Pecos hesitated indecisively for a moment and then, 'All right. I will come with you, but we must be careful. The one called Flame-Hair will kill us if we are caught by his warriors.'

'They will not catch us,' Kwanah snorted derisively. 'We will move like snakes through the grass, with only a ripple to speak of our passing.'

The two young Indians mounted their ponies, galloping toward the Edwards Plateau where Tierra Rosa sprawled, vast and awesome, over nearly a hundred and fifty thousand acres of West Texas. The brilliant summer sun overhead shone down upon the boys brightly, hotly; and the wind, rustling through their long, untamed manes of coal black hair as they raced across the arid, desertlike plains, was warm upon their copper-skinned faces. They laughed together gaily as they rode, Pecos's earlier fears subsiding as he caught the sense of anticipation and bravado sparkling in his brother's dark brown eyes; and their legs, tanned deeply, hugged the bare backs of their animals tightly. Like all Comanches they were graceful on horseback, their hands sure upon the looped strands of rope that served as their bridles, their knees guiding their mounts expertly over the rough terrain.

Time flew swiftly, as did their ponies' hooves, and soon they had reached the boundaries of Tierra Rosa. They did not understand how they knew this was so. They simply saw and felt instinctively the mark of the *taceboh* upon The Land. Their sharp, trained eyes noted the deep tracks of shod horses and herds of cattle. Their sensitive nostrils discerned the odor of manure that belonged not to buffalo, but to Gabriel North's stock. Their acute ears heard the faint lowing of a cow to her calf in the distance and then the rapidly pounding staccato of a horse's hooves over the hard, baked ground.

Quickly and silently the young Indians dismounted, secreting themselves and their ponies behind a cluster of rocks in the hills. Hidden from view, they crept forward to get a better look at the sweep of land below and the rider clattering toward them recklessly from the east.

'It is only a woman,' Pecos stated at last, slightly relieved, 'and it cannot be Eyes-Like-Summer-Rain, for her hair is black, like a moonless night. This woman is golden, like the tall grass of the prairies when the sun has burned it dry.'

'We will follow her anyway,' Kwanah decided firmly. 'It may be that she is the *beht* of the one called Flame-Hair and will lead us to Eyes-Like-Summer-Rain.'

The two boys remounted their ponies, stealthily setting out hastily after the woman they'd seen.

'Look, Kwanah!' Pecos pointed after giving chase some

miles. 'She goes to that wooden tipi there.'

'Yes, you are right, my brother. And look; there are two more god-dogs out front. We will wait here. Perhaps we may learn something.'

They watched as Cathy – for it *was* Gabriel's daughter, as the young Indians had surmised – entered Rosa Pequeño. She seemed highly agitated, and minutes later they heard her begin to scream. They nudged their ponies closer, hoping to get a glimpse inside the cabin, but could see nothing through the curtained windows.

'Let us go now, brother. A white woman screaming always means trouble, and I see no sign of Eyes-Like-Summer-Rain,' Pecos intoned a trifle anxiously.

Kwanah had just opened his mouth to reply when they heard the shots.

'Great-Spirit! What has happened?' he breathed.

'Brother,' Pecos repeated more urgently. 'Let us be gone from this place. Now! Before the warriors of the one called Flame-Hair are upon us—'

'Look!' Kwanah gasped, ignoring his brother. 'The woman has come out, and I can see Eyes-Like-Summer-Rain through the flap of the tipi. I will go to her—'

'No, brother! The sounds of the fire-stick echoed loudly through the hills. They will have been heard by the warriors of the one called Flame-Hair. Listen! Press your ear against the ground as our *ara* has taught you! Do you not hear and feel the nearing thunder of their god-dogs' hooves even now? We must go—'

'No! We will wait and see what it means.'

The boys sat stilly upon their ponies. Presently they saw Gabriel and his men appear.

'It is the one called Flame-Hair and his warriors.' Kwanah's eyes narrowed intently against the summer sun. 'They are taking Eyes-Like-Summer-Rain away. We must stop them.'

'No, Kwanah. We are too few, and they are too many, and

we have no fire-sticks. Look; they are carrying out a man now. He must be sick—'

'No, his spirit has left his shell. Do you not see all the blood, Pecos? Eyes-Like-Summer-Rain must have killed him with the fire-stick. Yes, that is why the other woman – the golden one – was screaming and why the one called Flame-Hair is taking Eyes-Like-Summer-Rain away.' Kwanah's eyes were proud and fierce and filled with hate as he gazed down at the men below. He swore under his breath, a horrible curse. 'He has no right to touch her. She is the *paraibo* of Brother-Of-The-Wolf, a Comanche warrior. Someday, Pecos, I will be a mighty war chief, and I will lead The People into battle against the White-Eyes and drive them from all *Comanchería*. Yes, I will learn the ways of the *tabeboh* and their fire-sticks, and I will fight to keep The Land free. Come, my brother. We must return to camp at once and tell Brother-Of-The-Wolf what has happened.'

The young Indians turned their ponies homeward, galloping swiftly and surely over the endless plains.

'Brother-Of-The-Wolf! Brother-Of-The-Wolf!' they called loudly upon attaining camp. 'Come! Come!'

Wolf, upon hearing the cries of the boys, strode quickly through the camp until he reached their lathered ponies.

'What is it, Kwanah? Pecos?' he asked.

Breathlessly, their faces flushed with exertion and excitement, they explained what they had seen as Wolf listened intently, his dark visage grim.

Storm had killed someone, they said, and Gabriel North had come with his men and taken her away. Wolf's heart lurched sickeningly in his breast at the news. Sweet Jesus! *Murder!* Who had she gunned down – and why? Oh, Christ! Why had he ever taught her how to shoot?

'They will have taken her into Santa Rosa,' he voiced the thought aloud, a muscle in his jaw working, his pulse racing.

'You must go to her, my brother,' Moon-Raider spoke gravely, placing one hand on Wolf's shoulder. 'If you love her still, you must go to her.'

'Yes, I must go.'

'They will kill you,' Crazy-Soldier-Boy said.

Wolf shrugged. 'That's a chance I'll just have to take.'

'It is one we will take with you, my brother,' Moon-Raider stated calmly.

After a moment Wolf nodded his thanks wordlessly. Then, his countenance set in hard, determined lines, he walked rapidly to his tipi and changed his clothes, donning the black silk accoutrements he wore always when not with the *Kweharehnuh*. Almost mechanically he checked his revolvers and his rifle and carbine. Then he mounted Pahuraix and headed south – to Santa Rosa.

Storm struggled valiantly against the lynch mob, but she was no match for their steely strength and crazed intentions. They dragged her sobbing figure from the bunk where she was cowered, yanking her from the jail and shoving her forward roughly. They laughed when she tripped and fell, sprawling in the dirt. She lay there in the road stunned for a moment, inhaling the grit, sputtering as it ground its way inside her mouth, gagging her. Oh, God! How could she, once the belle of five counties, have come to such an end? Then the men bent down, snatching her up from the earth, jeering at her, tearing at her garments, pawing her breasts beneath the shreds of her blouse and camisole as they passed her from man to man.

'You ain't so high 'n' mighty now, are you, bitch?'

'Filthy Injun's whore!'

'Why don'tcha give us a taste of whatcha wanted to give Joe Jack before you killed him?'

'Yeah. Jesus! Look at them titties! I'd like to git my hands on them!'

'Pass her over here, boys. My pecker's so hard it's about to bust the buttons off my britches.'

'Yeah? Well, you'll jest hafta wait yore turn, 'cause I mean to be first, see?'

Oh, God! It was horrible. Horrible! Storm wanted to die as

they pressed their tobacco-stained lips to hers, thrusting their foul-tasting tongues in her mouth, squeezing her exposed breasts, and pinching her nipples, laughing raucously all the while. *Sacré bleu*! Even old Pop Daniels was among the men who tormented and humiliated her so unmercifully, while Gabriel North watched from the shadows, grinning at the girl's terror and distress.

'Pass her around! Pass her around! Shit! Don't let her git away, you fools!'

'Who you callin' a fool?'

'Hell. She ain't goin' nowhere, are you, bitch? That's right; come on over here, and gimme a kiss, whore. Joe Jack might not of wanted you, but I shore do.'

'Git her down, boys, and spread her legs.'

'Yeah! I wanna see that sweet—'

'Gawddamned slut! Kicked me in the balls!'

The man so injured slapped Storm viciously several times after he'd recovered, then forced her down upon the hard, sandy road while the others hooted and howled encouragement.

'Somebody come hold her arms and legs. Jesus! What a hellcat!'

'Git her skirt up! Git her skirt up!'

'Come on, bitch. Stop fightin'. You want sumpin' to remember us by before we string you up, don'tcha?'

It was then a shot rang out, startling them all into frozen silence. They looked up disbelievingly at Wolf staring down at them murderously from Pahuraix's broad back.

'It's the half-breed!' someone hissed in the stillness.

'Yeah.' Wolf's lips curled up derisively in a mocking half-smile. 'And I'm going to give you bastards about one minute to let that lady go.'

'Lady! Shit! She ain't no lady! She's a Gawddamned whore; that's what!'

'You all unbuckle your gunbelts, and throw down your weapons. Real easy now; no sudden moves,' Wolf went on, ignoring the remark, 'and back off nice and slow. That way maybe I won't have to kill any of you.'

Somebody laughed, but it was a nervous sound. The lynch mob's bravado had gone. Their eyes shifted to one another's faces uneasily. In the shadows Gabriel North reached for his pistol.

'I wouldn't if I were you,' Wolf drawled, never turning from the crowd. 'You wouldn't want to leave Storm a rich widow now, would you, *Mr* North?' he sneered.

Gabriel dropped his hand. 'You really don't think you can get away with this, do you?' the rancher snapped curtly, enraged and mentally cursing the nagging gunslinger who seemed destined to haunt him. 'We'll catch you both before you get a mile from town!'

'Yeah, I know. That's why I wasn't planning on going anywhere. Your minute's up. Now tell your men to throw down their guns and back off before I decide to take my chances with Storm and kill you. I've got a real itchy trigger finger tonight.'

There was another tense silence for a moment, but at last Gabriel told his men to do as Wolf had ordered.

'Storm,' Wolf said coolly after the mob had dispersed warily some distance away, leaving their weapons strewn upon the ground. 'Throw the key to the jail up here, then take one of those pistols, and get back inside your cell.'

'But – but, why?' she gasped, horrified.

'Because I don't aim to be shot in the back helping you to escape. Now do as I say.' Trembling with shock and despair, the girl did as he instructed. 'Now,' Wolf continued icily, raising his voice so that the men could hear him. 'I'm going to ride out of here, up into those hills where my Comanche friends are waiting and where we're going to keep a close watch on that jail. The first time any one of you makes a move toward it, we're going to blow you away. Where's the jailor?'

Quivering, Luís stepped forward from where he'd been crouched in fear after having been aroused from his bed and giving in to the crowd's threatening demand for the key to the jail.

'Here – here I am, *señor*,' he stammered.

'Do you know who I am?'

'Oh, *sí. Sí, señor*. You are the one they call El Lobo, the – the *bandolero*.'

'That's right.' Wolf tossed down the key to the adope hut. 'I want you to take that, and lock Storm back in her cell. Then I want you to hand her the key through the window. Do you understand?'

'*Sí. Sí, señor*.' Luís nodded vigorously.

'Good. When you bring her her meals, you get the key from her the same way, then give it back to her each time after you lock the door. Do you understand?' Wolf asked again.

'*Sí. Sí, señor*.'

'You'd better, because if anything happens to her, I'm holding you personally responsible. If I don't see you come three times a day with her meals, I'll kill you. If I see anyone else go near that jail, I'll kill you. If you try to leave town, I'll kill you. If I can't find you, I'll kill your family. Now gather up those guns, and take them into your house. These – *bastards*,' Wolf spat the word through clenched teeth once more, 'can pick them up there later. If anyone tries to stop you from obeying my orders, you'd better shoot them, because your life and the lives of your family depend on you doing exactly what I've told you. Do you understand?'

'*Sí. Sí, señor*.'

'Get on with it then.'

'May I – may I call my sons to help me, *señor*?'

'Yeah, but you'd better not try anything funny.'

'Oh, no, *señor*. Antonio. Carlos. Francisco. Jorge. Miguel. Ricardo. Vicente. Come; come, and help your *pobre padre*. *Ahora, por favor*.'

The Mexican's seven sons came running quickly from the door of their *jacale* where they'd been standing, watching, ever since the mob had come for their father. Luís sighed with relief upon seeing them, then hurriedly waddled over to the adobe hut, locked Storm in, and handed her the key through the window. She clutched it to her breast convulsively, realizing at last that Wolf's way was the best way after all. They couldn't have outridden Gabriel's men. At least now she would get a trial. Wolf would see to that.

Oh, why had she ever accused him of murdering their son? Sent Wolf away when she'd needed him so and – and, yes, loved him still, in spite of everything? How horrible and hateful she'd been, and still he had come to her aid tonight when she'd needed him again so desperately. He loved her! He must! He wouldn't have done what he'd done otherwise. He might have been killed! She ran to the window once more, pulling herself up to be certain he'd made his escape safely. Yes, yes, he was galloping off, and Gabriel's men were standing around stupidly, glaring with mean intent at Wolf's rapidly retreating figure, then glancing up at the hills with narrowed eyes, wondering if his Comanche friends were indeed there, watching them – and waiting, as he'd said.

After a time, seeing that Gabriel had already left and muttering under their breath to themselves, they retrieved their weapons from a very nervous Luís and went back to Tierra Rosa.

In the hush that followed Storm laid down on the hard wooden bunk and cried herself to sleep.

36

Luís, evidently more afraid of Wolf than Gabriel North, had apparently kept several of the ranch hands' weapons against their intimidating protests and had posted himself right outside the jail, from whose door he left only to relieve himself. He was guarded constantly by his seven sons, who'd positioned themselves in various lookout points around town just in case the hated rancher or his men got any ideas about killing the Mexican. His two daughters, Elisa and Natividad, brought Storm's meals three times a day, setting the food down in the middle of the road and casting their anxious dark eyes about cautiously as their father rose to collect the covered baskets. His wife, Dolores, had kindly given Storm a change of clothes after her ordeal with the lynch mob.

Inside the jail the girl paced endlessly, wondering if she shouldn't try to escape; but there was no way to open the cell door from the inside, even with the key. Besides, if she set one foot outside, she was certain Gabriel's men would gun her down without mercy, for every day a few of them came into town to be sure she wouldn't cheat the hangman's rope. Already they had begun building the gallows, bringing wagonloads of wood and supplies to Santa Rosa. Storm could hear them barking orders to each other, the thuds of their unburdening the wagons and stacking the lumber. Later came the sawing, then the relentless hammering. The sounds seemed to pound their death knell right into her brain. Even at night, when the men had stopped working, she could still hear the horrible grinds and whacks drumming in her ears.

She pitied herself and Santa Rosa, whose quiet, peaceful existence had been torn asunder by the deadly battle between Wolf and Gabriel North. Storm knew the citizens of the small town blamed her for the disruption and the fear with which they now all lived. She thought if someway, somehow, she managed to survive, it would be a very long time before she would ever be able to show her face in Santa Rosa again.

The girl sighed and wiped the sweat from her brow tiredly. It didn't seem possible that only two weeks had passed since Joe Jack's death. It felt as though a year had come and gone since then. After a time she rose from the bunk and began her restless pacing once more. There was nothing else to do. Mentally she counted off the steps. She didn't have very far to go. The jail was only six-by-six feet square.

Luís rapped on the bars of the window. She glanced up eagerly, for it meant it was time to eat, and meals were the only bright spots of Storm's day. Luís's wife and daughters went to a great deal of trouble to prepare tempting dishes for the girl.

'*Señora*, it is Luís, with your lunch.' Quickly she passed him the key, and in moments he was placing her basket inside. '*Arroz con pollo* today, *señora*. My wife killed a chicken. It was a scrawny bird,' he apologized, 'but better than nothing, no?'

'Yes, Luís. Please tell your wife "thank you" for me. She's very kind. I know I'll enjoy lunch very much.'

'*Señora*—' Luís hesitated.

'Yes?'

'There is – there is something else. A – a lady came— At least I think she was a lady. She talked very grand, even though she was smoking a cigar and wearing a man's shirt and – and breeches—'

'Cathy!' Storm breathed.

'I – I am sorry, *señora*. I do not know her name, but she asked if I would give you this.' He held out a folded note.

Rapidly Storm scanned its contents, then looked up. 'Luís, please don't tell anyone you gave me this or from whom you got it.'

'No, oh, no, *señora*. The lady – she pay me very well not to say anything. I – I must go now, *señora*. *Señor* North's men – they get very angry if I spend too much time with you—'

'I understand, Luís. Thank you.'

As soon as he'd closed the door and handed her the key back through the window, Storm sat down and re-read the contents of Cathy's letter.

August 15, 1856

Dear Storm,

I know why you killed Joe Jack, and my conscience has been troubling me sorely ever since it happened. I feel in many ways responsible for what occurred by blurting out what he'd done to you the way I did, but I did not want to see you make a mistake you would regret for the rest of your life. I'm sorry.

Pa intends to see you hang; I know he does. That's why he insisted you be taken into Santa Rosa where the whole town fears him, rather than San Antonio where you might have gotten a fair trial. The circuit judge who is to try your case is an old acquaintance of pa's as well.

I know it's not much help, but I have taken the liberty of engaging a lawyer for you. His name is Elijah Randolph, and he used to be a very highly respected state legislator until he retired into practice. He should be arriving to see you within a few weeks. I hope you will let him aid you in any way he can. Please rest assured that I have taken care of his fee.

I know we have not been friends in the past, but please do not hesitate to let me know if there is anything more I can do.

Cathy

Tears stung Storm's eyes as she folded the note. Oh, if only things had been different, she and Cathy might have been friends. They were not, however, and Storm realized what it must have taken for Cathy to have arranged for a lawyer and smuggled the letter into the jail unbeknownst to her father. Certainly if Gabriel North discovered his daughter's perfidy, Cathy would suffer for it.

For the first time a tiny flicker of hope stirred in Storm's breast. With a good attorney she might stand a chance – a slim one, but a chance.

*　　*　　*

Several days went by and then the following week Elijah Randolph came. He was a very dapper gray-haired gentleman with a handlebar mustache that reminded Storm painfully of Brett Diamond when first she saw the lawyer standing impatiently in the middle of the road, Luís's rifle pointed straight at his heart.

'For heaven's sake, man,' Mr Randolph said, exasperated. 'I'm here to help Mrs North. How do you expect me to do that if I cannot even go inside to talk privately with her?'

'I am very sorry, *señor*, but I have my orders,' Luís answered firmly, refusing to move aside.

'Surely you can at least allow me to approach the window of the jail!' the attorney insisted.

'No, *señor*, I am very sorry, but I cannot. El Lobo, the notorious *bandolero* – he would see and shoot us both dead.'

'Luís. Luís.' Storm called from the window upon hearing the commotion. 'Is – is that *Monsieur* Randolph?'

'*Sí, señora.*'

'Oh, dear, and there's no way for him to come inside, is there?'

'Really, Mrs North!' Mr Randolph fumed to her barely visible face above the window sill. 'I have traveled several hundred miles to be of assistance to you only to be told I cannot even approach your window, lest I be gunned down by some ruffian. Just who is this gunslinger anyway? Miss – uh – no one told me anything about him!'

'He's – he's my – my— Oh, dear, this is all really very difficult to explain. I must find some way to get you inside. Luís, come get the key, and open the door.'

'But – but, *señora*—'

'Please, Luís.'

Hastily Storm tore a shred from the ruined blouse she'd tossed in one corner after Luís's wife had brought her the change of clothes. Once Luís had the door unlocked, she moved to stand very carefully just at its entrance, not daring to step even one foot outside as Gabriel's men suddenly ceased their tormentingly drawn-out work on the gallows and glanced up speculatively. Storm held the piece of white fabric as high as she could, waving it back and forth so that it fluttered eye-catchingly in the faint breeze that stirred in the stifling heat.

'Walk toward me very slowly, *Monsieur* Randolph,' the girl ordered uneasily, watching the far hills and wondering if Wolf could see her signal and understand its meaning. 'And please, please do not make any sudden moves.'

Finding it very difficult to swallow all of a sudden, the lawyer gazed up toward the knolls in the distance, feeling a slight amount of trepidation as he did as Storm had instructed him. When he finally reached the jail without mishap, an angry growl arose from Gabriel's men, who'd searched the swelling crests for Wolf and the Comanches the past weeks without result. With mean intent upon their faces they threw down their saws and hammers, starting determinedly toward the adobe hut. Immediately several warning shots slammed into the road, ricocheting in every direction. Two of Gabriel's men were hit, not seriously, but they fell where they'd stood, fearing to be killed otherwise. Storm breathed a huge sigh of relief at finding Wolf had not deserted her after all.

Quickly she stepped aside so that Mr Randolph might enter the cell, then told Luís to lock the door and bring her the key. The attorney stared with amazement and disbelief.

'Mrs North, may I ask why you are in control of the key to this – this pathetic little jail?' he questioned, wrinkling his nose with disgust and distaste at the stench in the adobe hut.

Storm flushed with embarrassment as she gave a covert glance at the old wooden bucket she'd had Luís bring her to serve as a slop jar, there being nothing else available. The Mexican emptied the pail every day, but unfortunately, although Luís had shoveled out the worst of the filthy dirt floor, the strong odor of the cell's previous inhabitants had persisted.

'I – I must apologize for the smell in here, *Monsieur* Randolph. I'm sure it's – it's not to what you are accustomed. I'm afraid I'm not used to it either, but—' She shrugged, dismissing the matter. '*C'est la vie*. Won't you sit down.' She indicated the lower bunk. 'Now, as to your question, I am in possession of the key to this jail for my own safety.'

'Mrs North, I'm afraid I don't understand any of this: how you came to murder your stepson – if indeed you did so, why a lady of your stature had been incarcerated in such a – a hovel, why your husband's men are apparently attempting to kill you before you can be brought to a just trial—'

'Please, *Monsieur* Randolph, allow me to explain. What I have to tell you is a very sad, shocking, and – and in many ways scandalous story.'

Then Storm started at the very beginning and told the lawyer everything. It was nearly four hours later when she had finished. Mr Randolph sighed, removed his spectacles, and rubbed his face with his hands. Then he cleaned the small silver-wire-trimmed glasses carefully with his handkerchief and put them back on after mopping his brow.

'Mrs North, I do not know that I can help you. You have no proof that Joe Jack North murdered your son, and though I am inclined to agree that he did indeed do so – and under orders from his father – unless Cathleen North agrees to testify to that fact, your defense will, for lack of evidence, be an extremely poor one. The judge and jury will have only your word against that of Gabriel North, a very rich and powerful man in these parts. Furthermore, the case is, in addition, complicated by numerous contributing factors.

'Firstly, you married Gabriel North not for love, but money, and apparently it was plain to his ranch hands that the two of you did not get along. Secondly, it was also obvious to said ranch hands that you intended to have or indeed had already instigated an affair between yourself and your stepson. Thirdly, your child was the illegitimate offspring of a gunslinger and sometime bounty hunter, who may

– or may not be, according to you – a half-breed Comanche. Whether Mr Lobo is or is not of mixed blood is irrelevant. The point is that unfortunately everyone *believes* him to be so, and thus it follows that your son was as well.

'Although I am sorry to say this, Mrs North, racial prejudice, especially against the Indians, as I'm sure you are aware, is rampant in the state of Texas. Even if Miss North can be persuaded – against her loyalty to her family name and her brother's memory – to corroborate your story that Joe Jack North, in collusion with his father, murdered your child, you may still discover little public sympathy for either yourself or the manner of your son's death. You must understand, Mrs North, that the circumstances of your original agreement to marry Gabriel North and the – in many people's eyes – scandalous intervening factors of your past that prevented the wedding from taking place until last summer, seven years later, will all be brought out during the trial. You may, quite possibly, find yourself branded as a scarlet woman, which will provide titillation for the tongues of every gossip in the state of Texas and may well cause a public outcry for your execution in light of the respect many persons hold for the North family.

'In addition, although I understand very well why you did so, there is the fact that you *did*, instead of prosecuting both Gabriel and Joe Jack North through the proper legal channels, take the matter of the law into your own hands. That in itself may be – if you will pardon a gentleman for the expression – damning to your case, no matter which way public opinion sways. Many *tejanos* can remember a time when there was no law and order in Texas, and the majority of decent citizens do *not* want a return of those days.'

'I – I see. *Monsieur* Randolph, are you – are you saying that no matter what happens I most certainly will hang?'

'No. I am simply trying to point out the difficulties presented by your defense. Naturally I will do the best I can for you, and there is always the chance that something unexpected or that we have overlooked will turn up. You mustn't give up hope, Mrs North. Judge Valerian is also an old acquaintance of *mine*, and I know him to be a fair man. I can assure you it will be his *own* conscience that dictates to him in the matter and not Gabriel North's, despite the fact that Mr North may think otherwise.'

'*Monsieur* Randolph, you – you don't like my husband, do you?'

'To be frank, Mrs North, no, I don't. I know him to be a crook and a black sheep from my legislator days. Furthermore, a very old and dear friend of mine who used to be a judge before he died, told me Gabriel North acquired the property known as Tierra Rosa in a most despicable fashion and undoubtedly murdered its rightful owners, although nothing could ever be proved. Now if you will have the door to this contemptible jail unlocked, I will bid you good afternoon. Chin up, Mrs North. You are a young woman of great courage and spirit, for which I like and admire you. I will not let the hangman have you if there is any way in which such a tragedy can possibly be avoided.'

Six weeks later Judge Valerian arrived, and Storm's trial began. It took place in Santa Rosa's humble, one-room adobe church, for there was no other building whose accommodations were suitable for the proceedings. The pews were packed with people who had come from far and wide to catch a glimpse of Gabriel North's notorious wife, the woman who had murdered her stepson and been the whore of a half-breed Indian. A hush fell over the buzzing crowd as Mr Randolph escorted Storm inside, both of them heavily guarded by Luís and his sons. The girl took a deep breath and held her head up proudly as she walked slowly down the aisle amidst the speculative murmurs that soon started up again. Her veiled face looked neither right nor left as she passed, and her figure, clothed in a striking gray-and-black ensemble that she had designed herself and that Cathy had obtained for her at great expense, was as rigid as a ramrod. The throng was angry at not being allowed a peek at Storm's pale lovely countenance and disappointed by her tasteful costume, for they had fully expected to see a cheap, brazen hussy clothed like a whore. There was a slight, breathless ripple of anticipation, however, as the girl inclined her head briefly to Cathy, sitting next to Ross Stuart, the foreman of the Chaparral – of all people! Really! To what were the Norths coming? – and then another eagerly expectant silence as Storm stared unflinchingly at Gabriel and his lawyer for a moment before turning aside. However, when nothing untoward occurred, the assemblage gave another collective, crestfallen grumble and resumed its low-voiced muttering of displeasure.

As soon as Storm had been seated in the front left pew, and Mr Randolph had drawn up the table provided on which to lay out his notes, Luís announced Judge Valerian. Everyone rose respectfully and remained standing until the judge had taken his place on the high stool behind the pulpit. Then Judge Valerian banged his gavel loudly, calling for order, and the court was in session.

It took three days for Mr Randolph and Ulysses Oakley, Gabriel's attorney, to agree on a jury, but at last Mr Randolph was satisfied that he'd managed to get at least a few decent citizens to hear Storm's case; and the actual trial itself ensued.

After that the proceedings dragged on and on, and they were horrible. Every morning when Storm arose and donned her gray silk and black satin outfit, she wasn't certain she could bring herself to face another awful, grueling, humiliating day. The gathering's hunger for juicy tidbits about her and her past seemed insatiable as one after another of Gabriel's witnesses took the chair on the altar to give damaging testimony about her to the jury.

'Now, Sheriff Martin, you're sure it was the gang known as the Barlow brothers who held up the stage on which Mrs

538

North – then Miss Lesconflair – was traveling?' Mr Oakley asked.

'Oh, yessir. There weren't a doubt in my mind about it. We follered their tracks to their hideout, see? And Mr North found some newspaper clippin's, tellin' about 'em, there in one of the cupboards.'

'And these newspaper clippings, they described *only* the activities of the Barlow brothers, rather like a scrapbook, you might say?' Mr Oakley continued.

'Yessir.'

'What did Mr North do then?'

'Oh, he tried to pay everybody to stay on and keep huntin' for his little fiancée, 'cause he were right taken with her, but of course we figgered the Barlows had gone into Gorda Vaca, and there weren't a one of us who were gonna set foot in *that* hellhole!'

'That was when Mr North told you to post the $5,000 reward for his fiancée or any information leading to her whereabouts?'

'Yessir.'

'Thank you, Sheriff Martin. That will be all.'

'You got any questions, Elijah?' Judge Valerian queried.

'No, your honor.'

'Next witness.'

Oh, how Storm remembered the terrible stagecoach hold-up, Mammy's bloodstained body lying sprawled in the dirt, the buzzards circling slowly overhead in the hot sun, Billy Barlow's arm about her waist, Ma Barlow's fearful punch, Gorda Vaca, and Wolf looking up her with his midnight blue eyes from the poker table . . .

'. . . so the first time you saw Mrs North – then Miss Lesconflair – Sheriff Yancey, she was with this half-breed Indian gunslinger El Lobo?'

'Objection,' Mr Randolph said. 'The Prosecution has not established the fact that Mr Lobo is a half-breed Indian.'

'Objection sustained,' Judge Valerian ruled. 'Ulysses, I'm

afraid you're going to have to rephrase your question.'

Storm fanned herself gently, and for a moment it was the wild dawn wind blowing through her tangled mass of black curls as she and Wolf rode out of Gorda Vaca toward Goliad, with Elijah Barlow's body bouncing along on the pack horse behind them. Then they were leaving Sheriff Yancey's office, and Wolf was counting out her share of the reward money before tipping his hat politely.

'. . . so the second time you saw Mrs North, Sheriff Yancey, she claimed to be the gunslinger's wife?'

'Yessir. Of course I doubted if they'd had a priest, him bein' sech a heathen and all—'

'Objection!' Mr Randolph broke in. 'The validity of Mrs North's marriage to Mr Lobo is pure speculation on the part of the witness.'

'Objection sustained. The jury will disregard the witness's last statement,' Judge Valerian instructed.

'And that was when you notified Mr North of his fiancée's whereabouts?' Mr Oakley went on, unruffled, for the point had been made.

'Yessir.'

'Thank you, Sheriff Yancey.'

'You got any questions, Elijah?'

'No, your honor.'

'Next witness.'

'Call Arthur Quigley to the stand.'

Luís shuffled forward laconically. 'Raise your right hand, and place your left hand on the Bible,' he droned. 'Do you solemnly swear to tell the truth, the whole truth, and nothing but the truth, so help you, God?'

'I do.'

Mr Oakley spread his jacket, glanced at his watch, then placed the timepiece back in his vest pocket. It was nearly suppertime, and he was hungry.

'Please state your full name and occupation for the jury.'

'Arthur Nelson Quigley. I'm the proprietor of a general

540

store in Goliad.'

Storm closed her eyes. A half-smile curved her lips beneath her filmy black veil as she saw again, in her memory, Wolf's mouth twitching – just that once – at the breathless, babbling explanation she'd given the impertinent little shopkeeper of their supposedly runaway love match . . .

A week went by and then another, and still the trial dragged on, as though Gabriel were taking an immense pleasure in shaming Storm before all Texas, in seeing her brought to her knees before the final *coup de grâce*.

'What's the stall?'

'Yeah! We don't need to hear all this shit! We all know the whore's guilty, don't we, boys?'

'Yeah! Guilty as sin! Let's git on with it! Hang the friggin' bitch!'

'Shut yore mouth! There're ladies present!'

'Somebody git a rope!'

'Look! Miss Cathy's swooned! It's the heat! Stand back! Stand back! Give her air. I said, give her some air, Gawddamnit!'

'Where's the friggin' rope? Let's git that whore strung up!'

'Yeah! Hang her! Hang her!'

'Order!' Judge Valerian banged his gavel thunderously. 'Order! There will be no lynchings while *I* am in charge here! Now I will have order in this court, or I will clear the courtroom, is that understood? Miss North, are you all right?' Cathy nodded weakly. 'Very well then. Ulysses, call your next witness.'

There were gasps of mortification and secret delight as Mimi La Roche, with her dyed flaming red hair and heavily made-up green eyes, traipsed up the aisle in a shockingly low-cut, hot-pink gown to explain how Storm and Wolf had slept together at her whorehouse and there brutally knifed to death and savagely–' Oh, yes, quite *savagely*; the sheriff said so,' Mimi swore, despite Mr Randolph's heated objections to the hearsay evidence – scalped one Zeke Barlow.

Mr Randolph did his best to point out that Zeke Barlow had been a hardened criminal, an armed robber and murderer wanted dead or alive, but Mimi's statement, although stricken from the record, had been made nevertheless, adding fuel to the already raging fire against Storm. As the madame of the Corpus Christi bordello left the stand, preening herself smugly, Gabriel shot Storm a triumphant smirk, certain the girl was as good as hung.

'Next witness.'

'. . . now, Gabriel, you say you showed Mr Sinclair a daguerreotype of Mrs North, whom Mr Sinclair immediately recognized as the notorious woman known as French Lightning, hostess of The Bon Ton saloon and its proprietor Brett Diamond's mistress.'

'*Objection*!' Mr Randolph roared, springing to his feet. 'The Prosecution has not established the fact that Mrs North was Mr Diamond's mistress.'

'Objection sustained. Ulysses, I'm going to have to remind you again to stick to the facts in this case.'

'I apologize, your honor. Gabriel' – the lawyer turned back to his client – 'if you knew all this about your wife, why did you marry her?'

'I . . . I just couldn't believe it. I loved her, and I just couldn't believe it.'

'That's a damned lie!' Storm spat, rising hotly, her fists clenched tightly, the first sign of emotion she'd displayed during the entire proceedings.

The crowd roared with glee as Gabriel flushed redly, and Mr Randolph yanked Storm back down into her seat, hissing quietly in her ear.

'Order! Order in the court!' Judge Valerian banged his gavel for the umpteenth time. 'Mrs North' – he looked at the girl sternly – 'another outburst like that, and I'm afraid I'll have to cite you for contempt of court. Proceed, Ulysses.'

Gabriel completed his testimony the following day. Mr Randolph examined him extensively at length afterward, but without success. Finally, after a swift, angry glance from the rancher, Mr Oakley stood and protested.

'Objection. Your honor, counsel for the Defense is badgering the witness. Mr North has already responded to the question.'

'Objection sustained. Elijah, if you don't have anything new to ask, the court would appreciate it if you'd conclude your examination. It's nearly time for lunch, and some of us' – he stared over at Luís, who was shoveling a plate of *frijoles* into his mouth – 'are finding it hard to wait.'

There was a ripple of laughter at this. Mr Randolph stiffened.

'Very well, your honor.'

'Court is in recess until one o'clock.'

When they had reconvened at the appointed hour, Judge Valerian instructed Mr Oakley to call his final witness. The throng leaned forward expectantly on the edges of their pews, tense with excitement as Gabriel's lawyer rose.

'Your honor, gentlemen of the jury, the Prosecution would like to call to the stand its star witness, a woman who actually saw Mrs North gun down her stepson in cold blood—'

'*Objection*!' Mr Randolph bellowed, spoiling Mr Oakley's elaborate introduction. 'The Prosecution has yet to establish that Mrs North did any such thing.'

'Objection sustained. The jury will disregard the Prosecution's final remark. Get on with it, Ulysses. There isn't any point in prolonging the suspense when we all know who you're about to call anyway.'

'Yes, your honor. My apologies to the court. The Prosecution calls Cathleen North to the stand.'

Cathy swallowed hard and got to her feet nervously. Ross squeezed her hand reassuringly, and she gave him a timid half-smile before walking up the aisle to be sworn in. She stood awkwardly in her unaccustomed dress and kid shoes as Luís held the Bible out and recited the oath, which she affirmed so quietly the assemblage had to strain to hear her.

Then she sat down on the chair on the altar.

'Now, Cathy,' Mr Oakley began, 'there's no need for you to be afraid, so I want you to speak right up, and tell the court in your own words what happened the day of your brother's death.'

Cathy was torn, oh, so horribly torn and undecided over what to say, what to do. She bit her lip, racking her brain feverishly. She could see now, with the way the trial was going, that even if she told the truth, Storm was likely to be hung anyway; Gabriel had done such a thorough job of blackening his wife's name and reputation by dredging up her scandalous past and exposing it to the jury. Cathy buried her face in her hands. It wasn't right. It just wasn't right! Joe Jack had murdered Storm's son, had killed a defenseless, six-year-old child! Dear God! Dear God! It just wasn't right that Storm should hang for shooting Joe Jack. She'd done what she'd done out of a mother's love and because no court in Texas would have punished Joe Jack for the dastardly deed. Gabriel's power and riches would have seen to that! But what could Cathy say or do that would spare her stepmother the gallows? Oh, God! Oh, God! Cathy needed more time; she needed more time to think. She hadn't been able to think clearly since the day her brother had died . . .

'Cathy.' Mr Oakley's voice seemed to be coming at her from a very great distance. 'Cathy, tell the court what happened the day of your brother's death.'

And Cathy, not knowing what else to say or do, cried, 'I – I don't remember!'

Then she fell off the witness stand in a dead faint.

37

Mr Randolph put Storm on the witness stand the next day. He had no other choice, since her word alone was her only defense. A doctor had been called when Cathy had swooned and had diagnosed her condition as hysterical amnesia. It was not known when or if she would be able to testify, and only Storm suspected the girl was lying about her loss of memory. But why? Why had Cathy kept silent all this time about what had happened that dreadful day? And what could the girl possibly hope to accomplish by refusing to tell? One way or another Storm was going to hang; she had litle doubt about that now. Gabriel North was dealing the deck, and the cards were stacked against her. Even the truth would not save her; Gabriel had so utterly tarnished her character that none would believe her anyway.

Nevertheless Storm tried her best to cheat the gallows. Calmly, coolly, like the marble statue she'd been all through the proceedings, with the exception of her one emotional outburst, she slowly lifted her veil so that the gathering got their first glimpse of her strikingly beautiful pale countenance. Those who had not previously seen her gasped with admiration, then quieted with the first respect they'd shown her as she began her incredible tale.

She started with her childhood at Belle Rive, painting a picture of a slow, languid, gracious way of life that many of the persons present recalled from their own pasts. Her voice broke with sorrow as she told about her parents' deaths and how she had gone to live at Vaillance. It throbbed with the hurt and anger of betrayal as she explained how her uncle had lost her inheritance and gambled her away to Gabriel North, a stranger to her, and how André-Louis had cast her aside because of it. She wept unashamedly over Mammy's death, and there was not a woman in the courtroom who did not feel her terror at being carried off by the Barlow brothers and share her horror of Ma Barlow. She told how they'd ridden into the hellhole called Gorda Vaca and how there Billy had wagered her away to El Lobo, the gunslinger, and how the Barlows had tried to kill her. Her chin lifted defiantly as she explained her decision to take up with Wolf, rather than remain with the cutthroat rabble inside the saloon; and her soft gray eyes lighted with hope when she saw no one present condemned her for her choice.

'I was alone and helpless, except for Wolf,' she said steadily. 'He was all I had, all I ever had. He took me in, and he taught me how to survive out West. He made me laugh again, gave me the strength to go on living. Gabriel North had destroyed all I'd ever loved. I could not go to him then, for time had not yet healed the wounds he'd given me.'

The rancher shifted uncomfortably on his pew at that, aware that the crowd was now staring at him thoughtfully, speculatively. He whispered urgently in Mr Oakley's ear, but the attorney shook his head, refusing to object.

Storm went on clearly, explaining that she and Wolf had stayed in Mimi La Roche's bordello because no decent hotel would admit Indians within its doors. She told how Zeke Barlow had attempted to rape her and how courageously Wolf had defended her honor.

The days passed, and still the girl talked, and all those who'd come to Santa Rosa listened – and learned.

They learned about a life of which they'd known nothing – the life of a sensitive, solitary man who'd turned gunslinger and bounty hunter because of his tragic, mysterious past.

They could almost envision the battle between Wolf and Rickie Lee Halfhand when Storm described it, and they felt as though they'd pried into something very private and special when she spoke of her love and passion for Wolf and how they had become one beneath a silvery Comanche moon.

They watched her face fill with joy when she told how Wolf had bought her the red satin dress and how she'd danced at *Señora* Ramirez's *fiesta*. They gasped with mortification when she explained how the remaining two Barlows had continued to pursue her, had tried to finish what their brother Zeke had started, and the courtroom actually cheered upon hearing how Wolf had blown Luther to smithereens with the black powder.

Gabriel North grew more and more uneasy as the days slipped by, and the tide of public opinion began to turn against him, as the women thought about what they would have done had they been in Storm's place and badgered their husbands to take pity on the poor girl.

The gathering understood for the first time what it meant to be an Indian in a white man's world as they saw the *Kwerharehnuh* – Tabenanika and his two wives, Masitaw-tawp, Moon-Raider, and all the rest – through Storm's eyes. They lowered their heads in shame and guilt as the girl told how the *tabeboh* had brought death and disease to proud The People who loved The Land so dearly and fought so fiercely to keep it free.

Every mother in the room dabbed at her eyes when Storm shared the wonderful experience of Chance's birth with them: how the man they'd thought a half-breed savage had massaged her aching back, had held her steady when her child had started to come, how he'd bathed the newborn infant so tenderly, and how lovingly he had placed the babe to her breast.

Not a one of them grudged what Wolf had done to Billy Barlow, and Storm's agony was their own when she explained her painful decision to leave Fin Terra and journey to San Francisco. Dear Lord! Were eggs *really* a dollar apiece out there? No wonder the poor girl had gone to work in a saloon. What? No law and order? Bodies just pitched in the Bay? Horrible! Simply horrible! And just what had become of the debonair Brett Diamond who'd been so kind to the girl?

547

Shocking! Just shocking! Someone had actually attempted to murder Mrs North in broad daylight! And the runaway buggy – how terrifying! It was a wonder the poor girl hadn't died of fright!

Gabriel North relaxed slightly as the opinion of the assemblage shifted again in his favor at hearing how bravely he'd rescued Storm and her son and brought them home to Tierra Rosa. Here too the girl's recital faltered, because she simply could not bring herself to speak to the crowd about what the rancher had done to her on their wedding night.

'I – I found I could not love him after all.' Storm wrung her hands anxiously in her lap. 'And so we – we did not live as – man and wife—'

'I think the court understands your meaning, Mrs North,' Mr Randolph stated kindly, giving her an encouraging smile. 'Please go on.'

'I – I was very much alone,' she continued, 'and even though I later discovered Wolf was alive, not dead, as Gabriel had told me, there was – was nothing left between us,' she lied, knowing she could not tell the throng how Wolf had come to her those nights, forcing himself on her unwilling body and soul. 'It – it was wrong of me, I know, but I turned to Joe Jack for companionship, for it appeared he was my only friend at Tierra Rosa. But he was only that – never my lover as has been implied in this courtroom.'

When at last she came to the part about the Comanches attacking the house, setting it afire, and Chance's death, Storm broke down and wept bitterly, and once more the gathering sympathized with her heartache and sorrow. There wasn't a woman in the courtroom who didn't shed tears over the image of Chance's pitiful little figure sprawled pathetically on the hard, frozen ground, his tiny carved dragon clutched tightly in his fist.

'I – I was a trifle mad those days following my son's death. Spring came, with its unfolding buds and new life. It depressed me. I – I did strange things, and I – I know people

548

talked about me— Only Joe – Joe Jack seemed to understand, to care that I was suffering deeply inside. All summer long we talked and rode the range together—'

'And then?' Mr Randolph prodded gently.

'And then—' Storm took a deep breath, and the assemblage leaned forward eagerly again on the edges of their pews. 'And then one day, the first of August, he asked me to meet him at Rosa Pequeño. We'd been playing poker, and he'd promised if I won, he'd leave me alone. He'd – he'd kept telling me he loved me, had grown more and more insistent about it. I'd reminded him several times that he was my stepson, that Gabriel was my husband, but it – it hadn't done any good. He'd still persisted in his attentions— Anyway I lost. He'd cheated me, and I – I told him I would come to Rosa Pequeño . . .'

'Go on, Mrs North.'

'And – and so I went. Cathy must have guessed what was happening, where we were going, because she – she followed us. She flung open the door and yelled, "Storm! You can't do it! You can't do it!" or something like that. Then Joe – Joe Jack started shouting at her real angrily, telling her to get out, but she wouldn't go. They – they began to – to argue—'

Here Storm broke down once more, and it was then Wolf opened the door of the adobe church. All eyes turned toward him gapingly. A sudden hush fell over the breathless crowd, and in the tense silence someone whispered,

'It's the half-breed.'

The murmur rustled through the throng, rising like a high wind.

'It's the half-breed.'

Cathy froze as she stared at Storm's lover, for there was something about him that nagged at her, just as it had her father, something in the back of her mind, something she couldn't quite place—

'Please continue, Mrs North. Cathy and her brother argued. What then?'

'Then Joe Jack hit her, trying to – to shut her up, but she – she kept on talking, saying that – that—'

'That what, Mrs North?'

'That – Gabriel had hated my son, that he'd wanted to see Chance dead, and that he'd promised to leave Joe Jack all Tierra Rosa if he'd kill the boy—'

'That's a friggin' lie, you bitch!' Gabriel yelled, jumping to his feet. 'Can't you see what she's doing?' He turned to the suddenly uproarious throng. 'She's trying to gain your sympathy and support by blackening my good name and tarnishing my son's memory! You all know me, and you all knew Joe Jack! Do you think I would have taken the child into my home if I'd wanted to kill him? Do you think Joe Jack would have murdered a defenseless boy?'

'Like hell!'

'No way, Boss!'

'My wife shot Joe Jack down in cold blood, I tell you,' the rancher continued to shout, urging the suddenly riotous mob on, 'because he honorably spurned her advances—'

'Shit! What are we waitin' fer then? Trial's over. Let's hang the whore!'

'Somebody git a rope—'

'Order! Order! I will have order in this courtroom!'

Oh, God! Oh, God! If only Gabriel hadn't spoken! If only he hadn't spoken! Storm had held the gathering in the palm of her hand, and now – now they'd never believe Joe Jack had murdered Chance, that Gabriel had promised his son all Tierra Rosa for the deed. It would take a miracle to save Storm now—

And suddenly, somehow in the *mêlée*, the miracle came.

Cathy stood up and screamed, 'I remember! I remember! I remember what happened!'

The assemblage that had gone crazy at Gabriel's words was just as suddenly so still they could have heard a pin drop at the sound of Cathy's voice. Still Judge Valerian banged his gavel just once for effect anyway.

'Call Cathleen North to the witness stand,' he said grimly.

Trembling all over, Cathy took the chair, giving a confused and apprehensive Storm a strange, warning, reassuring look with her eyes.

'Now, Miss North,' Judge Valerian went on, apparently having deciding to dispense with the formality of the lawyers. 'Why don't you tell this court just exactly what it is you now remember.'

Cathy faced the crowd defiantly, her glittering dark eyes oddly bright and unnatural.

'Pa *did* promise my brother all Tierra Rosa for killing Chance,' she stated flatly, 'and Joe Jack *did* murder the boy.'

'That's a Goddamned lie, and you know it, Cathy!' Gabriel roared. 'You've gone off your friggin' rocker; that's what!'

'That's funny, pa. That's what Joe Jack said before he admitted the truth!'

The throng burst out wildly again.

Judge Valerian banged his gavel so violently Storm thought surely the pulpit would collapse.

'Order! Order! I will have order in this courtroom! One more outburst like that, and I'll see you *all* behind bars!'

Once more the adobe church fell silent as Cathy began to speak again.

'It all happened that day just as Storm told you. I followed her and – and Joe Jack up to Rosa Pequeño and told her what he'd done. My brother *did* start hitting me, trying to shut me up, but I went on anyway, blurting out the truth. Storm went crazy of course. What mother wouldn't have? She ran at Joe Jack, screaming and crying and clawing at him like a madwoman, but she – she never shot my brother—'

A shocked murmur, quieter this time because they wanted to hear what Cathy had to say, soughed through the gathering. Storm gazed disbelievingly at her stepdaughter, stunned. Gabriel's shoulders slumped. He buried his face in his hands, as though he knew what was coming and still couldn't accept it.

'Joe Jack slapped my stepmother viciously, enraged,' Cathy continued, 'and – and all of a sudden I could tell he – he meant to kill her too. She – she would have talked, you know, told people what he and pa had done. I couldn't let him do it! I saw his gunbelt hanging on the bedpost. I – I yanked the pistol from his holster, and, God forgive me,' she sobbed, 'I fired again and again until he – he was dead.'

There was silence for a moment as the courtroom tried to absorb the girl's words, then, still weeping, Cathy turned quietly to her father.

'Do you want to hang me, pa?'

38

Ross Stuart drove Storm and Cathy back to Tierra Rosa together. It was late; night had long since fallen; and the two girls were silent, not knowing what to say to one another. Storm didn't ask why Cathy had suddenly claimed to remember what had happened (for Storm knew her stepdaughter's 'hysterical amnesia' had been but a pretense) and lied to the courtroom, wrongly taking the blame for her brother's death in order to save her stepmother from the hangman's rope; and Cathy didn't explain. It was enough that the trial was over, and they were both still alive.

'Good night, Ross. I'll see you tomorrow.'

'Don't you worry, darlin'. I'll be here bright and early.'

The house was quiet as Cathy closed the door, and Storm walked slowly up the winding staircase to pack her things. There were only a few treasures she wanted, cherished mementos of her past: her Comanche wedding ensemble, Chance's tiny carved dragon. She wrapped them up lovingly in a small bundle, then went downstairs to the salon where Cathy was sitting, just sitting in the shadowed darkness. Wordlessly Storm lit a single lamp.

'I'm leaving Tierra Rosa,' she said.

Cathy sighed. 'You're still pa's wife.'

'I know.'

There was silence for a moment, and then Cathy asked, 'Where will you go?'

Storm shook her head, empty and bereft and suddenly so tired, so very tired. 'I – I don't know.'

She looked for Wolf in the confusion after the trial, but he'd gone. He hadn't waited for her, and her heart had ached at knowing he had stayed to see her safe, then left her.

Hadn't he wanted her back? Hadn't he loved her after all?

Somewhere outside in the blackness a solitary wolf howled lonesomely, and strangely enough it was Cathy who first recognized the cry for what it really was.

'You know, Storm,' she spoke softly after a time. 'You and I are kind of like sunrise and tears. They can be sad – or joyful – depending on which road in life you choose to take. There's a man out there' – she indicated the endless prairie through the mullioned window – 'somewhere, who's waiting for you. If I were you, I'd put on my moccasins and follow him to the ends of the earth.'

The wolf bayed sorrowfully once more, and suddenly Storm knew. It was Wolf. He was too proud to come to her, too afraid all the love she'd once had inside for him had died that bitter rose dawn with Chance. Her eyes brimmed moistly as the sound died slowly away.

'How sad, Cathy,' she sobbed gently, 'that we've never been friends.'

'And never can be now.'

In unspoken agreement, hesitantly at first, the two women embraced, then clung to each other tightly, fiercely for a moment, as though daring the world to come between them. They had shared a something special together, an ordeal, a test of pride and strength; and they had come through it courageously, brave-heartedly. They parted at last, their eyes bright with unshed tears at what might have been had things been different.

'*Vaya con Dios*, Storm,' Cathy whispered. 'I'll always remember you.'

'And I, you, Cathy. You gave me my life.'

'And you set me free. Go on now. Hurry!'

Squaring her small shoulders proudly, Storm opened the front doors of Tierra Rosa, put on her moccasins, and began to run.

* * *

Hilton cleared his throat, hating to disturb the boss, but knowing it was necessary.

'She's goin', Mr North,' he said. 'Do you want me to stop her?'

'No, Hank. Let her go.'

Tiredly Gabriel got to his feet, moving deliberately to the window of his study from where he could see Storm's slight figure running wildly across the endless, flat plains. She had taken nothing with her but a small bundle, her Comanche clothes, no doubt. She'd wanted nothing from him, Gabriel North, the hated rancher, not even a horse. He sighed, pressing one hand to his eyes.

His wife, Storm, on her way to meet her half-breed Indian lover.

A ragged sob choked Gabriel's throat as Hilton left the room respectfully. God! How lovely she was. Even now, after all she'd been and done, lust for her ripped through the rancher's loins. She'd yanked off her bonnet and torn down her hair, tossing her head back joyously, sensuously as the cool night wind streamed through the cascading black mass caressingly. Her lips were parted – Gabriel could see the flash of her perfect white teeth in the moonlight – as though eagerly awaiting her lover's kisses.

In his mind the rancher imagined his wife running willingly to the half-breed's outstretched arms, saw the savage gunslinger crushing her fervently to his dark copper chest, his midnight blue eyes hungry with desire. He kissed her hard and demandingly, his tongue ravaging her mouth as impatiently he pressed her down upon the sweet, dying grass. Then he opened his eyes, lifting his gaze to Storm's languorous face. He smiled triumphantly as his hands began to undo the buttons of her gray silk and black satin costume. The girl's head was thrown back, her ebony tresses billowing about her like a cloud as El Lobo buried his visage in the thick, glossy tangle, inhaling the sweet rose fragrance of her deeply.

Gabriel's breath caught sharply. How well he remembered that fragrance! Even now it haunted him, seemed to waft to his nostrils tantalizingly.

The half-breed bared Storm's breasts. The pale ripe mounds gleamed softly beneath the silver of the stars. The girl's pink nipples flushed, hardened as the savage gunslinger teased them with his fingers, taunted them with his mouth.

Oh, God! Oh, God!

Storm was naked now, and El Lobo was making his way down her soft belly with his lips, spreading her inviting thighs with his hands. Then he was kissing her, there, upon the sweet, honeyed swell of her womanhood, tonguing her slowly as Storm moaned and writhed beneath his mouth, his exploring fingers. Her hands wrapped themselves in the half-breed's dark mane of shaggy hair, pulling him to her as she gasped raggedly again and again. And then the savage gunslinger was poising himself above her, entering her, driving down into her with hot, blinding ecstasy—

'Goddamn him!' Gabriel swore. 'Goddamn him to hell and back!'

'Goddamn who, pa?' Cathy asked quietly, crossing the shadowed study to stand at her father's side.

'That half-breed Indian! That's who! He's beaten me, the bastard! She and that son-of-a-bitch have won— Oh, Cathy. Cathy! Why? *Why*? For God's sake, why did you lie for her in that courtroom today?

'I didn't do it for her, pa. I did it for him.'

'Who?'

'Her lover.'

'But – but why? I don't understand— Oh, God! Oh, God! Who *is* he? Who is he that even now his midnight blue eyes haunt me so? Tormenting me, driving me crazy—'

Her voice strangely triumphant, as though she'd waited a long time to hear her father ask that question, Cathy told him. Then she left the room, closing the door firmly behind her. She

556

leaned against it, trembling for a moment, before walking slowly down the hall.

Thirty minutes later, like a sleepwalker, Gabriel North carefully unlocked his desk drawer, took out his Texas Patterson revolver, and blew his brains out all over his study.

Wolf was standing silently, staring down at Tierra Rosa in the moonlit darkness when Storm found him. His dark visage was closed, unreadable; his midnight blue eyes were clouded and distant, as though he were seeing something only he could see. Tentatively the girl approached him, for he did not turn to her, although she knew he sensed her presence. Hesitantly she laid her hand on his arm.

'Wolf?'

'So you came,' he said, still not looking at her.

'Yes.'

'Why?'

Storm swallowed hard. Had she been wrong? Did he not want her, love her after all?

'To – to ask your forgiveness, I guess, if nothing else, and to thank you for what you did for me that night in Santa Rosa. I was wrong, so terribly wrong about Chance. I know that now – now when maybe it's too – too late for us. Maybe it was always too late for us; maybe our love just wasn't enough; I don't know—' She broke off awkwardly, and the night was still once more.

Her heart pounded queerly in her breast as she gazed up at him pleadingly, only dimly aware of the cool, gentle sigh of the autumn-touched breeze that rippled softly over the plains, rustling the faded prairie grass and the leaves of the mesquite trees whisperingly. Somewhere in the distance an owl hooted, and a calf lowed plaintively for its mother. Storm's eyes filled with tears at the sound. *Maman. Maman.*

It was Wolf who first spoke again.

'Cathy lied, didn't she?' he asked. 'It was you who killed Joe Jack, wasn't it?'

'Yes.'

'Why?'

'A life for a life, you once told me. Is that not the Comanche way?'

He inhaled sharply.

'Yes, that is the Comanche way,' he responded finally, his voice low, then he paused. 'Did you – did you love him, Storm? Joe Jack, I mean.'

'No. No. I – I've never loved anyone but you. Oh, Wolf! Can you ever forget the things I said, the things I did? Can you ever forgive me for them? Can you – can you ever love me again? Will you – will you—' She bit her lip. She was a proud woman, but love has no pride, and her desire for Wolf was beyond shame. 'Will you ever take me back?' she beseeched him softly.

He looked down at her at last.

'Why?'

'Because I love you; I've never stopped loving you. I'll love you till the heavens meet the earth, and the stars fall in the sea.'

'That's a long time, Storm.'

'I'll wait. I'll wait just as long as it takes for you to want me again, and I'll go on loving you always, no matter what you say or do.'

'You're another man's wife!' he suddenly snarled harshly.

'I was yours once. Remember?'

She took his hand, turning his palm upward to reveal the faint scar of the knife that had sealed their Indian wedding vows. Then she took her own palm, marked in the same fashion, and laid it in his. His eyes darkened.

'I remember,' he breathed. 'I haven't changed, Storm,' he warned.

'Maybe I have.'

'Have you?'

'Yes.'

He turned, laying his hands on her shoulders.

'I'm not going to promise you anything. I don't know if I can ever forget and forgive. I love you. God knows, I do. But maybe that's not enough. Maybe it's never been enough for us, as you said. I don't know.'

'I'm not asking for anything, Wolf. Just let me stay with you. Please. Don't send me away.'

Wolf swore, and then suddenly he was pressing Storm down upon the sweet, dying grass – just as Gabriel North had imagined. His fingers were wrapped tightly in her mass of ebony hair; his breath was warm upon her face before he kissed her fiercely, possessively, then muttered, '*Bruja, bruja,*' hoarsely against her throat.

39

Cathy rode, proud and unafraid, into the autumn camp of the *Kwerharehnuh* just outside the vast boundaries of Tierra Rosa. Her back was as straight as a ramrod, and she looked neither right nor left at the curious, stoically faced Comanches who studied her silently, almost in awe as she passed. Strangely enough, no one made a move to halt her progress. When she had reached Wolf and Storm, she drew her gelding up slowly and dismounted. Tears filled her eyes as wordlessly she stretched out one hand to caress Wolf's face wonderingly. Storm watched, confused, as oddly enough Wolf permitted the half-searching, half-marveling touch of Cathy's slender fingers, then gently took the girl's hand and kissed it.

'All those years—' Cathy wept quietly. 'All those years ago – that dreadful day – you were that boy.'

'Yes,' Wolf said softly. 'I was that boy.'

'I – I think you've waited a long time for this.' She handed him a very old and yellowed scroll.

'Yes, a long time.' Wolf stared down at the faded parchment intently, but did not open it to read its contents.

Cathy hesitated briefly, then went on.

'Pa's dead,' she said flatly. 'He killed himself the night Storm left. He knew.' She answered the unspoken question in Wolf's eyes. 'In the end he knew. I – I told him.' Cathy paused, then announced defiantly, 'I – I'm going to marry Ross Stuart. I've taken what I wanted from the house—' She bit her lip. 'It – it's over now. It's all over now, isn't it?'

'Yes, it's over.'

'And we're – we're both free now, aren't we?'

'Yes, we're both free.'

Impulsively Cathy flung herself into Wolf's arms,

embracing him tightly for a moment.

'*Vaya con Dios*, El Lobo,' she whispered, her voice choked with sobs.

'May the Great-Spirit walk beside you and give you strength, Cathleen North,' he answered solemnly.

And then Cathy was gone as proudly as she had come.

Unspeakingly Wolf and Storm watched her brave-hearted figure go, galloping wildly – freely – over the fall-sun-touched plains, then questioningly Storm turned to Wolf by her side.

'What – what did she mean – *you were that boy*? What is that she gave you?'

Without even glancing at the aged scroll, his voice thick with emotion, Wolf replied, 'The deed to Tierra Rosa.'

'But – but why would Cathy give you such a thing?'

'Because she is a very great lady. A very great lady,' he murmured again.

Then quietly Wolf led Storm away to a sheltered place in the hills and told her what had happened that hot Indian summer's day twenty-three long years ago at Tierra Rosa.

'I was born Rafael Bautista Delgados y Aguilar,' he began, as though he had not said the name in a long, long time, then took Storm's hand in his, 'the only son of an *Aragonés* nobleman, *Don* Diego Ramón, and his beautiful *Castellano* wife, *Doña* Anna Maria. My father was much admired and respected, my mother much loved and adored, and we were happy in Spain where I was born and lived the first years of my young life. Aguila – my cousin – lived with us then, for his stepfather could not bear the sight of him, and every morning we rode our small *Andalusía* ponies into the mountains or on the beach along the sea. We knew little of the political unrest in our country, how it had divided itself into two factions, those who sided with King Ferdinand VII and those who wanted his brother, *Don* Carlos, to inherit the crown. *Mi padre* – my father – was one of the latter, for he saw that Ferdinand was a bad king.

'Aguila's stepfather, *Don* Manuel Vitorio de Zaragoza,

had always envied *mi padre*'s power and riches, and he and my father were bitter enemies. In time *Don* Manuel took advantage of the political unrest in our country to plot against *mi padre* and destroy him. Wrongfully and dishonorably *Don* Manuel denounced my father to King Ferdinand on trumped-up charges and had our family exiled from Spain.

'Proud, hurt, enraged, and impoverished, we came to the new world, with only the clothes on our backs and what few possessions we managed to salvage from our plight.' Wolf's midnight blue eyes were distant, recalling his family's flight across the ocean. 'I remember how bitterly I wept at parting from Aguila, for his stepfather forbade him to accompany us. I thought never to see him again.' He paused.

'But you did,' Storm spoke, recalling Aguila's dark brown eyes flashing in his lean, hawklike face.

'Yes, he grew to manhood, killed his stepfather in revenge for what *Don* Manuel had done to my family, among other things, and fled to the new world. But that is another story.'

'I'm sorry. I didn't mean to interrupt. Please go on,' the girl urged gently, deeply touched that at last Wolf was sharing his mysterious, shadowed past with her.

He sighed. 'How brave my mother was at leaving her friends and our home, the gardens where she'd tended her roses. And how strongly and honorably my father bore up under the disgrace of his old and noble family name. I remember how they stood together, their arms about each other lovingly, at the rail of the ship as we watched our beloved Spain disappear from sight, and then how courageously they set foot in the new world, determined to succeed, despite our poverty.

'We came to Texas, which was then a part of Mexico, where we thought we would be safe from the long arm of *Don* Manuel's vindictiveness, and there we settled on a vast, savagely wild and beautiful land my mother called *Tierra Rosa*, Rose Land.' Storm gasped, but Wolf continued calmly, ignoring the sound. '*Mi padre*, who had never labored physically in his life, built us a small adobe house; and *mi madre* planted a vegetable garden, tending it as lovingly as she had her roses. I went to the mission – the church at Santa Rosa and began my studies for the priesthood.

'I was seven years old that day Gabriel North came with his men and drove us away from our home. My father was very angry and indignant and vowed to take his grievance against the American usurper to the president of Mexico if necessary. We tried every government authority we could find, seeking help, for *mi padre* was a lawful and non-violent man, but everywhere our pleas for aid were turned aside. Santa Anna was already massing the Mexican army for the first of its attacks on the American colonists that Stephen Austin had brought to Texas, and no one had time to listen to us. We were just one family in thousands who'd had their property stolen by the American usurpers. Finally, five years later, we discovered an official, a Major Valdéz, who agreed to assist us. He drew up a deed for us, stamping it with a legal seal insuring that our claim to the land was valid.

'Victoriously we returned to the small house we'd taken in Santa Rosa and that summer rode out to Tierra Rosa to confront Gabriel North with our triumph. But our deed meant nothing to him. He spat upon us before his men and called my father a son-of-a-Mexican-whore! A greaser-pig! *Mi padre!*' Wolf's mouth tightened, and his nostrils flared whitely. '*Mi padre*, a Spanish *grandée* whose noble *Aragonés* blood had been undiluted for centuries! Then before my father even realized what was happening Gabriel North drew his pistol and gunned him down.'

'Oh, my God!' Storm breathed, beginning at last to understand the demons that had driven the only man she'd ever truly loved. 'Oh, my God!'

'My – my mother' – Wolf's voice broke, but he mastered himself manfully and went on – 'my gentle mother ran at Gabriel North, clawing at his face hysterically. He grabbed her and pinioned her arms behind her back roughly. A Mexican slut, her called her, she, who was a pure *Castellano*! And then –

and then he saw her eyes. Oh, Storm, her eyes – *mi madre* had the most beautiful eyes. Blue, like sapphires, they were. Gabriel North was ignorant of Spanish eyes and how they are not always brown, like Mexicans'. He thought my mother was white – an *Americana* – a white whore who'd married a greaser-pig. He forced her down upon the ground—'

'No!' Storm cried, tears by now streaming silently down her cheeks. 'No! I don't want to hear it! I don't want to hear it!'

But Wolf continued as though he hadn't heard her.

'He forced her down upon the ground, and he – he raped her brutally. Then he – he gave her to his men— She was – she was dead when they'd finished with her, and I was vomiting my guts out with shock and horror. Gabriel North's daughter, Cathy, saw the whole thing. I remember looking up and meeting her terrified eyes for just an instant before her father's men asked him if he wanted them to kill me too.

'"No, he's just a boy," Gabriel North said. "What can he do – tell all? Who'd believe him? A little half-breed bastard like that."

'*Half-breed*,' Wolf reiterated bitterly, 'Jesus! I never wanted to forget those two words as long as I lived.' He was silent for a time, then spoke again.

'After a while I managed to load my parents' bodies into our wagon. My – my mother was clutching her rosary in her hand. I took it, to remember her by, then buried her and my father in the hills. I don't recall much after that. I left the wagon, and I must have turned the horse loose, because I was on foot— I – I – I lost faith in my god and ran away, just kept on running until the *Kwerharehnuh* caught me.' He shook his head, thinking what a tragic waste it had all been.

'They were kind to me and raised me as their own. I stayed with them until Beloved-Of-The-Forest's death, then I left them to make my own way in the world. I thought – I thought I would never love again until I found you. That day I went back to Fin Terra and discovered you gone I—'

'You went back? You never told me that.'

'You never gave me a chance, Storm,' Wolf reminded her grimly. 'Yes, I went back, after Gabriel North and his men had hung me and left me for dead—'

'No! Oh, no!'

'Oh, yes, Storm,' Wolf went on relentlessly, taking off his beaded Indian collar so that she might see at last the dreadful scar around his throat.

'*Sainte Marie*! Forgive me! Forgive me! I didn't know! I didn't know! Gabriel – Gabriel said you'd argued with someone over a woman, tried to best one man too many, and that they'd hung you for it, but I – I never dreamed—'

'No, I know you didn't. It never even occurred to you that the woman was you, only you, always you – and that the other man was Gabriel North. I was lucky to be alive afterward, and it took me a long time to recover. That's why I didn't come back right away, and when I did, you were already gone. There wasn't any way for me to track you, so I rode north, to The People, hoping you'd look for me there, but you never did. You know the rest, Storm,' he ended, shrugging as though none of it really mattered anyway.

'Oh, if only I'd known!' The girl wept. 'If only I'd known! No wonder you hated him! No wonder you hated Gabriel North so! Oh, God! He murdered your parents! He nearly killed you! He bribed Joe Jack into – into murdering our son! Oh, Chance! Chance!' Storm buried her face in her hands, her body shaking pitifully with her racking sobs.

'Yeah,' Wolf said, studying her quietly, thoughtfully, 'I reckon Gabriel North caused us both a lot of grief and heartache. But it's over. It's all over now.' He let her cry it all out, then after a time he touched her gently on the shoulder. 'Come, Storm. There's something I want to show you.'

Somehow the girl knew, long before they ever reached the gently swelling crest overlooking the vast beauty of Tierra Rosa beneath the flaming October sun, where they were going. Her throat tightened as she unlocked her arms from Wolf's waist, slid from Pahuraix's broad back, and walked slowly toward the three special graves with their lovingly carved crosses. She knew now to whom they belonged: Wolf's parents and Chance. How ironic that Joe Jack had unwittingly brought her here that day. Had he known, somehow, someway?

'I wanted Chance to be here, you know,' the girl spoke quietly as she knelt down upon the hushed, grassy knoll. 'I used to come up here with flowers and pretend that he was, and now I find he really is. Do you think he senses our presence, Wolf? Do you think he knows how we still love him, wherever he is?'

'I'm sure he does, Storm.'

'Oh, Wolf! He was so young, too young to die!'

'I know.'

They were silent for a moment, each remembering the child conceived of their love and born upon a wild, fall-swept plain.

Would they ever love again as they had loved then? Storm wondered.

Wolf had accepted her presence that night on the prairie, had held her close and made love to her fiercely, tenderly as he'd done of old, had let her stay with him as she'd pleaded; but he had not spoken of their relationship since – nor of their future. She didn't even know if he still considered her his wife, and she had been afraid to ask him, afraid to learn that perhaps he could not forget and forgive the bittersweet past that lay between them after all.

He has forgiven, maman. *He has forgotten. Can you not see* Ap's *heart in his eyes?*

It was only the plaintive sighing of the cool autumn wind. Surely it was. And yet – and yet—

Storm turned, her heart leaping with sudden hope as she looked breathlessly into Wolf's midnight blue eyes.

He gazed back at her kneeling there beside their son's grave, and without warning a wave of love so strong it could not be denied suddenly washed over him as sweetly as the soft, soughing breeze gently touched his skin. He knew then what he wanted. He wanted to burn Gabriel North's house to the ground and build another in its stead, one that belonged to The Land. He wanted The People to know they would always have a place in his heart and home, a place where they could come and fulfill Tabenanika's dream of the future. And most of all he wanted Storm by his side, sharing the rest of his life with him for just as long as he lived. Yes, it was time now – time to put the past behind him, to hang up his guns for good, and to settle down at last with the woman he loved.

'*Paraibo*,' he breathed in a way that made the girl's heart soar wildly in her breast. 'I know a priest in Santa Rosa.'

Tears of incredulous joy filled Storm's eyes as she realized what Wolf was saying as he reached out to her just as he had done that rose dawn so long ago in the dusty road of Gorda Vaca.

'Thank you, Chance,' she whispered softly to the autumn wind. 'Thank you, my son.'

Then, running passionately to Wolf's side, Storm laid her palm in his and felt his hand close lovingly over hers for all time.

Author's Note

The history of Texas, one of the author's favorite states, is as violent as it is colorful and was in an almost constant state of turmoil during the time in which this novel is set. The difficulties began primarily in the early 1830s, when after leading a successful coup against the government then in power, Antonio López de Santa Anna assumed the presidency of Mexico. In addition to the country's pressing internal problems on the home front, skirmishes had already begun to develop in Texas between the American colonists, such as those brought to the state of Stephen Austin, and Mexican troops, to which Santa Anna immediately sent reinforcements in an attempt to quell the upheavals.

It is unfortunate but true that many of the Americans who first colonized the state of Texas stole their land from its Mexican settlers, who were unable to seek adequate redress because of the confusion that reigned at the time; and it is also fact that Mexican troops treated American colonists in a highly restrictive and tyrannical fashion. Since both Mexico and the United States laid claim to Texas, it is probable that the peoples of both nations considered themselves unanswerable to the government of the other and, in addition, felt justified in their actions against one another, however wrong those actions might have been. At any rate, there is no doubt that the abrasive dispute between the two countries contributed greatly to the growing unrest and prejudice among the state's inhabitants.

The disruption reached a head in 1836 at the famous siege of the Alamo, during the Texas revolution, in which both Jim Bowie and Davy Crockett were killed. 'Remember the Alamo!' was a cry that was not to be easily forgotten over the years, and continual raids by Mexico into the newly formed Republic of Texas and the subsequent Mexican War in 1846, did not help relations between the Americans and Mexicans.

Texas was also plagued by the problem of the Indians, the majority of whom were considered savage heathens by terrified and/or ignorant whites. In this novel, from the appalling ignorance of Mrs Thatcher, to the blind racial prejudice of Gabriel North, to Wolf's extensive knowledge and deep understanding of The People, the author has sincerely attempted to portray the Indians, primarily the Comanches, as they truly were: no better and no worse than any other tribe of people that has ever roamed the earth. In addition, the author has tried to provide the reader with an accurate picture of the Comanches' religion, customs, and way of life, much of which has sadly been lost or grossly distorted.

Contrary to popular belief, the gruesome practice of scalping did *not* originate with the Indians, but with the whites, who paid warring Indian tribes for each other's bodies and then just their scalps when the bodies became too numerous. Also to contrary popular belief, the majority of Indians were not sexually promiscuous until the arrival of the whites. Comanches, especially, placed great value on their women, who were generally virginal until after marriage. A Comanche wife who committed adultery and was discovered by her husband could expect either death or disfigurement for her crime, and the other man involved had to pay damages of the offended husband's choosing, provided the husband could force him to do so. Certainly no Comanche ever offered his wife to a white man. Incest was strictly forbidden (except among the *Waw'ai* band, who were scorned for the practice by the other Comanche bands); rape was almost unknown; and both crimes were punishable by death, as was murder.

It is interesting to note that in a time when white women and their property were by law virtual chattel of their husbands, Comanche women were generally treated with respect by their husbands, were protected to much extent by tribal law, and were property owners in their own right.

The Comanches, like most Indian tribes, had no written language, which has made translation difficult. The author has chosen to use the phonetic spelling of words, keeping in mind that all vowels, with the exception of those in combination with certain consonants (i.e. aw, eh, er, re, uh) are given the pronunciations of ah, aaa, eee, oh, ooh. The author apologizes for any errors that may have occurred in translation, but even the experts cannot agree on the definitions of various Comanche words, and the author has chosen to use those translations that seemed most appropriate for the context of her story. The reader may find the following pages containing a glossary of the Comanche terms employed herein of interest and benefit.

Lastly, the author would like very much to thank the Chambers of Commerce of the following cities, located in the state of Texas, which so graciously provided her with various information on historical background and physical descriptions during her lengthy research for this novel: Brackettville, Kinney County; Del Rio (San Felipe del Rio in the novel), Val Verde County; Eagle Pass, Maverick County; Laredo, Webb County; and Uvalde, Uvalde County.

The towns of Santa Rosa and Gorda Vaca, which the author has described in this novel, are fictional.

Rebecca Brandewyne

Glossary

A:heh: I claim it. A term used by warriors when counting coup or women when claiming buffalo killed by their husbands.

Aiee: An exclamation.

Ap': Father; a paternal uncle. A child's paternal cousins were considered his brothers and sisters. This was because upon a man's death, his brother would inherit his wives, and thus his children would become his brother's children.

Ara: A maternal uncle; the child of a man's sister. A child's *ara* was his special friend and teacher, and a child was allowed to take and use his *ara*'s possessions without permission whenever he wished.

Asenap: A proper name meaning 'Greyfoot.'

Awmawtawy: A pipe, more specifically a peace pipe.

Awyaw:t: A parfleche bag used for storing food.

Beht: Daughter.

Berdache: A homosexual. Indians believed that Mother-Moon appeared to young boys during their puberty and offered them either a bow or a woman's pack strap. If the boy hesitated when reaching for the bow, Mother-Moon handed him the pack strap, and thereafter he lived a feminine lifestyle. *Berdaches* acted as matchmakers and often went into battle to treat wounded warriors.

Black-Robes: The name given by the Comanches to Spanish priests.

Blue-Soldiers: The name given by the Comanches to members of the United States Army.

Chikoba: A proper name meaning 'Breaks-Something.'

Comanche: A term deriving from the Ute word '*Komantcía*,' meaning 'enemy.'

Comanchería: The vast, heart-shaped territory located in the

Great Plains, so called because it was there the Comanches ruled supreme.

Comanchero: Any person not of Comanche blood who traded goods and guns to the tribe. The life of a *comanchero* was noted for its risks, since the Comanches sometimes turned on such traders when displeased.

Dohate: A proper name meaning 'Owl-Prophet.'

Eh-haitsma: Literally, 'It is your close friend.' What a woman called from her tipi to her husband after giving birth to a baby boy.

Ehkaraw'ro: Literally, 'She blushes.' Also used as a proper name.

Ekakura: A proper name meaning 'Red-Buffalo.'

Ersamop'ma: Literally, 'It is a girl.' What a woman called from her tipi to her husband after giving birth to a baby girl.

Fire-stick: The name given by the Comanches to any type of white man's gun.

Fire-water: The name given by the Comanches to any type of white man's liquor.

God-dog: Horse. Horses were so highly treasured and cherished by Comanches that they had seventeen explicit words describing them. *Dunnia*, for example, meant a yellow horse with a black mane and tail. *Awdutsuhnaro* meant a sorrel pinto. *Ehkanaki* meant a horse with red ears. Unlike the Apaches, the Comanches *never* ate horsemeat unless they were starving to death, and on horseback there was no one equal to their superior riding ability.

Haints: Friend; the brother of a man's wife.

Herbi: A woman.

Herkiyani: A proper name meaning 'Carrying-Her-Sunshade.' Many Comanches, both men and women, carried sunshades against the glare of the prairie sun.

Hihites: Greetings.

Hisusanchis: A proper name meaning 'The-Little-Spaniard.'

Hu: An exclamation.

Idahi: Snake. Also used as a proper name. The movement of a snake going backwards was used in Indian sign language to indicate the Comanches. The state of Idaho may have derived its name from this word and/or another Comanche word, *Idaho*, meaning 'cold.'

Inde: A derogatory term given by the Comanches to the Apaches, whom the Comanches despised.

Ishatai: A proper name meaning 'Coyote-Droppings.' Coyote meat, as well as dog meat, pork, turkey, fish, and frogs were taboo for the Comanches.

Itehta'o: Burnt-Meat. A name given to one of the ten minor bands of Comanches.

Kumaxp: Husband.

Kusehtehmini: Literally, 'Asking about the buffalo.' A name given by the Comanches to the horned toad, whom the Comanches believed had the power to divine the location of buffalo herds.

Kutsuehka: Buffalo-Eaters. A name given to one of the seven major bands of Comanches. The buffalos were highly revered by the Comanches, who used every part of the beasts' carcasses, not leaving them to rot upon the plains as so many white hunters did.

Kwahadi and/or *Kwahiherkehnuh*: Literally, 'Sunshades on their backs,' or 'People with sunshades on their backs.' Names by which the *Kwerharehnuh* band of Comanches was also known.

Kwanah: A proper name meaning 'Sweet-Odor.' Kwanah, who was called Quanah Parker by the white man, was a half-breed Comanche, the son of Chief Peta-Nawkoni and Cynthia Ann Parker, a white woman captured by the *Kwerharehnuh* as a child. He became the last war chief of the Comanches ever to surrender and after settling down on a reservation in Oklahoma served as the main interpreter of white civilization to The People, encouraging them to learn the ways of the white world while maintaining their proud Comanche heritage.

Kwasia: A proper name meaning 'Eagle-Tail-Feather'.

Kwerharehnuh: Antelope. More specifically, Antelope-People. A name given to one of the seven major bands of Comanches. The *Kwerharehnuh* were the proudest and fiercest band of all those in *Comanchería* and were the last band ever to surrender.

Masitawtawp: A proper name meaning 'Bear-Claw-Marks-On-His-Shield.'

Mawtakwoip: Hand-Talk. The name given by the Comanches to sign language. Comanches were not very adept at sign language, since the majority of Plains Indians spoke the Comanche language.

Muwaw: A derogatory reference to a man.

Naibi: A young woman, usually in her teens.

Namaer'ernuh: Literally, 'Something together'. The name given by the Comanches to sexual intercourse.

Nanehwokuh: Damages. A man whose wife had committed adultery was legally entitled to demand damages from his rival. The offended husband collected, however, provided only that he could force the other man to pay.

Nanip'ka: Literally, 'Guess over the hill.' A game played by Comanche children, which was similar to hide-and-seek.

Narabuh: A derogatory reference to an old man.

Nat'sakerna: A Comanche man or woman's wardrobe case.

Naukwahip: Champion rider. Also used as a proper name.

Nawkoni: Literally, 'Those who turn back.' A name given to one of the seven major bands of Comanches. This band was also known by two other names: *Nawyehka*, 'Those-Who-Move-Often;' and *Dertsanawyehka*, 'Wanderers-Who-Make-Bad-Camps.'

Nayia: Slope. Also used as a proper name.

Nermernuh: The People. More specifically, True Human Beings. The term used by the Comanches to describe their tribe.

Ona: Infant or baby.

Pabi: Elder sister.

Padoponi: Literally, 'See how deep the water is.' Also used as a proper name.

Pana: A paternal aunt; the child of a woman's brother.

Pahuraix: Water-Horse. A name given to one of the ten minor bands of Comanches. This band was also known by the name, *Parkinaum*, 'Water-People.'

Paradadeha: Big boy. Also used as a proper name.

Paraibo: Chief wife.

Paria:bo: Peace Chief.

Pecos: Peanut. Also used as a proper name. Pecos was the brother of Kwanah.

Pehnaterkuh: Honey-Eaters. A name given to one of the seven major bands of Comanches. This band was also known by the names: *Teyuwit*, 'Hospitable;' *Tekapwai*, 'No-Meat;' *Kubaratpat*, 'Steep-climbers;' *Pehnaner*, 'Wasp,' 'Stinger,' or 'Raider;' and *Ho'is*, 'Timber-People.'

Peplum: A sash worn by Comanche women.

Peta-Nawkoni: See 'Nawkoni' above. Meaning of 'Peta' uncertain. Since Peta-Nawkoni was a chief of the *Kwerharehnuh*, an educated guess as to the meaning of his name might be 'One who refuses to turn back.' Peta-Nawkoni was the father of Kwanah.

Pia: Mother; a maternal aunt. Generally a Comanche man married women who were sisters, and so maternal aunts were considered mothers to their sisters' children.

Piamermpits: Big-Cannibal-Owl. A bogey with which Comanches frightened their children when the youngsters misbehaved.

Pianahuwait: Big doctoring.

Pianer'erpai'i: Big whip. The name given by Comanches to a bull whip.

Pitsikwina: White woman's dress.

Pohoi: Wild-Sage. The name of a band of Shoshoni Indians, cousins of the Comanches. This band is sometimes mistakenly believed to have been part of the Comanche tribe.

Posa: Crazy, especially in reference to 'crazy warriors,' so called because they would stand stock still in the middle of battles, humming to themselves, etc. They were believed to have very powerful medicine.

Puhakut: Shaman, medicine man, or spirit-talker.

Sehkwitsit-Puhitsit: Mud-Men. A bogey with which Comanches frightened their children when the youngsters misbehaved.